Friedrich Schiller

Wilhelm Tell - Schauspiel

Friedrich Schiller

Wilhelm Tell - Schauspiel

ISBN/EAN: 9783743644069

Printed in Europe, USA, Canada, Australia, Japan

Cover: Foto ©Andreas Hilbeck / pixelio.de

More available books at **www.hansebooks.com**

Wilhelm Tell

Schauspiel

von

Friedrich Schiller

EDITED WITH

INTRODUCTION, NOTES, AND VOCABULARY

BY

ARTHUR H. PALMER

Professor in Yale University

NEW YORK
HENRY HOLT AND COMPANY
1898

Schiller's Coat of Arms.

" The last great dramatic work of Schiller—and whether it be not the grandest production of his genius I leave to others to judge—is founded on the most remarkable and beneficent political revolution which, previous to our own, the world had seen,—an event the glory of which belongs solely to the Teutonic race—that ancient vindication of the great right of nationality and independent government, the revolt of Switzerland against the domination of Austria, which gave birth to a republic now venerable with the antiquity of five hundred years. He took a silent page from history, and, animating the personages of whom it speaks with the fiery life of his own spirit, and endowing them with his own superhuman eloquence, he formed it into a living protest against foreign dominion which yet rings throughout the world. Wherever there are generous hearts, wherever there are men who hold in reverence the rights of their fellow-men, wherever the love of country and the love of mankind coexist, Schiller's drama of ' William Tell' stirs the blood like the sound of a trumpet."—WILLIAM CULLEN BRYANT: Address at centennial celebration of Schiller's birth, in Cooper Union, New York City, 1859.

THIS edition of Schiller's *Wilhelm Tell*, intended especially for schools and colleges, has been made at the request of the publishers. An editor of this drama at the present time must in general move along the same lines with his many predecessors, as regards most of his Introduction and Notes. For these, then, the editor frankly acknowledges that he has made conscientious use of all accessible Schiller-literature —histories, biographies, editions, commentaries—and has drawn freely upon them, especially upon those contained in the Bibliography, Appendix, pp. 282–287.

In the Notes he has endeavored to be concise, to give translations only in cases where the average dictionary is inadequate, and not to stray into the fields of grammar and etymology. On the other hand, the comment in both Introduction and Notes on the structure and development of the plot and on the characters has been made considerably fuller than in any preceding edition. Here the unitary conception of the drama has been favored. Under this general head the editor acknowledges very direct and extensive indebtedness (although at the same time differing from him in important points of view) to H. Gaudig in his most excellent commentary on the drama, contained in the *Wegweiser durch die klassischen Schul-*

dramen, Vol. 5, Part 3 of *Aus deutschen Lesebüchern* by O. Frick and others.

Since *Wilhelm Tell* is so often the first classical German drama to be read in our schools, the first division of the Introduction is given to a sketch of some of the main outlines of the great classical period of German literature. The aim here is not so much to impart full information as to suggest the broad literary background before which *Tell* stands, and to awaken interest in the rich treasures of the literature of Germany.

The relations of fact and fiction in history and legend are set forth in the Introduction, more because of the intrinsic importance of the real history of Switzerland than because knowledge of these relations is essential to the understanding and enjoyment of Schiller's drama.

The Text is presented in the standard form, but with the Prussian official orthography. The punctuation retains somewhat freely the dash which Schiller employed so much.

The Vocabulary has been independently made from the text. It is believed that it will meet the desires and the needs of many schools.

A. H. P.

Yale University, September 18, 1898.

CONTENTS.

LIST OF PLATES.

vi

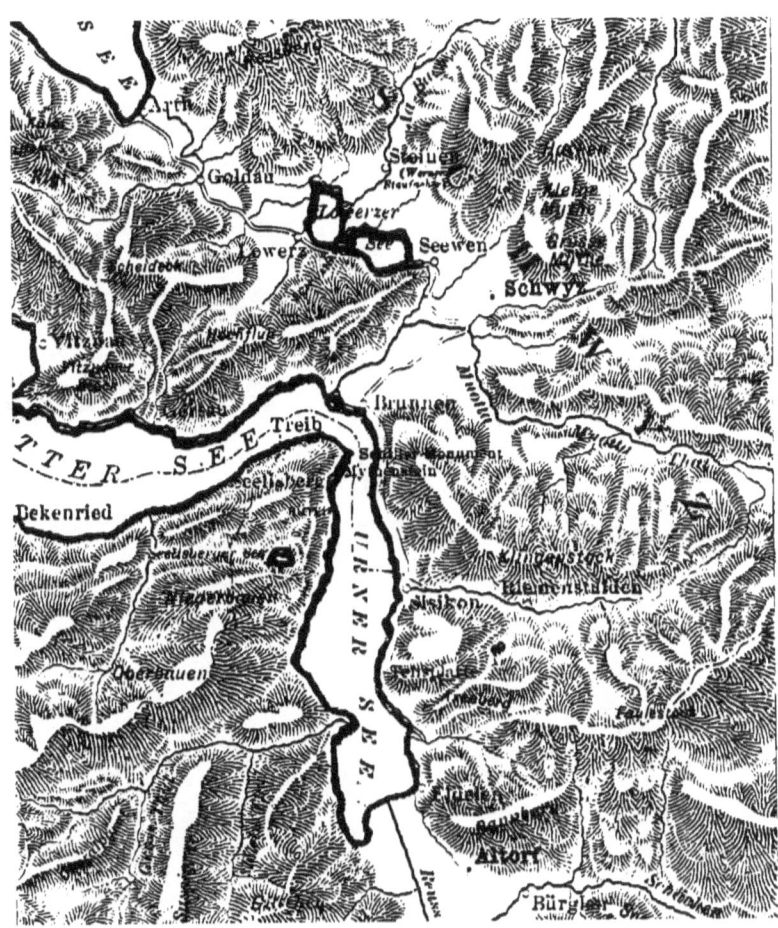

INTRODUCTION.

THE PLACE OF "WILHELM TELL" AND ITS AUTHOR IN GERMAN LITERATURE.

Wilhelm Tell is the most popular drama of that author who has been universally known and loved in his own country as no other writer. It opens before us the great classical period of German literature, leading us back to Weimar, where on February 18th, 1804, it was completed and on March 17th first performed.

The region of Thuringia where Weimar * lies has always been preeminent in favoring the spiritual and national interests of Germany. Landgrave Hermann of the Wartburg was in the thirteenth century a patron of poets, among whom were Wolfram von Eschenbach, the greatest epic poet of his age, and Walther von der Vogelweide, one of the sweetest and strongest lyric poets of all times and tongues; there in the fourteenth

---

* Cf. Scherer—*Geschichte der deutschen Litteratur*, 5th ed. pp. 526 ff., to which in general the editor acknowledges indebtedness, as also to Stein—*Ästhetik der deutschen Klassiker*, Julian Schmidt—*Geschichte der deutschen Litteratur*, and other current authorities.

century the drama proved its power, and there in the sixteenth century Luther, translating the New Testament, laid the foundations of the language of all later writers. The Weimar princes in the seventeenth century took part in organized movements to elevate and refine the language from the degradation and corruption of the Thirty Years' War, and towards the end of the eighteenth century Duchess Anna Amalia and her son, Duke Karl August, made the name of Weimar immortal as the home of the greatest writers of Germany's classical literature. This same large-minded Duke had also no small share in the revival of the truly national idea in German politics.

WIELAND * was the first of the great names in German literature to be permanently associated with the small city which soon came to be known as the

* CHRISTOPH MARTIN WIELAND, born 1733 near Biberach in Würtemberg, died 1813 in Weimar. 1752–60 in Switzerland ; 1760–69, official in Biberach ; 1769–72, professor in the University of Erfurt. His youthful writings, influenced by Klopstock and Plato, were followed by a period of revulsion from their pietistic strain to delight in the world and the pleasures of sense. Finding the golden mean, he was at the height of his power during the first decade of his residence in Weimar, after which time he occupied himself very largely with study and translation of the classic literature of ancient Greece and Italy. His notable novels are *Agathon*, 1766 ; *Die Abderiten*, 1774 ; and *Peregrinus Proteus*, 1791. He wrote many comic tales in verse, an epic-didactic poem, *Musarion*, 1768, and other shorter and longer epics in verse. He first naturalized Shakespeare in Germany, by translating in prose a large portion of his plays. Wieland's masterpiece is his romantic epic *Oberon*, 1780, in which chivalry, the Orient, and fairy-lore are attractively blended.

Athens of Germany. He was called thither in 1772 by Duchess Amalia as tutor of her sons, and remained until his death in 1813. As a writer of epic poems, romantic and comic, of philosophic novels, and as an editor, he made German style more fluent and elegant, won over the higher classes of the nation from French to German literature, popularized English and French philosophy, and remained withal a kindly, genial friend and patron of all men of letters.

GOETHE,* in Matthew Arnold's view "the greatest poet" and "the clearest, the largest, the most helpful thinker of modern times," came to Weimar in 1775, on the invitation of Duke Karl August, to make a visit of a few months, and—remained until his death

---

* JOHANN WOLFGANG VON GOETHE, born 1749 in Frankfurt-on-the-Main, died 1832 in Weimar. After a precocious boyhood in his native city, he studied at the universities of Leipzig and Strassburg, and lived again mostly in Frankfurt until he went to Weimar. From 1786 to 1788 Goethe was in Italy. Thereafter his residence at Weimar was uninterrupted, save by travel. Early and long he shared largely in the administration of the government of the Duchy. His writings are numerous and most varied. As a writer of short lyric poems he is unequaled. His chief dramatic works are *Götz von Berlichingen*, 1773; *Iphigenie auf Tauris*, 1787; *Egmont*, 1788; *Torquato Tasso*, 1790; and *Faust*, 1808–1832. His leading epic poems are *Reineke Fuchs*, 1793, and *Hermann und Dorothea*, 1797. In the field of the novel and of narrative prose his weightier productions are *Die Leiden des jungen Werthers*, 1774; *Wilhelm Meisters Lehrjahre*, 1795; *Wilhelm Meisters Wanderjahre*, 1821–29; *Die Wahlverwandtschaften*, 1809; and the wonderful autobiography, *Aus meinem Leben, Dichtung und Wahrheit*, 1811–1833. He wrote much in criticism of literature and art, and in the domain of natural science, where also he achieved greatness.

in 1832. Weimar was soon the chief of the small principalities, which now, as in 1517 and 1675, at once initiated and directed the intellectual movement of the age. Goethe more than any other man made Weimar the literary capital of Europe.

HERDER,* great personality and mighty prophet, was invited by the Duke, on the advice of Goethe, to come to Weimar in 1776 in an official capacity, and continued to reside there until his death in 1803. Of him Karl Hillebrand has said : "No one, Kant perhaps alone excepted, has contributed more to the stock of German thought, or has exercised greater or

---

*JOHANN GOTTFRIED HERDER, born 1744 near Königsberg, died 1803 in Weimar. As a student of philosophy and theology at Königsberg he was profoundly influenced by the great Kant, by Hamann, by the works of Rousseau and of Lessing. After alternately teaching, preaching, and traveling, he became in 1776 the head of the ecclesiastical affairs of the Duchy of Weimar. His purely original poetic productions are not important. It is in his prose works and his translations that his power lay. His critical writings were : *Fragmente über die neuere deutsche Litteratur*, 1766; *Kritische Wälder* [= Collections], 1769; and, in conjunction with Goethe, *Blätter von deutscher Art und Kunst*, 1773. In the field of religion and philosophy he wrote *Die älteste Urkunde des Menschengeschlechts*, 1774; *Vom Geist der ebräischen Poesie*, 1782–83; *Ideen zur Philosophie der Geschichte der Menschheit*, 1784–1791; and *Briefe zur Beförderung der Humanität*, 1793-1797. As translator his chief works were the *Stimmen der Völker in Liedern*, 1778–1779, and *Der Cid*, not published until 1805, after his death ; the former is a collection of folk-songs and popular ballads from all parts of the world, the latter is a free reproduction of a collection of Spanish ballads on the legendary history of the famous Don Rodrigo Diaz de Bivar, who lived in the eleventh century.

more lasting influence over an age, a nation, or the world at large, than Herder. Directly or indirectly he revolutionized learning, history, and literature, as Kant reconstructed philosophy."

It was Wieland, Herder, Goethe, and Schiller* who, aided by the somewhat older Klopstock† and Lessing,‡ recreated German literature and, by making a united intellectual, spiritual Germany, laid the necessary foundation of that united political Germany which was not fully realized until after 1870. How prophetic are Schiller's words in an early essay on the stage: "If we should come to have a real national

---

* SCHILLER was closely connected with Weimar from 1787 and resided there after 1799. In the Appendix is given a table of the more important dates of his life, for a detailed presentation of which and of the traits of his character and outward appearance the reader is referred to any one of the biographies in the list on pp. 282, 283.

† FRIEDRICH GOTTLIEB KLOPSTOCK, born 1724 in Quedlinburg, died 1803 in Hamburg. His fame rests upon his many lyric poems and mainly upon his masterpiece *Der Messias*, 1748–1773, a religious epic in twenty cantos, singing Christ's death, resurrection, and ascension, the chief beauties of which are also lyric in their nature.

‡ GOTTHOLD EPHRAIM LESSING, born 1729 in Kamenz in Upper Lusatia, died 1781 in Braunschweig, is the greatest critic of modern times and the founder of the modern German drama. His critical works were: *Briefe die neueste Litteratur betreffend*, 1759–60; *Laokoon*, 1766; *Hamburgische Dramaturgie*, 1767–68; and several small polemical writings relating to the history of art, philosophy, and theology. His epoch-making dramas were: *Miss Sara Sampson*, 1755; *Minna von Barnhelm*, 1767 (the first classic German comedy); *Emilia Galotti*, 1772 (the first classic German tragedy); and *Nathan der Weise*, 1779, a dramatic poem, which is his chief poetic production.

stage (or drama), then we should be a nation."
Indeed, geographical Germany may be annihilated,
but this foundation of the spiritual Germany of
Lessing, Goethe, and Schiller will last forever.

In Weimar, then, *Tell*—this drama of liberty and
national unity—was written and first played. Human
liberty, individual and national, is its theme. It is a
monument to the liberating and liberalizing power of
the ideal of humanism which was the common glory
of the great writers just mentioned,—above all of
Herder, Goethe, and Schiller,—and the realization of
which in literature and life was the inspiration of the
friendship of Goethe and Schiller, unparalleled in the
annals of literary history and interrupted only by
death.

The years of this friendship from 1794 to 1805 are
preeminently the period of Weimar's hegemony in
German literature. In the union of these two men
are focused all the previous thought and literature of
Germany, and from it radiate all the influences that
have determined the later literature. "For us of the
present time the golden age of classical idealism is
only seemingly past, although we call ourselves not
idealists, but realists. If we analyze the ideas which
underlie the ethics of to-day, we find them connected
by a thousand threads with classical idealism. The
true vital content of that golden age was faith in the
reality and harmony of the Good and the Beautiful,
the conviction that ideals grow on the earth like the
flowers of spring, that heaven is above the earth but
not outside of it, that man made in the image of God
has the right and the power to draw the divine from
his own breast." (Julian Schmidt.)

Goethe and Schiller had each in youth passed through a period of intensely revolutionary feeling; Goethe, ten years older than Schiller, in the eighth decade of the century and Schiller in the ninth. Residence and society in Weimar, unselfish labor, and study of natural science had in Goethe's case prepared the way for the completion by art during his travel and residence in Italy, 1786–88, of that strengthening and purifying which Schiller had gained by his study of history from 1787 on, and of Kant's philosophy, 1791 and later. Although Schiller in 1787, during Goethe's absence in Italy, had passed some months in Weimar, and through Goethe's influence had become professor of history in the University of Jena in 1789, it was not until 1794 that intimate relations were formed between them. It was an editorial project of the younger man that furnished the occasion—the publication for the year 1795 of a monthly, *Die Horen* ("The Hours"). A request to contribute brought from Goethe a kind answer; a personal meeting in Jena in May 1794 developed this beginning; correspondence and visits followed and favored the rapid flowering and fruition of this friendship. Of it Goethe said later: "It was for me a new springtime, in which all seeds shot up and gaily blossomed in my nature." Under its influence Schiller was yet to unfold his highest power.

The publication of *The Hours* was a publication of the fact that the authors of Weimar and the scholars of Jena now were the leaders in spiritual Germany and in the work of its unification. In his prospectus Schiller said: "The more the narrow interests of the present keep the minds of men on the stretch and subjugate while they narrow, the more imperious is the need to free them through the higher universal interest in that which is purely *human* and removed beyond the influence of time, and thus once more to reunite the divided political world under the banner of Truth and Beauty."

The ideals of *The Hours* were, however, too lofty to be realized immediately. The stupidity and envy of mediocre writers contributed to prevent the success of the journal, memorable though it be in the history of German literature. Yet what the journal failed in was soon accomplished by the *Xenien*, by the creation of new imperishable works of literary art and by the influence of the Weimar theater.

For the years 1796–1800 Schiller edited a *Musen-almanach*, an annual of poetry. The *Xenien* appeared in September, 1796, in the *Musenalmanach* for 1797. Suggested by the *Xenia* of the Latin poet Martial, they are about four hundred distichs, satirical, drastic, crushing, partly by Goethe, partly by Schiller, and partly by both, in which these authors deal with the bad writers and shallow critics of their time as Pope and Byron did with their contemporaries in the *Dunciad* and in *English Bards and Scotch Reviewers*. "The justness of the attack," says Scherer, "was brilliantly proven by the pitiableness of the defence." The outcome of the tremendous sensation produced was the confirmation of the leadership assumed in *The Hours*.

The movements just mentioned were, however, but a clearing of the way, a preparation for that creation and presentation of literature of the highest order, which culminated in the performance upon the

Weimar stage in the years from 1798 to 1804 of Schiller's great dramas under Goethe's direction. Goethe managed the Ducal Theater in Weimar from 1791 until 1817, and made it as much a national theater as any in Germany, especially in the years 1798–1804, when even that in Berlin was influenced by it. An ideal style and an ideal repertory were aimed at.

The period of Goethe's successful writing of dramas seemed now to be past, but in epic poetry, in the ballad, and in the novel he was yet to publish great and beautiful works. Since the appearance in 1774 of his novel, *The Sorrows of Young Werther*, which moved profoundly all Germany and twenty years later began to make him famous in England, he had published no narrative work, long or short, in prose or in verse, with the exception of a few ballads. But his greatest work in the form of the novel, *Wilhelm Meister's Apprenticeship*, which he had begun in 1777, now had its completion hastened under the stimulus of Schiller's sympathy, and came entire into the hands of the public in October 1796, simultaneously with the *Xenien*. This novel of culture, " a rich, manifold life brought close to our eyes," more than any other of his prose writings spread and confirmed his fame in Germany and has "entered into the training of Europe."

Goethe's most perfect long poem was his next work, begun immediately after he finished *Wilhelm Meister*, and completed in June 1797,—*Hermann and Dorothea*, an epic poem in hexameters. He had exercised himself in this form in his translation and reconstruction in 1793 of the Low-German *Reynard the Fox ;* he now used this verse in portraying German middle-class life with comprehensive, tender truthfulness and beauty that can never fade. In the Homeric spirit he most successfully realized the endeavor, in his own words, "in an epic crucible to free from its dross the purely human existence of a small German town and at the same time mirror in a small glass the great movements and changes of the world's stage."

But in this season of poetical ripening and reaping, due so largely to Schiller's fervent admiration, sympathy, and stimulating example, the lesser fruits and *Faust*, the greatest, were no less favored.

Before this time Schiller himself had not written many short poems that deserve to live. Superior to Goethe as a dramatic poet, he is not his peer in lyric poetry. His intellectual interest in philosophy and history does not leave room enough for that fullness of unreflecting passion and clearness of sensuous apprehension of nature and life, from which the finest lyrics freely spring. Schiller's lyrics are mostly lyrics of reflection, of thought; as such, not a few of his philosophic odes are masterpieces. It is by one of these, indeed, that next to his greatest dramas he is best known; for more than all the others it is charged with human emotion. This is *Das Lied von der Glocke*, finished in September, 1799. No other German lyric is more dear to the heart of the people than this Song of the Bell. Of it Wilhelm von Humboldt said: "In no language do I know of any poem that within so small a compass opens so wide a poetic horizon, traversing the scale of all deepest human emotion, and in altogether lyrical way displaying life with its most important events and epochs as an epos bounded by natural limits." The year 1797 was for both poets numerically *the* "Ballad Year"; that and the following years were rich in ballads and lyrics from both, productions of great power and depth of feeling and thought, and of most perfect art.

In the year 1797 also, Goethe, yielding to Schiller's kindly urgency, took in hand again his *Faust*, of which a small "Fragment" had been published in 1790, and, humanly speaking, the world owes to Schiller the existence in its present relatively complete form of this marvellous, unique work, the greatest in all modern literature since Shakespeare, presenting as it does with unsurpassed depth, power, and beauty all that Goethe's rare nature and experience could teach as to the spiritual meaning and end of life.

To Schiller we are also in a measure indebted that Goethe wrote his other works of these and later years, his autobiography *Fiction and Truth*, his novel *Elective Affinities*, his rich and varied *Wilhelm Meister's Journeymanship*, his many lyrics, both detached and in the collection *West-Östlicher Divan*. Without the second poetic spring beginning in 1795 could there have been this full harvest in these later years? And what more convincing testimony than Goethe's life and work during these ten years to the strength and elevation of Schiller's mind and heart!

The question arises: Why might there not have been twenty instead of only ten years of this noble friendship through an earlier beginning? When a young student, Schiller read Goethe, even then a famous author whose works not only directed his thought, but also challenged him to emulation. He saw Goethe when in 1779 Karl August and Goethe visited the Karlsschule; and when in 1787 Schiller's drama *Don Carlos* showed to all that his artistic power was well developed and much refined, the consciousness that he had some right to stand with the best authors of his day impelled him to go to Weimar to make the personal acquaintance of his present and future peers. He was heartily welcomed by Wieland, by Herder, by all, but—Goethe was in Italy. Schiller's frame of mind at this time we know from his letters to friends. "I am where I have so often longed to be and seem to myself to be moving in the plains of Greece." He will give his life to greatness, pre-eminence in the things of the spirit. He feels only one man to be his superior—Goethe. To this one man he feels called to draw near and give uplifting aid. But when their personal acquaintance formally begins in September 1788, all ground for this prophetic feeling seems to vanish, and he writes that his high opinion of Goethe has not been lowered, but that they will always stand far apart.

On Goethe's side, however, the reserve was more intense and conscious. Six years had to pass away before he could sufficiently overcome the aversion he felt towards the dramas of Schiller's youth and their author. Schiller stood before Goethe's mind as the representative of the excesses and errors of the Storm and Stress Period, of which he himself was now completely purged. Lofty ideals of simplicity, grandeur, repose possessed Goethe, the literary artist, on his return from the land of ideal art. He would give himself to art and science. How could he now take to his heart the author of *The Robbers?* "Schiller was odious to me," he says, "because his powerful but immature talent had poured out over my country in a full sweeping flood those very ethical and dramatic paradoxes from which I was endeavoring to keep myself free." Schiller had, to be sure, developed more than Goethe knew, but still more time and the experiences of the next few years were needed to make him fully worthy to be received by Goethe as he longed to be received.

What were these early works that still rose as a barrier between Schiller and Goethe? Schiller's dramatic production divides naturally into two well-defined periods or groups, at once separated and connected by years of study, thought, and writing, mainly in history and philosophy. To the first group, of the period of storm and stress in personal experience and of tumultuous, unclarified production, belong the three kindred prose dramas, *Die Räuber*, *Die Verschwörung des Fiesko*, *Kabale und Liebe*, and one in iambic blank verse, *Don Karlos*, completed in 1787, marking its author's rapid development and his passing over to history. These prose plays are satirical, republican, revolutionary. Their spirit of rebellion against all established order and social conventions sprang from the general conditions of the time and especially from the trials, the despotic tyranny and oppression which Schiller had himself experienced.

The Robbers, although the first, is the most remarkable of the early plays. It is the tragedy of the individual in conflict with the law and order of civilization, which he regards as based on wrong, until, made wise by experience, he resigns himself to his fate in submission to law. Technical dramatic skill, foreshadowing future perfection, strength and variety of the characters, great vigor of expression, are all manifest in it. There is much youthful exaggeration in thought and word, but also much genius and power in its whole plan and movement. "The brooding spirit of dissatisfaction and revolt had found a voice; and there was in *The Robbers* an appeal to the deeper nature of man, to the grander impulses of youth, an appeal that seldom fails."

The *Conspiracy of Fiesco* is a "Republican Tragedy," whose hero is the noble leader of an attempted political revolution in Genoa in the sixteenth century. It is interesting as being the first of Schiller's historical dramas, less extravagant in diction and more condensed in action than his first work, below which it falls far in creative force.

The third play, *Love and Intrigue*, is a tragedy of middle-class family life, torrent-like in the rush of its emotion, "a magnificent description, compressed into *one* action, of the conditions of the life of the time." It is, however, imperfect in many crudities, much unnaturalness, and no little false pathos.

Don Carlos marks transition in many respects. Originally conceived in 1782, it was not completed until 1787, after many interruptions and recastings. The life and death of this son of Philip II. of Spain have often been regarded as a fit theme for tragedy. Had Schiller treated it when fully matured, the drama might well have been inferior to no other he wrote, as it is on the whole much superior to his earlier works. Its weakness, due in part to the slowness of its completion, is lack of unity. In the first part of the play Prince Carlos is the hero, while in nearly all the rest of it the hero is the Marquis Posa, an embodiment of all the faith in man and the cosmopolitan ideals of the eighteenth century. This figure, a radiant and fascinating creation, together with the splendid diction of many elevated passages and the successful use of iambic verse, are what make the play live even to-day, imperfect yet great.

It is a long reach of twelve years forward to the completion of Schiller's next drama. There intervene varied trials and acute protracted illness, historical study and writing, editorial labors, absorbing interest in philosophy, literary criticism, lyrics, ballads, and epigrams. The two main streams of interest, however, are history and philosophy, with the watershed between them lying at the end of the year 1792. To this period belongs then naturally the greater portion of Schiller's non-dramatic prose writings, whose style is in general clear, full, rhetorical, often majestic. Among these are several critical essays, notably those on Goethe's *Egmont* and on Bürger's *Poems*. His *Philosophical Letters* are interesting for the light they shed on the development of his religious views. He attempted prose fiction in one uncompleted tale, *The Visionary*, extravagant in plot, but clear and broad in style.

Schiller's historical writings have real and great value, not as representing profound original investigation, but as uniquely successful in instructing and charming the ordinary reader. To him has been ascribed the creation of an artistic historical style in German. The first large work was the *History of the Revolt of the United Netherlands from Spanish Rule*, in some respects the best of his historical works, a vigorous, brilliant account of a portion of that great conflict for liberty, with much emphasis on ethical

values, much psychological penetration, and effective
analysis of character. It was again the theme of
liberty—spiritual, religious liberty—that led him to
write the *History of the Thirty Years' War*, in which
are well traced the broad outlines of this complicated
struggle. Among his numerous shorter historical
essays the most striking is his inaugural lecture as
professor on *What Is General History and To What
End Do We Study It?* It is important in the development of the philosophy of history, and indeed it
must be said that in all his historical writings philosophic connection is aimed at. He conceives history
in the broad sense as the history of civilization in all
its aspects.

As fruits of Schiller's philosopical study and reflection we have not a few essays on æsthetics. Here
belong also the *Letters on the Æsthetic Education of
Man.* Perhaps the most original and in its influence the most far-reaching of Schiller's prose writings was his essay *On Naïve and Sentimental Poetry*,
to which Goethe referred the introduction into modern literary criticism of the distinction between clas-
sicism and romanticism.

The years just after 1790 were for both Goethe and
Schiller years of slumbering poetic activity. In study
of history Schiller was broadening his knowledge, in
philosophic reflection he was deepening and refining
it, in both he was enriching himself for dramatic
creation. Their friendship led Goethe back from
plastic art and natural science to poetic production.
No less did it lead Schiller back from learning and
speculation to pure literature. The fruits of philosophy are most evident in his reflective lyrics. But

as he had passed from the drama to history, so now his study of the Thirty Years' War restored him to the drama, and between October 1796 and March 1799 he wrote what in bulk and weight of matter is his largest work and what many regard as all in all his most important dramatic production.

This is, in title, *Wallenstein, a Dramatic Poem*, but in reality one great tragedy of eleven acts, divided into a one-act prelude, *Wallenstein's Camp*, and two five-act plays, *The Piccolomini* and *Wallenstein's Death*. The time of the play is the last four days of Wallenstein's life in February 1634, but it brings before us with the utmost impressivness not only the tragedy of that great man's character and fate, but also the struggles, the sufferings, and the triumphs of the whole Thirty Years' War. This drama moulded the German drama for at least a generation. Tieck said thirty years later that all Germany felt that it established a new epoch.

When Schiller in December 1799 took up his residence in Weimar, he brought with him three acts of a new drama, also historical, the elaboration after the completion of *Wallenstein* of a long-cherished idea. This was his *Maria Stuart*, which was finished early in 1800 and first performed in June 1800. The familiar subject of the life and death of Mary, Queen of Scots, was modified in details, her character refined and brightened, Elizabeth's coarsened and darkened. The main theme is the moral elevation of the idealized character of the heroine. It is the most regularly constructed of all Schiller's plays,—technically a masterpiece and splendid in many passages of lofty thought and intense feeling. To Madame de Staël it seemed to be the most pathetic and best conceived of German dramas.

From the English-French atmosphere of Maria Stuart Schiller turned at once, as if seeking to maintain a proper balance of national interests, to the French-English scenes of his *Maid of Orleans*. This drama, *Die Jungfrau von Orleans*, was written between June 1800 and April 1801. It is in some sense less strictly historical than those just preceding, and as part of its title the author named it a Romantic Tragedy. Belonging to the Middle Ages, the subject involves miracles and idyllic elements. The simplicity of the Maid's character was especially congenial to Schiller, and hardly less so the grand and massive effects of warring armies. Purity in woman, the inspiring sway of religion and patriotism, with what power and beauty are these here portrayed !

Die Braut von Messina, our author's next drama, was completed in February 1803, after about a year's labor in working out a conception that extended back almost fifteen years. *The Bride of Messina* is a digression into the field of experiment from the main highway of Schiller's dramatic production, a digression due to the temptation of theory and perhaps partly to that unconscious desire of equilibrium suggested just above. For here Schiller attempted to pour modern spirit and feeling into the mould of the ancient Greek drama, to exalt the sway of destiny, to compress the action within the compass of but few characters, and to employ a chorus. The theme is Schiller's free invention, the tragic destruction of a family doomed by destiny through the love of two brothers for their own sister, unrecognized until it is

too late.   The attempt was as a whole unsuccessful.
The combination of the ancient and the modern elements is not sufficiently intimate, organic.   But in
stateliness of style and melody of diction, great por-
tions of it are unsurpassed by anything that Schiller
ever wrote.

The next and, alas! the last large drama of our
author was the one which is now before us, *Wilhelm
Tell*, the details of the writing of which are given
below, and elsewhere critical comment.   But the last
dramatic work which Schiller completed was the brief
lyrical play, *Homage of the Arts*, an allegory celebrat-
ing beauty and the function of the arts in ennobling
life.   How fitting that this noble expression of the
high office of art followed so immediately upon the
presentation to the nation of his *Tell*.

Of the group of great dramas which we have now
reviewed Richard Wagner said :   "Each of Schiller's
dramas from *Wallenstein* to *Tell* marks a conquest in
the domain of the unknown ideal."   *Wilhelm Tell* is
not only in the best sense the most popular of German
dramas, but also a work of art characteristic of the
classical age of German literature and a monument of
the cooperation of Goethe and Schiller.

Schiller's life has been called a drama more agitated,
attractive, and touching than any he wrote.   It is the
tragedy of the spirit, the ideal in conflict with the
material realities of earthly life, temporally seeming to
be conquered, but eternally triumphant.   The brilliant
historian Scherer has sketched it with these bold
strokes :

"Goethe, narrating the death of Achilles, makes
Athene say of him : 'Alas, that so early this fair form

shall fade from the earth, which far and wide rejoices in commonness!' And when Schiller was dead and Goethe celebrated him in song, he gave him this highest praise: 'Behind him lay in unsubstantial seeming that which subdues and fetters us all,—the common.'

"But we say: Not Achilles! Here is more than Achilles! No son of the gods, no favorite of the gods; no Thetis was his mother, no Athene protected him. In lowliness was he born, through lowliness did he drag his way for long years. Wild and vehement was his youth, rich in passion and catastrophes. His poetic talent rushed on unbridled by rule; revolutionary fury was his muse, and strong theatrical effect his guiding star. No one warned him on his way, the public hailed him with exultation, enthusiastic friendship cast itself upon his heart.

"To seek his fortune he came to Weimar. What he attained was not much,—a meager professorship in Jena, later limited means in Weimar. Soon sickness and wasting disease began to drain his physical strength.

"Yet Providence gave him three great goods—the friendship of Goethe, the love of a noble, single-hearted wife, and, what transcends even happiness in friendship and marriage, invincible elevation of soul. However long he waited, however hard he strove, however low he bowed, before one bright ray of good fortune fell upon him there still remained ever untouched within him something that had pinions and bore him safe aloft.

"The on-storming youth became a man of stable strength. First at a distance and then nearer and nearer he followed the steps of Goethe. But from the very beginning the difference between them was fundamental. Goethe found his ideals again in reality; Schiller measured reality by his ideals and found it too small. Above reality, the world of the senses, ordinary things, the commonplace, the prose of life,—above all this that Goethe named 'the common' (das Gemeine) Schiller ever sought to lift himself, and so did conquer it."

This loftiness in Schiller was so characteristic as to make ever memorable the words of the sculptor Dannecker, "I will make Schiller life-size—that is, colossal."

THE WRITING OF WILHELM TELL.

Liberty and national union are, abstractly stated, the theme of Schiller's *Wilhelm Tell*. On this theme and its beautiful treatment rests the universal and continued popularity of the drama. In it and in the origin of the play we may also find again both the union and the independence that characterized the friendship of Goethe and Schiller. The general notion of treating poetically the story of Tell was common to both poets, originating with Goethe and in some sense resigned by him in favor of Schiller, while their proposed modes of treatment were altogether independent.

When Goethe in 1797 for the third and last time traveled in Switzerland, he visited the country of the Forest Cantons, where the story of Tell impressed itself deeply upon his mind as being fit for fashioning into an epic poem. On October 14th he wrote to Schiller with keen interest, saying in part : "I feel almost sure

that the story of Tell could be treated epically, and if
I should succeed in what I contemplate, we shall have
a curious instance of a story first attaining its full
truth through poetry, instead of history being made a
fable, as generally happens.'' Schiller answered with
hearty approval, unconsciously prophetic of his own
future work : "Your idea with regard to Wilhelm Tell
is a very happy one. . . . This beautiful subject will
afford us a certain broad insight into human nature,
in the same way as between high mountains one may
often obtain a vista into the far distance." In Goethe's
letters there is further mention of the plan at intervals
until late in July, 1798, after which time other interests
seem to have suppressed this one.

In later years Goethe wrote several brief accounts
of his intended epic *Tell* and his relation to Schiller's
drama ; the italicized passages in the following quotation from Goethe's *Annals*, under the year 1804 (but
written much later), are especially important : "We
had entered into the new century. I had often talked
over the affair with Schiller, had often enough enter-
tained him with my lively description of those walls of
rock and the anguished lot of the people, *so that at
last this theme could not but shape and mould itself in
his mind according to his own fashion.* He too made
me acquainted with his views, nor did I wish to have
any part whatever in a material which had now for me
lost the charm of novelty and of immediate observation, but formally and with pleasure I resigned in his
favor all my rights and claims to the property. . . .
It will, moreover, clearly appear, when the above
representation is compared with Schiller's drama, that
the latter is wholly the author's production, and that he

*owes nothing to me except the incitement to the task and
a more vivid view of the situation than the simple legend
could have afforded him."*

Early in 1801, amid the universal curiosity as to
what dramatic subject Schiller would take up after his
now completed *Maria Stuart*, the report spread abroad
that he was writing a drama, *Tell*, while in fact he was
at work upon his *Jungfrau von Orleans*. How shall
we explain this report? Probably by assuming that
Schiller somewhat recently before this must have
expressed in conversation his strong interest in the
story of Tell and his opinion of its suitability for the
drama. At any rate we know that from December
1800 until December 1801 he had from the Weimar
Library the first two volumes of Müller's *History of
Switzerland*, containing the story of Tell. This rumor
caused many inquiries to be made of Schiller, by
publishers, theater-managers, and others, but we have
no recorded definite utterance from Schiller himself
before March, 1802, in letters to Goethe, Körner, and
his publisher, Cotta. To the latter, for example, he
then wrote, asking for an accurate map of the region
of the Forest Cantons, and added: "I have been
obliged to hear so often the false rumor that I was
writing a *Wilhelm Tell* that at last I have turned my
attention to this subject and studied Tschudi's *Chronicon Helveticum*. This work has attracted me so
much that I am now fully resolved to make a *Wilhelm
Tell*, and it shall become a play by which we shall get
honor." In September of the same year he wrote
to Körner: "Perhaps you heard it said as early as last
year that I was writing a *Wilhelm Tell*, for even
before my journey to Dresden [in August 1801]

inquiries were made of me about it from Berlin and Hamburg. I had never dreamt of it. As, however, the demand for this play was continually repeated, my attention was excited, and I began to study Tschudi's *History of Switzerland.* This was a revelation to me, for the author writes with such an honest Herodotean, nay, almost Homeric spirit that his work is able to put me into a poetic mood. . . . Although the story of Tell seems anything but favorable to dramatic treatment, since the action falls widely apart in place and in time, is mainly political, and—apart from the tale of the hat and the apple—hard to represent, still I have now so reconstructed it poetically that it has passed over from history into poetry. I need not tell you that it is a desperately hard task. . . . Yet the pillars of the building are already firmly set, and I hope to rear a substantial edifice."

In spite, however, of his interest in this subject, another one now had the first place, because of the charm of its novelty of form and because it seemed easier to finish rapidly,—*Die Braut von Messina*, written between August 1802 and February 1803. Then older subjects were once more taken up—one from the history of the Knights of Malta and one from that of the English Pretender Warbeck—and two comedies were translated from the French of Picard. These and other digressions filled up the following spring and summer and delayed the beginning of the actual writing of *Tell* until the 25th of August, 1803. During these months, Iffland, the director of the theater in Berlin, had repeatedly written to Schiller urging him to write plays of great scenic effect and appealing powerfully to the general public, and this consideration seems to have had no little weight in Schiller's final decision. Interesting extracts from his letters follow. To Iffland in July: "This work [*Tell*] shall, I hope, turn out to be in accordance with your wishes, and as a play for the people interest both the feelings and the senses." To Wilhelm von Humboldt in August: "This subject [*Tell*] is very refractory and is causing me great difficulty; but since in other respects it possesses great attraction and by reason of its popular character is so suitable to the stage, I do not shrink from the labor of mastering it." To Körner, September 12th: "I beg you to mention some good books on Switzerland, if you know of any. I am obliged to read much about the country, because the local conditions and coloring have such great significance in this subject, and I should like to have as many local features and touches as possible. If the gods are favorable to the execution of what I have in mind, it shall become a mighty work and shake the stages of Germany." To Iffland in November: "In *Tell* I am now living and moving. . . . A real play for the whole people, I promise you."

These extracts reveal to us the poet's delight in his subject, his difficulties and his desires. Having never been in Switzerland, he was obliged through laborious study of many books, maps, and illustrations to construct for his mind's eye vivid pictures of the Swiss landscape and life.* In this he was also aided by the

---

* For Swiss history and the story of Tell, Schiller's chief authority was Ägidius Tschudi's (1505–1572) *Chronicon Helveticum oder eigentliche Beschreibung der sowohl im H. Römischen Reich als besonders in einer löblichen Eidgenossenschaft vorgeloffenen Begegnussen*, which was not printed until

sympathetic descriptions which both his wife and
Goethe as eye-witnesses could give him. It was moreover not easy to mould the subject-matter into simplicity and unity, while further lesser difficulties were
caused him by ill health, by ordinary business and
social duties, by the death of Herder, and by the protracted visit in Weimar of the talented but loquacious
Frenchwoman, Madame de Staël. Favoring influences
withal were the performance in October of Shakespeare's *Julius Cæsar* and the visit in January 1804
of the Swiss historian Johannes von Müller.

But Schiller's genius and diligence were sure to
triumph over all obstacles. Early in January 1804
the first act (then containing also the first scene of
the present second act) was completed and sent to
Goethe on the 12th. February 18th saw the whole
work finished. In the middle of March it had its
first presentation, at Weimar, on the 17th, 19th, and
24th, while in the course of a few months it was performed with the greatest success at many of the best
theaters of the land. Of the performances in Berlin
in July, Iffland wrote that *Tell* had been received with

1734–36 by Iselin. But he also used freely Johannes von
Müller's *Geschichte der schweizerischen Eidgenossenschaft*,
1786, M. I. Schmidt's *Geschichte der Deutschen*, Petermann
Etterlin's *Kronika von der loblichen Eydtgnosschafft*, 1507, in
the edition of Spreng, 1752, and J. Stumpf's *Schwytzer
Chronik*, 1548. For the scenery of Switzerland and the
manners and customs of the people Schiller's principal
sources were Scheuchzer's *Naturgeschichte des Schweizer-
landes*, 1746, and its continuation of 1752, Fäsi's *Staats- und
Erdbeschreibung der ganzen helvetischen Eidgenossenschaft*,
1766, Meiner's *Briefe über die Schweiz*, 1792, and J. G. Ebel's
Schilderung der Gebirgsvölker der Schweiz, 1798–1802.

delight and that the crowds of spectators showed no
diminution. The success of the drama on the stage
was but the precursor of its wider and greater success
when issued in print. This did not occur until
October 1804, in the form of an *almanac* or annual,
adapted to serve as a Christmas or New Year's gift,
as may be seen from the facsimile of the title-page,
printed in this edition, immediately before the text.

The first edition numbered 7000 copies, of which
a portion contained one or more colored engravings.
But few months had passed before a new edition was
required ; this numbered 3000 copies. The later circulation we need not follow numerically ; in the editions of the poet's collected works, in separate editions, both German and foreign, it has gone wherever
the German language is read.* The universal and
complete success of the drama on the stage and
throughout the nation and the world then and since
is but the fulfillment of the hopes of its author and
publisher. To Körner Schiller wrote : " *Wilhelm Tell*
has produced a greater effect upon the stage than any
other play of mine " ; and to Cotta : " I have written
it with all my heart, and that which comes from the
heart will touch the heart." Cotta, returning to the
author the last proofs, wrote : " Here is the end of your
immortal *Tell*—in his time there lived real men " ;
and when the first edition was issued : " *Tell* now goes
into all the world."

Created and given to the German people when
destruction was threatened by Napoleonic tyranny,

* In the popular low-priced series of the *Universalbiblio-
thek*, published by Reclam in Leipzig, *Tell* leads by far in
circulation. More than 600,000 copies of it have been sold.

Schiller's drama *Wilhelm Tell* then and ever since
has most powerfully inspired the Germans in their
long struggle for the realization of the ideals of liberty
and union in righteousness. These ideals Schiller
himself expressed, contrasting them with the dangers
of wild revolution, in the lines with which he dedi-
cated a presentation-copy in manuscript to his friend
and patron Karl Theodor von Dalberg, Archbishop of
Mainz, Prince Elector :

> Wenn rohe Kräfte feindlich sich entzweien
> Und blinde Wut die Kriegesflamme schürt,
> Wenn sich im-Kampfe tobender Parteien
> Die Stimme der Gerechtigkeit verliert,
> Wenn alle Laster schamlos sich befreien,
> Wenn freche Willkür an das Heil'ge rührt,
> Den Anker löst, an dem die Staaten hängen :
> Da ist kein Stoff zu freudigen Gesängen.

> Doch wenn ein Volk das fromm die Herden weidet,
> Sich selbst genug, nicht fremden Guts begehrt,
> Den Zwang abwirft, den es unwürdig leidet,
> Doch selbst im Zorn die Menschlichkeit noch ehrt,
> Im Glücke selbst, im Siege sich bescheidet :
> Das ist unsterblich und des Liebes wert,
> Und solch ein Bild darf ich Dir freudig zeigen ;
> Du kennst's ; denn alles Große ist Dein eigen.

LEGEND, HISTORY, MYTH.

According to Schiller's own statement to Körner,
quoted above, it was the study of Tschudi's *Chronicon
Helveticum* that revealed to him the full poetic beauty
of the story of Tell. To this author he applies the
epithets " Herodotean," " Homeric," and that with far
greater right doubtless than he himself intended, since

Tschudi's unquestioning acceptance of legend and myth and his free use of constructive fancy are far greater than Schiller could have known them to be. Of himself Schiller moreover says that he so treated the subject-matter as to transfer it from history to poetry. From the hands of an Herodotus and of a dramatic poet of creative genius we hardly expect comprehensive, evenly balanced, accurate historical truth, and really knowledge of such historical truth is not at all necessary to the full understanding and appreciation of the drama *Wilhelm Tell* in its poetic beauty and power. But the great importance to the world of the achievement and maintenance of Swiss liberty prompts us to brief inquiry into its historical origin and basis.

LEGEND.

The popular tradition about the origin of the Swiss Confederation and the exploits of Tell is in its main outlines as follows : The land of the Forest Cantons was first settled in the time of the Romans by people who came from the far north, some from Frisia, but most from Sweden. These in time of dire famine had been chosen by lot to go forth from their beloved homes and find a new dwelling-place. They struggled on ever southward until they reached amid the Alps a lake where a storm compelled them to delay a while. On viewing the region, they were pleased with its resemblance in many features to their forsaken northern home—mountain and forest, lake and stream— and determined there to cease from wandering. The previously uninhabited shores of the lake thus became the home of freemen, the forefathers of the people of the Forest Cantons, who never acknowledged allegiance to any lord except the Emperor.* To him they ever rendered service gladly, as early as in the year 410, when they helped Emperor Alarich and the Pope to wrest Rome from heathen control, and as late as 1240 to Emperor Friedrich. But they were always honored by the Emperors and received from them many privileges and chartered liberties. In their internal affairs they governed themselves with absolute independence, except that certain matters of criminal law were left to a representative of the Emperor, who came into the land at their summons to exercise this penal jurisdiction. So free were these lands that they at times renounced all allegiance even to the Empire, thus early in the thirteenth century. Independent of each other, they were still united by treaties that were renewed at intervals. From the year 1240 on, when they of their own free will rejoined the Empire, they lived in full peace and security, until the Habsburg Duke Albrecht of Austria, on becoming German Emperor, began to attempt to make the three Cantons vassals of the Habsburg family. This he did in spite of remonstrances made by envoys from the Cantons, by sending representatives—governors, prefects, bailiffs

---

* The German sovereign, the head of the reestablished mediæval Roman-German Empire (*das Heilige Römische Reich Deutscher Nation*), in which the King of the Germans was also *ipso facto* King of Italy and Roman Emperor. In earlier times the coronation as German King took place in Aachen, as King of Italy in an Italian city, and as Emperor in Rome ; in later times there was but one coronation, in Frankfurt-am-Main. In this drama the titles *König* and *Kaiser* are both used without consistent observance of any distinction.

—who were nominally officers of the Empire, but in fact, serving only the interests of the Habsburg family, endeavored to pervert the relation of the Cantons to the Empire into a relation of vassalage to the Duke of Habsburg.

In the year 1304 Emperor Albrecht sent two such governors, one, Gessler, over Uri and Schwyz, and the other, Landenberg, over Unterwalden. The residences or strongholds of Gessler were Küssnacht in Schwyz and Altorf in Uri. Landenberg had his seat in the stronghold of Sarnen, and he placed a deputy named Wolfenschiessen in that of Rossberg. These three governors or bailiffs were all hard and cruel. Of their tyrannical outrages three typical extreme cases are recited.

In the autumn of the year 1306 Wolfenschiessen grievously insulted the wife of Baumgarten in the latter's absence, who on his return promptly killed with his axe the wicked bailiff.

In Unterwalden dwelt an intelligent and honorable freeman by the name of Heinrich von Melchthal, who had incurred the particular animosity of Landenberg. In the year 1307 his son Arnold von Melchthal committed an unimportant offence, for which Landenberg imposed upon the father as fine the loss of a yoke of oxen. Arnold, having resisted the servant who was sent for the oxen, having struck him and broken his finger, fled into Uri, where he was hidden by a relative. The governor sought him and ordered his father to deliver him up. And when the latter, through ignorance of his son's movements, was unable to do this, Landenberg caused both eyes of the aged Heinrich to be put out and confiscated much of his property.

The yeomanry were angered and Arnold planned vengeance.

While such things were happening in Unterwalden, Gessler was treating with similar harshness the people of Uri and Schwyz. In Altorf he compelled the people to aid with their own labor in the building of a stronghold with which he designed to keep the people down, and there also he set up a.pole with a hat on it, before which every passer-by was to bare his head and bow, while soldiers were stationed near to enforce obedience. This hat was the symbol of Austrian, not imperial, authority. In Schwyz, Gessler's arrogance was especially great towards the leading men of means and influence.

One of these, Werner Stauffacher, was urged by his wise wife Gertrud to form a league of his like-minded countrymen against the Austrian governors. He went to his friend Walther Fürst in Uri, where he found intense and wide-spread discontent. Here he agreed with Fürst and Arnold von Melchthal to rouse the people of the three Cantons to active resistance and the expulsion of the tyrants. These three representative leaders, each bringing ten worthy men of his own Canton, met on November 10, 1307, by night at a small meadow-clearing, the Rütli, and by solemn oath the thirty-three bound themselves to bring about a united general rising of the three lands against the governors on New Year's Day 1308, if possible without bloodshed, and in the mean time to offer no open resistance.

But on the 18th of December it chanced that a good, honest yeoman of Uri, by name Wilhelm Tell, who was a member of the Rütli-league, passed several times by the hat on the pole in Altorf without obeying the governor's order to bare his head and bow. He was therefore brought before Gessler for punishment. Now Tell was a fine marksman with the crossbow, and had handsome children whom he loved. These the governor sent for, and picking out a boy of six years, commanded Tell to hit with his arrow an apple placed on the boy's head, threatening him with loss of his life in case of refusal. On Tell's declaring that he would rather die than shoot, Gessler told him that he must shoot or both the boy and himself die. Under this cruel compulsion Tell, praying to God for protection, shot and succeeded. The governor was amazed at Tell's boldness and skill, but wondered also why Tell had placed a second arrow in readiness. To Gessler's inquiry about this Tell gave only evasive answer, until the governor assured him of his life in any event. On his then declaring that if he had hit his child with the first arrow, he would with the second have taken the governor's life, Gessler had him seized, bound, and placed in the boat with himself to be taken across the lake for life-long imprisonment in the dungeon of Küssnacht. Tell's weapons Gessler also caused to be brought into the boat, that he might keep them for himself. When now they were out on the lake a fearful storm arose and was near destroying the boat and all it carried. But one of the men told Gessler that Tell was a skillful oarsman and sailor and familiar with the lake. To Gessler's inquiry whether Tell believed he could help them out of this danger, Tell answered that with God's help he could, whereupon Gessler ordered him to be unbound and to save them. But Tell, watching his opportunity, soon seized his weapons and leaped ashore upon a projecting ledge of rock, thrusting the boat behind him out upon the tossing waves. Gessler and his men barely escaped with their lives, and landing set out on their way towards Küssnacht. Meanwhile Tell had hastened to place himself in ambush by a narrow defile of the way near Küssnacht, and here he shot Gessler through with an arrow so that the tyrant fell from his horse and died.

On New Year's Eve 1308 the plans of the Rütli-league were carried out. The strongholds Rossberg, Sarnen, and others, including the unfinished one at Altorf, were seized and destroyed, the governor Landenberg driven out, and the three lands completely freed from Habsburg-Austrian tyrants—all without bloodshed. On the following Sunday the three Waldstätte sent messengers each to the other two and swore a league for ten years, in all points identical with the original agreement between Stauffacher, Fürst, and Arnold von Melchthal.

Early in the year 1308, on May 1st, the Emperor, the Habsburg Duke Albrecht of Austria, was murdered by his nephew and certain accomplices, and the choice of a Luxemburger, Heinrich VII., as the next Emperor in place of a Habsburger, confirmed in security the reasserted liberties of the Forest Cantons.

Such in its main outlines is the popular tradition concerning the deliverance of the Forest Cantons from Austrian tyranny and the origin of the Swiss Confederation. But this popular tradition as Schiller received it, with the sanction of Tschudi and Johannes von Müller, is a blending of legend, myth, historical fact, and poetic fiction, of which all the striking features and details are unhistoric—the origin and character of the population of the Forest Cantons, their relation to the Empire, the disposition of Emperor Albrecht, the existence and mutual relations of Gessler and Tell, the sudden expulsion of tyrannous governors. The establishment of Swiss liberty and the formation of the Swiss Confederation was a slow and quasi-organic process, the essential facts of which, viewed in the light of history, are as follows.

HISTORY.

Of Switzerland or Helvetia in general the earliest inhabitants were the prehistorical hunters, cave-dwellers, and lake-dwellers, of whom numerous traces have been found. The later Celtic races were subjugated by the Romans, and during the early centuries of our era this joint population, dependent upon the Roman Empire, made some advance in civilization. From none of these peoples, however, did the population of the greater portion of historic Switzerland descend, but rather from Germanic ancestors, the Alemannic and Burgundian races. By the great waves of the migration of nations with which from the fourth to the seventh century A.D. the flood of the northern Germanic population swept against and inundated the Roman Empire, these races were carried toward the south. The heathen Alemanni were left about the year 406 in northeastern and the Christian Burgundians about the year 450 in southwestern Switzerland. The undisturbed persistence in southeastern Switzerland of the Roman-Celtic population, and the adoption on the part of the Burgundians of the Roman language and civilization, constitute the explanation of the Neo-Latin or Romance character of these parts of

the country.   But the cradle of Swiss liberty is to be
found within the limits of Germanic Switzerland.

The Alemanni maintained their customs, their language, their political institutions, and for a time their
heathen belief.   Their entire social life favored the
liberty of the individual and of the community rather
than the power of a central ruler, duke or king, and
we may almost affirm that this spirit has ever been the
soul of Swiss political life.   But the Alemanni did not
constitute a large and compactly united nation, and
therefore they could not maintain their external independence against the powerful Franks, and toward the
middle of the sixth century they became, together with
the Burgundian lands, a part of the Frankish or Merovingian kingdom.   During the following period of
Merovingian rule, the internal social life of the Alemanni remained essentially intact, except that they
became Christianized.   The Carolingian kings, however, imposed their royal authority more directly upon
the Swiss lands by subjecting them to the same administration as all the other provinces of the Frankish
realm, so that here no more liberty prevailed than
elsewhere.   By reason of the partition made in the.
year 843 the Alemannic territory became ultimately
part of the German Empire, as did Burgundian
Switzerland in the year 1032.

Moreover the three valleys of the later Forest
Cantons did not begin to be settled until after the
year 700, and not until about 850 does any authentic
document show the existence in this region of a
permanent population.   That these districts were
among the last in Switzerland to receive settlers
and be permanently inhabited was due to their in-

fertility and inaccessibility. But when the time for
settlement came, it took place under the influence
of the same causes and in the same way as elsewhere. History knows nothing of the sudden in-
trusion hither of some thousands of people, differing
in origin, character, and language from the population immediately adjacent. It rather knows that
this adjacent population supplied the earlier and the
later settlers, who gradually spread from better, lower,
more accessible sites to those that were less good,
higher, more inaccessible.

The settlement of the Forest Cantons was hastened
by three main influences: (1) that of the Emperor
through high vassals and officials; (2) that of monasteries and nobles; and (3) the enterprise of freemen,
singly or in groups. Since in URI the first of these
causes was most powerful, its population at first
consisted mostly of holders of land belonging to
the crown, who were nominally vassals, but still ap-
proached the condition of freemen. SCHWYZ was
settled mostly by freemen, who were nevertheless
subjects of the Empire, and by the side of whom there
appeared also many vassals of monasteries or of nobles.
UNTERWALDEN received its population chiefly through
the mediation of monasteries and of nobles, wherefore
there the freemen were fewer and the lesser nobility
more numerous and influential.

Thus when the three Cantons first entered into
history, they were by no means in possession of ancient and complete independence, but their political
and social condition was precisely similar to that of
the lands about them, and not until the middle of the
thirteenth century do we find any trace of any sort of

alliance between them. Between their emergence into
history and the end of the thirteenth century each of
the three districts developed independently of the
others into a more or less organized community, having a somewhat well-defined right to consider itself
free from all allegiance except to the Empire. This
development ran along continuously in opposition to
the increase of territorial possessions and power which
successive leading noble families endeavored with varying fortune to secure for themselves and their descendants. As part of the German Empire, that portion
of Switzerland with which we are now concerned
belonged to the Duchy of Alemannia or Swabia, and
was ruled by the Dukes of Zähringen until this
family died out in the year 1218. Had this family
lived and ruled a century or two longer, it is probable
that Switzerland would have become not a federal
republic, but a principality and later a kingdom.
In the struggle for the lands and power left by the
Zähringers the ducal dynasties of Savoy in the west,
of Kiburg and Habsburg in the east, took part until,
by inheritance, by marriage, by force, and by cunning,
the house of Habsburg absorbed the territory and
power of Kiburg and other lesser families, and, check-
ing the rise of Savoy, made itself, in the person of
Duke Rudolf, who was elected German Emperor in
the year 1273, the controlling influence in land and
power, notably in the regions all about and to a great
extent within the Forest Cantons.

If we now briefly review the historic growth of the
liberties of the Forest Cantons, we shall be prepared
to understand the final conflict between the Swiss and
the Habsburg power.

URI was chronologically the first to appear on the stage and to begin Swiss history in the narrower sense. In the year 853 Ludwig the German donated to the newly founded Abbey of Our Lady in Zürich all the crown-lands with their inhabitants in the district of Thurgau. This included the valley of Uri (*pagellus Uroniæ*). In his deed of gift Ludwig ordained that all the occupants of these lands should stand under the jurisdiction of the bailiffs or governors (Vögte) representing the Abbey and the realm which later became the German Empire. The larger portion of the population of Uri came thus to be vassals of the Abbey and at the same time to stand in a certain immediate relation to the crown. But to be vassal of an ecclesiastical foundation was to be nearly free. Moreover the entire population of Uri, however manifold its class-distinctions were, formed one large community in so far as it still, in the ancient Germanic manner, held and used all unfiefed land in common. To administer this land, regular although infrequent assemblies of the community occurred, in which gradually the consciousness of political as well as economic unity could hardly fail to develop. Here then are the two roots of the liberty and the unity of Uri.

Shortly after the year 1200 Uri began to act in matters of purely local interest somewhat as a self-governing community. Its budding liberty was threatened by the last Duke of Zähringen, who was the governor (Vogt) in the name of the Abbey and the Empire, but this danger was removed by the Duke's death in 1218. Immediately thereafter Emperor Friedrich seems to have taken the Abbey-lands in Uri for a time into direct dependence upon himself as Emperor, which relation would of itself sooner or later have led to complete political liberation. But before long we find Uri under the elder Duke Rudolf of Habsburg, to whom it was probably given by the Emperor as a fief in return for the Duke's promise of support. By this change Uri was in danger of losing its privileges of immunity from all jurisdiction except that of the Emperor, and of becoming a land subject to the Habsburgs as their hereditary possession.

Here we have the all-important distinction, so often referred to in the drama, between the immediate (unmittelbar) and the mediate (mittelbar) relation to the Empire. The Reichsunmittelbarkeit or dependence on the Emperor alone as liege lord was a loose bond of attachment and would not naturally lead to the hereditary lordship of any one family. On the other hand, the mediate relation to the Empire through direct dependence upon some lord who himself was, nominally at least, a vassal of the Emperor, involved very strict subjection to this lord, hereditary vassalage to his family and the prospect of no political liberties. This then was the question which received its final answer only after a long period of development and conflict: Will the Habsburgs, Dukes of Austria, be able by force or by guile to transform the loose and non-hereditary dependence of the Swiss territories upon themselves as Emperors (first Rudolf, 1273–1291, and then Albrecht, 1298–1308) into the relation of hereditary vassalage to themselves as Dukes of Austria?

Immediate danger of this subjection was removed from Uri by Heinrich, the son of Friedrich, who in the year 1231 redeemed the men of Uri from vassalage to the elder Rudolf of Habsburg, and by a formal charter engaged that they should forever remain in direct dependence upon the Empire, and never be separated therefrom, either by fief or by mortgage. This charter of Uri of the year 1231 is the real corner-stone of the constitutional liberty of Switzerland. A few years later we find in Uri an Ammann or chief-magistrate, chosen from its inhabitants, and in 1243 Uri employed an official seal. Shortly after his election as Emperor, Rudolf of Habsburg, in the year 1274, formally confirmed the rights and liberties of the charter of 1231, and these seem to have been enjoyed without any open and violent encroachments upon them during Rudolf's long reign until his death in 1291.

SCHWYZ could not long remain unaffected by the developments in Uri. Its inhabitants were mostly freemen, of strong and self-reliant character, who were not likely to view with indifference the large posses-sions of the Habsburgs in their valley, and the ill-defined, easily expansible rights of lordship which the latter assumed. In the year 1240 a favorable occasion seemed to the men of Schwyz to present itself. From Emperor Friedrich II., then at Faenza in Italy, they obtained a charter granting them the same privileges of dependence solely upon the Empire which the charter of 1231 had secured to Uri. This charter was never fully acknowledged by the Habsburgs, but in the year 1273 Rudolf of Habsburg, as Emperor, him-self granted by charter certain privileges to Schwyz, which was almost equivalent to recognizing it as a community dependent only upon the Empire. Yet for Schwyz also the danger of passing into complete hereditary vassalage to the Habsburg family was ever present until the death of Rudolf in the year 1291.

In UNTERWALDEN, owing to the relatively small number of freemen, to the partition of the land among a large number of petty nobles and ecclesiastical holdings, to the great variety of jurisdictions and to distinct rights of the Habsburgs to lordship there, the development of a community with privileges and rights was much delayed. Nevertheless the men of Unterwalden did take some part against the Habsburgs in the imperial-papal conflict of the middle of the thirteenth century. With Schwyz and Luzern they made a defensive league in 1246, which is the earliest known, and probably is the "ancient confederation" of which the treaty of 1291 makes mention. Indeed, it may be that the struggles during the last years of Emperor Friedrich's reign gave rise to the traditions of the Rütli-oath, the expulsion of the governors, and the destruction of castles, and furnished the immediate basis of the development of the Swiss Confederation. Unterwalden, however, at the death of Emperor Rudolf in 1291 had still no charter, and only with far greater fear than the men of Uri or Schwyz could its people view their relation to the Habsburgs, whose power seemed destined ever to increase.

All the previous political development of the Forest Cantons, their hopes and their fears, are centered in the league of 1291, the document declaring which is the written Magna Charta of Switzerland. Heretofore the Waldstätte had for the most part acted individually, henceforth they were federated for common action. The liberties which they all possessed although in different degrees, they now combined to defend and to secure equally for all. This feeling and purpose, intensified by the general fear, caused by the death of Emperor Rudolf, of a return of the dangers and struggles of the middle of the century, brought the two parts of Unterwalden into full sympathy with Schwyz and Uri. Only seventeen days after the Emperor's death, on August 1st, 1291, the representatives of the three Cantons concluded and signed their ever-memorable compact.*

But this document shows no such open rebellious, revolutionary spirit as the traditional story would lead us to expect. In principle it was indeed directed against the power and authority of the Habsburg family, and in spirit it was somewhat independent, but in form and tone it was very conservative and moderate. It declared the aim of the league to be the preservation of the existing conditions, and expressly enjoined obedience on the part of every one to his lawful lord. Neither the property-rights of the Habsburgs nor their rights of lordship were openly disputed. An alliance for defense and offense was formed, and the administration of justice was regulated in important respects; in particular it was

---

* The first lines (incomplete because of the width of the manuscript) of this remarkable document are here reproduced in facsimile. In the Appendix, pp. 287–289, may be found the Latin in full of these lines and an English translation of the whole. The venerable original—the cornerstone of the constitutional Confederation—is preserved in the archives of Schwyz. The older writers—even Tschudi —were unaware of its existence. It was published in 1760, but not appreciated by Müller or anyone before the labors of J. E. Kopp, 1835. The six-hundredth anniversary of its signing was solemnly celebrated in 1891.

agreed that the Cantons would accept no judge (i.e., Ammann) who was not one of their own people, and that they would themselves assume jurisdiction of criminal offenses. In these matters, indeed, limits were thus set to the sovereign rights of any lord. Herein and in the perpetual duration which was pledged to the obligations of the treaty was latent the character of a revolutionary declaration of independence, which was made effective, however, only by the conflicts and victories of subsequent years.

The immediate successor of Rudolf as German Emperor was not his son Albrecht nor any other Habsburg, but Adolf of Nassau, 1292–1298, with whom, however, Albrecht disputed the imperial throne. The Swiss sided naturally with Adolf, from whom in 1297 Schwyz and Uri obtained the confirmation of their liberties as granted by the charter given to Schwyz in 1240 by Friedrich II. But Adolf was unable to maintain his position, was deposed by the Electors, and killed in battle against Albrecht, who succeeded him as Emperor in 1298.

The accession of the Habsburg Albrecht, Duke of Austria, to the imperial throne made the situation of the Forest Cantons to be the same again as under Emperor Rudolf. Their natural defense against encroachments from Habsburg-Austria—the imperial authority—was now in the hands of the chief of the Habsburg family, to say nothing of the large private rights of this family in Switzerland. As Rudolf steadily but without gross violence had furthered the interests of his dynasty, so it was to be expected that Albrecht would endeavor energetically to widen and strengthen the hold of Habsburg upon Switzerland, to restrict and finally to annul the moderate liberties already won. The authentic history of his reign, 1298–1308, does not, however, show this to have taken place in any harsh and cruel way. He was, in the interest both of the Empire and of his family, a strict but not an unjust or violent ruler. He loved law and order and confirmed the liberties of various cities in Switzerland, but the charters of Adolf to Schwyz and Uri he did not renew. During his reign, however, nothing in any way extraordinary occurred between him and the Forest Cantons ; no trace of hateful rigor can be found in any of the places under his jurisdiction ; no change took place in the administration of the affairs of the Cantons, except indeed that Unterwalden arrived at the same measure of liberty and independence as Uri and Schwyz. In none of these Cantons did a foreign governor appear ; the chief-magistrate in each was an Ammann chosen from its inhabitants. Of direct or indirect tyrannous repression on the part of Albrecht and of rebellion on the part of the inhabitants of the Cantons the authentic history of the time knows nothing. Albrecht's bearing even to the end of his reign, and that of his sons immediately after his death, showed the fullest confidence in the friendliness of the Cantons, while the people of Uri no long time after his death declared themselves to be "good friends of their highnesses, the Dukes of Austria."

Nevertheless the reign of Albrecht, against whose great power they were unable to do anything, was for the Cantons a period of repression of their aspirations for greater freedom. From this painful situation they were released by the assassination of Emperor Albrecht, which was wrought not by any inhabitant of

the Cantons, but by his own nephew * and other
noblemen of his court.   The Forest Cantons thus
slipped once more from the house of Habsburg, as on
the death of Rudolf.   For Albrecht's successor,
Heinrich VII. of Luxemburg, was jealous of the great
power of the Habsburgs, and in the summer of 1309
at Constanz he confirmed the charters given by Friedrich II. and Adolf to Uri and Schwyz, and formally
extended their privileges to Unterwalden.   At the
same time he united the three lands under one governor, and granted them immunity from the jurisdiction of all courts outside their borders, with the exception of the imperial court, thus pledging to them
one of the most important constitutional rights of the
time.   The hopes of the alliance of the year 1291—
union and the greatest possible independence—thus
received the sanction of the Emperor.   The Dukes
of Austria could not consistently recognize this action,
and persistently urged their rights.   Heinrich VII.
died in 1313.   In 1314 Ludwig of Bavaria was chosen
Emperor by the majority and Friedrich of Austria by
the minority of the Electors.   The Forest Cantons at
once recognized the supremacy of Ludwig, as their
natural ally against Austria, and he displayed great
friendliness towards them.   In an edict issued by him
in 1315 we find the three Cantons designated for the
first time as a community and recognized as a distinct

---

* Johannes Parricida or Johannes von Schwaben, born in
1290, was son of Duke Rudolf II. of Swabia and grandson
of Emperor Rudolf of Habsburg.   Both his parents died
early and he grew up at the court of his mother's father,
Ottokar of Bohemia.   The account given of him in this
drama is essentially historical.

political union. But the power of Ludwig not being yet secure, Friedrich issued a decree assigning to his own family the possession of the Waldstätte. This decree Friedrich's brother, Leopold II., engaged to execute by force of arms. In October 1315 he assembled at Baden in Aargau a brilliant host of nobles and of burghers, and in November marched proudly forth, directing his attack chiefly against Schwyz. But on the 15th of November in the narrow defile of Morgarten the sturdy Swiss freemen, heroically defending their liberties, surprised and utterly destroyed the main body of the Austrian forces, while the rest, learning of this disaster, fled the land. Soon afterwards the Forest Cantons under date of December 9th, 1315, at Brunnen, renewed the compact of 1291, changing its character and scope as the changed conditions demanded and warranted. This victory and this treaty consummated the foundation of the Swiss Confederation.*

* The Confederation was confirmed by the famous victories of later generations, e.g., those alluded to in lines 2438 ff. and mentioned in the Notes thereto, and enlarged by the accession of the following Cantons in the years indicated: Lucerne, 1332; Zürich, 1351; Glarus, 1352; Zug, 1352; Bern, 1353. The preceding five with the original three Forest Cantons constituted *Die Acht Alten Orte* (*Cantons*). With these eight the following five made *Die Dreizehn Alten Orte* (*Cantons*), of which with eleven associated Cantons the Confederation consisted until the year 1798: Freiburg, 1481; Solothurn, 1481; Basel, 1501; Schaffhausen, 1501; Appenzell, 1501. The disturbances of the revolutionary and Napoleonic period found their conclusion in the adoption in 1814 of the present constitution, under which the Confederation consists of twenty-two Cantons.

We have now before us the main outlines, on the one hand, of the popular tradition, and, on the other, of the real facts as drawn from contemporary sources. It remains to indicate in general the stages of the former's growth.

As to all the picturesque dramatic features in which the legend here deviates from fact, all the contemporary annalists and chroniclers who touch upon Swiss affairs are absolutely silent. Oral tradition and the common imagination of the people require long periods of time in which to do their work of rearranging, reconstructing, embellishing, and so it is not until about a century after the battle of Morgarten, when its story had been retold by five or six generations, that we find the first addition of legendary matter and coloring in a written history.

Conrad Justinger of Bern wrote about the year 1420 a chronicle of Bern in which he gave also an account of the political origin of the Forest Cantons and of the causes of their liberation. In his conscientious but confused treatment of the main historical facts, as given above, he makes mention, evidently based on oral statements of the common people, of tyrannous and outrageous acts of foreign governors,—but all this in the most general terms. He also makes the liberties of these Cantons and their alliance to be of very ancient date.

It is also in the first half of the fifteenth century that first appears the attempt to construct a special genealogy and by their alleged remote and ancient origin to distinguish the inhabitants of the Forest

Cantons from their neighbors and to reinforce their claim to independence from time immemorial. Even if we suppose that a faint recollection remained of the migration of the Alemanni from the north nearly a thousand years before, still the specific form of the later legend is in every case plainly the arbitrary creation of learned men, whose ignorance and caprice were prompted by national vanity. In a chronicle which he is said to have written about 1414, Johann Püntiner of Uri made the inhabitants of the Forest Cantons to be descendants of the Goths. An official document of Schwyz dated 1443 formally indorses certain details of his statement. But what may be called the classical version of the legend of a Scandinavian origin, as accepted by Tschudi, Müller, and Schiller, is due to the imagination of Johannes Fründ of Schwyz, who felt himself called to defend his fellow-countrymen from the imputation of being common peasants. His account is richly adorned with picturesque details of incidents, names, and places. But the glory which the fancies of Fründ created for Schwyz necessarily evoked the destructive envy and the constructive imitation of others. Thus, for example, Felix Hemmerlin of Zürich, about 1450, declared the inhabitants of Schwyz to be the descendants of Saxon prisoners of war, transported thither by Karl the Great. Still others derived the population of the Cantons from Cimbrians, Tauricians, Ostro-Goths, Vikings, yes, that of Unterwalden even from Romans driven from home by civil war.

Hemmerlin appears also among the creators of the legendary account of the foundation of the Confederation itself. His historical ignorance is greater than

Justinger's, but he adds in incidents, in names of persons and localities, details which are borrowed from him literally in 1487 by Felix Faber of Zürich. Although the legend thus had begun to be more definite and concrete, none of these writers made mention of tyranny on the part of Albrecht, of outrages of his governors, of conspirators at the Rütli, of Tell. To Uri indeed Hemmerlin gave no place in his account of the Confederation.

Directly contradicting Hemmerlin, the *Tellenlied*, an historical ballad, written in Lucerne about 1470, ascribes to Uri and to Wilhelm Tell alone the creation of the Confederation. This " manifesto of Uri's claims," so distinctly fictitious and fanciful, is a striking example of the part played by individual caprice and partisan pride in the elaboration of the legend which we are considering. The specifically Urner version early received full development at the hands of Melchior Russ of Lucerne. His chronicle, written from 1482 to 1488, contains a literal repetition of Justinger's narrative, into the middle of which is inserted the story of Tell as given in the Lied, but with much expansion of detail. This Urner version is in plain conflict with that later generally accepted, which developed about the same time.

The first connected presentation of all the important features of this legendary cycle in a form similar to that universally accepted later was made in the so-called *White Book* of Sarnen, or of Obwalden. This is a chronicle written about 1470, probably by Hans Schriber of Obwalden, who may have copied an older manuscript now lost. This author had but slight knowledge of real facts, but great ability to distort, confuse, and invent. He was a literary artist in so far as that in reciting the examples of outrages on the part of the governors, he distributed them equally among the three Cantons and the three divisions of the Tenth Commandment—house, wife, ox. The story of Tell is introduced and amplified, but in subordination to the joint action of the Cantons under the leadership of Schwyz. Still the legend as given in the *White Book* lacks foundation and cohesion. No dates are given on which it may rest firmly. Few names occur, and those which are mentioned are very indefinite. There is much looseness, vagueness, and confusion,

The two conflicting—not to say contradictory—forms of the legend, the specific Uri-Tell form and the more general form of the *White Book*, existed long side by side, until both were finally modified and blended. The Uri-Tell form (adopted with arbitrary modifications by Diebold Schilling of Lucerne in 1512 and by Loriti of Glarus in 1515) was embellished with further details in a play written in Uri about the year 1512 and published in 1540, *Ein hüpsch spyl gehalten zu Ury in der Eydgenoszschaft von dem Wilhelm Thellen ihrem landtmann und ersten eydtgenossen.* About this time appeared the last learned author to write an account of the origin of the Confederation without connecting therewith the story of Tell, the outrages in Unterwalden, the person of Stauffacher, and the meeting at the Rütli. This was Mutz or Mutius of Basel in his chronicle published in 1539. He silently rejected much of the growing legends. On the other hand, Johann Stumpf of Zürich, in his chronicle published in 1548, following mainly the Uri version, freely accepted and modified the legends without agreeing with any of his predecessors nor indeed with himself entirely. He assigned Tell's deed to the year 1314.

But the contradictions, the variations, and the vagueness of the legends in their previous growth were to disappear under the hands of later writers, who gradually elaborated the canonical form of the entire legendary cycle out of the material furnished by the *White Book*. The first in this work was Petermann Etterlin of Lucerne, whose chronicle, published in 1507, first made the story of the manuscript *White Book* more widely known. In the main Etterlin copied his authority very closely, introducing, however, greater precision and probability in some details and in others making arbitrary, groundless changes. He names Gessler always Grissler. Instead of Tall he has Wilhelm Tell. For Rütli he has Betlin. He changed Melchi into Melchthal, thus confusing two entirely distinct and unlike localities.

Ägidius [Gilg] Tschudi of Glarus (1505–1572) substantially completed the condensing, clarifying, and unifying of the hitherto vague and discordant legends into the form whose main outlines are given above. He was a high official and a learned man, who devoted many years to writing his historical works, of which the most important was his Chronicon Helveticum. This was not printed until 1734–36, but was used in manuscript and closely followed by nearly all writers after him. "The circumstances, the dates, the persons are the three elements of the national legend which received from Tschudi a degree of precision which they had not previously attained. . . . By thus giving a natural impress and a self-evident reason to every detail, by endeavoring with captivating accuracy to arrange the events in definite sequence, by employing in his characterization of the situation, the rôle, the language of the persons a skillfully combined mixture of real and invented elements, he gave to the legend that degree of probability which brings the mind of the reader into unsuspecting repose and makes him accept all that is told him. Tschudi presents all his material with such richness of expression, such simplicity and candor that we are deceived thereby. The more he invents, the more readily do we believe him." (Rilliet.)

Tschudi's version was adopted by Heinrich Bullinger in his unprinted chronicle, and gained wide diffusion by the work of Josias Simler of Zürich, printed in 1576, *Vom Regiment der löblichen Eidgenossenschaft*. During the seventeenth and eighteenth centuries some unimportant details were added from various sources. With these additions and some independent modifications Tschudi's account received its modern popular form in the classical history of Johannes von Müller (1752–1809), *Die Geschichte Schweizerischer Eidgenossenschaft*, 1786.

MYTH.

The most beautiful part of this Swiss national tradition, whose growth has just been sketched, is that which was earliest discredited and which, as the most thorough investigations of the best scholars in recent time have shown, has the least foundation of historic fact—the person and the exploits of Tell. The Swiss historian Franz Guillimann of Freiburg in the year

1607 based his conviction that the story of Tell was a pure fable upon the now incontestable fact that as to the person of Tell not the slightest documentary proof existed. Other writers during the seventeenth and eighteenth centuries were similarly sceptical, although their attacks upon the general national credulity were repulsed for the time by a host of forged documentary "proofs," and finally by the overwhelming authority of Johannes von Müller. But the new historical spirit and methods of our century, through the conscientious labors of Kopp, Vischer, Wyss, Meyer von Knonau, Oechsli, Vaucher, Bernouilli, Rilliet, and others, have brought about an impartial, passionless, definitive separation of historic fact from legend and myth, and have assigned Tell and his shot to the realm of myth and poetry where he lives in immortal beauty.

The story of Tell is not found recorded until toward the end of the fifteenth century in the *Tellenlied* and the *White Book*. In the utter absence of other information or proof about Tell, the resemblance between this story and what is narrated by an earlier mediæval historian, whose work just before this time became known in Germany and Switzerland, is so close as to justify us in seeking no further for the source of this tale of the archer-hero. And that a most ancient myth is the ultimate source of this historian's account is proved by the existence in almost all parts of the world of similar stories—not only among all the Germanic peoples, in Germany, England, Scandinavia, Iceland, but also in Italy, Greece, Persia, India, and even in non-Aryan lands.

The historian just referred to was the Dane Saxo Grammaticus, who lived in the twelfth century and, nearly a hundred and fifty years before the alleged exploit of Tell, wrote his *Historia Danorum Regum Heroumque.* Saxo tells his story of a certain Toko (also Tokko, Palna Toko, and Palnatoki), a soldier in the army of King Harald Blaatand (Bluetooth) in the tenth century. Toko once boasted to his comrades at a feast that he was so skillful with the bow as to hit far off with the first arrow an apple ever so small, fastened on a stick. Envious rivals reported this utterance to the king, who wickedly ordered the apple to be laid on the head of Toko's own son, and declared that if the father did not hit the apple with the first arrow, his life should be forfeited as a punishment for his boasting. Toko had to obey, stationed his son, admonished him not to move his head at the noise of the arrow, and turned the boy's face from him. Then taking three arrows from his quiver, Toko placed one upon his bow and shooting hit the apple with this first arrow. To the king's inquiry hereupon why he had taken out three arrows, when he was required to shoot only one, he replied: "In order to kill you who give to others such cruel commands, that is, in case I had missed with the first shot." Toko was also an expert skater (as Tell a boatsman) and was forced by the king to a trial of his skill that endangered his life. Finally, in revenge for the wrongs and insults which the king had done him, Toko from an ambush mortally wounded the king with an arrow (as Tell slays Gessler).

Of all the numerous forms in which this archer-story appears with great variations in names and incidents, this Danish version is the only one which is altogether similar to the oldest Swiss form of the Tell story.

The conclusion is hard to resist, that Saxo's work, or the extract (containing the apple-story) made from it about 1430 by a German monk, Gheysmer, became known to some Swiss scholar of the fifteenth century, who simply transferred this archer-hero to Swiss soil and made him the champion of Uri's claims to the first place in the achievement of Swiss liberty. It is also possible that the ancient Germanic myth had been kept alive in some form by oral tradition among the common people, after having been brought by their ancestors from their northern home, and that this popular tradition, alone or through its adoption and reconstruction by some scholar acquainted with Saxo's history, was the origin of our Tell.*

The most natural explanation of both the relationship and the wide distribution of these archer-stories

---

* We have little fact and much conjecture as to the origin and significance of the name Wilhelm Tell. A noted Swiss historian is authority for the statement that the name Wilhelm perhaps does not occur a single time in the historical documents of the Forest Cantons. It is then not impossible that this name is due to the borrowing by some learned man of the name of the hero of the similar story told in the old English ballad of William of Cloudesly. The second name appears in various forms, Tell, Täll, Thell, Thall, Tall, of which the last seems to have been the earliest. In the *White Book* the definite article always stands before the form Thall or Tall, and the author evidently understood it to mean "foolish," "simple" (cf. 1. 1872). In this sense the word would be connected with the words *dalen* or *talen*, 'to talk or act foolishly,' and with *toll*, "mad" (*Eng.* "dull"). Jacob Grimm connected Tell in the sense of "archer" with the Latin word *telum*, "arrow"; it is also conceivable that a learned man of the fifteenth century should have made this fanciful construction.

is that they are all variant developments of one and the same primitive nature-myth. The oldest element of this myth is the sunbeam or the lightning-bolt conceived as an arrow and shot forth by the god Wotan or Odin, as sun-god or summer-god, in conflict with and destruction of storm-cloud and winter, conceived as the common enemies of mankind.

POETIC TREATMENT.

Schiller did not merely passively receive his material from Müller and Tschudi, but, as he himself said, he reconstructed it poetically.

For some features of this reconstruction he was indebted to earlier dramas. Of these the earliest were the old Urner play already mentioned and its revision by Jacob Ruef in the year 1545. Of the others, all written after 1760, the most important are these : the French tragedy, *Guillaume Tell*, in alexandrine verse of Lemierre in 1767 ; the four dramas of the Swiss J. J. Bodmer in 1775,—(1) *Wilhelm Tell oder der gefährliche Schuss*, (2) *Gesslers Tod oder das erlegte Raubtier*, (3) *Der alte Heinrich von Melchthal oder die ausgetretenen Augen*, (4) *Der Hass der Tyrannei und nicht der Person, oder Sarne durch List eingenommen ;* the three plays of Joh. Ludwig Am Bühl,—(1) *Der Schweizerbund*, 1779, (2) *Hans von Schwaben oder Kaiser Alberts Tod*, 1784, (3) *Wilhelm Tell, ein schweizerisches Nationalschauspiel*, 1792. Further may be mentioned J. I. Zimmermann's *Wilhelm Tell*, 1777, A. G. Meissner's *Johann von Schwaben* and F. R. Crauer's *Kaiser Albrechts Tod*, both in 1780, J. B. Petri's *Der Dreybund*, 1791. The detailed comparison of Schiller's drama with these its predecessors would only define without diminishing Schiller's originality. The following very general observations need only be made here. Of Melchthal, Stauffacher, and Fürst the essential traits occur in earlier plays. Attinghausen was elevated by Schiller, who also improved upon the earlier Rudenz. Of Bertha only the name occurred. Rudolf der Harras and the two soldiers who guard the hat were individualized by Schiller. Bodmer gave the name Hedwig to Tell's wife, who was introduced by Ruef and Lemierre. In the *Schweizerbund* of Am Bühl occurred the names Mechtilde, Stauffacher's wife ; Gertrud, Tell's wife ; and Bertha. These all reappear with Schiller, but are given to different characters.

Whether now Schiller drew his materials from legend, myth, historical and descriptive writings, earlier dramas, oral reports of others, or whencesoever, he so blended and transmuted them by the magic power of his poetic genius that his *Wilhelm Tell* is in the best sense his original creation. The archer-hero, the men of the Rütli, the liberty of the Forest Cantons, and the legendary origin of the Swiss Confederation, though dead to history, still live immortal "in the transfiguration into which Schiller has exalted them."

DRAMATIC STRUCTURE.

A drama is a scenic representation of an action (plot) of persons (characters) from its first inward inception to its final full accomplishment. This action ought to be *one* action, i.e., the drama ought to have unity of action. Since many critics have urged that

Schiller's *Tell* is especially defective in this chief respect, the question needs to be briefly considered.

It must indeed be granted that this play does not possess the simplest unity of having a single person as the all-dominating hero of a simple plot, for, in spite of the title, Tell is not in this sense its hero. The whole people of the Forest Cantons is the hero of this drama, and the one action which runs its course before our eyes is the achievement of deliverance from Austrian oppression and of united liberty. Since in this action all the people take part, the nobles must be represented no less than the yeoman or peasant class, both free and unfree. Moreover in such a struggle much room necessarily exists for the daring exploits of individual persons, which the single man Wilhelm Tell so beautifully exemplifies.

We are then in this drama to look for complex threefold unity : the *whole* people,—(1) as individuals exemplified by Tell, (2) in its sturdy yeomanry represented by those who enter into the Rütli-league, and (3) in its nobility represented by Attinghausen and Rudenz. In other words, the unity of action of this play is to be found in the blending of three partial plots,—the Tell-plot, the Yeomen-plot, and the Nobles-plot,—and in proportion as our conception of the play shall find these blended into unity shall we do justice to the play and its author.* This is the point of view

* What is here named the Nobles-plot has been most often called the Rudenz-plot or the Rudenz-Bertha plot, for which practice there is to be sure considerable justification in the author's manifest delight in the episode of the love of these two characters. But the designation "Nobles-plot" gives due importance to the rôle of Attinghausen, assigns a more fitting place to the persons and characters

of the following brief analysis, and of the running comment on action and character distributed through the Notes.

Schiller's *Wilhelm Tell* is a " Schauspiel," i.e., neither a tragedy nor a comedy but a serious drama, in which the hero is finally victorious. In construction, however, the serious drama does not differ essentially from the tragedy. According to the generally accepted view † the regular. drama is composed of five main parts, usually but not necessarily coinciding with the acts. These parts are :

1. The *Exposition*, in which we are acquainted with the place, the time, the leading characters, the nature and importance of that conflict of interest, in which every drama centers. The exposition naturally consists of an Initial Chord (or Dramatic Overture), a detailed scene (or scenes) of Exposition proper, and a transition to the Initial Impulse (see below).

2. The *Ascending Action*, in which the conflict of

of Rudenz and Bertha, and makes it easier to find the harmonious unity of all the parts of the drama (*cf. Notes, pp.* 259, 260). A careful review of the references to Attinghausen and of the scenes in which he appears can hardly fail to bring the conviction that he is, to say the least, not inferior in importance to Rudenz. A further weighty consideration is the difficulty of supposing that Schiller, in view of the very patent relation of the subject-matter of Tell to the political conditions of the poet's own time and country, could have intended to depict a national uprising and liberation in which the nobility had no equal part.

† This view is best presented in G. Freytag's *Technik des Dramas*, of which an English translation by E. J. MacEwan under the title *Technique of the Drama* is published by Scott, Foresman & Co., Chicago.

interest becomes, by one stage or by several stages, more clear and intense, until is reached

3. The *Climax*, in which the result of the ascending action distinctly appears, the conflict of interest is most intense, and something happens that we immediately perceive to be decisive for the final outcome of this conflict.

4. The *Descending Action*, in which by one or by several stages the conflict of interest sinks to its final adjustment. (In tragedy this is the decline of the hero's fortune.)

5. The *Catastrophe*, the final adjustment of the conflict of interest, the natural and effective ending of the action. (In tragedy this requires usually the death of the hero, by which the Catastrophe is sharply distinguished from the Descending Action. In *Tell* the Descending Action is more gradually resolved into the Catastrophe.)

Connecting these five main parts there may also be three less extensive but very intensive scenes :

1. The *Initial Impulse*, which brings the conflict of interest into active play.

2. The *Tragic Crisis*, some unexpected but reasonable result of previously known causes, occurring usually soon after the Climax and of decisive importance for the conflict of interest.

3. The *Final Reaction*, a last hindering or retarding of the subsidence of the conflict of interest. (In tragedy a brief reaction in favor of the hero's fortune.) Of these three minor parts the first is essential, the last two are not and indeed are not distinct in *Tell*.

The relation of the eight parts just described is exhibited thus :

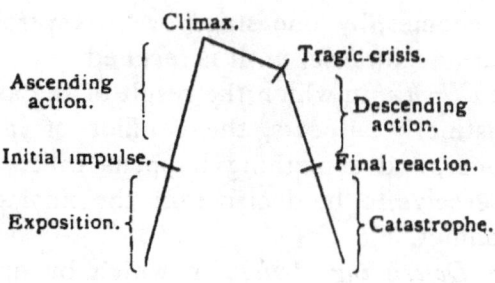

Since Act I would otherwise be too long, a part of the Exposition of *Wilhelm Tell* is found in Act II. The idyllic landscape and peaceful life with the quickly following storm strike strong and sweet the Initial Chord, the keynotes of the mood that suits this drama. The Exposition then quickly introduces the action proper, beginning with the

TELL-PLOT.

I. 1. EXPOSITION and transition to Initial Impulse, in the conversation of the men and Baumgarten's appeal.

INITIAL IMPULSE. Tell's rescue of Baumgarten keenly excites our interest in him personally, while it is plain that it will provoke the wrath of the governors against him.

I. 3. ASCENDING ACTION. *First Stage.* Conversation of Tell with Stauffacher in view of Keep Uri and the hat borne about upon the pole.

III. 1. *Second Stage.* Tell's home. Hedwig's forebodings. Tell's recital of his fateful meeting with Gessler and departure for Altorf, where we must expect Gessler to be.

III. 3. CLIMAX. The shooting at the apple.

TRAGIC CRISIS. This is here in some degree represented by Gessler's arresting Tell and taking him away for imprisonment, which is perhaps rather to be viewed as a preparatory stage of the descending action.

IV. 1. DESCENDING ACTION. *First Stage.* Tell's escape from the boat.

IV. 3. *Second Stage.* Tell's shooting Gessler.

FINAL REACTION. (Not represented.)

IV. 3 and V. 2, 3. CATASTROPHE. In some sense the Tell-plot ends with the death of Gessler, but we do not reach the final adjustment of his conflict until we see him permanently united in peace and happiness with his family and his people.

YEOMEN-PLOT.

I. 2. EXPOSITION. Conversation of Stauffacher with his wife Gertrud, in which her arguments and appeals are in contrast with the brief introductory words of Pfeifer. Stauffacher's decision to confer with Fürst and Attinghausen is the transition to the

I. 4. INITIAL IMPULSE. The blinding of Melchthal's father—this new unparalleled outrage—impels the three men who had come together only for counsel, to that action which is also the

ASCENDING ACTION. The formation of the alliance of Stauffacher, Fürst, and Melchthal and the plan of the Rütli-meeting.

II. 2. CLIMAX. The renewal at the Rütli of the old confederation to maintain their ancient liberty and to overthrow all tyranny.

TRAGIC CRISIS. (Not represented.)

III. 3. DESCENDING ACTION. *First Stage.* The behavior of the yeomen in connection with Tell's arrest and his shooting at the apple.

IV. 2. *Second Stage.* The nobles—in the persons of Attinghausen and Rudenz—recognize the independent action of the yeomen, while Rudenz and Melchthal resolve together to begin to execute the plans of the Rütli-meeting.

V. 1. *Third Stage.* Accomplishment of the Rütliplans to reassert and maintain their liberty in (*a*) the expulsion of the governors and the destruction of the strongholds, and (*b*) the death of the Emperor.

FINAL REACTION. (Not represented.)

V. 1 and 3. CATASTROPHE. These events and the concluding picture are a guarantee of permanent freedom, unity, and peace.

NOBLES-PLOT.

II. 1. EXPOSITION. After brief preliminary mention of Attinghausen in I. 1, 2, and 4, the exposition proper in II. 1. Schiller's original intention was to place it in I, but this would have made that act too long. The transition to the initial impulse is the purpose of Rudenz to go to Altorf, and his departure thither.

III. 2. INITIAL IMPULSE. The mutual explanation between Bertha and Rudenz makes clear to the latter the conflict of his interest in patriotism and love with the Austrian purposes which he has been blindly favoring.

III. 3. ASCENDING ACTION. Rudenz, representing the younger nobility, begins actively to place himself on the side of the yeomen, his countrymen.

IV. 2. CLIMAX. Attinghausen, dying, blesses the confederation of the yeomanry, prophesies and rejoices in the entrance of the nobility into it. Rudenz identifies his interest with that of the confederation and determines the immediate execution of its plans.

TRAGIC CRISIS. (Not represented.)

V. 1. DESCENDING ACTION. The action of Rudenz in taking and destroying the stronghold of Sarnen, and his being tacitly accepted by Melchthal as belonging to the confederation.

FINAL REACTION. (Not represented.)

V. 3. CATASTROPHE. Rudenz is united with Bertha, and in these two representatives the nobility enter also into the new order of freedom and unity.

The accompanying figure is intended to exhibit the outlines of the construction of these plots as here given.

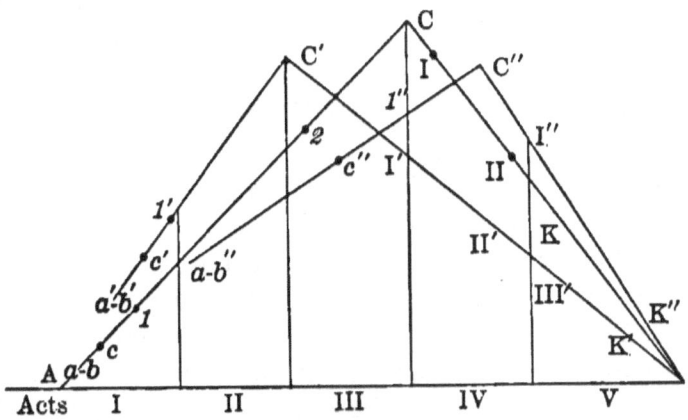

EXPLANATION: *A* = Initial Chord; *a-b* (Tell-plot), *a'-b'* (Yeomen-plot), *a"-b"* (Nobles-plot) = Exposition; *c, c', c"* = Initial Impulse; *1, 1', 1", 2, 2', 2"*, etc., = Stages of Ascending Action; *C, C', C"* = Climax; I, I', I", II, II, II", etc., = Stages of Descending Action; *K, K', K"* = Catastrophe.

VERSE. DICTION. STYLE.

While the predominating epic character of the subject-matter of *Tell* caused Schiller difficulties in respect
of dramatic unity which, as has been said, many
critics hold him not to have been wholly successful
in overcoming, all—ingenuous readers and captious
critics—agree in praising the verse, the diction, and in
general the poetic treatment.

The verse * does not differ essentially from the corresponding form in English. It is the blank verse,
i.e., the iambic line normally having five unaccented
and five accented syllables in regular alternation, and
without rhyme. The liberties taken in contracting
and expanding words, in varying the grammatical and
rhetorical accent, in the use of the hiatus, in the number and location of the unaccented syllables, in length-
ening or shortening the lines by increasing or diminishing the number of accents, and by employing after
the fifth accent an unaccented syllable, so that the
line has a feminine ending,—these liberties are just as
in English. Schiller's use of the cæsura—change or
pause in thought within the line, cutting it more or
less sharply—is excellent. The cæsura comes usually
after the second or the fourth accent, but may occur
at any point in the line after the first accent. Rhyme
is used with great effect to emphasize important passages and culminations of interest. Short poems in
lyric measures stand at the opening of Acts I and III
and at the end of Act IV. In all respects Schiller's
use of verse-form in Tell is noble, free, artistic.

* For minute details of versification reference is made to
E. Belling, *Die Metrik Schillers*, pp. 217 ff., and to Breul,
Schillers Tell, pp. xlix ff.

The diction of this drama is for the most part simple and popular in the best sense ; not without dignity and stateliness, but never consciously rhetorical, stilted. Its beauty is enhanced by the same licenses as are usual in English. Many words and phrases have been taken from the homely, vigorous, direct language of the old chroniclers ; with these harmonize fully the elements coming directly or indirectly from the Bible and from Homer. A poetical, rhythmical diction, since, as Schiller himself said, it treats all characters and situations according to one law, does not readily admit sharp distinctions and contrasts in the manner of speaking. Nevertheless many of the persons in the play are characterized and individualized in no small measure by their language. That the diction of this drama is at once simple and strong is shown by the very large number of popular quotations drawn from it, of which the commonest are printed in the Appendix, pp. 289, 290.

But not only the superficial fitness and beauty of the verse-form and language deserve high praise. Of the character-drawing in general Freytag says : " For more than half a century the splendid nobility of Schiller's characters ruled the German stage ; yet the weak imitators of his style did not understand that the fullness of his diction produced such great effects only because a wealth of dramatic life is covered by it as by costly gilding." Attention is called in the Notes to the prominent traits of the characters, which are not merely full of dramatic life, but wonderfully true to nature. Thus one of the earliest Swiss critics wrote : " One would readily make oath that Schiller had lived the greatest part of his life in Schwyz or

Uri among these simple, unpretending, vigorous people.
Such *are* these little known mountaineers in the hours
of trouble ; . . . thus do they think, thus act. . . .
It is almost incomprehensible how a man who has
perhaps never seen Switzerland, or at least only for a
short time, has by his genius been able to individualize
the thoughts and feelings of each of these people."

While perhaps somewhat long and detailed study
and comparison are necessary to appreciate Schiller's
poetic genius and dramatic art in respect of his unifying mastery of the materials he drew from legend and
history, and in respect of verse, diction, and character-
drawing, every reader or spectator feels at once and
forever that the poet brings Switzerland itself immediately before him. We all feel with Gustav Schwab,
who said that nature is so reflected in *Tell* that every
one who has earlier read the drama thinks on seeing
the country that he has already beheld it in dreamlike
transfiguration, or, better, with Carriere : " One who
has read *Tell* and then visits Switzerland feels as if
he had already seen it all, and that which seemed an
ideal picture of the imagination becomes actual and
living reality."

Schiller's genius and art are nowhere more splendidly
manifest * than in this creation of true men in that
true Switzerland, of which he makes Tell himself say
with suggestion of the vital relation between the land
and its people :

> *Das Haus der Freiheit hat uns Gott gegründet.*

* In the Appendix, pp. 291–295, may be found, in translation, passages of penetrating and sympathetic comment
on that which here is merely pointed out, from K. Heinrich
von Stein : *Goethe und Schiller. Beiträge zur Ästhetik der
deutschen Klassiker.*

FRIEDRICH SCHILLER.

Painted by Anton Graff. Engraved by Johann Gotthard Müller. Schiller sat for this picture in the spring of 1786 ; Graff, however, did not finish it until 1791. In 1794 Müller engraved the picture to Schiller's satisfaction. (*To face p.* 1.)

Wilhelm Tell

Schauspiel

von

Schiller.

———

Zum Neujahrsgeschenk

auf 1805.

———

Tübingen,
in der J. G. Cotta'schen Buchhandlung.
1804.

[Photographic reproduction of title-page to the first edition.]

Personen.

Hermann Geßler, Reichsvogt in Schwyz und Uri.
Werner, Freiherr von Attinghausen. Bannerherr.
Ulrich von Rudenz, sein Neffe.

Werner Stauffacher,
Konrad Hunn,
Itel Reding,
Hans auf der Mauer,   } Landleute aus Schwyz.
Jörg im Hofe,
Ulrich der Schmid,
Jost von Weiler,

Walther Fürst,
Wilhelm Tell,
Rösselmann, der Pfarrer,
Petermann, der Sigrist,   } aus Uri.
Kuoni, der Hirt,
Werni, der Jäger,
Ruodi, der Fischer,

Arnold vom Melchthal,
Konrad Baumgarten,
Meier von Sarnen,
Struth von Winkelried,   } aus Unterwalden.
Klaus von der Flüe,
Burkhart am Bühel,
Arnold von Sewa,

Pfeifer von Luzern.
Kunz von Gersau.
Jenni, Fischerknabe.
Seppi, Hirtenknabe.
Gertrud, Stauffachers Gattin.
Hedwig, Tells Gattin, Fürsts Tochter.
Bertha von Bruneck, eine reiche Erbin.

Armgard,
Mechthild,   } Bäuerinnen.
Elsbeth,
Hildegard,

Walther,   } Tells Knaben.
Wilhelm,

Frießhardt,   } Söldner.
Leuthold,

Rudolf der Harras, Geßlers Stallmeister.
Johannes Parricida, Herzog von Schwaben.
Stüssi, der Flurschütz.
Der Stier von Uri.
Ein Reichsbote.
Fronvogt.
Meister Steinmetz, Gesellen und Handlanger.
Öffentliche Ausrufer.
Barmherzige Brüder.
Geßlersche und Landenbergische Reiter.
Viele Landleute, Männer und Weiber aus den N..

Erster Aufzug.

Erste Scene.

Hohes Felsenufer des Vierwaldstättersees, Schwyz gegenüber.

Der See macht eine Bucht ins Land, eine Hütte ist unweit dem Ufer, Fischerknabe fährt sich in einem Kahn. Über den See hinweg sieht man die grünen Matten, Dörfer und Höfe von Schwyz im hellen Sonnenschein liegen. Zur Linken des Zuschauers zeigen sich die Spitzen des Haken, mit Wolken umgeben; zur Rechten im fernen Hintergrund sieht man die Eisgebirge. Noch ehe der Vorhang aufgeht, hört man den Kuhreihen und das harmonische Geläut der Herdenglocken, welches sich auch bei eröffneter Scene noch eine Zeit lang fortsetzt.

Fischerknabe (singt im Kahn).

Melodie des Kuhreihens.

Es lächelt der See, er ladet zum Bade,
Der Knabe schlief ein am grünen Gestade,
    Da hört er ein Klingen,
    Wie Flöten so süß,
    Wie Stimmen der Engel   5
    Im Paradies.
Und wie er erwachet in seliger Lust,
Da spülen die Wasser ihm um die Brust,
    Und es ruft aus den Tiefen:
    Lieb Knabe, bist mein!   10
    Ich locke den Schläfer,
    Ich zieh' ihn herein.

Hirt (auf dem Berge).

Variation des Kuhreihens.

Ihr Matten, lebt wohl,
Ihr sonnigen Weiden!
Der Senne muß scheiden,   15
Der Sommer ist hin.

Wir fahren zu Berg, wir kommen wieder,
Wenn der Kuckuck ruft, wenn erwachen die Lieder,
Wenn mit Blumen die Erde sich kleidet neu,
Wenn die Brünnlein fließen im lieblichen Mai.   20

Ihr Matten, lebt wohl,
Ihr sonnigen Weiden!
Der Senne muß scheiden,
Der Sommer ist hin.

Alpenjäger (erscheint gegenüber auf der Höhe des Felsen).

Zweite Variation.

Es donnern die Höhen, es zittert der Steg,   25
Nicht grauet dem Schützen auf schwindlichtem Weg;
Er schreitet verwegen
Auf Feldern von Eis;
Da pranget kein Frühling,
Da grünet kein Reis;   30
Und unter den Füßen ein nebliches Meer,
Erkennt er die Städte der Menschen nicht mehr;
Durch den Riß nur der Wolken
Erblickt er die Welt,
Tief unter den Wassern   35
Das grünende Feld.

(Die Landschaft verändert sich, man hört ein dumpfes Krachen von den
Bergen, Schatten von Wolken laufen über die Gegend.)

Ruodi, der Fischer, kommt aus der Hütte. Werni, der Jäger, steigt
bom Felsen. Kuoni, der Hirt, kommt mit dem Melknapf auf der
Schulter, Seppi, sein Handbube, folgt ihm,

Ruodi.

Mach' hurtig, Jenni! Zieh' die Naue ein!
Der graue Thalvogt kommt, dumpf brüllt der Firn,
Der Mythenstein zieht seine Haube an,
Und kalt her bläst es aus dem Wetterloch;   40
Der Sturm, ich mein', wird da sein, eh' wir's denken.

Kuoni.

's kommt Regen, Fährmann.   Meine Schafe fressen
Mit Begierde Gras, und Wächter scharrt die Erde.

Werni.

Die Fische springen, und das Wasserhuhn
Taucht unter.   Ein Gewitter ist im Anzug.   45

Kuoni (zum Buben.)

Lug, Seppi, ob das Vieh sich nicht verlaufen.

Seppi.

Die braune Lisel kenn' ich am Geläut.

Kuoni.

So fehlt uns keine mehr, die geht am weitsten.

Ruodi.

Ihr habt ein schön Geläute, Meister Hirt.

Werni.

Und schmuckes Vieh — Ist's euer eignes, Landsmann?   50

Kuoni.

Bin nit so reich — 's ist meines gnäd'gen Herrn,
Des Attinghäusers, und mir zugezählt.

Ruodi.

Wie schön der Kuh das Band zu Halse steht!

Kuoni.

Das weiß sie auch, daß sie den Reihen führt,
Und, nähm' ich ihr's, sie hörte auf zu fressen.   55

Ruodi.

Ihr seid nich klug!   Ein unvernünft'ges Vieh —

Werni.

Ist bald gesagt.   Das Tier hat auch Vernunft,
Das wissen w i r, die wir die Gemsen jagen.
Die stellen klug, wo sie zur Weide gehn,
'ne Vorhut aus, die spitzt das Ohr und warnet   60
Mit heller Pfeife, wenn der Jäger naht.

Ruodi (zum Hirten).

Treibt ihr jetzt heim?

Kuoni.

     Die Alp ist abgeweidet,

Werni.

Glückfel'ge Heimkehr, Senn!

Kuoni.

      Die wünsch' ich euch;
Von eurer Fahrt kehrt sich's nicht immer wieder.

Ruodi.

Dort kommt ein Mann in voller Hast gelaufen.   65

Werni.

Ich kenn' ihn, 's ist der Baumgart von Alzellen.

Konrad Baumgarten (atemlos hereinstürzend.)

Baumgarten.

Um Gottes willen, Fährmann, euren Kahn!

Ruodi.

Nun, nun, was giebt's so eilig?

Baumgarten.

Bindet los!

Ihr rettet mich vom Tode! Setzt mich über!

Kuoni.

Landsmann, was habt ihr?

Werni.

Wer verfolgt euch denn? 70

Baumgarten (zum Fischer).

Eilt, eilt, sie sind mir dicht schon an den Fersen!
Des Landvogts Reiter kommen hinter mir;
Ich bin ein Mann des Tods, wenn sie mich greifen.

Ruodi.

Warum verfolgen euch die Reisigen?

Baumgarten.

Erst rettet mich, und dann steh' ich euch Rede. 75

Werni.

Ihr seid mit Blut befleckt, was hat's gegeben?

Baumgarten.

Des Kaisers Burgvogt, der auf Roßberg saß —

Kuoni.

Der Wolfenschießen! Läßt euch der verfolgen?

Baumgarten.

Der schadet nicht mehr, ich hab' ihn erschlagen.

Alle (fahren zurück).

Gott sei euch gnädig! Was habt ihr gethan? 80

Baumgarten.

Was jeder freie Mann an meinem Platz!
Mein gutes Hausrecht hab' ich ausgeübt
Am Schänder meiner Ehr' und meines Weibes.

Kuoni.

Hat euch der Burgvogt an der Ehr' geschädigt?

Baumgarten.

Daß er sein bös Gelüsten nicht vollbracht,   85
Hat Gott und meine gute Axt verhütet.

Werni.

Ihr habt ihm mit der Axt den Kopf zerspalten?

Kuoni.

O, laßt uns alles hören, ihr habt Zeit,
Bis er den Kahn vom Ufer losgebunden.

Baumgarten.

Ich hatte Holz gefällt im Wald, da kommt   90
Mein Weib gelaufen in der Angst des Todes.
„Der Burgvogt lieg' in meinem Haus, er hab'
Ihr anbefohlen, ihm ein Bad zu rüsten.
Drauf hab' er Ungebührliches von ihr
Verlangt, sie sei entsprungen, mich zu suchen."   95
Da lief ich frisch hinzu, so wie ich war,
Und mit der Axt hab' ich ihm's Bad gesegnet.

Werni.

Ihr thatet wohl, kein Mensch kann euch drum schelten.

Kuoni.

Der Wüterich! Der hat nun seinen Lohn!
Hat's lang' verdient ums Volk von Unterwalden.   100

Baumgarten.

Die That ward ruchtbar; mir wird nachgesetzt —
Indem wir sprechen — Gott — verrinnt die Zeit —
(Es fängt an zu donnern.)

Kuoni.

Frisch, Fährmann — schaff' den Biedermann hinüber!

Ruodi.

Geht nicht. Ein schweres Ungewitter ist
Im Anzug. – Ihr müßt warten.

Baumgarten.

Heil'ger Gott! 105
Ich kann nicht warten. Jeder Aufschub tötet —

Kuoni (zum Fischer).

Greif an mit Gott! Dem Nächsten muß man helfen;
Es kann uns allen Gleiches ja begegnen.
(Brausen und Donnern.)

Ruodi.

Der Föhn ist los, ihr seht, wie hoch der See geht;
Ich kann nicht steuern gegen Sturm und Wellen. 110

Baumgarten (umfaßt seine Kniee).

So helf' euch Gott, wie ihr euch mein erbarmet —

Werni.

Es geht ums Leben, sei barmherzig, Fährmann!

Kuoni.

's ist ein Hausvater und hat Weib und Kinder!
(Wiederholte Donnerschläge.)

Ruodi.

Was? Ich hab' auch ein Leben zu verlieren,
Hab' Weib und Kind daheim wie er — Seht hin, 115
Wie's brandet, wie es wogt und Wirbel zieht
Und alle Wasser aufrührt in der Tiefe.
— Ich wollte gern den Biedermann erretten;
Doch es ist rein unmöglich, ihr seht selbst.

Baumgarten (noch auf den Knieen).

So muß ich fallen in des Feindes Hand, 120
Das nahe Rettungsufer im Gesichte!

—Dort liegt's!   Ich kann's erreichen mit den Augen,
Hinüberdringen kann der Stimme Schall;
Da ist der Kahn, der mich hinübertrüge,
Und muß hier liegen, hilflos, und verzagen!   125

Kuoni.

Seht, wer da kommt!

Werni.

Es ist der Tell aus Bürglen.
(Tell mit der Armbrust.)

Tell.

Wer ist der Mann, der hier um Hilfe fleht?

Kuoni.

's ist ein Alzeller Mann, er hat sein' Ehr'
Verteidigt und den Wolfenschieß erschlagen,
Des Königs Burgvogt, der auf Roßberg saß —   130
Des Landvogts Reiter sind ihm auf den Fersen.
Er fleht den Schiffer um die Überfahrt;
Der fürcht't sich vor dem Sturm und will nicht fahren.

Ruodi.

Da ist der Tell, er führt das Ruder auch,
Der soll mir's zeugen, ob die Fahrt zu wagen.   135

Tell.

Wo's not thut, Fährmann, läßt sich alles wagen.
(Heftige Donnerschläge, der See rauscht auf.)

Ruodi.

Ich soll mich in den Höllenrachen stürzen?
Das thäte keiner, der bei Sinnen ist.

Tell.

Der brave Mann denkt an sich selbst zuletzt;
Vertrau' auf Gott und rette den Bedrängten.   140

Ruodi.

Vom sichern Port läßt sich's gemächlich raten.
Da ist der Kahn und dort der See! Versucht's!

Tell.

Der See kann sich, der Landvogt nicht erbarmen.
Versuch' es, Fährmann!

Hirten und Jäger.

Rett' ihn! Rett' ihn! Rett' ihn!

Ruodi.

Und wär's mein Bruder und mein leiblich Kind,   145
Es kann nicht sein; 's ist heut' Simons und Judä,
Da rast der See und will sein Opfer haben.

Tell.

Mit eitler Rede wird hier nichts geschafft;
Die Stunde bringt, dem Mann muß Hilfe werden.
Sprich, Fährmann, willst du fahren?

Ruodi.

Nein, nicht ich!   150

Tell.

In Gottes Namen denn! Gieb her den Kahn!
Ich will's mit meiner schwachen Kraft versuchen.

Kuoni.

Ha, wackrer Tell!

Werni.

Das gleicht dem Weidgesellen!

Baumgarten.

Mein Retter seid ihr und mein Engel, Tell!

Tell.

Wohl aus des Vogts Gewalt errett' ich euch!   155
Aus Sturmes Nöten muß ein andrer helfen.

Doch besser ist's, ihr fallt in Gottes Hand
Als in der Menschen!
(Zu dem Hirten.)
Landsmann, tröstet ihr
Mein Weib, wenn mir was Menschliches begegnet.
Ich hab' gethan, was ich nicht lassen konnte.   160
(Er springt in den Kahn.)

Kuoni (zum Fischer).

Ihr seid ein Meister Steuermann. Was sich
Der Tell getraut, das konntet ihr nicht wagen?

Ruodi.

Wohl beßre Männer thun's dem Tell nicht nach,
Es giebt nicht zwei, wie der ist, im Gebirge.

Werni (ist auf den Fels gestiegen).

Er stößt schon ab. Gott helf' dir, braver Schwimmer! 165
Sieh, wie das Schifflein auf den Wellen schwankt!

Kuoni (am Ufer).

Die Flut geht drüber weg — Ich seh's nicht mehr.
Doch, halt, da ist es wieder! Kräftiglich
Arbeitet sich der Wackre durch die Brandung.

Seppi.

Des Landvogts Reiter kommen angesprengt.   170

Kuoni.

Weiß Gott, sie sind's! Das war Hilf' in der Not.
(Ein Trupp Landenbergischer Reiter.)

Erster Reiter.

Den Mörder gebt heraus, den ihr verborgen!

Zweiter.

Des Wegs kam er, umsonst verhehlt ihr ihn.

Kuoni und Ruodi.

Wen meint ihr, Reiter?

Erster Reiter (entdeckt den Nachen).

Ha, was seh' ich! Teufel!

Werni (oben).

Ist's der im Nachen, den ihr sucht? — Reit't zu! 　　175
Wenn ihr frisch beilegt, holt ihr ihn noch ein.

Zweiter.

Verwünscht! Er ist entwischt.

Erster (zum Hirten und Fischer).

Ihr habt ihm fortgeholfen.
Ihr sollt uns büßen — Fallt in ihre Heerde!
Die Hütte reißet ein, brennt und schlagt nieder!

(Eilen fort.)

Seppi (stürzt nach).

O meine Lämmer!

Kuoni (folgt).

Weh mir! Meine Heerde! 　　180

Werni.

Die Wütriche!

Ruodi (ringt die Hände).

Gerechtigkeit des Himmels!
Wann wird der Retter kommen diesem Lande?

(Folgt ihnen.)

Zweite Scene.

Zu Steinen in Schwyz. Eine Linde vor des
Stauffachers Hause an der Landstraße,
nächst der Brücke.

Werner Stauffacher, Pfeifer von Luzern kommen im Gespräch.

Pfeifer.

Ja, ja, Herr Stauffacher, wie ich euch sagte.
Schwört nicht zu Östreich, wenn ihr's könnt vermeiden.
Haltet fest am Reich und wacker wie bisher.   185
Gott schirme euch bei eurer alten Freiheit!
(Drückt ihm herzlich die Hand und will gehen.)

Stauffacher.

Bleibt doch, bis meine Wirtin kommt — ihr seid
Mein Gast zu Schwyz, ich in Luzern der eure.

Pfeifer.

Viel Dank! Muß heute Gersau noch erreichen.
— Was ihr auch Schweres mögt zu leiden haben   190
Von eurer Vögte Geiz und Übermut,
Tragt's in Geduld! Es kann sich ändern, schnell,
Ein andrer Kaiser kann ans Reich gelangen.
Seid ihr erst Österreichs, seid ihr's auf immer.
(Er geht ab. Stauffacher setzt sich kummervoll auf eine Bank unter
der Linde. So findet ihn Gertrud, seine Frau, die sich neben ihn stellt
und ihn eine Zeit lang schweigend betrachtet.)

Gertrud.

So ernst, mein Freund? Ich kenne dich nicht mehr.   195
Schon viele Tage seh' ich's schweigend an,
Wie finstrer Trübsinn deine Stirne furcht.
Auf deinem Herzen drückt ein still Gebresten;

Vertrau' es mir; ich bin dein treues Weib,
Und meine Hälfte fordr' ich deines Grams.   200

(Stauffacher reicht ihr die Hand und schweigt.)

Was kann dein Herz beklemmen, sag' es mir.
Gesegnet ist dein Fleiß, dein Glücksstand blüht,
Voll sind die Scheunen, und der Rinder Scharen
Der glatten Pferde wohlgenährte Zucht
Ist von den Bergen glücklich heimgebracht   205
Zur Winterung in den bequemen Ställen.
— Da steht dein Haus, reich, wie ein Edelsitz;
Von schönem Stammholz ist es neu gezimmert
Und nach dem Richtmaß ordentlich gefügt;
Von vielen Fenstern glänzt es wohnlich, hell;   210
Mit bunten Wappenschildern ist's bemalt
Und weisen Sprüchen, die der Wandersmann
Verweilend liest und ihren Sinn bewundert.

Stauffacher.

Wohl steht das Haus gezimmert und gefügt,
Doch, ach — es wankt der Grund, auf dem wir bauten. 215

Gertrud.

Mein Werner, sage, wie verstehst du das?

Stauffacher.

Vor dieser Linde saß ich jüngst, wie heut',
Das schön Vollbrachte freudig überdenkend,
Da kam daher von Küßnacht, seiner Burg,
Der Vogt mit seinen Reisigen geritten.   220
Vor diesem Hause hielt er wundernd an;
Doch ich erhob mich schnell, und unterwürfig,
Wie sich's gebührt, trat ich dem Herrn entgegen,
Der uns des Kaisers richterliche Macht
Vorstellt im Lande. „Wessen ist dies Haus?"   225

Fragt' er bösmeinend, denn er wußt' es wohl.
Doch schnell besonnen ich entgegn' ihm so:
„Dies Haus, Herr Vogt, ist meines Herrn des Kaisers,
Und eures, und mein Lehen" — Da versetzt er:
„Ich bin Regent im Land an Kaisers Statt   230
Und will nicht, daß der Bauer Häuser baue
Auf seine eigne Hand und also frei
Hinleb', als ob er Herr wär' in dem Lande;
Ich werd' mich unterstehn, euch das zu wehren."
Dies sagend, ritt er trutziglich von dannen,   235
Ich aber blieb mit kummervoller Seele,
Das Wort bedenkend, das der Böse sprach.

Gertrud.

Mein lieber Herr und Ehewirt! Magst du
Ein redlich Wort von deinem Weib vernehmen?
Des edeln Ibergs Tochter rühm' ich mich,   240
Des vielerfahrnen Manns.   Wir Schwestern saßen,
Die Wolle spinnend, in den langen Nächten,
Wenn bei dem Vater sich des Volkes Häupter
Versammelten, die Pergamente lasen
Der alten Kaiser, und des Landes Wohl   245
Bedachten in vernünftigem Gespräch.
Aufmerkend hört' ich da manch kluges Wort,
Was der Verständ'ge denkt, der Gute wünscht,
Und still im Herzen hab' ich mir's bewahrt.
So höre denn und acht' auf meine Rede!   250
Denn, was dich preßte, sieh, das wußt' ich längst.
— Dir grollt der Landvogt, möchte gern dir schaden,
Denn du bist ihm ein Hindernis, daß sich
Der Schwyzer nicht dem neuen Fürstenhaus
Will unterwerfen, sondern treu und fest   255
Beim Reich beharren, wie die würdigen

Altvordern es gehalten und gethan. —
Ist's nicht so, Werner? Sag' es, wenn ich lüge!

Stauffacher.

So ist's, das ist des Geßlers Groll auf mich.

Gertrud.

Er ist dir neidisch, weil du glücklich wohnst,   260
Ein freier Mann auf deinem eignen Erb'
— Denn er hat keins. Vom Kaiser selbst und Reich
Trägst du dies Haus zu Lehn; du darfst es zeigen,
So gut der Reichsfürst seine Länder zeigt;
Denn über dir erkennst du keinen Herrn   265
Als nur den Höchsten in der Christenheit —
Er ist ein jüngrer Sohn nur seines Hauses,
Nichts nennt er sein als seinen Rittermantel;
Drum sieht er jedes Biedermannes Glück
Mit scheelen Augen gift'ger Mißgunst an.   270
D i r hat er längst den Untergang geschworen —
Noch stehst du unversehrt — Willst du erwarten,
Bis er die böse Lust an dir gebüßt?
Der kluge Mann baut vor.

Stauffacher.

Was ist zu thun?

Gertrud (tritt näher).

So höre meinen Rat! Du weißt, wie hier   275
Zu Schwyz sich alle Redlichen beklagen
Ob dieses Landvogts Geiz und Wüterei.
So zweifle nicht, daß sie dort drüben auch
In Unterwalden und im Urner Land
Des Dranges müd' sind und des harten Jochs —   280
Denn, wie der Geßler hier, so schafft es frech

Der Landenberger drüben überm See —
Es kommt kein Fischerkahn zu uns herüber,
Der nicht ein neues Unheil und Gewalt=
Beginnen von den Vögten uns verkündet.   285
Drum thät' es gut, daß eurer etliche,
Die's redlich meinen, still zu Rate gingen,
Wie man des Drucks sich möcht' erledigen;
So acht' ich wohl, Gott würd' euch nicht verlassen
Und der gerechten Sache gnädig sein —   290
Hast du in Uri keinen Gastfreund, sprich,
Dem du dein Herz magst redlich offenbaren?

Stauffacher.

Der wackern Männer kenn' ich viele dort
Und angesehen große Herrenleute,
Die mir geheim sind und gar wohl vertraut.   295

(Er steht auf.)

Frau, welchen Sturm gefährlicher Gedanken
Weckst du mir in der stillen Brust! Mein Innerstes
Kehrst du ans Licht des Tages mir entgegen,
Und was ich mir zu denken still verbot,
Du sprichst's mit leichter Zunge kecklich aus.   300
— Hast du auch wohl bedacht, was du mir rätst?
Die wilde Zwietracht und den Klang der Waffen
Rufst du in dieses friedgewohnte Thal —
Wir wagten es, ein schwaches Volk der Hirten,
In Kampf zu gehen mit dem Herrn der Welt?   305
Der gute Schein nur ist's, worauf sie warten,
Um loszulassen auf dies arme Land
Die wilden Horden ihrer Kriegesmacht,
Darin zu schalten mit des Siegers Rechten
Und unterm Schein gerechter Züchtigung   310
Die alten Freiheitsbriefe zu vertilgen.

Gertrud.

Ihr ſeid auch Männer, wiſſet eure Axt
Zu führen, und dem Mutigen hilft Gott!

Stauffacher.

O Weib! Ein furchtbar wütend Schrecknis iſt
Der Krieg; die Herde ſchlägt er und den Hirten.   315

Gertrud.

Ertragen muß man, was der Himmel ſendet;
Unbilliges erträgt kein edles Herz.

Stauffacher.

Dies Haus erfreut dich, das wir neu erbauten.
Der Krieg, der ungeheure, brennt es nieder.

Gertrud.

Wüßt' ich mein Herz an zeitlich Gut gefeſſelt,   320
Den Brand wärf' ich hinein mit eigner Hand.

Stauffacher.

Du glaubſt an Menſchlichkeit! Es ſchont der Krieg
Auch nicht das zarte Kindlein in der Wiege.

Gertrud.

Die Unſchuld hat im Himmel einen Freund!
— Sieh vorwärts, Werner, und nicht hinter dich!   325

Stauffacher.

Wir Männer können tapfer fechtend ſterben;
Welch Schickſal aber wird das eure ſein?

Gertrud.

Die letzte Wahl ſteht auch dem Schwächſten offen,
Ein Sprung von dieſer Brücke macht mich frei.

Stauffacher (ſtürzt in ihre Arme).

Wer ſolch ein Herz an ſeinen Buſen drückt,   330
Der kann für Herd und Hof mit Freuden fechten,

Und keines Königs Heermacht fürchtet er —
Nach Uri fahr' ich stehnden Fußes gleich,
Dort lebt ein Gastfreund mir, Herr Walther Fürst,
Der über diese Zeiten denkt wie ich.   335
Auch find' ich dort den edeln Bannerherrn
Von Attinghaus — obgleich von hohem Stamm
Liebt er das Volk und ehrt die alten Sitten.
Mit ihnen beiden pfleg' ich Rats, wie man
Der Landesfeinde mutig sich erwehrt —   340
Leb' wohl — und, weil ich fern bin, führe du
Mit klugem Sinn das Regiment des Hauses —
Dem Pilger, der zum Gotteshause wallt,
Dem frommen Mönch, der für sein Kloster sammelt,
Gieb reichlich und entlaß' ihn wohlgepflegt.   345
Stauffachers Haus verbirgt sich nicht.   Zu äußerst
Am offnen Heerweg steht's, ein wirtlich Dach
Für alle Wandrer, die des Weges fahren.

(Indem sie nach dem Hintergrund abgehen, tritt Wilhelm Tell mit
Baumgarten vorn auf die Scene.)

Tell (zu Baumgarten.)

Ihr habt jetzt meiner weiter nicht von nöten.
Zu jenem Hause gehet ein; dort wohnt   350
Der Stauffacher, ein Vater der Bedrängten.
— Doch sieh, da ist er selber — Folgt mir, kommt!

(Gehen auf ihn zu; die Scene verwandelt sich.)

Dritte Scene.

Öffentlicher Platz bei Altorf.

Auf einer Anhöhe im Hintergrund sieht man eine Feste bauen, welche schon so weit gediehen, daß sich die Form des Ganzen darstellt. Die hintere Seite ist fertig, an der vorderen wird eben gebaut, das Gerüste steht noch, an welchem die Werkleute auf und nieder steigen; auf dem höchsten Dach hängt der Schieferdecker — alles ist in Bewegung und Arbeit.

Fronvogt. Meister Steinmetz. Gesellen und Handlanger.

Fronvogt (mit dem Stabe, treibt die Arbeiter).

Nicht lang' gefeiert, frisch! Die Mauersteine
Herbei, den Kalk, den Mörtel zugefahren!
Wenn der Herr Landvogt kommt, daß er das Werk   355
Gewachsen sieht — Das schlendert wie die Schnecken.
        (Zu zwei Handlangern, welche tragen.)
Heißt das geladen? Gleich das Doppelte!
Wie die Tagdiebe ihre Pflicht bestehlen!

Erster Gesell.

Das ist doch hart, daß wir die Steine selbst
Zu unserm Twing und Kerker sollen fahren!   360

Fronvogt.

Was murret ihr? Das ist ein schlechtes Volk,
Zu nichts anstellig, als das Vieh zu melken
Und faul herum zu schlendern auf den Bergen.

Alter Mann (ruht aus).

Ich kann nicht mehr.

Fronvogt (schüttelt ihn).

      Frisch, Alter, an die Arbeit!

Erster Gesell.

Habt ihr denn gar kein Eingeweid', daß ihr   365
Den Greis, der kaum sich selber schleppen kann,
Zum harten Frondienst treibt?

Meister Steinmetz und Gesellen.

'ß ist himmelschreiend!

Fronvogt.

Sorgt ihr für euch; ich thu', was meines Amts..

Zweiter Gesell.

Fronvogt, wie wird die Feste denn sich nennen,
Die wir da baun?

Fronvogt.

Zwing Uri soll sie heißen!   370
Denn unter dieses Joch wird man euch beugen.

Gesellen.

Zwing Uri!

Fronvogt.

Nun, was giebt's dabei zu lachen?

Zweiter Gesell.

Mit diesem Häuslein wollt ihr Uri zwingen?

Erster Gesell.

Laß sehn, wie viel man solcher Maulwurfshaufen
Muß über 'nander setzen, bis ein Berg   375
Draus wird, wie der geringste nur in Uri!

(Fronvogt geht nach dem Hintergrund.)

Meister Steinmetz.

Den Hammer werf' ich in den tiefsten See,
Der mir gedient bei diesem Fluchgebäude!

(Tell und Stauffacher kommen.)

Stauffacher.

O, hätt' ich nie gelebt, um das zu schauen!

Tell.

Hier ist nicht gut sein. Laßt uns weiter gehn.   380

Stauffacher.

Bin ich zu Uri, in der Freiheit Land?

Meister Steinmetz.

O Herr, wenn ihr die Keller erst gesehn
Unter den Türmen! Ja, wer die bewohnt,
Der wird den Hahn nicht fürder krähen hören.

Stauffacher.

O Gott!

Steinmetz.

Seht diese Flanken, diese Strebepfeiler,   385
Die stehn, wie für die Ewigkeit gebaut!

Tell.

Was Hände bauten, können Hände stürzen.
(Nach den Bergen zeigend.)
Das Haus der Freiheit hat uns Gott gegründet.
(Man hört eine Trommel, es kommen Leute, die einen Hut auf einer
Stange tragen; ein Ausrufer folgt ihnen, Weiber und Kinder dringen
tumultuarisch nach.)

Erster Gesell.

Was will die Trommel? Gebet acht!

Meister Steinmetz.

                                    Was für
Ein Fastnachtsaufzug, und was soll der Hut?   390

Ausrufer.

In des Kaisers Namen! Höret!

Gesellen.

                    Still doch! Höret!

Ausrufer.

Ihr sehet diesen Hut, Männer von Uri!
Aufrichten wird man ihn auf hoher Säule,

Mitten in Altorf, an dem höchsten Ort,
Und dieses ist des Landvogts Will' und Meinung: 395
Dem Hut soll gleiche Ehre wie ihm selbst geschehn.
Man soll ihn mit gebognem Knie und mit
Entblößtem Haupt verehren — Daran will
Der König die Gehorsamen erkennen.
Verfallen ist mit seinem Leib und Gut   400
Dem Könige, wer das Gebot verachtet.

(Das Volk lacht laut auf, die Trommel wird gerührt, sie gehen vorüber.)

Erster Gesell.

Welch neues Unerhörtes hat der Vogt
Sich ausgesonnen! Wir 'nen Hut verehren!
  ! Hat man je vernommen von dergleichen?

Meister Steinmetz.

Wir unsre Kniee beugen einem Hut!   405
Treibt er sein Spiel mit ernsthaft würd'gen Leuten?

Erster Gesell.

Wär's noch die kaiserliche Kron'! So ist's
Der Hut von Österreich; ich sah ihn hangen
Über dem Thron, wo man die Lehen giebt!

Meister Steinmetz.

Der Hut von Österreich! Gebt acht, es ist   410
Ein Fallstrick, uns an Östreich zu verraten!

Gesellen.

Kein Ehrenmann wird sich der Schmach bequemen.

Meister Steinmetz.

Kommt, laßt uns mit den andern Abred' nehmen.

(Sie gehen nach der Tiefe.)

Tell (zum Stauffacher).

Ihr wisset nun Bescheid. Lebt wohl, Herr Werner!

Stauffacher.

Wo wollt ihr hin? O, eilt nicht so von dannen.   415

Tell.

Mein Haus entbehrt des Vaters. Lebet wohl!

Stauffacher.

Mir ist das Herz so voll, mit euch zu reden.

Tell.

Das schwere Herz wird nicht durch Worte leicht.

Stauffacher.

Doch könnten Worte uns zu Thaten führen.

Tell.

Die einz'ge That ist jetzt Geduld und Schweigen.   420

Stauffacher.

Soll man ertragen, was unleidlich ist?

Tell.

Die schnellen Herrscher sind's, die kurz regieren.
—Wenn sich der Föhn erhebt aus seinen Schlünden,
Löscht man die Feuer aus, die Schiffe suchen
Eilends den Hafen, und der mächt'ge Geist   425
Geht ohne Schaden spurlos über die Erde.
Ein jeder lebe still bei sich daheim;
Dem Friedlichen gewährt man gern den Frieden.

Stauffacher.

Meint ihr?

Tell.

    Die Schlange sticht nicht ungereizt.
Sie werden endlich doch von selbst ermüden,   430
Wenn sie die Lande ruhig bleiben sehn.

Stauffacher.

Wir könnten viel, wenn wir zusammenstünden

Tell.

Beim Schiffbruch hilft der einzelne sich leichter.

Stauffacher.

So kalt verlaßt ihr die gemeine Sache?

Tell.

Ein jeder zählt nur sicher auf sich selbst.   435

Stauffacher.

Verbunden werden auch die Schwachen mächtig.

Tell.

Der Starke ist am mächtigsten allein.

Stauffacher.

So kann das Vaterland auf euch nicht zählen,
Wenn es verzweiflungsvoll zur Notwehr greift?

Tell (giebt ihm die Hand).

Der Tell holt ein verlornes Lamm vom Abgrund   440
Und sollte seinen Freunden sich entziehen?
Doch, was ihr thut, laßt mich aus eurem Rat,
Ich kann nicht lange prüfen oder wählen;
Bedürft ihr meiner zu bestimmter That,
Dann ruft den Tell, es soll an mir nicht fehlen.   445

(Gehen ab zu verschiedenen Seiten. Ein plötzlicher Auflauf entsteht um
das Gerüste.)

Meister Steinmetz (eilt hin).

Was giebt's?

Erster Gesell (kommt vor, rufend).

Der Schieferdecker ist vom Dach gestürzt.

(Bertha mit Gefolge.)

Bertha (stürzt herein).

Ist er zerschmettert? Rennet, rettet, helft —
Wenn Hilfe möglich, rettet, hier ist Gold —

(Wirft ihr Geschmeide unter das Volk.)

Meister.

Mit eurem Golde — Alles ist euch feil   450
Um Gold; wenn ihr den Vater von den Kindern
Gerissen und den Mann von seinem Weibe,
Und Jammer habt gebracht über die Welt,
Denkt ihr's mit Golde zu vergüten — Geht!
Wir waren frohe Menschen, eh' ihr kamt;   455
Mit euch ist die Verzweiflung eingezogen.

Bertha (zu dem Fronvogt, der zurückkommt).

Lebt er?

(Fronvogt giebt ein Zeichen des Gegenteils.)

O unglückfel'ges Schloß, mit Flüchen
Erbaut, und Flüche werden dich bewohnen! (Geht ab.)

Vierte Scene.

Walther Fürsts Wohnung.

Walther Fürst und Arnold vom Melchthal treten zugleich ein
von verschiedenen Seiten.

Melchthal.

Herr Walther Fürst —

Walther Fürst.

Wenn man uns überraschte!
Bleibt, wo ihr seid. Wir sind umringt von Spähern.   460

Melchthal.

Bringt ihr mir nichts von Unterwalden? nichts
Von meinem Vater? Nicht ertrag' ich's länger,
Als ein Gefangner müßig hier zu liegen.
Was hab' ich denn so Sträfliches gethan,
Um mich gleich einem Mörder zu verbergen?

Dem frechen Buben, der die Ochsen mir,
Das trefflichste Gespann, vor meinen Augen
Weg wollte treiben auf des Vogts Geheiß,
Hab' ich den Finger mit dem Stab gebrochen.

Walther Fürst.

Ihr seid zu rasch.   Der Bube war des Vogts;   470
Von eurer Obrigkeit war er gesendet.
Ihr wart in Straf' gefallen, mußtet euch,
Wie schwer sie war, der Buße schweigend fügen.

Meldthal.

Ertragen sollt' ich die leichtfert'ge Rede
Des Unverschämten: „Wenn der Bauer Brot   475
Wollt' essen, mög' er selbst am Pfluge ziehn!"
In die Seele schnitt mir's, als der Bub' die Ochsen,
Die schönen Tiere, von dem Pfluge spannte;
Dumpf brüllten sie, als hätten sie Gefühl
Der Ungebühr, und stießen mit den Hörnern;   480
Da übernahm mich der gerechte Zorn,
Und meiner selbst nicht Herr, schlug ich den Boten.

Walther Fürst.

O, kaum bezwingen wir das eigne Herz;
Wie soll die rasche Jugend sich bezähmen!

Meldthal.

Mich jammert nur der Vater — Er bedarf   485
So sehr der Pflege, und sein Sohn ist fern.
Der Vogt ist ihm gehässig, weil er stets
Für Recht und Freiheit redlich hat gestritten.
Drum werden sie den alten Mann bedrängen,
Und niemand ist, der ihn vor Unglimpf schütze.   490
—Werde mit mir, was will, ich muß hinüber.

Walther Fürst.

Erwartet nur und faßt euch in Gebuld,
Bis Nachricht uns herüber kommt vom Walde.
— Ich höre klopfen, geht — Vielleicht ein Bote
Vom Landvogt — Geht hinein — Ihr seid in Uri   495
Nicht sicher vor des Landenbergers Arm;
Denn die Tyrannen reichen sich die Hände.

Melchthal.

Sie lehren uns, was w i r thun sollten.

Walther Fürst.

Geht!

Ich ruf' euch wieder, wenn's hier sicher ist.

(M e l ch t h a l geht hinein.)

Der Unglückselige, ich darf ihm nicht   500
Gestehen, was mir Böses schwant — Wer klopft?
So oft die Thüre rauscht, erwart' ich Unglück.
Verrat und Argwohn lauscht in allen Ecken;
Bis in das Innerste der Häuser dringen
Die Boten der Gewalt; bald thät' es not,   505
Wir hätten Schloß und Riegel an den Thüren.

(Er öffnet und tritt erstaunt zurück, da W e r n e r S t a u f f a ch e r herein-
tritt.)

Was seh' ich? Ihr, Herr Werner! Nun, bei Gott!
Ein werter, teurer Gast — kein beßrer Mann
Ist über diese Schwelle noch gegangen.
Seid hoch willkommen unter meinem Dach!   510
Was führt euch her? Was sucht ihr hier in Uri?

Stauffacher (ihm die Hand reichend).

Die alten Zeiten und die alte Schweiz.

Walther Fürst.

Die bringt ihr mit euch — Sieh, mir wird so wohl,

Warm geht das Herz mir auf bei eurem Anblick.
— Setzt euch, Herr Werner — Wie verließet ihr   515
Frau Gertrud, eure angenehme Wirtin,
Des weisen Jbergs hochverständ'ge Tochter?
Von allen Wandrern aus dem deutschen Land,
Die über Meinrads Zell nach Welschland fahren,
Rühmt jeder euer gastlich Haus — Doch, sagt,   520
Kommt ihr soeben frisch von Flüelen her
Und habt euch nirgend sonst noch umgesehn,
Eh' ihr den Fuß gesetzt auf diese Schwelle?

Stauffacher (setzt sich).

Wohl ein erstaunlich neues Werk hab' ich
Bereiten sehen, das mich nicht erfreute.   525

Walther Fürst.

O Freund, da habt ihr's gleich mit e i n e m Blicke!

Stauffacher.

Ein solches ist in Uri nie gewesen —
Seit Menschendenken war kein Twinghof hier,
Und fest war keine Wohnung als das Grab.

Walther Fürst.

Ein Grab der Freiheit ist's. Ihr nennt's mit Namen. 530

Stauffacher.

Herr Walther Fürst, ich will euch nicht verhalten,
Nicht eine müß'ge Neugier führt mich her;
Mich drücken schwere Sorgen — Drangsal hab' ich
Zu Haus verlassen, Drangsal find' ich hier.
Denn ganz unleidlich ist's, was wir erdulden,   535
Und dieses Dranges ist kein Ziel zu sehn.
Frei war der Schweizer von uralters her,
Wir sind's gewohnt, daß man uns gut begegnet.

Ein solches war im Lande nie erlebt,
Solang' ein Hirte trieb auf diesen Bergen.   540
                    Walther Fürst.
Ja, es ist ohne Beispiel, wie sie's treiben!
Auch unser edler Herr von Attinghausen,
Der noch die alten Zeiten hat gesehn,
Meint selber, es sei nicht mehr zu ertragen.
                    Stauffacher.
Auch drüben unterm Wald geht Schweres vor,   545
Und blutig wird's gebüßt — Der Wolfenschießen,
Des Kaisers Vogt, der auf dem Roßberg hauste,
Gelüsten trug er nach verbotner Frucht;
Baumgartens Weib, der haushält zu Alzellen,
Wollt' er zu frecher Ungebühr mißbrauchen,   550
Und mit der Axt hat ihn der Mann erschlagen.
                    Walther Fürst.
O, die Gerichte Gottes sind gerecht!
— Baumgarten, sagt ihr? ein bescheidner Mann!
Er ist gerettet doch und wohl geborgen?
                    Stauffacher.
Euer Eidam hat ihn übern See geflüchtet;   555
Bei mir zu Steinen halt' ich ihn verborgen —
— Noch Greulichers hat mir derselbe Mann
Berichtet, was zu Sarnen ist geschehn;
Das Herz muß jedem Biedermanne bluten.
                    Walther Fürst (aufmerksam).
Sagt an, was ist's?
                    Stauffacher.
                    Im Melchthal, da, wo man   560
Eintritt bei Kerns, wohnt ein gerechter Mann,
Sie nennen ihn den Heinrich von der Halden,
Und seine Stimm' gilt was in der Gemeinde.

Walther Fürst.

Wer kennt ihn nicht! Was ist's mit ihm? Vollendet!

Stauffacher.

Der Landenberger büßte seinen Sohn   565
Um kleinen Fehlers willen, ließ die Ochsen,
Das beste Paar, ihm aus dem Pfluge spannen;
Da schlug der Knab' den Knecht und wurde flüchtig.

Walther Fürst (in höchster Spannung).

Der Vater aber — sagt, wie steht's um den?

Stauffacher.

Den Vater läßt der Landenberger fordern,   570
Zur Stelle schaffen soll er ihm den Sohn,
Und da der alte Mann mit Wahrheit schwört,
Er habe von dem Flüchtling keine Kunde,
Da läßt der Vogt die Folterknechte kommen —

Walther Fürst (springt auf und will ihn auf die andere Seite führen).

O, still, nichts mehr!

Stauffacher (mit steigendem Ton).

                    „Ist mir der Sohn entgangen, 575
So hab' ich dich!" — läßt ihn zu Boden werfen,
Den spitz'gen Stahl ihm in die Augen bohren —

Walther Fürst.

Barmherz'ger Himmel!

Melchthal (stürzt heraus).

                    In die Augen, sagt ihr?

Stauffacher (erstaunt zu Walther Fürst).

Wer ist der Jüngling?

Melchthal (faßt ihn mit krampfhafter Heftigkeit).

                    In die Augen? Redet!

Walther Fürst.

O der Bejammernswürdige!

Stauffacher.

Wer ist's?   580

(Da Walther Fürst ihm ein Zeichen giebt).

Der Sohn ist's? Allgerechter Gott!

Meldthal.

Und ich

Muß ferne sein! — In seine beiden Augen?

Walther Fürst.

Bezwinget euch! Ertragt es, wie ein Mann!

Meldthal.

Um m e i n e r Schuld, um m e i n e s Frevels willen!
— Blind also? Wirklich b l i n d und g a n z geblendet?   585

Stauffacher.

Ich sagt's. Der Quell des Sehns ist ausgeflossen,
Das Licht der Sonne schaut er niemals wieder.

Walther Fürst.

Schont seines Schmerzens.

Meldthal.

Niemals! niemals wieder!

(Er drückt die Hand vor die Augen und schweigt einige Momente; dann
wendet er sich von dem einen zu dem andern und spricht mit sanfter, von
Thränen erstickter Stimme.)

O, eine edle Himmelsgabe ist
Das Licht des Auges — Alle Wesen leben   590
Vom Lichte, jedes glückliche Geschöpf —
Die Pflanze selbst kehrt freudig sich zum Lichte.
Und e r muß sitzen, fühlend, in der Nacht,
Im ewig Finstern — ihn erquickt nicht mehr
Der Matten warmes Grün, der Blumen Schmelz;   595

Die roten Firnen kann er nicht mehr schauen —
Sterben ist nichts — doch l e b e n und nicht f e h e n,
Das ist ein Unglück — Warum seht ihr mich
So jammernd an? Ich hab' zwei frische Augen
Und kann dem blinden Vater keines geben,   600
Nicht einen Schimmer von dem Meer des Lichts,
Das glanzvoll, blendend mir ins Auge bringt. ——

Stauffacher.

Ach, ich muß euren Jammer noch vergrößern,
Statt ihn zu heilen — Er bedarf noch mehr!
Denn alles hat der Landvogt ihm geraubt;   605
Nichts hat er ihm gelassen, als den Stab,
Um nackt und blind von Thür zu Thür zu wandern.

Melchthal.

Nichts als den Stab dem augenlosen Greis!
Alles geraubt und auch das Licht der Sonne,
Des Ärmsten allgemeines Gut — Jetzt rede   610
Mir keiner mehr von Bleiben, von Verbergen!
Was für ein feiger Elender bin ich,
Daß ich auf m e i n e Sicherheit gedacht
Und nicht auf deine! — dein geliebtes Haupt
Als Pfand gelassen in des Wütrichs Händen!   615
Feigherz'ge Vorsicht, fahre hin — Auf nichts
Als blutige Vergeltung will ich denken.
Hinüber will ich — Keiner soll mich halten —
Des Vaters Auge von dem Landvogt fordern —
Aus allen seinen Reisigen heraus   620
Will ich ihn finden — Nichts liegt mir am Leben,
Wenn ich den heißen, ungeheuren Schmerz
In seinem Lebensblute kühle.   (Er will gehen.)

Walther Fürst.

Bleibt!

Was könnt ihr gegen ihn? Er sitzt zu Sarnen
Auf seiner hohen Herrenburg und spottet   625
Ohnmächt'gen Zorns in seiner sichern Feste.

Melchthal.

Und wohnt' er droben auf dem Eispalast
Des Schreckhorns oder höher, wo die Jungfrau
Seit Ewigkeit verschleiert sitzt — ich mache
Mir Bahn zu ihm; mit zwanzig Jünglingen,   630
Gesinnt, wie ich, zerbrech' ich seine Feste.
Und wenn mir niemand folgt, und wenn ihr alle,
Für eure Hütten bang und eure Herden,
Euch dem Thrannenjoche beugt — die Hirten
Will ich zusammenrufen im Gebirg,   635
Dort, unterm freien Himmelsdache, wo
Der Sinn noch frisch ist und das Herz gesund,
Das ungeheuer Gräßliche erzählen.

Stauffacher (zu Walther Fürst).

Es ist auf seinem Gipfel — Wollen wir
Erwarten, bis das Äußerste —

Melchthal.

          Welch Äußerstes   640
Ist noch zu fürchten, wenn der Stern des Auges
In seiner Höhle nicht mehr sicher ist?
— Sind wir denn wehrlos? Wozu lernten wir
Die Armbrust spannen und die schwere Wucht
Der Streitaxt schwingen? Jedem Wesen ward   645
Ein Notgewehr in der Verzweiflungsangst.
Es stellt sich der erschöpfte Hirsch und zeigt
Der Meute sein gefürchtetes Geweih,

Die Gemse reißt den Jäger in den Abgrund—
Der Pflugstier selbst, der sanfte Hausgenoß 650
Des Menschen, der die ungeheure Kraft
Des Halses duldsam unters Joch gebogen,
Springt auf, gereizt, wetzt sein gewaltig Horn
Und schleudert seinen Feind den Wolken zu.

Walther Fürst.

Wenn die drei Lande dächten wie wir drei, 655
So möchten wir vielleicht etwas vermögen.

Stauffacher.

Wenn Uri ruft, wenn Unterwalden hilft,
Der Schwyzer wird die alten Bünde ehren.

Melchthal.

Groß ist in Unterwalden meine Freundschaft,
Und jeder wagt mit Freuden Leib und Blut, 660
Wenn er am andern einen Rücken hat
Und Schirm — O fromme Väter dieses Landes!
Ich stehe, nur ein Jüngling, zwischen euch,
Den Vielerfahrnen — meine Stimme muß
Bescheiden schweigen in der Landsgemeinde. 665
Nicht, weil ich jung bin und nicht viel erlebte,
Verachtet meinen Rat und meine Rede;
Nicht lüstern jugendliches Blut, mich treibt
Des höchsten Jammers schmerzliche Gewalt,
Was auch den Stein des Felsen muß erbarmen. 670
Ihr selbst seid Väter, Häupter eines Hauses
Und wünscht euch einen tugendhaften Sohn,
Der eures Hauptes heil'ge Locken ehre
Und euch den Stern des Auges fromm bewache.
O, weil ihr selbst an eurem Leib und Gut 675
Noch nichts erlitten, eure Augen sich

Noch frisch und hell in ihren Kreisen regen,
So sei euch darum unsre Not nicht fremd.
Auch über euch hängt das Tyrannenschwert,
Ihr habt das Land von Östreich abgewendet; 680
Kein anderes war meines Vaters Unrecht,
Ihr seid in gleicher Mitschuld und Verdammnis.

Stauffacher (zu Walther Fürst).

Beschließet ihr! Ich bin bereit zu folgen.

Walther Fürst.

Wir wollen hören, was die edeln Herrn
Von Sillinen, von Attinghausen raten — 685
Ihr Name, denk' ich, wird uns Freunde werben.

Melchthal.

Wo ist ein Name in dein Waldgebirg'
Ehrwürdiger, als eurer und der eure?
An solcher Namen echte Währung glaubt
Das Volk, sie haben guten Klang im Lande. 690
Ihr habt ein reiches Erb' von Vätertugend
Und habt es selber reich vermehrt — Was braucht's
Des Edelmanns? Laßt's uns allein vollenden!
Wären wir doch allein im Land! Ich meine,
Wir wollten uns schon selbst zu schirmen wissen. 695

Stauffacher.

Die Edeln drängt nicht gleiche Not mit uns;
Der Strom, der in den Niederungen wütet,
Bis jetzt hat er die Höhn noch nicht erreicht —
Doch ihre Hilfe wird uns nicht entstehn,
Wenn sie das Land in Waffen erst erblicken. 700

Walther Fürst.

Wäre ein Obmann zwischen uns und Östreich,
So möchte Recht entscheiden und Gesetz.

Doch, der uns unterdrückt, ist unser Kaiser
Und höchster Richter — so muß Gott uns helfen
Durch unsern Arm — Erforschet ihr die Männer   705
Von Schwytz, ich will in Uri Freunde werben.
Wen aber senden wir nach Unterwalden? —

Melchthal.

Mich sendet hin — Wem läg' es näher an —

Walther Fürst.

Ich geb's nicht zu; ihr seid mein Gast, ich muß
Für eure Sicherheit gewähren!

Melchthal.

Laßt mich!   710
Die Schliche kenn' ich und die Felsensteige;
Auch Freunde find' ich gnug, die mich dem Feind
Verhehlen und ein Obdach gern gewähren.

Stauffacher.

Laßt ihn mit Gott hinüber gehn. Dort drüben
Ist kein Verräter — So verabscheut ist   715
Die Thrannei, daß sie kein Werkzeug findet.
Auch der Alzeller soll uns nid dem Wald
Genossen werben und das Land erregen.

Melchthal.

Wie bringen wir uns sichre Kunde zu,
Daß wir den Argwohn der Thrannen täuschen?   720

Stauffacher.

Wir könnten uns zu Brunnen oder Treib
Versammeln, wo die Kaufmannsschiffe landen.

Walther Fürst.

So offen dürfen wir das Werk nicht treiben

—Hört meine Meinung. Links am See, wenn man
Nach Brunnen fährt, dem Mythenstein grad' über,   725
Liegt eine Matte heimlich im Gehölz,
Das Rütli heißt sie bei dem Volk der Hirten,
Weil dort die Waldung ausgereutet ward.
Dort ist's, wo unsre Landmark und die eure (zu Melchthal).
Zusammengrenzen, und in kurzer Fahrt (zu Stauffacher).   730
Trägt euch der leichte Kahn von Schwyz herüber.
Auf öden Pfaden können wir dahin
Bei Nachtzeit wandern und uns still beraten.
Dahin mag jeder zehn vertraute Männer
Mitbringen, die herzeinig sind mit uns,   735
So können wir gemeinsam das Gemeine
Besprechen und mit Gott es frisch beschließen.

Stauffacher.

So sei's. Jetzt reicht mir eure biedre Rechte,
Reicht ihr die eure her, und so, wie wir
D r e i M ä n n e r jetzo unter uns die Hände   740
Zusammenflechten, redlich, ohne Falsch,
So wollen wir d r e i L ä n d e r auch zu Schutz
Und Trutz zusammenstehn auf Tod und Leben.

Walther Fürst und Melchthal.

Auf Tod und Leben!
(Sie halten die Hände noch einige Pausen lang zusammengeflochten
und schweigen.)

Melchthal.

Blinder, alter Vater!

Du kannst den Tag der Freiheit nicht mehr s c h a u e n ; 745
Du sollst ihn h ö r e n. — Wenn von Alp zu Alp
Die Feuerzeichen flammend sich erheben,

Die festen Schlösser der Thrannen fallen,
In deine Hütte soll der Schweizer wallen,
Zu deinem Ohr die Freudenkunde tragen,   750
Und hell in deiner Nacht soll es dir tagen.

(Sie gehen auseinander.)

Zweiter Aufzug.

Erste Scene.

Edelhof des Freiherrn von Attinghausen.

(Ein gotischer Saal, mit Wappenschildern und Helmen verziert. Der
Freiherr, ein Greis von fünfundachtzig Jahren, von hoher, edler Statur,
an einem Stabe, worauf ein Gemsenhorn, und in ein Pelzwams gekleidet.
Kuoni und noch sechs Knechte stehen um ihn her mit Rechen und
Sensen. Ulrich von Rudenz tritt ein in Ritterkleidung.)

Rudenz.

Hier bin ich, Oheim — Was ist euer Wille?

Attinghausen.

Erlaubt, daß ich nach altem Hausgebrauch
Den Frühtrunk erst mit meinen Knechten teile.

(Er trinkt aus einem Becher, der dann in der Reihe herumgeht.)

Sonst war ich selber mit in Feld und Wald,   755
Mit meinem Auge ihren Fleiß regierend,
Wie sie mein Banner führte in der Schlacht;
Jetzt kann ich nichts mehr, als den Schaffner machen,
Und kommt die warme Sonne nicht zu mir,
Ich kann sie nicht mehr suchen auf den Bergen.   760
Und so, in enger stets und engerm Kreis,
Beweg' ich mich dem engesten und letzten,

Wo alles Leben ſtillſteht, langſam zu.
Mein Schatte bin ich nur, bald nur mein Name.

    Kuoni (zu Rudenz mit dem Becher.)

Ich bring's euch, Junker.

  (Da Rudenz zaudert, den Becher zu nehmen.)

     Trinket friſch! Es geht 765
Aus einem Becher und aus einem Herzen.

    Attinghauſen.

Geht, Kinder, und wenn's Feierabend iſt,
Dann reden wir auch von des Lands Geſchäften.

  (Knechte gehen ab.)

  Attinghauſen und Rudenz.

    Attinghauſen.

Ich ſehe dich gegürtet und gerüſtet,
Du willſt nach Altorf in die Herrenburg? 770

    Rudenz.

Ja, Oheim, und ich darf nicht länger ſäumen —

    Attinghauſen (ſetzt ſich).

Haſt du's ſo eilig? Wie? Iſt deiner Jugend
Die Zeit ſo karg gemeſſen, daß du ſie
An deinem alten Oheim mußt erſparen?

    Rudenz.

Ich ſehe, daß ihr meiner nicht bedürft, 775
Ich bin ein Fremdling nur in dieſem Hauſe.

  Attinghauſen (hat ihn lange mit den Augen gemuſtert).

Ja, leider biſt du's. Leider iſt die Heimat
Zur Fremde dir geworden! — Uli! Uli!
Ich kenne dich nicht mehr. In Seide prangſt du,
Die Pfauenfeder trägſt du ſtolz zur Schau 780
Und ſchlägſt den Purpurmantel um die Schultern;

Den Landmann blickst du mit Verachtung an
Und schämst dich seiner traulichen Begrüßung.

Rudenz.

Die Ehr', die ihm gebührt, geb' ich ihm gern;
Das Recht, das er sich nimmt, verweigr' ich ihm.   785

Attinghausen.

Das ganze Land liegt unterm schweren Zorn
Des Königs — jedes Biedermannes Herz
Ist kummervoll ob der tyrannischen Gewalt,
Die wir erdulden — dich allein rührt nicht
Der allgemeine Schmerz — dich siehet man,   790
Abtrünnig von den Deinen, auf der Seite
Des Landesfeindes stehen, unsrer Not
Hohnsprechend, nach der leichten Freude jagen
Und buhlen um die Fürstengunst, indes
Dein Vaterland von schwerer Geißel blutet.   795

Rudenz.

Das Land ist schwer bedrängt — Warum, mein Oheim?
Wer ist's, der es gestürzt in diese Not?
Es kostete ein einzig leichtes Wort,
Um augenblicks des Dranges los zu sein
Und einen gnäd'gen Kaiser zu gewinnen.   800
Weh ihnen, die dem Volk die Augen halten,
Daß es dem wahren Besten widerstrebt!
Um eignen Vorteils willen hindern sie,
Daß die Waldstätte nicht zu Östreich schwören,
Wie ringsum alle Lande doch gethan.   805
Wohl thut es ihnen, auf der Herrenbank
Zu sitzen mit dem Edelmann — den K a i s e r
Will man zum Herrn, um k e i n e n Herrn zu haben.

Attinghausen.

Muß ich d a s hören und aus deinem Munde!

Rudenz.

Ihr habt mich aufgefordert, laßt mich enden!   810
— Welche Person ist's, Oheim, die ihr selbst
Hier spielt? Habt ihr nicht höhern Stolz, als hier
Landammann oder Bannerherr zu sein
Und neben diesen Hirten zu regieren?
Wie? Ist's nicht eine rühmlichere Wahl,   815
Zu huldigen dem königlichen Herrn,
Sich an sein glänzend Lager anzuschließen,
Als eurer eignen Knechte Pair zu sein
Und zu Gericht zu sitzen mit dem Bauer?

Attinghausen.

Ach, Uli, Uli! Ich erkenne sie,   820
Die Stimme der Verführung! Sie ergriff
Dein offnes Ohr, sie hat dein Herz vergiftet.

Rudenz.

Ja, ich verberg' es nicht — in tiefer Seele
Schmerzt mich der Spott der Fremdlinge, die uns
Den Bauernadel schelten — Nicht ertrag' ich's,   825
Indes die edle Jugend ringsumher
Sich Ehre sammelt unter Habsburgs Fahnen,
Auf meinem Erb' hier müßig still zu liegen
Und bei gemeinem Tagewerk den Lenz
Des Lebens zu verlieren — Anderswo   830
Geschehen Thaten, eine Welt des Ruhms
Bewegt sich glänzend jenseits dieser Berge —
Mir rosten in der Halle Helm und Schild;
Der Kriegsdrommete mutiges Getön,
Der Heroldsruf, der zum Turniere ladet,   835
Er bringt in diese Thäler nicht herein;

Nichts als den Kuhreihn und der Herdeglocken
Einförmiges Geläut' vernehm' ich hier.

Attinghausen.

Verblendeter, vom eiteln Glanz verführt!
Verachte dein Geburtsland! Schäme dich   840
Der uralt frommen Sitte deiner Väter!
Mit heißen Thränen wirst du dich dereinst
Heim sehnen nach den väterlichen Bergen,
Und dieses Herdenreihens Melodie,
Die du in stolzem Überdruß verschmähst,   845
Mit Schmerzenssehnsucht wird sie dich ergreifen,
Wenn sie dir anklingt auf der fremden Erde.
O, mächtig ist der Trieb des Vaterlands!
Die fremde, falsche Welt ist nicht für dich;
Dort an dem stolzen Kaiserhof bleibst du   850
Dir ewig fremd mit deinem treuen Herzen!
Die Welt, sie fordert andre Tugenden,
Als du in diesen Thälern dir erworben.
—Geh hin, verkaufe deine freie Seele,
Nimm Land zu Lehen, werd' ein Fürstenknecht,   855
Da du ein Selbstherr sein kannst und ein Fürst
Auf deinem eignen Erb' und freien Boden.
Ach, Uli! Uli! Bleibe bei den Deinen!
Geh nicht nach Altorf — O, verlaß sie nicht,
Die heil'ge Sache deines Vaterlands!   860
— Ich bin der Letzte meines Stamms — mein Name
Endet mit mir. Da hängen Helm und Schild;
Die werden sie mir in das Grab mitgeben.
Und muß ich denken bei dem letzten Hauch,
Daß du mein brechend Auge nur erwartest,   865
Um hinzugehn vor diesen neuen Lehenhof

Und meine edeln Güter, die ich frei
Von Gott empfing, von Östreich zu empfangen!

Rudenz.

Vergebens widerstreben wir dem König,
Die Welt gehört ihm; wollen wir allein   870
Uns eigensinnig steifen und verstocken,
Die Länderkette ihm zu unterbrechen,
Die er gewaltig rings um uns gezogen?
S e i n sind die Märkte, die Gerichte, f e i n
Die Kaufmannsstraßen, und das Saumroß selbst,   875
Das auf dem Gotthard ziehet, muß ihm zollen.
Von seinen Ländern wie mit einem Netz
Sind wir umgarnet rings und eingeschlossen.
—Wird uns das Reich beschützen? Kann es selbst
Sich schützen gegen Östreichs wachsende Gewalt? 880
Hilft Gott uns nicht, kein Kaiser kann uns helfen.
Was ist zu geben auf der Kaiser Wort,
Wenn sie in Geld= und Kriegesnot die Städte,
Die untern Schirm des Adlers sich geflüchtet,
Verpfänden dürfen und dem Reich veräußern?   885
—Nein, Oheim! Wohlthat ist's und weise Vorsicht,
In diesen schweren Zeiten der Parteiung
Sich anzuschließen an ein mächtig Haupt.
Die Kaiserkrone geht von Stamm zu Stamm,
D i e hat für treue Dienste kein Gedächtnis;   890.
Doch, um den mächt'gen Erbherrn wohl verdienen,
Heißt Saaten in die Zukunft streun.

Attinghausen.

Bist du so weise?

Willst heller sehn als deine edeln Väter,
Die um der Freiheit kostbarn Edelstein

Mit Gut und Blut und Heldenkraft gestritten? 895
—Schiff' nach Luzern hinunter, frage dort,
Wie Östreichs Herrschaft lastet auf den Ländern!
Sie werden kommen, unsre Schaf' und Rinder
Zu zählen, unsre Alpen abzumessen,
Den Hochflug und das Hochgewilde bannen 900
In unsern freien Wäldern, ihren Schlagbaum
An unsre Brücken, unsre Thore setzen,
Mit unsrer Armut ihre Länderkäufe,
Mit unserm Blute ihre Kriege zahlen—
—Nein, wenn wir unser Blut dran setzen sollen, 905
So sei's für uns—wohlfeiler kaufen wir
Die Freiheit als die Knechtschaft ein!

Rudenz

Was können wir,
Ein Volk der Hirten, gegen Albrechts Heere!

Attinghausen.

Lern' dieses Volk der Hirten kennen, Knabe!
Ich kenn's, ich hab' es angeführt in Schlachten, 910
Ich hab' es fechten sehen bei Favenz.
Sie sollen kommen, uns ein Joch aufzwingen,
Das wir entschlossen sind nicht zu ertragen!
—O, lerne fühlen, welches Stamms du bist!
Wirf nicht für eiteln Glanz und Flitterschein 915
Die echte Perle deines Wertes hin—
Das Haupt zu heißen eines freien Volks,
Das dir aus Liebe nur sich herzlich weiht,
Das treulich zu dir steht in Kampf und Tod—
Das sei dein Stolz, des Adels rühme dich— 920
Die angebornen Bande knüpfe fest,
Ans Vaterland, ans teure, schließ dich an,

Das halte fest mit deinem ganzen Herzen!
Hier sind die starken Wurzeln deiner Kraft;
Dort in der fremden Welt stehst du allein,   925
Ein schwankes Rohr, das jeder Sturm zerknickt.
O, komm, du hast uns lang' nicht mehr gesehn,
Versuch's mit uns nur e i n e n Tag — nur heute
Geh nicht nach Altorf — Hörst du? Heute nicht;
Den e i n e n Tag nur schenke dich den Deinen!   930
(Er faßt seine Hand.)

Rudenz.

Ich gab mein Wort — Laßt mich — Ich bin gebunden.

Attinghausen (läßt seine Hand los, mit Ernst).

Du bist gebunden — Ja, Unglücklicher,
Du bist's, doch nicht durch Wort und Schwur,
Gebunden bist du durch der Liebe Seile!
(Rudenz wendet sich weg.)

— Verbirg dich, wie du willst. Das Fräulein ist's,   935
Bertha von Bruneck, die zur Herrenburg
Dich zieht, dich fesselt an des Kaisers Dienst.
Das Ritterfräulein willst du dir erwerben
Mit deinem Abfall von dem Land — Betrüg dich nicht!
Dich anzulocken, zeigt man dir die Braut;   940
Doch deiner Unschuld ist sie nicht beschieden.

Rudenz.

Genug hab' ich gehört. Gehabt euch wohl!   (Er geht ab.)

Attinghausen.

Wahnsinn'ger Jüngling, bleib! Er geht dahin!
Ich kann ihn nicht erhalten, nicht erretten —
So ist der Wolfenschießen abgefallen   945
Von seinem Land — so werden andre folgen;
Der fremde Zauber reißt die Jugend fort,

Gewaltsam strebend über unsre Berge.
— O unglücksel'ge Stunde, da das Fremde
In diese still beglückten Thäler kam,   950
Der Sitten fromme Unschuld zu zerstören!
Das Neue dringt herein mit Macht, das Alte,
Das Würd'ge scheidet, andre Zeiten kommen,
Es lebt ein andersdenkendes Geschlecht!
Was thu' ich hier? Sie sind begraben alle,   955
Mit denen ich gewaltet und gelebt.
Unter der Erde schon liegt m e i n e Zeit;
Wohl dem, der mit der n e u e n nicht mehr braucht zu
      leben!

                          (Geht ab.)

Zweite Scene.

Eine Wiese von hohen Felsen und Wald umgeben.

Auf den Felsen sind Steige mit Geländern, auch Leitern, von denen man
nachher die Landleute herabsteigen sieht. Im Hintergrunde zeigt sich der
See, über welchem anfangs ein Mondregenbogen zu sehen ist. Den Prospekt schließen hohe Berge, hinter welchen noch höhere Eisgebirge ragen.
Es ist völlig Nacht auf der Scene, nur der See und die weißen Gletscher
leuchten im Mondlicht.

Melchthal, Baumgarten, Winkelried, Meier von Sarnen, Burkhardt am Bühel, Arnold von Sewa, Klaus
von der Flüe und noch vier andere Landleute, alle bewaffnet.

          Melchthal (noch hinter der Scene).

Der Bergweg öffnet sich, nur frisch m i r nach!
Den Fels erkenn' ich und das Kreuzlein drauf;   960
Wir sind am Ziel, hier ist das Rütli.

              (Treten auf mit Windlichtern.)

Winkelried.

Horch!

Sewa.

Ganz leer.

Meier.

's ist noch kein Landmann da. Wir sind
Die ersten auf dem Platz, wir Unterwaldner.

Melchthal.

Wie weit ist's in der Nacht?

Baumgarten.

Der Feuerwächter
Vom Selisberg hat eben zwei gerufen. 965

(Man hört in der Ferne läuten.)

Meier.

Still! Horch!

Am Bühel.

Das Mettenglöcklein in der Waldkapelle
Klingt hell herüber aus dem Schwyzerland.

Von der Flüe.

Die Luft ist rein und trägt den Schall so weit.

Melchthal.

Gehn einige und zünden Reisholz an,
Daß es loh brenne, wenn die Männer kommen. 970

(Zwei Landleute gehen.)

Sewa.

's ist eine schöne Mondennacht. Der See
Liegt ruhig da als wie ein ebner Spiegel.

Am Bühel.

Sie haben eine leichte Fahrt.

Winkelried (zeigt nach dem See).

Ha, seht!

Seht dorthin! Seht ihr nichts?

Meier.

Was denn? — Ja, wahrlich!
Ein Regenbogen mitten in der Nacht! 975

Melchthal.

Es ist das Licht des Mondes, das ihn bildet.

Von der Flüe.

Das ist ein seltsam wunderbares Zeichen!
Es leben viele, die das nicht gesehn.

Sewa.

Er ist doppelt; seht, ein blässerer steht drüber.

Baumgarten.

Ein Nachen fährt soeben drunter weg. 980

Melchthal.

Das ist der Stauffacher mit seinem Kahn,
Der Biedermann läßt sich nicht lang erwarten.

(Geht mit Baumgarten nach dem Ufer.)

Meier.

Die Urner sind es, die am längsten säumen.

Am Bühel.

Sie müssen weit umgehen durchs Gebirg,
Daß sie des Landvogts Kundschaft hintergehen. 985

(Unterdessen haben die zwei Landleute in der Mitte des Platzes ein
Feuer angezündet.)

Melchthal (am Ufer.)

Wer ist da? Gebt das Wort!

Stauffacher (von unten).

Freunde des Landes.

Alle gehen nach der Tiefe, den Kommenden entgegen. Aus dem Kahn
steigen Stauffacher, Itel Reding, Hans auf der Mauer,
Jörg im Hofe, Konrad Hunn, Ulrich der Schmid, Jost von
Weiler und noch drei andere Landleute, gleichfalls bewaffnet.

Alle (rufen).

Willkommen!

(Indem die übrigen in der Tiefe verweilen und sich begrüßen, kommt
Melchthal mit Stauffacher vorwärts.)

Melchthal.

O Herr Stauffacher! Ich hab' ihn
Gesehn, der mich nicht wiedersehen konnte!
Die Hand hab' ich gelegt auf seine Augen,
Und glühend Rachgefühl hab' ich gesogen   990
Aus der erloschnen Sonne seines Blicks.

Stauffacher.

Sprecht nicht von Rache! Nicht Geschehnes rächen,
Gedrohtem Übel wollen wir begegnen.
— Jetzt sagt, was ihr im Unterwaldner Land
Geschafft und für gemeine Sach' geworben,   995
Wie die Landleute denken, wie ihr selbst
Den Stricken des Verrats entgangen seid.

Melchthal.

Durch der Surennen furchtbares Gebirg,
Auf weit verbreitet öden Eisesfeldern,
Wo nur der heisre Lämmergeier krächzt,   1000
Gelangt' ich zu der Alpentrift, wo sich
Aus Uri und vom Engelberg die Hirten
Anrufend grüßen und gemeinsam weiden,
Den Durst mir stillend mit der Gletscher Milch,
Die in den Runsen schäumend niederquillt.   1005

In den einsamen Sennhütten kehrt' ich ein,
Mein eigner Wirt und Gast, bis daß ich kam
Zu Wohnungen gesellig lebender Menschen.
—Erschollen war in diesen Thälern schon
Der Ruf des neuen Greuels, der geschehn,   1010
Und fromme Ehrfurcht schaffte mir mein Unglück
Vor jeder Pforte, wo ich wandernd klopfte.
Entrüstet fand ich diese graden Seelen
Ob dem gewaltsam neuen Regiment;
Denn so wie ihre Alpen fort und fort   1015
Dieselben Kräuter nähren, ihre Brunnen
Gleichförmig fließen, Wolken selbst und Winde
Den gleichen Strich unwandelbar befolgen,
So hat die alte Sitte hier vom Ahn
Zum Enkel unverändert fort bestanden.   1020
Nicht tragen sie verwegne Neuerung
Im altgewohnten gleichen Gang des Lebens.
—Die harten Hände reichten sie mir dar,
Von den Wänden langten sie die rost'gen Schwerter,
Und aus den Augen blitzte freudiges   1025
Gefühl des Muts, als ich die Namen nannte,
Die im Gebirg dem Landmann heilig sind,
Den eurigen und Walther Fürsts — Was euch
Recht würde dünken, schwuren sie zu thun,
Euch schwuren sie bis in den Tod zu folgen.   1030
—So eilt' ich sicher unterm heil'gen Schirm
Des Gastrechts von Gehöfte zu Gehöfte —
Und als ich kam ins heimatliche Thal,
Wo mir die Vettern viel verbreitet wohnen —
Als ich den Vater fand, beraubt und blind,   1035
Auf fremdem Stroh, von der Barmherzigkeit
Mildthät'ger Menschen lebend —

Stauffacher.

Herr im Himmel!

Meldthal.

Da weint' ich nicht! Nicht in ohnmächt'gen Thränen
Goß ich die Kraft des heißen Schmerzens aus;
In tiefer Brust, wie einen teuren Schatz,   1040
Verschloß ich ihn und dachte nur auf Thaten.
Ich kroch durch alle Krümmen des Gebirgs,
Kein Thal war so versteckt, ich späht' es aus;
Bis an der Gletscher eisbedeckten Fuß
Erwartet' ich und fand bewohnte Hütten,   1045
Und überall, wohin mein Fuß mich trug,
Fand ich den gleichen Haß der Tyrannei;
Denn bis an diese letzte Grenze selbst
Belebter Schöpfung, wo der starre Boden
Aufhört zu geben, raubt der Vögte Geiz—   1050
Die Herzen alle dieses biedern Volks
Erregt' ich mit dem Stachel meiner Worte,
Und unser sind sie all'mit Herz und Mund.

Stauffacher.

Großes habt ihr in kurzer Frist geleistet.

Meldthal.

Ich that noch mehr. Die beiden Festen sind's,   1055
Roßberg und Sarnen, die der Landmann fürchtet;
Denn hinter ihren Felsenwällen schirmt
Der Feind sich leicht und schädiget das Land.
Mit eignen Augen wollt' ich es erfunden;
Ich war zu Sarnen und besah die Burg.   1060

Stauffacher.

Ihr wagtet euch bis in des Tigers Höhle?

Melchthal.

Ich war verkleidet dort in Pilgerstracht,
Ich sah den Landvogt an der Tafel schwelgen —
Urteilt, ob ich mein Herz bezwingen kann;
Ich sah den Feind, und ich erschlug ihn nicht.   1065

Stauffacher.

Fürwahr, das Glück war eurer Kühnheit hold.

(Unterdessen sind die anderen Landleute vorwärts gekommen und nähern
sich beiden.)

Doch jetzo sagt mir, wer die Freunde sind
Und die gerechten Männer, die euch folgten?
Macht mich bekannt mit ihnen, daß wir uns
Zutraulich nahen und die Herzen öffnen.   1070

Meier.

Wer kennte e u ch nicht, Herr, in den drei Landen?
Ich bin der Mei'r von Sarnen; dies hier ist
Mein Schwestersohn, der Struth von Winkelried.

Stauffacher.

Ihr nennt mir keinen unbekannten Namen.
Ein Winkelried war's, der den Drachen schlug   1075
Im Sumpf bei Weiler und sein Leben ließ
In diesem Strauß.

Winkelried.

Das war mein Ahn, Herr Werner.

Melchthal (zeigt auf zwei Landleute).

D i e wohnen hinterm Wald, sind Klosterleute
Vom Engelberg — Ihr werdet sie drum nicht
Verachten, weil sie e i g n e Leute sind   1080
Und nicht, wie wir, frei sitzen auf dem Erbe —
Sie lieben's Land, sind sonst auch wohl berufen.

Stauffacher (zu den beiden).

Gebt mir die Hand.　Es preise sich, wer keinem
Mit seinem Leibe pflichtig ist auf Erden;
Doch Redlichkeit gedeiht in jedem Stande.　　1085

Konrad Hunn.

Das ist Herr Reding, unser Altlandammann.

Meier.

Ich kenn' ihn wohl.　Er ist mein Widerpart,
Der um ein altes Erbstück mit mir rechtet.
— Herr Reding, wir sind Feinde vor Gericht;
Hier sind wir einig.　(Schüttelt ihm die Hand.)

Stauffacher.

　　　　　　Das ist brav gesprochen.　　1090

Winkelried.

Hört ihr?　Sie kommen.　Hört das Horn von Uri!
(Rechts und links sieht man bewaffnete Männer mit Windlichtern die
Felsen herabsteigen.)

Auf der Mauer.

Seht!　Steigt nicht selbst der fromme Diener Gottes,
Der würd'ge Pfarrer, mit herab?　Nicht scheut er
Des Weges Mühen und das Graun der Nacht,
Ein treuer Hirte für das Volk zu sorgen.　　1095

Baumgarten.

Der Sigrist folgt ihm und Herr Walther Fürst;
Doch nicht den Tell erblick' ich in der Menge.

Walther Fürst, Rösselmann, der Pfarrer, Petermann, der
Sigrist, Kuoni, der Hirt, Werni, der Jäger, Ruodi, der Fischer,
und noch fünf andere Landleute. Alle zusammen, dreiunddreißig an
der Zahl, treten vorwärts und stellen sich um das Feuer.

Walther Fürst.

So müssen wir auf unserm eignen Erb'
Und väterlichen Boden uns verstohlen

Zusammen schleichen, wie die Mörder thun,   1100
Und bei der Nacht, die ihren schwarzen Mantel
Nur dem Verbrechen und der sonnenscheuen
Verschwörung leihet, unser gutes Recht
Uns holen, das doch lauter ist und klar
Gleichwie der glanzvoll offne Schoß des Tages.   1105

Melchthal.

Laßt's gut sein! Was die dunkle Nacht gesponnen,
Soll frei und fröhlich an das Licht der Sonnen.

Rösselmann.

Hört, was mir Gott ins Herz giebt, Eidgenossen!
Wir stehen hier statt einer Landsgemeinde
Und können gelten für ein ganzes Volk.   1110
So laßt uns tagen nach den alten Bräuchen
Des Lands, wie wir's in ruhigen Zeiten pflegen;
Was ungesetzlich ist in der Versammlung,
Entschuldige die Not der Zeit. Doch Gott
Ist überall, wo man das Recht verwaltet,   1115
Und unter seinem Himmel stehen wir.

Stauffacher.

Wohl, laßt uns tagen nach der alten Sitte!
Ist es gleich Nacht, so leuchtet unser Recht.

Melchthal.

Ist gleich die Zahl nicht voll, das H e r z ist hier
Des ganzen Volks, die B e s t e n sind zugegen.   1120

Konrad Hunn.

Sind auch die alten Bücher nicht zur Hand,
Sie sind in unsre Herzen eingeschrieben.

Rösselmann.

Wohlan, so sei der Ring sogleich gebildet!
Man pflanze a u f die Schwerter der Gewalt!

Auf der Mauer.

Der Landesammann nehme seinen Platz,   1125
Und seine Weibel stehen ihm zur Seite!

Sigrist.

Es sind der Völker dreie. Welchem nun
Gebührt's, das Haupt zu geben der Gemeinde?

Meier.

Um diese Ehr' mag Schwyz mit Uri streiten;
Wir Unterwaldner stehen frei zurück.   1130

Melchthal.

Wir stehn zurück; wir sind die Flehenden,
Die Hilfe heischen von den mächt'gen Freunden.

Stauffacher.

So nehme Uri denn das Schwert; sein Banner
Zieht bei den Römerzügen uns voran.

Walther Fürst.

Des Schwertes Ehre werde Schwyz zu teil;   1135
Denn seines Stammes rühmen wir uns alle.

Rösselmann.

Den edeln Wettstreit laßt mich freundlich schlichten:
Schwyz soll im Rat, Uri im Felde führen.

Walther Fürst (reicht dem S t a u f f a c h e r die Schwerter).
So nehmt!

Stauffacher.

Nicht mir, dem Alter sei die Ehre!

Im Hofe.

Die meisten Jahre zählt Ulrich der Schmid.   1140

Auf der Mauer.

Der Mann ist wacker, doch nicht freien Stands;
Kein eigner Mann kann Richter sein in Schwyz.

Stauffacher.

Steht nicht Herr Reding hier, der Altlandammann?
Was suchen wir noch einen Würdigern?

Walther Fürst.

Er sei der Ammann und des Tages Haupt!   1145
Wer dazu stimmt, erhebe seine Hände!

(Alle heben die rechte Hand auf.)

Reding (tritt in die Mitte).

Ich kann die Hand nicht auf die Bücher legen,
So schwör' ich droben bei den ew'gen Sternen,
Daß ich mich nimmer will vom Recht entfernen.

*(Man richtet die zwei Schwerter vor ihm auf, der Ring bildet sich um ihn
her, Schwyz hält die Mitte, rechts stellt sich Uri und links Unterwalden. Er
steht auf sein Schlachtschwert gestützt.)*

Was ist's, das die drei Völker des Gebirgs   1150
Hier an des Sees unwirtlichem Gestade
Zusammenführte in der Geisterstunde?
Was soll der Inhalt sein des neuen Bunds,
Den wir hier unterm Sternenhimmel stiften?

Stauffacher (tritt in den Ring).

Wir stiften keinen neuen Bund; es ist   1155
Ein uralt Bündnis nur von Väter Zeit,
Das wir erneuern! Wisset, Eidgenossen!
Ob uns der See, ob uns die Berge scheiden
Und jedes Volk sich für sich selbst regiert,
So sind wir e i n e s Stammes doch und Bluts,   1160
Und e i n e Heimat ist's, aus der wir zogen.

Winkelried.

So ist es wahr, wie's in den Liedern lautet,
Daß wir von fernher in das Land gewallt?
O, teilt's uns mit, was euch davon bekannt,
Daß sich der neue Bund am alten stärke!　　　　1165

Stauffacher.

Hört, was die alten Hirten sich erzählen.
— Es war ein großes Volk, hinten im Lande
Nach Mitternacht, das litt von schwerer Teurung.
In dieser Not beschloß die Landsgemeinde,
Daß je der zehnte Bürger nach dem Los　　　　1170
Der Väter Land verlasse — Das geschah!
Und zogen aus, wehklagend, Männer und Weiber,
Ein großer Heerzug, nach der Mittagsonne,
Mit dem Schwert sich schlagend durch das deutsche Land,
Bis an das Hochland dieser Waldgebirge.　　　　1175
Und eher nicht ermüdete der Zug,
Bis daß sie kamen in das wilde Thal,
Wo jetzt die Muotta zwischen Wiesen rinnt —
Nicht Menschenspuren waren hier zu sehen,
Nur eine Hütte stand am Ufer einsam,　　　　1180
Da saß ein Mann und wartete der Fähre —
Doch heftig wogete der See und war
Nicht fahrbar; da besahen sie das Land
Sich näher und gewahrten schöne Fülle
Des Holzes und entdeckten gute Brunnen　　　　1185
Und meinten, sich im lieben Vaterland
Zu finden — Da beschlossen sie zu bleiben,
Erbaueten den alten Flecken S ch w y z
Und hatten manchen sauren Tag, den Wald
Mit weitverschlungnen Wurzeln auszuroden —　　　　1190

Drauf, als der Boden nicht mehr Gnügen that
Der Zahl des Volks, da zogen sie hinüber
Zum schwarzen Berg, ja, bis ans Weißland hin,
Wo, hinter ew'gem Eiseswall verborgen,
Ein andres Volk in andern Zungen spricht.   1195
Den Flecken S t a n z erbauten sie am Kernwald,
Den Flecken A l t o r f in dem Thal der Reuß —
Doch blieben sie des Ursprungs stets gedenk;
Aus all den fremden Stämmen, die seitdem
In Mitte ihres Lands sich angesiedelt,   1200
Finden die Schwyzer Männer sich heraus,
Es giebt das Herz, das Blut sich zu erkennen.

(Reicht rechts und links die Hand hin.)

Auf der Mauer.

Ja, wir sind e i n e s Herzens, e i n e s Bluts!

Alle (sich die Hände reichend).

Wir sind e i n Volk, und einig wollen wir handeln.

Stauffacher.

Die andern Völker tragen fremdes Joch,   1205
Sie haben sich dem Sieger unterworfen.
Es leben selbst in unsern Landesmarken
Der Sassen viel, die fremde Pflichten tragen,
Und ihre Knechtschaft erbt auf ihre Kinder.
Doch w i r, der alten Schweizer echter Stamm,   1210
Wir haben stets die Freiheit uns bewahrt.
Nicht unter Fürsten bogen wir das Knie,
Freiwillig wählten wir den Schirm der Kaiser.

Rösselmann.

Frei wählten wir des Reiches Schutz und Schirm;
So steht's bemerkt in Kaiser Friedrichs Brief.   1215

Stauffacher.

Denn herrenlos ist auch der Freiste nicht.
Ein Oberhaupt muß sein, ein höchster Richter,
Wo man das Recht mag schöpfen in dem Streit.
Drum haben unsre Väter für den Boden,
Den sie der alten Wildnis abgewonnen,   1220
Die Ehr' gegönnt dem Kaiser, der den Herrn
Sich nennt der deutschen und der welschen Erde,
Und, wie die andern Freien seines Reichs,
Sich ihm zu edelm Waffendienst gelobt;
Denn dieses ist der Freien einz'ge Pflicht,   1225
Das Reich zu schirmen, das sie selbst beschirmt.

Melchthal.

Was drüber ist, ist Merkmal eines Knechts.

Stauffacher.

Sie folgten, wenn der Heribann erging,
Dem Reichspanier und schlugen seine Schlachten.
Nach Welschland zogen sie gewappnet mit,   1230
Die Römerkron' ihm auf das Haupt zu setzen.
Daheim regierten sie sich fröhlich selbst
Nach altem Brauch und eigenem Gesetz,
Der höchste Blutbann war allein des Kaisers.
Und dazu ward bestellt ein großer Graf,   1235
Der hatte seinen Sitz nicht in dem Lande.
Wenn Blutschuld kam, so rief man ihn herein,
Und unter offnem Himmel, schlicht und klar,
Sprach er das Recht und ohne Furcht der Menschen.
Wo sind hier Spuren, daß wir Knechte sind?   1240
Ist einer, der es anders weiß, der rede!

Im Hofe.

Nein, so verhält sich alles, wie ihr sprecht,
Gewaltherrschaft ward nie bei uns geduldet.

Stauffacher.

Dem Kaiser selbst versagten wir Gehorsam,
Da er das Recht zu Gunst der Pfaffen bog.   1245
Denn als die Leute von dem Gotteshaus
Einsiedeln uns die Alp in Anspruch nahmen
Die wir beweidet seit der Väter Zeit,
Der Abt herfürzog einen alten Brief,
Der ihm die herrenlose Wüste schenkte —   1250
Denn unser Dasein hatte man verhehlt —
Da sprachen wir: „Erschlichen ist der Brief!
Kein Kaiser kann, was unser ist, verschenken;
Und wird uns Recht versagt vom Reich, wir können
In unsern Bergen auch des Reichs entbehren.‟   1255
— So sprachen unsre Väter! Sollen w i r
Des neuen Joches Schändlichkeit erdulden,
Erleiden von dem fremden Knecht, was uns
In seiner Macht kein Kaiser durfte bieten?
— Wir haben diesen Boden uns e r s c h a f f e n   1260
Durch unsrer Hände Fleiß, den alten Wald,
Der sonst der Bären wilde Wohnung war,
Zu einem Sitz für Menschen umgewandelt;
Die Brut des Drachen haben wir getötet,
Der aus den Sümpfen giftgeschwollen stieg;   1265
Die Nebeldecke haben wir zerrissen,
Die ewig grau um diese Wildnis hing,
Den harten Fels gesprengt, über den Abgrund
Dem Wandersmann den sichern Steg geleitet;
Unser ist durch tausendjährigen Besitz   1270
Der Boden — und der fremde Herrenknecht
Soll kommen dürfen und uns Ketten schmieden
Und Schmach anthun auf unsrer eignen Erde?
Ist keine Hilfe gegen solchen Drang?
     (Eine große Bewegung unter den Landleuten.)

Nein, eine Grenze hat Tyrannenmacht.   1275
Wenn der Gedrückte nirgends Recht kann finden
Wenn unerträglich wird die Last — greift er
Hinauf getrosten Mutes in den Himmel
Und holt herunter seine ew'gen Rechte,
Die droben hangen unveräußerlich   1280
Und unzerbrechlich wie die Sterne selbst —
Der alte Urstand der Natur kehrt wieder,
Wo Mensch dem Menschen gegenüber steht —
Zum letzten Mittel, wenn kein andres mehr
Verfangen will, ist ihm das Schwert gegeben —   1285
Der Güter höchstes dürfen wir verteid'gen
Gegen Gewalt — Wir stehn für unser Land,
Wir stehn für unsre Weiber, unsre Kinder!

     Alle (an ihre Schwerter schlagend.)

Wir stehn für unsre Weiber, unsre Kinder!

     Rösselmann (tritt in den Ring.)

Eh' ihr zum Schwerte greift, bedenkt es wohl!   1290
Ihr könnt es friedlich mit dem Kaiser schlichten.
Es kostet euch ein Wort, und die Tyrannen,
Die euch jetzt schwer bedrängen, schmeicheln euch.
— Ergreift, was man euch oft geboten hat,
Trennt euch vom Reich, erkennet Östreichs Hoheit —   1295

     Auf der Mauer.

Was sagt der Pfarrer? Wir zu Östreich schwören!

     Am Bühel.

Hört ihn nicht an!

     Winkelried.

        Das rät uns ein Verräter,
Ein Feind des Landes!

Reding.

Ruhig, Eidgenossen!

Sewa.

Wir Östreich huldigen, nach solcher Schmach!

Von der Flüe.

Wir uns abtrotzen lassen durch Gewalt,   1300
Was wir der Güte weigerten!

Meier.

Dann wären
Wir Sklaven und verdienten, es zu sein!

Auf der Mauer.

Der sei gestoßen aus dem Recht der Schweizer,
Wer von Ergebung spricht an Österreich!
— Landammann, ich bestehe drauf; dies sei   1305
Das erste Landsgesetz, das wir hier geben.

Melchthal.

So sei's! Wer von Ergebung spricht an Östreich,
Soll rechtlos sein und aller Ehren bar,
Kein Landmann nehm' ihn auf an seinem Feuer.

Alle (heben die rechte Hand auf).

Wir wollen es, das sei Gesetz!

Reding (nach einer Pause).

Es ist's.   1310

Rösselmann.

Jetzt seid ihr frei, ihr seid's durch dies Gesetz.
Nicht durch Gewalt soll Österreich ertrotzen,
Was es durch freundlich Werben nicht erhielt —

Joft von Weiler.

Zur Tagesordnung, weiter!

Reding.

Eidgenossen!

Sind alle sanften Mittel auch versucht?   1315
Vielleicht weiß es der König nicht; es ist
Wohl gar sein Wille nicht, was wir erdulden.
Auch dieses letzte sollten wir versuchen,
Erst unsre Klage bringen vor sein Ohr,
Eh' wir zum Schwerte greifen. Schrecklich immer,   1320
Auch in gerechter Sache, ist Gewalt.
Gott hilft nur dann, wenn Menschen nicht mehr helfen.

Stauffacher (zu Konrad Hunn).

Nun ist's an euch, Bericht zu geben. Redet!

Konrad Hunn.

Ich war zu Rheinfeld an des Kaisers Pfalz,
Wider der Vögte harten Druck zu klagen,   1325
Den Brief zu holen unsrer alten Freiheit,
Den jeder neue König sonst bestätigt.
Die Boten vieler Städte fand ich dort,
Vom schwäb'schen Lande und vom Lauf des Rheins,
Die all' erhielten ihre Pergamente   1330
Und kehrten freudig wieder in ihr Land.
Mich, euren Boten, wies man an die Räte,
Und die entließen mich mit leerem Trost:
„Der Kaiser habe diesmal keine Zeit;
Er würde sonst einmal wohl an uns denken.“   1335
—Und als ich traurig durch die Säle ging
Der Königsburg, da sah ich Herzog Hansen
In einem Erker weinend stehn, um ihn
Die edeln Herrn von Wart und Tegerfeld.

Die riefen mir und sagten: „Helft euch selbst!   1340
Gerechtigkeit erwartet nicht vom König.
Beraubt er nicht des eignen Bruders Kind
Und hinterhält ihm sein gerechtes Erbe?
Der Herzog fleht' ihn um sein Mütterliches,
Er habe seine Jahre voll, es wäre   1345
Nun Zeit, auch Land und Leute zu regieren.
Was ward ihm zum Bescheid? Ein Kränzlein setzt' ihm
Der Kaiser auf: Das sei die Zier der Jugend."

Auf der Mauer.

Ihr habt's gehört.   Recht und Gerechtigkeit
Erwartet nicht vom Kaiser!   Helft euch selbst!   1350

Reding.

Nichts andres bleibt uns übrig.   Nun gebt Rat,
Wie wir es klug zum frohen Ende leiten.

Walther Fürst (tritt in den Ring).

Abtreiben wollen wir verhaßten Zwang;
Die alten Rechte, wie wir sie ererbt
Von unsern Vätern, wollen wir bewahren,   1355
Nicht ungezügelt nach dem Neuen greifen.
Dem Kaiser bleibe, was des Kaisers ist;
Wer einen Herrn hat, dien' ihm pflichtgemäß.

Meier.

Ich trage Gut von Österreich zu Lehen.

Walther Fürst.

Ihr fahret fort, Östreich die Pflicht zu leisten.   1360

Jost von Weiler.

Ich steure an die Herrn von Rappersweil.

Walther Fürst.

Ihr fahret fort, zu zinsen und zu steuern.

Rösselmann.

Der großen Frau zu Zürch bin ich vereidet.

Walther Fürst.

Ihr gebt dem Kloster, was des Klosters ist.

Stauffacher.

Ich trage keine Lehen als des Reichs.　　　　　　　　1365

Walther Fürst.

Was sein muß, das geschehe, doch nicht drüber!
Die Vögte wollen wir mit ihren Knechten
Verjagen und die festen Schlösser brechen;
Doch, wenn es sein mag, ohne Blut. Es sehe
Der Kaiser, daß wir notgedrungen nur　　　　　　　　1370
Der Ehrfurcht fromme Pflichten abgeworfen.
Und sieht er uns in unsern Schranken bleiben,
Vielleicht besiegt er staatsklug seinen Zorn;
Denn bill'ge Furcht erwecket sich ein Volk,
Das mit dem Schwerte in der Faust sich mäßigt.　　　　1375

Reding.

Doch lasset hören! Wie vollenden wir's?
Es hat der Feind die Waffen in der Hand,
Und nicht fürwahr in Frieden wird er weichen.

Stauffacher.

Er wird's, wenn er in Waffen uns erblickt;
Wir überraschen ihn, eh' er sich rüstet.　　　　　　1380

Meier.

Ist bald gesprochen, aber schwer gethan.
Uns ragen in dem Land zwei feste Schlösser,
Die geben Schirm dem Feind und werden furchtbar,
Wenn uns der König in das Land sollt' fallen.
Roßberg und Sarnen muß bezwungen sein,　　　　　　1385
Eh' man ein Schwert erhebt in den drei Landen.

Stauffacher.

Säumt man so lang', so wird der Feind gewarnt;
Zu viele sind's, die das Geheimnis teilen.

Meier.

In den Waldstätten find't sich kein Verräter.

Rösselmann.

Der Eifer auch, der gute, kann verraten.   1390

Walther Fürst.

Schiebt man es auf, so wird der Twing vollendet
In Altorf, und der Vogt befestigt sich.

Meier.

Ihr denkt an e u ch.

Sigrist.

Und ihr seid ungerecht.

Meier (auffahrend).

Wir ungerecht! Das darf uns Uri bieten!

Reding.

Bei eurem Eide, Ruh'!

Meier.

Ja, wenn sich Schwyz   1395
Versteht mit Uri, müssen w i r wohl schweigen.

Reding.

Ich muß euch weisen vor der Landsgemeinde,
Daß ihr mit heft'gem Sinn den Frieden stört!
Stehn wir nicht alle für dieselbe Sache?

Winkelried.

Wenn wir's verschieben bis zum Fest des Herrn,   1400
Dann bringt's die Sitte mit, daß alle Sassen
Dem Vogt Geschenke bringen auf das Schloß;

So können zehen Männer oder zwölf
Sich unverdächtig in der Burg versammeln,
Die führen heimlich spitz'ge Eisen mit,   1405
Die man geschwind kann an die Stäbe stecken;
Denn niemand kommt mit Waffen in die Burg.
Zunächst im Wald hält dann der große Haufe,
Und wenn die andern glücklich sich des Thors
Ermächtiget, so wird ein Horn geblasen,   1410
Und jene brechen aus dem Hinterhalt.
So wird das Schloß mit leichter Arbeit unser.

Melchthal.

Den Roßberg übernehm' ich zu ersteigen,
Denn eine Dirn' des Schlosses ist mir hold,
Und leicht bethör' ich sie, zum nächtlichen   1415
Besuch die schwanke Leiter mir zu reichen;
Bin ich droben erst, zieh' ich die Freunde nach.

Reding.

Ist's aller Wille, daß verschoben werde?
(Die Mehrheit erhebt die Hand.)

Stauffacher (zählt die Stimmen).

Es ist ein Mehr von zwanzig gegen zwölf!

Walther Fürst.

Wenn am bestimmten Tag die Burgen fallen,   1420
So geben wir von einem Berg zum andern
Das Zeichen mit dem Rauch; der Landsturm wird
Aufgeboten, schnell, im Hauptort jedes Landes.
Wenn dann die Vögte sehn der Waffen Ernst,
Glaubt mir, sie werden sich des Streits begeben   1425
Und gern ergreifen friedliches Geleit,
Aus unsern Landesmarken zu entweichen.

Stauffacher.

Nur mit dem Geßler fürcht' ich schweren Stand,
Furchtbar ist er mit Reisigen umgeben;
Nicht ohne Blut räumt er das Feld; ja, selbst   1430
Vertrieben bleibt er furchtbar noch dem Land.
Schwer ist's und fast gefährlich, ihn zu schonen.

Baumgarten.

Wo's halsgefährlich ist, da stellt mich hin!
Dem Tell verdank' ich mein gerettet Leben.
Gern schlag' ich's in die Schanze für das Land,   1435
Mein' Ehr' hab' ich beschützt, mein Herz befriedigt.

Reding.

Die Zeit bringt Rat.   Erwartet's in Geduld!
Man muß dem Augenblick auch was vertrauen.
—Doch seht, indes wir nächtlich hier noch tagen,
Stellt auf den höchsten Bergen schon der Morgen   1440
Die glühnde Hochwacht aus — Kommt, laßt uns scheiden,
Eh' uns des Tages Leuchten überrascht.

Walther Fürst.

Sorgt nicht, die Nacht weicht langsam aus den Thälern.

(Alle haben unwillkürlich die Hüte abgenommen und betrachten mit stiller
Sammlung die Morgenröte.)

Rösselmann.

Bei diesem Licht, das uns zuerst begrüßt
Von allen Völkern, die tief unter uns   1445
Schwer atmend wohnen in dem Qualm der Städte,
Laßt uns den Eid des neuen Bundes schwören.
—Wir wollen sein ein einzig Volk von Brüdern,
In keiner Not uns trennen und Gefahr.

(Alle sprechen es nach mit erhobenen drei Fingern.)

—Wir wollen frei sein, wie die Väter waren,   1450
Eher den Tod, als in der Knechtschaft leben. (Wie oben.)

—Wir wollen trauen auf den höchsten Gott
Und uns nicht fürchten vor der Macht der Menschen.

(Wie oben. Die Landleute umarmen einander.)

Stauffacher.

Jetzt gehe jeder seines Weges still
Zu seiner Freundschaft und Genoßsame!   1455
Wer Hirt ist, wintre ruhig seine Herde
Und werb' im stillen Freunde für den Bund!
—Was noch bis dahin muß erduldet werden,
Erduldet's! Laßt die Rechnung der Thrannen
Anwachsen, bis ein Tag die allgemeine   1460
Und die besondre Schuld auf einmal zahlt.
Bezähme jeder die gerechte Wut
Und spare für das Ganze seine Rache;
Denn Raub begeht am allgemeinen Gut,
Wer selbst sich hilft in seiner eignen Sache.   1465

(Indem sie zu drei verschiedenen Seiten in größter Ruhe abgehen, fällt das
Orchester mit einem prachtvollen Schwung ein; die leere Scene bleibt noch
eine Zeit lang offen und zeigt das Schauspiel der aufgehenden Sonne über
den Eisgebirgen.)

Dritter Aufzug.

Erste Scene.

Hof vor Tells Hause.

Tell ist mit der Zimmeraxt, Hedwig mit einer häuslichen Arbeit beschäftigt. Walther und Wilhelm in der Tiefe spielen mit einer kleinen Armbrust.

Walther (singt).

Mit dem Pfeil, dem Bogen,
　　Durch Gebirg und Thal
　　Kommt der Schütz gezogen
　　Früh am Morgenstrahl.

Wie im Reich der Lüfte　　　　　　　　　　1470
　　König ist der Weih —
　　Durch Gebirg und Klüfte
　　Herrscht der Schütze frei.

Ihm gehört das Weite,
　　Was sein Pfeil erreicht,　　　　　　　1475
　　Das ist seine Beute,
　　Was da kreucht und fleugt.

(Kommt gesprungen.)

Der Strang ist mir entzwei.　Mach' mir ihn, Vater!

Tell.

Ich nicht.　Ein rechter Schütze hilft sich selbst.

(Knaben entfernen sich.)

Hedwig.

Die Knaben fangen zeitig an zu schießen.　　　1480

Tell.

Früh übt sich, was ein Meister werden will.

Hedwig.

Ach, wollte Gott, sie lernten's nie!

THE HUNTER'S SONG.

Reproduced from the original MS. in possession of Herrn Geheimen
Justizrats Lessing in Berlin. (To face p. 72)

Tell.

Sie sollen alles lernen. Wer durchs Leben
Sich frisch will schlagen, muß zu Schutz und Trutz
Gerüstet sein.

Hedwig.

Ach, es wird keiner seine Ruh'   1485
Zu Hause finden.

Tell.

Mutter, ich kann's auch nicht,
Zum Hirten hat Natur mich nicht gebildet;
Rastlos muß ich ein flüchtig Ziel verfolgen.
Dann erst genieß' ich meines Lebens recht,
Wenn ich mir's jeden Tag aufs neu' erbeute.   1490

Hedwig.

Und an die Angst der Hausfrau denkst du nicht,
Die sich indessen, deiner wartend, härmt.
Denn mich erfüllt's mit Grausen, was die Knechte
Von euren Wagefahrten sich erzählen;
Bei jedem Abschied zittert mir das Herz,   1495
Daß du mir nimmer werdest wiederkehren.
Ich sehe dich, im wilden Eisgebirg
Verirrt, von einer Klippe zu der andern
Den Fehlsprung thun, seh', wie die Gemse dich
Rückspringend mit sich in den Abgrund reißt,   1500
Wie eine Windlawine dich verschüttet,
Wie unter dir der trügerische Firn
Einbricht, und du hinabsinkst, ein lebendig
Begrabner, in die schauerliche Gruft —
Ach, den verwegnen Alpenjäger hascht   1505
Der Tod in hundert wechselnden Gestalten!
Das ist ein unglückseliges Gewerb',
Das halsgefährlich führt am Abgrund hin!

Tell.

Wer frisch umherspäht mit gesunden Sinnen,
Auf Gott vertraut und die gelenke Kraft,   1510
Der ringt sich leicht aus jeder Fahr und Not;
Den schreckt der Berg nicht, der darauf geboren.

(Er hat seine Arbeit vollendet, legt das Gerät hinweg.)

Jetzt, mein' ich, hält das Thor auf Jahr und Tag.
Die Axt im Haus erspart den Zimmermann.

(Nimmt den Hut.)

Hedwig.

Wo gehst du hin?

Tell.

Nach Altorf, zu dem Vater.   1515

Hedwig.

Sinnst du auch nichts Gefährliches?   Gesteh mir's!

Tell.

Wie kommst du darauf, Frau?

Hedwig.

Es spinnt sich etwas
Gegen die Vögte — Auf dem Rütli ward
Getagt, ich weiß, und du bist auch im Bunde.

Tell.

Ich war nicht mit dabei — doch werd' ich mich   1520
Dem Lande nicht entziehen, wenn es ruft.

Hedwig.

Sie werden dich hinstellen, wo Gefahr ist;
Das Schwerste wird dein Anteil sein, wie immer.

Tell.

Ein jeder wird besteuert nach Vermögen.

Hedwig.

Den Unterwaldner hast du auch im Sturme
Über den See geschafft — Ein Wunder war's,

Daß ihr entkommen — Dachtest du denn gar nicht
An Kind und Weib?

Tell.

Lieb Weib, ich dacht' an euch;
Drum rettet' ich den Vater seinen Kindern.

Hedwig.

Zu schiffen in dem wüt'gen See! Das heißt   1530
Nicht Gott vertrauen! Das heißt Gott versuchen!

Tell.

Wer gar zu viel bedenkt, wird wenig leisten.

Hedwig.

Ja, du bist gut und hilfreich, dienest allen,
Und wenn du selbst in Not kommst, hilft dir keiner.

Tell.

Verhüt' es Gott, daß ich nicht Hilfe brauche!   1535
(Er nimmt die Armbrust und Pfeile.)

Hedwig.

Was willst du mit der Armbrust? Laß sie hier!

Tell.

Mir fehlt der Arm, wenn mir die Waffe fehlt.
(Die Knaben kommen zurück.)

Walther.

Vater, wo gehst du hin?

Tell.

Nach Altorf, Knabe
Zum Ehni — Willst du mit?

Walther.

Ja, freilich will ich.

Hedwig.

Der Landvogt ist jetzt dort. Bleib weg von Altorf.   1540

Tell.

Er g e h t, noch heute.

Hedwig.

          Drum laß ihn erst fort sein!
Gemahn' ihn nicht an dich, du weißt, er grollt uns.

Tell.

Mir soll sein böser Wille nicht viel schaden,
Ich thue recht und scheue keinen Feind.

Hedwig.

Die recht thun, eben die haßt er am meisten.   1545

Tell.

Weil er nicht an sie kommen kann — Mich wird
Der Ritter wohl in Frieden lassen, mein' ich.

Hedwig.

So, weißt du das?

Tell.

          Es ist nicht lange her,
Da ging ich jagen durch die wilden Gründe
Des Schächenthals auf menschenleerer Spur,   1550
Und da ich einsam einen Felsensteig
Verfolgte, wo nicht auszuweichen war,
Denn über mir hing schroff die Felswand her,
Und unten rauschte fürchterlich der Schächen,

(Die Knaben drängen sich rechts und links an ihn und sehen mit gespannter
Neugier an ihm hinauf.)

Da kam der Landvogt gegen mich daher,   1555
Er ganz allein mit mir, der auch allein war,
Bloß Mensch zu Mensch, und neben uns der Abgrund.
Und als der Herre mein ansichtig ward
Und mich erkannte, den er kurz zuvor
Um kleiner Ursach' willen schwer gebüßt,   1560
Und sah mich mit dem stattlichen Gewehr
Daher geschritten kommen, da verblaßt' er,
Die Knie' versagten ihm, ich sah es kommen,

Daß er jetzt an die Felswand würde sinken.
— Da jammerte mich sein, ich trat zu ihm   1565
Bescheidentlich und sprach: Ich bin's, Herr Landvogt.
Er aber konnte keinen armen Laut
Aus seinem Munde geben — Mit der Hand nur
Winkt' er mir schweigend, meines Wegs zu gehn;
Da ging ich fort und sandt' ihm sein Gefolge.   1570

Hedwig.

Er hat vor dir gezittert — Wehe dir!
Daß du ihn schwach gesehn, vergiebt er nie.

Tell.

Drum meid' ich ihn, und er wird mich nicht suchen.

Hedwig.

Bleib heute nur dort weg. Geh lieber jagen!

Tell.

Was fällt dir ein?

Hedwig.

          Mich ängstigt's. Bleibe weg!   1575

Tell.

Wie kannst du dich so ohne Ursach' quälen?

Hedwig.

Weil's keine Ursach' hat — Tell, bleibe hier!

Tell.

Ich hab's versprochen, liebes Weib, zu kommen.

Hedwig.

Mußt du, so geh — nur lasse mir den Knaben!

Walther.

Nein, Mütterchen. Ich gehe mit dem Vater.   1580

Hedwig.

Wälti, verlassen willst du deine Mutter?

Walther.
Ich bring' dir auch was Hübsches mit vom Ehni.
(Geht mit dem Vater.)

Wilhelm.
Mutter, ich bleibe bei dir!

Hedwig (umarmt ihn.)
Ja, du bist
Mein liebes Kind, du bleibst mir noch allein!
(Sie geht an das Hofthor und folgt den Abgehenden lange mit den Augen.)

Zweite Scene.

Eine eingeschlossene wilde Waldgegend,
Staubbäche stürzen von den Felsen.

Bertha im Jagdkleid. Gleich darauf Rudenz.

Bertha.
Er folgt mir.   Endlich kann ich mich erklären.   1585

Rudenz (tritt rasch ein).
Fräulein, jetzt endlich find' ich euch allein,
Abgründe schließen ringsumher uns ein;
In dieser Wildnis fürcht' ich keinen Zeugen,
Vom Herzen wälz' ich dieses lange Schweigen —

Bertha.
Seid ihr gewiß, daß uns die Jagd nicht folgt?   1590

Rudenz.
Die Jagd ist dort hinaus — Jetzt oder nie!
Ich muß den teuren Augenblick ergreifen —
Entschieden sehen muß ich mein Geschick,
Und sollt' es mich auf ewig von euch scheiden.

—O, waffnet eure güt'gen Blicke nicht   1595
Mit dieser finstern Strenge —Wer bin ich,
Daß ich den kühnen Wunsch zu euch erhebe?
Mich hat der Ruhm noch nicht genannt; ich darf
Mich in die Reih' nicht stellen mit den Rittern,
Die siegberühmt und glänzend euch umwerben.   1600
Nichts hab' ich als mein Herz voll Treu und Liebe —

       Bertha (ernst und streng).

Dürft ihr von Liebe reden und von Treue,
Der treulos wird an seinen nächsten Pflichten?

       (Rudenz tritt zurück.)

Der Sklave Österreichs, der sich dem Fremdling
Verkauft, dem Unterdrücker seines Volks?   1605

       Rudenz.

Von euch, mein Fräulein, hör' ich diesen Vorwurf?
Wen such' ich denn als euch auf jener Seite?

       Bertha.

Mich denkt ihr auf der Seite des Verrats
Zu finden? Eher wollt' ich meine Hand
Dem Geßler selbst, dem Unterdrücker, schenken,   1610
Als dem naturvergeßnen Sohn der Schweiz,
Der sich zu seinem Werkzeug machen kann!

       Rudenz.

O Gott, was muß ich hören!

       Bertha.

         Wie? Was liegt
Dem guten Menschen näher als die Seinen?
Giebt's schönre Pflichten für ein edles Herz,   1615
Als ein Verteidiger der Unschuld sein,
Das Recht des Unterdrückten zu beschirmen?
—Die Seele blutet mir um euer Volk;

Ich leibe m i t ihm, denn ich muß es lieben,
Das so bescheiden ist und doch voll Kraft;   1620
Es zieht mein ganzes Herz mich zu ihm hin,
Mit jedem Tage lern' ich's mehr verehren.
— Ihr aber, den Natur und Ritterpflicht
Ihm zum geborenen Beschützer gaben,
Und der's v e r l ä ß t, der treulos übertritt   1625
Zum Feind und Ketten schmiedet seinem Land,
Ihr seid's, der mich verletzt und kränkt; ich muß
Mein Herz bezwingen, daß ich euch nicht hasse.

Rudenz.

Will ich denn nicht das Beste meines Volks?
Ihm unter Östreichs mächt'gem Scepter nicht   1630
Den Frieden —

Bertha.

    Knechtschaft wollt ihr ihm bereiten!
Die Freiheit wollt ihr aus dem letzten Schloß,
Das ihr noch auf der Erde blieb, verjagen.
Das Volk versteht sich besser auf sein Glück;
Kein Schein verführt sein sicheres Gefühl.   1635
Euch haben sie das Netz ums Haupt geworfen —

Rudenz.

Bertha!   Ihr haßt mich, ihr verachtet mich!

Bertha.

Thät' ich's, mir wäre besser — Aber den
Verachtet s e h e n und verachtungswert,
Den man gern lieben möchte —

Rudenz.

     Bertha! Bertha!   1640
Ihr zeiget mir das höchste Himmelsglück
Und stürzt mich tief in e i n e m Augenblick.

Bertha.

Nein, nein, das Edle ist nicht ganz erstickt
In euch! Es schlummert nur, ich will es wecken;
Ihr müßt Gewalt ausüben an euch selbst,   1645
Die angestammte Tugend zu ertöten;
Doch, wohl euch, sie ist mächtiger als ihr,
Und trotz euch selber seid ihr gut und edel!

Rudenz

Ihr glaubt an mich! O Bertha, alles läßt
Mich eure Liebe sein und werden!

Bertha.

      Seid,   1650
Wozu die herrliche Natur euch machte!
Erfüllt den Platz, wohin sie euch gestellt,
Zu eurem Volke steht und eurem Lande
Und kämpft für euer heilig Recht!

Rudenz.

      Weh mir!
Wie kann ich euch erringen, euch besitzen,   1655
Wenn ich der Macht des Kaisers widerstrebe?
Ist's der Verwandten mächt'ger Wille nicht,
Der über eure Hand tyrannisch waltet?

Bertha.

In den Waldstätten liegen meine Güter,
Und ist der Schweizer frei, so bin auch ich's.   1660

Rudenz.

Bertha, welch einen Blick thut ihr mir auf!

Bertha.

Hofft nicht, durch Östreichs Gunst mich zu erringen;
Nach meinem Erbe strecken sie die Hand,

Das will man mit dem großen Erb' vereinen.
Dieselbe Ländergier, die eure Freiheit   1665
Verschlingen will, sie drohet auch der meinen!
— O Freund, zum Opfer bin ich auserfehn,
Vielleicht, um einen Günftling zu belohnen —
Dort, wo die Falschheit und die Ränke wohnen,
Hin an den Kaiferhof will man mich ziehn,   1670
Dort harren mein verhaßter Ehe Ketten;
Die Liebe nur — die eure kann mich retten!

Rudenz.

Ihr könntet euch entschließen, hier zu leben,
In meinem Vaterlande mein zu sein?
O Bertha, all mein Sehnen in das Weite,   1675
Was war es, als ein Streben nur nach euch?
Euch sucht' ich einzig auf dem Weg des Ruhms,
Und all mein Ehrgeiz war nur meine Liebe.
Könnt ihr mit mir euch in dies stille Thal
Einschließen und der Erde Glanz entsagen —   1680
O, dann ist meines Strebens Ziel gefunden;
Dann mag der Strom der wildbewegten Welt
Ans sichre Ufer dieser Berge schlagen —
Kein flüchtiges Verlangen hab' ich mehr
Hinauszusenden in des Lebens Weiten —   1685
Dann mögen diese Felsen um uns her
Die undurchdringlich feste Mauer breiten,
Und dies verschloßne sel'ge Thal allein
Zum Himmel offen und gelichtet sein!

Bertha.

Jetzt bist du ganz, wie dich mein ahnend Herz   1690
Geträumt, mich hat mein Glaube nicht betrogen!

Rudenz.

Fahr' hin, du eitler Wahn, der mich bethört!
Ich soll das Glück in meiner Heimat finden.
Hier, wo der Knabe fröhlich aufgeblüht,
Wo tausend Freudespuren mich umgeben,   1695
Wo alle Quellen mir und Bäume leben,
Im Vaterland willst du die Meine werden!
Ach, wohl hab' ich es stets geliebt! Ich fühl's,
Es fehlte mir zu jedem Glück der Erden.

Bertha.

Wo wär' die sel'ge Insel aufzufinden,   1700
Wenn sie nicht hier ist in der Unschuld Land?
Hier, wo die alte Treue heimisch wohnt,
Wo sich die Falschheit noch nicht hingefunden,
Da trübt kein Neid die Quelle unsers Glücks,
Und ewig hell entfliehen uns die Stunden.   1705
—Da seh' ich dich im echten Männerwert,
Den Ersten von den Freien und den Gleichen,
Mit reiner, freier Huldigung verehrt,
Groß, wie ein König wirkt in seinen Reichen.

Rudenz.

Da seh' ich dich, die Krone aller Frauen,   1710
In weiblich reizender Geschäftigkeit,
In meinem Haus den Himmel mir erbauen
Und, wie der Frühling seine Blumen streut,
Mit schöner Anmut mir das Leben schmücken
Und alles rings beleben und beglücken!   1715

Bertha.

Sieh, teurer Freund, warum ich trauerte,
Als ich dies höchste Lebensglück dich selbst
Zerstören sah —Weh mir! Wie stünd's um mich,

Wenn ich dem stolzen Ritter müßte folgen,
Dem Landbedrücker, auf sein finstres Schloß!   1720
—Hier ist kein Schloß.   Mich scheiden keine Mauern
Von einem Volk, das ich beglücken kann!

Rudenz.

Doch, wie mich retten — wie die Schlinge lösen
Die ich mir thöricht selbst ums Haupt gelegt?

Bertha.

Zerreiße sie mit männlichem Entschluß!   1725
Was auch draus werde — steh zu deinem Volk!
Es ist dein angeborner Platz. (Jagdhörner in der Ferne.)

Die Jagd

Kommt näher — Fort, wir müssen scheiden — Kämpfe
Fürs Vaterland, du kämpfst für deine Liebe!
Es ist ein Feind, vor dem wir alle zittern,   1730
Und eine Freiheit macht uns alle frei! (Gehen ab.)

Dritte Scene.

Wiese bei Altorf. Im Vordergrund Bäume,
in der Tiefe der Hut auf einer Stange. Der
Prospekt wird begrenzt durch den Bannberg,
über welchem ein Schneegebirg emporragt.

Frießhardt und Leuthold halten Wache.

Frießhardt.

Wir passen auf umsonst. / Es will sich niemand
Heran begeben und dem Hut sein' Reverenz
Erzeigen. ('s war doch sonst wie Jahrmarkt hier;   )
Jetzt ist der ganze Anger wie verödet,   1735
Seitdem der Popanz auf der Stange hängt.

TELL STATUE AT ALTORF.

(*To face p.* 84.)

Leuthold.

Nur schlecht Gesindel läßt sich sehn und schwingt
Uns zum Verdrieße die zerlumpten Mützen.
Was rechte Leute sind, die machen lieber
Den langen Umweg um den halben Flecken,   1740
Eh' sie den Rücken beugten vor dem Hut.

Frießhardt.

Sie müssen über diesen Platz, wenn sie
Vom Rathaus kommen um die Mittagsstunde.
Da meint' ich schon, 'nen guten Fang zu thun,
Denn keiner dachte dran, den Hut zu grüßen.   1745
Da sieht's der Pfaff, der Rösselmann — kam just
Von einem Kranken her — und stellt' sich hin
Mit dem Hochwürdigen, grad' vor die Stange —
Der Sigrist mußte mit dem Glöcklein schellen;
Da fielen all' aufs Knie, ich selber mit,   1750
Und grüßten die Monstranz, doch nicht den Hut.

Leuthold.

Höre, Gesell, es fängt mir an zu deuchten,
Wir stehen hier am Pranger vor dem Hut;
's ist doch ein Schimpf für einen Reitersmann,
Schildwach' zu stehn vor einem leeren Hut —   1755
Und jeder rechte Kerl muß uns verachten.
— Die Reverenz zu machen einem Hut,
Es ist doch, traun, ein närrischer Befehl!

Frießhardt.

Warum nicht einem leeren, hohlen Hut?
Bückst du dich doch vor manchem hohlen Schädel.   1760

(Hildegard, Mechthild und Elsbeth treten auf mit Kindern und
stellen sich um die Stange.)

Leuthold.

Und du bist auch so ein dienstfert'ger Schurke
Und brächtest wackre Leute gern ins Unglück.
Mag, wer da will, am Hut vorübergehn,
Ich drück' die Augen zu und seh' nicht hin.

Mechthild.

Da hängt der Landvogt — habt Respekt, ihr Buben!   1765

Elsbeth.

Wollt's Gott, er ging' und ließ' uns seinen Hut;
Es sollte drum nicht schlechter stehn ums Land!

Frießhardt (verscheucht sie).

Wollt ihr vom Platz! Verwünschtes Volk der Weiber!
Wer fragt nach euch? Schickt eure Männer her,
Wenn sie der Mut sticht, dem Befehl zu trotzen_   1770
(Weiber gehen.)

(Tell mit der Armbrust tritt auf, den Knaben an der Hand führend.
Sie gehen an dem Hut vorbei gegen die vordere Scene, ohne darauf zu
achten.)

Walther (zeigt nach dem Bannberg).

Vater, ist's wahr, daß auf dem Berge dort
Die Bäume bluten, wenn man einen Streich
Drauf führte mit der Axt —

Tell.

           Wer sagt das, Knabe?

Walther.

Der Meister Hirt erzählt's — Die Bäume seien
Gebannt, sagt er, und wer sie schädige,   1775
Dem wachse seine Hand heraus zum Grabe.

Tell.

Die Bäume sind gebannt, das ist die Wahrheit.
—Siehst du die Firnen dort, die weißen Hörner,
Die hoch bis in den Himmel sich verlieren?

Walther.

Das sind die Gletscher, die des Nachts so donnern   1780
Und uns die Schlaglawinen niedersenden.

Tell.

So ist's, und die Lawinen hätten längst
Den Flecken Altorf unter ihrer Last
Verschüttet, wenn der Wald dort oben nicht
Als eine Landwehr sich dagegen stellte.   1785

Walther (nach einigem Besinnen).

Giebt's Länder, Vater, wo nicht Berge sind?

Tell.

Wenn man hinuntersteigt von unsern Höhen
Und immer tiefer steigt, den Strömen nach,
Gelangt man in ein großes, ebnes Land,
Wo die Waldwasser nicht mehr brausend schäumen,   1790
Die Flüsse ruhig und gemächlich ziehn;
Da sieht man frei nach allen Himmelsräumen,
Das Korn wächst dort in langen, schönen Auen,
Und wie ein Garten ist das Land zu schauen.

Walther.

Ei, Vater, warum steigen wir denn nicht   1795
Geschwind hinab in dieses schöne Land,
Statt daß wir uns hier ängstigen und plagen?

Tell.

Das Land ist schön und gütig, wie der Himmel;
Doch die's bebauen, sie genießen nicht
Den Segen, den sie pflanzen.

Walther.

Wohnen sie   1800
Nicht frei, wie du, auf ihrem eignen Erbe?

Tell.

Das Feld gehört dem Bischof und dem König.

Walther.

So dürfen sie doch frei in Wäldern jagen?

Tell.

Dem Herrn gehört das Wild und das Gefieder.

Walther.

Sie dürfen doch frei fischen in dem Strom?   1805

Tell.

Der Strom, das Meer, das Salz gehört dem König.

Walther.

Wer ist der König denn, den alle fürchten?

Tell.

Es ist der e i n e, der sie schützt und nährt.

Walther.

Sie können sich nicht mutig selbst beschützen?

Tell.

Dort darf der Nachbar nicht dem Nachbar trauen.   1810

Walther.

Vater, es wird mir eng im weiten Land;—
Da wohn' ich lieber unter den Lawinen.

Tell.

Ja, wohl ist's besser, Kind, die Gletscherberge
Im Rücken haben als die bösen Menschen.

(Sie wollen vorübergehen.)

Walther.

Ei, Vater, sieh den Hut dort auf der Stange! 1815

Tell.

Was kümmert uns der Hut? Komm, laß uns gehen!

(Indem er abgehen will, tritt ihm F r i e ß h a r d t mit vorgehaltener Pike
entgegen.)

Frießhardt.

In des Kaisers Namen! Haltet an und steht!

Tell (greift in die Pike).

Was wollt ihr? Warum haltet ihr mich auf?

Frießhardt.

Ihr habt's Mandat verletzt; ihr müßt uns folgen.

Leuthold.

Ihr habt dem Hut nicht Reverenz bewiesen. 1820

Tell.

Freund, laß mich gehen!

Frießhardt.

Fort, fort ins Gefängnis!

Walther.

Den Vater ins Gefängnis! Hilfe! Hilfe!

(In die Scene rufend.)

Herbei, ihr Männer, gute Leute, helft!
Gewalt! Gewalt! Sie führen ihn gefangen.

(R ö ß e l m a n n, der Pfarrer, und P e t e r m a n n, der Sigrist, kommen
herbei, mit drei anderen Männern.)

Sigrist.

Was giebt's?

Rösselmann.

Was legst du Hand an diesen Mann? 1825

Frießhardt.

Er ist ein Feind des Kaisers, ein Verräter!

Tell (faßt ihn heftig).

Ein Verräter, ich!

Rösselmann.

Du irrst dich, Freund.   Das ist
Der Tell, ein Ehrenmann und guter Bürger.

Walther (erblickt Walther Fürsten und eilt ihm entgegen).

Großvater, hilf! Gewalt geschieht dem Vater.

Frießhardt.

Ins Gefängnis, fort!

Walther Fürst (herbeieilend).

Ich leiste Bürgschaft, haltet!   1830
—Um Gottes willen, Tell, was ist geschehen?

(Melchthal und Stauffacher kommen.)

Frießhardt.

Des Landvogts oberherrliche Gewalt
Verachtet er und will sie nicht erkennen

Stauffacher.

Das hätt' der Tell gethan?

Melchthal.

Das lügst du, Bube!

Leuthold.

Er hat dem Hut nicht Reverenz bewiesen.   1835

Walther Fürst.

Und darum soll er ins Gefängnis? Freund,
Nimm meine Bürgschaft an und laß ihn ledig!

Frießhardt.

Bürg' du für dich und deinen eignen Leib!
Wir thun, was unsers Amtes — Fort mit ihm!

Meldthal (zu den Landleuten).

Nein, das ist schreiende Gewalt! Ertragen wir's,   1840
Daß man ihn fortführt, frech, vor unsern Augen?

Sigrist.

Wir sind die Stärkern. Freunde, duldet's nicht!
Wir haben einen Rücken an den andern.

Frießhardt.

Wer widersetzt sich dem Befehl des Vogts?

Noch drei Landleute (herbeieilend).

Wir helfen euch. Was giebt's? Schlagt sie zu Boden! 1845

(Hildegard, Mechthild und Elsbeth kommen zurück.)

Tell.

Ich helfe mir schon selbst. Geht, gute Leute!
Meint ihr, wenn ich die Kraft gebrauchen wollte,
Ich würde mich vor ihren Spießen fürchten?

Meldthal (zu Frießhardt).

Wag's, ihn aus unsrer Mitte wegzuführen!

Walther Fürst und Stauffacher.

Gelassen! Ruhig!

Frießhardt (schreit).

Aufruhr und Empörung!

(Man hört Jagdhörner.)

Weiber.

Da kommt der Landvogt!

Frießhardt (erhebt die Stimme).

Meuterei! Empörung!

Stauffacher.

Schrei, bis du berstest, Schurke!

Rösselmann und Meldthal.

Willst du schweigen?

Frießhardt (ruft noch lauter).

Zu Hilf', zu Hilf' den Dienern des Gesetzes!

Walther Fürst.

Da ist der Vogt! Weh uns, was wird das werden!

(Geßler zu Pferd, den Falken auf der Faust, Rudolf der Harras,
Bertha und Rudenz, ein großes Gefolge von bewaffneten Knechten,
welche einen Kreis von Piken um die ganze Scene schließen.)

Rudolf der Harras.

Platz, Platz dem Landvogt!

Geßler.

      Treibt sie auseinander! 1855
Was läuft das Volk zusammen? Wer ruft Hilfe?
     (Allgemeine Stille.)

Wer war's? Ich will es wissen. (Zu Frießhardt.)
      Du tritt vor!
Wer bist du, und was hältst du diesen Mann?
    (Er giebt den Falken einem Diener.)

Frießhardt.

Gestrenger Herr, ich bin dein Waffenknecht
Und wohlbestellter Wächter bei dem Hut. 1860
Diesen Mann ergriff ich über frischer That,
Wie er dem Hut den Ehrengruß versagte.
Verhaften wollt' ich ihn, wie du befahlst,
Und mit Gewalt will ihn das Volk entreißen.

Geßler (nach einer Pause).

Verachtest du so deinen Kaiser, Tell, 1865
Und mich, der hier an seiner Statt gebietet,
Daß du die Ehr' versagst dem Hut, den ich
Zur Prüfung des Gehorsams aufgehangen?
Dein böses Trachten hast du mir verraten.

Tell.

Verzeiht mir, lieber Herr! Aus Unbedacht,   1870
Nicht aus Verachtung eurer ist's geschehn.
Wär' ich besonnen, hieß' ich nicht der Tell,
Ich bitt' um Gnad', es soll nicht mehr begegnen.

Geßler (nach einigem Stillschweigen).

Du bist ein Meister auf der Armbrust, Tell,
Man sagt, du nehmst es auf mit jedem Schützen?   1875

Walther Tell.

Und das muß wahr sein, Herr, 'nen Apfel schießt
Der Vater dir vom Baum auf hundert Schritte.

Geßler.

Ist das dein Knabe, Tell?

Tell.

　　　Ja, lieber Herr.

Geßler.

Hast du der Kinder mehr?

Tell.

　　　Zwei Knaben, Herr.

Geßler

Und welcher ist's, den du am meisten liebst?   1880

Tell.

Herr, beide sind sie mir gleich liebe Kinder.

Geßler.

Nun, Tell! weil du den Apfel triffst vom Baume
Auf hundert Schritt, so wirst du deine Kunst
Vor mir bewähren müssen — Nimm die Armbrust —
Du hast sie gleich zur Hand — und mach' dich fertig,   1885
Einen Apfel von des Knaben Kopf zu schießen —
Doch will ich raten, ziele gut, daß du

Den Apfel treffest auf den ersten Schuß;
Denn fehlst du ihn, so ist dein Kopf verloren.

(Alle geben Zeichen des Schreckens.)

Tell.

Herr — Welches Ungeheure sinnet ihr   1890
Mir an? — Ich soll vom Haupte meines Kindes —
— Nein, nein doch, lieber Herr, das kommt euch nicht
Zu Sinn — Verhüt's der gnäd'ge Gott — Das könnt ihr
Im Ernst von einem Vater nicht begehren!

Geßler.

Du wirst den Apfel schießen von dem Kopf   1895
Des Knaben — ich begehr's und will's.

Tell.

                    Ich soll
Mit meiner Armbrust auf das liebe Haupt
Des eignen Kindes zielen? — Eher sterb' ich!

Geßler.

Du schießest, oder stirbst m i t deinem Knaben.

Tell.

Ich soll der Mörder werden meines Kinds!   1900
Herr, ihr habt keine Kinder — wisset nicht,
Was sich bewegt in eines Vaters Herzen.

Geßler.

Ei, Tell, du bist ja plötzlich so besonnen!
Man sagte mir, daß du ein Träumer seist
Und dich entfernst von andrer Menschen Weise.   1905
Du liebst das Seltsame — drum hab' ich jetzt
Ein eigen Wagstück für dich ausgesucht.
Ein andrer wohl bedächte sich — d u drückst
Die Augen zu und greifst es herzhaft an.)

Bertha.

Scherzt nicht, o Herr, mit diesen armen Leuten! 1910
Ihr seht sie bleich und zitternd stehn — so wenig
Sind sie Kurzweils gewohnt aus eurem Munde.

Geßler.

Wer sagt euch, daß ich scherze?
(Greift nach einem Baumzweige, der über ihn herhängt.)
Hier ist der Apfel.
Man mache Raum — Er nehme seine Weite,
Wie's Brauch ist — Achtzig Schritte geb' ich ihm — 1915
Nicht weniger, noch mehr — Er rühmte sich,
Auf ihrer hundert seinen Mann zu treffen —
Jetzt, Schütze, triff und fehle nicht das Ziel!

Rudolf der Harras.

Gott, das wird ernsthaft — Falle nieder, Knabe,
Es gilt, und fleh' den Landvogt um dein Leben! 1920

Walther Fürst (beiseite zu Melchthal, der kaum seine Ungeduld
bezwingt).

Haltet an euch, ich fleh' euch drum, bleibt ruhig!

Bertha (zum Landvogt).

Laßt es genug sein, Herr! Unmenschlich ist's,
Mit eines Vaters Angst also zu spielen.
Wenn dieser arme Mann auch Leib und Leben
Verwirkt durch seine leichte Schuld, bei Gott! 1925
Er hätte jetzt zehnfachen Tod empfunden.
Entlaßt ihn ungekränkt in seine Hütte,
Er hat euch kennen lernen; dieser Stunde
Wird er und seine Kindeskinder denken.

Geßler.

Öffnet die Gasse — Frisch, was zauderst du? 1930
Dein Leben ist verwirkt, ich kann dich töten;

Und sieh, ich lege gnädig dein Geschick
In deine eigne kunstgeübte Hand.
Der kann nicht klagen über harten Spruch,
Den man zum Meister seines Schicksals macht.   1935
Du rühmst dich deines sichern Blicks.   Wohlan!
Hier gilt es, S ch ü tz e , deine Kunst zu zeigen;
Das Ziel ist würdig, und der Preis ist groß!
Das Schwarze treffen in der Scheibe, d a s
Kann auch ein andrer; d e r ist mir der Meister,   1940
Der seiner Kunst gewiß ist überall,
Dem 's Herz nicht in die Hand tritt, noch ins Auge.

   Walther Fürst (wirft sich vor ihm nieder).

Herr Landvogt, wir erkennen eure Hoheit;
Doch lasset Gnad' vor Recht ergehen, nehmt
Die Hälfte meiner Habe, nehmt sie ganz!   1945
Nur dieses Gräßliche erlasset einem Vater!

   Walther Tell.

Großvater, knie nicht vor dem falschen Mann!
Sagt, wo ich hinstehn soll!   Ich fürcht' mich nicht.
Der Vater trifft den Vogel ja im Flug,
Er wird nicht fehlen auf das Herz des Kindes   1950

   Stauffacher.

Herr Landvogt, rührt euch nicht des Kindes Unschuld?

   Rösselmann.

O, denket, daß ein Gott im Himmel ist,
Dem ihr müßt Rede stehn für eure Thaten.

   Geßler (zeigt auf den Knaben).

Man bind' ihn an die Linde dort!

   Walther Tell.

      Mich binden!
Nein, ich will nicht gebunden sein.   Ich will   1955

Still halten, wie ein Lamm, und auch nicht atmen.
Wenn ihr mich bindet, nein, so kann ich's nicht,
So werd' ich toben gegen meine Bande.

Rudolf der Harras.

Die Augen nur laß dir verbinden, Knabe

Walther Tell.

Warum die Augen? Denket ihr, ich fürchte   1960
Den Pfeil von Vaters Hand? Ich will ihn fest
Erwarten und nicht zucken mit den Wimpern.
— Frisch, Vater, zeig's, daß du ein Schütze bist!
Er glaubt dir's nicht, er denkt uns zu verderben —
Dem Wütrich zum Verdrusse schieß und triff!   1965

(Er geht an die Linde, man legt ihm den Apfel auf.)

Melchthal (zu den Landleuten).

Was? Soll der Frevel sich vor unsern Augen
Vollenden? Wozu haben wir geschworen?

Stauffacher.

Es ist umsonst. Wir haben keine Waffen;
Ihr seht den Wald von Lanzen um uns her.

Melchthal.

O, hätten wir's mit frischer That vollendet!   1970
Verzeih's Gott denen, die zum Aufschub rieten!

Geßler (zum Tell).

Ans Werk! Man führt die Waffen nicht vergebens.
Gefährlich ist's, ein Mordgewehr zu tragen,
Und auf den Schützen springt der Pfeil zurück.
Dies stolze Recht, das sich der Bauer nimmt,   1975
Beleidiget den höchsten Herrn des Landes.
Gewaffnet sei niemand, als wer gebietet.
Freut's euch, den Pfeil zu führen und den Bogen,
Wohl, so will ich das Ziel euch dazu geben.

Tell (spannt die Armbrust und legt den Pfeil auf).

Öffnet die Gasse!   Platz!   1980

Stauffacher.

Was, Tell? Ihr wolltet — Nimmermehr — Ihr zittert,
Die Hand erbebt euch, eure Kniee wanken —

Tell (läßt die Armbrust sinken).

Mir schwimmt es vor den Augen!

Weiber.

Gott im Himmel!

Tell (zum Landvogt).

Erlasset mir den Schuß!   Hier ist mein Herz!
(Er reißt die Brust auf.)

Ruft eure Reisigen und stoßt mich nieder!   1985

Geßler.

Ich will dein Leben nicht, ich will den Schuß.
— Du kannst ja alles, Tell, an nichts verzagst du;
Das Steuerruder führst du wie den Bogen,
Dich schreckt kein Sturm, wenn es zu retten gilt.
Jetzt, Retter, hilf dir selbst — du rettest alle!   1990

(Tell steht in fürchterlichem Kampf, mit den Händen zuckend und die
rollenden Augen bald auf den Landvogt, bald zum Himmel gerichtet. —
Plötzlich greift er in seinen Köcher, nimmt einen zweiten Pfeil heraus und
steckt ihn in seinen Goller. Der Landvogt bemerkt alle diese Bewegungen.)

Walther Tell (unter der Linde).

Vater, schieß zu!   Ich fürcht' mich nicht.

Tell.

Es muß!

(Er rafft sich zusammen und legt an.)

Rudenz (der die ganze Zeit über in der heftigsten Spannung gestanden
und mit Gewalt an sich gehalten, tritt hervor).

Herr Landvogt, weiter werdet ihr's nicht treiben,
Ihr werdet n i c h t — Es war nur eine Prüfung —

Den Zweck habt ihr erreicht — Zu weit getrieben,
Verfehlt die Strenge ihres weisen Zwecks, 1995
Und allzustraff gespannt, zerspringt der Bogen.

Geßler.

Ihr schweigt, bis man euch aufruft!

Rudenz.

Ich will reden!

Ich darf's! Des Königs Ehre ist mir heilig;
Doch solches Regiment muß Haß erwerben.
Das ist des Königs Wille nicht — ich darf's 2000
Behaupten — Solche Grausamkeit verdient
Mein Volk nicht, dazu habt ihr keine Vollmacht.

Geßler.

Ha, ihr erkühnt euch!

Rudenz.

Ich hab' still geschwiegen
Zu allen schweren Thaten, die ich sah;
Mein sehend Auge hab' ich zugeschlossen, 2005
Mein überschwellend und empörtes Herz
Hab' ich hinabgedrückt in meinen Busen.
Doch länger schweigen wär' Verrat zugleich
An meinem Vaterland und an dem Kaiser.

Bertha (wirft sich zwischen ihn und den Landvogt).

O Gott, ihr reizt den Wütenden noch mehr 2010

Rudenz.

Mein Volk verließ ich, meinen Blutsverwandten
Entsagt' ich, alle Bande der Natur
Zerriß ich, um an euch mich anzuschließen —
Das Beste aller glaubt' ich zu befördern,
Da ich des Kaisers Macht befestigte — 2015
Die Binde fällt von meinen Augen — Schaudernd

Seh' ich an einen Abgrund mich geführt —
Mein freies Urteil habt ihr irr geleitet,
Mein redlich Herz verführt — Ich war daran,
Mein Volk in bester Meinung zu verderben.   2020

Geßler.

Verwegner, diese Sprache deinem Herrn?

Rudenz.

Der Kaiser ist mein Herr, nicht ihr — Frei bin ich
Wie ihr geboren, und ich messe mich
Mit euch in jeder ritterlichen Tugend.
Und stündet ihr nicht hier in Kaisers Namen,   2025
Den ich verehre, selbst wo man ihn schändet,
Den Handschuh wärf' ich vor euch hin, ihr solltet
Nach ritterlichem Brauch mir Antwort geben.
— Ja, winkt nur euren Reisigen — Ich stehe
Nicht wehrlos da, wie d i e — (auf das Volk zeigend)
                              Ich hab' ein Schwert, 2030
Und wer mir naht

Stauffacher (ruft).
Der Apfel ist gefallen!

(Indem sich alle nach dieser Seite gewendet und B e r t h a zwischen
R u d e n z und den Landvogt sich geworfen, hat T e l l den Pfeil
abgedrückt).

Rösselmann.

Der Knabe lebt!

Viele Stimmen.
Der Apfel ist getroffen!

(W a l t h e r   F ü r s t schwankt und droht zu sinken, B e r t h a hält ihn).

Geßler (erstaunt).

Er hat geschossen? Wie? Der Rasende!

Bertha.

Der Knabe lebt! Kommt zu euch, guter Vater!

Walther Tell (kommt mit dem Apfel gesprungen).

Vater, hier ist der Apfel — Wußt' ich's ja,   2035
Du würdest deinen Knaben nicht verletzen.

(Tell stand mit vorgebogenem Leib, als wollt' er dem Pfeil folgen — die
Armbrust entsinkt seiner Hand — wie er den Knaben kommen sieht, eilt er
ihm mit ausgebreiteten Armen entgegen und hebt ihn mit heftiger In=
brunst zu seinem Herzen hinauf; in dieser Stellung sinkt er kraftlos zusam=
men. Alle stehen gerührt.)

Bertha.

O güt'ger Himmel!

Walther Fürst (zu Vater und Sohn.)

Kinder! meine Kinder!

Stauffacher.

Gott sei gelobt!

Leuthold.

Das war ein Schuß! Davon
Wird man noch reden in den spätsten Zeiten.

Rudolf der Harras.

Erzählen wird man von dem Schützen Tell,   2040
So lang' die Berge stehn auf ihrem Grunde.

(Reicht dem Landvogt den Apfel.)

Geßler.

Bei Gott, der Apfel mitten durch geschossen!
Es war ein Meisterschuß, ich muß ihn loben.

Rösselmann.

Der Schuß war gut; doch wehe dem, der ihn
Dazu getrieben, daß er Gott versuchte!   2045

Stauffacher.

Kommt zu euch, Tell, steht auf, ihr habt euch männlich
Gelöst, und frei könnt ihr nach Hause gehen.

Rösselmann.

Kommt, kommt und bringt der Mutter ihren Sohn!

(Sie wollen ihn wegführen.)

Geßler.

Tell, höre!

Tell (kommt zurück).

Was befehlt ihr, Herr?

Geßler.

Du stecktest
Noch einen zweiten Pfeil zu dir — Ja, ja,   2050
Ich sah es wohl — Was meintest du damit?

Tell (verlegen).

Herr, das ist also bräuchlich bei den Schützen.

Geßler.

Nein, Tell, die Antwort laß' ich dir nicht gelten;
Es wird was anders wohl bedeutet haben.
Sag' mir die Wahrheit frisch und fröhlich, Tell!   2055
Was es auch sei, dein Leben sichr' ich dir.
Wozu der zweite Pfeil?

Tell.

Wohlan, o Herr,
Weil ihr mich meines Lebens habt gesichert —
So will ich euch die Wahrheit gründlich sagen.

(Er zieht den Pfeil aus dem Goller und sieht den Landvogt mit einem
furchtbaren Blick an.)

Mit diesem zweiten Pfeil durchschoß ich — euch,   2060
Wenn ich mein liebes Kind getroffen hätte,
Und eurer — wahrlich! hätt' ich nicht gefehlt.

Geßler.

Wohl, Tell! Des Lebens hab' ich dich gesichert,
Ich gab mein Ritterwort, das will ich halten —

Doch weil ich deinen bösen Sinn erkannt,   2065
Will ich dich führen lassen und verwahren,
Wo weder Mond noch Sonne dich bescheint,
Damit ich sicher sei vor deinen Pfeilen.
Ergreift ihn, Knechte! Bindet ihn! (Tell wird gebunden.)

Stauffacher.

                              Wie, Herr!
So könntet ihr an einem Manne handeln,   2070
An dem sich Gottes Hand sichtbar verkündigt?

Geßler.

Laß sehn, ob sie ihn zweimal retten wird.
—Man bring' ihn auf mein Schiff! Ich folge nach
Sogleich, ich selbst will ihn nach Küßnacht führen.

Rösselmann.

Das dürft ihr nicht, das darf der Kaiser nicht,   2075
Das widerstreitet unsern Freiheitsbriefen!

Geßler.

Wo sind sie? Hat der Kaiser sie bestätigt?
Er hat sie nicht bestätigt—Diese Gunst
Muß erst erworben werden durch Gehorsam.
Rebellen seid ihr alle gegen Kaisers   2080
Gericht und nährt verwegene Empörung.
Ich kenn' euch alle — ich durchschau' euch ganz —
Den nehm' ich jetzt heraus aus eurer Mitte;
Doch alle seid ihr teilhaft seiner Schuld.
Wer klug ist, lerne schweigen und gehorchen.   2085
(Er entfernt sich, Bertha, Rudenz, Harras und Knechte folgen.
Frießhardt und Leuthold bleiben zurück.)

Walther Fürst (in heftigem Schmerz).

Es ist vorbei; er hat's beschlossen, mich
Mit meinem ganzen Hause zu verderben!

Stauffacher (zum Tell).

O, warum mußtet ihr den Wütrich reizen!

Tell.

Bezwinge sich, wer meinen Schmerz gefühlt!

Stauffacher.

O, nun ist alles, alles hin! Mit euch   2090
Sind wir gefesselt alle und gebunden!

Landleute (umringen Tell).

Mit euch geht unser letzter Trost dahin!

Leuthold (nähert sich).

Tell, es erbarmt mich — doch ich muß gehorchen.

Tell.

Lebt wohl!

Walther Tell (sich mit heftigem Schmerz an ihn schmiegend).

O Vater! Vater! lieber Vater!

Tell (hebt die Arme zum Himmel).

Dort droben ist dein Vater! Den ruf' an   2095

Stauffacher.

Tell, sag' ich eurem Weibe nichts von euch?

Tell (hebt den Knaben mit Inbrunst an seine Brust.)

Der Knab' ist unverletzt; mir wird Gott helfen.

(Reißt sich schnell los und folgt den Waffenknechten.)

Vierter Aufzug.

Erste Scene.

Östliches Ufer des Vierwaldstättersees.

Die seltsam gestalteten schroffen Felsen im Westen schließen den Prospekt.
Der See ist bewegt, heftiges Rauschen und Tosen, dazwischen Blitze
und Donnerschläge.

Kunz von Gersau. Fischer und Fischerknabe.

Kunz.

Ich sah's mit Augen an, ihr könnt mir's glauben;
's ist alles so geschehn, wie ich euch sagte.

Fischer.

Der Tell gefangen abgeführt nach Küßnacht,   2100
Der beste Mann im Land, der bravste Arm,
Wenn's einmal gelten sollte für die Freiheit.

Kunz.

Der Landvogt führt ihn selbst den See herauf;
Sie waren eben dran, sich einzuschiffen,
Als ich von Flüelen abfuhr; doch der Sturm,   2105
Der eben jetzt im Anzug ist, und der
Auch mich gezwungen, eilends hier zu landen,
Mag ihre Abfahrt wohl verhindert haben.

Fischer.

Der Tell in Fesseln, in des Vogts Gewalt!
O, glaubt, er wird ihn tief genug vergraben,   2110
Daß er des Tages Licht nicht wieder sieht!
Denn fürchten muß er die gerechte Rache
Des freien Mannes, den er schwer gereizt!

Kunz.

Der Altlandammann auch, der edle Herr
Von Attinghausen, sagt man, lieg' am Tode.   2115

Fischer.

So bricht der letzte Anker unsrer Hoffnung!
Der war es noch allein, der seine Stimme
Erheben durfte für des Volkes Rechte!

Kunz.

Der Sturm nimmt überhand. Gehabt euch wohl!
Ich nehme Herberg' in dem Dorf; denn heut'   2120
Ist doch an keine Abfahrt mehr zu denken. (Geht ab.)

Fischer.

Der Tell gefangen und der Freiherr tot!
Erheb' die freche Stirne, Tyrannei,
Wirf alle Scham hinweg! Der Mund der Wahrheit
Ist stumm, das sehnde Auge ist geblendet,   2125
Der Arm, der retten sollte, ist gefesselt!

Knabe.

Es hagelt schwer. Kommt in die Hütte, Vater,
Es ist nicht kommlich, hier im Freien hausen.

Fischer.

Raset, ihr Winde! Flammt herab, ihr Blitze!
Ihr Wolken, berstet! Gießt herunter, Ströme   2130
Des Himmels, und ersäuft das Land! Zerstört
Im Keim die ungeborenen Geschlechter!
Ihr wilden Elemente, werdet Herr!
Ihr Bären, kommt, ihr alten Wölfe wieder
Der großen Wüste! euch gehört das Land.   2135
Wer wird hier leben wollen ohne Freiheit!

Knabe.

Hört, wie der Abgrund tost, der Wirbel brüllt,
So hat's noch nie gerast in diesem Schlunde!

Fischer.

Zu zielen auf des eignen Kindes Haupt,

Solches ward keinem Vater noch geboten! 2140
Und die Natur soll nicht in wildem Grimm
Sich drob empören — O, mich soll's nicht wundern,
Wenn sich die Felsen bücken in den See,
Wenn jene Zacken, jene Eisestürme,
Die nie auftauten seit dem Schöpfungstag, 2145
Von ihren hohen Kulmen niederschmelzen,
Wenn die Berge brechen, wenn die alten Klüfte
Einstürzen, eine zweite Sündflut alle
Wohnstätten der Lebendigen verschlingt!

(Man hört läuten.)

Knabe.

Hört ihr, sie läuten droben auf dem Berg. 2150
Gewiß hat man ein Schiff in Not gesehn
Und zieht die Glocke, daß gebetet werde. (Steigt auf eine
Anhöhe.)

Fischer.

Wehe dem Fahrzeug, das, jetzt unterwegs,
In dieser furchtbarn Wiege wird gewiegt!
Hier ist das Steuer unnütz und der Steurer, 2155
Der Sturm ist Meister, Wind und Welle spielen
Ball mit dem Menschen — Da ist nah und fern
Kein Busen, der ihm freundlich Schutz gewährte!
Handlos und schroff ansteigend starren ihm
Die Felsen, die unwirtlichen, entgegen 2160
Und weisen ihm nur ihre steinern schroffe Brust.

Knabe (deutet links).

Vater, ein Schiff! es kommt von Flüelen her.

Fischer.

Gott helf' den armen Leuten! Wenn der Sturm
In dieser Wasserkluft sich erst verfangen,
Dann rast er um sich mit des Raubtiers Angst, 2165

Das an des Gitters Eisenstäbe schlägt;
Die Pforte sucht er heulend sich vergebens;
Denn ringsum schränken ihn die Felsen ein,
Die himmelhoch den engen Paß vermauern.
(Er steigt auf die Anhöhe.)

Knabe.

Es ist das Herrenschiff von Uri, Vater,   2170
Ich kenn's am roten Dach und an der Fahne.

Fischer.

Gerichte Gottes!   Ja, er ist es selbst,
Der Landvogt, der da fährt — Dort schifft er hin
Und führt im Schiffe sein Verbrechen mit!
Schnell hat der Arm des Rächers ihn gefunden,   2175
Jetzt kennt er über sich den stärkern Herrn.
Diese Wellen geben nicht auf seine Stimme,
Diese Felsen bücken ihre Häupter nicht
Vor seinem Hute — Knabe, bete nicht!
Greif' nicht dem Richter in den Arm!   2180

Knabe.

Ich bete für den Landvogt nicht — Ich bete
Für den Tell, der auf dem Schiff sich mit befindet.

Fischer.

O Unvernunft des blinden Elements!
Mußt du, um einen Schuldigen zu treffen,
Das Schiff mitsamt dem Steuermann verderben!   2185

Knabe.

Sieh, sieh, sie waren glücklich schon vorbei
Am Buggisgrat; doch die Gewalt des Sturmes,
Der von dem Teufelsmünster widerprallt,
Wirft sie zum großen Axenberg zurück.
— Ich seh' sie nicht mehr.

Fischer.

Dort ist das Hackmesser,   2190
Wo schon der Schiffe mehrere gebrochen.
Wenn sie nicht weislich dort vorüberlenken,
So wird das Schiff zerschmettert an der Fluh,
Die sich gähstohig absenkt in die Tiefe.
— Sie haben einen guten Steuermann   2195
Am Bord; könnt' einer retten, wär's der Tell;
Doch dem sind Arm' und Hände ja gefesselt.

Wilhelm Tell mit der Armbrust.

(Er kommt mit raschen Schritten, blickt erstaunt umher und zeigt die heftigste Bewegung. Wenn er mitten auf der Scene ist, wirft er sich nieder, die Hände zu der Erde und dann zum Himmel ausbreitend.)

Knabe (bemerkt ihn).

Sieh, Vater, wer der Mann ist, der dort kniet?

Fischer.

Er faßt die Erde an mit seinen Händen
Und scheint wie außer sich zu sein.   2200

Knabe (kommt vorwärts).

Was seh' ich! Vater! Vater, kommt und seht!

Fischer (nähert sich).

Wer ist es? — Gott im Himmel! Was! der Tell?
Wie kommt ihr hieher? Redet!

Knabe.

                    Wart ihr nicht
Dort auf dem Schiff gefangen und gebunden?

Fischer.

Ihr wurdet nicht nach Küßnacht abgeführt?   2205

Tell (steht auf).

Ich bin befreit.

Fischer und Knabe.

        Befreit! O Wunder Gottes!

Knabe.

Wo kommt ihr her?

Tell.

Dort aus dem Schiffe.

Fischer.

Was?

Knabe (zugleich).

Wo ist der Landvogt?

Tell.

Auf den Wellen treibt er.

Fischer.

Ist's möglich? Aber ihr? Wie seid ihr hier?
Seid euren Banden und dem Sturm entkommen?   2210

Tell.

Durch Gottes gnäd'ge Fürsehung — Hört an!

Fischer und Knabe.

O, redet, redet!

Tell.

Was in Altorf sich
Begeben, wißt ihr's?

Fischer.

Alles weiß ich, redet!

Tell.

Daß mich der Landvogt fahen ließ und binden,
Nach seiner Burg zu Küßnacht wollte führen.   2215

Fischer.

Und sich mit euch zu Flüelen eingeschifft.
Wir wissen alles.   Sprecht, wie ihr entkommen?

Tell.

Ich lag im Schiff, mit Stricken fest gebunden,

Wehrlos, ein aufgegebner Mann — Nicht hofft' ich,
Das frohe Licht der Sonne mehr zu sehn,   2220
Der Gattin und der Kinder liebes Antlitz,
Und trostlos blickt' ich in die Wasserwüste —

Fischer.

O armer Mann!

Tell.

So fuhren wir dahin,
Der Vogt, Rudolf der Harras und die Knechte.
Mein Köcher aber mit der Armbrust lag   2225
Am hintern Gransen bei dem Steuerruder.
Und als wir an die Ecke jetzt gelangt
Beim kleinen Axen, da verhängt' es Gott,
Daß solch ein grausam mördrisch Ungewitter
Gählings herfürbrach aus des Gotthards Schlünden,   2230
Daß allen Ruderern das Herz entsank,
Und meinten alle, elend zu ertrinken.
Da hört' ich's, wie der Diener einer sich
Zum Landvogt wendet' und die Worte sprach:
„Ihr sehet eure Not und unsre, Herr,   2235
Und daß wir all' am Rand des Todes schweben —
Die Steuerleute aber wissen sich
Vor großer Furcht nicht Rat und sind des Fahrens
Nicht wohl berichtet — Nun aber ist der Tell
Ein starker Mann und weiß ein Schiff zu steuern.   2240
Wie, wenn wir sein jetzt brauchten in der Not?"
Da sprach der Vogt zu mir: „Tell, wenn du dir's
Getrautest, uns zu helfen aus dem Sturm,
So möcht' ich dich der Bande wohl entled'gen."
Ich aber sprach: „Ja, Herr, mit Gottes Hilfe   2245
Getrau' ich mir's und helf' uns wohl hiedannen."
So ward ich meiner Bande los und stand

Am Steuerruder und fuhr redlich hin;
Doch schielt' ich seitwärts, wo mein Schießzeug lag,
Und an dem Ufer merkt' ich scharf umher,　　2250
Wo sich ein Vorteil aufthät' zum Entspringen.
Und wie ich eines Felsenriffs gewahre,
Das abgeplattet vorsprang in den See —

Fischer.

Ich kenn's, es ist am Fuß des großen Axen,
Doch nicht für möglich acht' ich's — so gar steil　　2255
Geht's an — vom Schiff es springend abzureichen

Tell.

Schrie ich den Knechten, handlich zuzugehn,
Bis daß wir vor die Felsenplatte kämen,
Dort, rief ich, sei das Ärgste überstanden —
Und als wir sie frischrudernd bald erreicht,　　2260
Fleh' ich die Gnade Gottes an und drücke,
Mit allen Leibeskräften angestemmt,
Den hintern Granzen an die Felswand hin.
Jetzt, schnell mein Schießzeug fassend, schwing' ich selbst
Hochspringend auf die Platte mich hinauf,　　2265
Und mit gewalt'gem Fußstoß hinter mich

Schleudr' ich das Schifflein in den Schlund der Wasser —
Dort mag's, wie Gott will, auf den Wellen treiben!
So bin ich hier, gerettet aus des Sturms
Gewalt und aus der schlimmeren der Menschen.　　2270

Fischer.

Tell, Tell! ein sichtbar Wunder hat der Herr
An euch gethan; kaum glaub' ich's meinen Sinnen —
Doch saget!　Wo gedenket ihr jetzt hin?
Denn Sicherheit ist nicht für euch, wofern
Der Landvogt lebend diesem Sturm entkommt.　　2275

Tell.

Ich hört' ihn sagen, da ich noch im Schiff
Gebunden lag, er woll' bei Brunnen landen
Und über Schwyz nach seiner Burg mich führen.

Fischer.

Will er den Weg dahin zu Lande nehmen?

Tell.

Er denkt's

Fischer.

O, so verbergt euch ohne Säumen!   2280
Nicht zweimal hilft euch Gott aus seiner Hand.

Tell.

Nennt mir den nächsten Weg nach Arth und Küßnacht.

Fischer.

Die offne Straße zieht sich über Steinen;
Doch einen kürzern Weg und heimlichern
Kann euch mein Knabe über Lowerz führen.   2285

Tell (giebt ihm die Hand).

Gott lohn' euch eure Gutthat. Lebet wohl!
(Geht und kehrt wieder um.)
— Habt ihr nicht auch im Rütli mitgeschworen?
Mir deucht, man nannt' euch mir.

Fischer.

                          Ich war dabei
Und hab' den Eid des Bundes mit beschworen.

Tell.

So eilt nach Bürglen, thut die Lieb' mir an!   2290
Mein Weib verzagt um mich; verkündet ihr,
Daß ich gerettet sei und wohl geborgen.

Fischer.

Doch wohin sag' ich ihr, daß ihr geflohn?

Tell.

Ihr werdet meinen Schwäher bei ihr finden
Und andre, die im Rütli mitgeschworen —   2295
Sie sollen wacker sein und gutes Muts,
Der Tell sei frei und seines Armes mächtig;
Bald werden sie ein Weitres von mir hören.

Fischer.

Was habt ihr im Gemüt?   Entdeckt mir's frei

Tell.

Ist es gethan, wird's auch zur Rede kommen. (Geht ab.) 2300

Fischer.

Zeig' ihm den Weg, Jenni — Gott steh' ihm bei!
Er führt's zum Ziel, was er auch unternommen. (Geht ab.)

Zweite Scene.

Edelhof zu Attinghausen.

Der Freiherr, in einem Armsessel, sterbend. Walther Fürst,
Stauffacher, Melchthal und Baumgarten um ihn beschäftigt.
Walther Tell, knieend vor dem Sterbenden.

Walther Fürst.

Es ist vorbei mit ihm, er ist hinüber.

Stauffacher.

Er liegt nicht wie ein Toter — Seht, die Feder
Auf seinen Lippen regt sich!   Ruhig ist   2305
Sein Schlaf, und friedlich lächeln seine Züge.

(Baumgarten geht an die Thüre und spricht mit jemand.)

Walther Fürst (zu Baumgarten).

Wer ist's?

Baumgarten (kommt zurück).

Es ist Frau Hedwig, eure Tochter;
Sie will euch sprechen, will den Knaben sehn.

(Walther Tell richtet sich auf.)

Walther Fürst.

Kann ich sie trösten? Hab' ich selber Trost?
Häuft alles Leiden sich auf meinem Haupt?   2310

Hedwig (hereindringend).

Wo ist mein Kind? Laßt mich, ich muß es sehn —

Stauffacher.

Faßt euch! Bedenkt, daß ihr im Haus des Todes —

Hedwig (stürzt auf den Knaben).

Mein Wälti! O, er lebt mir!

Walther Tell (hängt an ihr).

Arme Mutter!

Hedwig.

Ist's auch gewiß? Bist du mir unverletzt?

(Betrachtet ihn mit ängstlicher Sorgfalt.)

Und ist es möglich? Konnt' er auf dich zielen?   2315
Wie konnt' er's? O, er hat kein Herz — Er konnte
Den Pfeil abdrücken auf sein eignes Kind!

Walther Fürst.

Er that's mit Angst, mit schmerzzerrißner Seele;
Gezwungen that er's, denn es galt das Leben.

Hedwig.

O, hätt' er eines Vaters Herz, eh' er's   2320
Gethan, er wäre tausendmal gestorben!

Stauffacher.

Ihr solltet Gottes gnäd'ge Schickung preisen,
Die es so gut gelenkt —

Hedwig.

Kann ich vergessen,
Wie's hätte kommen können? — Gott des Himmels!
Und lebt' ich achtzig Jahr' — ich seh' den Knaben ewig   2325
Gebunden stehn, den Vater auf ihn zielen,
Und ewig fliegt der Pfeil mir in das Herz.

Melchthal.

Frau, wüßtet ihr, wie ihn der Vogt gereizt!

Hedwig.

O rohes Herz der Männer! Wenn ihr Stolz
Beleidigt wird, dann achten sie nichts mehr;   2330
Sie setzen in der blinden Wut des Spiels
Das Haupt des Kindes und das Herz der Mutter

Baumgarten.

Ist eures Mannes Los nicht hart genug,
Daß ihr mit schwerem Tadel ihn noch kränkt?
Für seine Leiden habt ihr kein Gefühl?   2335

Hedwig (kehrt sich nach ihm um und sieht ihn mit einem großen Blick an).

Hast du nur Thränen für des Freundes Unglück?
— Wo waret ihr, da man den Trefflichen
In Bande schlug? Wo war da eure Hilfe?
Ihr sahet zu, ihr ließt das Gräßliche geschehn;
Geduldig littet ihr's, daß man den Freund   2340
Aus eurer Mitte führte — Hat der Tell
Auch so an euch gehandelt? Stand er auch
Bedauernd da, als hinter dir die Reiter
Des Landvogts drangen, als der wüt'ge See
Vor dir erbrauste? Nicht mit müß'gen Thränen   2345
Beklagt' er dich, in den Nachen sprang er, Weib
Und Kind vergaß er und befreite dich —

Walther Fürst.

Was konnten wir zu seiner Rettung wagen,
Die kleine Zahl, die unbewaffnet war!

Hedwig (wirft sich an seine Brust).

O Vater! Und auch du hast ihn verloren!   2350
Das Land, wir alle haben ihn verloren!
Uns allen fehlt er, ach, wir fehlen ihm!
Gott rette seine Seele vor Verzweiflung.
Zu ihm hinab ins öde Burgverließ
Dringt keines Freundes Trost — Wenn er erkrankte! 2355
Ach, in des Kerkers feuchter Finsternis
Muß er erkranken — Wie die Alpenrose
Bleicht und verkümmert in der Sumpfesluft,
So ist für ihn kein Leben als im Licht
Der Sonne, in dem Balsamstrom der Lüfte.   2360
Gefangen! Er! Sein Atem ist die Freiheit,
Er kann nicht leben in dem Hauch der Grüfte.

Stauffacher.

Beruhigt euch! Wir alle wollen handeln,
Um seinen Kerker aufzuthun.

Hedwig.

Was könnt ihr schaffen ohne ihn? — So lang'   2365
Der Tell noch frei war, ja, da war noch Hoffnung,
Da hatte noch die Unschuld einen Freund,
Da hatte einen Helfer der Verfolgte,
Euch alle rettete der Tell — Ihr alle
Zusammen könnt nicht seine Fesseln lösen!   2370

(Der Freiherr erwacht.)

Baumgarten.

Er regt sich, still!

Attinghausen (sich aufrichtend).

Wo ist er?

Stauffacher.

Wer?

Attinghausen.

Er fehlt mir,
Verläßt mich in dem letzten Augenblick!

Stauffacher.

Er meint den Junker — Schickte man nach ihm?

Walther Fürst.

Es ist nach ihm gesendet — Tröstet euch!
Er hat sein Herz gefunden, er ist unser.   2375

Attinghausen.

Hat er gesprochen für sein Vaterland?

Stauffacher.

Mit Heldenkühnheit.

Attinghausen.

Warum kommt er nicht,
Um meinen letzten Segen zu empfangen?
Ich fühle, daß es schleunig mit mir endet.

Stauffacher.

Nicht also, edler Herr! Der kurze Schlaf   2380
Hat euch erquickt, und hell ist euer Blick.

Attinghausen.

Der Schmerz ist Leben, er verließ mich auch.
Das Leiden ist, so wie die Hoffnung, aus.

(Er bemerkt den Knaben.)

Wer ist der Knabe?

Walther Fürst.

Segnet ihn, o Herr!

Er ist mein Enkel und ist vaterlos.   2385

(Hedwig sinkt mit dem Knaben vor dem Sterbenden nieder.)

Attinghausen.

Und vaterlos laß' ich euch alle, alle
Zurück — Weh mir, daß meine letzten Blicke
Den Untergang des Vaterlands gesehn!
Mußt' ich des Lebens höchstes Maß erreichen,
Um ganz mit allen Hoffnungen zu sterben!   2390

Stauffacher (zu Walther Fürst).

Soll er in diesem finstern Kummer scheiden?
Erhellen wir ihm nicht die letzte Stunde
Mit schönem Strahl der Hoffnung? — Edler Freiherr!
Erhebet euren Geist! Wir sind nicht ganz
Verlassen, sind nicht rettungslos verloren.   2395

Attinghausen.

Wer soll euch retten?

Walther Fürst.

Wir uns selbst. Vernehmt!
Es haben die drei Lande sich das Wort
Gegeben, die Tyrannen zu verjagen.
Geschlossen ist der Bund; ein heil'ger Schwur
Verbindet uns. Es wird gehandelt werden,   2400
Eh' noch das Jahr den neuen Kreis beginnt.
Euer Staub wird ruhn in einem freien Lande.

Attinghausen.

O, saget mir! Geschlossen ist der Bund?

Melchthal.

Am gleichen Tage werden alle drei
Waldstätte sich erheben. Alles ist   2405

Bereit und das Geheimnis wohlbewahrt
Bis jetzt, obgleich viel' Hunderte es teilen.
Hohl ist der Boden unter den Thrannen,
Die Tage ihrer Herrschaft sind gezählt,
Und bald ist ihre Spur nicht mehr zu finden.   2410

Attinghausen.
Die festen Burgen aber in den Landen?

Melchthal.
Sie fallen alle an dem gleichen Tag.

Attinghausen.
Und sind die Edeln dieses Bunds teilhaftig?

Stauffacher.
Wir harren ihres Beistands, wenn es gilt;
Jetzt aber hat der Landmann nur geschworen.   2415

Attinghausen.
(Richtet sich langsam in die Höhe mit großem Erstaunen.)

Hat sich der Landmann solcher That verwogen,
Aus eignem Mittel, ohne Hilf' der Edeln,
Hat er der eignen Kraft so viel vertraut —
Ja, dann bedarf es unserer nicht mehr;
Getröstet können wir zu Grabe steigen,   2420
Es lebt n a c h uns — durch andre Kräfte will
Das Herrliche der Menschheit sich erhalten.
(Er legt seine Hand auf das Haupt des Kindes, das vor ihm auf den
Knieen liegt.)

Aus diesem Haupte, wo der Apfel lag,
Wird euch die neue, beßre Freiheit grünen;
Das Alte stürzt, es ändert sich die Zeit,   2425
Und neues Leben blüht aus den Ruinen.

Stauffacher (zu W a l t h e r   F ü r st).
Seht, welcher Glanz sich um sein Aug' ergießt!

Das ist nicht das Erlöschen der Natur,
Das ist der Strahl schon eines neuen Lebens.

Attinghausen.

Der Adel steigt von seinen alten Burgen   2430
Und schwört den Städten seinen Bürgereid;
Im Üchtland schon, im Thurgau hat's begonnen,
Die edle Bern erhebt ihr herrschend Haupt,
Freiburg ist eine sichre Burg der Freien,
Die rege Zürich waffnet ihre Zünfte   2435
Zum kriegerischen Heer — es bricht die Macht
Der Könige sich an ihren ew'gen Wällen —

(Er spricht das Folgende mit dem Ton eines Sehers — seine Rede steigt
bis zur Begeisterung.)

Die Fürsten seh' ich und die edeln Herrn
In Harnischen herangezogen kommen,
Ein harmlos Volk von Hirten zu befriegen.   2440
Auf Tod und Leben wird gekämpft, und herrlich
Wird mancher Paß durch blutige Entscheidung.
Der Landmann stürzt sich mit der nackten Brust,
Ein freies Opfer, in die Schar der Lanzen!
Er bricht sie, und des Adels Blüte fällt,   2445
Es hebt die Freiheit siegend ihre Fahne.

(Walther Fürsts und Stauffachers Hände fassend.)

Drum haltet fest zusammen — fest und ewig —
Kein Ort der Freiheit sei dem andern fremd —
Hochwachten stellet aus auf euren Bergen,
Daß sich der Bund zum Bunde rasch versammle —   2450
Seid einig — einig — einig —

(Er fällt in das Kissen zurück — seine Hände halten entseelt noch die andern
gefaßt. Fürst und Stauffacher betrachten ihn noch eine Zeit lang
schweigend; dann treten sie hinweg, jeder seinem Schmerz überlassen. Unterdessen sind die Knechte still hereingedrungen, sie nähern sich mit Zeichen
eines stillern oder heftigern Schmerzens, einige knieen bei ihm nieder und
weinen auf seine Hand; während dieser stummen Scene wird die Burgglocke
geläutet.)

Rudenz zu den Vorigen.

Rudenz (rasch eintretend).

Lebt er? O saget, kann er mich noch hören?

Walther Fürst (deutet hin mit weggewandtem Gesicht).

Ihr seid jetzt unser Lehensherr und Schirmer,
Und dieses Schloß hat einen andern Namen.

Rudenz (erblickt den Leichnam und steht von heftigem Schmerz ergriffen).

O güt'ger Gott! — Kommt meine Reu' zu spät?   2455
Konnt' er nicht wen'ge Pulse länger leben,
Um mein geändert Herz zu sehn?
Verachtet hab' ich seine treue Stimme,
Da er noch wandelte im Licht — Er ist
Dahin, ist fort auf immerdar und läßt mir   2460
Die schwere, unbezahlte Schuld! — O, saget!
Schied er dahin im Unmut gegen mich?

Stauffacher.

Er hörte sterbend noch, was ihr gethan,
Und segnete den Mut, mit dem ihr spracht!

Rudenz (kniet an dem Toten nieder).

Ja, heil'ge Reste eines teuren Mannes!   2465
Entseelter Leichnam! hier gelob' ich dir's
In deine kalte Totenhand — Zerrissen
Hab' ich auf ewig alle fremden Bande;
Zurückgegeben bin ich meinem Volk,
Ein Schweizer bin ich, und ich will es sein   2470
Von ganzer Seele —— (Aufstehend.)
                    Trauert um den Freund,
Den Vater aller, doch verzaget nicht!
Nicht bloß sein Erbe ist mir zugefallen,
Es steigt sein Herz, sein Geist auf mich herab,
Und leisten soll euch meine frische Jugend,   2475

Was euch sein greises Alter schuldig blieb.
— Ehrwürd'ger Vater, gebt mir eure Hand!
Gebt mir die eurige! Melchthal, auch ihr!
Bedenkt euch nicht! O, wendet euch nicht weg!
Empfanget meinen Schwur und mein Gelübde.   2480

Walther Fürst.

Gebt ihm die Hand. Sein wiederkehrend Herz
Verdient Vertraun.

Melchthal.

Ihr habt den Landmann nichts geachtet.
Sprecht, wessen soll man sich zu euch versehn?

Rudenz.

O, denket nicht des Irrtums meiner Jugend!

Stauffacher (zu Melchthal).

Seid einig, war das letzte Wort des Vaters.   2485
Gedenket dessen!

Melchthal.

Hier ist meine Hand!
Des Bauern Handschlag, edler Herr, ist auch
Ein Manneswort! Was ist der Ritter ohne uns?
Und unser Stand ist älter, als der eure.

Rudenz.

Ich ehr' ihn, und mein Schwert soll ihn beschützen   2490

Melchthal.

Der Arm, Herr Freiherr, der die harte Erde
Sich unterwirft und ihren Schoß befruchtet,
Kann auch des Mannes Brust beschützen.

Rudenz.

                                        Ihr
Sollt meine Brust, ich will die eure schützen,

So sind wir einer durch den andern stark.   2495
— Doch wozu reden, da das Vaterland
Ein Raub noch ist der fremden Tyrannei?
Wenn erst der Boden rein ist von dem Feind,
Dann wollen wir's in Frieden schon vergleichen.

(Nachdem er einen Augenblick inne gehalten.)

Ihr schweigt?   Ihr habt mir nichts zu sagen?   Wie? 2500
Verdien' ich's noch nicht, daß ihr mir vertraut?
So muß ich wider euren Willen mich
In das Geheimnis eures Bundes drängen.
— Ihr habt getagt — geschworen auf dem Rütli —
Ich weiß — weiß alles, was ihr dort verhandelt,   2505
Und, was mir nicht von euch vertrauet ward,
Ich hab's bewahrt gleichwie ein heilig Pfand.
Nie war ich meines Landes Feind, glaubt mir,
Und niemals hätt' ich gegen euch gehandelt.
— Doch übel thatet ihr, es zu verschieben;   2510
Die Stunde bringt, und rascher That bedarf's —
Der Tell ward schon das Opfer eures Säumens —

Stauffacher.

Das Christfest abzuwarten, schwuren wir.

Rudenz

Ich war nicht dort, ich hab' nicht mitgeschworen.
Wartet ihr ab, ich handle.

Melchthal.

Was?   Ihr wolltet —   2515

Rudenz.

Des Landes Vätern zähl' ich mich jetzt bei,
Und meine erste Pflicht ist, euch zu schützen.

Walther Fürst.

Der Erde diesen teuren Staub zu geben,
Ist eure nächste Pflicht und heiligste.

Rudenz.

Wenn wir das Land befreit, dann legen wir   2520
Den frischen Kranz des Siegs ihm auf die Bahre.
O Freunde! eure Sache nicht allein,
Ich habe meine eigne auszufechten
Mit dem Tyrannen — Hört und wißt! Verschwunden
Ist meine Bertha, heimlich weggeraubt,   2525
Mit kecker Frevelthat aus unsrer Mitte!

Stauffacher.

Solcher Gewaltthat hätte der Tyrann
Wider die freie Edle sich verwogen?

Rudenz.

O meine Freunde! euch versprach ich Hilfe,
Und ich zuerst muß sie von euch erflehn.   2530
Geraubt, entrissen ist mir die Geliebte.
Wer weiß, wo sie der Wütende verbirgt,
Welcher Gewalt sie frevelnd sich erkühnen,
Ihr Herz zu zwingen zum verhaßten Band!
Verlaßt mich nicht, o, helft mir sie erretten —   2535
Sie liebt euch! o, sie hat's verdient ums Land,
Daß alle Arme sich für sie bewaffnen —

Walther Fürst.
Was wollt ihr unternehmen?

Rudenz.

             Weiß ich's? Ach!
In dieser Nacht, die ihr Geschick umhüllt,
In dieses Zweifels ungeheurer Angst,   2540
Wo ich nichts Festes zu erfassen weiß,
Ist mir nur dieses in der Seele klar:
Unter den Trümmern der Tyrannenmacht
Allein kann sie hervorgegraben werden;

Die Festen alle müssen wir bezwingen,   2545
Ob wir vielleicht in ihren Kerker dringen.

Melchthal.

Kommt, führt uns an! Wir folgen euch.   Warum
Bis morgen sparen, was wir heut' vermögen?
Frei war der Tell, als wir im Rütli schwuren,
Das Ungeheure war noch nicht geschehen.   2550
Es bringt die Zeit ein anderes Gesetz;
Wer ist so feig, der jetzt noch könnte zagen!

Rudenz (zu Stauffacher und Walther Fürst).

Indes bewaffnet und zum Werk bereit,
Erwartet ihr der Berge Feuerzeichen;
Denn, schneller als ein Botensegel fliegt,   2555
Soll euch die Botschaft unsers Siegs erreichen,
Und seht ihr leuchten die willkommnen Flammen,
Dann auf die Feinde stürzt wie Wetters Strahl
Und brecht den Bau der Thrannei zusammen! (Gehen ab).

Dritte Scene.

Die hohle Gasse bei Küßnacht.

Man steigt von hinten zwischen Felsen herunter, und die Wanderer werden,
ehe sie auf der Scene erscheinen, schon von der Höhe gesehen. Felsen um-
schließen die ganze Scene; auf einem der vordersten ist ein Vorsprung
mit Gesträuch bewachsen.

Tell (tritt auf mit der Armbrust.)

Durch diese hohle Gasse muß er kommen;   2560
Es führt kein andrer Weg nach Küßnacht — Hier
Vollend' ich's — Die Gelegenheit ist günstig.
Dort der Holunderstrauch verbirgt mich ihm,
Von dort herab kann ihn mein Pfeil erlangen;
Des Weges Enge wehret den Verfolgern.   2565

Mach' deine Rechnung mit dem Himmel, Vogt,
Fort mußt du, deine Uhr ist abgelaufen.

Ich lebte still und harmlos — das Geschoß
War auf des Waldes Tiere nur gerichtet,
Meine Gedanken waren rein von Mord —   2570
Du hast aus meinem Frieden mich heraus
Geschreckt; in gärend Drachengift hast du
Die Milch der frommen Denkart mir verwandelt;
Zum Ungeheuren hast du mich gewöhnt —
Wer sich des Kindes Haupt zum Ziele setzte,   2575
Der kann auch treffen in das Herz des Feinds.

Die armen Kindlein, die unschuldigen,
Das treue Weib muß ich vor deiner Wut
Beschützen, Landvogt! — Da, als ich den Bogenstrang
Anzog — als mir die Hand erzitterte —   2580
Als du mit grausam teuflischer Lust
Mich zwangst, aufs Haupt des Kindes anzulegen —
Als ich ohnmächtig flehend rang vor dir,
Damals gelobt' ich mir in meinem Innern
Mit furchtbarm Eidschwur, den nur Gott gehört,   2585
Daß meines nächsten Schusses erstes Ziel
Dein Herz sein sollte — Was ich mir gelobt
In jenes Augenblickes Höllenqualen,
Ist eine heil'ge Schuld — ich will sie zahlen.

Du bist mein Herr und meines Kaisers Vogt;   2590
Doch nicht der Kaiser hätte sich erlaubt,
Was du — Er sandte dich in diese Lande,
Um Recht zu sprechen — strenges, denn er zürnet —
Doch nicht, um mit der mörderischen Lust
Dich jedes Greuels straflos zu erfrechen;   2595
Es lebt ein Gott, zu strafen und zu rächen.

Komm du hervor, du Bringer bittrer Schmerzen,
Mein teures Kleinod jetzt, mein höchster Schatz —
Ein Ziel will ich dir geben, das bis jetzt
Der frommen Bitte undurchdringlich war —   2600
Doch dir soll es nicht widerstehn — Und du,
Vertraute Bogensehne, die so oft
Mir treu gedient hat in der Freude Spielen,
Verlaß mich nicht im fürchterlichen Ernst!
Nur jetzt noch halte fest, du treuer Strang,   2605
Der mir so oft den herben Pfeil beflügelt —
Entränn' er jetzo kraftlos meinen Händen,
Ich habe keinen zweiten zu versenden.

(Wanderer gehen über die Scene.)

Auf dieser Bank von Stein will ich mich setzen,
Dem Wanderer zur kurzen Ruh' bereitet —   2610
Denn hier ist keine Heimat — Jeder treibt
Sich an dem andern rasch und fremd vorüber
Und fraget nicht nach seinem Schmerz — Hier geht
Der sorgenvolle Kaufmann und der leicht
Geschürzte Pilger — der andächt'ge Mönch,   2615
Der düstre Räuber und der heitre Spielmann,
Der Säumer mit dem schwerbeladnen Roß,
Der ferne herkommt von der Menschen Ländern,
Denn jede Straße führt ans End' der Welt.
Sie alle ziehen ihres Weges fort   2620
An ihr Geschäft — und meines ist der Mord! (Setzt sich).

Sonst, wenn der Vater auszog, liebe Kinder,
Da war ein Freuen, wenn er wiederkam;
Denn niemals kehrt' er heim, er bracht' euch etwas,
War's eine schöne Alpenblume, war's   2625
Ein seltner Vogel oder Ammonshorn,
Wie es der Wandrer findet auf den Bergen —

Jetzt geht er einem andern Weidwerk nach,
Am wilden Weg sitzt er mit Mordgedanken;
Des Feindes Leben ist's, worauf er lauert.   2630
— Und doch an euch nur denkt er, liebe Kinder,
Auch jetzt — euch zu verteid'gen, eure holde Unschuld
Zu schützen vor der Rache des Tyrannen,
Will er zum Morde jetzt den Bogen spannen. (Steht auf.)

    Ich laure auf ein edles Wild — Läßt sich's   2635
Der Jäger nicht verdrießen, tagelang
Umherzustreifen in des Winters Strenge,
Von Fels zu Fels den Wagesprung zu thun,
Hinan zu klimmen an den glatten Wänden,
Wo er sich anleimt mit dem eignen Blut,   2640
— Um ein armselig Grattier zu erjagen.
Hier gilt es einen köstlicheren Preis,
Das Herz des Todfeinds, der mich will verderben.

    (Man hört von ferne eine heitere Musik, welche sich nähert.)

    Mein ganzes Leben lang hab' ich den Bogen
Gehandhabt, mich geübt nach Schützenregel;   2645
Ich habe oft geschossen in das Schwarze
Und manchen schönen Preis mir heimgebracht
Vom Freudenschießen — Aber heute will ich
Den Meisterschuß thun und das Beste mir
Im ganzen Umkreis des Gebirgs gewinnen.   2650

(Eine Hochzeit zieht über die Scene und durch den Hohlweg hinauf. Tell
betrachtet sie, auf seinen Bogen gelehnt; Stüssi, der Flurschütz, gesellt
sich zu ihm.)

            Stüssi.

Das ist der Klostermei'r von Mörlischachen,
Der hier den Brautlauf hält — ein reicher Mann,
Er hat wohl zehen Senten auf den Alpen.
Die Braut holt er jetzt ab zu Imisee,

Und diese Nacht wird hoch geschwelgt zu Küßnacht.   2655
Kommt mit! 's ist jeder Biedermann geladen.

Tell.
Ein ernster Gast stimmt nicht zum Hochzeithaus.

Stüffi.
Drückt euch ein Kummer, werft ihn frisch vom Herzen!
Nehmt mit, was kommt; die Zeiten sind jetzt schwer;
Drum muß der Mensch die Freude leicht ergreifen.   2660
Hier wird gefreit und anderswo begraben.

Tell.
Und oft kommt gar das eine zu dem andern

Stüffi.
So geht die Welt nun.   Es giebt allerwegen
Unglücks genug — Ein Ruffi ist gegangen
Im Glarner Land und eine ganze Seite   2665
Vom Glärnisch eingesunken.

Tell.
                        Wanken auch
Die Berge selbst?   Es steht nichts fest auf Erden.

Stüffi.
Auch anderswo vernimmt man Wunderdinge.
Da sprach ich einen, der von Baden kam.
Ein Ritter wollte zu dem König reiten,   2670
Und unterwegs begegnet ihm ein Schwarm
Von Horniffen; die fallen auf sein Roß,
Daß es vor Marter tot zu Boden sinkt,
Und er zu Fuße ankommt bei dem König.

Tell.
Dem Schwachen ist sein Stachel auch gegeben.   2675

(Armgard kommt mit mehreren Kindern und stellt sich an den Eingang
des Hohlwegs.)

Vierter Aufzug. 3. Scene.

Stüffi.

Man deutet's auf ein großes Landesunglück,
Auf schwere Thaten wider die Natur.

Tell.

Dergleichen Thaten bringet jeder Tag;
Kein Wunderzeichen braucht sie zu verfünden.

Stüffi.

Ja, wohl dem, der sein Feld bestellt in Ruh'   2680
Und ungekränkt daheim sitzt bei den Seinen.

Tell.

Es kann der Frömmste nicht im Frieden bleiben,
Wenn es dem bösen Nachbar nicht gefällt.

(Tell sieht oft mit unruhiger Erwartung nach der Höhe des Weges.)

Stüffi.

Gehabt euch wohl! Ihr wartet hier auf jemand?

Tell.

Das thu' ich.

Stüffi.

Frohe Heimkehr zu den Euren!   2685
— Ihr seid aus Uri? Unser gnäd'ger Herr,
Der Landvogt, wird noch heut' von dort erwartet.

Wanderer (kommt).

Den Vogt erwartet heut' nicht mehr. Die Wasser
Sind ausgetreten von dem großen Regen,
Und alle Brücken hat der Strom zerrissen. (Tell steht auf.) 2690

Armgard (kommt vorwärts).

Der Landvogt kommt nicht?

Stüffi.

Sucht ihr was an ihn?

Armgard.

Ach freilich!

Stüffi.

Warum stellet ihr euch denn
In dieser hohlen Gass' ihm in den Weg?

Armgard.

Hier weicht er mir nicht aus, er muß mich hören.

Frießhardt (kommt eilfertig den Hohlweg herab und ruft in die Scene).

Man fahre aus dem Weg — Mein gnäd'ger Herr,		2695
Der Landvogt, kommt dicht hinter mir geritten. (Tell
	geht ab.)

Armgard (lebhaft).

Der Landvogt kommt!

(Sie geht mit ihren Kindern nach der vorderen Scene. Geßler und
	Rudolf der Harras zeigen sich zu Pferd auf der Höhe des Wegs.)

Stüffi (zum Frießhardt).

Wie kamt ihr durch das Wasser
Da doch der Strom die Brücken fortgeführt?

Frießhardt.

Wir haben mit dem See gefochten, Freund,
Und fürchten uns vor keinem Alpenwasser.		2700

Stüffi.

Ihr wart zu Schiff in dem gewalt'gen Sturm?

Frießhardt.

Das waren wir. Mein Lebtag denk' ich dran —

Stüffi.

O, bleibt, erzählt!

Frießhardt.

Laßt mich, ich muß voraus,
Den Landvogt muß ich in der Burg verkünden. (Ab.)

Stüssi.

Wär'n gute Leute auf dem Schiff gewesen, 2705
In Grund gesunken wär's mit Mann und Maus;
Dem Volk kann weder Wasser bei noch Feuer. (Er sieht
sich um.)
Wo kam der Weidmann hin, mit dem ich sprach? (Geht ab)
(Geßler und Rudolf der Harras zu Pferd.)

Geßler.

Sagt, was ihr wollt, ich bin des Kaisers Diener
Und muß drauf denken, wie ich ihm gefalle. 2710
Er hat mich nicht ins Land geschickt, dem Volk
Zu schmeicheln und ihm sanft zu thun — Gehorsam
Erwartet er; der Streit ist, ob der Bauer
Soll Herr sein in dem Lande oder der Kaiser.

Armgard.

Jetzt ist der Augenblick! Jetzt bring' ich's an! 2715
(Nähert sich furchtsam.)

Geßler.

Ich hab' den Hut nicht aufgesteckt zu Altorf
Des Scherzes wegen, oder um die Herzen
Des Volks zu prüfen; diese kenn' ich längst.
Ich hab' ihn aufgesteckt, daß sie den Nacken
Mir lernen beugen, den sie aufrecht tragen — 2720
Das Unbequeme hab' ich hingepflanzt
Auf ihren Weg, wo sie vorbeigehn müssen,
Daß sie drauf stoßen mit dem Aug' und sich
Erinnern ihres Herrn, den sie vergessen.

Rudolf der Harras.

Das Volk hat aber doch gewisse Rechte — 2725

Geßler.

Die abzuwägen, ist jetzt keine Zeit!

— Weitschicht'ge Dinge sind im Werk und Werden;
Das Kaiserhaus will wachsen; was der Vater
Glorreich begonnen, will der Sohn vollenden.
Dies kleine Volk ist uns ein Stein im Weg —   2730
So oder so — es muß sich unterwerfen.

(Sie wollen vorüber. Die Frau wirft sich vor dem Landvogt nieder.)

Armgard.

Barmherzigkeit, Herr Landvogt!   Gnade! Gnade!

Geßler.

Was bringt ihr euch auf offner Straße mir
In Weg? — Zurück!

Armgard.

                    Mein Mann liegt im Gefängnis;
Die armen Waisen schrei'n nach Brot — Habt Mitleid,   2735
Gestrenger Herr, mit unserm großen Elend!

Rudolf der Harras.

Wer seid ihr?   Wer ist euer Mann?

Armgard.

                              Ein armer
Wildheuer, guter Herr, vom Rigiberge,
Der überm Abgrund weg das freie Gras
Abmähet von den schroffen Felsenwänden,   2740
Wohin das Vieh sich nicht getraut zu steigen —

Rudolf der Harras (zum Landvogt).

Bei Gott, ein elend und erbärmlich Leben!
Ich bitt' euch, gebt ihn los, den armen Mann!
Was er auch Schweres mag verschuldet haben,
Strafe genug ist sein entsetzlich Handwerk. (Zu der Frau.)   2745
Euch soll Recht werden — Drinnen auf der Burg
Nennt eure Bitte — hier ist nicht der Ort.

Armgard.

Nein, nein, ich weiche nicht von diesem Platz,
Bis mir der Vogt den Mann zurückgegeben!
Schon in den sechsten Mond liegt er im Turm   2750
Und harret auf den Richterspruch vergebens.

Geßler.

Weib, wollt ihr mir Gewalt anthun? Hinweg!

Armgard.

Gerechtigkeit, Landvogt! Du bist der Richter
Im Lande an des Kaisers Statt und Gottes.
Thu' deine Pflicht! So du Gerechtigkeit   2755
Vom Himmel hoffest, so erzeig' sie uns!

Geßler.

Fort! Schafft das freche Volk mir aus den Augen!

Armgard (greift in die Zügel des Pferdes).

Nein, nein, ich habe nichts mehr zu verlieren.
— Du kommst nicht von der Stelle, Vogt, bis du
Mir Recht gesprochen — Falte deine Stirne,   2760
Rolle die Augen, wie du willst — Wir sind
So grenzenlos unglücklich, daß wir nichts
Nach deinem Zorn mehr fragen. —

Geßler.

Weib, mach' Platz,
Oder mein Roß geht über dich hinweg.

Armgard.

Laß es über mich dahin gehn — Da —
(Sie reißt ihre Kinder zu Boden und wirft sich mit ihnen ihm in den Weg.)

Hier lieg' ich 2765
Mit meinen Kindern — Laß die armen Waisen
Von deines Pferdes Huf zertreten werden!
Es ist das Ärgste nicht, was du gethan —

Rudolf der Harras.

Weib, seid ihr rasend?

Armgard (heftiger fortfahrend).

Tratest du doch längst
Das Land des Kaisers unter deine Füße!   2770
— O, ich bin nur ein Weib! Wär' ich ein Mann,
Ich wüßte wohl was Besseres, als hier
Im Staub zu liegen —

(Man hört die vorige Musik wieder auf der Höhe des Wegs, aber
gedämpft.)

Geßler.

Wo sind meine Knechte?
Man reiße sie von hinnen, oder ich
Vergesse mich und thue, was mich reuet.   2775

Rudolf der Harras.

Die Knechte können nicht hindurch, o Herr,
Der Hohlweg ist gesperrt durch eine Hochzeit.

Geßler.

Ein allzu milder Herrscher bin ich noch
Gegen dies Volk — die Zungen sind noch frei,
Es ist noch nicht ganz, wie es soll, gebändigt —   2780
Doch es soll anders werden, ich gelob' es:
Ich will ihn brechen, diesen starren Sinn,
Den kecken Geist der Freiheit will ich beugen,
Ein neu Gesetz will ich in diesen Landen
Verkündigen — Ich will —

(Ein Pfeil durchbohrt ihn; er fährt mit der Hand ans Herz und will sinken.
Mit matter Stimme:)

Gott sei mir gnädig!   2785

Rudolf der Harras.

Herr Landvogt — Gott! Was ist das? Woher kam das?

Armgard (auffahrend).

Mord! Mord! Er taumelt, sinkt! Er ist getroffen!
Mitten ins Herz hat ihn der Pfeil getroffen!

Rudolf der Harras (springt vom Pferde).

Welch gräßliches Ereignis — Gott — Herr Ritter —
Ruft die Erbarmung Gottes an! Ihr seid   2790
Ein Mann des Todes!

Geßler.

Das ist Tell's Geschoß.

(Ist vom Pferd herab dem Rudolf Harras in den Arm gegleitet und
wird auf der Bank niedergelassen.)

Tell (erscheint oben auf der Höhe des Felsen).

Du kennst den Schützen, suche keinen andern!
Frei sind die Hütten, sicher ist die Unschuld
Vor dir, du wirst dem Lande nicht mehr schaden.

(Verschwindet von der Höhe. Volk stürzt herein.)

Stüssi (voran).

Was giebt es hier? Was hat sich zugetragen?   2795

Armgard.

Der Landvogt ist von einem Pfeil durchschossen.

Volk (im Hereinstürzen).

Wer ist erschossen?

(Indem die vordersten von dem Brautzug auf die Scene kommen, sind die
hintersten noch auf der Höhe, und die Musik geht fort.)

Rudolf der Harras.

Er verblutet sich.

Fort, schaffet Hilfe! Setzt dem Mörder nach!
—Verlorner Mann, so muß es mit dir enden;
Doch meine Warnung wolltest du nicht hören!   2800

Stüssi.

Bei Gott, da liegt er bleich und ohne Leben.

Viele Stimmen.

Wer hat die That gethan?

Rudolf der Harras.

Rast dieses Volk,
Daß es dem Mord Musik macht? Laßt sie schweigen!

(Musik bricht plötzlich ab, es kommt noch mehr Volk nach.)

Herr Landvogt, redet, wenn ihr könnt — Habt ihr
Mir nichts mehr zu vertrauen?

(Geßler giebt Zeichen mit der Hand, die er mit Heftigkeit wiederholt, da
sie nicht gleich verstanden werden.)

Wo soll ich hin?   2805
— Nach Küßnacht? Ich versteh' euch nicht — O, werdet
Nicht ungeduldig — Laßt das Irdische,
Denkt jetzt, euch mit dem Himmel zu versöhnen.

(Die ganze Hochzeitgesellschaft umsteht den Sterbenden mit einem fühllosen
Grausen.)

Stüffi.

Sieh, wie er bleich wird — Jetzt, jetzt tritt der Tod
Ihm an das Herz — die Augen sind gebrochen.   2810

Armgard (hebt ein Kind empor).

Seht, Kinder, wie ein Wüterich verscheidet!

Rudolf der Harras.

Wahnsinn'ge Weiber, habt ihr kein Gefühl,
Daß ihr den Blick an diesem Schrecknis weidet?
— Helft — leget Hand an — Steht mir niemand bei,
Den Schmerzenspfeil ihm aus der Brust zu ziehn?   2815

Weiber (treten zurück).

Wir ihn berühren, welchen Gott geschlagen!

Rudolf der Harras.

Fluch treff' euch und Verdammnis!

(Zieht das Schwert.)

Stüſſi (fällt ihm in den Arm).

Wagt es, Herr!
Eu'r Walten hat ein Ende. Der Tyrann
Des Landes iſt gefallen. Wir erbulden
Keine Gewalt mehr. Wir ſind freie Menſchen.   2820

Alle (tumultuariſch).

Das Land iſt frei!

Rudolf der Harras.

                    Iſt es dahin gekommen?
Endet die Furcht ſo ſchnell und der Gehorſam?
(Zu den Waffenknechten, die hereindringen.)
Ihr ſeht die grauſenvolle That des Mords,
Die hier geſchehen — Hilfe iſt umſonſt —
Vergeblich iſt's, dem Mörder nachzuſetzen.   2825
Uns drängen andre Sorgen — Auf, nach Küßnacht,
Daß wir dem Kaiſer ſeine Feſte retten!
Denn aufgelöſt in dieſem Augenblick
Sind aller Ordnung, aller Pflichten Bande,
Und keines Mannes Treu' iſt zu vertrauen.   2830
(Indem er mit den Waffenknechten abgeht, erſcheinen ſechs barm-
herzige Brüder.)

Armgard.

Platz! Platz! Da kommen die barmherz'gen Brüder.

Stüſſi.

Das Opfer liegt — die Raben ſteigen nieder.

Barmherzige Brüder (ſchließen einen Halbkreis um den Toten und
ſingen in tiefem Ton).

Raſch tritt der Tod den Menſchen an,
    Es iſt ihm keine Friſt gegeben;
Es ſtürzt ihn mitten in der Bahn,   2835
    Es reißt ihn fort vom vollen Leben.
Bereitet oder nicht, zu gehen,
    Er muß vor ſeinen Richter ſtehen!
(Indem die letzten Zeilen wiederholt werden, fällt der Vorhang.)

Fünfter Aufzug.

Erste Scene.

Öffentlicher Platz bei Altorf.

Im Hintergrunde rechts die Feste Zwing Uri mit dem noch stehenden Bau-
gerüste, wie in der dritten Scene des ersten Aufzugs; links eine Aussicht in
viele Berge hinein, auf welchen allen Signalfeuer brennen. Es ist eben
Tagesanbruch, Glocken ertönen aus verschiedenen Fernen.

Ruodi, Kuoni, Werni, Meister Steinmetz und viele andere
Landleute, auch Weiber und Kinder.

Ruodi.

Seht ihr die Feuersignale auf den Bergen?

Steinmetz.

Hört ihr die Glocken drüben überm Wald?   2840

Ruodi.

Die Feinde sind verjagt.

Steinmetz.

　　　　　Die Burgen sind erobert.

Ruodi.

Und wir im Lande Uri dulden noch
Auf unserm Boden das Thrannenschloß?
Sind wir die letzten, die sich frei erklären?

Steinmetz.

Das Joch soll stehen, das uns zwingen wollte?   2845
Auf, reißt es nieder!

Alle.

　　　Nieder! nieder! nieder!

Ruodi.

Wo ist der Stier von Uri?

Stier von Uri.

　　　　Hier. Was soll ich?

Ruodi.

Steigt auf die Hochwacht, blast in euer Horn,
Daß es weitschmetternd in die Berge schalle
Und, jedes Echo in den Felsenklüften   2850
Aufweckend, schnell die Männer des Gebirgs
Zusammenrufe.

(Stier von Uri geht ab. Walther Fürst kommt.)

Walther Fürst.

Haltet, Freunde! Haltet!
Noch fehlt uns Kunde, was in Unterwalden
Und Schwyz geschehen. Laßt uns Boten erst
Erwarten!

Ruodi.

Was erwarten? Der Thrann   2855
Ist tot, der Tag der Freiheit ist erschienen.

Steinmetz.

Ist's nicht genug an diesen flammenden Boten,
Die rings herum auf allen Bergen leuchten?

Ruodi.

Kommt alle, kommt, legt Hand an, Männer und Weiber!
Brecht das Gerüste! Sprengt die Bögen! Reißt   2860
Die Mauern ein! Kein Stein bleib' auf dem andern.

Steinmetz.

Gesellen, kommt! Wir haben's aufgebaut,
Wir wissen's zu zerstören.

Alle.

Kommt, reißt nieder!

(Sie stürzen sich von allen Seiten auf den Bau.)

Walther Fürst.

Es ist im Lauf. Ich kann sie nicht mehr halten.

(Melchthal und Baumgarten kommen.)

Melchthal.

Was? Steht die Burg noch, und Schloß Sarnen liegt 2865
In Asche, und der Roßberg ist gebrochen?

Walther Fürst.

Seid ihr es, Melchthal? Bringt ihr uns die Freiheit?
Sagt! Sind die Lande alle rein vom Feind?

Melchthal (umarmt ihn).

Rein ist der Boden. Freut euch, alter Vater!
In diesem Augenblicke, da wir reden,   2870
Ist kein Thrann mehr in der Schweizer Land.

Walther Fürst.

O, sprecht, wie wurdet ihr der Burgen mächtig?

Melchthal.

Der Rudenz war es, der das Sarner Schloß
Mit männlich kühner Wagethat gewann.
Den Roßberg hatt' ich nachts zuvor erstiegen.   2875
—Doch höret, was geschah. Als wir das Schloß,
Vom Feind geleert, nun freudig angezündet,
Die Flamme prasselnd schon zum Himmel schlug,
Da stürzt der Diethelm, Geßlers Bub, hervor
Und ruft, daß die Bruneckerin verbrenne.   2880

Walther Fürst.

Gerechter Gott!

(Man hört die Balken des Gerüstes stürzen.)

Melchthal.

            Sie war es selbst, war heimlich
Hier eingeschlossen auf des Vogts Geheiß.
Rasend erhub sich Rudenz —denn wir hörten
Die Balken schon, die festen Pfosten stürzen
Und aus dem Rauch hervor den Jammerruf   2885
Der Unglückseligen.

Walther Fürst.
Sie ist gerettet?

Meldthal.

Da galt Geschwindsein und Entschlossenheit!
— Wär' er nur unser Edelmann gewesen,
Wir hätten unser Leben wohl geliebt;
Doch er war unser Eidgenoß, und Bertha   2890
Ehrte das Volk — So setzten wir getrost
Das Leben dran und stürzten in das Feuer.

Walther Fürst.
Sie ist gerettet?

Meldthal.

          Sie ist's.   Rudenz und ich,
Wir trugen sie selbander aus den Flammen,
Und hinter uns fiel krachend das Gebälk.   2895
— Und jetzt, als sie gerettet sich erkannte,
Die Augen aufschlug zu dem Himmelslicht,
Jetzt stürzte mir der Freiherr an das Herz,
Und schweigend ward ein Bündnis jetzt beschworen,
Das, fest gehärtet in des Feuers Glut,   2900
Bestehen wird in allen Schicksalsproben —

Walther Fürst.
Wo ist der Landenberg?

Meldthal.

          Über den Brünig.
Nicht lag's an mir, daß er das Licht der Augen
Davontrug, der den Vater mir geblendet.
Nach jagt' ich ihm, erreicht' ihn auf der Flucht   2905
Und riß ihn zu den Füßen meines Vaters.
Geschwungen über ihm war schon das Schwert;
Von der Barmherzigkeit des blinden Greises

Erhielt er flehend das Geschenk des Lebens.
Urfehde schwur er, nie zurückzukehren;   2910
Er wird sie halten; unsern Arm hat er
Gefühlt.

Walther Fürst.

          Wohl euch, daß ihr den reinen Sieg
Mit Blute nicht geschändet!

      Kinder (eilen mit Trümmern des Gerüstes über die Scene).

                    Freiheit! Freiheit!

    (Das Horn von Uri wird mit Macht geblasen.)

Walther Fürst.

Seht, welch ein Fest! Des Tages werden sich
Die Kinder spät als Greise noch erinnern.   2915

(Mädchen bringen den Hut auf einer Stange getragen; die ganze Scene
füllt sich mit Volk an.)

Ruodi.

Hier ist der Hut, dem wir uns beugen mußten.

Baumgarten.

Gebt uns Bescheid, was damit werden soll.

Walther Fürst.

Gott! Unter diesem Hute stand mein Enkel.

Mehrere Stimmen.

Zerstört das Denkmal der Tyrannenmacht!
Ins Feuer mit ihm!

Walther Fürst.

          Nein, laßt ihn aufbewahren!   2920
Der Tyrannei mußt' er zum Werkzeug dienen,
Er soll der Freiheit ewig Zeichen sein!

(Die Landleute, Männer, Weiber und Kinder stehen und sitzen auf den
Balken des zerbrochenen Gerüstes malerisch gruppiert in einem großen
Halbkreis umher.)

Melchthal.

So stehen wir nun fröhlich auf den Trümmern
Der Thrannei, und herrlich ist's erfüllt,
Was wir im Rütli schwuren, Eidgenossen!   2925

Walther Fürst.

Das Werk ist angefangen, nicht vollendet.
Jetzt ist uns Mut und feste Eintracht not;
Denn, seid gewiß, nicht säumen wird der König,
Den Tod zu rächen seines Vogts und den
Vertriebnen mit Gewalt zurückzuführen.   2930

Melchthal.

Er zieh' heran mit seiner Heeresmacht!
Ist aus dem Innern doch der Feind verjagt;
Dem Feind von außen wollen wir begegnen.

Ruodi.

Nur wen'ge Pässe öffnen ihm das Land,
Die wollen wir mit unsern Leibern decken.   2935

Baumgarten.

Wir sind vereinigt durch ein ewig Band,
Und seine Heere sollen uns nicht schrecken!

(Rösselmann und Stauffacher kommen.)

Rösselmann (im Eintreten).

Das sind des Himmels furchtbare Gerichte.

Landleute.

Was giebt's?

Rösselmann.

In welchen Zeiten leben wir!

Walther Fürst.

Sagt an, was ist es? Ha, seid ihr's, Herr Werner?   2940
Was bringt ihr uns?

Landleute.

Was giebt's?

Rösselmann.

Hört und erstaunet!

Stauffacher.

Von einer großen Furcht sind wir befreit —

Rösselmann.

Der Kaiser ist ermordet.

Walther Fürst.

Gnäd'ger Gott!

(Landleute machen einen Aufstand und umdrängen den Stauffacher.)

Alle.

Ermordet! Was! Der Kaiser! Hört! Der Kaiser!

Melchthal.

Nicht möglich! Woher kam euch diese Kunde?   2945

Stauffacher.

Es ist gewiß. Bei Bruck fiel König Albrecht,
Durch Mörders Hand — ein glaubenswerter Mann,
Johannes Müller, bracht' es von Schaffhausen.

Walther Fürst.

Wer wagte solche grauenvolle That?

Stauffacher.

Sie wird noch grauenvoller durch den Thäter.   2950
Es war sein Neffe, seines Bruders Kind,
Herzog Johann von Schwaben, der's vollbrachte.

Melchthal.

Was trieb ihn zu der That des Vatermords?

Stauffacher.

Der Kaiser hielt das väterliche Erbe
Dem ungeduldig Mahnenden zurück;   2955

Es hieß, er denk' ihn ganz darum zu kürzen,
Mit einem Bischofshute ihn abzufinden.
Wie dem auch sei — der Jüngling öffnete
Der Waffenfreunde bösem Rat sein Ohr,
Und mit den edeln Herrn von Eschenbach,   2960
Von Tegerfelden, von der Wart und Palm
Beschloß er, da er Recht nicht konnte finden,
Sich Rach' zu holen mit der eignen Hand.

Walther Fürst.

O, sprecht, wie ward das Gräßliche vollendet?

Stauffacher.

Der König ritt herab vom Stein zu Baden,   2965
Gen Rheinfeld, wo die Hofstatt war, zu ziehn,
Mit ihm die Fürsten Hans und Leopold
Und ein Gefolge hochgeborner Herren.
Und als sie kamen an die Reuß, wo man
Auf einer Fähre sich läßt übersetzen,   2970
Da drängten sich die Mörder in das Schiff,
Daß sie den Kaiser vom Gefolge trennten.
Drauf, als der Fürst durch ein geackert Feld
Hinreitet — eine alte große Stadt
Soll drunter liegen aus der Heiden Zeit —   2975
Die alte Feste Habsburg im Gesicht,
Wo seines Stammes Hoheit ausgegangen —
Stößt Herzog Hans den Dolch ihm in die Kehle,
Rudolf von Palm durchrennt ihn mit dem Speer,
Und Eschenbach zerspaltet ihm das Haupt,   2980
Daß er heruntersinkt in seinem Blut,
Gemordet von den Seinen, auf dem Seinen.
Am andern Ufer sahen sie die That;
Doch, durch den Strom geschieden, konnten sie
Nur ein ohnmächtig Wehgeschrei erheben;   2985

Am Wege aber saß ein armes Weib,
In ihrem Schoß verblutete der Kaiser.

Melchthal.

So hat er nur sein frühes Grab gegraben,
Der unersättlich alles wollte haben!

Stauffacher.

Ein ungeheurer Schrecken ist im Land umher;   2990
Gesperrt sind alle Pässe des Gebirgs,
Jedweder Stand verwahret seine Grenzen;
Die alte Zürich selbst schloß ihre Thore,
Die dreißig Jahr' lang offen standen, zu,
Die Mörder fürchtend und noch mehr — die Rächer   2995
Denn, mit des Bannes Fluch bewaffnet, kommt
Der Ungarn Königin, die strenge Agnes,
Die nicht die Milde kennet ihres zarten
Geschlechts, des Vaters königliches Blut
Zu rächen an der Mörder ganzem Stamm,   3000
An ihren Knechten, Kindern, Kindeskindern,
Ja, an den Steinen ihrer Schlösser selbst.
Geschworen hat sie, ganze Zeugungen
Hinabzusenden in des Vaters Grab,
In Blut sich wie in Maientau zu baden.   3005

Melchthal.

Weiß man, wo sich die Mörder hingeflüchtet?

Stauffacher.

Sie flohen alsbald nach vollbrachter That
Auf fünf verschiednen Straßen auseinander
Und trennten sich, um nie sich mehr zu sehn —
Herzog Johann soll irren im Gebirge.   3010

Walther Fürst.

So trägt die Unthat ihnen keine Frucht!

Rache trägt keine Frucht!   Sich selbst ist sie
Die fürchterliche Nahrung, ihr Genuß
Ist Mord, und ihre Sättigung das Grausen.

Stauffacher.

Den Mördern bringt die Unthat nicht Gewinn;   3015
Wir aber brechen mit der reinen Hand
Des blut'gen Frevels segenvolle Frucht.
Denn einer großen Furcht sind wir entledigt;
Gefallen ist der Freiheit größter Feind,
Und wie verlautet, wird das Scepter gehn   3020
Aus Habsburgs Haus zu einem andern Stamm,
Das Reich will seine Wahlfreiheit behaupten.

Walther Fürst und mehrere.

Vernahmt ihr was?

Stauffacher.

Der Graf von Luxemburg
Ist von den mehrsten Stimmen schon bezeichnet.

Walther Fürst.

Wohl uns, daß wir beim Reiche treu gehalten;   3025
Jetzt ist zu hoffen auf Gerechtigkeit!

Stauffacher

Dem neuen Herrn thun tapfre Freunde not;
Er wird uns schirmen gegen Östreichs Rache.

(Die Landleute umarmen einander.)

(Sigrist mit einem Reichsboten.)

Sigrist.

Hier sind des Landes würd'ge Oberhäupter.

Rösselmann und mehrere.

Sigrist, was giebt's?

Sigrist.

Ein Reichsbot' bringt dies Schreiben.   3030

Alle (zu Walther Fürst).

Erbrecht und leset!

Walther Fürst (liest).

„Den bescheidnen Männern
Von Uri, Schwyz und Unterwalden bietet
Die Königin Elsbeth Gnad' und alles Gutes."

Viele Stimmen.

Was will die Königin?   Ihr Reich ist aus.

Walther Fürst (liest).

„In ihrem großen Schmerz und Witwenleid,   3035
Worein der blut'ge Hinscheid ihres Herrn
Die Königin versetzt, gedenkt sie noch
Der alten Treu' und Lieb' der Schwyzerlande."

Melchthal.

In ihrem Glück hat sie das nie gethan.

Rösselmann.

Still!   Lasset hören!   3040

Walther Fürst (liest).

„Und sie versieht sich zu dem treuen Volk,
Daß es gerechten Abscheu werde tragen
Vor den verfluchten Thätern dieser That;
Darum erwartet sie von den drei Landen,
Daß sie den Mördern nimmer Vorschub thun,   3045
Vielmehr getreulich dazu helfen werden,
Sie auszuliefern in des Rächers Hand,
Der Lieb' gedenkend und der alten Gunst,
Die sie von Rudolfs Fürstenhaus empfangen."

(Zeichen des Unwillens unter den Landleuten.)

Viele Stimmen.

Der Lieb' und Gunst!   3050

Stauffacher.

Wir haben Gunst empfangen von dem Vater;
Doch wessen rühmen wir uns von dem Sohn?
Hat er den Brief der Freiheit uns bestätigt,
Wie vor ihm alle Kaiser doch gethan?
Hat er gerichtet nach gerechtem Spruch   3055
Und der bedrängten Unschuld Schutz verliehn?
Hat er auch nur die Boten wollen hören,
Die wir in unsrer Angst zu ihm gesendet?
Nicht eins von diesem allen hat der König
An uns gethan, und hätten wir nicht selbst   3060
Uns Recht verschafft mit eigner mut'ger Hand,
Ihn rührte unsre Not nicht an — Ihm Dank?
Nicht Dank hat er gesät in diesen Thälern.
Er stand auf einem hohen Platz, er konnte
Ein Vater seiner Völker sein; doch ihm   3065
Gefiel es, nur zu sorgen für die Seinen.
Die er gemehrt hat, mögen um ihn weinen!

Walther Fürst.

Wir wollen nicht frohlocken seines Falls,
Nicht des empfangnen Bösen jetzt gedenken,
Fern sei's von uns! Doch, daß wir rächen sollten   3070
Des Königs Tod, der nie uns Gutes that,
Und die verfolgen, die uns nie betrübten,
Das ziemt uns nicht und will uns nicht gebühren.
Die Liebe will ein freies Opfer sein;
Der Tod entbindet von erzwungnen Pflichten,   3075
— Ihm haben wir nichts weiter zu entrichten.

Melchthal.

Und weint die Königin in ihrer Kammer,
Und klagt ihr wilder Schmerz den Himmel an,
So seht ihr hier ein angstbefreites Volk

Zu eben diesem Himmel dankend flehen —   3080
Wer Thränen ernten will, muß Liebe säen.

(Reichsbote geht ab.)

Stauffacher (zu dem Volk).

Wo ist der Tell?   Soll er allein uns fehlen,
Der unsrer Freiheit Stifter ist?   Das Größte
Hat e r gethan, das Härteste erduldet.
Kommt alle, kommt, nach seinem Haus zu wallen,   3085
Und rufet Heil dem Retter von uns allen!

(Alle gehen ab.)

Zweite Scene.

Tells Hausflur.

Ein Feuer brennt auf dem Herd.   Die offen stehende Thüre zeigt ins Freie.

Hedwig. Walther und Wilhelm.

Hedwig.

Heut' kommt der Vater.   Kinder, liebe Kinder!
Er lebt, ist frei, und wir sind frei und alles!
Und euer Vater ist's, der's Land gerettet.

Walther.

Und ich bin auch dabei gewesen, Mutter!   3090
Mich muß man auch mit nennen.   Vaters Pfeil
Ging mir am Leben hart vorbei, und ich
Hab' nicht gezittert.

Hedwig (umarmt ihn).

Ja, du bist mir wieder

Gegeben!   Zweimal hab' ich dich geboren!
Zweimal litt ich den Mutterschmerz um dich!   3095
Es ist vorbei — ich hab' euch beide, beide!
Und heute kommt der liebe Vater wieder!

(Ein Mönch erscheint an der Hausthüre.)

Wilhelm.

Sieh, Mutter, sieh — dort steht ein frommer Bruder;
Gewiß wird er um eine Gabe flehn.

Hedwig.

Führ' ihn herein, damit wir ihn erquicken ;   3100
Er fühl's, daß er ins Freudenhaus gekommen.

(Geht hinein und kommt bald mit einem Becher wieder.)

Wilhelm (zum Mönch).

Kommt, guter Mann! Die Mutter will euch laben.

Walther.

Kommt, ruht euch aus und geht gestärkt von dannen !

Mönch (scheu umherblickend mit zerstörten Zügen).

Wo bin ich? Saget an, in welchem Lande?

Walther.

Seid ihr verirret, daß ihr das nicht wißt?   3105
Ihr seid zu Bürglen, Herr, im Lande Uri,
Wo man hineingeht in das Schächenthal.

Mönch (zur Hedwig, welche zurückkommt).

Seid ihr allein? Ist euer Herr zu Hause?

Hedwig.

Ich erwart' ihn eben — doch was ist euch, Mann?
Ihr seht nicht aus, als ob ihr Gutes brächtet.   3110
— Wer ihr auch seid, ihr seid bedürftig, nehmt!

(Reicht ihm den Becher.)

Mönch.

Wie auch mein lechzend Herz nach Labung schmachtet,
Nichts rühr' ich an, bis ihr mir zugesagt —

Hedwig.

Berührt mein Kleid nicht, tretet mir nicht nah,
Bleibt ferne stehn, wenn ich euch hören soll !   3115

Mönch.

Bei diesem Feuer, das hier gastlich lodert,
Bei eurer Kinder teurem Haupt, das ich
Umfasse — (Ergreift die Knaben).

Hedwig.

Mann, was sinnet ihr?   Zurück
Von meinen Kindern! — Ihr seid kein Mönch! Ihr seid
Es nicht!   Der Friede wohnt in diesem Kleide;   3120
In euren Zügen wohnt der Friede nicht.

Mönch.

Ich bin der unglückseligste der Menschen.

Hedwig.

Das Unglück spricht gewaltig zu dem Herzen;
Doch euer Blick schnürt mir das Innre zu.

Walther (aufspringend).

Mutter, der Vater!   (Eilt hinaus.)

Hedwig.

O mein Gott!
(Will nach, zittert und hält sich an.)

Wilhelm (eilt nach).

Der Vater! 3125

Walther (draußen).

Da bist du wieder!

Wilhelm (draußen).

Vater, lieber Vater!

Tell (draußen).

Da bin ich wieder — Wo ist eure Mutter? (Treten herein.)

Walther.

Da steht sie an der Thür' und kann nicht weiter,
So zittert sie vor Schrecken und vor Freude.

Tell.

O Hedwig! Hedwig! Mutter meiner Kinder!   3130
Gott hat geholfen — uns trennt kein Tyrann mehr.

Hedwig (an seinem Halse).

O Tell! Tell! Welche Angst litt ich um dich!

(Mönch wird aufmerksam.)

Tell.

Vergiß sie jetzt und lebe nur der Freude!
Da bin ich wieder! Das ist meine Hütte!
Ich stehe wieder auf dem Meinigen!   3135

Wilhelm.

Wo aber hast du deine Armbrust, Vater?
Ich seh' sie nicht.

Tell.

Du wirst sie nie mehr sehn.
An heil'ger Stätte ist sie aufbewahrt;
Sie wird hinfort zu keiner Jagd mehr dienen.

Hedwig.

O Tell! Tell! (Tritt zurück, läßt seine Hand los.)

Tell.

Was erschreckt dich, liebes Weib?   3140

Hedwig.

Wie — wie kommst du mir wieder? — Diese Hand
— Darf ich sie fassen? — Diese Hand — o Gott!

Tell (herzlich und mutig).

Hat euch verteidigt und das Land gerettet;
Ich darf sie frei hinauf zum Himmel heben.

(Mönch macht eine rasche Bewegung, er erblickt ihn.)

Wer ist der Bruder hier?

Hedwig.

Ach, ich vergaß ihn!   3145
Sprich du mit ihm, mir graut in seiner Nähe.

Mönch (tritt näher).

Seid ihr der Tell, durch den der Landvogt fiel?

Tell.

Der bin ich, ich verberg' es keinem Menschen.

Mönch.

Ihr seid der Tell! Ach, es ist Gottes Hand,
Die unter euer Dach mich hat geführt.   3150

Tell (mißt ihn mit den Augen).

Ihr seid kein Mönch! Wer seid ihr?

Mönch.

                                    Ihr erschlugt
Den Landvogt, der euch Böses that — Auch ich
Hab' einen Feind erschlagen, der mir Recht
Versagte — Er war euer Feind, wie meiner —
Ich hab' das Land von ihm befreit.

Tell (zurückfahrend).

                                    Ihr seid —   3155
Entsetzen! — Kinder! Kinder, geht hinein!
Geh, liebes Weib! Geh, geh! — Unglücklicher!
Ihr wäret —

Hedwig.

Gott, wer ist es?

Tell.

                                    Frage nicht!
Fort, fort! Die Kinder dürfen es nicht hören.
Geh aus dem Hause — weit hinweg — du darfst   3160
Nicht unter einem Dach mit diesem wohnen.

Hedwig.

Weh mir, was ist das? Kommt! (Geht mit den Kindern).

Tell (zu dem Mönch).

Ihr seid der Herzog
Von Österreich — Ihr seid's! Ihr habt den Kaiser
Erschlagen, euern Ohm und Herrn.

Johannes Parricida.

Er war
Der Räuber meines Erbes.

Tell.

Euern Ohm   3165
Erschlagen, euern Kaiser! Und euch trägt
Die Erde noch! Euch leuchtet noch die Sonne!

Parricida.

Tell, hört mich, eh' ihr —

Tell.

Von dem Blute triefend
Des Vatermordes und des Kaisermords,
Wagst du zu treten in mein reines Haus?   3170
Du wagst's, dein Antlitz einem guten Menschen
Zu zeigen und das Gastrecht zu begehren?

Parricida.

Bei euch hofft' ich Barmherzigkeit zu finden;
Auch ihr nahmt Rach' an eurem Feind.

Tell.

Unglücklicher!
Darfst du der Ehrsucht blut'ge Schuld vermengen 3175
Mit der gerechten Notwehr eines Vaters?
Hast du der Kinder liebes Haupt verteidigt?
Des Herdes Heiligtum beschützt? das Schrecklichste,

Das Letzte von den Deinen abgewehrt?
— Zum Himmel heb' ich meine reinen Hände,   3180
Verfluche dich und deine That — Gerächt
Hab' ich die heilige Natur, die du
Geschändet — Nichts teil' ich mit dir — Gemordet
Hast du, ich hab' mein Teuerstes verteidigt.   X

Parricida.

Ihr stoßt mich von euch, trostlos, in Verzweiflung?   3185

Tell

Mich faßt ein Grausen, da ich mit dir rede.
Fort! Wandle deine fürchterliche Straße!
Laß rein die Hütte, wo die Unschuld wohnt!

Parricida (wendet sich zu gehen).

So kann ich, und so will ich nicht mehr leben!

Tell.

Und doch erbarmt mich deiner — Gott des Himmels!   3190
So jung, von solchem adeligen Stamm,
Der Enkel Rudolfs, meines Herrn und Kaisers,
Als Mörder flüchtig, hier an meiner Schwelle,
Des armen Mannes — flehend und verzweifelnd —
(Verhüllt sich das Gesicht.)

Parricida.

O, wenn ihr weinen könnt, laßt mein Geschick   3195
Euch jammern; es ist fürchterlich — Ich bin
Ein Fürst — ich war's — ich konnte glücklich werden,
Wenn ich der Wünsche Ungeduld bezwang
Der Neid zernagte mir das Herz — Ich sah
Die Jugend meines Vetters Leopold   3200
Gekrönt mit Ehre und mit Land belohnt,
Und mich, der gleiches Alters mit ihm war,
In sklavischer Unmündigkeit gehalten —

Tell.

Unglücklicher, wohl kannte dich dein Ohm,
Da er dir Land und Leute weigerte!   3205
Du selbst mit rascher, wilder Wahnsinnsthat
Rechtfertigst furchtbar seinen weisen Schluß.
— Wo sind die blut'gen Helfer deines Mords?

Parricida.

Wohin die Rachegeister sie geführt;
Ich sah sie seit der Unglücksthat nicht wieder.   3210

Tell.

Weißt du, daß dich die Acht verfolgt, daß du
Dem Freund verboten und dem Feind erlaubt?

Parricida.

Darum vermeid' ich alle offne Straßen;
An keine Hütte wag' ich anzupochen —
Der Wüste kehr' ich meine Schritte zu;   3215
Mein eignes Schrecknis irr' ich durch die Berge
Und fahre schaudernd vor mir selbst zurück,
Zeigt mir ein Bach mein unglückselig Bild.
O, wenn ihr Mitleid fühlt und Menschlichkeit —

(Fällt vor ihm nieder.)

Tell (abgewendet).

Steht auf! Steht auf!   3220

Parricida.

Nicht, bis ihr mir die Hand gereicht zur Hilfe.

Tell.

Kann ich euch helfen? Kann's ein Mensch der Sünde?
Doch stehet auf — Was ihr auch Gräßliches
Verübt — Ihr seid ein Mensch — ich bin es auch;
Vom Tell soll keiner ungetröstet scheiden —   3225
Was ich vermag, das will ich thun.

Parricida (auffspringend und seine Hand mit Heftigkeit ergreifend.)

　　　　　　　O Tell!
Ihr rettet meine Seele von Verzweiflung.

　　　　　　　Tell.

Laßt meine Hand los — Ihr müßt fort.　Hier könnt
Ihr unentdeckt nicht bleiben, könnt entdeckt
Auf Schutz nicht rechnen — Wo gedenkt ihr hin?　　3230
Wo hofft ihr Ruh' zu finden?

　　　　　　　Parricida.

　　　　　　　Weiß ich's?　Ach!

　　　　　　　Tell.

Hört, was mir Gott ins Herz giebt — Ihr müßt fort
Ins Land Italien, nach Sankt Peters Stadt!
Dort werft ihr euch dem Papst zu Füßen, beichtet
Ihm eure Schuld und löset eure Seele!　　　3235

　　　　　　　Parricida.

Wird er mich nicht dem Rächer überliefern?

　　　　　　　Tell.

Was er euch thut, das nehmet an von Gott!

　　　　　　　Parricida.

Wie komm' ich in das unbekannte Land?
Ich bin des Wegs nicht kundig, wage nicht
Zu Wanderern die Schritte zu gesellen.　　　3240

　　　　　　　Tell.

Den Weg will ich euch nennen, merket wohl!
Ihr steigt hinauf, dem Strom der Reuß entgegen,
Die wildes Laufes von dem Berge stürzt —

　　　　　　　Parricida (erschrickt).

Seh' ich die Reuß?　Sie floß bei meiner That.

Tell.

Am Abgrund geht der Weg, und viele Kreuze 3245
Bezeichnen ihn, errichtet zum Gedächtnis
Der Wanderer, die die Lawine begraben.

Parricida.

Ich fürchte nicht die Schrecken der Natur,
Wenn ich des Herzens wilde Qualen zähme.

Tell.

Vor jedem Kreuze fallet hin und büßet 3250
Mit heißen Reuethränen eure Schuld —
Und seid ihr glücklich durch die Schreckensstraße,
Sendet der Berg nicht seine Windeswehen
Auf euch herab von dem beeisten Joch,
So kommt ihr auf die Brücke, welche stäubet. 3255
Wenn sie nicht einbricht unter eurer Schuld,
Wenn ihr sie glücklich hinter euch gelassen,
So reißt ein schwarzes Felsenthor sich auf —
Kein Tag hat's noch erhellt — da geht ihr durch,
Es führt euch in ein heitres Thal der Freude — 3260
Doch schnellen Schritts müßt ihr vorüber eilen;
Ihr dürft nicht weilen, wo die Ruhe wohnt.

Parricida.

O Rudolf! Rudolf! Königlicher Ahn!
So zieht dein Enkel ein auf deines Reiches Boden!

Tell.

So immer steigend, kommt ihr auf die Höhen 3265
Des Gotthards, wo die ew'gen Seen sind,
Die von des Himmels Strömen selbst sich füllen.
Dort nehmt ihr Abschied von der deutschen Erde,
Und muntern Laufs führt euch ein andrer Strom

Ins Land Italien hinab, euch das gelobte —   3270

(Man hört den Kuhreihen von vielen Alphörnern geblasen.)

Ich höre Stimmen.   Fort!

Hedwig (eilt herein).

Wo bist du, Tell?

Der Vater kommt!   Es nahn in frohem Zug
Die Eidgenossen alle —

Parricida (verhüllt sich).

Wehe mir!

Ich darf nicht weilen bei den Glücklichen.

Tell.

Geh, liebes Weib!   Erfrische diesen Mann,   3275
Belad' ihn reich mit Gaben, denn sein Weg
Ist weit, und keine Herberg' findet er.
Eile!   Sie nahn.

Hedwig.

Wer ist es?

Tell.

Forsche nicht!

Und wenn er geht, so wende deine Augen,
Daß sie nicht sehen, welchen Weg er wandelt!   3280

(Parricida geht auf den Tell zu mit einer raschen Bewegung; dieser
aber bedeutet ihn mit der Hand und geht.   Wenn beide zu verschiedenen
Seiten abgegangen, verändert sich der Schauplatz, und man sieht in der

Letzten Scene.

den ganzen Thalgrund vor Tells Wohnung, nebst den Anhöhen, welche
ihn einschließen, mit Landleuten besetzt, welche sich zu einem malerischen
Ganzen gruppieren.   Andere kommen über einen hohen Steg, der über den
Schächen führt, gezogen.   Walther Fürst mit den beiden Knaben,
Melchthal und Stauffacher kommen vorwärts, andere drängen
nach; wie Tell heraustritt, empfangen ihn alle mit lautem Frohloden.)

THE SCHILLER STONE (DER MYTHENSTEIN)
ON LAKE LUCERNE.
(*To face p.* 162.)

Alle.

Es lebe Tell, der Schütz und der Erretter!

(Indem sich die vordersten um den Tell drängen und ihn umarmen, erscheinen noch Rudenz und Bertha, jener die Landleute, diese die Hedwig umarmend. Die Musik vom Berge begleitet diese stumme Scene. Wenn sie geendigt, tritt Bertha in die Mitte des Volks.)

Bertha.

Landleute! Eidgenossen! Nehmt mich auf
In euern Bund, die erste Glückliche,
Die Schutz gefunden in der Freiheit Land.
In eure tapfre Hand leg' ich mein Recht;   3285
Wollt ihr als eure Bürgerin mich schützen?

Landleute.

Das wollen wir mit Gut und Blut.

Bertha.

Wohlan!
So reich' ich diesem Jüngling meine Rechte,
Die freie Schweizerin dem freien Mann!

Rudenz.

Und frei erklär' ich alle meine Knechte.   3290

(Indem die Musik von neuem rasch einfällt, fällt der Vorhang.)

NOTES.

DRAMATIS PERSONÆ.

HERMANN GESSLER, imperial governor (or prefect or bailiff) of the Cantons of Schwyz and Uri. Tradition makes him a member of the noble family of the Gesslers von Bruneck (or Brunegg), a castle of which the ruins may still be seen in Aargau, south of Brugg, between Lenzburg and Mellingen. The historical facts are that this castle did not come into the possession of the Gessler family before the end of the fourteenth century, and that no Gessler was ever Reichsvogt in Uri.

The word Vogt (Reichsvogt and Landvogt being used in the same sense) was borrowed from the mediæval Latin *vocatus* in the sense of *advocatus* or "advocate." In the middle ages a rich variety of special applications developed from this general notion of advocate, protector, guardian, defender, representative. In this play both the simple and the compound forms of the word are used of the representatives of the authority and the interests of the Empire or the Emperor.

The Gessler of the drama is the typical harsh tyrant, cruel, cunning, inflexible, ready to sacrifice any or all who are under his authority, in order to aggrandize his Emperor and himself.

BARON WERNER VON ATTINGHAUSEN, *Banneret* (cf. n. l. 336), is an historical personage from an ancient noble family. He was Landammann or chief-magistrate of Uri from 1294 to 1317. Schiller makes him much older than he really was, and deviates also from historical fact in making him the last of his family and in placing his death before the accomplishment of Swiss liberty. He is the representa-

165

tive, more narrowly, of the patriarchal nobility whose epoch is now passing away, and, more broadly, of the part taken by the nobles in freeing the land.

ULRICH VON RUDENZ, a fictitious character. Tschudi mentions a von Rudenz as a nephew of Stauffacher, and the castle of this name belonged to the Attinghausen family. We should expect the name Rudenz to be accented on the second syllable, but in the play the verse-stress falls on the first syllable more often. Ulrich is the bold young noble, misled at first by his ambition, but regained through love of Bertha to the cause of his country. Together with his uncle he typifies the attitude of the nobility, without whom the overthrow of the hated foreign rule is not accomplished.

WERNER STAUFFACHER, an historical character in so far as there was a Landammann, of this name, descendant of an ancient family, in the years 1313 and 1314, who lived as late as the year 1341. A chapel at Steinen, built in 1400, is said to be on the site of his house. The Stauffacher of the drama is a man in the full maturity of his powers. Rich and childless, cautious, deliberate, a man of counsel, knowing all the history of his country, an able speaker, he is the predestined founder and soul of the confederation. He represents the Canton Schwyz.

CONRAD HUNN, an historical character, sometime Landammann, mentioned officially as early as 1251.

ITEL REDING. This family was long famous in Swiss history; a Rudolf Reding planned the successful movements of the battle of Morgarten in 1315; Itel Reding was a worthy Landammann of the early portion of the fifteenth century. Cf. n. l. 1086.

HANS AUF DER MAUER.

JÖRG (George) IM HOFE.

ULRICH DER SCHMID (Smith).

JÖST (Jöbst, contracted from Jodöcus) VON WEILER. The last four names are taken with unessential modifications from a document of the year 1282, relating to Conrad Hunn.

WALTHER FÜRST, the traditional father-in-law of Tell, is an historical character, in so far as Tschudi mentions him as a well-known, wise, and honorable man of means, living at Attinghausen. In the drama he represents the Canton Uri, and respected, cautious, conservative old age.

WILHELM TELL. (See Introduction, pp. lix–lxiii and Notes *passim*.

RÖSSELMANN, *the Priest*.

PETERMANN, *the Sacristan*. The last two names are genuine Swiss names, but not here derived from definite historical characters. Among those who fell at Sempach a Petermann is mentioned ; it is also possible that Schiller used the name of Petermann Etterlin (see Introd. p. lviii), just as that of Am Bühl below and of Johannes von Müller in l. 2948. These characters are typical of influential classes.

KUONI (pronounce KŪ'(ŏ)ni), *the Herdsman*. Kuoni is the familiar abbreviation of Konrad.

WERNI, *the Huntsman*. Werni, from Werner.

RUODI (-Ū'(ŏ)- as in Kuoni), *the Fisherman*. Ruodi, from Ruodolf = Rudolf. The typical nature of these three characters is self-evident.

ARNOLD VOM MELCHTHAL, an historical character. Tschudi names him Arnold von Melchthal, Müller names him Erni (= Arnold) an der Halden, from the Melchthal. This family name is given to his father in l. 562. The family flourished until modern times. Melchthal, as he is called in the drama, represents the Canton Unterwalden, and bold, impetuous youth.

CONRAD BAUMGART(EN), historical on the authority of Tschudi, living at Alzellen.

MEIER VON SARNEN (cf. n. l. 1072), a name taken from Tschudi.

STRUTH (or Struthan) VON WINKELRIED. Tschudi states that a Winkelried was present at the Rütli. Schiller took the name of the traditional hero described in the note to l. 1075. Arnold von Winkelried was the hero of the battle of Sempach in 1336.

KLAUS VON DER FLÜE (= precipice), famous as a hermit

and political peacemaker in the second half of the fifteenth century.

BURKHART AM BÜHEL (= hill). In the document of 1282 relating to Conrad Hunn, Schiller found the names Ulrich am Berge and Burkhart von Ybach ; of these he made Burkhart am Bühl, commemorating also Joh. Ludwig am Bühl, author of a drama *Wilhelm Tell* (1792). (See Introd. p. lxiii.)

ARNOLD VON SEWA, a name derived from the document just mentioned. The real Sewa was in Schwyz, not in Unterwalden.

PFEIFER OF LUCERNE, unhistorical. The name is that of an old and notable family of Lucerne, of which a contemporary of Schiller was a distinguished representative.

KUNZ OF GERSAU, a fictitious character. Kunz is a familiar shortening of Konrad. Gersau is a hamlet on the lake S.E. of the Rigi.

JENNI, *Fisherman's Boy*. The name, pronounced "Yenni," is abbreviated from Johann.

SEPPI, *Herdsman's Boy*. The name from Joseph.

GERTRUD, *Stauffacher's Wife*. The wife of Stauffacher was by late tradition named Margaretha Herlö'big. Schiller makes her (l. 240) to be the daughter of Konrad ab Iberg, Landammann of Schwyz in 1311.

HEDWIG, *Tell's Wife*. The historians make Tell a son-in-law of Walther Fürst. For the names Gertrud, Hedwig, and (below) Mechthild, see Introd. p. lxiv.

BERTHA VON BRUNECK, a fictitious character, the name from the castle mentioned above.

ARMGARD, MECHTHILD, ELSBETH, HILDEGARD, are arbitrarily chosen names. Mechthild = Mathilde, Elsbeth = Elisabeth.

WALTHER and WILHELM. These names are given by Müller to Tell's sons on the authority of the old chronicler Klingenberg, in the order Wilhelm and Walther. Schiller makes the older bear his grandfather's name.

FRIESSHARDT and LEUTHOLD are of course fictitious. The names Friesshardt and the following Rudolf der Harras are derived from Müller's account of the battle of Sempach. Friesshardt means "fearful and bold"; Leuthold seems to mean "kind to people," but originally it meant "ruling the people."

RUDOLF DER HARRAS, *Gessler's Master of the Horse*, in this connection fictitious. "Harras" is generally taken to mean Master of the Horse, and to be derived from the mediæval Latin *haracium*, "stud of horses."

JOHANN THE PARRICIDE, *Duke of Swabia.* See Introd. p. lii.

STUSSI, *the Ranger*, fictitious. The name, found in Müller, is the familiar abbreviation of Justus.

THE BULL (= *Hornblower*) *of Uri*. See note to l. 1091.

OVERSEER (or *Taskmaster*).

BROTHERS OF MERCY. See n. *139 on p. 266.

HORSEMEN (or *Troopers*) *of Gessler and of Landenberg*. See n. l. 72.

ACT I.

ARGUMENT.—The *first* scene is opened on the shore of the lake with three songs by a fisher-boy, a herdsman, and a hunter. An approaching storm gathers them in conversation with the fisherman at the latter's hut. Baumgarten, pursued by horsemen of the governor of Unterwalden, enters breathless, and begs to be ferried over. He has killed the bailiff Wolfenschiessen for having attempted to dishonor his wife. While all are refusing in fear to help Baumgarten, Tell appears and bravely delivers Baumgarten from pursuit by rowing him across. The baffled horsemen destroy the herds and the hut of the herdsman and fisherman.

In the *second* scene we are before the handsome house of Stauffacher, a well-to-do yeoman of Steinen in Schwyz. Gertrud, his wife, shares his anxious fears for himself and their country, and inspires him to initiate a common movement against Austrian oppression. As Stauffacher is about to set out for Uri, there to confer with like-minded friends,

Tell brings the rescued Baumgarten to him for secret shelter.

The *third* scene presents at Altorf in Uri the erection, under orders of the cruel governor Gessler, of a stronghold and prison. While Tell and Stauffacher are discussing it, a public crier proclaims the governor's outrageous edict that a pole is to be set up and on top of this a hat placed, to which the people shall do obeisance. Stauffacher vainly endeavors to persuade Tell actively to join with him in planning for a common uprising. Just as they leave, a roofer is killed by a fall. The noblewoman Bertha von Bruneck, who sympathizes with the Swiss, utters against the building the righteous malediction, that voices the feeling of all.

The *fourth* scene shows the youth Arnold vom Melchthal, a refugee from the wanton oppression of the governor of Unterwalden, in the house of the aged Walther Fürst in Altorf. As they are conversing on the wrongs Melchthal has suffered and those he fears may be inflicted on his father, Stauffacher comes and the young man conceals himself. Stauffacher, ignorant of the presence of Melchthal in Altorf, recites to Fürst the vengeance which the governor has wreaked, by blinding Melchthal's father and robbing him of everything. Young Arnold, hearing this from the adjoining room, rushes in, unable to contain himself, and with impassioned eloquence utters his despair and grief and vehement vows of vengeance. These three men, conscious that the crisis is at hand, form an alliance, offensive and defensive, in representation of their three cantons. They agree, each bringing ten trusty men of his own canton, to met at the Rütli, there to conclude a more formal union.

SCENE I.

* **Aufzug**, 'act,' from **aufziehen**, first used only of the 'raising' of the curtain. The synonym **Akt** is also much used, derived not from the French *acte*, but from the Latin *actus*.

* **Scene**, from French *scène*, is used throughout this drama and in „Die Räuber." In all his other plays Schiller uses the word Auftritt. As in English usage a new Scene implies a change of place and stage-setting, while there is a new Auf=tritt whenever a character, excepting insignificant messengers and the like, makes an entry or an exit.

The four scenes of Act I are on October 28, 1307; the first scene is late in the forenoon at a place on the western shore of the Lake of Lucerne near Treib in the Canton Uri. The German name of this lake,

* **Bierwaldstättersee,** 'Lake of the Four Forest Cantons,' is made up of the noun See and an indeclinable adj. of place in =er (Wh. 415, 5), formed from the numeral vier and Walb=stätte, the archaic plural of Walbstat[t], lit. 'wood-stead.' The Swiss Cantons were first called Stätte and then Orte until the gradual introduction after the middle of the sixteenth century of the word Kanton from the French. The four Cantons that gave the name to the lake were Uri, Schwyz, Unterwalden, and Luzern, the first three being the original Walb=stätte. This lake was the natural means of communication of the inhabitants of these districts, and at this place we are in Uri, not far from the boundary of Unterwalden, while to the east, just across the lake, about half a mile distant, lies the Canton

* **Schwyz,** to be pronounced as if spelled Schwiez.

* **unweit** is now regularly construed with the gen. or von.

* **Matten,** in general, mountain 'meadow, mead,' to which it is an etymological parallel; a specifically Alemannic word, but since the middle of the eighteenth century of wide use in poetic diction. Die Weide is any piece of land where cattle can eat standing grass, whether cultivated or wild; die Wiese is always a field of cultivated grass and especially one lying low and well-watered; die Matte may be an uncultivated surface, but strictly should be one on which the grass can be mowed with the scythe; der Anger is an untilled piece of land covered with grass, mostly lying high and dry, while die Trift is properly a fallow field used temporarily for pasturage, although the word is employed also of any pasturage, especially by poets.

* **liegen,** inf. obj. of **ſieht.** A number of verbs govern an infinitive in the manner of a second object, along with their ordinary object; these are **heißen, nennen, lehren, helfen, machen, laſſen,** and, denoting perception by the senses, **ſehen, hören, fühlen, finden.**

* **die Spitzen des Haken** (**Hacken** or **Haggen**), 'Hook.' The poet conceives the two **Mythen** to be parts of the **Hafen,** as a group of mountains, in the Canton Schwyz, northeast of the town of the same name. Now the name **Hafen** is no longer used as a collective designation, and a distinction is made between the three peaks, **der Hafen, die große Mythe** and **die kleine Mythe.**

* **Eisgebirge,** in the Canton Glarus, which with poetic license are assumed to be visible.

* **Kuhreihen** (the common Swiss form is **Kühreihen,** also **Kühreigen**), lit. 'cow-dance,' 'cow-line,' or 'cow-song,' but best rendered by transferring the word, *Kuhreihen.* It is not properly a song, but a modulated succession of simple tones without words, formed in the throat, but sometimes blown through the long alp-horn (cf. the stage-direction following line 3270). Its real purpose is to call together the cows at milking-time, when they may be widely scattered over the mountains, but it is also sounded to the driving-out of the herd at other times. **Reihen** is here the old German designation for a dance in line or rank, which general meaning also appears in the French equivalent term, *ranz* (= **Rang**) *des vaches.* Some prefer to derive it from a Swiss verb **reihen** = **holen, heimholen,** but this seems to be a secondary development from the former meaning. While the *Kuhreihen* is in some sense uniform in its general type, it has countless variations. It is said to be heard in greatest purity and originality in the Canton Appenzell.

1. **Es,** very often the neuter nominative **es,** as the indefinite grammatical subject, serves the purpose of a mere device for shifting the true subject to a position after the verb, and is itself untranslatable.—Note the personification of the lake.

ladet, in modern prose the compound **ladet — ein,** is more usual, while the older language preferred the simple verb.

It is also to be noted that in poetry the simple forms are often preferred to the compound forms of prose.

4. **Flöten,** plural of **Flöte,** not infin. used as substantive.

8. **die Wasser,** poetic plural, as in ll. 35 and 117.

9. **es ruft,** 'there's a call': es is the subject, indefinite and impersonal, and so suggesting mystery. Cf. lines 40, 116, 2835-6, and mark the difference between this use of es and that in l. 1.

10. **Lieb,** in old German, in poetry and to some extent colloquially, the adj. ending is sometimes omitted in the masc. and fem., as well as frequently in the neut. nom. and acc. There are in this play many instances of the omitted neut. ending.

(du) bist, note the colloquial omission of the subject pronoun, which is common in the songs and familiar speech of the people, and often used by Schiller to produce that effect.

m e i n, the use of spaced or separated type, as in this word, is for emphasis like that of *italics* in English.

11-12. This song was suggested to Schiller by the legend narrated by Scheuchzer, that Lake Calandari (known now as **der Schwellisee),** in the district of Schams near Chur, possessed the power of drawing into its depths people who fell asleep near it. The sweet strong attraction that beautiful water has for all men has, however, from the earliest times been a favorite subject of legend and poetry; cf. the ancient story of the Argonaut Hylas and the modern ballad **Der Fischer** by Goethe.

15. **Der Senne,** the 'cow-keeper' or 'herdsman' of an Alpine dairy; he drives the cows to the **Alp(e),** fem., i.e. mountain pasture which is not mowed, and tends them there. The cows begin to be driven up to the **Alpen** at the end of May or early in June, but the highest pastures are not reached until in July; the return in reverse order is earlier or later, according to the weather. For a large herd and pasture there may be the following **Alpknechte** or **Älpler;** a **Senn(e),** a **Zusenn(e),** i.e. assistant to the **Senn(e),** a **Hirt(e)** or **Küher,** and a **Handbub,** i.e. a 'boy' usually of twelve or four-

teen years ; when there are so many, the Senn(e) is the re-
sponsible head of all, including the dairy-production, while
the Hirt(e) has charge only of the cows.

17. zu Berg (or, more strictly, zu Alp) fahren is the technical
expression for the ascent with cows to the high pastures.
The present, used for the future, has reference to the following spring, and

wir kommen wieder is an explanatory repetition of the first
half of the line.

fahren, here in its old meaning of 'go' = ziehen, wandern, as
also in l. 348.

20. Springs that flow in May because of the melting snow,
but are dry in autumn.

25. Es, cf. note to 1.

donnern, i.e. with the fall of avalanches and the bursting
of glaciers ; cf. l. 38 and ll. 1780–1.

Steg, here probably ' path,' but different in l. 1269.

26. The verb is impersonal, with omission of the grammatical subject es and with the logical subject in the dat.

schwindlichtem and (l. 31) neblichtes, the adj. termination
-icht is now generally replaced by -ig.

30. Reis, neut.; distinguish this from der Reis.

31. Meer, accus. used absolutely, as if governed by *with*
or *having* understood.

35. Wassern, the same as Meer of l. 31 and Wolken of l. 33,
and not the torrents and waterfalls on the mountain-sides,
as many commentators interpret.

* verändert sich, said only of the aspect of the landscape.

* dumpfes Krachen, cf. ll. 25 and 38.

The opening of this scene is a dramatic overture of
striking beauty. The romantic scenery transports us at
once into the world of this drama. The idyllic songs
portray the peaceful, joyous existence of an innocent,
harmless people. Short as are these songs of (as yet
unnamed) representatives of the three leading occupa-
tions of the Swiss, they make us know that this people
is bound by strong and intimate ties to its land, is self-
reliant, courageous, tried and proved in danger.

Upon this brightness and happiness there now begins
to gather the darkness of a violent storm. Thus the
note of conflict is struck. These men have no unreasonable fear of the natural storm. How will this
people bear itself under the moral storm-clouds of
oppression? †

* 𝔐𝔢𝔩𝔨𝔫𝔞𝔭𝔣, ' milk-pail.'

* 𝔥𝔞𝔫𝔡𝔟𝔲𝔟𝔢, ' boy ' in the sense of 'assistant'; cf. English
' handmaid.'

37. 𝔐𝔞𝔠𝔥' 𝔥𝔲𝔯𝔱𝔦𝔤 (adv.), ' Be quick,' ' Make haste.'

𝔑𝔞𝔲𝔢, ordinarily a freight boat from 40 to 60 feet long,
but here, borrowed from Etterlin, in the sense of 𝔉𝔦𝔰𝔠𝔥𝔢𝔯𝔟𝔬𝔬𝔱,
𝔎𝔞𝔥𝔫 ; a loan-word, Latin *navis*, early imported into Switzerland and Southern Germany.

38. 𝔇𝔢𝔯 𝔤𝔯𝔞𝔲𝔢 𝔗𝔥𝔞𝔩𝔳𝔬𝔤𝔱, lit. ' the gray dale-governor ' or
' the gray lord of the valley'; personification as a storm-
spirit (cf. l. 425) of the wind driving dark clouds before it.
The expression is from Scheuchzer, who reports it of the
people of Engelberg. **Cf.** Introd. n. pp. xxxi, xxxii.

𝔉𝔦𝔯𝔫, ' glacier,' primarily the old snow of the high Alps
that remains unmelted from year to year and gradually
becomes solid ice ; then also glacier or, as in l. 1778, a
mountain-top covered with such snow and ice.

39. 𝔇𝔢𝔯 𝔐𝔶𝔱𝔥𝔢𝔫𝔰𝔱𝔢𝔦𝔫, really a rock in the Lake of Lucerne,
rising only about eighty feet above its surface (cf. n. l.
725). Either Schiller uses it here of one or both of the
peaks which he regarded as constituting the Haken (see p.
3 and note), or he misapprehended the size or location of
the Mythenstein proper. The line refers to the gathering
of a cloud-cap about a mountain-peak as a sign of storm.

40. 𝔚𝔢𝔱𝔱𝔢𝔯𝔩𝔬𝔠𝔥, ' weather-hole,' a designation not infrequently used in mountainous districts of deep, narrow
caves and crevices, with or without an upper outlet, from
which in summer a cold wind proceeds, while in winter the
temperature is higher within than without and the draft is

---

† For the running notes on the plot and characters the editor has drawn
freely on the commentary of H. Gaudig in ' Aus deutschen Lesebüchern,'
cf. Preface, p. iii.

reversed. According to Schiller's authority Scheuchzer the line should read Unb lau her etc., for he says: „auß ben Wetterlöchern, b. h. Höhlen ober Bergspalten, bläst es kalt wenn baß Wetter bauernb schön bleibt, lau unb bünstig bei eintretenbem Sturm unb Regen."

42. 'ß for eß on account of the meter, in order to make 'ß kommt but one syllable; cf. l. 51.

Meine Schafe . . . Graß, implies that, after having been grazing all the morning, the sheep are feeding as if they had had nothing.

43. Wächter, lit. 'watcher,' is the speaker's dog = English 'Watch.' Kuoni's weather-signs are those natural to the herdsman.

44, 45. Werner's signs are those of the hunter.

46. lugen (with long u, or in Swiss pronunciation ue) = sehen, essentially a South German and Swiss word; an etymological parallel to English 'look.'

verlaufen is past part. with the auxiliary hat omitted, as is so frequently done.

47. Lisel, with long i, is a popular diminutive of Elisabeth. Each cow has her own name. These names are sometimes women's names, but usually are taken from physical characteristics: Scheck 'dappled,' Muša (mouse-colored), Stoß (with horns bent sharply upward).

am Geläut, by the tinkling of her bell.

49. Geläute, here 'set of bells.' Every Senne has a Geläute, which consists of three or at least two bells, harmonizing with one another and with the sounds of the Kuhreihen.

Meister, honorary title of the upper herdsman.

50. Landsmann, to be distinguished from Landmann.

51. Bin, see note on bist, l. 10.

nit, popular and dialectic for nicht, in Central and especially in Southern Germany and Switzerland.

52. Des Attinghäusers = bes Freiherrn von Attinghausen, cf. p. 166. Attinghäuser is the adj. formed from Attinghaus or Attinghausen, cf. ll. 128, 282, 717, 2880.

This mention of Baron Attinghausen is preparatory to the full exposition of the Nobles-plot, which is de-

layed by reason of the great length of Act I until Scene
I of Act II.

jugejäblt, ' told off to' ; it is implied that different herds,
each of definite number, were rented by the baron to different shepherds.

53. **der Ruh** (dat.). . . . **ju Halfe fteht.** ftehen, in the meaning ' become,' ' suit' governs the dat., commonly taking an
adverb, **gut, fchlecht, fchön,** etc., and often also an adverbial
phrase, **ju** with the dat., indicating the part of the face or
body especially affected.

54. **Reihen,** ' line,' cf. note on **Ruhreihen,** p. 172.

55. This and what is told of the chamois just below is
based on facts of common experience, according to Schiller's
authorities.

56. **Ihr feid nicht flug!** ' you are crazy,' but not too seriously said.

57. **(Das) ift bald** (= leicht) **gefagt** ; in effect, it's easy to say
that, if you have no regard for the facts of the case ; cf. l.
1381.

59. **Die,** in place of the personal pronoun of the third
person used emphatically.

60 **'ne,** for **eine,** colloquial ; cf. ll. 375, 403, 1876.

Vorhut, ' sentinel,' usually ' vanguard.'

61. **Mit heller Pfeife,** in effect, ' with sharp hissing' ; **Pfeife**
for **pfeifenähnlicher Ton,** which is said to be „**ein heiferer, fchneidender,
etwas gezogener Ton, der wahrfcheinlich aus den Vorderzähnen geht.**"

62. **Alp,** see note on **Der Senne,** l. 15.

abgeweidet, ' grazed bare.'

63. **Glückfel'ge,** in the older language synonymous with
glücklich, as here, but now distinguished from it in prose.

64. **fehrt fich's . . . wieder,** ' one returns' or ' there is a
return.' An intransitive reflexive (or an intransitive passive), used impersonally to express the action without
reference to some particular subject, is a rather frequent
idiom in German.

65. **gelaufen,** past part. used in the sense of a pres. part.
after a verb of motion, to express the mode of motion.

66. **der Baumgart,** colloquially shortened form of the name

𝕭aumgarten, l. 549; cf. 𝕭olfenſ𝔥ieſſen, l. 78, with the form in l. 129. Note the familiar use of the def. art. with the proper name.

𝖀lzellen, a village in Unterwalden, four hours distant from the lake, near to Wolfenschiessen; see map.

> The clouds, the thunders, and the lurid lightnings of oppression are indeed near.

68. was (acc.) giebt's (baß) ſo eilig (iſt)? 'why this haste?'

70. was (acc.) 𝔥abt i𝔥r? what is the matter with you?

benn, not to be translated, but in effect, 'I should like to know.'

72. 𝕷anbvogt, 'governor' or 'prefect,' the title of the chief ruler of a district, canton, or country, appointed by the Emperor and representing him; in this case it was Beringer von Landenberg, governor of Unterwalden. There are several occurrences of the word 𝖁ogt in compounds in this play: 𝕽eic𝔥svogt, cf. n. p. 165; 𝕭urgvogt, l. 77; 𝕿𝔥alvogt, l. 38.

73. ein 𝕸ann beß 𝕿obß, i.e. 'a dead man.' In this phrase 𝕸ann has the old sense of 'vassal,' 'bondsman,' and death is personified as a conqueror or lord, cf. l. 2791. Frequently the word 𝕸ann is omitted from this phrase.

74. bie 𝕽eiſigen, 'horsemen,' 'troopers'; this word is now used only in poetry and elevated diction.

75. ſte𝔥' i𝔥 eu𝔥 (dat.) 𝕽ebe, 'I will give you an account of myself.' In this phrase, jemanbem (zur) 𝕽ebe ſte𝔥en, the word 𝕽ebe has quite distinctly its original meaning of a reckoning or accounting, primarily in regard to money, but then also in regard to other responsibilities.

> At this point we must understand that Ruodi goes aside to his boat, to make it ready and to untie it; he returns just before l. 103.

77. 𝕭urgvogt, ordinarily 'castellan,' but here rather 'governor' or 'burggrave.'

𝕽o𝔰berg (or 𝕽o𝔰berg), a castle in Unterwalden, three miles west of Stanz, on that part of the lake of Lucerne which is called Lake Alpnach. The 𝕷anbvogt, Landenberg, had given over the stronghold, of which ruins are still to be seen, to

Wolfenschiessen, a man of an important noble family in
Unterwalden, who had adopted the cause of Austria.

faß, 'had his seat,' 'lived'; ſißen in this sense is archaic
and poetic.

78. euch, obj. of verfolgen, or to be translated as the subject
of it, taken passively.

79. The first individual act of redress has been performed
by Baumgarten.

81. Complete the line with gethan hätte, or with thun würbe.

82. Hausrecht, 'household right.' Both the Roman and
the ancient German law gave to the injured husband the
right to kill the violator or paramour of his wife.

85. bös, see note to Lieb, l. 10.

89. er = Ruodi.

91. Angſt des Todes, for prose Todesangſt.

92. The effect of Baumgarten's agitation is enhanced by
the omission of the words ſie rief or ſie ſagte, to introduce his
wife's report, and in this the subjunctives of indirect statement, lieg', hab', hab', ſei.

93. rüften, archaic, now poetic.

94. "Then he made improper proposals to her."

96. friſch hinzu, "quickly thither," i.e. to my house; for
this use of friſch, cf. ll. 103, 176, 364, 765.

97. hab' ich ihm's (= das) Bad geſegnet, lit., 'I blessed his
bath for him,' an ironical phrase, derived from the mediæval
custom that the servant wished the bather well. Both the
simple ſegnen and the compound geſegnen are used in this
phrase.

100. Hat's = er hat es.

um, 'from.'

This line gives the political disposition of the people
of Unterwalden.

101. ruchtbar, the current present form is ruchbar.

mir wird nachgeſeßt, impersonal passive; only in this way
can a passive be formed of verbs that govern the dative
alone; rendered by personal passive in English.

102. With or immediately after this line Ruodi returns
from his boat, having decided not to attempt to use it.

103. **hinüberſchaffen** (weak) = überſetzen, 1. 69.

104. **(Es) geht nicht,** 'it can't be done'; cf. English, 'it's no go.'

107. **Dem Nächſten,** 'neighbor' in the biblical sense.

109. **Der Föhn iſt los,** 'the Föhn has broken loose.' Föhn, probably from Latin Favonius as a loan-word, is the southeast to south wind, warm and dry, which blows in Central Switzerland from time to time, most frequently in spring and autumn, lasting sometimes only a few hours and again a week or longer. The older view that this wind originated in Africa, as the sirocco, is now rejected by the best authorities, who refer it to general meteorological conditions, affecting the Atlantic Ocean and the northern part of Europe as well. This wind is to Switzerland a source of important benefits as well as of dangers; it makes plants wither, animals fret and chafe, men inactive, and may be very destructive on both land and water, but it melts away the snow, hastening spring, and later dries the hay and ripens the grapes.

111. **mein,** poetic for meiner, gen. of ich.

112. **Es geht ums Leben,** 'it's a matter of life (and death),' or 'his life is at stake'; in usual prose, **Es gilt das Leben.**

114. Cf. ll. 1528-9.

115. **Kind** in this phrase is the old plural.

121. **Rettungsufer,** cf. note on **Meer,** l. 31. It was but little over half a mile distant.

124. **hinübertrüge,** pret. subjunctive, potential.

125. **(ich) muß.**

126. **der Tell,** cf. note on **der,** l. 66.

Bürglen, a village at the entrance of the valley of the Schächen, half an hour's distance above Altorf in Uri.

127. Characteristically Tell's first utterance is of help.

128. **Alzeller,** cf. note on l. 52.

129. Cf. note on l. 72.

130. **Königs,** cf. Introduction, n. pp. xxxv, xxxvi.

133. **fürcht't,** such elision is characteristic of old German and of present Alemannic dialects; cf. ll. 175, 1389.

136. **zeugen,** for prose, **bezeugen.**

𝔷𝔲 𝔴𝔞𝔤𝔢𝔫 (𝔦𝔰𝔱). In German the active infin. with 𝔷𝔲 is often used in dependence on a form of 𝔰𝔢𝔦𝔫, with the logical value of a passive infin.

136. 𝔩ä𝔰𝔱 𝔰𝔦𝔠𝔥 𝔞𝔩𝔩𝔢𝔰 𝔴𝔞𝔤𝔢𝔫, 'everything can be ventured.'

137. 𝔥ö𝔩𝔩𝔢𝔫𝔯𝔞𝔠𝔥𝔢𝔫, 'jaws of death' (*lit.*, hell).

139. 𝔟𝔯𝔞𝔳𝔢, not merely in a narrow sense 'brave,' but as always in the broader sense of 'good,' 'worthy.'

141. 𝔓𝔬𝔯𝔱, only poetic, prose 𝔥𝔞𝔣𝔢𝔫.

𝔩ä𝔰𝔱 𝔰𝔦𝔠𝔥'𝔰 𝔤𝔢𝔪ä𝔠𝔥𝔩𝔦𝔠𝔥 𝔯𝔞𝔱𝔢𝔫, 'advice can (very) comfortably (*or* easily) be given.'

143. In translation take 𝔢𝔯𝔟𝔞𝔯𝔪𝔢𝔫 after 𝔰𝔦𝔠𝔥.

* 𝔥𝔦𝔯𝔱𝔢𝔫 = Kuoni and Seppi.

145. 𝔲𝔫𝔡 (𝔴ä𝔯'𝔰) 𝔪𝔢𝔦𝔫 𝔩𝔢𝔦𝔟𝔩𝔦𝔠𝔥 (= 𝔢𝔦𝔤𝔢𝔫𝔢𝔰) 𝔎𝔦𝔫𝔡.

146. After 𝔍𝔲𝔡ä (Latin genitive of 𝔍𝔲𝔡𝔞𝔰) understand 𝔗𝔞𝔤. October 28th is St. Simon's and St. Jude's day. Ruodi finds a pretext in the superstition that the lake demanded on this day the sacrifice of a human life. This belief is often held concerning lakes and rivers and midsummer-day. This line gives us definitely the date of the opening of the drama.

148. 𝔪𝔦𝔱 𝔢𝔦𝔱𝔩𝔢𝔯 𝔯𝔢𝔡𝔢 = 𝔪𝔦𝔱 𝔟𝔩𝔬ß𝔢𝔯 𝔯𝔢𝔡𝔢 𝔬𝔥𝔫𝔢 𝔗𝔥𝔞𝔱, 'with idle words,' cf. l. 2511.

149. 𝔴𝔢𝔯𝔡𝔢𝔫, poetic for prose 𝔷𝔲 𝔗𝔢𝔦𝔩 𝔴𝔢𝔯𝔡𝔢𝔫. Cf. l. 645.

155. 𝔴𝔬𝔥𝔩, 'indeed,' as also in l. 163.

156. 𝔢𝔦𝔫 𝔞𝔫𝔡𝔢𝔯𝔢𝔯, = 𝔊𝔬𝔱𝔱.

158. 𝔡𝔢𝔯 𝔪𝔢𝔫𝔰𝔠𝔥𝔢𝔫, *gen. plur.* depending on 𝔥𝔞𝔫𝔡 understood.

159. 𝔴𝔢𝔫𝔫 ... 𝔟𝔢𝔤𝔢𝔤𝔫𝔢𝔱, here euphemism for 𝔴𝔢𝔫𝔫 𝔦𝔠𝔥 𝔰𝔱𝔢𝔯𝔟𝔢; cf. in Latin : si quid mihi humanitus accidisset.

160. 𝔩𝔞𝔰𝔰𝔢𝔫, 'let be,' 'leave undone.'

161. 𝔪𝔢𝔦𝔰𝔱𝔢𝔯 𝔰𝔱𝔢𝔲𝔢𝔯𝔪𝔞𝔫𝔫, virtually a compound with the chief accent on 𝔪𝔢𝔦𝔰𝔱𝔢𝔯; the meaning is, in effect, boatman by calling, professional boatman.

168. 𝔎𝔯ä𝔣𝔱𝔦𝔤𝔩𝔦𝔠𝔥, old and Biblical form of 𝔨𝔯ä𝔣𝔱𝔦𝔤, an infrequent adverb in modern German.

170. 𝔞𝔫𝔤𝔢𝔰𝔭𝔯𝔢𝔫𝔤𝔱, cf. note on 𝔤𝔢𝔩𝔞𝔲𝔣𝔢𝔫, l. 65.

172. Complete the line with 𝔥𝔞𝔟𝔱.

173. 𝔡𝔢𝔰 𝔴𝔢𝔤𝔰, 'this way,' *adv. gen.* That 𝔡𝔢𝔰 here has

very strong demonstrative force is shown by its accent, which is indicated by the spacing of the type.

175. Reit, contraction for reitet, 2d *plur. imper.*, cf. fürcht't, l. 133 ; reitet ju, ' ride on hard.'

176. Wenn ihr frisch beilegt, ' if you hasten quickly,' ' if you bestir yourselves briskly'; beilegen seems here to be intended to be a boatman's expression of rapid movement used mockingly; if so, Schiller mistook its meaning, which is really ' to heave to,' ' to lay to'; beilegen, as an intrans. verb, in the sense of sich baran halten, nicht müde werden, i.e. ' to keep on,' ' to lay on,' is not otherwise known.

178. uns, ethical dative, untranslatable.

büßen, ' suffer for it.'

182. diesem Lande = den brei Walbstätten.

The second part of this scene is a drama in miniature whose title might be " Tell, the Rescuer." Upon the exposition of Baumgarten's situation and danger the plot proper follows in the refusal of Ruodi and the readiness of Tell to rescue him. The vigorous movement of the dialogue is noteworthy. One typical outrage of a most sacred relation and right, which has been attempted in Unterwalden, is exhibited to us in the narrative and the person of Baumgarten, while the scene ends with wanton robbery and destruction in Uri. Nevertheless one rescue has been effected before our very eyes, and that by a man of unique power (l. 164). May he not be the savior of the country, for whom Ruodi despairingly prays as the scene closes?

Tell's character is drawn in some of its main lines with bold strokes. He is quick to see need of help in others; he is quick in decision ; he is unselfish; he trusts in God, even to the risking of his life ; he excels in physical strength and skill. But he seems not inclined to deliberation and counsel ; his eyes are not open to the general dangers that threaten from the governors ; it is the fate of Ruodi as an individual, and not the collective interest of the Swiss, that moves him ; he acts also solely as an individual. Herein lies now the

great importance—often underestimated—of this scene
for the Tell-plot. It insures our enthusiastic admiration of Tell, upon which our confidence in him shall
rest unshaken during Scene 3 of this Act and his later
absence (Act II. Sc. 2) from the meeting of the Rütli.

ACT I. SCENE 2.

* **Steinen,** a village northwest of the town Schwyz, near
Lake Lowerz.

* **Stauffacher,** see note, p. 166.

* **Pfeifer,** see note, p. 168.

184. **Östreich,** the longer form Österreich is used also where
metrical convenience requires, as in l. 194.

185. **Reich,** the Empire as distinguished from Austria;
see Introd. p. xlvi.

187. **doch,** for emphasis, as often, 'do' or 'pray.'

Wirtin, old German for Hausfrau; cf. ll. 238 and 516.

188. This line is Homeric; cf. *Iliad,* vi. 224-5.

189. **Gersau,** a hamlet in the Canton Schwyz, on the lake
beneath the Rigi.

190. **Was ... auch Schweres,** 'whatever hardship.' The
adj. is used substantively with the indefinite pronoun was,
whose indefinite character is increased, as very often, by
the insertion of auch (nur or immer are likewise used).

190-192, cf. ll. 492, 1437, 1458-9.

193. **Ein andrer Kaiser,** = ein Kaiser von einem anderen Hause als
das habsburgische. The imperial office was elective, not hereditary; see l. 3023 and n.

194. The first clause is the condition, the second is the
conclusion.

erst = einmal.

The conversation between Pfeifer and Stauffacher—
a brief introduction to the main portion of the scene—
makes it evident that those parts of Switzerland which
are under (as Lucerne since the year 1291) the immediate authority of the Duke of Austria are no less
sorely oppressed and would gladly return to their former liberty in allegiance to the Empire.

* **Gertrud,** see note, p. 168.

The conversation between Stauffacher and Gertrud rests on Tschudi's narrative. In tone and in some details it resembles the dialogue of Brutus and Portia in Shakespeare's *Julius Cæsar*, Act II. Sc. 1.

198. **Gebreſten** (here neut.), 'sorrow,' a word borrowed by Schiller from Tschudi, and by this passage introduced into literature as a noble, poetic term, with this figurative meaning and also the original one of 'want,' 'defect.'

203 ff. These lines are reminiscent of Homer : cf. *Odyssey,* xx. 212 and ix. 425.

207. **Edelſitz,** 'nobleman's seat,' 'manor-house.'

208. **neu ;** the building was new, not rebuilt.

209. Homeric, cf. *Odyssey,* v. 245 and xxi. 44.

Richtmaß, Heyne in the Grimm *Wörterbuch,* viii. 901, says this : Winkelmaß, um etwas ſenkrecht zu richten; we may then render it by '(carpenter's) square,' or more loosely by 'rule and measure.'

210. 'Its many windows are bright with light and comfort.'

211, 212. This use of coats-of-arms and wise sayings, mostly in rhyme, was very widespread in Europe and may still be seen on many German and Swiss houses, high up on the gable ends and over the doors ; a date and the owner's name are often also given ; colored glass windows were often similarly treated ; the lines generally contained a religious sentiment, but were sometimes humorous.

214. **wohl,** as in l. 155, 'indeed,' 'it is true.'

219, 220. The governor is Hermann Gessler (see p. 165), whose residence was the castle of Küssnacht, of which ruins are still to be seen near the village of that name in the Canton Schwyz, at the northernmost end of the lake.

221. **wundernd,** personal intransitive, while at present this verb is used only impersonally or reflexively, and here one would have to say ſich wundernd.

226. **bösmeinend,** 'with evil intent.'

227. **ſchnell beſonnen,** 'with quick presence of mind.'

229. **eures** may be regarded as in construction parallel

to meines, so that Stauffacher says in effect: This house belongs to the Emperor who is your sovereign as well as mine, and I hold it in fief from him. It is also possible to make eures neut. nom. sg. agreeing with Haus understood ; then the meaning will be : This house belongs to the Emperor and, as far as you represent him, it belongs to you, but I hold it in fief. The expression is given by Tschudi with this same ambiguity, which is probably not unintentional.

232. auf feine eigne Hand, 'on his own account,' 'independently.'

233. Hinleb', 'live on,' 'live along.'

234. sich unterstehen, old for unternehmen.

235. trutiglich, for modern tropig.

We know now that the Austrian governors do grievous wrong in Uri, Unterwalden, and Lucerne, and our thoughts have followed Tell across the Lake to Schwyz, which seemed the abode of peace and plenty as the play opened. How is it here? The keynote of the answer has been given by Pfeifer's words, which encouraged Stauffacher to persist in opposition to all encroachment, and reminded him of his impending personal danger. Even the honorable, upright, wealthy man, a leader in the community, is no more secure from insult and injury than the meanest. Gertrud has long divined her husband's sorrow and fear, which she now leads him to state explicitly. Stauffacher's attitude toward Gessler is characteristic of the natural disposition of the Swiss toward the governors, to whom as representatives of the Emperor they feel respectful submission to be due.

238. Herr und Ehewirt, 'lord and husband,' cf. note to Wirtin, l. 187.

240. Cf. note to GERTRUD, p. 168.

rühm' ich mich (ju fein), Homeric naïve expression of self-esteem without conceit.

244. Pergamente, 'parchments,' on which were written

the charters of their liberties granted by the Emperors; cf. l. 1331.

254. **Schwyzer,** sg. for plural = primarily the inhabitants of the Canton Schwyz.

nicht, not to be translated. This use of the negative, after another negative, or a word containing the idea of negation, is widespread and historic in German, although sometimes theoretically objected to as a pleonasm. Cf. ll. 803–4, 1535.

Fürstenhaus and **Reich,** l. 256, same distinction as in ll. 184 and 185.

257. **gehalten und gethan** (haben), 'steadily did.'

258. **wenn ich lüge,** 'if what I say is not so.'

262. Gessler and Landenberg, being younger sons, had neither a castle of his own.

264. **Reichsfürst,** 'Prince of the Empire,' the lord holding any territory as an immediate vassal of the Emperor as such.

266. **den Höchsten in der Christenheit.** In the title Kaiser des heiligen römischen Reiches deutscher Nation, the German Emperor claimed the world-sovereignty of the ancient Roman Emperors, which claim received added sanction within Christendom from his being crowned by the Pope. Cf. ll. 305, 870.

267–8. As younger son he had no right to any landed inheritance, but only to the title of knight.

372. **erwarten** = warten or abwarten.

273. **gebüßt** (hat) = gestillt, befriedigt.

277. **Ob** as a preposition with gen. or dat. is obsolete except in poetry and elevated diction; in usual prose über with the acc., or wegen with gen.

Wüterei = ruchlose Tyrannei.

279. **Urner,** an inhabitant of Uri, or as here an adj. = 'of Uri.'

281. **schafft es** (indef. object) = treibt es, 'is acting,' 'is doing,' in the most general sense.

282. **Der Landenberger,** Beringer von Landenberg, cf. l. 72.

überm See, in Unterwalden.

284-5. Gewalt-Beginnen, as a rather loose compound in a play intended to be spoken, is divided between the end of one line and the beginning of the next, a thing which can usually be done only in comic poetry for humorous effect.

Beginnen, as the verb beginnen is quite frequently used in the sense of machen, thun, so its infinitive used as a noun, as here, often has the sense of That, Thun.

286. eurer, lengthened form of euer, gen. plur. of the personal pronoun du, dependent as a partitive genitive on etliche. For other instances of this form of the gen. pl. cf. ll. 1871, 2062, 2419.

288. erledigen, more common in this sense is now entledigen, cf. ll. 2244, 3018.

289. so, 'then.'

acht(e), in the general sense of meinen, denken, as here, is archaic, Biblical.

nicht, only with verlassen, not with gnädig sein.

291. gastfreund, 'intimate friend,' cf. Greek ξένος and Latin *hospes*.

294. angesehen(e) große Herrenleute, 'distinguished and important men of standing.' As here Schiller very often leaves undeclined the first of two adjectives modifying the same noun. By Herrenleute are meant rich landowners who in manner of living, esteem, and influence vie with the nobility.

295. geheim is obsolete in this sense of 'familiar,' 'intimate.'

vertraut, 'reliable,' 'trusty.'

Resistance to the designs and the acts of Austria, in order to be successful, must be the united resistance of the whole people. The first prompting to this comes from a woman of large mind and noble heart. If she represents the free-born women of Switzerland, there is indeed hope for the land. Though resting on a broad foundation of historical knowledge and of great political insight, the *immediate* motive of Gertrud is purely individual, her husband's personal danger.

" She thinks as a statesman, she feels as a woman, she wills as a heroine."

299. ſtill, modifies Denken, not verbot.

303. friedgewohnte = an den Frieden gewöhnte.

304. wagten, preterite subjunctive, 'do you mean to say that we should venture ?' etc.

305. Herrn der Welt, see note on l. 266.

306. Der gute Schein, 'a good pretext.' They are only waiting for the *appearance* of things to be in their favor (*good*).

312–329. Note the vigorous animated movement of the dialogue in alternating distichs.

312. Axt. The Streitart was the ancient German weapon of foot-soldiers along with the Morgenſtern (a club with an iron head having numerous projecting spikes) and the Hellebarde.

315. Die Herde ſchlägt er und die Hirten, biblical, cf. Matt. xxvi. 31 and Zechariah xiii. 7.

324. Cf. l. 2367.

331. Herd und Hof, may be fittingly duplicated by 'hearth and home'; an alliterative phrase like the standard Haus und Hof and countless others ; cf. ll. 742–3, 895, 1484, 2706, 3287. Many of these formulas have come down essentially unchanged from the oldest times, when perhaps the chief characteristic of poetic form was alliteration.

Freuden, dat. pl., but equivalent to the sg. in English. The pl. is very commonly used in such adverbial phrases with a preposition, when no adjective modifies the noun.

332. Heermacht = usual Heeresmacht.

Stauffacher is a man of strong character ; he has a vivid sense of justice and is strictly conscientious. Therefore he deliberates and is not hasty in deciding upon action, though we may expect him to be of resolute, intense energy when he has once committed himself. Gertrud's clear thinking and almost inspired feeling enlighten and strengthen Stauffacher's mind and heart, until his last shrinking—that from the horrors of war—is overcome.

333. **fahr'**, probably in the general sense of ' go,' 'travel' as in ll. 17, 348, and usually in this drama, and this even if we suppose him to go by boat part of the way.

ſtehnden Fußes, 'immediately,' an adverbial genitive imitated from the Latin ablative absolute *stante pede*. The tautology of ſtehnben Fußes gleich is natural to Stauffacher's present impatient haste.

334. **mir**, dat. of interest, equivalent to possessive adj., 'of mine.'

Walther Fürſt, see p. 167.

336. **Bannerherr**, ' banneret,' or ' lord of the banner,' was the bearer of the chief standard of the armed forces of the canton or district when marching against an enemy. Men of dignity and position were chosen for this office.

337. **von Attinghaus**, see p. 165.

The interview, here intended, is omitted later because of the intervention of Melchthal; cf. especially ll. 692-5.

341. **weil**, in the old original sense of ' while,' dieweil, wäh= rend.

343. **Gotteshauſe**, probably the monastery at Einsiedeln; see the note to l. 519.

346. **zu äußerſt**, adv. of place, ' way out,' ' far out.'

347. **Heerweg**, ' highway,' for usual Heerſtraße.

This scene has been the exposition of the Yeomenplot. In the steady onward flow of the dialogue between husband and wife has been developed the decision which is to put into action the power of an entire people. In contrast with the appeals which Scene 1 made to the outer eye, it is here chiefly the inner vision before which a soul-drama is unfolded. The more epic elements of narration and description are made to serve dramatic ends.

The appearance of Tell with Baumgarten assures us of the successful issue of the struggle with nature and man with which Scene 1 ends; it thus aptly binds the two scenes together and prepares for the following scene.

Act I. Scene 3.

* **Altorf** (**Altdorf**), chief town of the Canton Uri, half an hour from the southern end of the lake, at which its port is Flüelen.

* **gediehen** = vorgerückt.

* **Fronvogt,** ' taskmaster,' ' overseer.' **Frone** was compulsory labor for a feudal lord.

* **Gesellen und Handlanger,** ' workmen and (under)laborers.'

353. **Nicht lang' gefeiert,** ' no long rest .' ; **gefeiert,** as also **zugefahren** in the next line, is the past participle used elliptically for the imperative. This substitution, like that of the infinitive or indicative, is commonly emphatic.

356. **Das** is sometimes used in a contemptuous or humorous way of persons, one or more, ' those fellows.'

357. **Heißt das geladen?,** ' do you call that a load?' (lit. ' is that called loaded?') ; with verbs of calling, the past participle, as originally in predicate apposition, is used with the sense of the infinitive or a verbal noun.

358. Neither **Tagdiebe** nor the verb **bestehlen,** which it suggested, can be literally rendered by ordinary English terms; yet as the German expression is unusual and poetic, the literal translation would be scarcely any more bold; otherwise **bestehlen** = ' shirk.'

360. **Twing** originally meant ' jurisdiction,' ' authority;' but is here equivalent to **Twinghof, Herrenhof,** or ' dungeon,' ' keep.' In l. 370 the form **Zwing** with same meaning, for modern **Zwinger.**

362. **anstellig** = brauchbar, geschickt, tüchtig.

365. **Eingeweid(e),** figuratively for **Herz, Gefühl** ; cf. English Biblical expression ' bowels of compassion.'

367. **'s ist himmelschreiend** = es schreit zum Himmel ; cf. Genesis iv. 10.

368. **Amts,** predicate possessive genitive ; complete the line with **ist** or with **Pflicht ist.**

370. **Zwing Uri** ; cf. l. 360 and note. Some ten miles above Altorf near Amstäg lie on a low hill the ruins of a

castle. Tschudi, whom Schiller follows, places it at Altorf
and relates that Gessler, on being asked its name, replied,
Zwing Uri unber die Stägen, i.e. 'Keep Uri under the yoke (?).'
We may imitate the play on the meaning of Zwing and zwingen by using 'keep' and 'keep down.'

375. 'nander = einander, cf. note to 1. 60.

378. Fluchgebäude = verfluchtes Gebäude, cf. ll. 457–8.

380. Hier ist nicht gut sein, common negative form of the
Biblical phrase, Matt. xvii. 4.

381. Uri is the 'land of freedom,' because this canton was
the first to attain immediate dependence upon the Empire.

384. ‚fürder,' etymological parallel to English 'further,'
obsolete, except in archaistic or elevated diction; nicht fürder, 'nevermore.'

385. Stauffacher's exclamation is spoken at the same time
with this line.

Flanken. The precise meaning of this word here is not
easy to determine; as a technical term of the art of forti-
fication it means the side wall of a bastion or of a bastion-
like projection at the corner of a large structure, but this
sense seems hardly large enough here; in a passage in
Scheuchzer, which probably was in Schiller's mind, it means
side, flank, or is synonymous with Strebepfeiler; on the whole,
it seems best to regard Flanken as standing here for Seiten or
Mauern, and to render 'these walls, these buttresses.'

388. A natural thought, and also suggested by Scheuchzer,
who says, e.g., 'Our fortresses ... are our high mountains,
placed ... by the omnipotent wisdom of God;' and again,
'I have now several times named the mountains buildings
(Gebäue). ... The foundations of the mountains are very
strong layers (courses or underpinning), upon which the
main pillars rest. The Blanken or Planggen [i.e., the Flanken
of l. 385] are like to the *anteridibus* or buttresses.'

The several somewhat distinct parts of this scene are
made one by the locality in which they are naturally
presented, and by their relation to the collective
liberty of the people. The ways of Tell returning home
and of Stauffacher going to Walther Fürst lead through

Altorf. By this means this scene is connected with the preceding.

The acts of violence and oppression which the preceding scenes depicted were directed against individuals, and the least important was the one in Uri at the end of Scene I. Furthermore the last scene encouraged us to hope for active and successful resistance against the tools of Austria. Now here in Uri we begin to realize how profoundly dangerous the situation is. The most sacred collective interests of the whole people are threatened. We see, as it were, the very execution of the Austrian plan to keep down this people and bury its liberty. But we see also the liberty-loving spirit of the people and their growing impatience of oppression.

390. **Faſtnachtsaufzug,** 'carnival procession.'

393. **Aufrichten** . . . **auf hoher Säule,** an unusual expression in the words aufrichten for aufpflanzen, and Säule for Stange.

394. **in Altorf,** as Tschudi has it; but Act III. Sc. 3, p. 84, has **bei Altorf.**

407. **noch,** 'at least' or 'only.'
    So, 'in this case' or 'as things are.'

408. **Der Hut von Öſterreich,** the ducal coronet of Austria, a crown adorned with twelve golden balls and surmounted by an orb. From l. 403 it would seem that quite an ordinary hat was intended; here is plainly prominent the crown. The relation between the two is not defined.

Note again the pervading distinction in ll. 407–411 between the Empire and Austria, i.e. the House of Habsburg, as in ll. 184–5.

408–9. **Thron.** It was the castle called the Stein zu Baden on the Limmat in the Canton Aargau, which was the residence of Emperor Albrecht when in Switzerland as head of the Habsburg family. Here were granted to Swiss vassals the fiefs of the House of Habsburg. This castle was destroyed by the Swiss in 1415.

411. Obeisance to the hat might be interpreted as formal acknowledgment of Austria in place of imperial authority.

* **Tiefe** (ber Bühne), 'background.'

As the Keep threatens physical liberty, so the hat and the edict of obeisance to it threaten spiritual liberty. They are designed to degrade and break the very spirit of the people ; by one and the same act the Swiss are to accept insult, arbitrary cruelty, and allegiance to Austria. The last two lines reveal the intention of the plain people and their means to its accomplishment ; the lines are as it were the introduction of the *motif* of Act II. Sc. 2.

The Crier on his rounds through the Canton appears now naturally enough in Altorf.

414. **Ihr wiffet nun Befcheid,** 'Now you know all about it.' We are in doubt as to the presence of Tell and Stauffacher since l. 387, so that the reference in these words is not definite, whether to the state of affairs in Uri, or to Tell's opinion, or to the particular fact of the building of the Zwing. Note the vigor of the dialogue in pregnant one-line speeches, the stichomythy of the Greek drama.

416. The genitive is now construed with **entbehren** only in poetic or elevated diction.

420. **einz'ge** = einzig mögliche, 'only possible.'

422. **fchnellen,** partly with the older meaning of 'violent,' 'rash,' and partly as a serious word-play in connection with furz. The line is modelled on the common proverb Geftrenge Herren regieren nicht lange.

424. This is still a strict legal requirement especially in Uri. Kuenen states that disregard of it in January, 1879, was the cause of the conflagration which consumed the greater part of the town of Meiringen in the Haslithal.

431. **Die Lande,** the Cantons. The oldest plural of Land was Land; then from the fourteenth century at least Länder came into use and is now the sole form in common use; the form Lande arose in the seventeenth century, in poetic and elevated diction, and is established as an ordinary prose word only in this present sense of the parts of a political whole.

438–9. Contain a clear indication of the plan of self-liberation.

442. **was,** for **was auch,** 'whatever.'

442–5. The rhymes are employed here after Shakespeare's example to emphasize the conclusion of the dialogue and the importance of Tell's words, which disclose to us Tell's character and provide us with an explanation of his non-appearance in Act II. Sc. 2.

445. **es soll an mir nicht fehlen,** 'I shall not be found wanting.'

This forceful dialogue between Stauffacher and Tell presents to us in further measure and with great definiteness their standpoints and their characters. Stauffacher is resolutely in favor of collective action by the people, and of previous joint deliberation. Tell will have nothing to do with any such general conference or council. At first he rejects the thought of any uprising at all against the governors, but afterwards he declares his readiness to do any individual deed to which the need of his country shall summon him. This conversation explains Tell's absence from the meeting at the Rütli in Act II. Sc. 2.

Tell has commonly been described by critics and commentators as laconic, taciturn. But the man who here speaks appears to be very ready to express himself on general interests, not only vigorously but fluently; there is here no lack of words, on occasion. He seems to be given to reflection and discussion, of which the fruits are pregnant, proverb-like sayings, wherein this conversation (as others of Tell also) so abounds. In concrete cases he does not always think clearly; several of the proverb-like utterances in which he here states his present view of his own case are shown by his later experience to be very wrong. He is a man of action, rather than of council.

This brief glimpse of Bertha von Bruneck (a relative of Gessler, who, as we shall learn in Act II. Sc. 1, has a residence in Altorf), and the earlier allusions to the

Baron von Attinghausen are preparing for the full exposition of the Nobles-plot. Here is a lady of noble birth whose sympathy is with the oppressed, and for whom the symbol of tyranny now rising before us is accursed.

This scene is one of the three (the others being Act III. Sc. 3 and Act IV. Sc. 2) in which representatives of all three plots appear, but here without concentration.

446. **Was giebt's?** Counts as an entire line because of the pause in speech amid the running and excitement.

447. The fall shows us that Zwing Uri is in fact a **Fluch=gebäube**, as the master-mason named it in l. 378.

450. **Mit eurem Golde** = **Fort** (*or* **Geht**) **mit eurem Golde. Mit** is not infrequently used in this way with omitted verb (or adverb) of motion to express surprise, vexation, or anger.

euch, 'for you,' 'in your opinion.' **euch** and **ihr** in the following lines are plural, referring to the Austrian nobles, with whose sentiments the master-mason wrongly identifies those of Bertha.

ACT I. SCENE 4.

* **Walther Fürst** and **Arnold von Melchthal,** see p. 167.

466. **Dem frechen Buben,** dative instead of possessive genitive with **Finger,** l. 469, as also **mir** with **Ochsen. Bube,** as in **Handbube,** page 4, foot, both here and in l. 470 is 'boy' in the sense of 'servant'; he is afterward called **Bote** and **Knecht.**

468. **Vogts.** It was Beringer von Landenberg, not Gessler. Cf. ll. 72, 282.

auf u.f.w., cf. l. 2882.

471. **Von eurer Obrigkeit,** "by one in authority over you."

473. **Wie schwer fie (auch) war,** cf. note on **was (auch),** l. 190. **Buße,** in the old legal sense of 'fine,' 'penalty.'

478. **spannen,** construed with **von,** 'unhitch.'

483. **wir (Alten),** emphatic contrast to **Jugend,** l. 484.

487. **gehässig,** here in the obsolete active sense of 'full of hatred,' while now the word is restricted to the sense of

'producing hate,' 'hateful,' or to the full passive sense of ‚verhaßt.'

490. ſchütze, subjunctive of characteristic.

491. hinüber (gehen), over the mountains from Uri to Unter-walden.

492. Cf. ll. 190-2, 1437, 1458-9.

493. Walde, i.e. the Kernwald (l. 1196), by which the Canton Unterwalden is divided into two parts, ob (above) dem Wald and nid (below) dem Wald; cf. ll. 545, 717. Melchthal's home was near Kerns on the border of this forest. In Unterwalden unter has the meaning of zwiſchen, among; in official documents in Latin the inhabitants are called *Intramontani.*

497. ſich = einander.

501. ſchwanen, to have forebodings like the swan, which in legend is a prophetic bird.

502. rauſcht = raſſelt, ein Geräuſch macht.

505. thät' and hätten, l. 506, subjunctive, to soften the positiveness of the assertion, 'it may soon be necessary,' (Wh. § 332, 3a.)

506. In the less populous mountain districts of Switzer-land, as also of Norway, even now bolts and locks are little used; simplicity and confidence are so universal and com-plete.

513. Sieh, as a general interjection, 'Oh!'

mir wird ſo wohl, 'I begin to feel so happy.'

514, geht—auf, 'opens,' 'expands.'

516. Wirtin, cf. note to l. 187.

519. (Sankt) Meinrads Zell is the present monastery of Our Lady at Einsiedeln, founded by St. Meinrad (Meinard, Meginhard), who, according to the legend, belonged to the Hohenzollern family and was born about 800 A.D. He came first as a monk from the monastery at Reichenau to the foot of the mountain Ezel in Schwyz, and there built him a hermit's cell in the year 832, where in January, 861, he was murdered by two robbers. In 946 Otto the Great founded the monastery on that spot. It has ever since the building of that first cell been a place of pilgrimage, and is now visited by about 200,000 pilgrims annually.

Welſchland, here = Italy.

521. **Flüelen** (pronounce Flülen), see note on Altorf, *21.

524. **erſtaunlich(es) neues Werk,** cf. ll. 379 and following.

526. **es,** i.e. the whole story, all our trouble.

528. **ſeit Menſchendenken,** for usual ſeit Menſchengedenken, 'since time immemorial.'

529. **feſt war keine Wohnung** = keine Wohnung hielt feſt, 'held captive.'

530. **Mit Namen** = mit dem rechten Namen.

531. **verhalten,** for usual vorenthalten, verhehlen, or verſchweigen, 'keep from you.'

536. **Ziel,** in the now less common sense of Grenze, Ende.

537. **von uralters her,** 'from the most ancient times.' The usual phrase is von alters her, in which alters is an adverbial genitive used as object of a preposition. The prefix ur- has its usual strengthening force.

540-1. **Treiben,** in two different meanings: **trieb** (540) has as its object ſeine Herde understood, while **treiben** (541), with the indefinite obj. **es,** means 'to drive (things),' 'to carry on,' 'to act.'

542-4. A definite statement of the attitude of the nobility, as to which we are thus led to expect the further information that is given to us by the completion of the exposition in II. 1.

547. **hauſte,** here probably in the neutral sense of 'resided.'

549. **Alzellen,** in Nid dem Wald ; cf. l. 66.

550. 'He tried to wrong with shameful impropriety.'

553. **beſcheidner,** here in the older sense of instructed, informed, and hence 'sensible,' 'discreet,' 'prudent,' rather than the modern 'modest.'

554. Cf. l. 2292.

555. **Eidam,** now obsolete in ordinary prose, = Schwieger-ſohn.

556. As Walther Fürst concealed Melchthal. The oppressed, no less than the tyrants (l. 497), aid one another.

558. **Sarnen,** the chief town of Ob dem Wald and the residence of Landenberg.

563. **gilt was,** 'has no little weight'; **was** for **etwas.**

565. **büßte,** 'fined,' 'punished,' here active in meaning.

569. **wie steht's um den?** = wie steht's mit ihm?

572. **Zur Stelle schaffen** (bringen) = 'produce,' 'bring forward.'

586. **ist ausgeflossen,** 'has ceased to flow,' 'has emptied itself.'

588. **Schmerzens.** This form of the genitive of **Schmerz** is no longer usual, except as it is retained in compound words of which it is the first member.

589–602. Compare the opening lines of Book III of Milton's *Paradise Lost.*

593. **fühlend,** not 'feeling his way' or 'groping,' but rather sein Unglück empfindend, 'feeling (conscious of) all his loss,' in contrast with the plants and animals just alluded to.

595. **Schmelz,** 'enamel,' because of the brilliant and variegated hues of the flowers that so often cover Alpine fields.

596. **roten Firnen,** here 'red snow-peaks,' glowing with the first light of the rising or the last of the setting sun; the well-known 'Alpine glow,' Alpenglühen.

599. **jammernd,** for bejammernd, mitleidig.

frische, 'sound.'

613. **denken,** used with **auf,** implies wish, aspiration, desire, volition, while with **an** it is purely intellectual, although both are expressed in English by 'think of.'

622–3. **Wenn . . . kühle,** 'if only I may cool,' etc.

The participants in this scene, Melchthal, Stauffacher (in whose person this scene is connected with Scene 3), and Fürst, are respectively representatives, in origin, of the three Cantons, in years, of youth, mature manhood, and old age, in personality of passionate energy, manly prudence and counsel, and of anxious caution. The portion of the scene which here culminates in Melchthal's outburst of feeling—a lyric lament of great power and beauty—belongs technically to the general exposition. The outrages committed by the governors are reviewed and a new extreme case detailed. The third governor, Landenberg, is seen to be no less en-

vious, rapacious and cruel than Gessler. The tyrannical oppression is rising in intensity and the governors
assist one another. The distress is common to all the
land and all its inhabitants. Is there no hope? The
resentment of the people is rising too. The conversation
between Stauffacher and Fürst is charged with noble
indignation and passion, while Melchthal's feeling
knows no bounds.

625. **auf . . . Herrenburg,** 'in his lordly keep.'

627. **wohnt',** pret. subj. in conditional clause.

628. The Schreckhorn (13,386 feet high) and the Jungfrau
(13,671 feet high) are two peaks of the Bernese Alps. They
were regarded as inaccessible until ascended, the latter in
1811 and the former in 1861.

629. **verschleiert** has commonly been understood by commentators of clouds, but this seems hardly adequate and
the present editor would prefer to understand it of the snow
as a white virginal veil, with suggestion also of inaccessibility.

ich mache, the pres. indic., with future meaning, substituted
in the conclusion for the pret. subj. to make the thought
more emphatic.

639. **Es,** the state of affairs, the evil, the tyranny.

auf seinem Gipfel, 'at its apex,' 'at its worst.'

641. **Augenstern** is used of the pupil of the eye and by
poets of the whole eye.

645. **ward,** see note on line 149.

646. **Notgewehr,** lit. 'weapon in need,' 'weapon for self-
defense.'

647. **stellt sich,** 'takes his stand,' 'stands at bay.'

649. Cf. ll. 1499–1500. The thought is that in the frenzy
of its extreme danger the chamois dashes back over the
hunter or between him and the wall of rock and pushes
him over the edge. That this is cool self-defense is hardly
a fact, although firmly believed by the Swiss; but instances
of its being blindly done cannot be denied.

652. **duldsam,** for prose geduldig.

653. **(wenn er) gereizt (wird).**

654. 𝖘𝖈𝖍𝖑𝖊𝖚𝖉𝖊𝖗𝖙 . . . 𝖏𝖚, sep. verb, 'hurls towards.'

655. 𝕷𝖆𝖓𝖉𝖊, cf. note to l. 431.

657-8. Uri is represented by Fürst, Unterwalden by Melchthal, while Stauffacher is from Schwyz.

𝖉𝖎𝖊 𝖆𝖑𝖙𝖊𝖓 𝕭ü𝖓𝖉𝖊, see Introd. pp. xxxvi, xlviii, and xlix.

659. 𝕱𝖗𝖊𝖚𝖓𝖉𝖘𝖈𝖍𝖆𝖋𝖙, in its older sense of 𝕭𝖊𝖗𝖜𝖆𝖓𝖉𝖙𝖘𝖈𝖍𝖆𝖋𝖙, 'kindred'; 'I have many kinsmen,' etc., cf. ll. 1034 and 1455.

661. 𝕽ü𝖈𝖐𝖊𝖓, in the sense of 𝕽ü𝖈𝖐𝖍𝖆𝖑𝖙, 'support,' 'backing' is a favorite expression with Schiller; here derived perhaps from Tschudi.

662. 𝖋𝖗𝖔𝖒𝖒𝖊 = gute.

665. 𝕷𝖆𝖓𝖉𝖘𝖌𝖊𝖒𝖊𝖎𝖓𝖉𝖊 = 𝕷𝖆𝖓𝖉𝖊𝖘𝖛𝖊𝖗𝖘𝖆𝖒𝖒𝖑𝖚𝖓𝖌, 'assembly of the canton'; the annual meeting of all the citizens of the canton to deliberate as to its interests and to elect its magistrates.

668-9. 𝖒𝖎𝖈𝖍 𝖙𝖗𝖊𝖎𝖇𝖙, belongs to the two contrasted subjects 𝕭𝖑𝖚𝖙 and 𝕲𝖊𝖜𝖆𝖑𝖙, which in prose would have 𝖘𝖔𝖓𝖉𝖊𝖗𝖓 between them.

670. 𝖂𝖆𝖘 𝖆𝖚𝖈𝖍, 'that which even.'

673-4 𝖊𝖍𝖗𝖊 and 𝖇𝖊𝖜𝖆𝖈𝖍𝖊, see note on 𝖘𝖈𝖍ü𝖙𝖊, l. 490.

677. 𝖋𝖗𝖎𝖘𝖈𝖍, as in l. 599.

𝕶𝖗𝖊𝖎𝖘𝖊𝖓, 'orbits,' 'sockets.'

682. 𝖎𝖓 𝖌𝖑𝖊𝖎𝖈𝖍𝖊𝖗 𝕸𝖎𝖙𝖘𝖈𝖍𝖚𝖑𝖉 𝖚𝖓𝖉 𝕭𝖊𝖗𝖉𝖆𝖒𝖒𝖓𝖎𝖘, 'in equal joint guilt and condemnation'; in part a reminiscence of Luke xxiii. 40.

683. His attitude is as in l. 658.

685. 𝕾𝖎𝖑𝖑𝖎𝖓𝖊𝖓 (now 𝕾𝖎𝖑𝖊𝖓𝖊𝖓), accent on the first syllable; the village is 2½ hours above or south of Altorf, on the right bank of the Reuss. There remains one tower of the old castle.

𝕬𝖙𝖙𝖎𝖓𝖌𝖍𝖆𝖚𝖘𝖊𝖓, see p. 165.

687. 𝖉𝖊𝖒 𝖂𝖆𝖑𝖉𝖌𝖊𝖇𝖎𝖗𝖌, in effect 𝖉𝖊𝖓 𝖂𝖆𝖑𝖉𝖘𝖙ä𝖙𝖙𝖊𝖓.

688. Probably Melchthal addresses first Fürst and then Stauffacher.

689. 𝖊𝖈𝖍𝖙𝖊 𝖂ä𝖍𝖗𝖚𝖓𝖌, 'sterling value.'

692. 𝖜𝖆𝖘, with force of 𝖜𝖆𝖗𝖚𝖒. Melchthal does not trust the nobility, because the younger nobles, of whom Rudenz

is representative, may hold to Austria, as we shall learn in Act II. Sc. 1.

694. **wären**... **Land**!, ordinarily understood as a wish that there were no nobles; but it might be 'What if we were after all alone in the land!'

699. **entstehn,** in the old and poetic sense of fernstehen, mangeln.

701. **Obmann,** i.e. ein Mann, der über den Parteien steht, 'arbitrator,' 'umpire'; the ordinary term is Schiedsrichter.

704-5. With this bold declaration, which is the more forcible because uttered by the cautious Walther Fürst, the alliance is formed in the persons of these three representative men.

710. **gewähren,** intrans. in the sense of Gewähr leisten, bürgen, einstehen; the commoner trans. meaning of gestatten occurs in l. 713.

711. **Schliche,** here in the literal original sense of 'secret paths,' 'by-paths,' not in the ordinary figurative meaning of 'tricks,' 'artifices.'

717. **der Alzeller** = Baumgarten, cf. l. 66 and note, and also note to l. 52.

nid dem Wald, see note to l. 493.

721. See map and notes of Act I. Sc. 1.

725. **Mythenstein** is a single column of rock about eighty feet high, projecting from the lake a little south of Brunnen. On it there was placed, right after the centennial anniversary of the poet's birth, the inscription Dem Sänger Tells, Friedrich Schiller, die Urkantone, 1860. Cf. note to l. 39

grad' über = gerade gegenüber.

727. **Das Rütli** (long ü), also Grütli, derived from the Swiss form of the verb reuten, North German roden, to clear, to root out, is a meadow-clearing on the western shore of the lake, a little south of Selisberg, surrounded by rocky walls, trees, and bushes. This traditional cradle of Swiss liberty is now the property of the nation, having been bought by subscription of the school-children of Switzerland.

729. Distinguish carefully die Mark (two meanings), die Marke, and das Mark.

735. **herzeinig,** ' one at heart.'

736. **gemeinfam das Gemeine,** ' in common—the common good'; effective repetition for emphasis.

734–737. The precise time of meeting and the watchword are not discussed ; it is assumed that an agreement as to these can easily be had by means of messengers.

738. Speaks first to Walther Fürst.

741. **zufammenflechten,** for prose in einander legen.

742–3. **zu Schutz und Trutz,** ' for defense and defiance,' ' for offense and defense.'

746 ff. The realization of this prophetic outburst is seen in the Fifth Act. **erheben** and **fallen** are both in the clause of condition. Rhyme is again used in these important lines that conclude the act, cf. note to l. 442–5.

747. This custom is most ancient and universal. Cf. ll. 1421, 1422.

749. Cf. l. 3085 and Act V. Sc. 3.

751. ' In thy night shall be the bright day' (of liberty).

The first portion of the scene was charged with feeling, the second is dominated by the will, and culminates in the alliance of the three representative men, with faith in God, and in behalf of the three Cantons. Melchthal leads the way with moving eloquence, at first blindly vehement, then calmer, clear, and convincing. Fürst is at the opposite pole of reserve and caution. Stauffacher occupies the less conspicuous but more reasonable middle ground. The three men show three typical forms of the relations existing between the people and the nobility. Fürst has the standpoint of the era now closing, that the interests of both are one, that the people can do nothing without the nobles. Melchthal, viewing the two classes in radical opposition, rejects all thought of aid from the nobility. Stauffacher, seeing things more as they really are, desires a voluntary rising of the people, but hopes that the nobles will make the cause of the people their own. Fürst finally acknowledges the necessity of independent action, and now displays resolute decision and wisdom in planning.

The conference concludes with the solemn vow of union, wherein our inner vision sees the powers of the entire people united. Again, in Melchthal's prophecy of the day of freedom does a broad band of hope break in upon the gloom.

So far as Act I contains the exposition (see Introd. pp. lxiv–lxxi) it answers to Schiller's own definition of the best sort of exposition, for it also develops the plot.

The condition of land and people under the lawless arbitrary rule of the Austrian governors is presented to us partly in narration and partly in acts which we behold. One governor has attempted to violate the sanctity of the family ; another with revolting cruelty has outraged the right and person of a respected old man ; a third, Gessler, is planning to destroy the rights and liberties of the whole people. All three are avaricious, proud, unscrupulous. But the real oppressor is the Emperor, the Duke of Austria, who, faithless to his duty as emperor, desires to make the Swiss Cantons own allegiance to the House of Austria, and is angered by their refusal, whether expressed or tacit.

The Swiss spirit of liberty and some promise of their power of resistance is also revealed to us in the plans and the acts of individuals, both as such and as symbolizing the popular feeling and will.

Act I is given in part to the exposition of the Tellplot, but chiefly to that of the Yeomen-plot. The climax of the act is therefore the alliance of Fürst, Stauffacher, and Melchthal in Scene 4. The movement leading to this climax starts in the relation of Gessler to Stauffacher as realized by the latter in Scene 2. Gessler hates Stauffacher's patriotism, covets his property, and means to ruin him. No individual alone can prevent such ruin in his own case ; there must be common action of the whole land. In order to secure common action there must be previous counselling. Thus does Gertrud Stauffacher urge upon her husband the end and

the means of the Yeomen-plot.   The foundation of the
league is in part individual self-defense and self-preser-
vation ; but it rests also on the common cause, the cause
of country, the cause of liberty, and by this it is hallowed.

For the Tell-plot this act introduces the title-hero.
Scene 1 prepares for Scene 3, this for Act III. Sc. 3,
and leading qualities in Tell's character are strongly
drawn.

In passing mention of Attinghausen and the brief
appearance of Bertha von Bruneck hints are given of
the Nobles-plot.

SEAL OF URI, 1291.

ACT II.

ARGUMENT.—The *first* scene is in the great hall of the baronial manor of Attinghausen. The aged patriotic Swiss Baron, feeling that his death is not remote, reproaches his young nephew and heir, Rudenz, with deserting the cause of his native land for the vain pomp of the Austrian court. Rudenz is blinded by his love for Bertha, whom he mistakenly supposes to be Austrian in sentiment, and can see power and honor only in allegiance to Austria. He therefore will not heed his uncle's wise and heartfelt remonstrances, but, starting to go to Gessler in Altorf, he leaves the Baron in despair of the national cause.

The *second* scene makes us witnesses of the midnight meeting at the Rütli and the formal organization of the confederation. The Unterwaldeners, led by Melchthal, come first, then Stauffacher and they of Schwyz. While these all are waiting for the men of Uri, Melchthal tells of his movements and his seeing his blind father. When the men of Uri are come, the assembly is duly constituted. Stauffacher recites the origin, history, and liberty of the Swiss, and Conrad Hunn tells of the formal refusal of the Emperor to confirm their liberty. Since now it is plain that only the way of forcible resistance is open, the assembly decides upon an uprising at Christmas, for the sake of capturing the strongholds and expelling the Austrian governors. Before separating, these representatives of the three Forest Cantons swear a solemn oath to remain united and free, in reliance on God and fearlessness of man.

SCENE I.

The two scenes of this act occur on one and the same day, the first in the morning, the second in the night. This day is probably about midway between October 28 and November 19; Tschudi makes it November 8.

* **Edelhof.** On a hill near Attinghausen, a little south of Altorf on the left bank of the Reuss, may still be seen the ruins of the baronial residence Schweinsberg.

* **Freiherrn von Attinghausen,** see p. 165.

* **Kuoni,** see p. 167 and Act I. Sc. 1.

* **Ulrich von Rudenz,** see p. 166.

* **Mit Rechen und Sensen.** In the Alps second-growth hay is cut very late in the valley-bottoms, but hardly so late as November. Cf. also l. 1913.

754. **Frühtrunk,** 'early draught,' 'morning-cup.' The word is not else in use, and its meaning is undefined. Schiller probably understood it to consist of wine or cider.

757. Cf. l. 911.

758. **den Schaffner (= Verwalter) machen,** 'act the part of steward.'

761. **in enger stets und engerm Kreis,** 'within a narrower and ever narrower circle,' ' within a circle ever closing in upon me '; thus he indicates the narrowing of his activity from the wide world successively to his estate, his castle, his room, and finally to the center of repose, l. 762, in the coffin. Note that the declensional ending is expressed with only one of the comparatives.

765. **Ich bring's euch,** 'I drink your health,' 'I pledge you.'

Junker, ' young squire.'

Es geht [comes] (bei uns) ... **Herzen** = wie wir ein Herz sind, so trinken wir auch aus einem Becher.

767. **Kinder,** ' boys.'

wenn's Feierabend ist, ' when the evening-rest has come.' The locality of this scene pictures to us the life of the nobility, as the houses of Stauffacher and Fürst that of well-to-do yeomen. We see first in this brief introduction the patriarchal character of the generation of nobles now just passing away, while the bearing of Rudenz betrays a different spirit.

770. **Herrenburg,** cf. note to l. 625. Gessler had temporary quarters in a tower at Altorf, while Zwing-Uri was building ; of this tower Attinghausen is made to speak as a well-equipped castle or château. The residence proper of Gessler was in Küssnacht.

772. **Hast du's so eilig?** = Hast du solche Eile?

773-4. **fie erſparen an,** 'save it out of,' 'gain it at the expense of.'

778. **Zur Fremde,** 'a strange place, 'foreign.' With werben the predicate noun is often put in the dative after zu.

Uli, diminutive of **Ulrich.**

779. **In Seide.** Silk costumes were used at court festivals, while leather was the ordinary outer dress of the knights of the time.

780. 'You proudly display the peacock's feather.' This was a symbol of attachment to Austria, because the Austrian dukes were wont to wear peacock's feathers.

781. **Purpurmantel.** Red was the color of Austria; its coat-of-arms had a red field with a silver bar.

782. **Landmann,** cf. note to l. 50. The Baron noticed in silence the rejection by Rudenz of the **Frühtrunf,** but now he speaks. This and the **wir** and **unſer** of lines 789 and 792 place him clearly on the side of the people.

785. **fich nimmt,** 'takes to himself,' 'assumes,' is emphatic.

797. Supply **hat** at end of line.

798. **foſtete,** pret. subj. for **würde koſten.**

ein einzig(es) leichtes Wort, viz. the "Yes" of allegiance to Austria.

801-2. Aimed at his uncle.

halten = zuhalten, 'hold shut,' 'keep closed.'

804. **nicht,** see note on **nicht,** l. 254.

805. **Wie — alle — doch gethan,** cf. l. 3054.

806. **Wohl thut es ihnen,** 'it makes them feel good.'

Herrenbant, 'nobles' bench.' In court and legislative sessions knights and free peasants had equal vote and equal right, which would not so continue under Austrian rule.

808. They were so remote from the Emperor, as such, as not to feel his power.

811. **Perſon,** 'rôle,' 'part.'

813. **Landammann,** '*chief-magistrate* of a canton,' chosen annually by the people. **Ammann** is a form of **Amtmann.**

Bannerherr, see l. 336 and note.

817. **Lager,** for **Hoflager,** 'court' of a prince.

818. **Pair** (pronounced **Pär**), 'peer.' In the Germanic feudal state 'peers' were originally such vassals as could be judged in matters of their fiefs only by their equals.

819. **zu Gericht zu sitzen,** 'to hold court.'

824. **Fremdlinge,** 'foreigners,' the Austrian knights of the retinues of the governors.

825. **Bauern=adel,** 'peasant-nobility.'

826–7. Albrecht I. fought in 1301 against Count Rudolf of the Palatinate, in 1304 against King Wenzel of Bohemia, and in 1307 against Friedrich of Thuringia.

833. **Halle,** 'hall,' the great room of the castle.

834. **Drommete** is an archaic and poetical form of **Trompete.**
In its unitary character this scene is comparable to Act I. Sc. 2 and Act III. Sc. 2. All three are dialogues in which one participant desires to move the other to a decision. Here Attinghausen seeks to win the soul of his nephew and heir, but apparently in vain, since love and ambition seem to prevail over the ideals of liberty and country. This first portion of the dialogue between Attinghausen and Rudenz consists of the former's accusations and the latter's defense. The charges are that Rudenz is a stranger to his home, a renegade to his country, intent on frivolous pleasure and princely favor; the defense is that the leaders of the people are controlled only by self-interest in their resistance to Austria, and that only on the side of Austria can Rudenz obtain the honors that befit him. As he speaks, we are strongly impressed with the power and wealth of the Duke of Austria. Rudenz is young and, we fear, hasty, weak, unwise. Has the school of experience naught in store for him?

843. **Heim sehnen,** 'feel homeward longing.' Proverbial is the homesickness of the Swiss, especially on hearing the Kuhreihen in any land however remote.

844. **Herdenreihen** = **Kuhreihen.**

846. **Schmerzenssehnsucht** = schmerzliche Sehnsucht or Schmerz und Sehnsucht.

847. **dir anklingt,** 'strikes your ear.'

848. **der Trieb des Vaterlands,** 'the (instinctive) love of country.'

855. **Fürstenknecht,** 'servant (or slave) of a prince.'

856. **Da** (doch), 'while,' adversative.

Selbstherr, 'your own master.'

861. **der Letzte.** Not historical, since the family line continued half a century longer. The change is for dramatic impressiveness.

863. **mitgeben,** in accordance with custom, he being the last male member of his house.

865. **brechend**(es), lit. 'breaking,' while in English we must say 'failing' or 'closing.'

866. This line has six feet.

Lehenhof, 'court of fiefs,' the court at which fiefs were bestowed upon vassals.

867-8. Rudenz would give away his inheritance to Austria, and receive it back as a fief to be held by him as a vassal.

870. **Die Welt gehört ihm,** in so far as in the title of Emperor the kings of Germany laid claim to the world-sovereignty of the ancient Roman Empire; cf. note on l. 266.

871. 'be stiffly and stubbornly obstinate in.'

872. **Länderkette.** Schiller made the following note on the effort of Albrecht as Count of Habsburg and Duke of Austria to increase the territorial possessions of his family:

„Kreis von Ländereien . . . die er um die Waldstätte herumschlingt:

Zug	Unter Schweiz	Einsiedeln
Luzern	Uri	Glarus
Entlibucher	Wald Ursern	Disentis

Um diese kostspieligen Käufe zu machen, muß er alle seine Länder schwer beschatzen und besteuern."

874-5. The poet follows Tschudi and Müller, who state that Albrecht forced the people to attend the weekly markets in Lucerne and Zug, upon which he levied duties, while on the traffic by pack-horse over the Gotthard-pass he levied tolls. The courts were his, because he appointed the judges.

881. **fein Kaifer,** i.e. no Emperor not a member of the Habsburg family.

882. **Was ift zu geben auf,** 'what reliance is to be placed on.'

884. **des Adlers** = des Reichsadlers, the symbol of the Empire.

885. The mortgaging and alienating from the Empire of rights, domains, and offices, cities and countries, was frequent and disastrous. Adolf von Nassau mortgaged the Abbey of Essen to the Prince Elector of Cologne, and other ecclesiastical foundations to the Archbishop of Trèves. Ludwig the Bavarian mortgaged in 1315 the free city Eger to Johann of Bohemia, and the city was never thereafter redeemed.

891. Prose **doch, fich um den mächtigen Erbherrn wohl verdient machen,** 'to deserve well at the hands of the powerful hereditary lord.'

892. **Heißt** = ift.

889–892. The thought is: the emperors are unable permanently to reward services, since the office passes from one family to another by election, but whoever serves well the hereditary power of some one family, sows seed for future harvests.

893. **Willft,** 'do you claim.'

896–7. The disposition of Lucerne we know from Pfeiffer's words at the opening of Sc. 2 of Act I. Lucerne had been sold in 1291 by the Abbey of Murbach in Alsace to the Habsburg family.

900. 'forbid the hunting of the higher game, both bird and beast.'

901. **Schlagbaum,** 'toll-bar,' 'toll-gate.'

903. **Mit unfrer Armut,** i.e. with money extorted from us, poor as we are.

904. **Mit unferm Blute,** i.e. as soldiers in Austrian service.

906. **wohlfeiler.** The price is the same in either case, but Freiheit is an infinitely greater good than Knechtschaft.

909. The Baron calls Rudenz „Knabe" in return for the latter's scornful „Ein Volk der Hirten."

911. **Favenz,** German form of Faenza, Fayence, a city in Italy a little southwest of Ravenna. It was conquered in 1240–41 by the Emperor Friedrich II., to whose help the Forest Cantons sent 600 men, in return for a charter (referred to in the next scene) and payment in advance. The presence of the Baron is Schiller's invention, possible because of his increased age ; see p. 165.

919. **zu,** 'by.'

920. **Das** and **des,** both emphatic as demonstrative pronouns, 'this.'

927. **lang' nicht mehr,** 'not for a long time now.'

934. **der Liebe Seile,** 'cords of love,' Biblical, Hosea xi. 4.

935. **Fräulein,** in the original sense of 'noble young lady'; so also **Ritterfräulein,** l. 938, which can hardly be rendered differently.

942. **deiner Unschuld,** 'for your innocence,' i.e. for you in your innocence (simplicity, inexperience, unsuspecting guilelessness). Cf. ll. 1662–1672.

944. **erhalten** = 'zurückhalten,' 'check,' 'restrain.'

948. **strebend** modifies **Jugend,** l. 947.

958. This line has six feet.

The second portion of the conversation, which is the climax of the scene, turns on the thoughts of liberty and native land. The noble patriarch strives to lead Rudenz to appreciation of the value of these grand realities and ideals. His solemn rebukes and exhortations Attinghausen concludes by disclosing his knowledge that the goal of Rudenz' mistaken efforts is Bertha and her love, and that Rudenz is but a blind tool of Austrian plans.

Attinghausen's final monologue, in lament and in prophecy, is most pathetic. But the question comes to us : May not the "new" era be a better era ?

Act II. Scene 2.

* **Eine Wiese,** the **Rütli,** see note to l. 727.
* **Mondregenbogen,** 'lunar rainbow.'
. * For the names see pp. 165–168.

959. **nach** = nachgefolgt in the sense of the imperative.

960. **Den Fels,** i.e. the Selisberg beneath which the Rütli lies. **Seli** is the diminutive of **See.**

* **Windlichtern,** 'torches,' Fackeln, die im Winde nicht verlöschen.

962. **Landmann,** here = Landsmann, 'man of the Canton.'

964. **Feuerwächter,** rare for prose Nachtwächter.

965. **Selisberg,** here referring to a little village on the height of the same name.

966. **Mettenglöcklein,** 'matin-bell.' The line has six feet.

967. **Schwyzerland,** 'Schwyz,' the Canton.

969. **Gehn, zünden an,** subjunctive as imperative.

984. **weit umgehen,** 'make a wide circuit.' In this sense um'gehen is a separable compound with accent on the first syllable, although the rhythm accents here the second syllable.

985. **Kundschaft,** 'spies,' collective abstract singular for concrete plural Kundschafter.

986. **Wort,** for prose Losungswort, or die Losung.

* **nach der Tiefe,** see note on Tiefe, *24.

* **drei andere Landleute.** This would seem to be a mistake of the poet in writing, or a misprint, for vier, since otherwise only ten men of Schwyz are present, including Stauffacher, and there would be only thirty-two in all, in place of the thirty-three expressly mentioned after line 1097.

992. Note the strength of Stauffacher's leadership in repressing at once all personal revengefulness and thus giving to the conference the character of calm deliberation.

995. **für gemeine Sach',** for für die gemeine Sache, on account of the meter.

998. **Surennen,** here with accent on the second syllable, although the form in general use is Surenen, name of a mountain ridge and pass between Uri and Unterwalden, the pass leading from Altorf to Engelberg.

1000. **Lämmergeier,** 'läm'mergeir,' see this word in Webster's Dictionary. The statement that this bird is now extinct in Switzerland is without foundation.

1001. **Alpentrift,** '(Alpine) pasture,' see note on Matten, *3.

1002. **Engelberg,** name of a valley, a village, and a monastery of the Canton Unterwalden.

1004. **mit der Gletscher Milch** = mit der Milch der Gletscher, for mit milchweißem Gletscherwasser. The water flowing from beneath glaciers is very often whitish, because carrying pulverized stone in suspension.

1005. **Runsen** (die Runse), in origin an Allemannic word, for Rinnsal, 'channels,' 'gullies'; now rather freely used in literature.

1006. **einsamen,** because the herdsmen must long before this have gone down from the highest pastures.

1011. **Ehrfurcht** is object.

1013. **Entrüstet** modifies as predicate **Seelen.**

1014. **Ob,** see note on l. 277.

1017. This comparison was suggested by Ebel's observation of a certain regularity in the winds over all lakes that lie in the direction of transverse valleys at the foot of the Alps on either the northern or the southern side.

1021. **tragen,** for prose ertragen.

1034. **mir die** = meine.
Vettern, 'relatives,' cf. l. 659.

1036. **auf fremdem Stroh,** for auf dem Stroh von Fremden.

1038. Cf. l. 2345.

1042. **Krümmen,** on account of the meter for prose Krümmungen.

1043. In translation insert 'but that' before ich spähte. This idiomatic expression, quite common in German, is ordinarily explained as a confusion of two constructions: (1) Jedes Thal, wie versteckt es auch war, ich spähte es aus; and (2) Kein Thal war so versteckt, daß ich es nicht ausspähte.

1053. **mit Herz und Mund,** 'with heart and tongue (lit. mouth),' i.e. in feeling (thought) and in word, secretly and openly, about equivalent to mit Herz und Hand.

1056. **Roßberg,** see note to l. 77.
Sarnen. The village of this name lies at the northern end of Lake Sarnen in Unterwalden; on a hill near the village stood the castle of Beringer of Landenberg.

1068. **gerechten,** here about = 'good,' von rechter Art, reblich, bieber.

1072. **Mei(e)r,** here to be taken as a proper family name. The word means literally 'steward,' 'manager,' 'overseer'; and since this office in the case of large estates often became hereditary, the name of the office easily became a family name. In origin the word is a loan-word from Latin *major*, from which come also Eng. major, major-dome, and mayor.

1075. Struthan von Winkelried had distinguished himself in 1240 before Fayence (Favenz). Having thereafter been exiled for murder, he is said by tradition to have secured permission to return to his country, through promising to kill a dragon living near *Wyler* (Weiler = hamlet, small village). He slew the monster, but was poisoned to death by its blood. See also n. to Dramatis Personæ.

1076. **Weiler,** precisely Obweiler, in a valley near Alpnach not far from Rossberg, where the cave of the dragon is still pointed out.

1077. **Strauß,** for usual prose Kampf.

1078. **hinter,** 'beyond,' i.e. in Obwalden.

Klosterleute vom Engelberg = Leute (people, vassals) des Klosters vom Engelberg.

1080. **eigne** (owned) **Leute** = Leibeigne, 'serfs.' In general the serfs of a religious community had better conditions than those of a lay lord.

1082. **sind ... wohl berufen,** 'are of good repute,' for prose stehen ... in gutem Rufe.

1084. **Mit seinem Leibe pflichtig** ('bound,' 'subject'), 'in servitude,' 'a serf,' = leibeigen.

Erden. Formerly many feminine nouns of this declension took the ending in the gen. and dat. sg., like the masculines.

1086. **Reding.** The Reding family is notable in Swiss history; J. von Müller mentions Itel Reding as Landammann of Schwyz early in the fifteenth century; in Schiller's own time Aloys von Reding was a leader of his Canton Schwyz in the struggles against the French, 1798–1802, and from 1803 Landammann.

Altlandammann = 'ex-landammann,' 'former chief-magistrate.' In Switzerland alt⸗ is thus prefixed to the designation of an office, a profession, a calling, to indicate that it is now given up, no longer held or followed; Altratsherr, Alt⸗bürgermeister, Altapotheker.

1091. **das Horn von Uri.** The battle-horn of Uri, supposed to be made of a horn of the 'ure-ox,' Aurochse, now extinct, from which word in its old form Ur(ochse) tradition derives the name of Uri. The specially appointed bearer and blower of this horn was called der Stier von Uri, cf. l. 2847.

1096. **Sigrist,** 'sacristan,' 'sexton,' Alemannic for ordinary Küster or Mesner.

1097. The reason is given in ll. 442–5. Baumgarten can never forget Tell; cf. l. 1434.

1102. **sonnenscheuen,** 'sun-shunning.'

1106. **Laßt's gut sein!** 'Never mind!'

1106-7. **Was ... Sonnen,** an adaptation of the German proverb, one of whose forms is Es ist nichts so fein gesponnen, Es kommt ans Licht der Sonnen.

1107. **Sonnen** is gen. singular, cf. n. l. 1084.

The word "imposing" has been given as a characteristic epithet to this scene, the introduction of which ends here. It is imposing in its scenery, in the symbolized presence of the whole people, in the moral forces that control it, and in the decisions in which it culminates. The scenery is as it were the nocturnal counterpart of that on which the curtain first rose. Solemn grandeur, silence and repose, mysterious yet natural—how harmonious with the human action of which it is the ground! The double rainbow is no more unique in nature than is in human history the event of this night.

This Rütli-scene is a so-called ensemble-scene. The confederates stand for the whole people (ll. 1119–20); the character of these representatives is our warrant that the great national idea will move the masses also; nor is there any one overshadowingly prominent hero present. The unity of the meeting is the organic unity of three in one. Within each of the three groups two

characters are in some degree prominent: Stauffacher
and Reding, Fürst and Rösselmann, Melchthal and
Meier von Sarnen.   The real leader in the business of
the assembly is Stauffacher.

Melchthal's report deepens the impression produced
by the presence of these more than thirty men. We learn
through him that all the people of Unterwalden stand
back of him and his ten companions, and what we know
of this Canton we infer to be true of the others.   The
recital also characterizes further Melchthal himself and
the Swiss people.   The little scene before the arrival
of the men of Uri displays the power of this popular
movement, since in it the freeman and the serf, no less
than contestants at law, are united.

1108. Cf. l. 3232.

Eidgenoffen, 'confederates.' This word did not enter until
rather late into the official language of the Swiss, although
in a document of 1291 there is mention of *conjurati et com-
provinciales;* not until 1315 do we have eitgenoze.   The present name of the Federation is Die Schweizerische Eidgenossenschaft.

1109. Landsgemeinde, see note on l. 665.

1111. tagen, 'hold a diet,' 'hold a meeting, 'deliberate.'
Tagen in this sense = einen Tag halten, auf einen bestimmten Tag
zusammen kommen und sich beraten.

1113. ungesetzlich, rather 'unconstitutional' than 'illegal.'
It was not a legally constituted Landsgemeinde, in three respects : (1) they were only thirty-three self-appointed men,
l. 1119; (2) they met by night, l. 1118; (3) the old statute-
books and records were not present, l. 1121.

1118. Ist es gleich Nacht = Obgleich es Nacht ist.   Same use of
inversion in ll. 1119 and 1121.

1123 ff. For such a Landsgemeinde the Landammann took his
seat upon a pulpit-like platform a few feet high, the 'Stuhl,'
on either side of which a large battle-sword was placed
upright ; by his side stood the Weibel, 'beadles' or 'sum-
moners,' and the clerk, before whom lay the great 'Land-
buch,' in which all the action was recorded ; the assembled
citizens formed a great semi-circle, 'Ring,' before him.

1126. **Weibel** is the name given in Switzerland to the servants of magistrates, judges, and other officials. The term is obsolete elsewhere.

1127. **dreie,** rare old form of **drei**.

1130. **frei** = freiwillig.

1132. **Die** is rel. pron.

1134. **Römerzüge,** the processions or journeys in state of the German King and Emperor-elect to Rome in order to receive there imperial coronation from the Pope. All members of the Empire were expected to be represented, and thus also the Swiss, cf. ll. 1230–1.

uns is dative.

1136. Tradition makes **Schwyz** to have been first occupied by settlers, and derives therefrom the collective name of the whole country and people, **Schweiz** being but a later form of **Schwyz**; cf. ll. 1166–1202, particularly 1187 ff.

1141. **wacker,** 'good,' 'worthy,' 'excellent.'

1142. **eigner,** see note on l. 1080.

1145. **des Tages Haupt,** 'chief (or president) of the diet.'

1148. The prose order would be **bei den ew'gen Sternen droben**.

The main action of the scene begins at line 1108 with the organization of the Assembly. This is not a mere external formality, but a form necessary to the nature of the meeting. As representatives of the whole people they have the right to use the lawful forms of the Assembly of any individual canton. What they are seeking is only right and justice, and these forms are our warrant that the foundations of law and justice will not be abandoned.

1152. **Geisterstunde,** 'hour when spirits walk,' in a loose, general sense, since we know the time to be long after midnight.

1155. It was in order for each speaker to step forward within the ring and face the presiding officer.

1156–7. Cf. n. l. 658.

Väter, gen. plur.; cf. l. 1248.

1153. **Ob** = obgleich.

1162. **in den Liedern,** the so-called East Frisian Lay, of the seventeenth century, current in the Haslithal. Schiller follows Müller's prose abstract.

1167. **hinten im Lande,** colloquial, 'far back,' 'far away.' Sweden is not named, but is unmistakably described.

1168. **Nach Mitternacht** (zu) = gegen Norden.

1172. For prose **Und es zogen aus u.f.w.**

1173. **Heerzug,** 'marching army (host).' **Mittagsonne,** for usual **Mittagsonne,** 'southern sun.'

1174. **sich schlagend,** 'fighting (or forcing) their way.'

1178. **die Muotta** (two syllables, uo practically as English *oo*, cf. **Kuoni,** n. p. 167) empties into the lake near Brunnen.

1181. **warten,** in archaic construction with gen., 'to tend,' 'take care of.'

1190. **auszuroden,** see note on l. 727.

1191. **g(e)nügen that** = genügte.

1192. **hinüber,** that is over the Lake.

1193. **Zum schwarzen Berg,** the Brünig (**Brauneck**), between Unterwalden and Bern.

Weißland, so called because of its snow and glaciers, the Oberhasli valley of the Bernese Oberland, south of the Brünig.

1195. In the Canton Wallis (Valais) French is spoken, and in Tessin (Ticino) Italian.

1196. **Stanz,** the chief town of Nid dem Wald; see n. l. 493.

1198. **gedenk,** poetic for eingedenk.

1199. **fremden Stämmen,** i.e. Alemanni and Burgundians; see Introd. pp. xxxv, xli–xliii.

1200. **In Mitte,** arises from **in der Mitte** under the influence of inmitten.

Here ends the first of the three chief divisions of the transactions of the organized Assembly. These divisions correspond to the three themes of the oath pronounced by Rösselmann, ll. 1448–1453: union, liberty, self-help with faith in God.

The representatives of the three peoples are united in a common aim; but this union has a natural foundation, in that the three are one people in origin. To quicken the consciousness of this underlying unity is Stauffacher's object in his narration of the immigration of the Schwyzer.

1205. Die andern Völker, the people in the other cantons, of different descent.

1208. Saſſe, 'settler,' 'tenant,' here for Hinterſaſſe, 'vassal,' 'bondman,' which comes from the older German phrase hinter einem ſitzen, 'to be settled under a lord.' The Hinterſaſſe was not a freeman ; he had to be represented by his lord and to render certain service to his lord.

fremde Pflichten = Pflichten gegen Fremde, or von Fremden auferlegte Pflichten.

1213–1215. Freiwillig, according to the view of the older historians, who understood certain phrases in the charter of Friedrich II., 1240, as if the Schwyzer constituted a community apart from and by the side of the German Empire and had voluntarily entered into union with the Empire.

1218. wo = bei dem (relative).

ſchöpfen = finden, 'obtain,' 'get.'

1222. welſchen, Italian.

1224. gelobt, from geloben.

1227. Knechts = eigenen Mannes ; 'serf,' 'bondman.'

1228. Heribann, archaic form of Heerbann, 'army-summons,' the call to arms originally of all freemen able to bear arms, later of vassals to put their forces at the service of the Emperor.

1229. ſeine = des Kaiſers, to whom ihm in l. 1231 also refers.

1230. gewappnet, for present prose gewaffnet.

1234. Der höchſte Blutbann, 'the highest criminal jurisdiction,' involving capital punishment, belonged originally only to the Emperor and King in Germany, unless expressly conferred by him upon an inferior lord.

allein, here limits Blutbann ; i.e. only in this one thing did the Emperor participate in their government.

1236. That he might be impartial, and that no concession might be made to imperial authority in any other regard.

1244. **Kaiser,** Heinrich V. (1106–1125 A.D.), who in 1114 at Basel rendered a decision in favor of the monastery.

1245. **Pfaffen,** not at all contemptuous as now.

1246. **Gotteshaus,** 'monastery.' The story here told is taken from Müller. Gerhard, Abbot of Einsiedeln, cf. n. l. 519, in the year 1114 at a diet in Basel accused the people of Schwyz of pasturing their cattle on the land of the monastery; for the increasing herds of the subjects of the monks in wandering out met the herds of people of Schwyz on lands which the latter had inherited from their ancestors. The Abbot appealed to a charter of the Emperor Henry II. in the year 1018, which granted to the Abbey the **herrenlose Wüste,** l. 1250; that there were settlers there, the Emperor had not known and the predecessor of Gerhard had not disclosed. Henry V. decided against the Schwyzer, but they held their ground, and they were undisturbed until 1144, when Konrad III. threatened them with the ban of the Empire, and they declared their withdrawal from the Empire, to which they returned in 1152 on invitation of Friedrich I.

1248. **beweidet** (hatten), 'had grazed over.'

1249. **herfürzog,** archaic for **hervorzog**; cf. ll. 2211 and 2230.

1258. **dem fremden Knecht** = dem österreichischen Landvogt, i.e. Gessler and his like; so also in l. 1271.

1264. There are many legends of dragons in Switzerland, cf. l. 1075 and note.

1266. That is by clearing the land and making it arable.

1269. **Steg,** 'bridge,' cf. n. l. 25.   [xxxv. xli–xliii.

1270. **tausendjährig,** as a round number.   See Introd. pp.

1272. Cf. l. 1626.

1277–8. **greift ... Himmel,** 'with confident spirit he reaches up to heaven.'

1282. **Urstand** = Urzustand, i.e. the original state of individual maintenance of one's rights, of self-defense, by force if necessary.

1284. **Zum letzten Mittel,** 'as the last means.'

1285. **verfangen,** 'avail.'

1286. **der Güter höchstes** = das höchste der Güter, 'our liberty.'

1294-5. First motion made by Rösselmann, not seriousl;·, but to test the general feeling and to bring the confederates to a final declaration of their will to remain free.

1296. **wir ... ſchwören,** an elliptical expression, with ſollen or ſollten understood ; so also ll. 1299 and 1300.

1308. **bar** = verluſtig, 'deprived of,' 'stripped of.'

The second chief division of the transactions of the Assembly extends from l. 1205 through l. 1313. Its theme is liberty. Stauffacher aims to guide his countrymen to the determination never to accept the yoke of Austria. Their resistance must be the more quick, intense, and lasting, in proportion as their liberty shall appear to be a previously unquestioned national possession. Their right to liberty Stauffacher therefore proves from history, and that their forefathers even created this habitation out of the wilderness. The right of resistance is plain, for the governors by their lawlessness have overthrown the reign of law and order, and brought back the state of nature, wherein the individual, relying only on his own strength, has recourse to self-defense.

1317. **wohl gar ... nicht,** 'probably indeed ... not,' 'very probably not.'

1318-1320. Second motion, made by Reding ; it is also rejected.

1323. **Nun iſt's an euch** = Nun iſt die Reihe an euch, 'Now it's your turn.'

1324. **Rheinfeld(en),** a town in Aargau on the left bank of the Rhine, and on the road from Basel to Zürich.

Pfalz, here = 'residence' or 'court,' not necessarily a palace.

1326. See note on l. 911, and Introd. p. xlvii.

1329. **ſchwäb(i)ſch,** adj. from Schwaben (Swabia), 'Swabian.'

1330. **Die,** demonstrative for personal 'they.'

1335. **ſonſt einmal wohl,** 'at some other time doubtless.'

1337. **Hanſen,** obsolete accus. of Hans, the familiar abbreviation of Johannes; Duke John of Swabia, nephew of Emperor Albrecht. See p. 169.

1338. **Erfer**(fenſter), ‘bay-window.’

1339. **Herrn,** usually **Herren.** See l. 2961.

1343. **hinterhält** = zurückhält.

1344. **ſein Mütterliches** (Erbe, or Erbteil, or Erbgut).   He claimed the County of Kyburg which the Emperor Rudolf had given to his mother, while his paternal inheritance was the Dukedom of Swabia, cf. l. 2954.

1345. **habe** and **wäre,** subjunctive of indirect statement. **habe ſeine Jahre voll** = ſei volljährig.

1346. Cf. l. 3205.

1347. **Was ... Beſcheid,** ‘What answer did he receive?’

In the third and last main division of the doings of the meeting, the theme is self-help. Stauffacher pointed out before that the way of violence is the only means to the preservation of their liberty. But any people will shrink from a violent uprising, the more it is accustomed to respect law and order. Hunn's recital convinces the confederates and us that active, even violent self-defense is necessary, because it alone is possible.

1357. Cf. Mark xii. 17: **Gebet dem Kaiſer, was des Kaiſers iſt,** and also l. 1364.

1358. **Wer einen Herrn hat** = ‘whoever is vassal (holds a fief) of a foreign lord.’

1359. **Ich trage ... zu Lehen,** ‘I hold ... in fief.’

1360. **fahret fort,** indicative as imperative; so also in ll. 1362 and 1364.

1361. **ſteure,** ‘pay tribute,’ or taxes.

Rappersweil for present **Rapperſchwyl,** town in the Canton St. Gallen on Lake Zürich.

1363. ‘To the Great Lady at Zürich I am bound by oath.’ The reference seems to be most direct to the powerful abbess of the **Frauenmünſter** (nunnery) at Zürich, though it may be to the convent itself as bearing the name of the Virgin Mary, ‘Our Lady,’ French *Notre-Dame.* This was founded and endowed by Ludwig the German in 853 for his two daughters.

1367–69. Third motion, made by Fürst, and accepted.

1373. **ſtaatsklug,** 'in a politic way,' 'as a prudent statesman.'

In the person of the aged Walther Fürst the people of their own accord set limits to their rising. Such self-determination is most noble.

1381. **Iſt bald geſprochen,** see note on Iſt bald geſagt, l. 57.

1382. **uns,** dat. of interest = gegen uns.

1385. **Roßberg und Sarnen,** see notes on ll. 77 and 1056.

1389. **ſind't,** see note on l. 133.

1391. **Twing,** see note on l. 360.

1394. **Das darf uns Uri bieten!** lit., 'May Uri offer us this (insult)!' = 'Shall we suffer this from Uri!'

1395. **Bei eurem Eide,** the oath of allegiance to the constitution, which every Swiss citizen had to take not later than his sixteenth year, in order to be enfranchised. Schiller read in Ebel that every Swiss readily yielded to an appeal to this oath.

1397. **weiſen,** for verweiſen, zurechtweiſen.

1400. **Feſt des Herrn,** 'Festival of our Lord' = Chriſtfeſt, 'Christmas.' This date is given by some of the chroniclers, while others say New Year's Day.

1401. **bringt's die Sitte mit** (ſich), 'it is customary,' or 'custom requires.'

Saſſen, here = Inſaſſen, Einwohner, 'tenants' or 'dwellers,' not as in l. 1208.

1402. **Schloß,** i.e. Sarnen.

1407. **kommt** = darf kommen.

1408. **Zunächſt,** 'close by' or 'at first,' 'to begin with.'
der große Haufe, 'the main body.'

1410. **Ermächtiget,** for bemächtigt (haben).

1414. **Dirne,** here in good sense, = Mädchen, Dienerin.

1416. **Leiter** = Strickleiter.

1417. **Bin ich,** condition; **zieh' ich,** conclusion.

1418. **daß (es) verſchoben werde,** 'that there be postponement.'

1419. **Mehr** = Mehrheit der Stimmen, 'majority,' in this sense a long-used and frequent word in Switzerland, while elsewhere not so fixed and current.

In the debate on the execution of the plan the situation of Unterwalden is essentially different from that of
the two other cantons, because of the two strongholds
Rossberg and Sarnen, while in Uri the Keep is not
yet finished, and in Schwyz there is none at all. Hence
the difference of opinion and the decision to postpone
the rising.

1421-2. Cf. l. 747 and note. Very likely immediately
suggested by a passage in Scheuchzer: "Another and a
political advantage which the Swiss have from their mountains consists in this, that by means of fire, discharging of
cannon, and other similar signals, the so-called $\mathfrak{Hochwachten}$,
passing from one mountain to another, this whole nation
can come to arms within a day or two." Schiller uses the
word $\mathfrak{Hochwacht}$ in l. 1441.

1422-3. $\mathfrak{der\ Landsturm} \ldots \mathfrak{Landes,}$ 'the summons, calling
the country to arms, will be given quickly in the chief town
of every canton.'

1425. $\mathfrak{sich\ begeben,}$ with the gen. $= \mathfrak{aufgeben, verzichten\ auf.}$

1428. $\mathfrak{Stand} = \mathfrak{Widerstand, Kampf.}$ This mention of Gessler
is important in the development of the plot.

1433. $\mathfrak{halsgefährlich} = \mathfrak{lebensgefährlich.}$

1435. $\mathfrak{in\ die\ Schanze\ schlagen} = \mathfrak{aufs\ Spiel\ setzen,}$ 'stake,'
'risk,' lit. 'throw it into the chance.' $\mathfrak{Schanze,}$ in this sense,
is the French *chance* borrowed, which is itself derived from
the Latin *cadentia*, 'fall' (of the dice).

1437. $\mathfrak{Die\ Zeit\ bringt\ Rat.}$ The German proverb is, $\mathfrak{Kommt}$
$\mathfrak{Zeit, kommt\ Rat.}$

The Ammann cuts off, perhaps not unreasonably,
protracted discussion of Gessler's case. The confederates, under Stauffacher's guidance, have done all that
the most careful deliberation and counselling can do;
they cannot foresee all the possible difficulties in
execution. Something must be left to presence of mind
and quick decision in the moment of greatest need.
Tell is preeminent in these qualities.

$\mathfrak{erwartet\ u.s.w.,}$ cf. ll. 190-2, 492, 1458-9.

1439. Note the word-play in **nächtlich** and **tagen,** and cf. note on l. IIII.

1441. **Hochwacht,** cf. note on ll. 1421–22.

* **Sammlung,** ‘ meditation ,’ ‘ devotion.’

1448. **einzig,** not **einig,** to which it is often changed in popular quotation of this line.

* **mit erhobenen drei Fingern,** a symbol of the Holy Trinity.

1451. **den Tod,** obj. of **wollen,** l. 1450, in parallel construction with **sein** and **leben.**

1455. **Freundschaft,** cf. l. 659 and note.

die Genoßfame = **die Genossenschaft,** ‘ community’; as a collective noun = **Genossen.** Uri is even now divided politically into **Genossenschaften.**

1458–9. Cf. ll. 190–2, 492, 1437.

1464–5. Since every act of private vengeance would diminish the total collective guilt to be avenged in common.

* **mit einem prachtvollen Schwung,** ‘ with a stately movement.’

The scene and the act close with rhyme.

The swearing of the oath of confederation is the solemn conclusion. Moved by the grand spectacle of nature’s daily awakening—a sensuous spectacle not inferior in sublimity to the moral spectacle we have just witnessed—all stand as if in prayer. A religious consecration rests upon the whole proceeding. The sun of liberty is indeed rising, after the night of resignation to tyranny. The alliance of three individual men at the end of Act I has grown into a confederation of the three cantons with definite aims.

In construction Act II is very unlike Act I, in which all four scenes were somewhat closely linked together. Here the two scenes have no formal connection, unless we find it in contrast. Scene 1 is the exposition of the Nobles-plot ; Scene 2 is the climax of the Yeomen-plot ; the Tell-plot is not taken up at all. The time of Scene 1 is early morning, of Scene 2 the middle of the night. Scene 1 shows us in Attinghausen the nobles of an age now passing away, in Rudenz the nobles of the new age now opening. Rudenz is typical of the young nobles in their temptations and dangers from Austria. To these he at first yields, and the scene leaves us in fear lest the union of the nation may not include its young men of noble birth. While thus in Scene 1 the danger becomes visible which from within threatens the liberty of Switzerland, Scene 2 displays the concentration of the power of the yeomanry (at least) to protect this liberty. On the one hand an impending breach and a craving for innovation; on the other, impressive unity and the fixed resolve to preserve the old order. On both sides that bond is loosened which heretofore has joined nobles and yeomen. Can this bond—perhaps in a new form—be renewed? The final answer to this question, and to the questions of the fear which Scene 1 inspires, is given in Act IV. Scene 2.

SEAL OF SCHWYZ, 1291.

ACT III.

ARGUMENT.—The home of Tell at Bürglen is the *first* scene. That their two young boys delight to play with the bow and to sing of hunting leads his wife Hedwig to speak of the anxious fear which she, as wife and mother, has of the hunter's life. But there is a foreboding of greater evil which she cannot refrain from urgently expressing, when Tell prepares to go to Altorf; for in Altorf is their enemy Gessler. To no avail does Tell try to console her, as he sets out for the house of Walther Fürst in Altorf, taking with him his older boy Wilhelm and his cross-bow.

The *second* scene is a meeting, in the seclusion of the forest, of Rudenz and Bertha, as they are separated for a few moments from the chase. In mutual explanation of their sentiments, Bertha opens the eyes of Rudenz to his weak faithlessness to his country, wins him back from his fancied Austrian ambitions, and gains him for the cause of Swiss liberty.

In the *third* scene, at Altorf, the hat on the pole is before us, guarded by two soldiers, who complain that the people show it no reverence. Tell comes talking with his boy and inadvertently fails to do obeisance to the hat. He is arrested by the soldiers, and in the midst of the tumult which this new outrage causes among his friends and those of the populace who are present, Gessler enters. The opportunity for him to humiliate and crush Tell, whom he hates for his independence, is at hand. He seizes it and demands, in spite of the entreaties of the Swiss and the remonstrances of Rudenz, that Tell shoot an apple from the head of his son Walther, threatening both father and son with instant death if Tell refuse. After torturous conflict with himself in mind and heart, Tell composes himself and makes the shot successfully, to Gessler's complete surprise and consternation. But Tell had placed a second arrow in readiness, wherewith to shoot Gessler dead in case he missed the apple and harmed his son. By deceiving Tell, Gessler leads him to confess this purpose, and then has him arrested and led off to imprisonment. By these cruel outrages and the loss of Tell, the Swiss are plunged into dull despair for the time being, while Tell alone has confident hope and trust in God.

SCENE I.

This act and the next fall on November 19th. This scene at Bürglen begins about noon, since Tell reaches Altorf, only about a mile distant, early in the afternoon.

* Zimmerart, 'carpenter's axe.'

* Hedwig, see note p. 168.

* Walther und Wilhelm, see note p. 168.

Walther's song, the Schützenlied, is very popular in Germany. It was set to music in 1804 by B. A. Weber.

1469. 'in the early morning light.'

1471. Der Weih (or die Weihe). In the dialects all large birds of prey have this name; here probably the 'eagle' is meant.

1474. das Weite, 'the wide expanse.'

1477. Was da, 'whatever.'

kreucht und fleugt, archaic for kriecht and fliegt.

1478. Mach', 'mend,' 'fix.'

1481. was = wer; neuter used for collective indefinite. Cf. note on l. 356.

1484. Schutz und Trutz, see note to ll. 741-2.

1485. keiner (von den beiden Knaben).

1486. zu Hause, i.e. as herdsman rather than as hunter.

1489-90. Cf. the lines in Goethe's *Faust*, Part II :

> ' He only earns his freedom and existence
> Who daily conquers them anew.'

1493. Knechte, 'boys,' or ' men,' in the sense of servants; possibly Tell's own, as he may have considerable possessions.

1494. Wagefahrten, 'daring expeditions,' formed after the analogy of Wagestück.

1499. Fehlsprung thun, 'making a false leap,' 'missing your leap'; cf. Fehltritt and l. 649.

1500. **rückspringen** = zurückspringen, but occurs only in forms written as one word.

1501. **Windlawine.** The distinction between this sort of an avalanche, which is also called Staublawine, and the Schlag=lawine (l. 1781) is made clear by the following extract from Scheuchzer: "There are in general two sorts of ava-lanches. The one is called Windlawine, in part because they are often aroused by the wind, which moves the freshly fallen snow along from high places and thus occasions its fall, and in part because of their effects, since they pass swiftly along like a wind, and by their fall produce so strong a wind that this overthrows everything even at a distance, breaks in two the largest trees, etc. The second sort has the name Schloß= und Schlag=Lawinen, because they overwhelm everything they meet not so much by the wind moving with them as by their own weight, and not only con-sist of snow, to wit, old firmly compacted snow, but en-velop also trees, rocks, stones, yes, the very ground be-neath, drag these along with them, all-destroying." Cf. the extract from Symonds, *Our Life in the Swiss High-lands*, Appendix, pp. 295–300.

1502. **Firn,** see note to l. 38.

1511. **Fahr,** archaic and poetic for Gefahr.

1513. **auf Jahr und Tag,** 'for a year and a day' = 'many a long day,' 'long enough.'

1515. **zu dem Vater,** i.e. her father, Walther Fürst.

1517. **Es spinnt sich etwas,** 'some web is being spun.'

1525. **Den Unterwaldner** = Baumgarten; cf. l. 151 ff.

1535. **nicht,** see note on nicht, l. 254.

1539. **Ehni,** Alemannic diminutive of Ahn (compare Wälti from Walther, Etti from Att = Vater, Muetti = Mutter), meaning properly Altervater, 'great-grandfather,' but here Großvater.

1544. Compare the proverb, Thue recht und scheue niemand.

1545. **Die recht thun, eben die,** 'Those who do right, just them,'

1548 ff. This incident of the previous meeting of Tell and Gessler was invented by the poet in order to explain Gessler's hate, and also to show that Tell is not a murderer for personal vengeance.

1549. $\mathfrak{Gründe}$, 'gorges,' 'ravines.'

1550. The valley of the Schächen, Tell's native valley, extends from Altorf about twelve miles eastward.

1551. $\mathfrak{Felsensteig}$ = felsiger Steig.

1558. $\mathfrak{Herre}$, older form of $\mathfrak{Herr}$.

$\mathfrak{mein\ ansichtig\ ward}$, 'caught sight of me.'

1560. $\mathfrak{gebüßt}$ (hatte), see note on l. 565.

1561. $\mathfrak{Gewehr}$, in its original meaning of weapon, in general, here applied to the crossbow.

1562. $\mathfrak{verblaßt}$', used in the eighteenth century without distinction from erblaſſen whose present sense it has in this place. Verblaſſen tends now to be restricted to a permanent loss of color and so to be used of things only.

1563. $\mathfrak{versagten\ ihm}$ (den Dienſt), 'failed him.'

1565. $\mathfrak{sein}$, gen. of er.

1567. $\mathfrak{keinen\ armen}$ = nicht einmal den geringſten, ' not the slightest,' ' not a miserable (or sorry or pitiful).'

1574. $\mathfrak{dort\ weg}$ = von dort weg.

1575. $\mathfrak{Was\ fällt\ dir\ ein?}$ ' What are you thinking of?'

1577. Just because she can give no ground for her anxiety, she regards it as a sure presentiment of coming danger.

1581. $\mathfrak{Wälti}$, abbreviation of $\mathfrak{Walther}$.

1582. $\mathfrak{auch}$ = aber auch.

This scene makes us acquainted with Tell's home and individual life, while in relation to the third scene of this act it explains Tell's presence in Altorf with his son and his crossbow, and makes clear the origin and intensity of Gessler's hate of Tell. It has two main parts, the first ending with l. 1514.

The first part opens as an idyllic picture of family life. The song and the playing with the bow show on what the boys' minds are bent. This turn of their minds is the father's delight, the mother's sorrow. For here too Tell is above all the free-spirited, self-reliant man, dexterously able to do for himself. He intends that his

children shall also learn to do everything possible, since
the more a man individually can do, the more independent is he. Hedwig's character is in strong yet
beautiful contrast with Tell's and also with Gertrud
Stauffacher's. Hedwig, a loving mother and anxiously
tender wife, whose home is rightly her world, typifies
the great multitude of Swiss women whose most sacred
interests, whose peace and happiness in the life of the
home are bound up with the freedom of the land.
Gertrud, of broad mind and knowledge, and childless,
is the exceptional woman, who leads and who is able
to rejoice in the prospect of sacrificing herself for her
country. In contrast with Tell, Hedwig desires a calm
evenly flowing life, he a life that is every day a new
battle to be fought and won; she knows only the dangers of the hunter's life, he the means of safety, vigorous use of his powers, confidence in God and himself.

The second part of the scene clouds with foreboding
the sunshine of its opening. Hedwig mistrusts the
purpose of Tell's going, his preparations, his destination, his taking Walther along. Her fear of a collision
with Gessler Tell tries to dispel by means of two reasons which only confirm her in it. With feminine intuition she forebodes evil, and in the touching picture
with which the scene ends, our hearts are with her
while in thought we follow Tell to Altorf.

Throughout this scene also Tell uses many proverb-
like sententious expressions, yet his description of his
meeting Gessler is fluent and detailed. Thus are characterized his habits of thought and speech.

ACT III. SCENE 2.

* **Staubbäche,** 'brooks dashing in spray.' Staubbäche are
waterfalls whose water in its long downward plunge is divided by the resistance of the air into fine spray ('dust').
Most famous is the one in the valley of Lauterbrunnen near
Interlaken.

* **Bertha,** see note p. 168.

* 𝕽𝖚𝖇𝖊𝖓𝖟, see note p. 166.

1600. 𝖊𝖚𝖈𝖍 𝖚𝖒𝖜𝖊𝖗𝖇𝖊𝖓, 'pay court to you,' 'sue for your hand'; the word implies a number of assiduous suitors.

1603. 𝖙𝖗𝖊𝖚𝖑𝖔𝖘, usually construed with dative and no preposition.

𝖜𝖎𝖗𝖉. A verb agreeing with a relative is put in the third person even when the antecedent of the relative is a pronoun of the first or second person (or a vocative), unless that pronoun be repeated after the relative.

1611. 𝖓𝖆𝖙𝖚𝖗𝖛𝖊𝖗𝖌𝖊𝖋𝖋(𝖊)𝖓𝖊𝖓 (one of those infrequent expressions in which the past participle has active force) = 𝖉𝖊𝖗 𝖉𝖎𝖊 natürlichen Pflichten vergessen hat, 'unnatural,' 'degenerate.'

1612. 𝖋𝖊𝖎𝖓𝖊𝖒, i.e. Gessler's.

1626. Cf. l. 1272.

1629. 𝖉𝖆𝖘 𝕭𝖊𝖋𝖙𝖊 and 𝖉𝖊𝖓 𝕱𝖗𝖎𝖊𝖉𝖊𝖓, l. 1631, are direct objects of 𝖂𝖎𝖑𝖑. Cf. note on 𝖉𝖊𝖓 𝕿𝖔𝖉, l. 1451.

1632. 𝕾𝖈𝖍𝖑𝖔𝖘, here 'stronghold.'

1638. 𝕿𝖍ä𝖙' ... 𝖇𝖊𝖋𝖋𝖊𝖗 = 𝖂𝖊𝖓𝖓 𝖎𝖈𝖍 𝖊𝖘 𝖙𝖍ä𝖙𝖊, 𝖋𝖔 𝖜ä𝖗𝖊 𝖊𝖘 𝖇𝖊𝖋𝖋𝖊𝖗 𝖋ü𝖗 𝖒𝖎𝖈𝖍.

1646. 𝖆𝖓𝖌𝖊𝖋𝖙𝖆𝖒𝖒𝖙𝖊, 'inborn,' 'that is your heritage.'

1649–50. 𝖆𝖑𝖑𝖊𝖘 ... 𝖜𝖊𝖗𝖉𝖊𝖓 = 𝖊𝖚𝖗𝖊 𝕷𝖎𝖊𝖇𝖊 𝖑ä𝖘𝖙 ('makes,' 'enables') 𝖒𝖎𝖈𝖍 𝖆𝖑𝖑𝖊𝖘 𝖋𝖊𝖎𝖓 𝖚𝖓𝖉 𝖜𝖊𝖗𝖉𝖊𝖓.

1650–51. 𝕾𝖊𝖎𝖉 (𝖉𝖆𝖘) 𝖜𝖔𝖟𝖚.

1657. 𝖉𝖊𝖗 𝖁𝖊𝖗𝖜𝖆𝖓𝖉𝖙𝖊𝖓, primarily Gessler, whom Schiller makes a relative, both being called 𝖛𝖔𝖓 𝕭𝖗𝖚𝖓𝖊𝖈𝖐.

1659–60. The Bruneck family were native in Aargau, but her estates are placed in the Forest Cantons, and from the parallel she draws between her fate and that of Switzerland it would appear that her estates are immediate fiefs of the Empire.

1661. 𝕭𝖑𝖎𝖈𝖐, 'vista,' 'prospect.'

1664. 𝖉𝖊𝖒 𝖌𝖗𝖔𝖘𝖘𝖊𝖓 (𝕳𝖆𝖇𝖘𝖇𝖚𝖗𝖌𝖊𝖗) 𝕰𝖗𝖇𝖊.

1665. 𝕷ä𝖓𝖉𝖊𝖗𝖌𝖎𝖊𝖗, 'greed for territory.'

1671. = 𝕯𝖎𝖊 𝕶𝖊𝖙𝖙𝖊𝖓 𝖊𝖎𝖓𝖊𝖗 𝖛𝖊𝖗𝖍𝖆𝖘𝖘𝖙𝖊𝖓 𝕰𝖍𝖊 𝖍𝖆𝖗𝖗𝖊𝖓 𝖒𝖊𝖎𝖓 (genitive of 𝖎𝖈𝖍) 𝖉𝖔𝖗𝖙.

1664–72. As soon as intenser emotion appears we find rhyme, and this scene being largely lyrical, rhyme is most frequent in it.

1675. **Sehnen in das Weite,** 'longing for the wide world.'

1685. **des Lebens Weiten,** 'the distant realms of life.'

1688. The meaning is, **zum Himmel allein.**

1689. **gelichtet,** really = **mit Licht versehen**; render it by 'clear,' or 'bright,' or 'made bright.'

1690. Note the change from **ihr** to **du.**

ahnend, 'prophetic.'

1694. 'Here where the flower of happy boyhood opened.'

1695. **Freudespuren,** 'joyous memories.'

1696. They live for him because as a child he dwelt with them and they entered into his life.

1699. **fehlte,** preterite subjunctive. In effect, 'Without it no earthly happiness would be complete.'

1700. **sel'ge Insel.** Allusion to the legendary Isles of the Blessed, where perfect happiness prevails. They were often alluded to by the ancient Greek and Latin writers, and usually located in the Atlantic Ocean west of the Pillars of Hercules. Such classical allusions occur only three times in this drama; here and in lines 3116-7 and 3209. They are not out of place from the lips of nobles.

1719. **dem stolzen Ritter,** it may be Gessler.

1720. **Landbedrücker** = **Bedrücker des Landes.**

1726. **Was auch d(a)raus werde,** 'whatever may come of it.'

A scene of romantic love in a romantic locality. Of Bertha we had a glimpse in Act I. Sc. 3, while the scene (Act II. Sc. 1) between Attinghausen and Rudenz gave us some insight into the aspirations and sentiments of Rudenz. The present scene answers, in part at least, the questions which that one left with us. As Gertrud inspired Stauffacher to action, so here Bertha, the young noblewoman, clears the mental vision of Rudenz, the young nobleman—inspires and leads him. Among the nobility we may expect to find no fewer Berthas than Gertruds among the yeomanry. All classes, all ages, both sexes are entering into the movement whose cause and aim Bertha forcefully states in the last two lines of the scene.

This meeting both Bertha and Rudenz have long desired, with the same purpose of a final declaration, and it is to be decisive for both. The main portion of the scene from l. 1602 through l. 1702 has two parts, in the first of which Bertha discloses her real self to Rudenz, while in the second Rudenz begins to recover his real self. For him what Bertha says about herself is a surprising revelation; for Bertha, the real nature of Rudenz to which he now returns is what she has always had faith in and loved.

Rudenz is indeed as yet no hero. Doubtless the poet's execution of this character-portrait falls much short of his intention. Ambition and love seem to sway Rudenz too easily, and duty and true honor to be but faint within him. Nevertheless let us remember that he is a growing, developing character, let us find our ideal conception of him in Bertha's knowledge of him, as expressed in lines 1643–1648, 1650–1651, 1690–1691, and 1725–1727, and let us look forward with confident hope of his bearing in the future.

Act III. Scene 3.

The time of this scene is shortly after that of the first scene of this act, of which it is a continuation. The place is said to be a meadow or common *near* Altorf, while in line 394 it is said to be mitten in Altorf, with which location the statements of lines 1740 and 1742–3 more easily agree.

* Bannberg. This high hill lies on the eastern side of the village Altorf. In line 900, bannen is used of the prohibition of hunting; this Bannberg is so named because it is forbidden to cut any wood on it, lest an avalanche be started.

* Frießhardt, see note p. 168.

* Leuthold, see note p. 168.

1735. Anger, see note on Matten, * 3.

1738. Verdrieß, archaic form of Verdruß, frequently used by Luther.

1739. **Was rechte Leute sind, die,** 'all who are respectable people, they.' Their action seems to be in execution of the agreement of l. 413.

1741. **beugten,** preterite subjunctive.

1743. **um die Mittagsstunde.** The time is then early in the afternoon.

1746 ff. The priest carrying the Host (das Hochwürdige or das Venerabile—the consecrated wafer) was coming from a dying person to whom he had administered the sacraments of death, the Lord's Supper, and extreme unction. The ringing of the bell is the sign that the Host is approaching, and in Catholic lands the pious kneel to its passing.

1751. **die Monstranz,** 'the monstrance.' This is the transparent pyx or case, usually surrounded by rich ornamentation in cross-shape, in which the priest holds up to view the Host before the congregation in church. It is never carried to the sick, the closed case then used being called the ciborium, a cup provided with a cover. Devout Roman Catholics regard the action of Rösselmann as highly unbecoming.

1752. **deuchten,** also däuchten.

1758. **traun,** interjection, 'in truth.'

* **Hildegard, Mechthild und Elsbeth,** see note p. 168.

1763. **wer Da,** cf. was da, l. 1477.

1765. **habt Respekt,** said mockingly.

1766. **und ließ' uns** (nichts als) **seinen Hut.**

1767. 'The country would not be any the worse for that.'

1768. **Volk der Weiber** = Weibervolk.

1770. **Mut** here in the sense of Verlangen, Begierde.

sticht, 'pricks,' 'spurs,' 'prompts.'

The conversation of the two soldiers is the first part of the threefold introduction to this scene. As exposition, it explains the grave danger impending from the hat, and shows the attitude of the people toward it, for vagabonds and women mock, while decent men avoid it. In Shakespeare's manner we have in the talk of the two mercenaries and the women some bright touches of humor, to set off the tragic gloom to follow.

1771-2. That trees thus bleed is a very ancient widespread popular belief. Cf. Vergil, *Æneid*, iii. 22-34. It has often been used in literature, as by Ovid, Dante, Ariosto, Tasso, Spenser.

1773. führte, preterite subjunctive.

1775. gebannt. We may render this here and in line 1777 by 'under a ban,' but the meaning in the first case is 'charmed,' 'enchanted,' 'bewitched,' and in the second case 'sacred,' 'forbidden,' cf. note on Bannberg, * 84.

1778. die Firnen, see note on l. 38.

Hörner, here snow-clad sharp peaks, although more usually applied to bare peaks of rock rising above snow and ice.

1781. Schlaglawinen, 'avalanches,' or 'mass-avalanches,' see note on l. 1501 and App. p. 296.

1785. Landwehr, here in the older sense of Wehr, Damm, Schuß für das Land, 'bulwark.'

1787 ff. The description is put, no doubt intentionally, in such general terms that one may think of Germany, of Upper Italy (i.e. Lombardy), or possibly of France. On the whole it is easiest to refer it to Germany, since one following the streams from Tell's home would be led by the Schächen to the Reuss, then to the Aar, and then to the Rhine. Those who refer it to Italy suppose Tell's thoughts to go on in the same direction from the snow-mountains south of Altorf, of which he has just spoken ; they also find difficulty in applying to Germany ll. 1794, 1798, and 1810.

1790-1794. Rhyme, as it were involuntarily.

1792. nach allen Himmelsräumen, 'towards all quarters of the heavens,' 'in all directions.'

1802. Bischof and König, both with collective meaning = ecclesiastical and secular lords.

1804. Gefieder, usually 'plumage'; here Wild und Gefieder = 'bird and beast.'

1806. das Salz ; the sale of salt was a royal monopoly.

1811. es wird mir eng (narrow) im weiten (broad) Land ; this oxymoron like 'eloquent silence,' 'open secret,' can hardly be duplicated in English. The meaning is, 'I begin to feel oppressed in that broad land'; one might perhaps say, 'I begin to feel that broad land narrow about me.'

1812. **Da,** 'then,' 'if. that is so.'

unter, 'among,' or possibly 'below the (threatening) avalanches.'

1813–1814. Cf. ll. 157–8.

The second well-defined introductory incident is the talk of father and son, in which the course of Tell's thoughts is chiefly guided by the questions of the curious boy, that carry the father far away from what is immediately about him. We may note, however, in passing, that as, in Scene 1, Tell desired his sons to have all bodily skill and independence, so here he will not let Walther rest in dull superstition, and he teaches love of liberty and native land.

Tell's action and words in this part of the scene have been judged in most opposite ways, diverging in the interpretation of line 1816. One view is that Tell knows about the hat and the edict, and intends not to notice it or do obeisance ; another view holds that Tell does not yet know anything about either hat or edict. The second of these two interpretations we must reject, because it is difficult, if not impossible, to conceive of Tell's being present in Act I. Sc. 3 without seeing the hat and hearing the proclamation ; furthermore, Tell himself in lines 1870–1 explains his action by *heedlessness* rather than ignorance. Again, these words of Tell, together with what we already know of his peaceable disposition, render impossible also the view first mentioned above. We must rather understand that Tell knows about the hat and the edict, but having just passed it without noticing it, because absorbed in talk with Walther, and being now in his thoughts far away, he does not at the moment remember anything about the hat and the edict, and absent-mindedly answers line 1816. This is only the easier to comprehend if we recall how large an ele-

ment there is in Tell of reflection, visionariness ; thus
Gessler says, line 1904, „Man ſagte mir, daß Du ein Träumer
ſeiſt.“

* **greift in,** 'seizes upon.'

* **In die Scene rufend,** 'calling behind the scenes.'

1825. The second **Was** = **Warum.**

* **Fürſten,** see note on **Hanſen,** l. 1337.

1833. **erkennen** = anerkennen.

1834. **Das hätt' der Tell gethan,** 'Do you mean to say that
Tell has done that?' In this not infrequent idiom a past
subjunctive is used interrogatively to question or dispute
something supposed to have been asserted.

Bube, here = 'knave,' 'scoundrel.'

1839. **unſers Amtes,** cf. note on l. 368.

1840. **ſchreiende,** 'flagrant,' 'outrageous'; the common form
is **himmelſchreiende** as in line 367 ; see note.

1843. See l. 661 and note.

1846. **ſchon,** not of time, but for emphasis, = 'never fear,
I'll,' etc., or 'I'll help myself all right.'

The introductory portion of the scene culminates in
this third part,—the arrest. It is full of dramatic life.
What happens is for Tell and his friends like a thunder-
bolt from the clear sky. His conscience acquits him of
the charge made by Friesshardt, and his consciousness
of innocence keeps him from using or allowing violent
resistance.

1852. **berſteſt** is not subjunctive, but indicative ; **berſten** is
now commonly of the weak conjugation in the present tense.

* **Geßler,** see note p. 165.

* **den Falken,** absolute accusative, cf. note on **Meer,** l. 31.

* **Rudolf der Harras,** see note p. 169.

* **Bertha und Rudenz,** cf. the preceding scene. The hunt
is now ended and they have rejoined the hunting-party.

1858. **was** = warum.

* **Er giebt den Falken einem Diener;** i.e. on assuming the
character of judge.

1859. **geſtrenger Herr,** lit. 'Stern Sir,' or 'Dread Sir,' but
to be rendered by 'Your Worship'; in this use **geſtreng** was

originally a title given to nobles or officials of a prince having penal jurisdiction.

1859. Friesshardt here uses bu to Gessler. This bu of emotion is more freely employed in this drama than else- where by Schiller, and transitions back and forth between ifr and bu are very frequent.

Waffenknecht, 'man-at-arms.'

1860. **wohlbeſtellter** (or wohlbeſtallter), 'duly appointed.'

1861. **über** (for usual auf) **friſcher That,** 'in the very act.'

1862. **Ehrengruß,** 'salute of honor.'

1865. **Deinen Kaiſer.** In fact the hat is not the symbol of *imperial* authority.

Tell is recognized by Gessler at once.

1869. **Trachten,** infin. as noun, lit. 'desiring,' 'longing,' 'aspiring' = 'disposition.'

1870. **Aus Unbedacht,** 'from thoughtlessness,' 'without intention.'

1871. **eurer,** see note on l. 286.

1872. See Introd. p. lxii.

1873. **nicht mehr begegnen,** for prose nicht wieder geſchehen.

1875. **nehmſt,** subjunctive of indirect statement.

es mit jemandem aufnehmen, 'to cope with,' 'to compete with,' 'to be a match for.' In this phrase es stands for the old collective das Waffen, 'arms,' 'weapons,' the phrase originating from the custom of laying the weapons on the ground in case of a duel, in order to test their similarity and thereafter taking them up to fight; for es are also sub- stituted Kampf, Streit, Wette, Handſchuh, the last supported also by the use of the glove in challenging.

1877. **dir,** ethical dative, pleonastic; 'Father will shoot you an apple,' etc.

Schritte, plural (as also in l. 1915), but in l. 1883 the more usual invariable form Schritt. Masculine and neuter nouns used as units of measurement generally are invariable after numerals.

1892. **nein doch** = emphatic nein.

1893. **Zu Sinn,** usually in den Sinn.

1899. A very important line in regard to the plot and to Tell's character.

1908. **wohl bedächte sich,** 'would doubtless deliberate (or hesitate).'

drückst die Augen zu, figuratively = willst die Gefahr nicht sehen.

1909. **greifst es ... an,** 'attack it,' 'go at it.'

The main action of this scene begins with the arrival of Gessler, and its first division, the dialogue between Gessler and Tell, ends here.

Already known by reputation and feared by us, announced by horns, the cries of women, and Fürst's anxious words, coming proudly on horseback from one cruel sport to another yet more cruel, there now appears the only one of the Austrian governors whom we actually behold, the very incarnation of all the oppression that threatens the land,—Gessler. Our suspense is heightened by the critical nature of the moment, and the presence of the strong retinue of men-at-arms. In talk with Tell Gessler first accuses him and then introduces the assignment of a feat by which he means publicly to humiliate Tell. What feat he may have had in mind before Walther's words decided him we cannot say. When Tell in his horror is unable to believe that the governor is in earnest, Gessler repeats his command, and finally closes every way of escape by means of the awful dilemma: "Either you will try the shot or both you and your boy shall die!" to which with cruellest delight he adds his taunts.

1912. **Kurzweils,** here gen. sing. masc. or neut. 'jesting'; it is usually feminine.

1913. **Hier ist der Apfel.** It is by poetic license that apples are still on the trees after the middle of November. Cf. note on **Rechen und Sensen,** * 40.

1917. **ihrer,** partitive genitive depending on **hundert.**

1920. **Es gilt.** This impersonal exclamation, as used here in cases of danger and conflict, is not precisely paralleled in English; compare Engl. slang 'for all you are worth'; we may say, 'Life is at stake,' 'Now's the time,' 'It boots.'

1921. **Haltet an euch,** 'restrain yourself.'

1924. **Leib und Leben,** 'life and limb.'

1925. **verwirkt** (hätte).

1928. **kennen lernen** = kennen gelernt. The modal auxiliaries and a few other verbs—laſſen, heißen, helfen, hören, ſehen, and sometimes lehren and lernen—when construed with another verb in the infinitive, form their compound past tenses by adding the infinitive instead of the participle to the auxiliary; this apparent infinitive form is, however, historically itself a participle.

1930. **die Gaſſe öffnen,** here = Plaꜩ machen in Gaſſenform, form a double line with open space between, 'make a passage.'

1931. **verwirkt.** But has Tell directly violated the mandate?

1933. **kunſtgeübte,** 'practical,' trained,' 'skillful.'

1937. **gilt es,** 'it's worth your while.'

1939. **das Schwarze,** 'the bull's eye.'

1942. **Dem** (da)s **Herz,** etc. 'Whose emotion does not make his hand tremble nor cloud his eye.'

1948. **hinſtehn,** Swiss for hintreten, ſich hinſtellen. Cf. l. 2838, vor ſeinen Richter ſtehn.

1950. The ambiguity of this line may be excused on the ground of its being spoken by a boy. It can strictly mean only, 'He will not miss in shooting at the heart of his child,' i.e. he will surely hit the heart. But the intended meaning must be, 'He will not miss and hit the heart,' etc.; even so there is difficulty in having Herz rather than Haupt, unless we take Herz as very general in the sense of center of life.

1954–62. Walther's bearing and words resemble those of Prince Arthur in Shakespeare's *King John*, Act IV. Sc. 1.

1967. Cf. ll. 1447 ff.

1970, **mit friſcher That,** 'with swift action,' 'without delay,' cf. ll. 1400 ff.

1972. **vergebens,** 'in vain,' 'to no purpose,' 'for nothing'; i.e. if one carries weapons, he must expect to use them. The word cannot mean 'with impunity.'

1975. Cf. l. 785.

1978. **Freut's euch,** conaritional.

In this second division of the main action of this scene Tell is completely silent, overcome by emotion. Bertha, true to her noble soul, is the first to speak in behalf of reason and mercy ; thereafter Fürst, Harras indirectly, Rösselmann, Walther Tell, and Melchthal either intercede for Tell or speak defiance to Gessler. But the tyrant heeds none of them ; for him no one is present but Tell. His purpose is to goad Tell on towards the shooting ; not that he intends that Tell shall shoot, he only desires Tell to feel as most acute torture the conflict of his father-love with the temptation to shoot. Gessler eagerly hopes he may in this way break Tell's pride as an archer and his spirit as a man. The reason why Gessler does this is his experience in that earlier meeting (described by Tell in the first scene of this act) in which he felt the tyrant's fear of the mortal missile. Tell's omission to do reverence to the hat is only a pretext to Gessler, who has long since formed the purpose of humiliating and crushing Tell and now thinks he has an ideal opportunity. The feat he demands of Tell is fitted with cruellest nicety to Tell's character. From it Tell cannot escape by surrender of his own life alone.

1983. **Mir schwimmt es vor den Augen,** ' my head swims.'

1988. Mocking allusion to the rescue of Baumgarten.

1989. **Wenn . . . gilt,** ' when it's a question of saving.'

1990. **jetzt . . . selbst,** biblical, cf. Matt. xxvii. 40, 42; Luke xxiii. 25 ; Mark xv. 29.

du rettest alle. Again a mocking allusion to the past; you save every one, you are always saving people.

* **Der** (better **das**) **Goller** (also **Koller**) is a leather doublet or jacket.

1991. **Es muß** (geschehen).

1992 ff. Cf. ll. 1723-31.

1996. Cf. the proverb **Wer den Bogen überspannt, der zersprengt ihn.**

1998. **Ich darf's,** ' I have the right to.'

2006. **'überschwellend.** Not infrequently in poetry when

two adjectives are connected by unb the declensional ending is omitted with the first one.

2013. **euch**, Gessler or the Austrians in general.

2019. **baran**, 'on the point of,' 'about to.'

The events of the third division of the main body of this scene show that Gessler was mistaken in his confident calculation that Tell would be unable to make the shot. Tell's first attempt to aim fails, then Gessler's mocking refusal to accept his life in exchange for the shot brings Tell into most intense conflict of soul. Suddenly he places in his doublet the arrow with which, if need be, he will take Gessler's life, and as his boy calls to him encouragement, he becomes conscious of the dreadful necessity (cf. l. 136) of saving his boy's life, collects and composes himself, and aims. Parallel with Tell's aiming and getting full command of himself there now runs Rudenz' defiance of Gessler. Love has cleared Rudenz' vision and inspired him, but it is the cruelty of the unspeakable soul-torture which Gessler inflicts upon Tell that calls out the first nobly heroic act on the part of Rudenz. Reckless of himself, with hand on sword, he denounces and defies Gessler. As he is about to draw his sword, Stauffacher's cry rings out: "The apple has fallen"!

Can we explain Tell's shooting by reasonable psychological motives? The question has been only too often answered in the negative. Why did Schiller take the affirmative?

The one comprehensive motive which might lead Tell to refuse to shoot is the father's love of his son. That Tell's affection is deep and strong is sufficiently empasized not only in this scene but both earlier and later, so much so that some regard his shooting as on this account alone unintelligible, psychologically impossible.

In examining the motives for the act, we feel at once a difficulty in that Tell's words shed little light on his thoughts and feelings, while Gessler is goading him on.

A later line—2328—does give us some clue to the fact that Tell's pride as an archer, his inmost spirit as a man, is provoked, and his heart bids him do what his boy—his true *alter ego*—urges in lines 1963-5. Tell feels himself goaded by Gessler to a deed, not of vainglory, but of righteous self-assertion ; Gessler calls in question not only his skill as a marksman, but all those elements in his character on which his skill chiefly depends and which are a large part of that which makes life for him worth living. Tell has heretofore known and felt himself to be the man who, wherever it is necessary, can boldly try any venture and be sure of his skill always and everywhere, because he is master of all his powers. If he shoot at the apple resting on his child's head, he will assert before the governor and himself his control of his nerves, his head, his heart. What motive could be stronger than this ? Doubtless a father's true love ! And Tell will do grievous wrong to himself no less than to his boy if, in conflict with his love, he yield to this pride. But here this conflict does not exist. Because of the certainty that Gessler will execute his threat—"You will shoot or die *with* your boy !"—Tell has only to choose between delivering his boy and himself into the merciless hands of Gessler and taking his son's and his own fate into his own skillful hands. He makes the shot, therefore, with utter certainty.

Some critics will not restrict Tell's choice to the dilemma just stated. They urge a third possibility, that Tell might purposely have missed in shooting and thus have forfeited his own life, and a fourth, that he might at once have shot Gessler dead. But as to the first of these suggestions, it must be said that Tell's character does not admit of purposed missing, that Gessler would not have accepted such a shot, and that it would not have brought any safety to the boy Walther. Secondly, if Tell had shot Gessler, both his boy and himself, together with many or all of his

friends there present, would have been killed immediately by Gessler's men-at-arms, who surround the
entire company.

2035. **Wußt' ich's ja,** inverted order for emphasis, 'Why,
I knew.'

2046–7. **ihr ... gelöft,** 'you have manfully freed yourself,'
'you have quit yourself like a man.'

The main action of the scene ends in its brief fourth
division with the expression of the effects of the successful shot on those present. Amazement is common
to them all, excepting Walther. Gessler's first exclamation makes it clear that he did not expect Tell to
shoot. Tell's friends have also sympathy and joy. The
judgment of the value of the shot is given by a soldier,
by Rudolph der Harras, by Gessler himself, and by
Rösselmann, who utters also a righteous imprecation on
its instigator.

2049–50. **Du ftedteft ... zu dir,** 'you placed in your doublet'; see stage-direction after l. 1990.

2052. **bräuchlich,** archaic and poetic for **gebräuchlich.**

2053. **laff' ... gelten,** lit. 'I do not allow to pass,' 'I do
not accept.'

2054. The future indicative is sometimes used to state
a claimed present probability, and the future perfect—as
here—to state a claimed past probability.

2055. **frisch und fröhlich,** 'at once and cheerfully.'

2060. **durchschoß ich;** the preterite indicative used for emphasis in place of the pluperfect subjunctive.

2062. **eurer,** gen. with **fehlen;** cf. note on l. 286.

2071. Stauffacher regards the success of the shot as a
judgment of God in Tell's favor.

2076. The charters prohibited foreign imprisonment. By
that of 1291 the Forest Cantons were secured against foreign judges, and hence against execution of sentence in a
foreign place. Küssnacht was in the Canton Schwyz.

2077. Cf. ll. 1324–1335.

* **Bertha, Rudenz ... folgen.** The explanation of this action, which otherwise is improbable, especially on the part

of Rudenz, is given by the stage-direction inserted at this
point in the Hamburg MS. : „Inbem er [Geßler] abgeht, ergreift er
bie Hanb ber Bertha unb führt fie mit fich. Rubenz will ihr folgen, bie
Weiber werfen fich in ben Weg. Weiber : ‚O rettet ihn, Herr Freiherr!
Rettet ihn!‘ Rubenz reißt fich los unb folgt ber Bertha.“ Bertha is
thus compelled to go with Gessler, and Rudenz follows in
order to protect her.

2086. Cf. and contrast l. 3096.

2088. **warum mußtet ihr,** ‘ why had you to,’ ‘ why could you
not keep from.’

The main action of the scene led through great fear
and sorrow to highest joy. Its conclusion brings a
revulsion from this joy to intense fear and sorrow.
Tell is now a prisoner in the hands of his mortal enemy,
who is prompted to this new outrage by the fearful
foreboding of the truth of lines 2575-6. We look forward to see the free son of the mountains in a dungeon.
Gessler seems to be finally triumphant. Very striking
is the utter dejection of Stauffacher and the Swiss.
Tell's heart is full of faith in God, whom Gessler with
impious defiance has challenged. With Tell's faith we
therefore still hope.

In spite of its many characters and incidents this
scene is unitary, since everything has reference to
Tell's fate.

Between the three scenes of Act III there is external
connection in that Tell passes from the first, and Bertha
and Rudenz from the second to the third. But they are
also inwardly connected. The first really serves as exposition to the third, while the second, although more
complete in itself, contains also the explanation of Rudenz' bearing in the third, for what he there resolved
is here done.

Scene 1 has been called an idyll of the family, and 2
an idyll of the heart, while the tragic 3d scene has
been regarded as standing in direct contrast with 1 and
2. But Tell's narrative of his meeting with Gessler,

and Hedwig's forebodings cast tragic shadows on the idyllic brightness of 1, while 2 closes with the prospect of tragic conflict.

Of the three plots, the Tell-plot has in 1 the second stage of its ascending action, and in 3 rises irresistibly to its climax and the immediately following tragic crisis. The Nobles-plot has its initial impulse in 2, and its ascending action in 3. The Yeomen-plot—without any active movement—has the first stage of its descending action in 3, in which scene all three plots are united in one place and concentrated.

SEAL OF UNTERWALDEN, 1291.

ACT IV.

ARGUMENT.—In the *first* scene we see from the eastern shore of the lake a violent storm. Kunz von Gersau tells to the fisherman Ruodi and the boy Jenni what has happened at Altorf, and that the Baron von Attinghausen is dying. He leaves, and the others see and describe to us how Gessler's boat is driven about on the lake. Soon Tell appears and narrates to them that Gessler had been forced by fear to free him and to put him in command of the boat, and that by a hazardous leap ashore he had saved himself and left the boat adrift. Tell asks the fisherman to carry a message to his wife, and then the boy leads him the shortest way to Küssnacht, Gessler's destination.

The *second* is the scene of Attinghausen's death in his castle. Hedwig comes, to find her son Walther and her father. She reproaches her absent husband and his present friends for what has occurred. Attinghausen laments that Rudenz has not come to receive his dying blessing. Stauffacher and Fürst make his last hour radiantly joyous by telling of Rudenz' change of heart and of the confederation of the yeomanry of the three cantons. The Baron blesses Walther, prophesies the future freedom and glory of Switzerland, and dies while admonishing the Swiss ever to remain united. Rudenz appears, and grieves that he has come too late. He convinces Stauffacher, Fürst, and Melchthal that the nobles must make common cause with them in defense of the land and its liberty. He and Melchthal decide upon immediate action.

The *third* scene is the narrow defile through which Gessler must now pass. Tell appears, and as we through his monologue see his very mind and heart, we realize that he now will and must kill Gessler. Tell converses with Stüssi as a wedding procession passes. Gessler enters in conversion with Rudolf der Harras and separated from his retinue by the wedding party. A poor woman, Armgard, petitions Gessler for mercy toward her husband, an innocent victim of official cruelty. While Gessler, thus angered, is in the midst of vehement declaration that he will break the spirit of the Swiss and crush their liberties, Tell's arrow pierces his heart. Gessler recognizes and Tell confesses that Tell is the author of the shot. The people declare their joy in their beginning deliverance from the Austrian yoke. The friars, who remove Gessler's body, sing a solemn hymn, with which the act ends.

SCENE I.

The time is the afternoon of the same day as in the preceding act; the third scene is late in the same afternoon. The place is on the eastern shore of the southern arm of the lake, not far from the village Sissigen between Flüelen and Brunnen.

* **Kunz von Gersau,** see note p. 168.

* **Fischer** = Ruodi of Act I. Sc. I.

* **Fischerknabe** = Jenni of Act I. Sc. I. There is really no doubt about this identification, although the point has been much discussed. The boy is named in l. 2301; Ruodi is ferryman as well as fisherman, and as such must have shelter on both sides; in l. 115 he speaks of his home as being not where he then is; according to l. 2289 this fisherman was present at the Rütli, as was Ruodi, see stage-direction after l. 1097. At the close of Sc. I of Act I his hut on the western shore was destroyed and he has now moved across the lake (at least temporarily).

2102. 'If liberty is ever at stake.'

2104. **d(a)ran,** see note on l. 2019.

2113. **Des freien Mannes,** condensed for **des Mannes, wenn er jetzt frei wäre.**

2115. **am Tode liegen** for more usual **auf den Tod liegen** or **im Sterben liegen.**

2120. **Dorf** = Sissigen or Sisikon; see note above.

2124. **Der Mund der Wahrheit** = Attinghausen.

2125. **Das sehnde Auge** = Attinghausen. To refer this expression, as some do, to Heinrich von der Halden, Melchthal's father, or to Rudenz, seems quite inadmissible;

neither has done anything important and widely known in opposition to tyranny, nor are they alluded to elsewhere in this connection. Those who do refer these words to Rudenz find support for their view in the expressions ll. 2005 and 839.

2126. Der Arm = Tell.

2128. kommlich, Swiss for bequem, angenehm.

hausen = sich aufhalten, 'to stay.'

2129 ff. These lines echo the famous outburst in Shakespeare's *King Lear*, Act III. Sc. 2, 'Blow, winds, and crack your cheeks! rage! blow!' etc.

2135. Wüste, here = Wildnis; gen. dependent on Wölfe. Such separation is poetical. This and the preceding line allude to the legend as given in ll. 1260 ff.

2140. geboten, past part. of gebieten.

2144. Eisestürme = Türme von Eis.

2147-8. Wenn die alten Klüfte einstürzen, not clear, but probably = 'if the old gorges close up,' i.e. by the falling in together of their sides.

2152. daß (es) gebetet werde, 'that prayer may be offered,' i.e. by all who hear the bell.

2158. Busen, = 'bay' or 'cove.'

2159. Handlos, 'handless,' 'inaccessible.'

2161. This line has six feet.

2163 ff. In his fear of the elements and lack of self-reliance Ruodi is as he was in Act I. Sc. 1.

2164. Wasserkluft, 'gorge of water,' 'gorge above the water.'

sich erst verfangen (hat), 'has once become caught.'

2170. Herrenschiff, say 'governor's boat.' The word is formed like Herrenburg, Herrenbank.

am roten Dach, render either 'by its red awning (or roof or top)' or 'by its red deck.' The boat may have had a sort of deck-house or shelter of which the roof was painted with the Austrian color, cf. l. 781, or its deck proper may have been painted red.

2177. geben nicht auf, usually transitive, geben nichts auf, 'do not heed (or regard, or obey).'

2180. **Greif' nicht in** . . . 'do not stay.'

2185. **mitſamt,** pleonastic and hence emphatic, = zuſammen mit.

2187 ff. **Buggisgrat and Hackmeſſer** are steep cliffs of the **Axenberg** on the eastern shore of the lake between Flüelen and Brunnen ; **Teufelsmünſter** is a perpendicular rock on the western shore. Note the meanings of the compounds Hackmeſſer and Teufelsmünſter.

2191. **gebrochen,** poetic for geſcheitert (ſind).

2193. **Fluh** (Flüh, Flue) = ſteile Felſenwand, a Swiss word.

2194. **gähſtoßig,** a Swiss word = 'precipitously'; gäh = jäh, and ſtoßig is an adj. from Stoß, 'vertical declivity.'

In the short time intervening between Acts III and IV Gessler has embarked, after previously arranging the abduction of Bertha ; also the news of Tell's arrest and Attinghausen's dying has spread.

It is a master-stroke of dramatic art that in this introductory portion of the scene we are witnesses through the eyes of Ruodi and Jenni of the fearful passage of the boat on which Gessler is conducting Tell away, and that Tell appears in the very moment when we think he must be lost. Ruodi's impassioned eloquence is hardly his own. It is rather as if the very mind and heart of the common people were, under poetic inspiration, expressing, with most intense lyric fervor, sorrow and despair, joy in the sympathizing wrath of nature, and appeal to the judgment of God in nature.

2199. In joyous gratitude for having solid ground beneath him after being rescued from danger by water.

2208. Cf. l. 2268.

2211. **Fürſehung,** archaic for Vorſehung.

2214. **fahen,** archaic and poetic for fangen.

2219. **aufgegebner,** 'lost,' 'abandoned,' 'a man given up.'

2222. **Waſſerwüſte,** 'waste of waters.'

2226. **der Granſen** (also Grans), a South-German word = Schiffsſchnabel; here **hintern Granſen** = 'stern.'

2228. The **kleine Axen** is south of the **große Axen**, both being parts of the Axenberg.

2230. **gählings** = jählings.

herfürbrach, archaic for **hervorbrach**.　Cf. note on l. 109.

2233. **der Diener einer** = einer von den Dienern.

2237–8. **wissen sich . . . nicht Rat,** 'are at their wits' end,' 'know not what to do.'

2239. **nicht wohl berichtet** = unkundig, 'not well informed,' 'not skilled.'

2241. The construction of the genitive **sein** (of **er**) with **brauchen** is poetical.

2242–3. **wenn du dir's getrautest** = wenn du dir (e)s zutrautest, 'if you were confident.'

2246. **hiedannen,** archaic for von dannen, von hier weg.

2248. **redlich,** here in the archaic sense of 'stoutly,' 'steadily,' not at all with the common meaning of 'honestly.'

2249. **Schießzeug,** 'shooting implements,' 'bow and quiver.'

2256. **angehen,** here = 'go up,' 'ascend.'

abreichen, unusual = erreichen.

2257. **handlich zuzugehen.**　In South-German usage **handlich** = rüstig, tapfer, 'stoutly,' 'vigorously'; **zugehen** here has the sense of 'to go at,' 'to lay on.'　Schiller used **zugehen** here because in Tschudi's expression „handlich zuginb" he mistook the latter word to be a form, zugiengen, of the verb zugehen, while it really = zögen from ziehen, 'to pull.'

2258. **Felsenplatte,** 'rocky ledge,' 'flat rock.'

2262. **angestemmt,** render by pres. part. 'pressing,' 'bearing on.'

2266. **Fußstoß,** 'thrust of my foot.'

2268. Cf. l. 2208.

2278. **über Schwyz,** across (by way of) Schwyz, to Sewen, Steinen, Arth, and Immensee, and then to Küssnacht.

2282. **Arth,** a large village at the southern end of Lake Zug, at the foot of the Rossberg.

2283. **Steinen,** Stauffacher's home ; cf. Act. I. Sc. 2.

2285. **Lowerz** is on the western shore of Lake Lowerz, to the east of which Steinen lies.

2290. **So,** 'then.'

thut . . . an, 'do me the kindness.'

2292. Cf. l. 554.

2294. **Schwäher,** usually = **Schwager,** 'brother-in-law,' but here in its original sense of **Schwiegervater,** 'father-in-law'; obsolescent, but still occurring in South Germany.

2300. **zur Rede kommen,** for usual **zur Sprache kommen,** 'to be talked about.'

2302. **was auch,** 'whatever.'

unternommen (**hat** or **haben mag**).

Again an effective rhymed conclusion of a scene.

It is with tremendous dramatic effect that Tell suddenly comes before us, and our hoping against hope is turned to joy in fulfillment. With no little fluency and aptness of speech, and with great dramatic vigor and clearness, does Tell narrate his deliverance. He recites, indeed, a miniature drama, playing between himself on one side, and on the other Gessler and his men. Tell is a second time at the helm of a boat threatened with destruction ; again he displays his skill and self-reliance, and again does God, whom Gessler but just now has defied, deliver Tell.

Some have attempted to criticise Tell's escape as being on his part a grave moral wrong. They claim that he commits a breach of confidence toward Gessler, because he first promises to help the governor and his men, and then breaks this promise. To brush away this criticism as utterly baseless, we need only call to mind the real facts of the situation, that Gessler by his words and acts has established a state of war between himself and Tell, that Tell makes no promise, and that Gessler, in foolish blindness to his own selfish interests, really forces upon Tell the duty of escaping. Even if one insist upon the fact of a promise on Tell's part, the subsequent safety of all who were on the boat is its fulfillment.

The conclusion of the scene, in particular lines 2282, 2298, and 2300, makes us anticipate that Gessler's cruelty has caused a fateful change and determination in Tell's soul, as to whose precise nature the scene leaves us in dramatic suspense.

ACT IV. SCENE 2.

The place is the same as in Act II. Scene 1. The time is nearly the same as that of the preceding scene.

2303. hinüber(gegangen), 'passed over,' a euphemism for geſtorben.

2304–5. On the lips of one dying or believed to be dead a downy feather is placed, in order that the breath may move it if life be present.

2313–4. mir, ethical dative, hardly to be translated.

2319. es galt das Leben, 'life was at stake,' 'it was a question of life and death.'

2325–27. As a phantom of her excited imagination she cannot help seeing the boy bound; she does not know that he stood free and called upon his father to shoot, and that Gessler threatened both with death, if Tell did not shoot.

2331. ſetzen = einſetzen, aufs Spiel . . . ſetzen, 'stake,' 'risk.'

*mit einem großen Blick, 'with wondering, reproachful gaze.'

2345. erbrauſte, 'rose roaring.'

Thränen, cf. l. 1038.

2355. erkrankte, preterite subjunctive.

2357. Alpenroſe. This so-called 'Alpine rose' is not really a rose but a rhododendron, growing on the mountains between the levels of four and of six thousand feet above the sea.

2360. in dem Balſamſtrom der Lüfte, 'in balmy streams of air.'

2367. Cf. l. 324.

2369. rettete, preterite subjunctive.

This scene has three very distinct parts, of which the first ends with the awakening of the Baron. In the first Hedwig is the leading character; in the second,

Attinghausen ; in the third, Rudenz and Melchthal.
With these leading characters in each case the leaders
of the Rütli-confederates are connected. But the construction of the scene is loose, and as a whole it hardly
possesses organic unity. It is, for example, not plain
why the Rütli-leaders and Walther Tell are present here
and now, nor how Hedwig knows that her boy is here.
We must overlook these relatively unimportant imper-
fections, for the sake of the beautiful symbolism of the
presence of representatives of all three plots at Attinghausen's death, for the sake of the inspiring grandeur
of the prophecy of the second part, and for the sake of
the noble action of Rudenz and Melchthal in the third
part.

The introduction of the scene belongs chiefly to the
Tell-plot, but the Yeomen-plot is represented in the
leaders who defend Tell and themselves against the
charges of the misinformed, home-loving Hedwig,
while the Nobles-plot furnishes both place and occasion.
Charmingly characteristic of Hedwig are her feelings,
their changeful play, and culmination in irrepressible
pride in Tell. Her last words are almost as if she had
some intuition of Tell's escape.

2373. **den Junker,** = Rudenz ; cf. note on l. 765.

2375. **Er hat sein Herz gefunden,** i.e. true love of country
has revived in his heart; a biblical phrase, cf. II. Sam. vii.
27. Cf. ll. 2006–7 and 2481.

2377. **Mit Heldenkühnheit,** see ll. 1992–2031.

2382. Sense of pain is a proof of the presence of life, and
absence of pain often a sign that death is near.

2397. **sich,** reciprocal = einander.

2409. Biblical phrase, Daniel v. 26.

2414. **wenn es gilt,** 'when the struggle is on.'

2416. **verwogen** is past participle of verwegen (verwägen), obsolete in this sense of 'to venture,' 'to be bold.'

2417. **eignem Mittel,** the plural is more usual.

2419. **unserer** = unser; see note on eurer, l. 286.

2421. **Es lebt nach uns** may be rendered 'there will be life after us,' or 𝔈𝔰 may be regarded as expletive and 𝔡𝔞𝔰 𝔥𝔢𝔯𝔯𝔩𝔦𝔠𝔥𝔢 as the subject of both 𝔩𝔢𝔟𝔱 and 𝔴𝔦𝔩𝔩, or again 𝔈𝔰 may be taken as = 𝔡𝔞𝔰 𝔥𝔢𝔯𝔯𝔩𝔦𝔠𝔥𝔢.

𝔞𝔫𝔡𝔯𝔢 𝔎𝔯ä𝔣𝔱𝔢, i.e. the burghers of free cities and the free yeomanry.

2422. 𝔡𝔞𝔰 𝔥𝔢𝔯𝔯𝔩𝔦𝔠𝔥𝔢 𝔡𝔢𝔯 𝔐𝔢𝔫𝔰𝔠𝔥𝔥𝔢𝔦𝔱, 'the glory of mankind,' i.e. freedom.

2423–26 and 2430–46. In the tone of the seer, prophetically.

𝔄𝔲𝔰 𝔡𝔦𝔢𝔰𝔢𝔪 𝔥𝔞𝔲𝔭𝔱𝔢 𝔲.𝔰.𝔴. Unless we find in these lines reference to Walther Tell as representing the younger generation of the yeomanry in the fairer union of whom with the nobility and the burghers the "glory of mankind" is to be conserved and perpetuated, we must have recourse to the general view that the meaning is rather merely that the incident of Tell's shot is, as it were, the seed of liberty.

2430–1. After the Crusades many nobles took up residence in the cities.

2432. Ü𝔠𝔥𝔱𝔩𝔞𝔫𝔡, formerly a name of the district between the Jura Mountains and the Bernese Alps, comprising the Canton Freiburg and part of the Canton Bern; ü𝔠𝔥𝔱 meant 'morning twilight.'

𝔗𝔥𝔲𝔯𝔤𝔞𝔲 was then larger than the present Canton of this name; it embraced all the northeastern part of Switzerland, east of Aargau.

2433. 𝔇𝔦𝔢, feminine because 𝔖𝔱𝔞𝔡𝔱 is understood. Bern and Freiburg were in Üchtland.

𝔥𝔢𝔯𝔯𝔰𝔠𝔥𝔢𝔫𝔡. Bern has ever been of commanding importance in Swiss affairs.

2435–6. 𝔷ü𝔯𝔦𝔠𝔥 was in Thurgau; it has always been commercially active, and the guilds were early instituted and influential, although not constitutionally recognized until the year 1336.

2436. 𝔷𝔲𝔪, 'as a,' 'to form a.'

2437. Probably of the victorious defense of the city of Zürich against Duke Albrecht and Emperor Charles IV. in 1345 and against the former in 1351 and 1352; but 𝔦𝔥𝔯𝔢𝔫 may be taken to refer to all these cities.

2438 ff. The notable battles, here alluded to, of the wars in defense against the Austrians and the Burgundians were those of Morgarten (a pass on the border between Schwyz and Zug) in 1315, Laupen in 1339, Sempach in 1386, Näfels (a pass in Glarus) in 1388, St. Jacob in 1444, Granson and Murten in 1476.

2443-6. Allusion to the traditional heroic act of Arnold von Winkelried, an Unterwaldner, in the battle of Sempach.

2444. Ein freies Opfer, cf. l. 3074.

2448. Ort, see Introd. p. liii and note on Vierwaldstättersee, p. 171.

* Burgglocke, 'castle-bell.'

The main portion of this scene consists of the 2d and 3d distinct parts and contains the climax of the Nobles-plot. In the 2d part, ending here, the dying nobleman, Attinghausen, blesses the confederation of the yeomanry and becomes its prophet, while in the following 3d part his nephew and heir, the young nobleman Rudenz, allying himself by solemn vow with the leaders of the confederation, commences the active fulfillment of Attinghausen's prophecy.

When we took leave of Attinghausen in Act II. Sc. 1 his soul was filled with pain at Rudenz' defection, and with sorrow because of the passing of the old and the coming of a new order of things. His death-hour takes from him this pain and sorrow. He hears of Rudenz' return to the holy cause of country, and his sorrow changes into joy as he looks forward to a brilliant future for his country. With prophetic vision he foretells the historic glory of Switzerland in the maintenance of liberty, and recognizes the new freedom—of the confederation of an independent yeomanry, an independent burgher-class, and an independent nobility—as the better freedom. The dying admonition to unity is our most solemn assurance that the cause of the nobles is one with the cause of the whole people.

2453. A freeman like Walther Fürst might hold fiefs in addition to property of his own.

2454. In so far only as it has another owner. It is now das Schloß von Rudenz (instead of Werner) auf Attinghausen.

2464. An inference from ll. 2377-8.

2477. Vater = Walther Fürst.

2478. die eurige, addressed to Stauffacher.

2482. The line has six feet. (für) nichts geachtet, 'regarded as nought,' 'despised.'

2483. weſſen . . . verſehn, 'what are we to expect from you?

2484. denken, with genitive instead of the usual an with the accusative.

2487. Handſchlag, 'hand-clasp,' as sealing a pledge.

2488. Ein Manneswort, 'an honest man's word.'

2489. Stand, 'class,' 'rank.'

2492. ſich is dative.

2498. Cf. ll. 2868-9.

2507. Pfand, 'pledge,' 'trust.'

2511. Cf. l. 149.

2515. wartet ab, imperative.

2525. Bertha must have resided in a castle in the land; she says herself that her estates are in Switzerland. Her intercession in the Gessler-scene revealed to the governor her real sentiments.

2528. vermogen, see note on l. 2416.

2532. der Wütende, as dem Thrannen, l. 2524, is Gessler.

2533. 'What outrage and violence they will boldly use.' ſie = Gessler, his companions and his creatures.

2534. zum verhaßten Band, see ll. 1667 ff., esp. 1671.

2538. Cf. l. 3231.

2546. Before Ob is an ellipsis of um zu verſuchen or um zu ſehen.

2548. ſparen for aufſparen in the sense of aufſchieben.

2551. Time as it moves on brings with it a change of circumstances, which requires a change of rules, laws and enactments.

2555. Botenſegel, 'messenger's sail' = 'messenger-boat.'

2558. **Wetters Strahl,** for usual **Wetterstrahl;** **Wetter** here = **Gewitter.**

* Rudenz grieves that he has not come in time to receive his uncle's dying blessing. But assured of Attinghausen's forgiveness, he soon turns to the new duties
devolving upon him. A most solemn vow does he take
that with all his soul he has given himself to his country
and his Swiss fellow-countrymen, and that he will live
in the spirit with which Attinghausen died. Fürst and
Stauffacher have confidence in Rudenz and accept his
vow, but Melchthal at first mistrusts him. In this way
Rudenz and Melchthal, the nobleman and the yeoman,
are distinctly marked as the leading characters in the
remainder of this scene. Melchthal alone represents
the proud self-consciousness which Attinghausen saw
in the bold action of the Rütli-meeting; in his words
ring a high sense of manhood and power and a strong
class-feeling. The yeomanry will defend itself and
stand independent and free by the side of the nobility.
This and his mistrust of the nobles are expressed in
lines 2482-3, 2488-9, and 2491-3. In answer—lines 2493-5
—the nobleman, with full acceptance of the new order
and in the spirit of Attinghausen's prophecy, admits
the full equality of the yeoman-class. Then after a
pause in which he realizes that this is not enough, he
proves that he merits full confidence, in that he has
treated his knowledge of the Rütli-meeting as a sacred
secret. To this negative proof Rudenz now adds con-
clusive positive proof by urging immediate execution
of the Rütli-plans and by declaring that, since he is not
bound by the decision there reached as to the time of
the rising and its joint character, he will act at once.

At this point it is to be noted that after his exclama-

---

* The view here taken is that of Bocksch in the ' Zeitschrift für den
deutschen Unterricht,' Bd. X. S. 185 ff.—It is certainly much more just to
Schiller's intention and to unitary conception of the drama than the commonly received view, which gives such romantic, extravagant importauce
to Rudenz' love for Bertha.

tion in line 2515 Melchthal says nothing until he pro-
nounces the momentous lines 2547–52. His exclamation shows that he is the first and the only one to realize
the full import of Rudenz' words and position: the
knights, the nobles, in voluntary alliance with us yeomen for action against the tyrants and their oppression.
And when now Rudenz further discloses that he and
his betrothed are victims of just such a personal outrage
as so many yeomen have suffered, and that he must
fight in his own self-interest, then the last vestige of
Melchthal's mistrust disappears, and in lines 2547–52 he
leads for the yeomanry in accepting the alliance of the
nobility and in committing himself to immediate joint
action with Rudenz.

The full content of Melchthal's thought is this: With
the powerful help of the nobles there can now (l. 2548)
be successfully accomplished the rising which we yeomen, when alone at the Rütli, decided could not be
undertaken until later. Since our meeting there, the
enormous double outrage on Tell has been perpetrated,
and now the nobles are with us in active alliance. Time
has changed these essential conditions and thus imposed upon us the law of immediate execution of the
Rütli-plans.

Thus in the persons of Rudenz and Melchthal is realized that participation of the nobles in the confederacy
which is later formally declared in l. 2890 and sealed as
described in lines 2898–2901.

ACT IV. SCENE 3.

* **Die hohle Gaſſe,** 'the hollow way,' 'the deep defile,' about
three quarters of an hour long, led from Imisee or Immensee, a small place on Lake Zug, past Gessler's castle to the
village of Küssnacht, see Map. Tell has come as quickly as
possible from where he was at the end of Scene 1, and from
Arth at the southern end of Lake Zug has reached this
pass. The time is late in the afternoon of the same day.
The road is now entirely changed, the defile having been

filled up. The traditional place is marked by a memorial chapel to Tell.

2563. **Holun'derstrauch,** 'elder-bush.'

2567. **Uhr.** The figure is taken from an hour-glass or sand-clock.

2572. **gärend Drachengift,** lit. 'fermenting dragon's-poison,' say 'rankling venom.'

2573. **Die Milch der frommen Denkart,** lit. 'The milk of good (pious) disposition,' is equivalent to Lady Macbeth's 'the milk of human kindness.'

2579. **Da,** anticipating **Damals** of l. 2584. **Bogenstrang,** 'bow-string.'

2583. **ohnmächtig,** here not 'swooningly,' but 'impotently,' 'unavailingly.'

2590. **meines Kaisers Vogt,** 'governor representing my Emperor.'

2592. **Was du** (dir erlaubt hast).

2594-5. **mit . . . erfrechen,** 'with delight in murder to do in insolence and with impunity every abominable outrage.'

2597. **Bringer bittrer Schmerzen,** addressed to the arrow, an Homeric expression, *Iliad*, iv. 117 and xv. 451.

2603. **in der Freude Spielen,** 'in joyous sports,' cf. l. 2648.

2606. **herben,** an Homeric epithet.

2608. It is difficult to assume that Tell has but one arrow, and the meaning of the line probably is, Ich werde keine Gelegenheit haben einen zweiten Pfeil zu versenden.

2609. **auf dieser Bank,** the dative of rest instead of the accusative with mich setzen in the sense of Platz nehmen, ausruhen.

2611-2. **jeder . . . vorüber,** 'Each hurries past the other swiftly and as a stranger.'

2614-5. **leicht geschürzte,** 'lightly girt,' not burdened with the wares and the cares of the merchant.

2616. **Spielmann,** 'minstrel,' 'musician.'

2617. **Säumer** = Führer der Saumrosse, 'driver,' 'carrier.'

2619. **Denn u.s.w.,** in explanation of ferne herkommt in the preceding line. For every road makes connection somehow with the remotest parts of the world.

2624. In translation insert 'but that' before **er bracht**; see note l. 1043.

2626. **Ammonshorn**, 'ammonite,' lit. 'Ammon's horn,' a fossil shell related to the nautilus, resembling somewhat a ram's horn in shape. Ammon was an appellation of Jupiter as represented with the horns of a ram.

2628. **Weidwerk**, here 'game' = **Wild** in l. 2635.

2635-6. **Läßt sich 's . . . verdrießen**, inversion for emphasis, not conditional : 'Why, the hunter does not let it discourage (daunt) him.'

2638. **Wagesprung**, 'daring leap'; cf. note l. 2874.

2640. Based on a passage in Scheuchzer, to the effect that in extreme need the chamois-hunter cuts the skin of the balls of his feet in order that the thickening adhesive blood may serve to prevent his slipping on smooth sloping rocks or narrow standing-places. This is now generally regarded as purely a matter of legend.

2641. **Grattier**, 'chamois,' or 'crag-deer,' living on the highest rocky ridges and peaks of the mountains, lighter reddish brown and smaller than the ordinary chamois, or **Walbtier**.

2648. **Freudenschießen**, usually a salute fired to celebrate some joyous event, but here = **Schützenfest**, 'shooting-match.'

2649. **das Beste**, 'the first prize.'

* **Eine Hochzeit**, 'a wedding party.'

* **gelehnt** = English present participle.

* **Flurschütz**, 'ranger.'

This scene divides naturally into two main parts, of which each in turn has two subdivisions ; after Tell's monologue and the conversations in which Stüssi appears, Gessler's appearance marks the beginning of the second part, which is cut across sharply by Tell's shot.

The poet's skill in arousing, sustaining, and heightening dramatic suspense is inimitable. Tell's very first words make us know what is to happen, so that our thought is ever intent upon this one thing. Gessler has not yet appeared, but he has been before our mind's eye every instant.

The monologue permits us to look Tell's soul through and through before his fateful act. Such insight is the more necessary as we do not yet have anything like real knowledge of the revolution which took place in Tell's inner being during the apple-shooting. It is a reflective monologue, altogether natural for a man of Tell's character, who is at no loss for words in which to clothe his thoughts when he desires to express them, and who is given to thoughtful meditation. He is to be sure not a Hamlet with resolution sicklied o'er with the pale cast of thought ; he will not long weigh pros and cons, and hesitate when choice is urgent, but he is disposed to reflect on the causes and the righteousness of such a decision as this. As regards the form of the monologue it is to be noted that it three times approaches dialogue, as Tell in thought addresses Gessler, then his arrow and bow-string, and lastly his children.

As if right to Gessler's face, Tell explains his ability, his necessity, his right to kill the tyrant. Because Gessler's cruelty has changed his heart and filled it with rankling venom, Tell has both the power and the will to do the deed that ordinarily is murder. But what he can do and wills to do is also what he must do. The necessity is multiple : he must protect his children, his wife, himself ; he must perform the vow he made, with his next shot to reach the governor's heart, and he must thus avenge upon Gessler the sanctity of nature that Gessler outraged in demanding that he shoot at his own son. The right to kill Gessler rests for Tell upon these same reasons, together with the fact that Gessler has violated the laws of man and of God ; Tell is but the executor of God's righteous judgment.

Now Tell prepares for the final moment, addressing his arrow and bow-string, until the passing of travelers diverts him. His words mentioning murder in lines 2621, 2629, and 2630 are not to be understood as expressing any shrinking from the deed ; they are simple reflections on a settled, rightful fact.

The tones with which the monologue closes, lines 2635–2650, vibrate, as it were, with the archer's supreme joy. Consciousness of his right, and hatred of Gessler, overcome the shrinking of the natural man from bloodshed, and the marksman's delight in a master-shot leaps forth.

The effectiveness of the contrast made by the wedding-procession and its music needs no comment. The wedding-party also explains the later separation of Gessler from his retinue and secures the presence upon the scene of the common people.

2651. **Kloſtermei(e)r,** 'monastery-steward,' i.e. the manager (see note to l. 1072) of the farm which the Monastery of Engelberg owned near the village of Mörlischachen on the Lake not far from Küssnacht. **Schachen** is an Alemannic word for a tongue of land projecting into water.

2652. **Brautlauf,** 'wedding-procession,' or 'wedding'; an obsolete word for **Hochzeit,** because the custom of competing for a future wife in a race died out long ago.

2653. **Sente,** a herd of cows, not less than twenty in number.

2654. **Imiſee** (or **Immenſee**), a hamlet on Lake Zug, a quarter of an hour's distance from the „hohle Gaſſe.“

2659. **Nehmt mit, was kommt,** 'take along whatever comes,' = English slang, 'take in (enjoy) whatever comes along.'

2660. **leicht ergreifen,** 'quickly grasp,' 'hasten to lay hold of.'

2661. 'Here there's marrying and elsewhere burying.'

2664. **Ruffi,** a Swiss word = **Bergſturz,** 'landslide.'

gegangen = **losgegangen.**

Glarner, adj., 'of Glarus,' the Canton.

2666. **Glärniſch,** name of a group of mountain-peaks in the Canton of Glarus, several of which are over 9000 feet high.

2669. **Da ſprach ich einen,** ' I just spoke with a man.'

Baden, see note on l. 409.

* **Armgard,** see note p. 168.

2676. **Man deutet's auf,** ' They interpret it with refer- —
ence to.'

2682. Note contrast with l. 428.

2690. **Der Strom,** the Muotta.

2691. **an ihn,** unusual for **bei ihm,** as if there stood here
Habt ihr ein Anſuchen an ihn?, or **Habt ihr ein Geſuch an ihn zu richten?**

> Still Gessler is not present in person, but we think of
> him every moment during these conversations, by which
> the dramatic suspense has been not only maintained,
> but even quickened. The underlying meaning of Tell's
> answers, of which Stüssi is unconscious, keeps our
> mind on the governor, while all the others mention him,
> either denying or affirming his coming. Again do we
> have the characteristic proverb-like substance and form
> of Tell's utterances.

2702. **Mein Lebtag,** ' all my days,' for either **meinen Lebtag**
or **meine Lebtage.**

2706. ' It would have sunk to the bottom with every living thing on board '; see note to l. 331.

2707. **Dem Volk,** ' This sort of people.'

Dem, with emphasis, is demonstrative pronoun.

kann ... bei (kommen), ' can ... get at ' (i.e. affect, hurt).

2710. **drauf denken,** see note on l. 613.

2712. **ihm (= dem Volk) ſanft zu thun,** ' to be agreeable to it.'

2715. **bring' ich's an,** ' I will present it ' (i.e. my request,
petition).

2726. **Die,** demonstrative pronoun.

2727. **im Werk und Werden,** ' on foot and in progress '; the
alliteration can hardly be duplicated in English.

2728. The Habsburgers aspired especially to increase
their power as a dynasty and in territory.

Der Vater is Rudolph I., Emperor from 1273 to 1291.

2729. **Der Sohn** is Albrecht I., Emperor from 1298 to 1308.

2731. **So oder ſo,** ' this way or that way,' i.e. whether it
will or not.

2735. **Waifen,** ' fatherless children '; sometimes indeed the English word ' orphan ' is applied to a child bereft of only one parent.

2736. **Geſtrenger,** see note on l. 1859.

2738. **Wildheuer,** ' gatherer of wild hay,' explained by the next lines.

Rigiberg, the famous Rigi, group of mountains between the lakes of Lucerne, Zug, and Lowerz.

2749. **den Mann,** ' my husband.'

2750. **in den ſechſten Mond** (poetic for **Monat**), lit. ' into the sixth month,' ' more than five months.'

2755. **So,** ' as.'

2760. **Recht geſprochen,** ' done justice.'

2763. **nach . . . fragen,** ' care for.'

2772. **was = etwas.**

2774. **Man . . . hinnen,** ' Let her be hurried away.'

2780. **wie es (ſein) ſoll.**

* **fährt mit der Hand,** ' puts his hand.'

2791. **Ein Mann des Todes!** ; see l. 73 and note.

* **gegleitet,** weak participle. This verb is usually of the strong conjugation, but in modern usage there is a tendency to make it weak.

2794. Cf. l. 79.

* **die Muſik geht fort,** ' the music continues.'

2810. **gebrochen,** see note on **brechend,** l. 865.

2814. **leget Hand an,** ' set about it.'

2817. **Wagt es, Herr (auf eure Gefahr)!;** a warning.

2830. **Treu',** dative case governed by **vertrauen.**

* **barmherzige Brüder.** The introduction of the friars of this particular order is an anachronism, as the order of the ' Brothers of Mercy' was not founded until the year 1540 in Seville by San Juan di Dio.

2832. **die Raben,** with the rude wit of common people, an allusion to the black garb of the friars.

2835. **Es** (as also in next line), an indefinite and impersonal subject ; best rendered in English by the passive.

2838. **ſtehen,** see note on l. 1948.

When Gessler is seen, Tell is invisibly present. In

Act III. Scene 3, Gessler revealed himself but in slight
degree as an antagonist of the people. Now his conversation with Rudolf der Harras fully discloses his
political plans, his ends, and his means, and also the
ultimate reason of his action. The scene with Armgard is very powerful and highly dramatic in construction. It not only brings before us again Gessler's cruel
outrages upon individuals and his violation of justice,
but it also culminates in his vow to break the liberty-
loving spirit of the Swiss people, and the arrow smites
him in this precise instant of his intensest antagonism,
individual and collective.

Gessler recognizes the missile as Tell's, and Tell
acknowledges his deed. The three lines 2792–4 have
been mistakenly criticised as untrue and merely theatrical. They are, however, not aimless boasting over
a dead man, but the expression of justifiable joy in the
re-established safety of the land, addressed to the still
living tyrant. Nor are these words intended by the
poet to deepen the impression that avenging Providence is here controlling. They have rather this other
very important purpose. The motives which in the
beginning of this scene impel Tell to kill Gessler all
lie in his individual relation to the governor; the
thought of delivering and saving the country is not
there evident. Lines 2793–4, however, make it plain that
this motive has since become decisive. So in line 3143
Tell seems to say the same thing. In the same sense
must be understood the later praise of Tell as the rescuer and savior of his country. After the monologue,
in which his personal motives are fully reviewed, Tell
is witness of the scene between Gessler and Rudolf
der Harras, and above all of the scene with Armgard.
And now he realizes that not only his cottage but all
the homes of the land, not only his innocent children
but innocence, not only himself but the whole land are
involved. The Gessler at whom he sends his arrow is
not only his personal enemy, but the enemy of his country.

In the conclusion of the scene the cold, unpitying horror of the people is significant. The immediate effect of Gessler's death is shown in Stüssi's bearing and words ; Tell's deed gives higher courage to the common man, who by the side of the dead tyrant declares his final rejection of the yoke of tyranny. The hymn of the friars, like a Greek chorus, expressing a general reflection based on this concrete case, brings calm and comfort to the agitated minds and hearts of all.

Act IV brings in Scene 1, for the Tell-plot, the first stage of the descending action, in Tell's escape from the boat ; in Scene 2, for the Yeomen-plot the second stage of the descending action, and for the Nobles-plot the climax, while the Tell-plot is passively represented ; and in Scene 3, for the Tell-plot the second stage of the descending action.

SEAL OF LUCERNE, 1314.

ACT V.

ARGUMENT.—The *first* scene shows us the destruction of Keep Uri. Gessler's death has been the signal for a general rising to expel the Austrian governors, and signal-fires on the mountains announce its universal success. Melchthal narrates the capture of Sarnen by Rudenz, and his own seizure of Rossberg and rescue there of Bertha. While all are rejoicing, Rösselmann brings the news of the death of Emperor Albrecht at the hands of his nephew, Duke Johann of Swabia, and the latter's friends. This news and the report that the next emperor will not be elected from the Habsburg family complete the joy of the Swiss, since they are thereby freed from all fear of Austrian vengeance. A messenger from the Empress arrives with the request that the Swiss assist her in punishing the murderers, but they are unanimous in feeling that they have no duty or desire so to do. Stauffacher summons all to go to Tell's home and extol him as their savior.

The *second* scene is the interior of Tell's house, where Hedwig and the two boys rejoice in the near coming of Tell. A man in the garb of a monk approaches. From his wild looks Hedwig is shrinking with foreboding of evil, when Tell arrives. On learning that it is Tell, the monk reveals himself to him as Duke Johann of Swabia. At first Tell gives way to his horror, but soon takes pity on the guilty youth, advises him to go to Rome and seek absolution from the Pope, and describes to him the way thither.

As he departs, the *third* scene shows us the valley and heights about Tell's house, with Tell's countrymen come from all quarters to hail him their savior and defender. Rudenz and Bertha come too. Bertha asks to be admitted into the confederation, and gives her hand in promise of marriage to Rudenz, who closes the act and the drama by liberating all his serfs.

Scene I.

The place is the same as in Act I. Scene 3. The time is two or three days later than that of Act IV, i.e. the 21st or 22d of November. The Sarner stronghold was taken during the night preceding the dawn with which this scene opens, while in l. 2875 Melchthal says that Rossberg was taken the night before. At least one day, therefore, must elapse between Acts IV and V.

* **Signalfeuer** and, l. 2839, **Feuersignale**, compare ll. 1421-2, 2554, and 2557.

2841. **Die Burgen**, Rossberg and Sarnen.

2845. **Joch**, see l. 370 and note.

2847. **Stier von Uri**, see note to l. 1091.

2848. **Hochwacht**; this word, which we have already had in ll. 1441 and 2449 in the sense of beacon-fire, designates also the guard placed on a height, or, as here, the height itself, 'mountain' or 'watch-tower' or 'signal-height.'

2862. **Gesellen**, 'workmen' or 'men.'

2862-3. Cf. l. 387.

2864. **Es ist im Lauf**, 'It is under full headway.'

2866. **gebrochen**, 'destroyed.'

2868. **die Lande** (see note to l. 431) and, l. 2871, **der Schweizer Land** both mean here only the three ancient Cantons, the **Waldstätte**.

rein u.s.w., cf. l. 2498.

2874. **mannlich**, archaic for **männlich**.

Wagethat, poetic newly coined word, 'deed of daring'; for similar compounds see ll. 1494 and 2638.

2875. **nachts zubor**, i.e. the night from the 19th to the 20th of November.

2877. **angezündet** [**hatten, und als**].

2879. **Bub**, see note to l. 466.

2880. **die Bruneckerin**, i.e. Bertha of Bruneck, 'my lady of Bruneck.'

2882. **auf u.s.w.**, cf. l. 468.

2887. **Da galt**, see notes to ll. 1920 and 1989.

Geschwindsein, 'quickness.'

2888. 𝕰𝖉𝖊𝖑𝖒𝖆𝖓𝖓, here = 𝕷𝖊𝖍𝖊𝖓𝖘𝖍𝖊𝖗𝖗, as in l. 245

2894. 𝖋𝖊𝖑𝖇𝖆𝖓𝖉𝖊𝖗, here 'together'; lit. 'I and one other.'

2901. 𝕾𝖈𝖍𝖎𝖈𝖋𝖆𝖑𝖘𝖕𝖗𝖔𝖇𝖊𝖓, 'tests (or trials) of fate.'

2902. 𝖚𝖇𝖊𝖗 𝖉𝖊𝖓 𝕭𝖗𝖚𝖓𝖎𝖌, see note to l. 1193. This mountain lies south of Sarnen; historically Landenberg fled northward towards Lucerne.

2905. 𝕹𝖆𝖈𝖍 . . . 𝖎𝖍𝖒, poetic emphatic inversion for 𝖎𝖈𝖍 𝖏𝖆𝖌𝖙𝖊 𝖎𝖍𝖒 𝖓𝖆𝖈𝖍.

2910. 𝖀𝖗𝖋𝖊𝖍𝖉𝖊, 'solemn oath.' This word means in full 'an oath not to seek vengeance for wrong suffered.'

2918. 𝖀𝖓𝖙𝖊𝖗, only in a very general sense, for in Act III. Scene 3 Walther stood not close by the pole, but under the linden-tree.

2922. The hat or cap is in so far a symbol of liberty as the right to cover one's head has always been regarded as a sign of liberty

The first scene of this final act shows us that the morning of a festival of deliverance is dawning in Switzerland. What line 387 prophesied for the common people is now fulfilled, and we behold the average man doing his part in the spirit of Stüssi's words in lines 2818–20. The destruction of the scaffolding and of the building has the significance of an effective declaration of liberty. The signals from Schwyz and the bells from Unterwalden proclaim the end of tyranny there, while here in Uri we see the yoke destroyed. The alliance of Rudenz and Melchthal, as was emphasized in the notes to Act IV. Sc. 2, has the deepest and widest symbolical importance; it is the reunion, on an independent footing of equality, of the yeomanry and the nobility. That the Swiss people in this union of all classes in these three Cantons has thus successfully realized its declaration of liberty, and, while rejoicing, shows noble moderation and self-restraint, gives us all the assurance that can be derived from the character of this people as to its continued freedom and happiness in the future. But the real antagonist of their rights and liberties, though distant, may still continue to threaten. What of the Emperor? Must he still and always be feared?

2946. **Brud**, or **Brugg**, is a small town on the river Aar in the Canton of Aargau.

2948. This line is the poet's homage to the noted historian Johannes von Müller, who was born at Schaffhausen in 1752, and died at Kassel in 1809. See Introd. p. lix.

2952. See lines 1336–1348 and notes thereto.

2953. **Batermord** = **Verwandtenmord**, 'parricide'; Albrecht was his uncle and guardian.

2954. **das väterliche Erbe** was the Duchy of Swabia; see l. 1344 and note.

2957. 'To compromise with him by giving him (To put him off with) a bishopric.'

Often the younger sons of great families have been made to have an ecclesiastical career, because high ecclesiastical station has implied a rich and influential position, while it was not necessary to take from the fortune of the eldest son anything for the benefit of the younger.

2958. **Wie dem auch sei**, 'Be that as it may.'

2965. **Der Stein zu Baden**, cf. l. 2669 and note l. 409.

2966. **Gen** (= **Gegen**) **Rheinfeld**, see note to l. 1324.

Hofstatt, 'court'; compare **Lager** (for **Hoflager**) in l. 817 and **Pfalz** in l. 1324, and notes thereto.

2967. **Hans** = Johann von Schwaben, l. 2952.

Leopold, Albrecht's second son, defeated at Morgarten in 1315.

2974. **alte große Stadt**, the Roman Vindonissa (now the village Windisch), an important frontier fortress against the Germans; it was destroyed by Childebert II. in the year 594.

2975. **Heiden**, 'pagans,' 'heathen,' i.e. the Romans.

2976. The Habsburg, originally Habichtsburg, was built about 1020 by Count Radbod of Altenburg on the wooded height of the Wülpelberg, which descends steeply towards the Aar. Count Werner II. in 1075 was the first to use the name Habsburg. The castle is now a ruin, twenty minutes' distance above Schinznach.

2982. 'Murdered by his own kinsmen (or adherents) on his own territory.'

2992. **Stand,** render by 'district' or 'canton'; it = precisely **Reichsstand,** '.estate,' which might be a county, or duchy, or canton, or free city, or bishopric, etc.

2996. **Bannes,** 'ban,' commonly used only of excommunication from the church, but here mainly of outlawry or banishment from the empire.

2997 ff. Agnes was the eldest of the five daughters of Albrecht; her husband, King Andreas III. of Hungary, had died in 1301, leaving her childless; she died in 1364, 83 years old, in the convent of Königsfelden founded by her and the Empress Elizabeth on the site of the murder, with the confiscated property of the families of the murderers. Tradition, which is not supported by modern historical research, makes her vengeance unparalleled in ferocity and relentlessness.

3003. **Zeugungen** = **Geschlechter,** 'generations.'

3005. The chroniclers relate such vows of the queen and their fulfillment. Bullinger states that after the surrender of Farwangen, the chief castle of Rudolf von Palm, she caused 63 men, some being nobles, to be beheaded in the forest before her face, and exclaimed, 'Now I am bathing in May dew.' This expression is explained perhaps by the fact that it was in May that Albrecht was killed.

3007. **alsbald** here has accent on first syllable, although usually on the second.

3012. **Sich,** dative; 'It is its own dreadful nourishment.'

3023. **was** = **etwas.**

The freedom of election of the Empire was maintained by the Electors choosing on November 29, 1308, not a member of the House of Habsburg, but the Count of Luxemburg, who, as Heinrich VII., reigned until his death in 1313. He confirmed the liberties of the Forest Cantons and protected them against Austria.

3024. **mehrsten** = **meisten.** This superlative from the comparative was early formed, and used through the eighteenth century, but much less than **meist;** it is now to be avoided.

* 𝕽𝖊𝖎𝖈𝖍𝖘𝖇𝖔𝖙𝖊, 'imperial messenger.'

3031. 𝖇𝖊𝖘𝖈𝖍𝖊𝖎𝖉(𝖊)𝖓𝖊𝖓, same meaning as in l. 553 ; see note.

3033. 𝕰𝖑𝖘𝖇𝖊𝖙𝖍 = Elizabeth, daughter of Meinhard, Duke of Carinthia, Count of Tyrol and Görtz, which countries she brought to Austria. She was married in 1282 and died in 1313 at Vienna.

𝖆𝖑𝖑𝖊𝖘 𝕲𝖚𝖙𝖊𝖘, for present usual 𝖆𝖑𝖑𝖊𝖘 𝕲𝖚𝖙𝖊.

3036. 𝖂𝖔𝖗𝖊𝖎𝖓 = 𝖜𝖔 𝖍𝖎𝖓𝖊𝖎𝖓 = 𝖎𝖓 𝖜𝖊𝖑𝖈𝖍𝖊.

𝕳𝖎𝖓𝖘𝖈𝖍𝖊𝖎𝖉, *m.* 'decease,' more common is 𝖉𝖆𝖘 𝕳𝖎𝖓𝖘𝖈𝖍𝖊𝖎𝖇𝖊𝖓.

3038. 𝕾𝖈𝖍𝖜𝖞𝖟𝖊𝖗𝖑𝖆𝖓𝖉𝖊 = 𝖉𝖎𝖊 𝖉𝖗𝖊𝖎 𝖂𝖆𝖑𝖉𝖘𝖙ä𝖙𝖙𝖊.

3040 and 3050. Incomplete lines, as often. The pause of the missing part of the line is filled by appropriate action. Here in the first case the crowd settles into quiet, and in the second a murmur perhaps runs through it.

3041. 𝖛𝖊𝖗𝖘𝖎𝖊𝖍𝖙, see note to l. 2483 ; here the genitive is replaced by the 𝖉𝖆𝖘 clause following.

3053. Cf. ll. 1324 and following.

3054. 𝖂𝖎𝖊 — 𝖆𝖑𝖑𝖊 — 𝖉𝖔𝖈𝖍 𝖌𝖊𝖙𝖍𝖆𝖓, cf. l. 805.

3062. 𝖗ü𝖍𝖗𝖙𝖊 . . . 𝖆𝖓 = 𝖜ü𝖗𝖉𝖊 𝖆𝖓𝖌𝖊𝖗ü𝖍𝖗𝖙 𝖍𝖆𝖇𝖊𝖓.

3067. 𝖌𝖊𝖒𝖊𝖍𝖗𝖙, 'aggrandized,' 'increased (in wealth and power)'; a mocking allusion to the phrase in the German version of the title of the Emperor, ,𝖆𝖑𝖑𝖊𝖟𝖊𝖎𝖙 𝕸𝖊𝖍𝖗𝖊𝖗 𝖉𝖊𝖘 𝕽𝖊𝖎𝖈𝖍𝖊𝖘,' which was a mistranslation of the Latin '*Imperator semper Augustus*,' the last word being taken as immediately from *augere*, 'to increase.'

3068. 𝖋𝖗𝖔𝖍𝖑𝖔𝖈𝖐𝖊𝖓, here with genitive, but usually with über and accusative.

3073. 𝖜𝖎𝖑𝖑 . . . 𝖓𝖎𝖈𝖍𝖙 = '𝖉𝖆𝖗𝖋 𝖓𝖎𝖈𝖍𝖙' or '𝖐𝖆𝖓𝖓 𝖓𝖎𝖈𝖍𝖙.'

3074. 𝖜𝖎𝖑𝖑 = 𝖒𝖚ß.

𝖋𝖗𝖊𝖎𝖊𝖘 𝕺𝖕𝖋𝖊𝖗, cf. l. 2444.

3076. 'We have no further duty to discharge to him (i.e. the dead Emperor).'

3077 and 3078. 𝖀𝖓𝖉, followed by inverted order = 'and while,' 'and though.'

3079. 𝖘𝖔, here adversative, 'still on the other hand.'

3081. Proverbial of tears of sympathy.

3085. Cf. l. 749 and Act V. Sc. 3.

The second division of this scene, beginning with

the appearance of Rösselmann and Stauffacher, gives us the assurance that the Swiss have nothing more to fear. The Emperor, who embodied in himself the hostile designs óf the Habsburg family, is dead, and the next Emperor will not belong to that dynasty, but will rather be a friend of Switzerland. The account of the Emperor's death is given with much epic breadth. Rösselmann's comment in l. 2938 is as if he had in mind the Rütli-vow, l. 1452. The letter of the Queen supplements Stauffacher's narration, and the conclusion of the scene exhibits the natural law that controls the relations between rulers and subjects. Stauffacher's thought of Tell and summons to all to go to him prepare for the last scene.

Act V. Scene 2.

The scene is the interior of Tell's house, of which we saw the exterior in Act III. Sc. 1.

The $\mathfrak{H}$ausflur in such a Swiss house was the 'main room,' into which one entered directly from the outside, and which was kitchen, sitting-room, and entrance-hall all in one.

*zeigt ins Freie, lit. 'points into the open air' = 'shows a view of the open country.'

The time is the same as in the preceding scene.

3089. der's = der das.

3092. Ging . . . vorbei, 'went close by my life.'

3096. Cf. and contrast l. 2086.

3101. ins Freudenhaus = 'into a house of rejoicing.'

*mit zerstörten (for usual verstörten) Zügen = 'with a wild and troubled look.'

3108. Herr, archaic for Gatte.

3109. was ist euch, 'what is the matter with you.'

3112. Wie auch, 'however much.'

3116-7. Such appeal to the hearth and to the heads of beloved persons is ancient and classical; compare Homer, *Odyssey*, vii. 153, xiv. 159, xv. 260-1, *Iliad*, ii. 15 and 665, Vergil, *Æneid*, vi. 364, x. 524.

3124. **ſchnürt mir das Innre zu,** 'stifles (smothers, or chokes, lit., laces up) my inmost feelings.'

* **hält ſich an,** 'checks (or contains) herself,' or 'leans against the door-post.'

3138. A religious custom of ancient times which passed on into the Middle Ages.

> The main portion of this scene is introduced by these three incidents, whose motives are of great beauty, but which are merely touched and not elaborated ; the joy of the mother and the sons in the father and his coming, the appearance of the monkish figure, with Hedwig's intuitive shrinking, and the coming of Tell with its throng of emotions, in part strongly conflicting.

3158. **Ihr wäret,** 'Do you mean to say that you are'; see note l. 1834.

3162-3. **Herzog von Öſterreich;** his title is more precisely given in l. 2952.

* **Johannes Parricida,** 'John the Parricide.' Schiller himself directed that the costume of the Duke should be a monk's white cowl, but that underneath should be a knight's costly attire with a jewelled girdle, which should become visible in connection with his being recognized by Tell.

3168. **eh' ihr** (richtet).

3169. **Vatermordes,** see note to l. 2953.

3170. **Du,** instead of ihr, probably in contempt.

3191. **So jung,** the real Johannes was only eighteen years old at the time of the crime.

3194. **Des armen Mannes,** genitive in apposition with the genitive of the personal pronoun implied in the possessive adjective **meiner** of the preceding line.

3197. **konnte** and (3198) **bezwang** ; see note on l. 2060.

3200. **Leopold,** see l. 2060 and note.

3205. Cf. l. 1346.

3207. **Schluß** for usual **Entſchluß.**

3209. **Rachegeiſter,** lit. 'spirits of vengeance,' = 'Furies'; see note to l. 1700.

3212. Complete the line with **biſt.** The language is that of Emperor Heinrich's formal decree of outlawry, as re-

ported by Tschudi : Die Täter ſeyen Jren Fründen verbotten (forbidden), Jren Vienden erloubt (allowed, given over).

3215. **Wüſte,** as in l. 2135.

3222. **ein Menſch der Sünde,** for ein ſünbiger Menſch, 'a sinful
mortal.'

3229. **entdeckt,** past part. used elliptically, 'if discovered';
cf. l. 653.

3231. Cf. l. 2538.

3232. Cf. l. 1108.

3235. **löſet,** 'redeem'; cf. Mark viii. 37. Ober was kann der
Menſch geben, damit er ſeine Seele löſe? According to tradition he
received absolution from Pope Clement V. at Rome and
died as an Augustine monk at Pisa.

3241 ff. The opening of the drama displayed the magnificent scenery about the Lake of the Four Forest Cantons ;
here now in conclusion is pictured the bold St. Gotthard pass.
which in the Middle Ages was the main highway from Germany across the Alps. The same descriptive material for
which he was chiefly indebted to Goethe, Joh. v. Müller,
and Meiner's *Briefe über die Schweiz,* Schiller used in one
of his best lyric poems, Das Berglied.

3243. **wildes** (usually wilden) **Laufes,** adverbial genitive of
manner.

3244. **Seh' ich** = Soll ich . . . ſehen. Cf. l. 2969.

3247. **begraben (hat).**

3252. **die Schreckensſtraße,** 'the road of horror,' is the wild
gorge Schöllenen, extending the distance of an hour and a
half from the village Göschenen to the Devil's Bridge.

3253. **Windeswehen,** here = Winblawinen, 'drift-avalanches';
see note to l. 1501.

3254. **Joch,** here = 'ridge,' 'saddle,' connecting two peaks
and dividing two valleys.

3255. **die Brücke, welche ſtäubet,** 'the bridge that hangs in
drizzling spray' (Th. Martin). This is, according to some,
the so-called ſtäubende Brücke, a hanging bridge of beams and
boards, swinging on chains across the deep gorge of the
Reuss above the Teufelsbrücke, and constantly wet with spray ;
others take it to be the Teufelsbrücke itself, which, however,

was not built until long after the time in which the drama plays ; of course the poet was free to carry back his own time into the past, as he does in l. 3258 and elsewhere.

3258. **Felfenthor,** 'rocky gate,' the so-called **Urnerloch,** 'hole of Uri.' An anachronism, as it was not until the year 1707 that this tunnel, more than 200 feet long, was made through the rock.

3260. **Thal der Freude** = Urferenthal.

3264. **deines Reiches Boden,** i.e. Italy including the Canton Tessin (Ticino), as part of the Holy Roman Empire.

3266. On the St. Gotthard are a number of small lakes, according to Bädeker about thirty. Of seven of these, near the Hospice, Scheuchzer states that during the whole year they remain unchanged in depth ; hence the epithet **ewig.**

3267. **von des Himmels Strömen,** i.e. from snow and rain.

3269. **ein andrer Strom,** i.e. the river Tessin (Ticino).

3270. **euch das gelobte (Land),** 'for you the Promised Land'; where you will find peace. The participle **gelobt** in this standing designation of the Holy Land belongs historically to the verb **geloben,** 'to promise, to vow,' but is commonly felt now as belonging to the verb **loben** in the sense of 'to praise.'

* **bedeutet ihn mit der Hand,** 'makes a sign to him with his hand.'

　　　In this interview between Tell and Parricida Schiller's intention seems to have been twofold : to bring before us with utmost vividness the reality of the death of the Emperor, and to show Tell after the shooting of Gessler as not only altogether without remorse, but serenely confident and rejoicing in it as an act of divine justice. But here again the poet's execution diverges from his intention, and our interest in Parricida and our sympathy are so aroused as seriously to interfere with Schiller's design. The scene is in itself strong and beautiful.

* **Letzte Scene,** cf. ll. 749, 3085.

3286. **Bürgerin,** here = 'fellow-citizen.'

　　　While Scene 1 belongs mainly to the Yeomen-plot,

although we learn too about Rudenz and Bertha, and
Scene 2 belongs exclusively to the Tell-plot, this 3d and
final scene unites the representatives of all three plots
in a picture symbolical of liberty, union, and happiness,
and of the nation's gratitude to Tell, the savior of his
country. In the last lines we find further fulfillment of
Attinghausen's prophecy. The noblewoman, seeking
legal protection, asks to be received into the Confederation. Rudenz abolishes serfdom, and with that
the form of civilization which depended on it. Thus
we see a twofold movement beginning with these
representatives of the nobility; on the one hand the
nobles move down towards the middle class, the
yeomen and burghers, while on the other the serfs
are lifted up into full citizenship. The drama 'ends
with the full harmony of liberty, equality, fraternity.

Act V is not superfluous, for this work is not a
tragedy but a "Schauspiel," a serious drama, which
must give us an harmonious adjustment of its conflict
of interest and confidence in the permanence of peace
and joy.

The Tell-plot, regarded as a purely tragic plot, does
indeed have its catastrophe and end in the death of
Gessler in Act IV. Sc. 3, but after all we are not recon-
ciled until we see Tell with his family and his people
in Act V. Scenes 2 and 3, which thus contain the conclusion of the catastrophe. With the end of Act IV
the two other plots imperatively demand continuation.
The Yeomen-plot has the conclusion of its descending
action and its catastrophe in Act V. Scenes 1 and 3.
The Nobles-plot has its descending action and its
catastrophe in the same scenes. Without them we
should have no assurance as to the fate of Bertha and
the relations of the nobility to the yeomanry, and the
Rütli plans would seem to have come to naught so far
as concerns the active participation of the common
people. The execution of the Parricida scene is, how-

ever, misleading, and the act is as a whole more epic,
picturesque, than dramatic.

SEAL OF ZÜRICH, 1291.

APPENDIX.

PRINCIPAL DATES OF THE LIFE

OF

Johann Christoph Friedrich [von] Schiller.

1759, Nov. 10. Birth at Marbach in Würtemberg.

1765–1768. Family resided in Lorch.

1768–1773. Pupil of Latin School in Ludwigsburg. Preparation for theology.

1772, Easter. Confirmation.

1773–1780. Pupil of the "Karlsschule," until 1775 in the Château Solitude, thereafter in Stuttgart. Law and medicine. Military surgeon. Early poems and *Die Räuber.*

1781, May. Publication of *Die Räuber.*

1782, Sept. 22. Flight from Stuttgart.

1782–1785. Wanderings and residence in Mannheim, Oggersheim, Bauerbach, and Mannheim.

1782. *Fiesko* written ; published in 1783.

1782–1783. *Kabale und Liebe* written ; published in 1784.

1783–1787. *Don Karlos* written ; published in 1787.

1785–1787. Residence in Leipzig and Dresden. Study of history.

1787–1789. Residence in Weimar and in Volkstedt near Rudolstadt.

1788. Publication of *Geschichte des Abfalls der vereinigten Niederlande von der spanischen Regierung.*

1789. Appointed professor in the university of Jena, where he now resided.

1790, Feb. 22. Married to Charlotte von Lengefeld.

1790 and thereafter. Writing of *Geschichte des dreissigjährigen Krieges*, published complete in 1793. Editorial labors. Study of philosophy.

1794. Beginning of friendship with Goethe.

1795. *Briefe über die ästhetische Erziehung des Menschen.*

1796. *Xenien.*

1797. Ballads and short poems.

1797–1799. *Wallenstein* written : *W.'s Lager* first performed in October 1798, *Die Piccolomini* in January 1799, and *W.'s Tod* in April 1799; the whole published in June 1800.

1799–1800. *Maria Stuart* written ; published in 1801.

1799, Dec. Removal to Weimar.

1800–1801. *Die Jungfrau von Orleans* written ; published end of 1801.

1802. Patent of nobility.

1802–1803. *Die Braut von Messina* written ; published 1803.

1803–1804. *Wilhelm Tell* written ; published 1804.

1805, May 9. Death.

BIBLIOGRAPHY.

This list contains only what is of more immediate and practical importance. An exhaustive bibliography may be found in Goedeke's *Grundriss zur Geschichte der deutschen Dichtung*, 2te Aufl. Bd. V. ss. 97–237. There is an annual review of the current Schiller-literature in Lyon's *Zeitschrift für den deutschen Unterricht* and in the *Jahresbericht für neuere deutsche Litteraturgeschichte*. Nevinson's *Life of Schiller* contains as an appendix a bibliography which treats with especial fullness the English translations and criticism.

LIVES OF SCHILLER.

K. Hoffmeister. Schillers Leben, Geistesentwickelung und Werke im Zusammenhang. 5 Bde. Stuttgart. 1838–1842.

H. Viehoff. Schillers Leben, Geistesentwickelung und Werke auf Grundlage der Karl Hoffmeisterschen Schriften neu bearbeitet. 3 Bde. Stuttgart. 1875.

E. Palleske. Schillers Leben und Werke. 2 Bde. Berlin. 1858–9. 13te Aufl. bearbeitet von Hermann Fischer. Stuttgart. 1891.

H. Düntzer. Schillers Leben. Leipzig. 1881.

R. Weltrich. Friedrich Schiller. Geschichte seines Lebens und Charakteristik seiner Werke. Unter kritischem Nachweis der biographischen Quellen. Stuttgart. 1885–9. [Incomplete, only a portion of the first volume yet issued.]

O. Brahm. Schiller. Berlin. 1888–92. [Only two vols. out of four yet issued.]

J. Minor. Schiller. Sein Leben und seine Werke dargestellt. Berlin. 1890—. [When finished in four or five vols. this work, of which only two vols. have been published, will be the fullest biography of Schiller.]

J. Wychgram. Schiller, dem deutschen Volke dargestellt. Bielefeld u. Leipzig. 1896. [A most excellent popular life with abundant illustrative material.]

T. Carlyle. The Life of Friedrich Schiller. London. 1825. 2d Ed. 1845, Supplement, 1872.

E. Palleske. Schiller's Life and Works. Transl. 2 vols. London.

J. Scherr. Schiller and his Times. Transl. Phila. 1881.

H. H. Boyesen. Goethe and Schiller. Their Lives and Works. New York. 1879.

H. Düntzer. The Life of Schiller. Transl. London. 1883.

J. Sime. Schiller. London. 1882. [In the series, Foreign Classics for English Readers. Brief but very good.]

H. W. Nevinson. Life of Friedrich Schiller. London. 1889. [In the series, Great Writers. Brief and unsatisfactory.]

EDITIONS OF "WILHELM TELL."

CRITICAL.

Wilhelm Tell. Schauspiel von Schiller. Zum Neujahrsgeschenk auf 1805. Tübingen, Cotta. 1804. [This was the first edition and the only one which Schiller

corrected. The play has been published since in num-
berless editions, complete or partial, of the poet's
works, of which only those of the following editors
deserve mention.]

M. Carriere. Mit Einleitung, dem alten Volksschauspiel
von Uri und Erläuterungen. Leipzig. 1872.

H. Oesterley. In Bd. XIV von K. Goedeke's Historisch-
Kritische Ausgabe von Schillers Sämmtlichen Schriften. Stuttgart. 1872.

W. v. Maltzahn. In Bd. VI von Schillers Werken in
Hempels Deutschen Klassikern. Berlin. 1879.

W. Vollmer. Mit einer Einleitung und kritischen Noten.
Stuttgart. 1879.

L. Bellermann. Schillers Werke. Kritisch durchgesehene
und erläuterte Ausgabe. Leipzig. 1895–1897.

FOR SCHOOL USE

German.

Denzel. Mit Anmerkungen. Stuttgart. 1865. 1879.

J. Naumann. Mit vollständigem Kommentar. Leipzig.
1876. 2d Ed., 1884. Map.

A. Funke. Mit ausführlichen Erläuterungen. Paderborn.
1880. 6th Ed., 1893. Map.

J. Pölzl. Wien, 1883. 2d Ed., 1888. Map.

O. Kallsen. [Mit Erläuterungen.] Gotha. 1884.

F. Prosch. Mit Einleitung und Anmerkungen. Wien.
[1884.] Map.

A. Thorbecke. [Mit Einleitung und Anmerkungen.] Bielefeld u. Leipzig. [1889.] Map.

A. Florin. Tell-Lesebuch. Davos. 1891. Map.

English.

(All with notes, etc.)

H. Müller-Strübing and **R. H. Quick.** With Companion
containing a complete (?) Vocabulary and Notes and
an Historical Introduction. 2d Ed. London. 1874.
Map.

C. A. Buchheim. Oxford. 1871. 7th Ed., 1886. Map,
—— (Abridgment of above as) School Edition. 2d Ed.,
1887. Map.
J. S. Bevir. London. 1886.
G. E. Fasnacht. London. 1887. Map.
K. Breul. Cambridge. 1890. 2 Maps.
—— (Abridgment of above as) School Edition. 1890.
Map.
R. W. Deering. Boston. 1894. Map.

French.

Th. Fix. Paris. 1849. [Repeatedly reissued.]
H. A. Birmann. Paris.
E. Hallberger. Paris. 1886.
B. Levy. Paris. 1886.
Ch. Kochersperger. Paris. 1891.

COMMENTARIES.

W. E. Weber. Schillers Tell. Zum Schul- und Privat-
gebrauch erläutert. Bremen. 1839. 2d Ed., 1878.
J. Meyer. Schillers Wilhelm Tell, auf seine Quellen
zurückgeführt und sachlich und sprachlich erläutert.
Nürnberg. 1840. 1858.—Nach des Verfassers Tod neu
herausgegeben und mit Anhängen versehen von H.
Barbeck. Nürnberg. 1876.
H. Düntzer. Schillers Wilhelm Tell. Erläutert. Leipzig.
1872. 5th Ed., 1892.
C. Gude. Erläuterungen deutscher Dichtungen. Bd. I.
Leipzig. 1874. 7th. Ed., 1881.
E. Kuenen. Die deutschen Klassiker, erläutert und gewür-
digt. I. Bändchen. Mühlheim. 1874. 3d Ed., Leip-
zig, 1889.
A. Florin. Die unterrichtliche Behandlung von Schillers
Wilhelm Tell. Davos. 1891.
L. Bellermann. Schillers Dramen. Beiträge zu ihrem
Verständnis. 2 Bde. Berlin. 1888–1891.
H. Gaudig. Aus deutschen Lesebüchern. Epische, lyrische
und dramatische Dichtungen erläutert. 5ter Band.

Wegweiser durch die klassischen Schuldramen. Bearbeitet von O. Frick und H. Gaudig. 3te Abteilung. Friedrich Schillers Dramen. II. Bearbeitet von H. Gaudig. Gera und Leipzig. 1894.

MISCELLANEOUS.

J. Keller. Litterarische Parallelen zu Schillers Wilhelm Tell. In " Pädagogische Blätter," Bd. 15. 1886. Pp. 145–165.

G. Roethe. Die dramatischen Quellen des Schillerschen Tells. In " Forschungen zur deutschen Philologie." Festgabe für Rudolf Hildebrand zum 13. März, 1894. Pp. 224–276.

H. Stickelberger. Parallelstellen bei Schiller. Beilage zum Jahresbericht über das Gymnasium in Burgdorf. Burgdorf. 1893.

K. H. v. Stein. Goethe und Schiller. Beiträge zur Ästhetik der deutschen Klassiker. Leipzig. (Reclams Universal-Bibliothek.)

E. Belling. Die Metrik Schillers Breslau. 1883.

E. Vogt. Schulwandkarte zu Schillers Wilhelm Tell. 2 Blätter in sechsfachem Farbendruck. Breslau. 1896.

B. Rein. Karte zu Schillers Wilhelm Tell. Gotha. (F. A. Pertes.)

HISTORY AND LEGEND.

(The two works first mentioned contain detailed bibliographies.)

K. Dändliker. Geschichte der Schweiz. 3 Bde. Bd. I. 3d Ed. Zürich. 1893.

J. Dierauer. Geschichte der schweizerischen Eidgenossenschaft. 2 Bde. Gotha. 1887–1892.

W. Oechsli. Die Anfänge der schweizerischen Eidgenossenschaft. Zürich. 1891.

A. Rilliet. Les Origines de la Confédération Suisse, Histoire et Legende. Genève. 2d Ed. 1869.

——— Der Ursprung der schweizerischen Eidgenossen-

FACSIMILE OF TEXT OF THE LEAGUE OF 1291.

(To face p. 287.)

schaft, Geschichte und Sage. 2d Ed. Ins Deutsche
übertragen von C. Brunner. Aarau. 1873.

E. L. Rochholz. Tell und Gessler in Sage und Geschichte.
Heilbronn. 1877.

TEXT OF THE LEAGUE OF 1291.

LATIN OF THE FACSIMILE.

(The bracketed words do not appear in the facsimile.)

In nomine domini Amen. Honestati consulitur et utilitati
publice providetur, dum [pacta quietis et pacis statu debito
solidantur. Noverint igitur universi, quod homines vallis
Uranie, universitasque] vallis de *Switz*, ac communitas
hominum *intramontanorum vallis inferioris*, [maliciam tem-
poris attendentes, ut se et sua magis defendere valeant et
in statu debito melius conservare, fide] bona promiserunt,
invicem sibi assistere auxilio, consilio quolibet ac favore
[personis et rebus, infra valles et extra, toto posse, toto
nisu, contra omnes ac singulos, qui eos vel alicui de ipsis
aliquam] intulerint violenciam, molestiam, aut iniuriam, in
personis et rebus malum [quodlibet machinando, ac in
omnem eventum quelibet universitas promisit alteri accur-
rere, cum necesse fuerit ad succerrendum] et in expensis
propriis, prout opus fuerit, contra inpetus malignorum
resistere, iniurias vindicare, [prestito super hiis corporaliter
iuramento, absque dolo servandis, antiquam confedera-
tionis formam iuramento vallatam presentibus innovando,]
Ita tamen, quod quilibet homo iuxta sui nominis con-
ditionem domino suo convenienter subesse tene[atur et
servire.] . . .

ENGLISH TRANSLATION OF THE WHOLE
DOCUMENT.

In the name of the Lord, Amen! It is honorable and of
benefit to the public weal that compacts of safety and peace
be fittingly confirmed. Know all men therefore that the
men of the valley Uri, the community of the valley of
Schwyz, and the communities of the men of the lower valley

of Unterwalden, in view of the evil times, in order that they
may be better able to protect and keep in good condition
themselves and their property, have in good faith promised
mutually to assist each other with aid, counsel, and good
will, whether persons or things be involved, both within
the valleys and without, with all power and with all zeal,
against all and every one who may do them or any of theirs
any violence, oppression, or injury in respect of property
or person; and each community has promised to assist the
others in every case, and to come to their aid as soon as it
may be necessary and this at its own expense, as far as it
is necessary to resist the attacks of malevolent persons, to
avenge injuries; they have pledged themselves to this agreement by an oath with raised hands, that they will keep it
without guile; they renew by these presents and with a
sacred oath confirm the ancient confederation; but in this
sense that every man according to his condition shall be
held to be duly subject to his lord and to serve him.   With
common counsel we have unanimously promised, decreed,
and ordained that in the above-mentioned valleys we do
not and never will accept a judge who has gained his office
by favor or by money, or who is not our fellow-inhabitant
or fellow-citizen.   If, however, a dispute should arise
between any of the parties to this league, then shall the
more prudent [representatives] of the parties meet together,
to adjust the difference amicably, as shall seem expedient
to them, and whichever party shall reject their decision,
the other parties shall oppose.   But above all there exists
among them the law that, whoever shall have slain another
murderously and without cause—if he be seized—shall lose
his life, in case he is not able to prove his innocence of
such an offence, and if he escapes, he shall never be allowed to return.   But whosoever receives or shelters such
an evil-doer, shall be banished from our valleys, until
he be with good reason recalled by the parties to this
league.   But whoever shall injure by fire another in the
league, by day or by night, treacherously and secretly, he
shall never be held to be a fellow-citizen.   And whoever
protects and shelters such an evil-doer within our valleys

shall give satisfaction to the injured man. If further any one in the league shall rob or injure in any way the things of another, and the property of the guilty man can be seized within our valleys, it shall be used in just compensation of the injury. Further, no one shall take as security the property of another, unless he be proven debtor or guarantor, and then it shall be done only with the sanction of the proper judge. Moreover, every one shall obey his own judge, and—if it should be necessary—determine his own judge within the land, before whom he shall answer for himself. And if any one should show disobedience to this judge, or if by his contumacy any one in the league should be injured, then all in the league shall be bound to compel the aforesaid delinquent to render the satisfaction adjudged. But if between one and another of the parties to the league war or discord should break out, and one party be unwilling to render right or satisfaction, then shall the other parties be bound to shelter and protect the other party.—The above-written agreements, wisely ordained for the common weal, shall, God willing, be perpetual. In testimony of which the present instrument at the request of the afore-mentioned was drawn up and confirmed by the seals of the three afore-mentioned communities and valleys. Done in the year of the Lord MCCLXXXX and first, in the beginning of the month of August.

FAMILIAR QUOTATIONS FROM "WILHELM TELL."

1. Greif an mit Gott! Dem Nächsten muß man helfen. (Kuoni, l. 107.)
2. Wo's not thut, läßt sich alles wagen. (Tell, l. 136.)
3. Der brave Mann denkt an sich selbst zulegt. (Tell, l. 139.)
4. Vom sichern Port läßt sich's gemächlich raten. (Ruodi, l. 141.)
5. Ich hab' gethan, was ich nicht lassen konnte. (Tell, l. 160.)
6. Der kluge Mann baut vor. (Gertrud, l. 274.)
7. Dem Mutigen hilft Gott. (Gertrud, l. 313.)
8. Unbilliges erträgt kein edles Herz. (Gertrud, l. 317.)
9. Die Unschuld hat im Himmel einen Freund. (Gertrud, l. 324.)
10. Was Hände bauten, können Hände stürzen. (Tell, l. 387.)
11. Das schwere Herz wird nicht durch Worte leicht. (Tell, l. 418.)

12. Die schnellen Herrscher sind's, die kurz regieren. (Tell, l. 422.)

13. Dem Friedlichen gewährt man gern den Frieden. (Tell, l. 428.)

14. Die Schlange sticht nicht ungereizt. (Tell, l. 429.)

15. Beim Schiffbruch hilft der einzelne sich leichter. (Tell, l. 433.)

16. Ein jeder zählt nur sicher auf sich selbst. (Tell, l. 435.)

17. Verbunden werden auch die Schwachen mächtig. (Stauffacher, l. 436.)

18. Der Starke ist am mächtigsten allein. (Tell, l. 437.) ×

19. O, mächtig ist der Trieb des Vaterlands! (Attinghausen, l. 848.)

20. Ans Vaterland, ans teure schließ dich an,
Das halte fest mit deinem ganzen Herzen!
Hier sind die starken Wurzeln deiner Kraft. (Attinghausen, ll. 922–4.)

21. Es lebt ein andersdenkendes Geschlecht. (Attinghausen, l. 954.)

22. Redlichkeit gedeiht in jedem Stande. (Stauffacher, l. 1085.)

23. Eine Grenze hat Tyrannenmacht. (Stauffacher, l. 1275.)

24. Schrecklich immer,
Auch in gerechter Sache, ist Gewalt. (Reding, ll. 1320–1.)

25. Man muß dem Augenblick auch was vertrauen. (Reding, l. 1438.)

26. Wir wollen sein ein einzig Volk von Brüdern,
In keiner Not uns trennen und Gefahr. (Rösselmann, ll. 1448–9.)

27. Früh übt sich, was ein Meister werden will. (Tell, l. 1481.)

28. Die Axt im Haus erspart den Zimmermann. (Tell, l. 1514.)

29. Ein jeder wird besteuert nach Vermögen. (Tell, l. 1524.)

30. Wer gar zu viel bedenkt, wird wenig leisten. (Tell, l. 1532.)

31. Der ist mir der Meister,
Der seiner Kunst gewiß ist überall. (Gessler, ll. 1940–1.)

32. [Und] allzustraff gespannt, zerspringt der Bogen. (Rudenz, l. 1996.)

33. Das Alte stürzt, es ändert sich die Zeit,
Und neues Leben blüht aus den Ruinen. (Attinghausen, ll. 2425–6.)

34. Seid einig — einig — einig. (Attinghausen, l. 2451.)

35. Es bringt die Zeit ein anderes Gesetz. (Melchthal, l. 2551.)

36. [Mach' deine Rechnung mit dem Himmel, Vogt,
Fort mußt du,] deine Uhr ist abgelaufen. (Tell, ll. 2566–7.)

37. Es lebt ein Gott, zu strafen und zu rächen. (Tell, l. 2596.)

38. Ich habe keinen zweiten zu versenden. (Tell, l. 2608.)

39. Dem Schwachen ist sein Stachel auch gegeben. (Tell, l. 2675.)

40. Es kann der Frömmste nicht im Frieden bleiben,
Wenn es dem bösen Nachbar nicht gefällt. (Tell, ll. 2682–3.)

41. Rache trägt keine Frucht. (Fürst, l. 3012.)

42. Die Liebe will ein freies Opfer sein. (Fürst, l. 3074.)

43. Wer Thränen ernten will, muß Liebe säen. (Melchthal, l. 3081.)
44. Das Unglück spricht gewaltig zu dem Herzen. (Hedwig, l. 3123.)

From K. Heinrich von Stein : *Goethe und Schiller, Beiträge zur Ästhetik der deutschen Klassiker*, pp. 99 ff.

The very subject-matter of Tell suggested that the processes of nature be drawn into direct participation in the action. The simplest conceivable means of giving poetic life could here be chosen, viz., that of bringing upon the stage the great phenomena of nature, which of themselves speak to the feelings and in so far are truly poetical. This was in the present case possible and necessary because the subject-matter is an event produced by the particular conditions of the land.

When the curtain rises for the drama *Tell* we ought to see with our own eyes the picture of a wonderful landscape : the scene of the action, Lake Uri, from the shore of Unterwalden, Schwyz opposite, in the distance to the right the shore of Flüelen. Songs are heard, first from the lake, then from the heights. These songs ought to be sung with great expression, in long, full notes. The landscape must speak to us, make itself known to us ; eye and ear must have time enough to become familiar with it. The character of this picture unfolded before us at the beginning, is deep peace, fullest beauty and loveliness :

> „Es lächelt der See, er ladet zum Bade ;
> Der Knabe schlief ein am grünen Gestade,
> Da hört er ein Klingen, wie Flöten so süß,
> Wie Stimmen der Engel im Paradies."

Into this land murder enters. Clouds have gathered, a storm is rising ; now Baumgarten rushes in, with his horrible, necessary, just accomplished deed in his every look and gesture. This is the problem of the drama : the tremendous possibilities of human action disturb the peace of nature. Malice and wickedness have made their abode in this pastoral paradise. A fearful struggle is to be fought out before us. Will the deep, healthy basis of what is

solidly and originally natural be stronger than the arbitrary
will of degenerate men? Most earnest is the conflict;
three times in the course of the drama is the decisive act
an assassination. As the depths of the lake are brought
up, surging and storming before us, so is it in *Tell* with the
relation of man to nature. Shall we reach the other shore,
—repose and peace in higher and safer form? This is the
question, this the problem. This is also in this very scene
the first task in which Tell proves himself. We feel, this
is the man with whose aid the anxious passage will be
made and that great struggle decided.

Afterwards it is again a storm that delivers Tell from
Gessler. It is one of these sudden Föhn-storms which are
peculiar to Lake Uri. Because Tell knows them, how they
come and go, he is freed from his fetters and placed at the
helm. The essential character of this natural phenomenon
becomes the occasion of all his following success. . . .

The broad foundation of the whole work of liberation is
the meeting at the Rütli. Again we have the action preceded by a detailed description of the landscape. A moonlight night; lake and glacier gleam and shimmer, they
alone; all the rest, the rocky precipices, the alpine meadows
are veiled in darkness. . . . While Melchthal is talking
with his companions, they suddenly catch sight of a lunar
rainbow above the lake. "Es leben viele, die das nicht
gesehn"—that is, a very special phenomenon, bordering on
the miraculous. One might doubt for an instant whether
this accumulation of detail might not involve surrender to
the mere material spectacle of the beauty of natural scenery.
But this accumulation is rather the representation of the
poetic intention, that we are to feel distinctly that Nature,
in expression and in action, is cooperating in the work
which is commencing before us. The sunrise at the end of
the Rütli-scene is the grandest element in this participation
of external nature. . . . The poet prescribes that, the
stage having first been left entirely empty, our entire
attention shall be attracted and held fast by the spectacle
of the sun rising above the snow-clad mountains.

This is the background before which the drama plays,

or, better, the soil from which it grows. For the human occurrences of the drama are themselves represented as great natural phenomena in breadth, fullness, and weight. A collective whole, the Swiss people, is the hero of the piece. This we learn above all in the scene of whose natural setting we just spoke. At the Rütli a conspiracy occurs. When Goethe gathered from his conversations with Schiller that the latter would represent the whole people in his play, he caused Shakespeare's *Julius Cæsar* to be played for his friend, thus affording the latter the finest and most grateful stimulus, as Schiller himself assures us. If we compare *Tell* and *Cæsar* in respect of the organization of the conspiracy, we find a great contrast. In *Cæsar* the feeling is that of a sultry, stormy night : the. gloomy pondering of Brutus, a fate ensnaring his every step and drawing him inextricably into its nets, this is chiefly what we learn of the origin of the enterprise. The conspirators are almost all selfishly interested ; after the deed, they are at variance with one another. . . . And now we pass from this to the Rütli, into that clear, moonlight night : the morning breeze is rising from the lake and above the mountains the sun announces his coming. All these men stand here in the conviction of their right. In *Cæsar* the common purpose is purely negative, the murder of the tyrant. Here it is quite different. The negation involved is indeed mentioned, but is not made the main issue ; Rösselmann, the priest, by the episode of his interruption makes hostility to Austria an element of the great work. This itself, however, is altogether positive—the foundation of the confederation, the constitution of a community embracing all the Cantons. This is the chief action of the Rütli-scene. Stauffacher leads up to this constitution by his narrative of the common origin of the inhabitants of the Cantons here represented. On natural foundations, on a common ground, is the work to rest. The history of this people as a whole we are to hear ; the deed of this people we are to witness.—In this regard the thought of the poet requires the fifth act to be represented as the highest climax of the drama. The ringing of the bells, the signal-fires, the destruction of Keep Uri—all this must crowd upon the spectator with impressive power ; we must *see* the people in its deed, in its success.

Tell himself is understood only if we give heed to the gravity, the weight of his decisions and his deed ; this very greatness or breadth of the inner processes of Tell's soul is what makes him to be the representative of the collective Swiss nation. Why does he not at once shoot the governor when the latter demands the shot at the apple ? Why does Tell speak so much, when, fully resolved upon his deed, he awaits Gessler ? Just in his having so much to say to himself at this moment does his character consist. That only an extreme case, not Gessler's demand —" er ist mein Herr und meines Kaisers Vogt "—but only the possible death of his son enables him to slay the tyrant, —just in this does the character of Tell's deed consist. If Gessler had not been his lord and master in that strict, religious sense, which his obedience to that awful command reveals, Tell could not by killing Gessler become a deliverer; Gessler's power is an actual authority, whose seat is not in the lances of his men-at-arms—" eure Macht ist aus " is the cry of the people after Gessler's death—but in the conscience of the Swiss people, in Tell's conscience. Only of the supreme need of such faithful, intense souls can the actual deed of deliverance be born.

This deed of deliverance is, however, a murder, which necessarily burdens the conscience with bonds, whose breaking we are now likewise to witness. Tell returns— without his crossbow—to his wife and children. Into the joy of their meeting no reproach really enters, for Tell is able to answer every reproach of Hedwig, but there does enter into it serious sadness. This sadness is intensified by the appearance of Parricida; it is not dispelled until at the end, by the appearance of the rejoicing people. The significance of this scene is that of Tell's absolution. "Above and beyond man (the individual) there is only one thing higher: mankind," says Wagner. Tell as an individual we could not conceive as living quietly on after his deed, however righteous it was ; but we can thus conceive him as the father of his children, in the midst of his own people. The spirit of this people wrought the deed by means of his arm ; now at the end the love of the assembled people absolves him.

Herewith we behold the spirit of the people, the community of the people achieving a victory over wickedness and arbitrariness, and restored to harmony with the calm, healthy foundations of its natural home. This victory is an ideal. . . .

. . . .

A common state, to which the individual may rightly and joyously sacrifice his personal being, is the highest form of existence which we can conceive. . . .

The gain for all time which is to be had from such a poetic production as *Tell* we would designate as confidence in the ideal. Such a work realizes the reconciling power of a highly intensified consciousness, and this power assures us of the noblest possibilities in the collective life of mankind. The height and breadth of such a work inspires in us certainty of feeling, definiteness of our ideal hope. . . . For Schiller the ideal is nature itself, truth itself. There are no phenomena of reality before which it pales into mere seeming. There are no forces in the world before which it loses its original, natural power. In poetic figure, just this is the theme of *Tell*. Here the ideal rises up like one of those snow-clad Swiss mountains, whence proceed the liberty and all noble significance of the people that has sprung from them.

From John Addington Symonds : *Our Life in the Swiss Highlands* (1892), pp. 64 ff.—The title of this essay, written in the summer of 1888, is *Snow, Frost, Storm, and Avalanche.*

There are several sorts of avalanches, which have to be distinguished and which are worthy of separate descriptions. One is called *Staub-Lawine* or Dust-Avalanche. This descends when snow is loose and has recently fallen. It is attended with a whirlwind, which lifts the snow from a whole mountain-side and drives it onward through the air. It advances in a straight line, overwhelming every obstacle, mowing forests down like sedge, "leaping" (as an old peasant once expressed it in my hearing) "from hill to hill," burying men, beasts, and dwellings, and settling down at last into a formidable compact mass without color and without outline.   The snow which forms these Staub-Lawinen is dry and finely powdered.   When it comes to rest upon the earth, it immediately hardens into something very like the consistency of ice, wrapping the objects which have been borne onward by its blast tightly round in a firm implacable clasp.   A man or horse seized by a Staub-Lawine, if the breath has not been blown out of his body in the air, has it squeezed out by the even clinging pressure of consolidating particles. . . .

Another sort of avalanche is called the *Schlag-Lawine*, or Stroke-Avalanche.   It falls generally in springtime, when the masses of winter snow have been loosened by warm winds or sodden by heavy rainfalls.   The snow is not whirled into the air, but slips along the ground, following the direction given by ravines and gullies, or finding a way forward through the forest by its sheer weight.   Lumbering and rolling, gathering volume as they go from all the barren fells within the reach of their tenacious undermining forces, these "slogging" avalanches push blindly onward till they come to rest upon a level.   Then they spread themselves abroad, and heap their vast accumulated masses by the might of pressure from behind up into pyramids and spires.   They bear the aspect of a glacier with its seracs, or of a lava-stream with its bristling ridges ; and their skirts are plumed with stately pine-trees, nodding above the ruin they have wrought.   Woe to the fragile buildings, to the houses and stables, which they meet upon their inert groveling career !   These are carried with them, incorporated, used as battering-rams.   Grooving like the snout of some behemoth, the snow dislodges giants of the forest, and forces them to act like ploughs upon its path. You may see tongues and promontories of the avalanche protruding from the central body, and carried far across frozen lakes or expanses of meadow by the help of some huge pine or larch.   The *Schlag-Lawine* is usually grayish white and softer in substance than its more dreadful sister, the Staub-Lawine—that daughter of the storm, with the breath of the tornado in her brief delirious energy. It is often distinguished by a beautiful bluish color, as of opaque ice, in the fantastically toppling rounded towers which crown it ; whereas the Staub-Lawine looks like marble of Carrara, and presents a uniform curved surface after it has fallen. Though the Schlag-Lawine closely resembles a glacier at first sight, practiced eyes detect the difference at once by the dulled hue which I have mentioned and by the blunted outlines of the pyramids. It might be compared to a glacier which had been sucked or breathed upon by some colossal fiery dragon. Less time has gone to make it ; it is composed of less elaborated substance, it has less of permanence in its structure than a glacier ; and close inspection shows that it will not survive the impact of soft southern winds in May. In extent these Schlag-Lawinen are enormous. I have crossed some which measured a thousand feet in breadth and more than sixty feet in depth. All road-marks, telegraph-posts, parapets, etc., are, of course, abolished. The trees, if trees there were upon their track, have been obliterated. Broken stumps, snapped off like matches, show where woods once waved to heaven. Valleys are made even with the ridges which confined them. Streams are bridged over and converted into temporary lakes by the damming up of water.

A species of the *Schlag-Lawine* may be distinguished, to which the name of *Grund-Lawine*, or Ground-Avalanche, shall be given. There is no real distinction between *Schlag-* and *Grund-Lawine*. I only choose to differentiate them here because of marked outward differences to the eye. The peculiarity of a *Grund-Lawine* consists in the amount of earth and rubbish carried down by it. This kind is filthy and disreputable. It is colored brown or slaty-gray by the rock and soil with which it is involved. Blocks of stone emerge in horrid bareness from the dreary waste of dirty snow and slush of water which compose it ; and the trees which have been so unlucky as to stand upon its path are splintered, bruised, rough-handled in a hideous fashion.

The Staub-Lawine is fury-laden like a fiend in its first swirling onset, flat and stiff like a corpse in its ultimate repose of death, containing men and beasts and trees entombed beneath its stern unwrinkled taciturnity of marble. The Schlag-Lawine is picturesque, rising into romantic spires and turrets, with erratic pine-plumed firths protruding upon sleepy meadows. It may even lie pure and beautiful, heaving in pallid billows at the foot of majestic mountain-slopes where it has injured nothing. But the Grund-Lawine is ugly, spiteful like an asp, tatterdemalion like a street Arab; it is the worst, the most wicked of the sisterhood. To be killed by it would mean a ghastly death by scrunching and throttling, as in some grinding machine, with nothing of noble and impressive in the winding-sheet of foul snow and débris heaped above the mangled corpse.

I ought to mention a fourth sort of avalanche, which is called *Schnee-Rutsch* or Snow-Slip. It does not differ materially from the Schlag-Lawine except in dimension, which is smaller, and in the fact that it may fall at any time and in nearly all kinds of weather by the mere detachment of some trifling mass of snow. The Schnee-Rutsch slides gently, expanding in a fan-like shape upon the slope it has to traverse, till it comes to rest upon a level. Small as the slip may be, it is very dangerous; for it rises as it goes, catches the legs of a man, lifts him off his feet, and winds itself around him in a quiet but inexorable embrace.

. . .

A special form of the snow-slip is known as *Wind-Schild*. When the force of the wind has drifted a mass of snow together on an overhanging slope, or heaped it up all along the ledges of a beetling precipice, the mass, too heavy to sustain itself in that position, slips downward like snow from a steep roof. This is called a Wind-Schild, and the sudden fall of such a snow-slip may overwhelm men, horses, and sledges, if it strikes them at a point where they can be carried off their legs and borne beyond the barriers of the road. The Wind-Schild gives no warning of its approach.

. . .

I have frequently mentioned the blast which avalanches

bring with them, and which runs before the snow-mass like a messenger of death. This phenomenon of the "Lawinen-Dunst," as it is called, deserves some illustration. The fact is well authenticated, but its results seem almost incredible. Therefore I will confine myself to details on which I can positively rely. A carter, whom I knew well for an honest fellow, told me that he was driving his sledge with two horses on the Albula Pass when an avalanche fell upon the opposite side of the gorge. It did not catch him. But the blast carried him and his horses and the sledge at one swoop over into the deep snow, whence they emerged with difficulty. . . . In order to understand the force of the Lawinen-Dunst, we must bear in mind that hundreds of thousands of tons of snow are suddenly set in motion in contracted chasms. The air displaced before these solid masses acts upon objects in their way like breath blown from a pea-shooter. From certain appearances in the torn and mangled trees which droop disconsolately above ravines down which an avalanche has thundered, it would also appear that the draught created by its passage acts like a vortex, and sucks in the stationary vegetation on either hand.

I will follow up these general details with a circumstantial account of what occurred here on February 6th last [1888]. The Fluela Pass, which connects Davos with the Lower Engadine, was closed to traffic on that day. But a man with whom I was acquainted, called Anton Broher (nicknamed the "Schaufel-Bauer" or "Knave of Spades," because of his black bushy beard), had started for the pass before this fact was generally known. Just before noon an avalanche caught him at a spot where avalanches rarely, if ever, fall, within a short distance of the inn at Tschuggen. An eye-witness saw him carried by the blast, together with his horse and sledge, 200 yards in the air across the mountain stream. The snow which followed buried him. He was subsequently dug out dead, with his horse dead, and the sledge beside him. The harness had been blown to ribbons in the air, for nothing could be found of it except the headpiece on the horse's neck. . . . When I reached the avalanche which carried Anton Broher across the water and killed him, I was astonished by its smallness and by the space he had traversed in the air. Yet there was the hole upon the other side, close to the stream, out of which his corpse, with horse and sledge, had been excavated.

VOCABULARY.

This Vocabulary contains all the words in the text of the drama, excepting the names of persons in the list of *dramatis personae*. The references are to the consecutive line-number in the case of speeches, but in the case of stage-directions to the page, the number being then preceded by an asterisk. The line-numbering of some editions varies by one or two from that here adopted, in consequence of different treatment of certain exclamatory utterances, containing two syllables. But this variation need cause no serious trouble in use of this vocabulary with texts thus different in numbering.

For the more usual meanings, references are made to the first three occurrences, but for unusual meanings, to all cases.

Of nouns the gender, the genitive singular (except of feminines), and the nominative plural, if the word has a plural, are indicated. Thus **Abgrunb**, *m.* -ᷤ, -ünbe, masculine noun, genitive singular **Abgrunbᷤ**, nominative plural **Abgründe**.

Of verbs the principal parts and other necessary forms are given whenever they are strong (old) or irregular. All other verbs are understood to be weak (new) and regular. The verbs are to be conjugated with **haben** unless the auxiliary is indicated by **j.** (jein) or by **h** and **j.** (**haben** and **jein**). The verbs are also marked as *tr.* (transitive), *intr.* (intransitive), or *refl.* (reflexive), and compound verbs, when necessary, as *sep.* (separable) or *insep.* (inseparable). Thus **abfahren, fuhr, gefahren, fährt,** *intr.* **j.,** is a separable. intransitive, strong verb with auxiliary **jein**; **abführen.** *tr.,* is a separable. weak, transitive verb with **haben**.

For the other parts of speech and other statements customary abbreviations are used as indicated in the following list. Since most adjectives are also used in the uninflected form as adverbs, no express mention is made of the adverbial use.

Accents are occasionally marked. A dash (—) indicates the repetition of the title-word or of some obvious portion of it. Cognates (words of the same or similar origin) are printed in full-faced letters, when it seems natural and helpful that this be done.

TABLE OF CUSTOMARY CONTRACTIONS.

acc., accusative
act., active (voice)
adj., adjective
adv., adverb
Amer., American
art., article
aux., auxiliary
cf., confer (compare)
col., colloquial (ly.)
collect., collective (ly)
comp., comparative
conj., conjunction
dat., dative
decl., declined
def., definite
demon., demonstrative
Eng., English
exclam., exclamation
f., feminine
fr., from
Fr., French
gen., genitive
geog., geographical
Ger., German
Gr., Greek
h., haben
imper., imperative
impers., impersonal
ind., indicative
indec., indeclinable
indef., indefinite
inf., infinitive
insep., inseparable
interj., interjection
interrog., interrogative
intr., intransitive
irreg., irregular

Ital., Italian
l., line
Lat., Latin.
lit., literally
m., masculine
n., *neut.*, neuter
N., Note
neg., negative
nom., nominative
num., numeral
obj., object
obso., obsolete
p., page
part., participle or participial
pass., passive (voice)
pers., person or personal
pl., plural
poet., poetical
poss., possessive
p. pts., principal parts
prec., preceding
pref., prefix
prep., preposition
pres., present
pron., pronoun
prop., proper
refl., reflexive
reg., regular
rel., relative
f., fein
sep., separable
sing., singular
subjunc., subjunctive
subst., substantive (ly)
superl., superlative
tr., transitive

VOCABULARY.

A.

ab, *adv. and sep. pref.*, **off**, away, down.

abbrechen, brach, gebrochen, bricht, *intr.*, **break off**, stop short, *138.

abdrücken, *tr. lit.*, **press off**; let fly (an arrow), shoot, *100, 2317.

aber, *conj.*, but, however, 236, 327, 569, *etc.*

abfahren, fuhr, gefahren, fährt, *intr.* [., drive **off**; set out, depart, set sail, 2105.

Abfahrt, *f.* -en, driving **off**; departure, setting sail, 2108, 2121.

Abfall, *m.* -s, -älle, **falling off**, desertion, defection, revolt, 939.

abfallen, fiel, gefallen, fällt, *intr.* [., **fall off**, desert, turn recreant, 945.

abfinden, fand, gefunden, *tr.*, satisfy, put **off**, 2957.

abführen, *tr.*, lead **off**, carry away, conduct, convey, 2100, 2205.

abgehen, ging, gegangen, *intr.* [., go **off**, *or* away; leave (the stage), withdraw, *exit* or *exeunt*, *14, *20, *26, *etc.*; *pres. part. as noun in dat. plur.* *78.

abgewinnen, gewann, gewonnen, *tr.*, win from (*dat.*), 1220.

Abgrund, *m.* -s, -ünde, **abyss**, chasm, precipice, 440, 649, 1268, *etc.*

abholen, *tr.*, **fetch from**, bring away, 2654.

ablaufen, lief, gelaufen, läuft, *intr.* [., **run down**, 2568; deine (Sand)= Uhr ist abgelaufen = your time is up, your hour has come.

abmähen, *tr.*, **mow**, cut **off**, 2740.

abmessen, maß, gemessen, mißt, *tr.*, **measure off**, survey and portion out, 899.

abnehmen, nahm, genommen, nimmt, *tr.*, take **off**, *70.

abplatten, *tr.*, **flatten** down *or* **off**; 2253, *past part. equivalent to adj.*, flat, level.

Abrede, *f.* -n, agreement; — nehmen, take counsel, act in concert, 413.

abreichen, *tr.*, **reach**, 2256; erreichen is more usual.

Abscheu, *m.* -s, abhorrence, aversion, loathing, 3042.

Abschied, *m.* -s, -e, departure, leave; parting, 1495; — nehmen, take leave, 3268.

absenken, *refl.*, **sink** down, descend, 2194.

abſtoßen, ſtieß, geſtoßen, ſtößt, *intr.,* push off (a boat from shore), 165.

Abt, *m.* -es, Äbte, abbot, 1249.

abtreiben, trieb, getrieben, *tr.,* drive off; throw off, shake off, 1353.

abtroßen, *tr.,* extort defiantly, *col.,* bully one out of, 1300.

abtrünnig, *adj.,* apostate; recreant, faithless (to, von), 791.

abwägen, wog, gewogen, *tr.,* weigh, consider carefully, 2726.

abwarten, *tr.,* await, wait for, 2513; *intr.,* or *without an expressed object,* wait passively, 2515, *imper. 2d pl.*

abwehren, *tr.,* ward off, avert, 3179.

abweiden, *tr.,* graze on *or* over; *past part.,* 62, grazed bare.

abwenden, *tr.,* turn off *or* away, avert, *159; alienate, estrange, 680.

abwerfen, warf, geworfen, wirft, *tr.,* throw *or* cast off, 1371.

ach, *interj.* ah! oh! alas! 215, 603, 1485, *etc.*

Acht, *f.* outlawry, ban, 3211.

achten, *tr.,* deem, judge, think, 289, 2255, *etc.;* esteem, regard, heed, 2330; *intr.* (*with prep.* auf), take notice of, attend to, heed, 250, *86, *etc.*

acht' geben, gab, gegeben, giebt, *sep. intr.,* pay attention, give heed, 389, 410.

achtzig, *cardinal num.,* eighty, 1915, 2325.

ackern, *tr.,* till, plough, 2973.

Abel, *m.* -s, nobility, 920; *collect.* 2430.

adelig, *adj.,* noble, 3191.

Abler, *m.* -s, —, eagle; 884, as symbol of the Empire.

Agnes. Agnes (1281–1364), eldest daughter of Emperor Albrecht I, and wife of King Andreas III of Hungary, who died in 1301; 2997.

Ahn, *m.* -en, -en, ancestor, forefather, grandsire, grandfather, 1019, 1077, 3263.

ahnen, *tr. and intr.* (*impers.*), anticipate, forebode, divine; 1690, *pres. part.,* prophetic.

Albrecht. Emperor Albrecht I (born 1250, Emperor from 1298 to his death in 1308), Duke of Austria, oldest son of Rudolf von Habsburg; 908, 2946.

all, *adj. and pron.,* all, whole, entire; each, every, any; *7, 88, 108, 117, etc.;* alles, *neut. sing.,* used collect., all (persons), everybody, *21, 3088, everything, 450.

allein', *indec. adj.,* alone, 437, 693, 694, 789, etc.; *adv.,* only; *conj.,* but, only.

allerwegen, *adv.* everywhere, 2663.

allgemein', *adj.,* common, general, universal, public, 610, 790, 1460, *etc.*

allgerecht, *adj.,* all righteous, altogether just, 581.

allzu, *adv.*, all too, too, 2778.

allzustraff, *adv.*, too tensely, too tightly, too far, 1996.

Alp(e), *f.* -en, mountain pasture, 62, 899, 1015, *etc.;* mountain, 746; *pl.*, Alps.

Alpenblume, *f.* -n, alpine *or* mountain flower, 2625.

Alpenjäger, *m.* -s, —, alpine hunter, mountain huntsman, *4, 1505.

Alpenrose, *f.* -n, alpine-rose, 2357; *it is really a rhododendron.*

Alpentrift, *f.* -en, mountain-pasture, 1001. *Cf. N.* to Matten, *3.

Alpenwasser, *n.* -s, —, alpine-water, mountain stream. 2700.

Alphorn, *n.* -es, -örner, alphorn, cowherd's horn, *162. *Cf. N.* to Kuhreihen, *3.

als, *conj.*, as, than, when; (*after comp.*), than; (*after neg.*), but, except, 266, 268; (*with past tenses*), when, as; (*before inverted clause*), as if; als wie = wie, as, 972.

alsbald, *adv.*, forthwith, immediately, 3007.

also, *adv.*, so, thus, as follows, 232, 1923, *etc.;* 2380, Nicht also, Nay indeed; *conj.*, then, so, therefore, 585, *etc.*

alt (*comp.*, älter, *superl.*, ält(e)st), *adj.*, old, aged, ancient, former, 186, 245, 311, *etc.;* 364, *m. nom. sing. as noun*, old man; 952, *n. nom. sing. as collect. noun.*

Alter, *n.* -s, —, age, old age, 1139, 2476, 3202.

altgewohnt, *part. adj.*, old (and) accustomed, 1022.

Altlandammann, *m.* -s, -e and -änner, ex-landammann, former chief-magistrate, 1086, 1143. 2114. In Switzerland Alt= is prefixed to terms of office or occupation to indicate that a person once was such an official or pursued such an occupation.

Altorf. Altorf *or* Altdorf, chief town of the Canton Uri, a little south of the southern end of the Lake of the Four Forest Cantons; *21, 394, 770, *etc.*

Altvordern, *m. pl.*, ancestors, forefathers, 257.

Alzellen, Alzellen, village in Unterwalden in the valley of the Engelberger Aa; 66, 549.

Alzeller, *m.* -s, —. Alzeller, inhabitant of Alzellen, 717; *as adj. indec.*, 128.

Ammann, *m.* -s, -e, and -änner, magistrate, ammann, 1145.

Ammonshorn, *n.* -es, -örner, *lit.* horn of Ammon; ammonite, a fossil shell, 2626.

Amt, *n.* -(e)s, Ämter, office; 368, *predicate pos. gen.*, was meines Amts (ist), what is my business; *so also* 1839.

an, *prep.* (*dat. or acc.*), *sep. pref.*, *adv.*, at, on, to, by, near, of, towards; 445, in respect to; 1323,

Nun ist'8 an euch (*dat.*), Now it is your turn; a:a = an dem.

anbefehlen, befahl, befohlen, befiehlt, *tr.*, command. order, 93.

Anblick, *m.* -es, -e, sight, view, 514.

anblicken, *tr.*, look at, regard, 782.

anbringen, brachte, gebracht, *tr.*, bring forward, present (a request), 2715.

andächtig, *adj.*, devout, 2615.

ander, *adj.*, other, different, next, following, second, 156, 193, 413, *etc.*

ändern, *tr. and refl.*, change, alter, 192, 2425, 2457.

anders, *adv.*, otherwise, different-(ly), 1241, 2781.

andersdenkend, *part. adj.*, thinking otherwise, of different mind, 954.

anderswo, *adv.*, elsewhere, 830, 2661, 2668.

anfangen, fing, gefangen, fängt, *intr.* (*and tr.*), begin, commence, 1480, 2926; *impers.*, *8, 1752.

anfangs, *adv.* (*gen.*), in the beginning, at first, *48.

anfassen, *tr.*, seize, grasp, 2199.

anflehen, *tr.*, implore, 2261.

anführen, *tr.*, lead, command, lead on, 910, 2547.

anfüllen, *refl.*, to be filled, *144.

angeboren, *part. adj.* inborn, native, hereditary, 921, 1727.

angehen, ging, gegangen, *intr.* f., ascend, stretch upward (*unusual*), 2256.

angenehm, *adj.*, pleasant, kind, 516.

Anger, *m.* -8, —, green, field, 1735; properly an untilled piece of land covered with grass.

angesehen, *part. adj.*, respected, esteemed, distinguished, 294.

angestammt, *part. adj.*, hereditary, natural, 1646.

angreifen, griff, gegriffen, *tr.*, undertake, attempt, set about, 107, 1909.

Angst, *f.* Ängste, anguish, anxiety, fear, 1491, 1923; 91, Angst des Todes = Todesangst, mortal terror.

angstbefreit, *part. adj.*, delivered from anguish *or* fear, 3079.

ängstigen, *tr.*, alarm, distress, frighten; 1575 *impers.* = *pass.*; *refl.*, to be distressed, live in anxiety, 1797.

ängstlich, *adj.*, anxious, *115.

anhalten, hielt, gehalten, hält, *intr.*, halt, 221, 1817; *refl.*, check, restrain, contain one's self, *154.

Anhöhe, *f.* -n., height, hill, *21, *107, *108.

anhören, *tr.*, hear, listen to, 1297, 2211.

Anker, *m.* -8, —, anchor, 2116.

anklagen, *tr.*, accuse, impeach, indict, 3078.

anklingen, klang, geklungen, *intr.*, begin to sound, strike the ear, 847.

ankommen, kam, gekommen, *intr.* f., come to, approach, arrive, 2674.

anlegen, *tr.*, **lay on**; 2814, 2859, Hand —, set about; *intr.*, aim *98, 2582.

anleimen, *refl.*, glue one's self **on** or fast, stick fast, 2640.

anliegen, lag, gelegen, *intr.*, lie near, concern, interest, 708.

anlocken, *tr.*, allure, entice, decoy, 940.

·Anmut, *f.*, charm, grace, 1714.

annehmen, nahm, genommen, nimmt, *tr.*, accept, receive, 1837, 3237.

anpochen, *intr.*, knock, 3214.

anrufen, rief, gerufen, *tr.*, call (to), hail, 1003; invoke, implore, 2095, 2790.

anrühren, *tr.*, touch, 3113; 3062, *pret. subjunc.*, touch, move (*of the feelings, unusual in this sense*).

ansagen, *tr.*, speak, **say on**, 560, 2940, 3104.

anschließen, schloß, geschlossen, *refl.*, join or attach one's self to, 817, 888, 922.

ansehen, sah, gesehen, sieht, *tr.*, look at, *or* **on**, *or* upon, 196, 269, 598, *etc.*

ansichtig, *adj.*, — werden, get sight of (*with gen.*), 1558.

ansiedeln, *refl.*, settle, 1200.

ansinnen, sann, gesonnen, *tr.*, ask of, demand of, impute to, 1890.

ansprengen, *intr.* f., gallop up *or* **on**; 170, *past. part. for Eng. pres. part.*

Anspruch, *m.* -s, -üche, claim; in — nehmen, claim, lay claim to, 1247.

ansteigen, stieg, gestiegen, *intr.* f., rise, ascend, 2159.

anstellig, *adj.*, apt, fit, useful, 362.

anstemmen, *tr.*, push, press against; 2262, *past part. equivalent to Eng. pres. part.*

Anteil, *m.* -s, -e, portion, lot, 1523.

anthun, that, gethan, *tr.*, do (to), show, offer, commit, 1273, 2290, 2752.

Antlitz, *n.* -es, -e, face, 2221, 3171.

antreten, trat, getreten, tritt, *tr.*, approach, 2833.

Antwort, *f.* -en, answer, 2028, 2053.

anwachsen, wuchs, gewachsen, wächst, *intr.* f., grow up *or* **on** and on, increase, 1460.

anziehen, zog, gezogen, *tr.*, draw *or* pull **on**, 39, 2580.

Anzug, *m.* -s, -üge, approach; im —, approaching, 45, 105, 2106.

anzünden, *tr.*, kindle, set fire to, 969, *50, 2877.

Apfel, *m.* -s, Äpfel, apple, 1876, 1882, 1886, *etc.*

Arbeit, *f.* -en, work, labor, toil, *21, 364, 1412, *etc.*

arbeiten, *refl.*, work one's way, 169.

Arbeiter, *m.* -s, —, workman, laborer, *21.

arg (*comp.* ärger, *superl.* ärgſt), *adj.*, bad, evil; 2259, 2768, *neut. superl.* used as *noun*, the worst (thing).

Argwohn, *m.* -s, suspicion, mistrust, 503, 720.

arm (*comp.* ärmer, *superl.* ärmſt), *adj.*, poor, miserable, 307, 1567, 1910, *etc.*; 610, *masc. superl.* used as *noun*.

Arm, *m.* -es, -e, arm, *19, 496, 705, 1537.

Armbruſt, *f.* -üſte, cross-bow, *10, 644, *72 *etc.*

armſelig, *adj.*, poor, paltry, miserable, 2641.

Armſeſſel, *m.* -s, —, arm-chair, *114.

Armut, *f.* poverty, 903.

Arth. Arth, large village at southern end of Lake Zug, at the foot of the Rossberg, 2282.

Aſche, *f.* -n (*rare*), ashes, 2866.

Atem, *m.* -s, breath, 2361.

atemlos, *adj.*, breathless, out of breath, *6.

atmen, *intr.*, breathe, 1446, 1956.

Attinghaus(en). Attinghausen, village near Altorf, and site of the castle of the baronial family von Attinghausen; *1, 337, 542, *etc.*

Attinghäuſer, *m.* -s, —. He of Attinghausen, Baron von Attinghausen, 52.

auch, *adv.*, also, even, too, *3, 54, 57, *etc.*; was . . . auch, whatever; wie . . . auch, however; wo . . .

auch), wherever; wenn . . . auch), even if; ſo (*adj.*) . . . auch), however (*adj.*); auch nicht, not even, not . . . either,

Aue, *f.* -n, fertile plain, 1793.

auf, *prep.* (*dat. or acc.*), on, upon, at, to, toward, for; *sep. pref. and adv.*, up, upon, upwards, open; *interj.*, up ! 2826, 2846.

aufbauen, *tr.*, build up, erect, 2862.

aufbewahren, *tr.*, preserve, keep, 2920, 3138.

aufbieten, bot, geboten, *tr.*, summon, call up *or* out, 1423.

aufblühen, *intr.* ſ., begin to bloom, grow up, 1694.

auffahren, fuhr, gefahren, fährt, *intr.* ſ., start up, fly into a passion, become vehement, *68, *137.

auffinden, fand, gefunden, *tr.*, find out, discover, 1700.

auffordern, *tr.*, call upon, invite, 810.

aufgeben, gab, gegeben, giebt, *tr.*, give up as lost, abandon, 2219.

aufgehen, ging, gegangen, *intr.* ſ., go up, rise, *3, *71, *etc.*; open, 514.

aufhalten, hielt, gehalten, hält, *tr.*, hold up, delay, detain, 1818.

aufhangen, hing, gehangen, hängt, *tr.*, hang up, 1868. (*This verb is not now used in the present tense, but* aufhängen.)

aufheben, hob, gehoben, *tr.*, lift up, raise, *58, *64.

aufhören, *intr.*, cease, 55, 1050.

auflachen, *intr.*, break into a laugh, laugh out, *24.

Auflauf, *m.* -ß, -äufe, uproar, tumult, *26.

auflegen, *tr.*, lay on, put on, *97, *98.

auflösen, *tr.*, loosen, undo, annul, 2828.

aufmerken, *intr.*, attend, give heed, listen carefully, 247.

aufmerksam, *adj.*, attentive, *31, *155.

aufnehmen, nahm, genommen, nimmt, *tr.*, take up, receive, 1309, 3282; 1875, es ... aufnehmen, compete, be a match for.

aufpassen, *intr.*, watch, 1732.

aufpflanzen, *tr.*, set up, fix in place, 1124.

aufrauschen, *intr.* f., rise (in roaring waves), *10.

aufrecht, *adj.*, upright, 2720.

aufreißen, riß, gerissen, *tr.*, tear open, *98; *refl.*, open suddenly, 3258.

aufrichten, *tr.*, put up, set up, 393, *58; *refl.*, get up, rise, *115, *118.

aufrufen, rief, gerufen, *tr.*, call upon, summon, ask, 1997.

Aufruhr, *m.* -ß, -e, tumult, rebellion, insurrection, 1850.

aufrühren, *tr.*, stir up, 117.

aufschieben, schob, geschoben, *tr.*, delay, postpone, 1391.

aufschlagen, schlug, geschlagen, schlägt, *tr.*, cast up, open, 2897.

Aufschub, *m.* -ß, -übe, delay, postponement, 106, 1971.

aufsetzen, *tr.*, put *or* place upon, 1347.

aufspringen, sprang, gesprungen, *intr.* f., spring up, leap up, *32, 653, *154, *etc.*

Aufstand, *m.* -ß, -ände, tumult, commotion, *146.

aufstecken, *tr.*, stick up, put up, 2716, 2719.

aufstehen, stand, gestanden, *intr.* f., stand up, get up, rise, *18, 2046, *109, *etc.*

auftauen, *intr.* f., thaw, 2145.

aufthun, that, gethan, *tr.*, open, 1661, 2364; *refl.*, open, offer, present itself, 2251.

auftreten, trat, getreten, tritt, *intr.* f., enter, appear, *48, *86, *etc.*

aufwecken, *tr.*, awake, 2851.

Aufzug, *m.* -ß, -üge, drawing up (of the curtain), act, *3, *etc.*

aufzwingen, zwang, gezwungen, *tr.*, force upon, 912.

Auge, *n.* -ß, -n, eye, 122, 270, 467, *etc.*

Augenblick, *m.* -ß, -e, moment, instant, 1438, 1592, *etc.*

augenblicks, *adv.* (*gen.*), instantly, 799.

augenlos, *adj.*, eyeless, sightless, 608.

aus, *prep.* (*dat.*), out of, from, of, because of; *adv.*, out, forth, over, at an end, 2383, 3034; *sep. pref. with similar meanings.*

ausbreiten, *tr.*, stretch out, extend, *101, *109.

auseinanderfliehen, floh, geflohen, *intr.* f., flee apart, scatter in flight, 3007-8.

auseinandergehen, ging, gegangen, *intr.* f., disperse, *40.

auseinandertreiben, trieb, getrieben, *tr.*, drive apart, disperse, scatter, 1855.

aus'ersehen, fah, ausersehe(e)n, fieht, *tr.*, choose, destine, 1667; *this verb having a sep. before an insep. pref. is used only in forms with both prefixes standing before the verb.*

ausfechten, focht, gefochten, ficht, *tr.*, fight out, 2523.

ausfließen, floß, gefloßen, *intr.* f., flow out, cease to flow, empty itself, 586.

ausgehen, ging, gegangen, *intr.*, f., go forth, proceed, issue, 2977.

ausgießen, goß, gegoffen, *tr.*, pour out, 1039.

ausliefern, *tr.*, deliver (up), surrender, 3047.

auslöschen, *tr.*, extinguish, put out, 424.

ausreuten, *tr.*, root out *or* up, clear away, 728.

ausroden, *tr.*, root out *or* up, clear away, 1190,

Ausrufer, *m.* -8, —, crier, *2, *23.

ausruhen, *intr. and refl.*, rest, *21, 3103.

aussehen, fah, gefehen, fieht, *intr.*, look, appear, 3110.

außen, *adv.*, out, without, abroad, 2933.

außer, *prep.* (*dat.*), without, out, except; außer fich, beside one's self, 2200.

äußerst, (*superl.* of äußer), *adj.*, utmost, outermost, last, extreme; 640, *neut. as noun*, extremity; *adv.*, 346, zu äußerst, way out, far out. [*140.

Aussicht, *f.* -en, view, prospect,

aussinnen, fann, gefonnen, *refl. with dat.*, devise, contrive, 403.

ausspähen, *tr.*, spy out, search out, 1043.

aussprechen, sprach, gesprochen, spricht, *tr.*, speak out, utter, 300.

ausstellen, *tr.*, put out, post, station, 59, 1440, 2449, *etc.*

aussuchen, *tr.*, seek out, pick out, choose, 1907.

austreten, trat, getreten, tritt, *intr.* f., step out, come forth; 2689, overflow.

ausüben, *tr.*, execute, exercise, do, 82, 1645.

ausweichen, wich, gewichen, *intr.* f., step aside, evade, 1552, 2694.

ausziehen, zog, gezogen, *intr.* f., march out, go forth, set out, 1172, 2622.

Aye, *m.* -n, ⎫ Axenberg *or*
Ayenberg, *m.* -8, ⎭ Axen, a mountain or its two main parts, along the eastern shore near the south-end of the Lake of the Four Forest Cantons; 2189, 2228, 2254.

Axt, *f.* -Äxte, **ax**, 86, 87, 97, *etc.;* 312, battle-ax.

B.

Bach, *m.* -es, Bäche, **brook**, 3218.

Bad, *n.* -es, Bäder, **bath**, 1, 93, 97, *etc.*

Baden. Baden, a town on the Limmat in the Canton Aargau, about 15 miles NW. of Zürich; 2669, 2965.

baden, *refl.*, **bathe**, 3005.

Bahn, *f.* -en, **path, way, course**, 630, 2835.

Bahre, *f.* -n, **bier**, 2521.

bald, *adv.*, **soon, easily**, 57, 764, 1381, *etc.;* bald . . . bald, **now . . . now**, *98.

Balken, *m.* -s, —, **beam, timber**, *142, 2884.

Ball, *m.* -(e)s, Bälle, **ball**, 2157.

Balsamstrom, *m.* -s, -öme, **balmy stream** or **current**, 2360.

Band, *n.* -es, Bänder, **ribbon, band**, 53.

Band, *n.* -es, Bande, **bond, tie, fetter**, 921, 1958.

bändigen, *tr.*, **tame, subdue**, 2780.

bang(e), *adj.*, **afraid, fearful, anxious**, 633.

Bank, *f.* Bänke, **bench, seat**, *14, 2609, *137.

Bann, *m.* -es, **ban, outlawry, excommunication**, 2996. *Cf. N.*

Bannberg, *m.* -s, Bannberg, a high hill east of Altorf; *84, *86.

bannen, *tr.*, **put under the ban**, 900, 1777; **enchant**, 1775.

Banner, *n.* -s, —, **banner**, 757, 1133.

Bannerherr, *m.* -n, -en, **banneret, lord of the banner**, *1, 336, 813. *Cf. N.* 336.

bar, *adj.*, **bare, naked, destitute, stripped** (of, *gen.*), 1308.

Bär, *m.* -en, -en, **bear**, 1262, 2134.

barmher'zig, *adj.*, **merciful**, 112. 578; *2, *139, barmherzige Brüder, "Brothers of Mercy."

Barmher'zigkeit, *f.* -en, **mercy, pity, charity**, 1036, 2732, 2908, *etc.*

Bau, *m.* -s, -e *and* Bauten, **building, edifice, structure, fabric**, 2559, *141.

bauen, *tr.*, **build, construct, rely**, 215, 231, *21, *etc.*

Bauer, *m.* -s, -n, **peasant, farmer, yeoman**, 231, 475, 819, *etc.*

Bäuerin, *f.* -innen, **peasant-woman**, *2.

Bauernadel, *m.* -s, **peasant-nobility** (*sarcastic*), 825.

Baugerüst, *n.* -es, -e, **scaffolding**, *140.

Baum, *m.* -es, Bäume, **tree**, 1696, *84, 1877.

Baumzweig, *m.* -s, -e, **branch of a tree**, *95.

Becher, *m.* -s, -, **beaker, cup**, *40, *41, 766, *etc.*

be-, *insep. pref.*, *never accented*, *Eng.* **be-**.

bebauen, *tr.*, **till, cultivate**, 1799.

bedauern, *tr.*, pity, deplore, be sorry for, 2343.

bedenken, bedachte, bedacht, *tr.*, think over, consider, 237, 246, 301, *etc.; refl.*, bethink one's self, hesitate, 1908, 2479.

bedeuten, *tr.*, mean, signify, 2054; beckon, direct, *162.

bedrängen, *tr.*, oppress, afflict, distress, 489, 796, 1293, *etc.; m. past part. as noun*, the oppressed, 140, 351.

bedürfen, beburfte, beburft, bebarf, *intr. (with gen.) and tr.*, be in need of, need, 444, 485, 604, *etc.*

bedürftig, *adj.*, needy, in want, 3111.

beeisen, *tr.*, cover with ice, 3254.

Befehl, *m.* -s, -e, command, order, 1758, 1770, 1844, *etc.*

befehlen, befahl, befohlen, befiehlt, *tr. (dat. of pers.)*, command, order, 1863, 2049.

befestigen, *tr.*, strengthen, 2015; *refl.*, strengthen, establish one's self, 1392.

befinden, befand, befunden, *refl.*, find one's self, be, 2182.

beflecken, *tr.*, spot, stain, 76.

beflügeln, *tr.*, furnish with wings, wing, 2606.

befolgen, *tr.*, follow, 1018.

befördern, *tr.*, further, promote, 2014.

befreien, *tr.*, free, deliver, rescue, 2206, 2347, 2520, *etc.*

befriedigen, *tr.*, satisfy, 1436.

befruchten, *tr.*, make fertile, fructify, 2492.

begeben, begab, begeben, begiebt, *refl.*, repair, betake one's self, go, come, 1733; happen, 2213; (*with gen.*), renounce, give up, forego, 1425.

begegnen, *intr.* f., meet, encounter, 933, 2671, 2933; happen, come to pass, befall, 108, 159, 1873; use, treat, 538.

begehen, beging, begangen, *tr.*, commit, perpetrate, 1464.

begehren, *tr.*, desire, demand, ask for, 1894, 1896, 3172.

Begeisterung, *f.*, inspiration, transport, ecstasy, *121.

Begierde, *f.* -n, desire, eagerness, 43.

beginnen, begann, begonnen, *intr.*, begin, 2432; *tr.*, 2401, 2729.

begleiten, *tr.*, accompany, *163.

beglücken, *tr.*, make happy, bless, 950, 1715, 1722, *etc.*

begraben, begrub, begraben, begräbt, *tr.*, bury, 955, 2661, *etc.; m. past part. as noun*, 1504.

begrenzen, *tr.*, bound, limit, close, *84.

begrüßen, *tr.*, greet, 1444; *refl. reciprocal*, *51, greet one another.

Begrüßung, *f.* -en, greeting, salutation, 783.

beharren, *intr.*, continue, persist, adhere (to, bei), 256.

behaupten, *tr.*, maintain, assert, 2001, 3022.

bei, *prep.*, *adv. and sep. pref.*, by, near, at, with, in, among, at the house of; 2707, = beifommen, get at, affect.

beidjten, *tr.*, confess, 3234.

beibe, *adj. pl.*, both, two, 339, 582, 1055, *etc.*

beilegen, *intr.*, hasten, bestir one's self, 176 (*unusual, cf. N.*).

beifei'te, *adv.*, aside, *95.

Beifpiel, *n.* -8, -e, example, precedent, 541.

Beiftanb, *m.* -8, -änbe, assistance, support, 2414.

beiftehen, ftanb, geftanben, *intr.*, assist, help, 2301, 2814.

beizählen, *tr.*, number with, count among, 2516.

bejammernswürbig, *adj.*, lamentable, wretched; *m. as noun*, 580.

befannt, *part. adj.*, known, acquainted, 1069, 1164.

beflagen, *tr.*, pity, 2346; *refl.*, complain, 276.

beflemmen, *tr.*, oppress, afflict, grieve, 201.

befriegen, *tr.*, make war upon, 2440.

belaben, belub, belaben, *tr.*, load, 3276.

beleben, *tr.*, animate, enliven, cheer, 1715.

belebt, *part. adj.*, animate, living, 1049.

beleibigen, *tr.*, offend, insult, affront, 1976, 2330.

belohnen, *tr.*, reward, 1668, 3201.

bemalen, *tr.*, paint, 211.

bemerfen, *tr.*, mark, notice, observe, *98, *109; remark, state, 1215.

bequem, *adj.*, convenient, comfortable, 206.

bequemen, *refl.*, submit, 412.

beraten, beriet, beraten, berät, *refl.*, counsel, deliberate together, 733.

berauben, *tr.*, rob, plunder, despoil, 1035, 1342.

bereit, *adj.*, ready, prepared, 683, 2406, 2553, *etc.*

bereiten, *tr.*, make ready, prepare, 525, 1631, 2610, *etc.*

Berg, *m.* -e8, -e, mountain, *4, 17 (*cf. N.*), etc.

bergen, barg, geborgen, birgt, *tr.*, save, shelter, secure, 554, 2292.

Bergweg, *m.* -8, -e, mountain way or path, 959.

Bericht, *m.* -e8, -e, report, information, 1323.

berichten, *tr.*, report, 558; 2239, *past part.*, informed, skilled.

Bern. The city Bern, capitol of the Canton Bern, 2433.

berften, barft, geborften, *intr.* f., burst, 1852 (*pres. ind.*, *2nd sing.*), 2130.

berufen, *part. adj.*, reputed, of repute, 1082.

beruhigen, *refl.*, calm one's self, become quiet, 2363.

berühren, *tr.*, touch, 2816, 3114.

befchäftigen, *tr.*, busy, employ, occupy, *72, *114.

Beſcheid, *m.* -8, -e, information, knowledge, direction, answer, 1347, 2917; — wiſſen, know all about, 414.

beſcheiden, beſchied, beſchieden, *tr.*, assign, destine, 941.

beſcheiden, *adj.*, modest, 665, 1620, *etc.;* discreet, prudent, 553, 3031.

beſcheidentlich, *adv.*, modestly, 1566.

beſcheinen, beſchien, beſchienen, *tr.*, shine upon, 2067.

beſchirmen, *tr.*, protect, defend, 1226, 1617.

beſchließen, beſchloß, beſchloſſen, *tr.*, determine, decide, resolve, 683, 737, 1169, *etc.*

beſchützen, *tr.*, protect, guard, defend, 879, 1436, 1809, *etc.*

Beſchützer, *m.* -8, —, protector, guardian, defender, 1624.

beſchwören, beſchwor, beſchworen, *tr.*, swear to, 2289, 2899.

beſehen, beſah, beſehen, beſieht, *tr.*, view, inspect, examine, 1060, 1183.

beſetzen, *tr.*, occupy, fill, cover, *163.

beſiegen, *tr.*, conquer, subdue, 1373.

Beſinnen (*inf. as subst.*), *n.* -8, reflection, *87.

Beſitz, *m.* -es, possession, 1270.

beſitzen, beſaß, beſeſſen, *tr.*, possess, 1655.

beſonder, *adj.*, particular, individual, 1461.

beſonnen, *part. adj.*, prudent, circumspect, discreet, having presence of mind, 227, 1872, 1903, *etc.*

beſprechen, beſprach, beſprochen, beſpricht, *tr.*, talk over, discuss, 737.

beſſer (*comp. of* gut), **better,** 157, 163, 508, *etc.; neut. as noun,* 2772.

beſt (*superl. of* gut), **best,** 567, *etc.; m. pl. as noun,* 1120; *neut. sing. as noun,* 802, 1629, 2014, good, interest; 2649, first prize.

beſtätigen, *tr.*, confirm, 1327, 2077, 2078, *etc.*

beſtehen, beſtand, beſtanden, *intr.*, last, endure, exist, 1020, 2901; insist upon (auf), urge, 1305.

beſtehlen, beſtahl, beſtohlen, beſtiehlt, *tr.*, steal from, rob, shirk, 358.

beſtellen, *tr.*, appoint, 1235; till, 2680.

beſteuern, *tr.*, tax, assess, 1524.

beſtimmt, *part. adj.*, fixed, appointed, definite, 444, 1420.

Beſuch, *m.* -8, -e, visit, call, 1416.

beten, *intr.*, pray, offer prayer, 2152, 2179.

bethören, *tr.*, befool, delude, beguile, 1415, 1692.

betrachten, *tr.*, look at, view, contemplate, *14, *70, *115, *etc.*

betrüben, *tr.*, trouble, distress, 3072.

betrügen, betrog, betrogen, *tr.*, deceive, 1691; *refl.*, deceive one's self, be deceived, mistaken, 939.

beugen, *tr.*, bend, bow, 371, 405, 1741, *etc.; refl.*, 634, 2916.

Beute, *f.* booty, 1476.

bewachen, *tr.*, watch, guard. 674.

bewachſen, bewuchs, bewachſen, be=
wächſt, *tr.*, cover with growth,
overgrow, *126.

bewaffnen, *tr.*, provide with weapons, arm, *48, *51, *55, *etc.*

bewahren, *tr.*, keep, preserve,
guard, 249, 1211, 1355, *etc.*

bewähren, *tr.*, prove, verify, show
(by trial), 1884.

bewegen, *refl.*, move, stir, agitate,
762, 832, 1902, *etc.*

Bewegung, *f.* -en, movement, stir,
commotion, *21, *62, *98, *etc.*

beweiden, *tr.*, graze on *or* over,
1248.

beweiſen, bewies, bewieſen, *tr.*,
show, do, make, 1820, 1835.

bewohnen, *tr.*, inhabit, 383, 458,
1045, *etc.*

bewundern, *tr.*, wonder at, ad-
mire, 213.

bezähmen, *tr.*, tame, curb, subdue,
restrain, 484, 1462.

bezeichnen, *tr.*, mark, designate,
3024, 3246.

bezwingen, bezwang, bezwungen,
tr. and refl., overcome, subdue,
master, 483, 583, 1064, *etc.*

bieder, *adj.*, honest, true, 738, 1051.

Biedermann, *m.* -s, -männer, good
man, worthy man, 103, 118,
269, *etc.*

biegen, bog, gebogen, *tr.*, bend,
warp, 397, 652, 1212, *etc.*

bieten, bot, geboten, *tr.*, offer,
1259, 1294, 1394, *etc.*

Bild, *n.*, -es, -er, image, 3218.

bilden, *tr.*, form, make, 976, 1123,
etc.; *refl.*, be formed, *58.

billig, *adj.*, reasonable, just, righteous, 1374

Binde, *f.* -n, bandage, 2016.

binden, band, gebunden, *tr.*, bind,
931, 932, 934, *etc.*

bis, *adv., prep.* (*acc.*) *and conj.*, to,
as far as, till, until, 89, 187, 273,
etc.

Biſchof, *m.* -s, -öfe, bishop, 1802.

Biſchofshut, *m.* -s, -üte, (bishop's)
miter, 2957.

bisher, *adv.*, hitherto, 185.

Bitte, *f.* -n, petition, request, en-
treaty, 2600, 2747.

bitten, bat, gebeten, *tr.*, ask, beg,
pray, 2743; *intr.*, (for, um),
1873.

bitter, *adj.*, bitter, sharp, 2597.

blaſen, blies, geblaſen, bläſt, *tr.
and intr.*, blow, 40, 1410, 2848.

blaß, (*comp.*, bläſſer, *superl.*, blä=
ſeſt, *now usually without* Umlaut),
adj., pale, 979.

bleiben, blieb, geblieben, *intr.* ſ.,
remain, stay, tarry, 187, 236, 431,
etc.; 611, *inf. as neut. noun.*

bleich, *adj.*, pale, wan, white, 1911,
2801, 2809.

bleichen, blich, geblichen, *intr.*, turn
pale, fade, 2358.

blenden, *tr.*, blind, 585, 602, 2125,
etc.

Blick, *m.* -es, -e, look, glance,
sight, 526, 991, 1595, *etc.*; view,
prospect, vista, 1661.

bliden, *intr.*, look, 2222.
blind, *adj.*, blind, 585, 600, 607, *etc.*
Blitz, *m.* -es, -e, lightning, flash,
*105, 2129.
blitzen, *intr.*, lighten, flash, gleam,
1025.
bloß, *adj.*, bare, naked, mere; *adv.*,
merely, only, simply, 1557, 2473.
blühen, *intr.*, bloom, blossom,
flourish, 202, 2426.
Blume, *f.* -n, flower, 19, 595, 1713,
etc.
Blut, *n.* -es, blood, 76, 660, 668,
etc.
Blutbann, *m.* -s, penal jurisdiction,
1234.
Blüte, *f.* -n, flower, 2445.
bluten, *intr.*, bleed, 559, 795, 1618,
etc.
blutig, *adj.*, bloody, 546, 617, 2442,
etc.
Blutschuld, *f.* -en, blood-guiltiness,
capital crime, 1237.
blutsverwandt, *part. adj.*, related
by blood; 2011 *m. dat. plu. as
noun*, relatives, kinsmen.
Boden, *m.* -s, —, bottom, ground,
soil, earth, 857, 1049, *etc.;* zu
Boden, to the ground, down, 576,
1845, *etc.*
Bogen, *m.* -s, —(*or* Bögen), bow,
1467, 1978, 1988, *etc.;* arch, 2860.
Bogensehne, *f.* -n, bow-string (lit.
sinew), 2602.
Bogenstrang, *m.* -s, -änge, bow-
string, 2579.
bohren, *tr.*, bore, 577.

Bord, *m. and n.*, -es, -e, board,
ship-board, edge; am Bord, on
board, 2196.
bös, böse, *adj.*, bad, evil, wicked,
ill, 85, 273, *etc.; m. as noun*,
evil *or* wicked man, 237; *neut. as
noun*, evil, wickedness, harm,
501, 3069, 3152.
bösmeinend, *part. adj.*, meaning
evil, with evil intent, 226.
Bote, *m.* -n, -n, messenger, 482,
494, 505, *etc.*
Botensegel, *n.* -s, —, messenger-
sail, messenger-boat, 2555.
Botschaft, *f.* -en, message, report,
2556.
Brand, *m.* -es, -ände, brand, fire-
brand, 321.
branden, *intr.*, break (as waves),
surge, seethe, 116.
Brandung, *f.* breakers, surges, surf,
169.
Brauch, *m.* -es, -äuche, usage, custom, 1111, 1233, 1915. *etc.*
brauchen, *tr.*, want, need, 958,
1535, *etc.; intr. impers. (with
gen.)*, 692; use, make use of
(*with gen.*), 2241.
bräuchlich, *adj.*, usual, customary,
2052, (*poetic for* gebräuchlich).
braun, *adj.*, brown, 47.
brausen, *intr.*, roar, rush, 1790;
inf. as noun, *9, roaring.
Braut, *f.* -äute, betrothed (woman),
future wife, 940, 2654; bride.
Brautlauf, *m.* -s, -äufe, wedding-
procession, wedding, 2652.

Brautzug, *m.* -8, -üge, wedding-procession, *137.

brav, *adj.*, worthy, good, honest, gallant, 139, 165, 1090, *etc.;* 2101, *superl.;* **brave.**

brechen, brach, gebrochen, bricht, *tr.*, break, tear down, destroy, 469, 1368, 2782, *etc.;* pluck, gather, 3016; *intr.* j. and h., break, 2116, 2147, *etc.;* dash forth, 1411; (of the eye in death), fail, grow dim, close, 865, 2810.

breiten, *tr.*, spread, extend, 1687.

brennen, brannte, gebrannt, *intr.* (*and tr.*), burn, 970, *140, *152.

Brief, *m.* -es, -e, letter, charter, 1215, 1249, 1252, *etc.*

bringen, brachte, gebracht, *tr.*, bring, 453, 461, *etc.;* 765 (of drinking health to one), pledge.

Bringer, *m.* -8, —, bringer, bearer, 2597.

Brot, *n.*, -es, -e, bread, 475, 2735.

Bruck. Bruck *or* Brugg, a small town on the river Aar in the Canton Aargau, 20 miles NW. of Zürich, 2946. [902, *etc.*

Brücke, *f.* -n, bridge, *14, 329,

Bruder, *m.* -8, -über, brother, 145, 1342, *etc.;* *2, *etc.*, barmherzige Brüder, Brothers of Mercy, (an order of friars).

brüllen, *intr.*, roar, bellow, low, 38, 479, 2137, *etc.*

Bruneck, castle of this name in Aargau, south of Brugg, (between Lenzburg and Mellingen).

Bruneckerin, *f.* my lady of Bruneck; 2880.

Brünig, *m.* -8. The mountain Brünig, between Unterwalden and Bern; 2902, *cf.* 1193.

Brunnen, *m.* -8, —, spring, well, 1016, 1185.

Brunnen. Brunnen, village and landing-place in the Canton Schwyz, on the eastern shore of the Lake of the Four Forest Cantons, at the mouth of the Muotta; 721, 725, 2277. [20.

Brünnlein, *n.* -8, —, (little) spring,

Brust, *f.* -üste, breast, 8, 297, 1040, *etc.*

Brut, *f.* -en, brood, 1264.

Bube, *m.* -n, -n, boy, servant, *5, 466, 470, 1765, 2879, *etc.;* knave, scoundrel, 1834.

Buch, *n.* -es, Bücher, book, 1121.

Buchhandlung, *f.* -en, (book-)publishing house; on facsimile of title-page of 1st ed.

Bucht, *f.* -en, bight, bay, cove, *3.

bücken, *tr. and refl.*, bow, duck, stoop, 1760, 2143, 2178, *etc.*

Buggisgrat, *m.* -8. Buggisgrat, a steep cliff of the Axenberg; 2187.

Büh(e)l, *m.* -8, —, hill, (South German word); as part of proper name, *1, *etc.*

buhlen, *intr.* (*with* um), court, woo, 794.

Bund, *m.* -es, Bünde, covenant, alliance, league, confederation, 658, 1153, 1155, *etc.*

Bündnis, *n.* -ffeß, -ffe, covenant, alliance, league, 1156, 2899.

bunt, *adj.*, bright, gay-colored, variegated, motley, 211.

Burg, *f.* -en, castle, stronghold, 219, 1060, 1404, *etc.*

bürgen, *intr.*, give bail *or* security, 1838.

Bürger, *m.* -ß, —, citizen, freeman, 1170, 1828.

Bürgereid, *m.* -ß, -e, citizen's oath, 2431.

Bürgerin, *f.* -nen, (female) citizen. fellow-citizen, 3286.

Burgglocke, *f.* -n, castle bell, *121.

Bürglen. Bürglen, village at the lower end of the valley of the Schächen, just east of Altorf; 126, 2290, 3106.

Bürgschaft, *f.*, bail, security, 1830, 1837.

Burgverließ, *n.* -eß, -e, castle keep *or* dungeon, 2354.

Burgvogt, *m.* -ß, -ögte, governor, burggrave, bailiff, 77, 84, 92, *etc.*

Busen, *m.* -ß, —, bosom, 330, 2007, *etc.*; bay, cove, inlet, 2158.

Buße, *f.* -n, punishment, fine, penalty, 473.

büßen, *tr. and intr. with* für, pay for, suffer for, atone, expiate, 178, 546, 3250, *etc.*; satisfy, 273; fine, punish, 565, 1560.

C.

Christenheit, *f.* christendom, 266.

Christfest, *n.* -ß, -e, Christmas, 2513.

D.

da, *adv. of place,* there, here, 29, 30, 41, *etc.*; *adv. of time,* then, 3, 8, 90, *etc.*; then, in that case, 1812; *conj.*, when, while, in that, 856, 2015, 2496, 3186, 3205; since, as.

dabei, *adv.*, thereby, thereat, present, 1520, 2288, *etc.*; therein, in that, 372.

Dach, *n.* -eß, Dächer, roof, 347 *21, 447, *etc.*; 2170, awning, top, *or* deck, *cf. N.*

dagegen, *adv.*, against it *or* them, 1785.

daheim, *adv.*, at home, 115, 427, 1232, *etc.*

daher, *adv. and sep. pref.*, thence, along, 219, 1555, 1562, *etc.*

dahin, *adv. and sep. pref.*, thither, there, along, away, 732, 734, *etc.*; biß dahin, till then, 1458; gone, departed, dead, 2460; to this, 2821.

damals, *adv.*, then, at that time, 2584.

damit, *adv.*, therewith, with it *or* that *or* them, 2917; *conj.*, that, in order that, 2068, 3100.

dämpfen, *tr.*, quench, subdue, muffle, *136.

Dank, *m.* -es, thanks, gratitude, 189, 3062, 3063.

danken, *intr.* (*dat.*), return thanks, thank, 3080.

dann, *adv.*, then, thereupon, 75, *33, *40, *etc.*

dannen, *adv. in* von —, from thence, thence, away, 235, 415, 3103.

daran, *adv.*, thereon, therein, on *or* in *or* by that *or* it *or* them, 398, 905, *etc.*; daran sein, be engaged in, on the point of, 2019, 2104.

darauf, *adv.*, thereupon, thereon, upon *or* to it *or* that *or* them, 960, 1512, *86; thereafter, 94, 1191, *78.

daraus, *adv.*, thereout, thereof, out of *or* from it *or* that *or* them; d(a)raus werden, come of it, *or* that, 376, 1726.

darin, *adv.*, therein, in it *or* that *or* them, 309.

d(a)rob, *adv.*, thereat, on that account, 2142.

darreichen, *tr.*, reach forth, stretch out, offer, 1023.

darstellen, *refl.*, be displayed, be evident, *21.

d(a)rüber, *adv.*, thereover, over *or* beyond it *or* that *or* them, 167, 979, 1227, *etc.*; at that; in the meantime.

darum, *adv.*, thereabout, around it *or* that *or* them; 2956, of it; therefore, on that account, 98, 269, 286, *etc.*

d(a)runter, *adv.*, thereunder, under (*or* among) it *or* that *or* them, 980, 2975.

Dasein, *n.* -s, presence, existence, 1251.

daß, *conj.*, that, so that, in order that, 54, 85, 231, *etc.*

davon, *adv. and sep. pref.*, therefrom, thereof, of it *or* that *or* them, 1164, 2038; away.

davontragen, trug, getragen, trägt, *tr.*, carry off *or* away, 2904.

dazu, *adv.*, thereto, to *or* for it *or* that *or* them, 1146, 1235, 2002.

dazwischen, *adv.*, between *or* among them; at intervals, *105.

decken, *tr.*, cover, close, 2935.

dein, *poss. adj. and pron.*, thy, thine, your; *pl. as noun*, your people, 791, 858.

Denkart, *f.* -en, way of thinking, sentiment, disposition, 2573, *cf.* N.

denken, dachte, gedacht, *tr. or intr.* (*gen. or usually* an, *but also* auf *and* über, *with acc.*), think, think of, 41, 139, 248; remember, 1929, 2484.

Denkmal, *n.* -s, -äler, monument, 2919.

denn, *adv.*, then, therefore, 70, 151, *etc.; conj.* (*first word in its clause*), for, because, 226, *etc.*

der (die, das), *def. art.*, the; *demon. adj. or pron.*, this, that, this *or* that one, he, she, it; *rel. pron.*, who, which, that; 97, ihm's = ihm das (*art.*).

dereinſt, *adv.*, once, at some future time, hereafter, 842.

dergleichen, *indec. adj. and pron.*, such, like, the like, 404, 2678.

derſelbe (dieſelbe, dasſelbe), *adj.*, the same, 557, 1016, 1399, *etc.*

deuchten, *impers.* (*with dat. or acc.*), seem, appear, 1752, 2288.

deuten, *intr.*, point, *107, *122; *tr.*, explain, interpret, 2676.

deutſch, *adj.*, German, 518, 1174, 1222.

dicht, *adj.*, dense, compact, close; *adv.*, close, 71, 2696.

dienen, *intr.* (*dat.*), serve, 378, 1358, 1533, *etc.*

Diener, *m.* -ß, —, servant, 1092, 1853, 2233, *etc.*

Dienſt, *m.* -eß, -e, service, 890, 937.

dienſtfertig, *adj.*, officious, 1761.

dies (dieſer, dieſe, dieſes), *adj. and pron.*, this, that, this one, that one, the latter, 182, 221, 225, *etc.*

diesmal, *adv.*, this time, 1334.

Diethelm, *m.* -ß, Diethelm (man's name), 2879.

Ding, *n.* -eß, -e, thing, 2727.

Dirne, *f.* -n, maiden, lass, girl, 1414.

doch, *adv. and conj.*, yet, however, nevertheless, but, though, 119, 157, 168, 222, *etc.*; surely, really, I hope, 554, etc.; (*for emphasis*), Why, indeed, 187, 2769. *etc.*

Dolch, *m.* -eß, -e, dagger, 2978.

donnern, *intr.*, thunder, 25, *8, *etc.*; *inf. as noun*, *9, *etc.*

Donnerſchlag, *m.* -ß, -äge, clap or burst or peal of thunder, *9, *10, *105.

doppelt, *adj.*, double, 979; *neut. as noun*, 357.

Dorf, *n.* -eß, Dörfer, village, hamlet, *3, 2120.

dort, *adv.*, there, yonder, 65, 122, 142, *etc.*

dorthin, *adv.*, thither, that way, 974.

Drache, *m.* -n, -n, dragon, 1075, 1264.

Drachengift, *n.* -ß, -e, dragon's poison, venom, 2572.

dran, see daran.

Drang, *m.* -eß, oppression, distress, 280, 536, 799, *etc.*

drängen, *tr.*, press (upon), oppress, afflict, 696, *etc.*; *refl.*, press, crowd, force one's way, *76, 2503, *etc.*

Drangſal, *n.* -ß, -e, oppression, misery, 533, 534.

drauf, see darauf.

draus, see daraus.

draußen, *adv.*, without, outside, *154.

drei, *num.*, three, 655, *51; *decl. nom. pl.*, 1127.

dreißig, *num.*, thirty, 2994.

dreiunddreißig, *num.*, thirty-three, *55.

dringen, brang, gedrungen, *intr.* ┊, press, urge, force one's way, throng, 149, 504, 602, *etc.*

drinnen, *adv.*, within, inside, 2746.

dritt, *num. adj.*, third, *21, *72, *etc.*

drob, see darob.

droben, *adv.*, above, up there, on high, in heaven, 627, 1148, 1280, *etc.*

drohen, *tr. or intr. (dat. of person)*, threaten, 993, 1666, *etc.;* be near to, be about to, *100.

drüben, *adv.*, over there *or* yonder, across there, 278, 282, 545, *etc.*

drüber, see darüber.

Druck, *m.* -es, -e, pressure, oppression, 288, 1325.

drücken, *tr.*, press, oppress, *14, 330, *etc.; masc. past. part. as noun*, 1276; *intr.*, press *or* weigh heavily, 198.

drum, see darum.

drunter, see darunter.

dulden, *tr.*, endure, tolerate, suffer, 1243, 1842, 2842, *etc.*

duldsam, *adj.*, patient, 652.

dumpf, *adj.*, dull, heavy, hollow, muffled, *4, 38, 479, *etc.*

dunkel, *adj.*, dark, 1106.

dünken, *intr. (dat.)*, seem, appear, 1029.

durch, *prep., adv., sep. and insep. pref.*, through, throughout, during, by, because of, 33, 169, 418, *etc.*

durchboh'ren, *insep., tr.*, bore through, pierce, transfix, *136.

durchren'nen, durchra'nnte, durch-ra'nnt, *insep., tr.*, run through, 2979.

durchschau'en, *insep., tr.*, look through, penetrate, fathom, 2082.

durchschie'ßen, durchschoß', durch-schof'fen, *insep., tr.*, shoot through, 2060 (*pret. ind. for pluperf. subjunc.*), 2796.

dürfen, durfte, gedurft, darf, *intr. and modal aux.*, be permitted, have a right, may, 263, 723, 771, *etc.*

Durst, *m.* -es, thirst, 1004.

düster, *adj.*, gloomy, sullen, 2616.

E.

eben, *adj.*, even, level, smooth, 972, 1789; *adv.*, even, just, just now, *21, 965, *etc.*

Echo, *n.* -s, -s, echo, 2850.

echt, *adj.*, genuine, pure, sterling, real, 689, 916, 1210, *etc.*

Ecke, *f.* -n, corner, angle, edge, 503, 2227.

edel, *adj.*, noble, 240, 317, 336, *etc.; m. pl. as noun*, nobles, nobility, 696, 2413, *etc.; neut. as noun*, 1643; *fem. sing. as noun*, 2528.

Edelhof, *m.* -s, -öfe, manor-house, baronial hall, *40, *114.

Edelmann, *m.* -s, *pl.* -männer *or* -leute, nobleman, 693, 807, 2888, *etc.*

Edelsitz, *m.* -es, -e, nobleman's seat, manor-house, baronial hall, 207.

Edelstein, *m.* -s, -e, precious stone, jewel, 894.

ehe, *conj.*, before, ere, *3, 41, 455, etc.

Ehe, *f.* -n, marriage, wedlock, 1671.

eher, *adv.* (*comp. of* ehe), sooner, rather, before, 1176, 1451, 1609, etc.

Ehewirt, *m.* -s, -e, husband, 238.

Ehni, *m.* -s, (*a Swiss word*) grandfather, 1539, 1582.

Ehre, *f.* -n, honor, 83, 84, 128, etc.

ehren, *tr.*, honor, respect, 338, 658, 673, etc.

Ehrengruß, *m.* -es, -üße, salute of honor, 1862.

Ehrenmann, *m.* -s, -änner, man of honor, worthy man, gentleman, 412, 1828.

Ehrfurcht, *f.* veneration, reverence, respect, 1011 (*acc.*), 1371.

Ehrgeiz, *m.* -es, ambition, 1678.

Ehrsucht, *f.* ambition,, 3175,

ehrwürdig, *adj.*, venerable, worthy, sacred, 688 (*comp.*), 2477.

ei, *interj.*, why! oh!, 1795, 1815.

Eid, *m.* -es, -e, oath, 1395, 1447.

Eidam, *m.* -s, -e, son-in-law, 555.

Eidgenoß(e), *m.* -n, -n, confederate, 1108, 1157, 2890, etc.

Eidschwur, *m.* -s, -üre, oath, 2585.

Eifer, *m.* -s, zeal, 1390.

eigen, *adj.*, own, proper, peculiar, 50, 261, etc.; 232, auf eigene Hand, on one's own account; 1080, eigne Leute, (owned people), bondmen, serfs, 1142; 1907, peculiar, unique.

eigensinnig, *adj.*, stubborn, obstinate, 871.

eilen, *intr.* f. *or* h., hasten, 71, 415, 1031, etc.

eilends, *adv.*, hastily, 425, 2107.

eilfertig, *adj.*, hasty, *132.

eilig, *adj.*, hasty; 68, why this haste?; 772, Are you in such haste?

ein, *indef. art. and num.*, a, an, one; so —, solch —, *or* -solcher, such a(n); der -e, the one; 60, 'ne = eine, 403, 1744, 1876, 'nen = einen.

ein, *sep. pref.*, in, into; down; asleep.

einander, *indec. pron.*, one another, each other; 375 ('nander = einander), *71, *149. *Often printed as one word with a prep. as in* auseinander, *etc.*

einbrechen, brach, gebrochen, bricht, *intr.* f., break, give way, 1503, 3256.

einfallen, fiel, gefallen, fällt, *intr.* f., fall in, (of music) begin, strike in, *71, *163; 1575, occur to, enter one's mind.

einförmig, *adj.*, uniform, monotonous, 838.

Eingang, *m.*, -s, -änge, entrance, *130.

eingehen, ging, gegangen, *intr.* f., go in, enter, 350.

Eingeweide, *n.* -s, —, bowels, entrails; heart, feelings, 365.

einholen, *tr.*, overtake, catch, 176.

einig, *adj.,* one, united, 1090, 1204, 2451, *etc.;* some (*especially in pl.*), *33, *39, 969, *87, *etc.*

einkaufen, *tr.,* buy, purchase, 906–7.

einkehren, *intr.* f., turn in, put up (as at an inn), lodge, 1006.

einmal, *adv.,* one time, once, sometime, 1335, 2102, *etc.;* auf —, (all) at once, together, 1461.

einreißen, riß, geriffen, *tr.,* tear *or* break down, 178, 2860.

einfam, *adj.,* solitary, lonely, alone, 1006, 1180, 1551, *etc.*

einfchiffen, *refl.,* take ship, embark, sail, 2104, 2216.

einfchlafen, fchlief, gefchlafen, fchläft, *intr.* f., fall asleep, 2.

einfchließen, fchloß, gefchloffen, *tr.,* shut in, confine, enclose, surround, 878, *78, 1587, *etc.*

einfchränken, *tr.,* bar in, bound, confine, 2168.

einfchreiben, fchrieb, gefchrieben, *tr.,* write in *or* on, inscribe, engrave, 1122.

Einfiedeln. Einsiedeln, town and monastery, in the Canton Schwyz, NE. of the Lake of the Four Forest Cantons and about 5 miles S. of Lake·Zürich; 1247, *cf. N.* 519.

einfinken, fank, gefunken, *intr.* f., sink in, settle, subside, 2666.

einftürzen, *intr.* f., fall *or* tumble in *or* down; 2148, close up, *cf. N.*

Eintracht, *f.,* unity, concord, union, 2927.

eintreten, trat, getreten, tritt, *intr.* f., enter, make one's entrance, *27, 561, *40, *etc.; inf. as noun,* *145.

einzeln, *adj.,* single, individual, 433.

einziehen, zog, gezogen, *tr.,* draw in, pull in, 37; *intr.* f., enter, come in, make one's entrance, 456, 3264.

einzig, *adj.,* only, single, alone, but one, sole, 420, 798, 1225, *etc.*

Eis, *n.* –es, ice, 28.

eisbedeckt, *part. adj.,* ice-covered, 1044.

Eifen, *n.* –s, —, iron, 1405.

Eifenftab, *m.* –s, –äbe, iron rod *or* bar, 2166.

Eisesfeld, *n.* –es, –er, field of ice, 999.

Eisesturm, *m.* –s, –ürme, tower of ice, 2144.

Eiseswall, *m.* –s, –älle, wall of ice, 1194.

Eisgebirge, *n.* –s, —, ice-mountains, mountains covered with ice and snow, *3, *48, *71, *etc.*

Eispalaft, *m.* –s, –äfte, ice-palace, 627.

eitel, *adj.,* vain, empty, 839, 915, *etc.;* idle, mere, nothing but, 148.

Element, *n.* –s, –e, element, 2133, 2183.

Elend, *n.* –s, misery, 2736.

elend, *adj.,* wretched, miserable, 2232, 2742, *etc.; masc. as noun,* wretch, 612.

Elsbeth. Elisabeth, wife of Emperor Albrecht, daughter of Meinhard, Duke of Carinthia; 3033.

empfangen, empfing, empfangen, empfängt, *tr.*, receive, 868, 2378, 2480, *etc.*

empfinden, empfand, empfunden, *tr.*, feel, experience, 1926.

emporheben, hob, gehoben, *tr.*, lift up, *138.

emporragen, *intr.*, project, tower (above, über), *84.

empören, *tr.*, stir up, revolt, shock (the feelings), 2006; *refl.*, revolt, rebel, rise, 2142.

Empörung, *f.* –en, sedition, rebellion, revolt, 1850, 1851, 2081, *etc.*

Ende, *n.* –s, –n, end, issue, limit, conclusion, 1352, 2619, 2818, *etc.*

enden, *intr.*, end, come to an end, 810, 862, 2379, *etc.*

endigen, *intr.*, end, cease, *163.

endlich, *adj.*, final; *adv.*, finally, at last, 430, 1585, 1586, *etc.*

eng(e), *adj.*, narrow, 761, 762, 2169, *etc.*; 1811, es wird mir eng, I begin to feel oppressed, *cf. N.*

Enge, *f.* –n, narrowness, 2565.

Engel, *m.* –s, —, angel, 5, 154.

Engelberg. Engelberg, valley, village and monastery in the Canton Unterwalden; 1002, 1079.

Enkel, *m.* –s, —, grandchild, descendant, 1020, 2385, 2918, *etc.*

ent=, *insep. pref.*, *never accented.*

entbehren, *intr.* (*gen.*), be without, in want of, 416; do without, dispense with, 1255.

entbinden, entband, entbunden, *tr.*, free, release, 3075.

entblößen, *tr.*, bare, uncover, 398.

entdecken, *tr.*, discover, descry, *13, 1185, *etc.*; disclose, reveal, 2299.

entfernen, *refl.*, withdraw, retire, *72, *103, *etc.*; depart, deviate, differ from, 1149, 1905.

entfliehen, entfloh, entflohen, *intr.* ſ., flee away, fly (of time), 1705.

entgegen, *prep.* (*following its noun in dat.*) *and sep. pref.*, towards, against, to, to meet, up along, *51, 3242.

entgegeneilen, *intr.* ſ., hasten to meet, *90, *101.

entgegenkehren, *tr.*, turn towards or against, 298.

entgegenstarren, *intr.*, stand (motionless) before, 2159.

entgegentreten, trat, getreten, tritt, *intr.* ſ., step towards, advance before, 223, *89.

entgegnen, *tr.*, reply, rejoin, 227.

entgehen, entging, entgangen, *intr.* ſ., escape, 575, 997.

entkommen, entkam, entkommen, *intr.* ſ., escape, 1527, 2210, 2217, *etc.*

entlassen, entließ, entlassen, entläßt, *tr.*, dismiss, let go, 345, 1333, 1927, *etc.*

entledigen, *tr.*, set free, release, deliver (from, *gen.*), 2244, 3018.

entreißen, entriß, entriffen, _tr._, snatch away, seize, wrest, 1864, 2531.

entrichten, _tr._, discharge, pay, 3076.

entrinnen, entrann, entronnen, _intr._ ſ., fly from, 2607.

entrüſten, _tr._, anger, provoke, enrage, 1013.

entſagen, _intr._ (_dat._), renounce, give up, 1680, 2012.

entſcheiden, entſchieb, entſchieben, _tr. and intr._, decide, determine, 702, 1593.

Entſcheidung, _f._ -en, decision, 2442.

entſchließen, entſchloß, entſchloſſen, _refl._, resolve, decide, determine, 913, 1673.

Entſchloſſenheit, _f._, resoluteness, decision, 2887.

Entſchluß, _m._ -es, -üſſe, resolution, resolve, 1725.

entſchuldigen, _tr._, excuse, justify. 1114.

entſeelt, _part. adj._, lifeless, dead, *121, 2466.

Entſetzen, _n._ -s, horror, 3156.

entſetzlich, _adj._, horrible, terrible, 2745.

entſinken, entſank, entſunken, _intr._ ſ., sink down, drop from, *101, 2231.

entſpringen, entſprang, entſprungen, _intr._ ſ., spring _or_ run away, escape, 95; _inf. as noun_, 2251.

entſtehen, entſtand, entſtanden, _intr._ ſ., arise, *26; fail, be wanting, 699.

entweichen, entwich, entwichen, _intr._ ſ., withdraw, retire, 1427.

entwiſchen, _intr._ ſ., escape, slip off, 177.

entziehen, entzog, entzogen, _refl._, avoid, forsake, 441, 1521.

entzwei, _adv._, in two, asunder, broken, 1478.

er, _pron._, he, it; _frequent._

er, _insep. pref._, _never accented._

erbarmen, _tr._, move to pity, 670; _refl._ (_with gen._), take pity, have mercy (on), 111, 143; _impers._ (_with acc._ [_and gen._]), es erbarmt mich, I am sorry, 2093, 3190.

erbärmlich, _adj._, pitiable, miserable, 2742.

Erbarmung, _f._ -en, mercy, pity, 2790.

erbauen, _tr._, build, build up, erect, 318, 458, 1188, _etc._

Erbe, _n._ -s, inheritance, heritage, 261, 691, 828.

erbeben, _intr._ ſ., shake, tremble, 1982.

erben, _intr._ ſ., descend by inheritence (to, auf), 1209.

erbeuten, _tr._, get as booty, capture, acquire, 1490.

Erbherr, _m._ -n, -en, hereditary lord _or_ ruler, 891.

Erbin, _f._ -innen, heiress, *2.

erblicken, _tr._, behold, discover, catch sight of, 34, 700, 1097, _etc._

erbrauſen, _intr._ ſ., rise roaring, 2345.

erbrechen, erbrach, erbrochen, er=
bricht, *tr.*, **break** open, open,
3031.

Erbſtück, *n.* -8, -e, inheritance, inherited piece of land, 1088.

Erbe, *f.* -n, **earth**, ground, soil,
land, 19, 43, 426, *etc.; dat.* -n,
1084, 2667; *gen.* -n, 1699.

erbulden, *tr.*, suffer, endure, tolerate, 535, 789, 1257, *etc.*

Ereigniß, *n.* -niſſes, -niſſe, event,
occurrence, 2789.

ererben, *tr.*, get by inheritance, in-
herit, 1354.

erfaſſen, *tr.*, lay hold of, grasp,
2541.

erflehen, *tr.*, implore, 2530.

erforſchen, *tr.*, search out, sound,
705.

erfrechen, *refl.* (*with gen.*), dare,
do insolently, 2595.

erfreuen, *tr.*, delight, gladden, 318,
525.

erfriſchen, *tr.*, refresh, give refreshment to, 3275.

erfüllen, *tr.*, **fill**, **fulfill**, 1493,
1652, 2924.

Ergebung, *f.* submission, 1304.

ergehen, erging, ergangen, *intr.* ſ.,
go forth, be issued, 1228; 1944,
let mercy go forth before (take
the place of) right.

ergießen, ergoß, ergoſſen, *refl.*, pour
forth, flow forth, 2427.

ergreifen, ergriff, ergriffen, *tr.*,
seize, move, touch, 821, 846, *etc.;*
1294, embrace, accept.

erhalten, erhielt, erhalten, erhält,
tr., check, restrain, 944; receive,
get, obtain, 1313, 1330, *etc.;* preserve, save, uphold, 2422.

erheben, erhob *and* erhub, erhoben,
tr., raise, lift up, 1146, 1386, *etc.;*
refl., rise, arise, 222, 423, 747, *etc.*

erhellen, *tr.*, light up, brighten,
2392, 3259.

erinnern, *refl.* (*gen. or* an *with*
acc.), remember, 2724, 2915.

erjagen, *tr.*, get by hunting, hunt
down, 2641.

erkennen, erkannte, erkannt, *tr.*,
perceive, recognize, acknowledge,
32, 265, 399, *etc.*

Erker, *m.* -8, —, bay-window, 1338.

erklären, *tr.*, declare, 3290; *refl.*,
declare one's self, 2844, explain
one's self, 1585.

erkranken, *intr.* ſ., become ill, 2355,
2357.

erkühnen, *refl.*, become bold, 2003;
(*with gen.*) boldly use, dare to
do, 2533.

erkunden, *tr.*, spy out, reconnoiter,
explore, 1059.

erlangen, *tr.*, reach, 2564.

erlaſſen, erließ, erlaſſen, erläßt, *tr.*,
remit, exempt from, excuse from,
let off from, 1946, 1984.

erlauben, *tr.*, allow, 753, (ſich), *dat.*)
2591, 3212.

erleben, *tr.*, experience, undergo,
meet with, 539, 666.

erledigen, *refl.*, free one's self from
(*gen.*), 288.

erleiden, erlitt, erlitten, *tr.*, suffer, endure, 676, 1258.

erlöſchen, erloſch, erloſchen, erliſcht, *intr.* ſ., go out, be extinguished, die away, 991; *inf. as noun*, 2428.

ermächtigen, *refl.* (*with gen.*), take possession of, 1410; *for usual* ſich bemächtigen.

ermorden, *tr.*, murder, 2943, 2944.

ermüden, *intr.* ſ., grow weary, 430, 1176.

erneuern, *tr.*, renew, 1157.

Ernſt, *m.* -es, seriousness, gravity, earnestness, *47, 1424, 1894, *etc.*

ernſt, *adj.*, earnest, serious, grave, 195, *79, 2657, *etc.*

ernſthaft, *adj.*, earnest, serious, 406, 1919.

ernten, *tr.*, reap, gather, harvest, 3081.

erobern, *tr.*, conquer, 2841.

eröffnen, *tr.*, open, *3.

erquicken, *tr.*, refresh, 594, 2381, 3100.

erregen, *tr.*, stir up, arouse, 718, 1052.

erreichen, *tr.*, reach, 122, 189, 698, *etc.*

erretten, *tr.*, save, rescue, deliver, 118, 155, 944, *etc.*

Erretter, *m.* -s, -, savior, deliverer, 3281.

errichten, *tr.*, set up, erect, 3246.

erringen, *tr.*, obtain (by strenuous effort), win, 1655, 1662.

erſäufen, *tr.*, drown, flood, 2131.

erſchaffen, *tr.*, create, 1260.

erſchallen, erſcholl, erſchollen, *intr.* ſ., sound, resound, spread abroad, 1009.

erſcheinen, erſchien, erſchienen, *intr.* ſ., appear, make one's appearance, come in sight, *4, *126, *137, *etc.*

erſchießen, erſchoß, erſchoſſen, *tr.*, shoot (to death), kill (by a shot), 2797.

erſchlagen, erſchlug, erſchlagen, erſchlägt, *tr.*, slay, kill, 79, 129, 551, *etc.*

erſchleichen, erſchlich, erſchlichen, *tr.*, obtain by fraud, fraudulently, 1252.

erſchöpfen, *tr.*, exhaust, spend, wear out, 647.

erſchrecken, erſchrak, erſchrocken, erſchrickt, *intr.* ſ., be startled, start with fear, *160.

erſchrecken, *tr.*, frighten, alarm, 3140.

erſparen, *tr.*, spare, save, 1514; (*with* an), save out of, gain at the expense of, 774.

erſt, *num. adj.*, first, *3, *5, *etc.*: *adv.*, first, 75, *etc.*; only, but, once, 194; not until.

erſtaunen, *intr.* ſ., be astonished, *29, *32, *100, 2941, *etc.*

Erſtaunen, *n.* -s, astonishment, *120.

erſtaunlich, *adj.*, astonishing, amazing, wonderful, 524.

erſteigen, erſtieg, erſtiegen, *tr.*, climb, scale, 1413, 2875.

erſticken, *tr.*, choke, suffocate, stifle, *33, 1643.

ertönen, *intr.*, sound, ring, *140.

ertöten, *tr.*, kill, deaden, 1646.

ertragen, ertrug, ertragen, erträgt, *tr.*, bear, endure, suffer, tolerate, 316, 317, 421, *etc.*

ertrinken, ertrank, ertrunken, *intr.* ſ., drown, be drowned, 2232.

ertrotzen, *tr.*, gain by defiance, 1312.

erwachen, *intr.* ſ., awake, wake, 7, 18, *117, *etc.*

erwarten, *tr*, wait, await, expect, look for, 272, 492, 502, 1045, *etc.*

Erwartnng, *f.* –en, expectation, *131.

erwecken, *tr.*, awaken, excite, 1374.

erwehren, *refl.* (*with gen.*), keep *or* ward off, defend one's self against, 340.

erwerben, erwarb, erworben, er= wirbt, *tr.*, acquire, get, gain, 853. 938, 1999, *etc.*

erzählen, *tr.*, tell, relate, recount, 638, *etc.;* (ſich, to one another), 1166, 1494, *etc.*

erzeigen, *tr.*, show, render, do, 1734, 2756.

erzittern, *intr.* ſ., tremble, shake, 2580.

erzwingen, erzwang, erzwungen, *tr.*, force, enforce, 3075.

eß, 'ß, *pron.*, it, he, she; something; so. *As expletive and when representing a clause it is often untranslatable.*

Eſchenbach. Walther von Eschenbach, friend and accomplice of Herzog Johannes von Schwaben; 2960, 2980.

eſſen, aß, gegeſſen, ißt, *tr.*, eat, 476.

etlich (*adj. and*) *pron.*, some, 286.

etwas, *indec. pron.* (*and adj.*), some, something, somewhat, 656, 1517, 2624, *etc.*

euer, *poss. adj. and pron.* (*corresponding to* ihr, *you*), your, yours, 50, 64, 67; *pl.*, 2685, your family and friends.

eurig (der, die, das –e), *poss. pron.*, yours, 1028, 2478.

ewig, *adj.*, eternal, everlasting, perpetual, 594, 851, 1148, *etc.;* *adv.*, ever, forever.

Ewigkeit, *f.*'–en, eternity, 386, 629.

F.

fahen, *archaic and poetic form of* fangen, *tr.*, catch, seize, 2214.

Fahne, *f.* –n, standard, banner, flag, 827, 2171, 2446, *etc.*

Fahr, *f.* –en (*archaic and poetic form for* Gefahr), danger, 1511.

fahrbar, *adj.*, navigable, practicable, 1183.

Fähre, *f.* –n, ferry, ferry-boat, 1181, 2970.

fahren, fuhr, gefahren, fährt, *intr.* ſ., move, go, row, sail, 17, 133, 150, 333, *etc.;* 2238, *inf. as noun,*

sailing, steering; *136, mit ber
Hand —, move, put one's hand;
refl., row about, *3.

Fährmann, *m.* -ß, -männer, -leute,
ferryman, 42, 67, 103, *etc.*

Fahrt, *f.* -en, passage, journey,
course, way, wandering, 64, 135,
730, etc.

Fahrzeug, *n.* -ß, -e, vessel, craft,
boat, 2153.

Falke, *m.* -n, -n, falcon, *92.

Fall, *m.* -ß, Fälle, fall, 3068.

fallen, fiel, gefallen, fällt, *intr.* f.,
fall, tumble, drop, 120, 157, 178
(in = upon), *etc.*; 472, in Strafe
—, incur a penalty; 1384, in bas
Land —, fall upon, invade the
land.

fällen, *tr.*, fell, 90.

Fallstrick, *m.* -ß, -e, snare, trap,
411.

falsch, *adj.*, false, 849, 1947.

Falsch, *n.* -eß, falsehood, deceit,
guile, 741 (*archaic and poetic*).

Falschheit, *f.* -en, falsehood, deceit,
guile, 1669, 1703.

falten, *tr.*, fold, wrinkle, knit,
2760.

Fang, *m.* -eß, Fänge, catch, capture, haul, 1744.

fangen, fing, gefangen, fängt, *tr.*,
catch, capture,; *past part. as adj.
or noun*, captive, imprisoned, prisoner, 463, 1824, 2100, 2122.

fassen, *tr.*, seize, grasp, lay hold of,
*32, *47, *90, *etc.*; *refl.*, compose
one's self, 492, 2312.

fast, *adv.*, almost, 1432.

Fastnachtsaufzug, *m.* -ß, -üge,
carnival procession, 390.

faul, *adj.*, lazy, idle, 363.

Faust, *f.* Fäuste, fist, hand, 1375,
*92.

Favenz. Faenza, Fayence, city of
Italy, SW. of Ravenna, 911.

fechten, focht, gefochten, ficht, *intr.*,
fight, 326, 331, 911, *etc.*

Feder, *f.* -n, feather, 2304.

fehlen, *intr.* (*dat.*), fail, be wanting *or* lacking, 48, 1537, 1699,
2352, *etc.*; 445, es soll an mir
nicht fehlen, I shall not be found
wanting; — auf (*acc.*), 1950, *cf.*
N., miss and hit; 2062 (*with
gen.*), miss, fail of hitting; *tr.*,
miss, 1889, 1918.

Fehler, *m.* -ß, —, fault, 566.

Fehlsprung, *m.* -ß, -ünge, false
leap; — thun, miss one's leap,
1499.

Feierabend, *m.* -ß, -e, evening
rest, 767.

feiern, *intr.*, rest, be idle, 353, *past
part. used for imper.*

feig, *adj.*, coward, cowardly, 612,
2552.

feigherzig, *adj.*, faint-hearted,
cowardly, 616.

feil, *adj.*, for sale, to be bought,
purchasable, 450.

Feind, *m.* -eß, -e, enemy, 120,
654, 712.

Feld, *n.* -eß, -er, field, 28, 36,
755, *etc.*

Fels (Felsen), *m.* –en (–ens), *acc. sing.,* Fels, *pl.,* –en, rock, cliff, *4, *12, 670, *etc.; archaic dat.,* von Fels zu Fels, 2638.   [2850.

Felsenkluft, *f.* –üfte, rocky chasm,

Felsenplatte, *f.* –n, shelf *or* ledge of rock, 2258.

Felsenriff, *n.* –s, –e, reef *or* ledge of rock, 2252.

Felsensteig, *m.* –s, –e, rocky path, path among *or* over rocks, 711, 1551.

Felsenthor, *n.* –s, –e, gate of rocks, rocky gateway *or* door, 3258.

Felsenufer, *n.* –s, —, rocky shore, *3.

Felsenwall, *m.* –s, –älle, rampart *or* wall of rock, 1057.

Felsenwand, *f.* –änbe, wall of rock, precipice, 2740.

Felswand, *f.* –änbe, wall of rock, precipice, 1553, 1564, 2263, *etc.*

Fenster, *n.* –s, —, window, 210.

fern, *adj.,* far, far off, distant, *3, *etc.*

fern(e), *adv.,* far, far off, at a distance, away, 341, 486, 582, 2618.

Ferne, *f.* –n, distance, *49, *84, *140.

ferner, *adv.,* from afar, 1163.

Ferse, *f.* –n, heel, 71, 131.

fertig, *adj.,* ready, prepared, finished, done, *21, 1885.

Fessel, *f.* –n, fetter, 2109, 2370.

fesseln, *tr.,* fetter, shackle, bind, attach, 320, 937, 2091, *etc.*

fest, *adj.,* fast, tight, firm, fixed, strong, secure, 185, 255, 529, *etc.; neut. as noun,* 2541.

Fest, *n.* –s, –e, feast, festival, 2914; 1400, — des Herrn, 'festival of our Lord,' 'Christmas.'

Feste, *f.* –n, stronghold, fortress, prison, *21, 369, 626, *etc.*

festhalten, hielt, gehalten, hält, *tr.,* hold fast, cling to, 923; *intr.,* hold firm, unbroken, 2605; hold fast, cleave, (to, an), 185.

festknüpfen, *tr.,* tie, bind, knit firmly, 921.

feststehen, stand, gestanden, *intr.,* stand firm, be stable, 2667.

feucht, *adj.,* damp, dank, 2356.

Feuer, *n.* –s, —, fire, 424, *50, *55, *etc.*

Feuersignal', *n.,* –s, –e, fire-signal = signal-fire, 2839.

Feuerwächter, *m.* –s, —, fire-watcher, = night-watchman, 964.

Feuerzeichen, *n.* –s, —, fire-sign, fiery signal, signal fire, 747, 2554.

finden, fand, gefunden, *tr.,* find, *14, 336, 534, *etc.; refl.,* be found, exist, be, 1187, 1389.

Finger, *m.* –s, —, finger, 469, *70.

finster, *adj.,* dark, gloomy, 197, 1596, *etc.; neut. as noun,* gloom, darkness, 594.

Finsternis, *f.* –nisse, darkness, gloom, 2356.

Firn, *m.* –es, –en, snow, glacier, snow-capped mountain, 38 (*cf. N.*), 596, 1502, *etc.*

Fiſch, *m.* -es, -e, fish, 44.

fiſchen, *intr.*, fish, 1805.

Fiſcher, *m.* -s, —, fisher, fisherman, *1, *4, *7, *etc.*,

Fiſcherkahn, *m.* -s, -ähne, fisherman's boat, 283.

Fiſcherknabe, *m.* -n, -n, fisherboy, fisherman's boy, *2, *3.

Flamme, *f.* -n, flame, 2557, 2878, 2894, *etc.*

flammen, *intr.*, flame, blaze, 747, 2129, 2857.

Flanke, *f.* -n, flank, side, wall, 385, (*cf. N.*).

Flecken, *m.* -s, —, town, 1188 1196, 1197, *etc.*

flehen, *intr.*, pray, implore, supplicate, (for, um), 127, 1131 (*pres. part. as noun*), 1344; *tr.* 132.

Fleiß, *m.* -es, diligence, industry, 202, 756, 1261, *etc.*

fliegen, flog, geflogen, *intr.* ſ. or h., fly, 1477 (*archaic pres. ind. 3rd sing.*, fleugt), 2327, 2555.

fliehen, floh, geflohen, *intr.* ſ., flee, 2293

fließen, floß, geflossen, *intr.* ſ. or h., flow, 20, 1017, 3244.

Flitterſchein, *m.*, -s, tinsel-luster, false luster, 915.

Flöte, *f.* -n, flute, 4.

Fluch, *m.* -es, -üche, curse, 457, 458, 2817, *etc.*

Fluchgebäude, *n.* -s, —, accursed building, 378.

Flucht, *f.* -en, flight, 2905.

flüchten, *tr.*, save by flight, rescue, 555; *refl.*, flee, take refuge, 884.

flüchtig, *adj.*, flying, fugitive, fleeting, transient, 568, 1488, 1684, *etc.*

Flüchtling, *m.* -s, -e, fugitive, 573.

Flüe, *f.* -n, = Fluh; as part of proper name, *1.

Flüelen. Flüelen (pron. Flūlen), village in the Canton Uri, at southern end of the Lake of the Four Forest Cantons; 521, 2105, 2162, *etc.*

Flug, *m.* -es, -üge, flight; im Fluge, on the wing, 1949.

Fluh, *f.* -en, wall of rock, precipice, 2193.

Flurſchütz, *m.* -en, -en, ranger, field-guard, *2, *129.

Fluß, *m.* -es, -üſſe, river, 1791.

Flut, *f.* -en, flood, billows, waves, 167.

Föhn, *m.* -es, -e, Föhn, south wind, storm, 109, 423.

folgen, *intr.* ſ., (*dat.*), follow, *4, *13, *etc.*; *neut. pres. part. as noun*, *121.

Folterknecht, *m.* -s, -e, rack-man, torturer, 574.

fordern, *tr.*, demand, 200, 619, *etc.*; — laſſen, send for, summon, 570.

Form, *f.* -en, form, *21.

forſchen, *intr.*, search, inquire, 3278.

fort, *adv. and sep. pref.*, forth, away, gone, 1541, 2460; on, continue to, keep on, 1015, 1020, *etc.*

forteilen, *intr.* f., hasten away, *13.

fortfahren, fuhr, gefahren, fährt, *intr.* h., continue, go on, 1360, 1362, *136, *etc.*

fortführen, *tr.*, lead *or* carry away *or* off, 1841, 2698.

fortgehen, ging, gegangen, *intr.* f., go away, 1570; go on, continue, *137.

forthelfen, half, geholfen, hilft, *intr.* (*dat.*), help one to escape, 177.

fortreißen, riß, gerissen, *tr.*, tear away, 2836, carry away *or* along, 947.

fortsetzen, *refl.*, be continued, *3.

fortziehen, zog, gezogen, *intr.* f., move on, proceed, 2620.

fragen, *tr.*, ask, inquire (for, nach), question, 226, 896, 1769, *etc.*; with nach, care for, 2763, *etc.*

Frau, *f.* -en, woman, lady, wife, *14, 296, *etc.*; 1363, "Great Lady" *or* "Our Lady" (said of a convent, *cf. N.*).

Fräulein, *n.* -s, —, nobleman's daughter, noble lady, lady, 935, *etc.*; (in address) my lady, 1586. 1606, *etc.*

frech, *adj.*, shameless, bold, insolent, impudent, 281, 466, 550, *etc.*

frei, *adj.*, free, 81, 232, 261, 1216 (*masc. superl. as noun*), *etc.*; 2740, free, unowned, common; voluntary, spontaneous, 1130, 1214, 2444, 3074, *etc.*; *neut. as*

noun, open air, open country, 2128, *152.

Freiburg. The city Freiburg, capital of the Canton Freiburg; 2434.

freien, *intr.* (*with* um), woo, marry, 2661.

Freiheit, *f.* -en, liberty, freedom, privilege, 186, 381, 388, *etc.*

Freiheitsbrief, *m.* -s, -e, charter (of liberty), 311, 2076.

Freiherr, *m.* -n, -en, baron, *1, *40, 2898.

freilich, *adv.*, certainly, to be sure, indeed, 1539, 2692.

freiwillig, *adj.*, of free will, voluntary, 1213.

fremd, *adj.*, foreign, alien, strange, 678, 847, 849, *etc.*; *neut. as subst.*, 949.

Fremde, *f.*, foreign country, 778.

Fremdling, *m.* -s, -e, foreigner, stranger, 776, 824, 1604, *etc.*

fressen, fraß, gefressen, frißt, *tr.*, eat (*of beasts*), 42, 55.

Freude, *f.* -n, joy, pleasure, delight, 331, 660, 793, *etc.*

Freudenhaus, *n.* -es, -häuser, house of rejoicing, 3101.

Freudenkunde, *f.* -n, joyous tidings, glad news, 750.

Freudenschießen, *n.* -s, —, *usually* a firing of guns for joy, a salute, *but in* 2648 = Schützenfest, shooting-match.

Freudespur, *f.* -en, joyous memory, 1695.

freudig, *adj.*, glad, joyful, joyous, 218, 592, 1025, *etc.*

freuen, *tr.*, give joy *or* pleasure, 1978; *refl.*, rejoice, 2869; *inf. as noun*, 2623, 2869, rejoicing.

Freund, *m.* -es, -e, friend, 195, 324, 441, *etc.*

freundlich, *adj.*, friendly, kind, 1137, 1313, 2158, *etc.*

Freundschaft, *f.* -en, friendship; 659 *and* 1455 *in older sense,* kindred.

Frevel, *m.* -s, —, outrage, crime, offence, 584, 1966, 3017, *etc.*

freveln, *intr.*, commit crime, outrage, do violence, 2533.

Frevelthat, *f.* -en, act of violence, outrage, 2526.

friedgewohnt, *adj.*, accustomed to peace, peaceful, 303.

Friede(n), *m.* -ns, -n, peace, 428, 1378, 1398, *etc.*

friedlich, *adj.*, peaceable, peaceful, 1291, 1426, 2306, *etc.; masc. as noun*, 428.

Friedrich. Emperor Friedrich II, born 1194, Emperor from 1212 till his death in 1250; 1215.

frisch, *adj.*, fresh, new, brisk, lively, gay; quick, quickly, 96, 103, 176 (briskly), 1963, 2055 (at once); 521, newly, directly; 599, whole, well, unharmed; 1861, über frischer That, in the very act; 1970, mit frischer That, with prompt action, without delay.

frischrudernd, *part. adj.*, rowing briskly, 2260.

Frist, *f.* -en, space of time, period, respite, 1054, 2834.

froh, *adj.*, glad, joyous, happy, 455, 1352, 2220, *etc.*

fröhlich, *adj.*, joyful, glad, gay, 1107, 1232, 1694, *etc.*

froh'locken, frohlockte, gefrohlockt, *intr.*, exult, 3068 (in = *gen.* instead of usual über with acc.); *inf. as noun*, exultation, *163.

fromm (*comp.*, frömmer, *superl.*, frömmst), *adj.*, good, worthy, pious, 344, 662, 674, *etc.; masc.*, *superl. as noun*, 2682.

Fronbienst, *m.* -es, -e, (compulsory) labor, servile toil, 367.

Fronvogt, *m.* -s, -vögte, overseer, taskmaster, *2, 21, 369.

Frucht, *f.* -üchte, fruit, 548, 3011, 3012. [*etc.*

früh, *adj.*, early, 1469, 1481, 2988,

Frühling, *m.* -s, -e, spring, 29, 1713.

Frühtrunk, *m.* -s, early draught, morning-cup, 754, *cf. N.*

fügen, *tr.*, join, fit together, 209, 214, *etc.; refl.*, accommodate one's self, submit to, acquiesce in, 473.

fühlen, *tr.*, feel, be sensible of, 593, 914, 1698, *etc.*

fühllos, *adj.*, unfeeling, cold, *138.

führen, *tr.*, lead, conduct, guide, 54, *etc.;* handle, wield, manage, bear, 134, 313, 1972; deal (a blow), 1772.

Fülle, f. fullness, abundance, plenty, 1184.

füllen, refl., be filled, 3267.

fünf, num., five, *55, 3008.

fünft, num. adj., fifth, *140, etc.

fünfundachtzig, num., eighty-five, *40.

für, prep. (acc.), for, 344, 348, etc.; — sich, to one's self, aside; was —, what sort or kind of, 389, etc.; — sich, by itself, independently, 1159.

furchen, tr., furrow, 197.

Furcht, f. fear, terror, dread, fright, 1239, 1374, 2238, etc.

furchtbar, adj., fearful, dreadful, terrible, 314, 998, 1383, etc.

fürchten, tr., fear, dread, 332, 641, 648, etc.; refl., be in fear, be afraid of, 133, 641, etc.

fürchterlich, adj., frightful, awful, terrible, 1554, *98, 2604, etc.

furchtsam, adj., timid, *133.

fürder, adv., archaic, further; nicht —, nevermore, 384.

Fürsehung, f., archaic = Vorsehung, providence, 2211.

Fürst, m. -en, -en, prince, 856, 1212, 2438, etc.

Fürstengunst, f. -ünste, favor of princes, court-favor, 794.

Fürstenhaus, n. -es, -äuser, princely house or family, dynasty, 254, 3049.

Fürstenknecht, m. -s, -e, servant or slave of a prince, 855.

fürwahr, adv., in truth, indeed, forsooth, 1066, 1378.

Fuß, m. -es, Füße, foot, 31, 523, etc.; stehenden Fußes, instantly, without delay, 333; zu Fuße, on foot, 2674.

Fußstoß, m. -es, -öße, push or thrust with the foot, kick, 2266.

G.

Gabe, f. -n, gift, 3099, 3276.

gählings, adv., abruptly, suddenly, 2230.

gähstotzig, adj., precipitously, 2194.

Gang, m. -es, Gänge, course, movement, 1022.

ganz, adj., whole, entire, all, 786, etc.; adv., wholly, entirely, quite, very, 535, 585; neut. as noun, (the) whole, *21, 1463, *163.

gar, adv., quite, entirely, very, with neg., at all; 295, 365, 1317, etc.

gären, gor, gegoren, intr., ferment; 2572, pres. part. in figurative sense, rankling.

Garten, m. -s, Gärten, garden, 1795.

Gasse, f. -n, (narrow) street, path, road, *126; double line, passage, 1930, 1980.

Gast, m. -es, Gäste, guest, 188, 508, 709, etc.

Gastfreund, m. -s, -e, guest-friend, intimate friend, 291, 334.

gastlich, adj., hospitable, 520, 3116.

Gaſtrecht, *n.* -ŝ, -e, right of hospitality, 1032, 3172.

Gattin, *f.* -innen, wife, *2, 2221.

ge, *insep. pref., never accented.*

Gebälk, *n.* -ŝ, -e, beams, timbers, 2895.

gebären, gebar, geboren, gebiert, *tr.*, bear, give birth to, 1512, 1624, 2023.

geben, gab, gegeben, giebt, *tr.*, give, 151, *etc.;* auf etwas geben, place reliance on, 882; ſich ʒu erkennen geben, make one's self known *or* felt, 1202; auf etwas geben, regard, heed, 2177; *impers. (acc.),* es giebt, es gab, es hat gegeben, u. ſ. w., there is, are, was, were, has been, have been, *etc.,* 68, 76, *etc.*

gebieten, gebot, geboten, *tr.,* command, rule, govern, 1866, 1977, 2140, *etc.*

Gebirg(e), *n.*-(e)ŝ, -e, (chain of) mountains, 164, 635, 984, *etc.*

Gebot, *n.* -ŝ, -e, command, order, 401.

gebrauchen, *tr.,* use, 1847.

Gebreſten, *n.* -ŝ, —, want, defect, sorrow, 198.

gebühren, *intr. (dat.),* be due, belong to, 784, 1128, 3073; *refl.,* be fit, becoming, proper, 223.

Geburtsland, *n.* -eŝ, -änder, native land, 840.

Gedächtnis, *n.* -niſſeŝ, -niſſe, memory, remembrance, 890, 3246.

Gedanke, *m.* -nŝ, -n, thought, 296, 2570.

gedeihen, gedieh, gediehen, *intr.* ſ., thrive, prosper, advance, *21, 1085.

gedenk, *adj.,* mindful, 1198.

gedenken, gedachte, gedacht, *intr.* (*gen.* or an *with acc.*), think of, be mindful of, 2486, 3037, 3048, *etc.;* intend, purpose, 2273, 3230.

Geduld, *f.* patience, 192, 420, 492, *etc.*

geduldig, *adj.,* patient, forbearing, 2340.

Gefahr, *f.* -en, danger, 1449, 1522.

gefährlich, *adj.,* dangerous, 296, 1432, *etc.;* neut. as noun, 1516.

gefallen, gefiel, gefallen, gefällt, *intr. (dat.),* please, 2683, 2710, 3066.

Gefängnis, *n.*-niſſeŝ,-niſſe, prison, 1821, 1822, 1830, *etc.*

Gefieder, *n.* -ŝ, plumage; 1804, birds.

Gefolge, *n.* -ŝ, —, train, retinue, attendants, *26, 1570, *92, *etc.*

Gefühl, *n.* -ŝ, -e, feeling, 479, 1026, 1635, *etc.*

gegen, *prep. (acc.),* against, in comparison with, contrary to, towards, about, 110, 624, 880, *etc.*

Gegend, *f.* -en, region, country, *4.

Gegenteil, *n.* -ŝ, contrary, *27.

gegenüber, *prep. (dat.) and adv.,* opposite (to), *3, *4, 1283, *etc.*

gehaben, gehub, gehabt, *refl.,* fare, 942, 2119, 2684, *etc.*

gehäſſig, *adj.,* full of hatred, 487.

geheim, *adj.,* familiar, intimate, 295; *usually* = secret.

Geheimnis, *n.* –niſſes, –niſſe, secret, 1388, 2406, 2503, *etc.*

Geheiß, *n.* –es, command, bidding, 468, 2882.

gehen, ging, gegangen, *intr.* ſ., **go,** 48, 59, *etc.;* succeed, go on well, do, 104; zu Rate —, take counsel together, 287; *impers. with* um, concern, be a matter of, 112; get loose, 2664.

Gehöft, *n.* –es, –e, farm, 1032.

Gehölz, *n.* –es, –e, wood, copse, 726.

gehorchen, *intr.* (*dat.*), obey, 2085, 2093.

gehören, *intr.* (*dat.*), belong, 870, 1474, 1802, *etc.*

gehorſam, *adj.,* obedient, submissive; *pl. as noun,* 399.

Gehorſam, *m.* –s, obedience, allegiance, 1244, 1868, 2079, *etc.*

Geißel, *f.* –n, scourge, 795.

Geiſt, *m.* –es, –er, spirit, soul, mind, 425, 2394, 2474, *etc.*

Geiſterſtunde, *f.* –n, ghostly hour, 1152.

Geiz, *m.* –es, avarice, greed, 191, 277, 1050, *etc.*

Geländer, *n.* s, —, rail, railing, *48.

gelangen, *intr.* ſ., get to, arrive at, reach, 193, 1001, 1789, *etc.*

gelaſſen, *part. adj.,* calm, quiet, 1850.

Geläut(e), *n.* –s, ringing (of bells), *3, 838, *etc.;* set of bells, 47, 49, *etc.*

Geldnot, *f.* –nöte(n), want of money, distress for money, 883.

Gelegenheit, *f.* –en, occasion, opportunity, 2562.

Geleit, *n.* –es, –e, conduct, escort, 1426.

gelenk, *adj.,* pliant, supple, agile, 1510.

geliebt, *part. adj.,* **loved,** beloved; *fem. sing. as noun,* 2531.

geloben, *tr.,* promise, pledge, vow, 2466, 2584, 2587, *etc.; refl.,* pledge one's self, 1224; 3270, das gelobte Land, the Promised Land.

gelten, galt, gegolten, gilt, *intr.,* be worth *or* of value, be valid, have weight *or* influence, pass (für, for, as), count, be at stake, 563, 1110, 2053, *etc.;* 1920, 1937, es gilt, it's worth your while, *etc., cf. N.;* it's a question of (*inf.*), 1989, (für *with acc.*), 2102.

Gelübde, *n.* –s, –, vow, 2480.

Gelüſten, *n.* –s, desire, longing, 85, 548.

gemächlich, *adj.,* easy, comfortable, 141, 1791.

gemahnen, *tr.,* remind (of, an *with acc.*), 1542.

gemein, *adj.,* common, general, 434, *etc.;* common, ordinary, mean, 829, *etc.; neut. as noun,* 736.

Gemeinde, *f.* –n, community, 563, *etc.;* assembly, 1128, *etc.*

gemeinfam, *adj.*, common, joint, in common, 736, 1003.

Gemfe, *f.* -n, chamois, wild goat, 58, 649, 1499, *etc.*

Gemfenhorn, *n.* -8, -örner, chamois-horn, *40.

Gemüt, *n.* -8, -er, mind, soul, heart, 2299.

gen, *contraction of* gegen, 2966.

genießen, genoß, genoffen, *tr.*, enjoy, 1489, 1799.

Genoß *or* -ffe, -en, -en, companion, associate, comrade, 718.

Genoßfame, *f.* -n, community, 1455.

genug, *adv., indec. adj. or noun,* enough, 712 (gnug), 942, 1922, *etc.*

G(e)nügen, *n.* -8, sufficiency; — thun, suffice for (*dat.*), 1191.

Genuß, *m*, -e8, -üffe, enjoyment, satisfaction, 3013.

gerade, *adj.*, straight, right, upright, honest, 1013, *etc.; adv.*, right, directly, just, 725, 1748, *etc.*

Gerät, *n.* -8, -e, tool, tools, *74.

gerecht, *adj.*, righteous, just, upright, good, 290, 310, 481, 1068, *etc.*

Gerechtigkeit, *f.* -en, justice, 181, 1341, 1349, *etc.*

Gericht, *n.* -8, -e, judgment, 552, *etc.;* court, 819, 874, *etc.*

gering, *adj.*, little, small, mean, 376.

gern(e), *adv.*, gladly, willingly; *with verbs*, like to, be glad to, 118, 252, 428, *etc.*

Gersau. Gersau, a hamlet in the Canton Schwyz, on the Lake SE. of the Rigi; *1, 189.

Gerüft(e), *n.* -e8, -e, scaffolding, *21, *26, 2860.　　　　[2621.

Geschäft, *n.* -8, -e, business, 768,

Geschäftigkeit, *f.*, activity, occupation, 1711.

geschehen, geschah, geschehen, geschieht, *intr.* f., (*used in 3rd pers. only*), happen, occur, be done, 396, 558, 831, *etc.; neut. past part. as noun,* 992.

Geschenk, *n.* -8, -e, present, gift, 1402, 2909.

Geschick, *n.* -8, -e, fate, destiny, lot, 1593, 1932, 2539, *etc.*

Geschlecht, *n.* -8, -er, generation, 954, 2132, *etc.;* sex, 2999.

Geschmeide, *n.* -8, jewelry, *26.

Geschöpf, *n.* -8, -e, created being, creature, 591.

Geschoß, *n.* -e8, -e, dart, missile, arrow, 2568, 2791.

geschwind, *adj.*, quick, speedy, swift, 1406, 1796.

Geschwindfein, *n.* -8, swiftness, promptness, 2887.

Gefell(e), *m.* -en, -en, workman, *2, *21, 2862, *etc.;* comrade, 1752, *etc.*

gefellen, *tr.*, associate, join, 3240; *refl.*, join, *129.

gefellig, *adj.*, sociable, in society, 1008.

Gefetz, *n.* -e8, -e, law, 702, 1233, 1310, *etc.*

Gefidht, *n.* -8, sight, view, 121, 2976, *etc.; pl.* -er, face, countenance, *122, *etc.*

Gefindel, *n.* -8, rabble, vagabonds, 1737.

gefinnt, *adj.*, minded, disposed, 631.

Gefpann, *n.* -8, -e, span, yoke, 467.

gefpannt, *part. adj.*, eager, intense, *76.

Gefpräch, *n.* -8, -e, talk, conversation, *14, 246.

geßlerifdh, *adj.*, Gessler's, of Gessler; *2.

Geftade, *n.* -8, —, bank, shore, 2, 1151.

Geftalt, *f.* -en, form, shape, 1506.

geftaltet, *part. adj.*, formed, shaped, *105.

geftehen, geftand, geftanden, *tr.*, confess, 501, 1516.

Gefträudh, *n.* -8, shrubs, bushes, *126.

geftreng, *adj.*, stern, dread; — Herr, your worship, 1859, *cf. N.*, 2736.

gefund, *adj.*, sound, healthy, well, uninjured, 637, 1509.

Getön, *n.* -8, sounding, 834.

getrauen, *refl.* (fidh, *dat.*), trust one's self, dare, 162, 2243, 2246, *etc.*

getreulidh, *adv.*, faithfully, 3046.

getroft, *adj.*, confident, courageous, 1278, 2891.

gewahren, *tr.*, perceive, 1184; *intr.* (*gen.*), 2252.

gewähren, *tr.*, grant, allow, 428, 713, *etc.; intr.*, render security, answer for, 710.

Gewalt, *f.* -en, power, authority, violence, 155, 505, 669, *etc.*

Gewaltbeginnen, *n.* -8, deed of violence, 284.

Gewaltherrfchaft, *f.* -en, rule of violence, despotism, 1243.

gewaltig, *adj.*, powerful, mighty, great, vast, 653, 873, 2266, *etc.*

gewaltfam, *adj.*, violent, forcible, 948, 1014.

Gewaltthat, *f.* -en, deed of violence, outrage, 2527.

Gewehr, *n.* -8, -e, weapon, 1561.

Geweih, *n.* -8, -e, horns, antlers, 648.

Gewerbe, *n.* -8, —, trade, business, 1507.

Gewinn, *m.* -8, -e, gain, advantage, 3015.

gewinnen, gewann, gewonnen, *tr.*, gain, get, take, 800, 2650, 2874, *etc.*

gewiß, *adj.*, sure, certain, some, 1590, 1941, 2151, *etc.*

Gewitter, *n.* -8, —, (thunder)storm, 45.

gewöhnen, *tr.*, accustom, 2574.

gewohnt, *adj.*, used, accustomed, (to, *acc. or gen.*), 538, 1912.

giftgefchwollen, *part. adj.*, swollen with venom, 1265.

giftig, *adj.*, poisonous, venomous, malignant, 270.

Gipfel, *m.* -8, —, top, pitch, climax, 639.

Gitter, *n.* -8, —, grating, 2166.

Glanz, *m.* -e8, brightness, splendor, glory, glitter, 839, 915, 1680, *etc.*

glänzen, *intr.*, be bright, shine, 210, *etc.; pres. part.* as *adj.*, brilliant, radiant, 817, 1600, *etc.*

glanzvoll, *adj.*, full of brightness, splendor, radiance, 602, 1105.

Glarner, *adj.*, of Glarus, the Canton, 2665.

Glärnisch, *m.* -e8, Glärnisch, a group of mountain peaks in Glarus, 2666.

glatt, *adj.*, smooth, sleek, 204, 2639.

Glaube(n), *m.* -n8, -n, belief, faith, 1691.

glauben, *tr.* (*dat. pers.*), believe, trust, 322, 689, 1425, *etc.*

glaubenswert, *adj.*, worthy of belief, trustworthy, 2947.

gleich, *adj.*, like, equal, even, same, 108 (*neut.* as *noun*), 396, 465, 1707 (*dat. pl. as noun*), *etc.; adv.* (= sogleich), at once, immediately, 333, 357, *etc.; conj.*, though, although, 1118, 1119.

gleichen, glich, geglichen, *intr.* (*dat.*), be like, 153.

gleichfalls, *adv.*, likewise, *51.

gleichförmig, *adj.*, uniform, even, 1017.

gleichwie, *conj.*, (like) as, 1105, 2507.

gleiten (*usually strong, but here weak*), *intr.* f. or h., glide, slip, fall, *137.

Gletscher, *m.* -8, —, glacier, *48, 1004, 1044, *etc.*

Gletscherberg, *m.* -8, -e, glacier-mountain, 1813.

Glocke, *f.* -n, bell, 2152, *140.

Glöcklein, *n.* -8, —, (little) bell, hand-bell, 1749.

glorreich, *adj.*, glorious, 2729.

Glück, *n.* -8, fortune, prosperity, happiness, 269, 1066, 1634, *etc.*

glücklich, *adj.*, fortunate, successful, happy, 205, 260, 591, *etc.; pl. as noun*, 3274; *fem. sing.* as *noun*, 3283.

glückselig, *adj.*, successful, happy, 63.

Glücksstand, *m.* -8, state of fortune, fortune, condition, 202.

glühen, *intr.*, glow, 990, 1441.

Glut, *f.*, -en, glow, heat, flame, 2900.

Gnade, *f.* -n, mercy, grace, favor, 1873, 1944, 2261, *etc.*

gnädig, *adj.*, gracious, merciful, favorable, 51, 80, 290, *etc.*

Gold, *n.* -e8, gold, 449, 450, 451, *etc.*

Goller, *m.* -8, —, doublet, *98, *102.

gönnen, *tr.*, grant, not grudge, 1221.

gotisch, *adj.*, gothic, in gothic *or* pointed style, *40.

Gott, *m.* -e8, Götter, god, God, 67, 80, 86, *etc.*

Gotteshaus, *n.* -e8, -häuser, house of God, church, monastery, 343, 1246.

Gotthard, *m.* -s, Saint Gotthard, a mountain-group and a pass, at the borders of the Cantons Uri, Wallis (Valais), Tessin (Ticino) and Graubünden (Grisons), 876, 2230, 3266.

Grab, *n.* -es, Gräber, grave, 529, 530, 863, *etc.*

graben, grub, gegraben, gräbt, *tr.*, dig, 2988.

grade, see gerade.

Graf, *m.* -en, -en, count, 1235.

Gram, *m.* -s, grief, sorrow, 200.

Gransen, *m.* -s, —, (bow *or*) stern of a boat, 2226, 2263.

Gras, *n.* -es, Gräser, grass, 43, 2739.

gräßlich, *adj.*, horrible, terrible, dire, 2789; *neut. as noun*, 638, 1946, 2339.

Grattier, *n.* -s, -e, crag-deer, chamois, 2641, *cf. N.*

grau, *adj.*, gray, 38, 1267.

grauen, *intr. impers. with dat.*, dread, fear, feel horror, 26, 3146; *inf. as noun*, horror, 1094.

grauenvoll, *adj.*, horrible, awful, 2949, 2950.

grausam, *adj.*, cruel, fierce, 2229, 2581.

Grausamkeit, *f.* -en, cruelty, 2001.

Grausen, *n.* -s, horror, terror, dread, 1493, *138, 3014, 3186.

grausenvoll, *adj.*, horrible, awful, 2823.

greifen, griff, gegriffen, *tr.*, gripe, grasp, seize, 73, *etc.; intr. (with*

zu, in, nach, u. f. w.), have recourse to, 439, 1290, 1320; reach, 1277, 1356, *etc.;* lay hold of, arrest, stay, check, 2180.

greis, *adj.*, gray, hoary, 2476.

Greis, *m.* -es, -e, old man, 366, 608, *40, *etc.*

Grenze, *f.* -n, bound, limit, confine, border, 1048, 1275, 2992, *etc.*

grenzenlos, *adj.*, boundless, infinite, 2762.

Greuel, *m.* -s, —, atrocity, outrage, 1010, 2595.

greulich, *adj.*, horrible, shocking, monstrous; *neut. comp. as noun*, 557.

Grimm, *m.* -s, fury, rage, 2141.

Groll, *m.* -s, ill-will, enmity, spite, 259.

grollen, *intr. (dat.)*, bear a grudge against, be angry with, 252, 1542.

groß (*comp.* größer, *superl.* größt), *adj*, great, big, large, 294, 659, *etc.; neut. as noun*, 1054; *-after* 2336, mit einem großen Blick, with eyes wide open; *superl. neut. as noun*, 3083.

Großvater, *m.* -s, -äter, grandfather, 1829, 1947.

Gruft, *f.*, Grüfte, cavern, cavity, grave, vault, 1504, 2362.

grün, *adj.*, green, *3, 2, *etc.*

Grün, *n.* -s, green (color), 595.

Grund, *m.* -es, Gründe, ground, base, foundation, 215, 2041, *etc.;* gorge, ravine, 1549; bottom, 2706.

grünben, *tr.*, found, establish, 388.

grünblich, *adj.*, thorough, 2059.

grünen, *intr.*, become **green**, thrive, flourish, 30, 2424; *pres. part. as adj.*, green, verdant, 36.

gruppieren, *tr.*, **group**, *144; *refl.*, form groups, be grouped, *163.

grüßen, *tr.*, **greet**, salute, 1745, 1751, *etc.*; *refl.*, greet one another, exchange greetings, 1003, *etc.*

Gunft, *f.*, favor, 1245, 1662, 2078, *etc.*

günftig, *adj.*, favorable, 2562.

Günftling, *m.* -s, -e, favorite, 1668.

gürten, *tr.*, gird, 769.

gut (*comp.* beſſer, *superl.* beſt), **good**, excellent, kind, right, 82, 86, 380, *etc.*; *masc. as noun*, 248; *neut. as noun*, 3071, 3110; Laßt's gut ſein, never mind, 1106; *adv.*, well, 1887; ſo gut, as well (as), 264.

Gut, *n.* -es, Güter, property, possession, **goods**, estate, 320, 400, 610, *etc.*

Güte, *f.*, kindness, 1301.

gütig, *adj.*, kind, gracious, 1595, 1798, 2037, *etc.*

Gutthat, *f.* -en, charitable act, kindness, 2286.

H.

ha, *interj.*, ha!, ah!, 153, 174, 973, *etc.*

Habe, *f.*, property, possessions, 1945.

haben, hatte, gehabt, *tr.*, **have**, possess, 49, 57, *etc.*; was habt ihr? what is the matter with you? 70.

Habsburg, *f.* Habsburg, the castle, near Brugg and Schinznach, whence the famous Habsburg family took its name; 827, 2976, 3021.

Hackmeſſer, *n.* -s. Hackmesser (*lit.* chopping-knife), a steep cliff of the Axenberg; 2190.

Hafen, *m.* -s, Häfen, **haven**, port, harbor, 425.

hageln, *intr. impers.*, hail, 2127.

Hahn, *m.* -es, Hähne, cock, 384.

Hake, *m.* -n. Haken, a mountain NE. of the town Schwyz; *3.

halb, *adj.*, **half**, 740.

Halbkreis, *m.* -es, -e, semi-circle, *139, *144.

Halde, *f.* -n. Name given to a steep mountain slope. Heinrich von der Halden (*archaic dat.*) is the name of the father of Arnold vom Melchthal; 562.

Hälfte, *f.* -n, **half**, 200, 1945.

Halle, *f.* -n, **hall**, 833.

Hals, *m.* -es, -e, neck, 53, 652, *155.

halsgefährlich, *adj.*, perilous, with danger to life, 1433, 1508.

halt, *interj.*, hold, halt, stop, 168.

halten, hielt, gehalten, hält, *tr.*, **hold**, keep, 257, 556, *58, *84, *etc.*; hold, restrain, 618; hold shut, keep closed, 801; hold,

celebrate, 2652; *intr.*, hold, hold
fast, 185, 3025; an ſich —, restrain one's self, 1921, *98; keep,
1956; halt, stop, 1408, 2852;
last, 1513.

Hammer, *m.* -8, Hämmer, hammer, 377.

Hand, *f.* Hände, hand, 120, 157,
*13, *etc.;* auf eigne —, on one's
own account, independently, 232;
zur Hand, at hand, present, 1121.

Handbube, *m.* -n, -n, boy, servant,
*4.

handeln, *intr.,* act, 1204, 2070,
2342, *etc.*

handhaben, handhabte, gehandhabt,
tr., handle, manage, wield, 2645.

Handlanger, *m.* -8, —, laborer, *2,
*21, *etc.*

handlich, *adj.*, (*here* =) stout, vigorous, 2257, *cf. N.*

handlos, *adj.*, handless, inaccessible, 2159.

Handſchlag, *m.* -8, -äge, hand-
clasp, 2487.

Handſchuh, *m.* -8, -e, glove, gaunt-
let, 2027.

Handwerk, *n.* -8, -e, business, occupation, 2745.

hangen, hing, gehangen, hängt,
intr., hang, *21, 408, 679, *etc.*

hängen (*tr. and*) *intr.*, hang, 862.

Hans, *m.* -en. Hans, abbreviation
of Johann(es); 1337, 2967, 2978.

härmen, *refl.*, grieve, sorrow, 1492.

harmlos, *adj.*, harmless, inoffen-
sive, 2440, 2568.

harmoniſch, *adj.*, harmonious, *3.

Harniſch, *m.* -e8, -e, armor, suit of
armor, 2439.

Harras, *m.* master of the horse, *2,
etc. From mediæval Lat. haracium,
"stud of horses."

harren, *intr.* (*with gen. or* auf *and*
acc.), wait for, await, 1671, 2414,
2751.

hart (*comp.* härter, *superl.* härteſt),
adj., hard, harsh, 280, 359, 367,
etc.; superl. neut. as noun, 3084;
adv., close, 3092.

härten, *tr.*, harden, temper, 2900.

haſchen, *tr.*, catch, seize, 1505.

Haß, *m.* -e8, hate, hatred, 1047,
1999.

haſſen, *tr.*, hate, 1545, 1628, 1637,
etc.

Haſt, *f.* haste, 65.

Haube, *f.* -n, cap, hood, 39.

Hauch, *m.* -e8, -e, breath, air, 864,
2362.

Haufe(n), *m.* -n8, -n, heap, crowd,
body (of men), 1408.

häufen, *refl.*, be heaped, piled,
massed, 2310.

Haupt, *n.* -e8, Häupter, head, chief,
leader, 243, 398, 614, *etc.*

Hauptort, *m.* -e8, -örter, chief place
or town, 1423.

Haus, *n.* -e8, Häuſer, house, home,
family, 92, *14, 207, *etc.;* zu
Hauſ(e), at home, 534, 1486;
nach Hauſe, to one's home, home,
2047.

hauſen, *intr.*, reside, be, 547, 2128.

Hausflur, f. -en, entrance-hall, main-room, *152, cf. N.

Hausfrau, f. -en, house-wife, wife, 1491.

Hausgebrauch, m. -s, -äuche, family custom, 753.

Hausgenoß(e), m. -en, -en, family companion, 650.

haushalten, hielt, gehalten, hält, intr., keep house, reside, dwell, 549.

Häuslein, n. -s, —, small house, 373.

häuslich, adj. domestic, household, *72.

Hausrecht, n. -s, -e, household right, family right, 82.

Hausthür(e), f. -en, house-door, 153.

Hausvater, m. -s, -väter, father of a family, 113.

heben, hob, gehoben, tr., lift, raise, 1277, *101, *104, etc.

Heer, n. -es, -e, host, army, 908, 2436, 2937, etc.

Heeresmacht, f. -mächte, military force, troops, 2931.

Heermacht, f. -mächte, military force, army, 332.

Heerweg, m. -es, -e, highway, 347.

Heerzug, m. -es, -züge, host, 1173.

heftig, adj., violent, vehement, fierce, furious, *10, 1182, 1398, etc.

Heftigkeit, f. violence, vehemence, *32, *138, *160.

Heide, m. -n, -n, heathen, pagan, 2975.

Heil, n. -es, health, welfare, as interj., hail!, 3086.

heilen, tr., heal, 604.

heilig, adj., holy, hallowed, sacred, 105, 673, 860, etc.

Heiligtum, n. -s, -ümer, sanctuary, 3178.

heim, adv. and sep. prep., home, homeward, 62, 843.

Heimat, f. -en, home, native place or land, 777, 1161, 1693, etc.

heimatlich, adj., native, 1033.

heimbringen, brachte, gebracht, tr., bring home, 205, 2647.

heimisch, adj., native, at home, 1702.

Heimkehr, f., return home, 63, 2685.

heimkehren, tr., return home, 2624.

heimlich, adj., secret, 726, 1405, 2284, etc.

heischen, tr., ask, demand, 1132.

heiser, adj., hoarse, 1000.

heiß, adj., hot, 622, 842, 1039, etc.

heißen, hieß, geheißen, intr., be called or named, 370, 727, etc.; be, 357, 1530, 1531, etc.; es hieß, 2956, it was said, people said.

heiter, adj., serene, bright, cheerful, merry, 2616, *129, 3260.

Heldenkraft, f. -kräfte, heroic force or might, 895.

Heldenkühnheit, f., heroic boldness, 2377.

helfen, half, geholfen, hilft, intr. (dat.), help, 107, 111, 156, etc.

Helfer, m. -es, —, helper, 2368, 3208.

hell, adj., clear, bright, *3, 893, etc.; clear, shrill, 61, etc.

Helm, m. -es, -e, helmet, *40, 833, 862, etc.

her, adv. and sep. pref., here, hither, this way, (towards the speaker). Often not to be translated. 40, 151, 537, *40, etc.; lang(e) her, long since, 1548.

herab, adv. and sep. pref., down from, down, 2129, 2564, 2965, etc.; with acc. preceding, down along, *132.

herabsteigen, stieg, gestiegen, intr. f., descend, *48, *55, 1092, etc.

heran, adv. and sep. pref., hither, near, up to, up, 1733.

heranziehen, zog, gezogen, intr. f., march on, draw near, 2439, 2931.

herauf, adv. and sep. pref., up here, up, upwards; with acc. preceding, up along, 2103.

heraus, adv. and sep. pref., out here, out of, out, from, forth, *32, 620, 2571, etc.

herausfinden, fand, gefunden, refl. reciprocal, find out or recognize one another, 1201.

herausgeben, gab, gegeben, giebt, tr., give up, deliver up, 172.

herausnehmen, nahm, genommen, nimmt, tr., take out, draw forth, take away, *98, 2083.

heraustreten, trat, getreten, tritt, intr. f., step out, appear, *163.

herauswachsen, wuchs, gewachsen, wächst, intr. f., grow up or forth, 1776.

herb, adj., bitter, 2606.

herbei, adv. and sep. pref., hither, near by, up, this way, 354, 1823.

herbeieilen, intr. f., hasten hither or up, *90, *91.

herbeikommen, kam, gekommen, sep. intr. f., come hither, or up or along, *89.

Herberg(e), f. -en, shelter, quarters, inn, 2120, 3277.

Herd, m. -es, -e, hearth, 331, *152.

Herde, f. -n, herd, flock, 178, 180, 315, etc.

Herde(n)glocke, f. -n, herd-bell, bell of a herd or flock, *3, 837.

Herdenreihen, m. -s, render by Kuhreihen, cf. N. *3, 844.

herein, adv. and sep. pref., in hither, in, 12, etc.

hereinbringen, brang, gebrungen, intr. f., press, crowd, force one's way, 836, 952, *115, etc.

hereineilen, intr. f., hasten in, appear hastily, *162.

hereinführen, tr., lead in, bring in, 3100.

hereinrufen, rief, gerufen, tr., call in, summon, 1237.

hereinstürzen, intr. f., rush in, *6 *26, *137, etc.; inf. as noun, *137.

hereintreten, trat, getreten, tritt, intr. f., step in, enter, *29, *154.

herein,ziehen, zog, gezogen, tr., draw in, 12.

herführen, tr., lead or bring here, 511, 532.

herfür, adv. and sep. pref., archaic form of hervor.

herfürbrechen, brach), gebrochen, bricht, intr. f., break out, 2230.

herfürziehen, zog, gezogen, tr., draw forth, display, 1249.

herhangen, hing, gehangen, hängt, intr. f., hang towards or down, *76, *95.

Heribann, m. -s, army-summons, call to arms, 1228. Archaic for Heerbann.

herkommen, kam, gekommen, intr. f., come hither or here, 521, 2618.

Heroldsruf, m. -s, -e, herold's call or summons, 835.

Herr, m. -n, -en, lord, Lord, gentleman, Mister or Sir, 51, 183, 223, etc.; 1558, Herre, archaic form; 'master, 482, 2133; husband, 3108.

herreichen, tr., reach, extend, 739.

Herrenbank, f. -bänke, nobles' bench, 806.

Herrenburg, f. -en, lordly keep or castle, 625, 770, 936, etc.

Herrenknecht, m. -s, -e, servant to a lord, servile vassal, 1271.

Herrenleute, pl., men of standing, 294, cf. N.

herrenlos, adj., without a lord, 1216; unowned, unclaimed, 1250.

Herrenschiff, n. -s, -e, lord's ship, governor's boat, 2170.

herrlich, adj., magnificent, glorious, splendid, excellent, 1651, 2441, etc.; neut. as noun, glory, 2422.

Herrschaft, f. -en, lordship, dominion, rule, 897, 2409.

herrschen, intr., rule, govern, reign, 1473, 2433.

Herrscher, m. -s, —, ruler, governor, sovereign, 422, 2778.

herschicken, tr., send hither or here, 1769.

herüber, adv. (and sep. pref.), over hither, to this side, across, 283, 493, 731, etc.

herum, adv. and sep. pref., around, round about, about, 363, etc.

herumgehen, ging, gegangen, intr. f., go or be passed around, *40.

herunter, adv. and sep. pref., down, downwards, 1279.

heruntergießen, goß, gegossen, intr., pour or rush down, 2130.

heruntersinken, sank, gesunken, intr. f., sink down, 2981.

heruntersteigen, stieg, gestiegen, intr. f., descend, *126.

hervor, adv. and sep. pref., forth, forward, out, 2885.

hervorgraben, grub, gegraben, gräbt, tr., dig (forth) from under (unter), 2544.

hervorkommen, kam, gekommen, intr. f., come forth, 2597.

hervorstürzen, intr. f., rush forth or out, 2879.

hervortreten, trat, getreten, tritt, *intr.* f., step forward, *98.

Herz, *n.*-ens, *acc.* Herz, -en, heart, 198, 201, 249, *etc.*

herzeinig, *adj.*, one at heart, 735.

herzhaft, *adj.*, courageous, bold, 1909.

herzlich, *adj.*, hearty, cordial, warm, *14, 918, *155, *etc.*

Herzog, *m.* -s, -öge, and -oge, duke, *2, 1337, 1344, *etc.*

heulen, *intr.*, howl, scream, roar, 2167.

heute, *adv.*, today, 146, 189, 217, *etc.*

hiebannen, *adv.*, out, away from here, 2246. *Archaic for* von bannen, von hier weg.

hieher, *adv.*, hither, here, 2203.

hier, *adv.*, here, 125, 127, 148, *etc.*

Hilfe, *f.* help, 127, 149, 171, *etc.*

hilflos, *adj.*, helpless, 125.

hilfreich, *adj.*, helpful, 1533.

Himmel, *m.* -s, —, heaven, sky, 181, 316, 324, *etc.*

himmelhoch, *adj.*, high as heaven, to the sky, 2169.

himmelschreiend, *part. adj.*, es ist —, it cries to heaven, 367.

Himmelsdach, *n.* -s, canopy of heaven, 636.

Himmelsgabe, *f.* -n, gift of heaven *or* of God, 589.

Himmelsglück, *n.* -s, heavenly happiness, 1641.

Himmelslicht, *n.* -s, -er, light of heaven, 2897.

Himmelsraum, *m.* -s, -räume, space *or* region *or* quarter of the heavens *or* sky, 1792.

hin, *adv. and sep. pref.*, hence, thither, that way, there, along, away, gone, (from the speaker). *Often not to be translated.* 115, 1508, *etc.;* 16, 2090, *etc.*, gone; 415, *etc.*, wo . . . hin, whither.

hinab, *adv. and sep. pref.*, down, downwards, 2354, 3269, *etc.*

hinabdrücken, *tr.*, press down, repress, 2007.

hinabsenden, sandte, gesandt, *tr.*, send down, 3004.

hinabsinken, sank, gesunken, *intr.* f., sink down, 1503.

hinabsteigen, stieg, gestiegen, *intr.* f., descend, 1796.

hinan, *adv.*, up, up along, 2639.

hinauf, *adv. and sep. pref.*, up, 1277, *76, *101, 2265, *etc.*

hinaufsteigen, stieg, gestiegen, *intr.* f., ascend, 3242.

hinaus, *adv. and sep. pref.*, out, hence, away, 1591, *etc.*

hinauseilen, *intr.* f., hasten out, make a hurried exit, *154.

hinaussenden, sandte, gesandt, *tr.*, send out, 1685.

hindern, *tr.*, hinder, prevent, 803.

Hindernis, *n.* -nisses, -nisse, hindrance, obstacle, 253.

hindurch, *adv.* (*and sep. pref.*), through, 2776.

hineilen, *intr.* f., hasten thither *or* away, *26.

hinein, *adv. and sep. pref.*, in, into, into it, 321, *140, *etc.*

hineingehen, ging, gegangen, *intr. ſ.*, go in, enter; 495, *29, *153, of entrance into another room *or* the house.

hinfahren, fuhr, gefahren, fährt, *intr. ſ.*, go away *or* hence; 616, 1692, *imper.*, farewell! go hence!; 2248, sail *or* steer along.

hinfallen, fiel, gefallen, fällt, *intr. ſ.*, fall down, 3250.

hinfinden, fand, gefunden, *reſl.*, find one's way, 1703.

hinflüchten, *reſl.*, seek refuge, 3006.

hinfort, *adv.*, henceforth, 3139.

hingehen, ging, gegangen, *intr. ſ.*, go thither *or* there, 854, 866, *etc.;* Wo gehſt du hin?, where are you going?, 1515, 1538, *etc.*

hinkommen, kam, gekommen, *intr. ſ.*, come there, get to, arrive at; Wo kam ... hin?, what became of, 2708.

hinleben, *intr.*, live on, pass one's life, 233.

hinnen, *adv.*, in here; von hinnen, hence, 2774.

hinpflanzen, *tr.*, plant *or* set there, 2721.

hinreichen, *tr.*, reach out, hold out, *60.

hinreiten, ritt, geritten, *intr. ſ.*, ride along, 2974.

Hinſcheid, *m.* -s, death, decease, 3036.

hinſchiffen, *intr. ſ.*, sail along, 2173.

hinſehen, ſah, geſehen, *intr.*, look thither *or* that way, 115, 1764.

hinſenden, ſandte, geſandt, *tr.*, send thither, 708.

hinſtehen, ſtand, geſtanden, *intr.*, stand, take one's place, 1948, *cf. N.*

hinſtellen, *tr.*, put, place, station, 1433, 1522, *etc.; reſl.*, station one's self, take one's stand, 1747, *etc.*

hinten, *adv.*, behind, *126; back, far away, 1167.

hinter, *adj.*, hind, hinder, back, rear, *21, 2226, 2263, *etc.*

hinter, *prep. (dat. or acc.), adv., sep. and insep. pref.*, behind, after, back, down, 72, 325, *48, *etc.;* beyond, 1078.

hintergeh'en, hinterging', hinter-gan'gen, *insep. tr.*, deceive, delude, 985.

Hintergrund, *m.* -s, -ünde, background, rear, *3, *20, *21, *etc.*

Hinterhalt, *m.* -s, ambush, 1411.

hinterhal'ten, hinterhielt', hinter-hal'ten, hinterhält', *insep. tr.*, withhold, keep back, 1343.

hinterſt, *adj. (superl. of* hinter), hindmost, last, *137.

hinüber, *adv. and sep. pref.*, over, across, beyond, 491, 618, 714, *etc.;* 2303, (passed) over, *i. e.* dead.

hinüberdringen, drang, gedrungen, *intr. ſ.*, reach across, 123.

hinüberſchaffen, *tr.*, take across, get over, 103.

hinübertragen, trug, getragen, trägt, *tr.*, carry over, bear across, 124.

hinunter, *adv. and sep. pref.*, down, downwards.

hinunterſchiffen, *intr.* ſ., sail down, 896.

hinunterſteigen, ſtieg, geſtiegen, *intr.* ſ., descend, 1787.

hinweg, *adv. and sep. pref.* away, forth, off, aside, *3, 2752, 2764, *etc.*

hinweglegen, *tr.*, lay aside, *74.

hinwegtreten, trat, getreten, tritt, *intr.* ſ., step aside, *121.

hinwegwerfen, warf, geworfen, wirft, *tr.*, throw away, cast aside, 2124.

hinwerfen, warf, geworfen, wirft, *tr.*, throw away, cast aside, 915, throw down, 2027.

hinziehen, zog, gezogen, *tr.*, draw towards, attract, 1621.

hinzu, *adv. and sep. pref.*, towards, thither, up to, up, 96.

Hirſch, *m.* -es, -e, stag, 647.

Hirt, *m.* -en, -en, herdsman, *1, *4, 49, *etc.*

Hirtenknabe, *m.* -n, -n, herdsman's boy *or* assistant, *2.

hoch (*comp.* höher, *superl.* höchſt), *adj.* (*when declined,* hoher, *etc.*), high, tall, lofty, great, *as adv.*, highly, very; *3, 109, 266, *etc.*

Hochflug, *m.* -s, (*lit.* high flight), larger and rarer game-birds, 900; *cf. N., and second word below.*

hochgeboren, *part. adj.*, high-born, 2968.

Hochgewilde, *n.* -s, larger and rarer game-animals, 900, *cf. N.;* den Hochflug und das Hochgewilde = the higher game, both bird and beast.

Hochland, *n.* -s, -länder, highland, upland, 1175.

hochſpringen, ſprang, geſprungen, *sep. intr.* ſ., leap high, 2265.

hochverſtändig, *adj.*, highly intelligent, 517.

Hochwacht, *f.* -en, beacon-fire, signal-fire, 1441, 2449; watch-tower, signal tower, signal-height, 2848, *cf. N.*

hochwürdig, *adj.*, highly venerable; das Hochwürdige, the host, the consecrated wafer, 1748.

Hochzeit, *f.* -en, wedding, wedding procession, *129, 2777.

Hochzeitgeſellſchaft, *f.* -en, wedding party, *138.

Hochzeithaus, *n.* -es, -häuſer, house of marriage, 2657.

Hof, *m.* -s, Höfe, yard, farm, courtyard, court, *1, *3, *72, *etc.;* Herd und Hof, hearth and home, 331.

hoffen, *tr.*, hope, 1662, 2219, 2756, *etc.*

Hoffnung, *f.* -en, hope, 2216, 2366, 2383, *etc.*

Hofstatt, *f.*, court, 2966.

Hofthor, *n.* -s, -e, yard-gate, *78.

Höhe, *f.* -n, height, top, eminence, *4, 25, 698, *etc.;* in die —, up, upward, *120.

Hoheit, *f.* -en, highness, greatness, sovereignty, 1295, 1943, 2977, *etc.*

hohl, *adj.*, hollow, empty, 1759, 1760, 2408, *etc.;* hollow, deep, *126.

Höhle, *f.* -n, hollow, hole, cavity, socket, den, 642, 1061.

Hohlweg, *m.* -s, -e, hollow way, narrow pass, defile, *129, *130, *132.

hohnsprechen, sprach, gesprochen, spricht, *sep. intr.*, mock, deride, 793.

hold, *adj.*, favorable, kind, sweet, gentle, 1066, 1414, 2632, *etc.*

holen, *tr.*, fetch, get, bring, secure, 440, 1104, 1326, *etc.*

Höllenqual, *f.* -en, hellish pain, infernal torment, 2588.

Höllenrachen, *m.* -s, —, mouth or jaw of hell, 137.

Holunderstrauch, *m.* -s, -äuche *and* -äucher, elder bush, 2563.

Holz, *n.* -es, Hölzer, wood, 90, 1185.

horchen, *intr.*, hearken, listen, 961, 966.

Horde, *f.* -n, horde, 308.

hören, *tr.* hear, *3, 3, *4, 247, *etc.*

Horn, *n.* -s, Hörner, horn, point, peak, 480, 653, 1091, *etc.*

Hornisse, *f.* -n, hornet, 2672. (*Here accented on first syllable, but now usually on the second.*)

hübsch, *adj.*, pretty, nice; *neut. as noun*, 1582.

Huf, *m.* -es, -e, hoof, 2767.

huldigen, *intr.*, render homage, give allegiance, 816, 1299.

Huldigung, *f.* -en, homage, 1708.

hundert, *num.*, hundred, 1506, 1877, 1883, *etc.*

hurtig, *adj.*, quick, 37.

Hut, *m.* -es, Hüte, hat, *23, 390, 392, *etc.*

Hütte, *f.* -n, hut, cottage, *3, *4, 179, *etc.*

J.

Jberg. Konrad ab (von) Iberg, Landammann of Schwyz, of whom Schiller makes Stauffacher's wife to be a daughter; 240, 517.

ich, *pron.*, I, 11, 12, 334, *etc.; gen.* mein, 111, 1671; meiner, 349, 444, *etc.*

ihr, *pron.*, ye, you, 13, 14, 21, *etc.*

ihr, *adj.* (*poss. corresponding to* sie), her, hers, its, their, 178, 213, 358, *etc.* Jhr, (*corresponding to* Sie), your.

Jmisee, *m.* -s. Imisee *or* Immensee, a hamlet on Lake Zug; 2654.

immer, *adv.*, always, ever, still, 64, 194, 1320, *etc.*

immerdar, *adv.*, always, ever, 2460.

in, *prep.* (*dat. and acc.*), in, into, to, within, at, *1, *3, 6, *etc.;* in8 = in ba8, im = in bem, *and occasionally* in = in bem, *as in* 305, 2706, 2734.

Inbrunft, *f.,* ardor, fervor, *101, *104.

inbem, *adv.,* meanwhile; *conj.,* while, when, as, 102, *20, *51, *etc.*

inbe8, inbeffen, *adj.,* meanwhile, 1493, 2553; *conj.,* while, 794, 826, 1439, *etc.*

Inhalt, *m.* -8, content, tenor, purport, substance, 1153.

inne, *adv.,* within; inne halten, hold in, stop, pause, *124.

inner, *adj.,* inner, interior; *neut. as noun,* heart, soul, 2584, 3124; the interior (of a land), 2932.

innerft, *adj.,* inmost, innermost; *neut. as noun,* inmost self, 297; innermost part, 504.

Infel, *f.* -n, isle, island, 1700.

irbifch, *adj.,* earthly, temporal; *neut. as noun,* 2807.

irr(e), *adj.,* astray, 2018.

irren, *intr.,* wander, 3010, 3216; *refl.,* be mistaken, 1827.

Irrtum, *m.* -8, =tümer, error, mistake, fault, 2484.

Italien, *n.* -8, Italy; 3233, 3270.

J.

ja, *adv.,* yea, yes, surely, indeed, certainly, you know, 108, 183, 383, *etc.*

Jagb, *f.* -en, chase, hunt, 1590, 1727, 3139.

Jagbhorn, *n.* -8, =hörner, hunting-horn, *84, *91.

Jagbfleib, *n.* -8, -er, hunting-dress or costume, *78.

jagen, *tr. and intr.,* hunt, chase, pursue, 58, 793, 1549, *etc.*

Jäger, *m.* -8, —, hunter, huntsman, *1, *4, 61, *etc.*

Jahr, *n.* -e8, -e, year, *40, 1140, 1345, *etc.;* Jahr unb Tag, a year and a day, a long time, 1513.

Jahrmarkt, *m.* -8, =märfte, fair, 1734.

Jammer, *m.* -8, misery, calamity, grief, 453, 603, 668, *etc.*

jammern, *tr. and impers., and intr.* (*with gen.*), grieve, cause pity to, pity, 485, 599, 1565, 3196.

Jammerruf, *m.* -8, -e, lamentation, wail, 2885.

je, *adv.,* always, ever, each time, 404; *distributive before numerals,* every, 1170.

jeber (jebe, jebe8), *adj. and pron.,* each, every, each one, every one, 81, 106, 269, *etc.*

jebweber (jebwebe, jebwebe8), *adj. and pron., archaic* = jeber, 2992.

jemanb, *pron.,* somebody, some one, *114, 2684.

jener (jene, jene8), *adj. and pron.,* yon, yonder, that, that one, he, the former, 350, 1411, 1607, *etc.*

jenſeitß, *adv. and prep.* (*with gen.*), on the other side, beyond, 832.

jcৡo, *adv., archaic* = jeৡt, 740, 1066, 2607.

jeৡt, *adv.,* now, 62, 349, 420, *etc.*

Joĉ, *n.* -eß, -e, yoke, 280, 371, 652, *etc.;* ridge (connecting mountain-peaks), 3254.

Jugenb, *f.,* youth, 484, 772, 826, *etc.*

jugenbliĉ, *adj.,* youthful, 668.

jung (*comp.* jünger, *superl.* jüngſt), *adj.,* young, 267, 666, 3191; jüngſt, *superl. as adv.,* recently, 217.

Jungfrau, *f.* Jungfrau, the famous peak of the Bernese Alps; 628.

Jüngling, *m.* -ß, -e, youth, young man, 579, 630, 663, *etc.*

Junſer, *m.* -ß, —, young squire, 765, 2373.

juſt, *adv.,* just, 1746.

Ǥ.

Ǥaĥn, *m.* -ß, Ǥäĥne, boat, *3, 67, 89, *etc.*

Ǥaiſer, *m.* -ß, —, emperor, 77, 193, 224 *etc.*

Ǥaiſerĥauß, *n.* -eß, -ĥäuſer, impe-rial house *or* family, 2728.

Ǥaiſerĥof, *m.* -ß, -ĥöfe, imperial court, 850, 1670.

Ǥaiſerᵏrone, *f.* -n, imperial crown, 889.

ᵏaiſerliĉ, *adj.,* imperial, 407.

Ǥaiſermorb, *m.* -ß, -e, murder of an emperor, 3169.

Ǥalᵏ, *m.* -eß, -e, lime, 354.

ᵏalt, *adj.,* cold, 40, 434, 2467, *etc.*

Ǥammer, *f.* -n, chamber, room, 3077.

Ǥampf, *m.* -eß, Ǥämpfe, contest, conflict, struggle, battle, 305, 919, *98, *etc.*

ᵏämpfen, *intr.,* combat, fight, struggle, 1654, 1727, 1728, *etc.*

ᵏarg, *adj.,* sparing, niggardly, stin-gy, 773.

Ǥaufmann, *m.* -ß, -leute *and* -män-ner, merchant, 2614.

Ǥaufmannßſĉiff, *n.* -ß, -e, mer-chant-ship, trading ship, 722.

Ǥaufmannßſtraৡe, *f.* -n, highway of commerce, 875.

ᵏaum, *adv.,* scarcely, hardly, 366, 483, *95.

ᵏecᵏ, *adj.,* bold, 2526, 2783, *etc.*

ᵏecᵏliĉ, *adv.,* boldly, 300.

Ǥeĥle, *f.* -n, throat, 2978.

ᵏeĥren, *refl.,* turn, 592.

Ǥeim, *m.* -eß, -e, germ, embryo, 2132.

ᵏein, (ᵏeine, ᵏein), *adj.,* no, none, not any, not a, 29, 30, *etc.*

ᵏeiner, (ᵏeine, ᵏein), *pron.,* no one, none, not any, 48, 138, 600, *etc.*

Ǥeller, *m.* -ß, —, cellar, 382.

ᵏennen, ᵏannte, geᵏannt, *tr.,* know, be acquainted with, 46, 66, 195, *etc.*

Ǥerᵏer, *m.* -ß, —, jail, prison, dun-geon, 360, 2356, 2364, *etc.*

Serl, *m.* -8, -e, fellow, 1756.

Rern8. Kerns, hamlet in Unterwalden, 2 miles west of Sarnen;
561.

Sernwald, *m.* -e8. Kernwald, the
forest in Unterwalden, 1196; *cf.*
N. 493.

Rette, *f.* -n, chain, 1272, 1626,
1671, *etc.*

Rind, -e8, -er, child, 113, 115, 145,
etc.; boys, 767.

Rindestind, *n.* -e8, -er, grandchild;
pl., children's children, 1929,
3001.

Rindlein, *n.* -8, —, little child,
baby, infant, 323, 2577.

Riffen, *n.* -8, —, cushion, pillow,
*121.

Rlage, *f.* -n, complaint, grievance,
1319.

flagen, *intr.,* complain, 1325, 1934,
(of, über).

Rlang, *m.* -e8, Rlänge, sound, ring,
302, 690.

flar, *adj.,* clear, bright, plain, 1104,
1238, 2542, *etc.*

Rleid, *n.* -e8, -er, garment, dress,
garb, habit, 3114, 3120.

fleiben, *tr.,* clothe, dress, attire,
40; refl., 19.

flein, *adj.,* little, small, petty, slight,
566, *72, 1560, *etc.*

Rleinod, *n.* -8, -ien, *or* -e, jewel,
treasure, ornament, 2598.

flimmen, flomm, geflommen, (also
flimmte, geflimmt,) *intr.* f., climb,
2639.

flingen, flang, geflungen, *intr.,*
sound, 967; *inf. as noun,* 3.

Rlippe, *f.* -n, cliff, crag, rock, 1498.

flopfen, *intr.,* beat, knock, rap, 494,
501, 1012, *etc.*

Rlöfter, *n.* -8, Rlöfter, convent,
monastery, nunnery, 344, 1364.

Rlofterleute, *pl.,* people (vassals,
serfs) of a monastery, 1078.

Rloftermei(e)r, *m.* -8, —, monastery-steward, 2651, *cf. N.*

Rluft, *f.* Rlüfte, cleft, chasm, gorge,
1472, 2147.

flug, (*comp.* flüger, *superl.* flügft),
adj., prudent, wise, sensible,
shrewd, 56, 59, 247, *etc.*

Rnabe, *m.* -n, -n, boy, lad, youth,
*2, 2, 10, *etc.*

Rnecht, *m.* -8, -e, servant, farm-
servant, man, vassal, slave, 568,
*40, 754, *etc.*

Rnechtschaft, *f.* bondage, servitude,
slavery, 907, 1209, 1451, *etc.*

Rnie, *n.* -8, -e, knee, *9, 397, *etc.*

fnieen, *intr.,* kneel, 1947, *114.

Röcher, *m.* -8, —, quiver, *98, 2225.

fommen, fam, gefommen, *intr.* f.,
come, arrive, get, 17, *4, *etc.;* hit
(upon, auf), think of, 1517; zu
fich —, come to one's self, collect
one's self, 2034, 2046.

fommlich, *adj.,* comfortable, pleasant, 2128. (*A Swiss word.*)

Rönig, *m.* -8, -e, king, 130, 332,
399, *etc.*

Röniging, *f.* -innen, queen, 2997,
3033.

königlid, *adj.*, kingly, royal, 816, 2999, 3263.

Königsburg, *f.* en, royal castle, 1337.

können, konnte, gekonnt, kann, *tr.* *and modal aux.*, can, be able, may, 98, 106, 108, *etc.;* 2707, kann... bei(kommen), can get at (affect *or* hurt).

Kopf, *m.* -s, Köpfe, head, 87, 1886, 1889, *etc.* [1793.

Korn, *n.* -s, Körner, corn, grain,

kostbar, *adj.*, costly, precious, 894.

kosten, *tr.*, cost, 798, 1292.

köstlich, *adj.*, costly, precious, 2642.

krachen, *intr.*, crash, crack, roar, 2895; *inf. as noun,* *4.

krächzen, *intr.*, croak, 1000.

Kraft, *f.* Kräfte, strength, force, power, 152, 651, 924, *etc.*

kräftiglich, *adv.*, strongly, power-fully, 168.

kraftlos, *adj.*, powerless, weak, *101, 2607.

krähen, *intr.*, crow, 384.

krampfhaft, *adj.*, convulsive, *32.

krank (*comp.* kränker, *superl.* kränk(e)st), *adj.*, sick, ill; *masc. as noun,* 1747.

kränken, *tr.*, hurt (one's feelings), grieve, wound, 1627, 2334.

Kranz, *m.* -es, Kränze, garland, wreath, 2521.

Kränzlein, *n.* -s, —, little garland, wreath, 1347.

Kraut, *n.* -s, Kräuter, herb, plant, 1016.

Kreis, *m.* -es, -e, circle, circut, sphere, 761, *92, *etc.;* orbit, socket, 677; round, revolution, 2401.

Kreuz, *n.* -es, -e, cross, 3245, 3250.

Kreuzlein, *n.* -s, —, little cross, 960.

kriechen, kroch, gekrochen, *intr.* f. *or* h., creep, crawl, 1042; kreucht, *archaic. pres. ind.*, 1477.

Krieg, *m.* -es, -e, war, 315, 319, 322, *etc.*

kriegerisch, *adj.*, warlike, martial, 2436.

Kriegesmacht, *f.* -mächte, military power *or* forces, army, 308.

Kriegesnot, *f.* -nöte, distress *or* misery of war, 883.

Kriegsbrommme'te, *f.* -n, war trumpet, 834.

Krone, *f.* -n, crown, 407, 1710 (= pearl).

krönen, *tr.*, crown, 3201.

Krümme, *f.* -n, winding, turning, 1042.

Kuckuck, *m.* -s, -e, cuckoo, 18.

Kuh, *f.* Kühe, cow, 53.

kühlen, *tr.*, cool, 623.

kühn, *adj.*, bold, 1597, 2874.

Kühnheit, *f.* -en, boldness, 1066.

Kuhreihen, *m.* -s, *lit.*, cow-dance, cow-line *or* cow-song, *but best rendered, by transferring the word,* Kuhreihen. *It is a melody sung or played, in calling cows together;* *3, *cf. N.,* *4, 837, *etc.*

Kulm, *m.* -8, ~e, top, peak, 2146.

Kummer, *m.* -8, sorrow, grief, anxiety, 2391, 2658.

kümmern, *tr.*, concern, regard, 1816.

kummervoll, *adj.*, sorrowful, grieved, anxious, *14, 236, 788, *etc.*

Kunde, *f.* -n, information, intelligence, knowledge, 573, 719, 2853, *etc.*

kundig, *adj.*, having knowledge, acquainted, familiar, 3239.

Kundschaft, *f. collect.*, spies, 985.

Kunst, *f.* Künste, art, skill, 1883, 1937, 1941, *etc.*

kunstgeübt, *part. adj.*, practised, trained, skilful, 1933.

kurz (*comp.* kürzer, *superl.* kürzeft), *adj.*, short, 422, 730, 1054, *etc.*

kürzen, *tr.*, shorten, curtail, deprive (of, um), 2956.

Kurzweil, *n. or m.* -8 (*usually feminine*), pastime, amusement, jest, 1912.

Küßnacht. Küssnacht, village and castle in Schwyz, at the northernmost end of the Lake of the Four Forest Cantons; 219, 2074, 2100, *etc.*

L.

laben, *tr.*, refresh, 3102.

Labung, *f.* -en, refreshment, 3112.

lächeln, *intr.*, smile, 1, 2306.

lachen, *intr.*, laugh, 372.

laden, lud, geladen, *tr.*, load, 357.

laden, lud, geladen, *tr.*, invite, summon, 1, 835, 2656.

Lager, *n.* -8, —, camp; 817, court.

Lamm, *n.* -e8, Lämmer, lamb, 180. 440, 1956.

Lämmergeier, *m.* -8,—, *lit.*, lamb's vulture, lammergeir, 1000.

Land, *n.* -e8, Länder *or* Lande, land, country, *3, 182, 225, *etc.*; zu Lande, by land, 2279; *with pl.*, Lande, canton, 431, 655, 805, 1071, 1423, 2411, 2868.

Landammann, *m.* -8, -e *and* -änner, chief-magistrate, landammann, 813, 1305, *etc.*

Landbedrücker, *m.* -8, —, oppressor of the land, 1720.

landen, *intr.* f., land, 722, 2107, 2277, *etc.*

Landenberg(er). Beringer von Landenberg, governor of Unterwalden; 282, 496, 2902, *etc. cf.* N, 72.

landenbergisch, *adj.*, Landenberg's, of Landenberg, *2, *12.

Ländergier, *f.*, greed for territory, 1665.

Länderkauf, *m.* -8, -käufe, purchase of land, territorial acquisition, 903.

Länderkette, *f.* -n, chain of lands, 872.

Landesammann = Landammann, 1125.

Landesfeind, *m.* -8, -e, enemy of the land *or* country, 340, 792.

Landesmark, *f.* -en, boundary, border of a country, 1207, 1427.

Landesunglück, *n.* -s, -e, misfortune, calamity of *or* to the land, 2676.

Landleute, *pl.*, country-people, peasants, men, *1, *2, *48, *etc.*

Landmann, *m.* -s, *pl.*, Landleute, countryman, peasant, 782, 1027, 1056, *etc.;* 962, = Landsmann, man of the canton.

Landmark, *f.* -en, boundary, border of a land, 729.

Landschaft, *f.* -en, landscape, scenery, *4.

Landsgemeinde, *f.* -n, assembly of the land *or* canton, 665, 1109, 1169, *etc.*

Landsgesetz, *n.* -es, -e, law of the land, 1306.

Landsmann, *m.* -s, *pl.*, Landsleute, fellow-countryman, compatriot, 50, 70, 158, *etc.*

Landstraße, *f.* -n, highway, *14.

Landsturm, *m.* -s, general levy of the people, reserves, 1422.

Landvogt, *m.* -s, =vögte, governor, prefect, 72, 131, 143, *etc.* Cf. *N.* on Reichsvogt, *1.

Landwehr, *f.* -en, defense, bulwark, rampart of the land, 1785.

lang (*comp.* länger, *superl.* längst), long, 242, *etc.;* lang, *adv. with preceding acc.*, during, for, *3, *14, *39, *etc.;* lang(e), *adv.*, long, for a long time, 100, 353, *41, *etc.;* längst, *adv.*, very long, long ago, 251, 271, 1782, *etc.*

langen, *tr.*, reach, take, 1024.

langsam, *adj.*, slow, 763, 1443, *120, *etc.*

Lanze, *f.* -n, lance, 1969, 2444.

lassen, ließ, gelassen, läßt, *tr.*, let alone, leave, give up, cease from, 160, 441, 606, *etc.;* let, permit, allow, have, cause, 78, 88, 136 (läßt sich) . . . wagen, can be risked), *etc.*

Last, *f.* -en, load, burden, weight, 1277, 1783.

lasten, *intr.*, weigh, press heavily, 897.

lauern, *intr.*, lurk, lie in wait, watch (for, auf), 2630, 2635.

Lauf, *m.* -s, Läufe, course, current, 1329, 3243; im Lauf, under way, in full course, 2864.

laufen, lief, gelaufen, läuft, *intr.* f. *and* h., run, pass swiftly, *4, *etc.;* 65, 91, *etc.*, past part. for *Eng. pres. part.*

lauschen, *intr.*, lurk, lie in wait, 503.

laut, *adj.*, loud, aloud, *24, *92, 163.*

Laut, *m.* -es, -e, sound, 1567.

lauten, *intr.*, sound, purport, run, say, 1162.

läuten, *tr. and intr.*, ring, *49, *107, 2150, *etc.*

lauter, *adj.*, clear, pure, plain, 1104.

Lawi'ne, *f.* -n, avalanche, 1782, 1812, 3247.

leben, *intr.*, live, 334, 2275, *etc.;* leb(e) wohl, lebt wohl, *and* leben Sie wohl, farewell, 13, *etc.*

Leben, *n.* -8, —, life, 112, 114, 621, *etc.*

leben'big, *adj.*, living, alive, 1503; *pl. as noun*, 2149.

Lebensblut, *n.* -8, life-blood, 623.

Lebensglück, *n.*-8, happiness of life, 1717.

lebhaft, *adj.*, lively, eager, *132.

Lebtag, *m.* -8, -e, day *or* time of one's life, all the days of one's life, 2702.

lechzen, *intr.*, languish, pant, 3112.

ledig, *adj.*, free, 1837.

leer, *adj.*, empty, void, vacant, vain, 962, 1333, *71, *etc.*

leeren, *tr.*, empty, clear, 2877.

legen, *tr.*, lay, put, place, 989, 1147, 1724, *etc.*

Leh(e)n, *n.* -8, —, fief, 229, 263, 409, *etc.*

Lehenhof, *m.* -8, -höfe, court of fiefs, 866.

Lehensherr, *m.* -n, -en, liege lord, 2453.

lehnen, *intr.*, lean, *129.

lehren, *tr.*, teach, 498.

Leib, *m.* -es, -er, body, person, life, 400, 660, 675, *etc.*

Leibeskraft, *f.* -kräfte, strength *or* force of body, 2262, (with might and main).

leiblich, *adj.*, bodily, one's own, 145.

Leichnam, *m.* -8, -e, dead body, corpse, *122, 2466.

leicht, *adj.*, light, easy, ready, nimble, 300, 418, 433, *etc.*

leichtfertig, *adj.*, light, wanton, loose, 474.

leiden, litt, gelitten, *tr. and intr.*, suffer, endure, 190, 1168, 1619, *etc.*

Leiden, *n.* -8, —, suffering, 2310, 2335.

leider, *interj.*, alas!, 777.

leihen, lieh, geliehen, *tr.*, lend, 1103.

leisten, *tr.*, do, render, perform, fulfill, 1054, 1360, 1830 furnish, *etc.*

leiten, *tr.*, lead, conduct, guide, 1269, 1352, 2018, *etc.*

Leiter, *f.* -n, ladder, *48; (rope-) ladder, 1416.

lenken, *tr.*, turn, govern, rule, order, 2323.

Lenz, *m.* -es, -e, spring, springtime, prime, 829.

Leopold. Leopold, second son of Emperor Albrecht; 2967, 3200.

lernen, *tr.*, learn, 643, 909, 1482, *etc.*

lesen, las, gelesen, liest, *tr.*, read, 213, 244, 3031, *etc.*

letzt, *adj.*, last, final, 328, 762; *masc. as noun*, 861; *neut. as noun*, 3179.

leuchten, *intr.*, light, shine, gleam, *48, 1118; *inf. as noun*, 1442.

Leute, *pl.*, people, men, persons, *23, 406, 1080, *etc.*

Licht, *n.* -es, -er, light, 298, 587, 590, *etc.*

lichten, *tr.*, light, provide with light, 1689.

lieb, *adj.*, dear, beloved, 10, 238, 1528, *etc.*

Liebe, *f.*, love, 918, 934, 1601, *etc.*; kindness, favor, 2290.

lieben, *tr.*, love, 338, 614, 1082, *etc.*

lieber, *adv. (comp. of* lieb, *used as comp. of* gern), rather, 1574, 1739.

lieblich, *adj.*, lovely, 20.

Lied, *n.* -es, -er, song, ballad, poem, 18, 1162.

liegen, lag, gelegen, *intr.* h. (*and* f.), lie, be situated, be, *3, 92, 122, *etc.*; nichts liegt mir am Leben, life is of no importance to me, I care nought for my life, 621; nicht lag's an mir, it did not lie with me, it was no fault of mine, 2903.

Linde, *f.* -n, lime-tree, linden-(tree), *14, 217, *etc.*

link, *adj.*, left; die Linke, the left hand; zur Linken, at the left, *3.

links, *adv.*, on the left, 724, *55, *58, *etc.*

Lippe, *f.* -n, lip, 2305.

Lisel, Lisel (= Lizzie), diminutive of Elisabeth; 47.

loben, *tr.*, praise, 2038, 2043, *etc.*

Locke, *f.* -n, lock (of hair), 673.

locken, *tr.*, allure, entice, tempt, 11.

lodern, *intr.*, blaze, 3116.

loh, *adj.*, blazing, bright, 970.

Lohn, *m.* -es, Löhne, reward, pay, 99.

lohnen, *tr.*, reward, requite, 2286.

los, *adj.*, loose, free, rid of, 109, 799, 2247, *etc.; sep. pref.*, loose, off, away, *etc.*

Los, *n.* -es, -e, lot, chance, fate, destiny, 1170, 2333.

losbinden, band, gebunden, *tr.*, untie, unfasten, 68, 89.

lösen, *tr.*, loosen, free, 1723, 2370, *etc.; refl.*, 2047.

losgeben, gab, gegeben, giebt, *tr.*, set free, release, 2743.

loslassen, ließ, gelassen, läßt, *tr.*, let loose, let go, 307, *47, *155, *etc.*

losreißen, riß, gerissen, *refl.*, break loose *or* away, *104.

Lowerz. Lowerz, village on western shore of Lake Lowerz; 2285.

Luft, *f.* Lüfte, air, breeze, 968, 1470.

lugen, *intr.*, look, 46. (*A South-German word*).

lügen, log, gelogen, *intr.*, lie, 258, (say wrong), 1834.

Lust, *f.* Lüste, desire, lust, pleasure, joy, 7, 273, 2581, *etc.*

lüstern, *adj.*, wanton, 668.

Luxemburg, Graf von. Count Heinrich IV von Luxemburg, as Emperor Heinrich VII; 3023.

Luzern. The city Lucerne, capitol of the Canton Lucerne, at the NW. end of the Lake of the Four Forest Cantons; *1, 188, 896, *etc.*

M.

machen, *tr.*, make, *3, 329, *etc.;* 758, act (the part of); 1478, mend, fix; *intr.*, make, act, 37.

Macht, *f.* **Mächte**, **might**, power, authority, 224, 952, 1259, *etc.*,

mächtig, *adj.*, **mighty**, powerful, strong, 425, 436, 437, *etc.; with gen.*, master of, 2297, 2872.

Mädchen, *n.* -8, —, girl, **maiden**, *144.

mahnen, *tr.*, remind, demand, dun; *pres. part. as noun*, 2955.

Mai, *m.* -e8, -e, *and* -en, **May**, 20.

Maientau, *m.* -8, **May-dew**, 3005.

malerisch, *adj.*, picturesque, *144, *163.

man, *pron. nom. sing.*, one, they, people, you, we; *often to be rendered by passive*; *3, *4, 107, *etc.*

mancher, (**manche**, **manches**), *adj. and pron.*, **many** a, many, many a one, 247, 1189, 1760, *etc.*

Mandat, *n.* -8, -e, **mandate**, order, 1819.

Mann, *m.* -e8, **Männer**, **man**, *2, 65, 73, *etc.;* husband, 2734, 2749.

Männerwert, *m.* -8, **manly worth**, dignity, 1706.

Manneswort, *n.* -8, -e, **word** of a man, man's word, 2488.

männlich, *adj.*, **manly**, valiant, brave, 1725, 2046; 2874, *archaic, form*, mannlich.

Mantel, *m.* -8, **Mäntel**, **mantle**, cloak, 1101.

Markt, *m.* -e8, **Märkte**, **market**, market-place, 874.

Marter, *f.* -n, torment, torture, 2673.

Maß, *n.* -e8, -e, measure, limit, 2389.

mäßigen, *refl.*, be moderate, control one's self, 1375.

matt, *adj.*, faint, feeble, *136.

Matte, *f.* -n, meadow, mead, *3 (*cf. N.*), 13, 595, *etc.*

Mauer, *f.* -n, wall, *1, 1687, 1721, 2861, *etc.*   [stone, 353.

Mauerstein, *m.* -8, -e, (building-)

Maulwurfshaufe(n), *m.* -ns, -n, mole-hill, 374.

Maus, *f.* **Mäuse**, **mouse**, 2706.

Meer, *n.* -e8, -e, sea, ocean, 31, 601, 1806, *etc.*

mehr, *adj.*, **more**; *adv. with* nicht *or other neg.*, no more, no longer, 32, 48, 79, *etc.*

Mehr, *n.* -e8, majority, 1419.

mehren, *tr.*, increase (in wealth and power), aggrandize, 3067.

mehrere, *adj.*, *only in pl.*, several, 2191, *130, *144.

mehrst, *adj.*, *archaic for* meist, most, 3024.

Mehrheit, *f.* -en, majority, *69.

meiden, mied, gemieden, *tr.*, avoid, shun, 1573.

Meier, *m.* -8, —, steward, manager; *as proper name*, *1, 1072, *etc.; cf. N.*, 1072.

mein, *adj. and pron.*, **my, mine**, 10, 42, 51, *etc.*

meinen, *tr. and intr.*, think, **mean,**
intend, 41, 174, 287, *etc.*

meinig (ber, bie, baš -e), *pron.*,
mine; *neut. as noun*, my own
(land *or* property), 3135.

Meinrab. Saint Meinrad (Meinard, Meginhard), born about 800
A.D., founder of the monastery
Einsiedeln, in legend a Hohenzollern; 519.

Meinung, *f.*, -en, opinion, **meaning,** intention, 395, 724, 2020, *etc.*

meiſt, *adj.*, **most,** 1140, 1545, 1880,
etc.

Meiſter, *m.* -š, —, **master,** *2,
49, 161, *etc.*

Meiſterſchuß, *m.*-eš, -üſſe, **master-
shot,** 2043, 2649.

Melchthal, *n.* -š. The Melchthal,
valley of the Melchaa, in the
southern part of Unterwalden,
east of Sarnen; from it Arnold
vom Melchthal is named; *1, 560.

melken, *tr.*, **milk,** 362.

Melknapf, *m.* -š, -näpfe, milk-
pail, *4.

Melobie', *f.* -bi'en, **melody,** *3,
844.

Menge, *f.* -n, **multitude, crowd,**
1097.

Menſch, *m.* -en, -en, **man,** human
being, person, 32, 98, 158, *etc.*

Menſchenbenken, *n.* -š, **man's
thinking;** ſeit —, since time immemorial, 528, *cf. N.*

menſchenleer, *adj.*, unpeopled, de-
serted, 1550.

Menſchenſpur, *f.* -en, **trace of
man,** human trace, 1179.

Menſchheit, *f.*, **man**kind, humanity,
2422.

menſchlich, *adj.*, **human;** *neut. as
noun*, 159, (et)was Menſchliches,
something human, belonging to
the lot of man, *euphemistic for*
accident *or* death.

Menſchlichkeit, *f.*, humanity, hu-
maneness, 322, 3219.

merken, *tr.*, **mark,** note, 3241.

Merkmal, *n.* -š, -e, **mark, sign,**
characteristic, 1227.

meſſen, maß, gemeſſen, mißt, *tr.*,
measure, scan, scrutinize, 773,
*156; *refl.*, vie with, compete
with, 2023.

Mettenglöcklein, *n.* -š, —, **matin-
bell,** 966.

Meute, *f.* -n, **pack of hounds,** 648.

Meuterei', *f.* -en, **mutiny, riot,**
1851.

Milch, *f.*, **milk,** 1004, 2573.

milb, *adj.*, **mild,** gentle, indulgent,
2778.

Milbe, *f.*, **mildness, gentleness,**
2998.

milbthätig, *adj.*, charitable, 1037.

mißbrau'chen, *tr. insep.*, abuse, mis-
use, 550.

Mißgunſt, *f.*, **envy, ill-will,** 270.

mit, *prep.* (*dat.*), *adv. and sep.
pref.*, **with,** together with, along
with, along, *3, 19, *4, *etc.*; 1520,
mit babei, present with the
rest.

mitbringen, brachte, gebracht, *tr.*, **bring** along with (one), 735, 1401 (require), 1582, *etc.*

mitführen, *tr.*, carry *or* bring along with (one), 1405, 2174.

mitgeben, gab, gegeben, giebt, *tr.*, **give,** to take along with one, *or* put with the rest, 863.

mitkommen, kam, gekommen, *intr.* f., come along, 2656.

Mitleid, *n.* -s, sympathy, compassion, pity, 2735, 3219.

mitnehmen, nahm, genommen, nimmt, *tr.*, take along, "take in," enjoy, 2659.

mitsamt, *prep. (dat.),* together with, 2185.

Mitschuld, *f.* -en, joint guilt, complicity, 682.

mitschwören, schwor, geschworen, *intr.*, **swear** *or* take an oath with (others), 2287, 2295, 2514.

Mittagsonne, *f.*, **midday-sun,** southern sun, south, 1173.

Mittagsstunde, *f.* -n, noon-hour, 1743.

Mitte, *f.* -n, middle, midst, center, *50, *58, 1200, *etc.*

mitteilen, *tr.*, communicate, impart, 1164.

Mittel, *n.* -s, —, means, way, expedient, 1284, 1315, 2417, *etc.*

mitten, *adv.*, **midway,** in the middle *or* midst, 394, 975, 2042, *etc.*

Mitternacht, *f.* =nächte, midnight, north, 1168.

mitziehen, zog, gezogen, *intr.* f., march along with (others), 1230.

mögen, mochte, gemocht, mag, *tr. and modal aux.*, **may,** be able, can, like, 190, 238, 252, *etc.*

möglich, *adj.*, possible, 449, 2209, 2255, *etc.*

Moment, *n.* -s, -e, moment, *33.

Mönch, *m.* -s, -e, monk, 344, 2615, *153, *etc.*

Mond, *m.* -es, -e, moon, 976, 2067, *etc.; pl.* -e *or* -en, month, 2750.

Mondennacht, *f.* =nächte, moonlight night, 971.

Mondlicht, *n.*, -s, moonlight, *48.

Mondregenbogen, *m.* -s, =bögen, lunar rainbow, *48.

Monstranz, *f.* -en, monstrance, pyx, 1751, *cf. N.*

Mord, *m.* -es, -e, murder, 2570, 2621, 2634, *etc.*

morden, *tr. and intr.*, murder, 2982, 3183.

Mörder, *m.* -s, —, murderer, 172, 465, 1100, *etc.*

mörderisch, *adj.*, murderous, 2229, 2594.

Mordgedanke, *m.* -ns, -n, thought of murder, 2629.

Mordgewehr, *n.* -s, -e, weapon of murder, 1973.

Morgen, *m.* -s, —, morning, 1440.

morgen, *adv.*, tomorrow, 2548.

Morgenröte, *f.* -n, dawn, daybreak, *70.

Morgenstrahl, *m.* -ß, -en, morning-ray *or* light, 1469.

Mörlischachen. Mörlischachen, village on the Lake, about 2 miles SW. of Küssnacht; 2651.

Mörtel, *m.* -ß, —, mortar, 354.

müde, *adj.*, tired, weary, 280.

Mühe, *f.* -n, trouble, pains, toil, 1094.

Müller, Johannes. In compliment to the noted historian Johannes von Müller (1752–1809) his name is given to a man mentioned in *l.* 2948.

Mund, *m.* -eß, -e, mouth, lips, 809, 1053 (tongue, *cf. N.*), 1568, *etc.*

munter, *adj.*, cheerful, blithe, gay, 3269.

murren, *intr.*, murmur, mutter, grumble, 361.

Muotta. Muotta (*pronounce Mu'otta, dissyllabic, the -o- being nearly inaudible*), river, east of the Lake of the Four Forest Cantons, into which it empties at Brunnen; 1178.

Musik', *f.*, music, *129, *136, *137, *etc.*

müssen, mußte, gemußt, muß, *intr. and modal aux.*, must, be obliged to, have to, 15, 105, 107, *etc.*

müßig, *adj.*, idle, 463, 532, 828, *etc.*

mustern, *tr.*, muster, inspect, examine, *41.

Mut, *m.* -eß, **mood,** humor, (frame of) mind, courage, 1026, 1278, *etc.*; desire, longing, 1770.

mutig, *adj.*, courageous, bold, 340, 834, 1809, *etc.; masc. as noun,* 313.

Mutter, *f.* Mütter, mother, 1486, 2048.

Mütterchen, *n.* -ß, —, dear mother, good mother, 1580.

mütterlich, *adj.*, motherly, maternal; *neut. as noun,* mother's estate, inheritance from one's mother, 1344.

Mutterschmerz, *m.* -eß, -en, mother's pangs, 3095.

Mütze, *f.* -n, cap, 1738.

Mythenstein, *m.* -ß. Mythenstein. This name is used by Schiller of one of the peaks of the Haken, *l.* 39, and also of the rock, properly bearing the name, in the Lake a little south of Brunnen, *l.* 725. Perhaps he confounded the two.

N.

nach, *prep. (dat.), adv. and sep. pref.,* after, behind, towards, to, according to, along, by, at, for, about, 209, 333, *20, *etc.*

Nachbar, *m.* -ß (*or* -n), -n, neighbor, 1810, 2683.

nachdem, *conj.*, after, *124.

nachdrängen, *intr.*, press *or* crowd after, *163.

nachbringen, brang, gebrungen, intr. ſ., press or crowd after, *23.

nacheilen, intr. ſ., hasten after, *154.

Nachen, m. -s, —, (small) boat, *13, 175, 980, etc.

nachfolgen, intr. ſ., follow after, 2073.

nachgehen, ging, gegangen, intr. ſ., follow, pursue, 2628.

nachher, adv., afterwards, *48.

nachjagen, intr. ſ. and h., chase, hunt, pursue, 2905.

nachkommen, kam, gekommen, intr. ſ., come after, follow, come up (with), *138.

Nachricht, f. -en, news, information, 493.

nachſetzen, intr., set after, follow, pursue, 101, 2798, 2825, etc.

nachſprechen, ſprach, geſprochen, ſpricht, tr., repeat, speak, say (after one), *70.

nächſt, adj., superl. of nah(e), next, nearest, 1603, 2282, etc.; 107, masc. as noun, neighbor.

nächſt, prep. (dat.), next, close to, *14.

nachſtürzen, intr. ſ., rush after, *13.

Nacht, f. Nächte, night, 242, 593, 751, etc.; des Nachts (irreg. gen.), in the night, at night, 1780.

nachthun, that, gethan, tr. (dat. of pers.), do after, imitate, 163.

nächtlich, adj., nightly, nocturnal, by night, 1415, 1439.

nachts, adv., at night, in the night, 2875.

Nachtzeit, f. -en, night-time, 733.

nachziehen, zog, gezogen, tr., draw after, 1417.

Nacken, m. -s, —, neck, 2719.

nackt, adj., naked, 607, 2443.

nah(e) (comp. näher, superl. nächſt), adj., near, nigh, near by, close, 121, *17, 708, etc.

Nähe, f., nearness, neighborhood, presence, 3146.

nahen, intr. ſ., approach, draw near, 61, 1070, 2031, etc.

nähern, refl., approach, draw near, *54, *104, *109, etc.

nähren, tr., foster, feed, nourish, support, 1016, 1808, 2081, etc.

Nahrung, f. -en, nourishment, food, 3013.

Name(n), m. -ns, —, name, 151, 391, 530, etc.

närriſch, adj., foolish, queer, 1758.

Natur', f. -en, nature, 1282, 1487, 1623, etc.

naturvergeſſen, part. adj., unnatural, degenerate, 1611.

Naue, f. -n, boat, 37, cf. N.

Nebeldecke, f. -n, cover of mist, veil of fog, 1266.

neben, prep. (dat. and acc.), beside, by the side of, by, *14, 814.

neb(e)licht, adj., misty, foggy, cloudy, 31.

nebſt, prep. (dat.), together with, *163.

Neffe, m. -n, -n, nephew, *1, 2951.

nehmen, nahm, genommen, nimmt, *tr.*, take, receive, accept, 55, 413, *41, etc.

Neid, *m.* –es, envy, 1704, 3199.

neidisch, *adj.*, envious, 260.

nein, *adv.*, no, 1840, 2784.

nennen, nannte, genannt, *tr.*, name, call, 268, 530, etc.; *refl.*, be named *or* called, 369.

Netz, *n.* –es, –e, net, 877, 1636.

neu, *adj.*, new, fresh, modern, 19, 208, 254, etc.; *neut. as noun*, 952; von neuem, anew, *163; aufs neu', anew, afresh, 1490.

Neuerung, *f.* –en, innovation, 1021.

Neugier, *f.*, curiosity, 532, *76.

Neujahrsgeschenk, *n.* –s, –e, New-Year's present; *on facsimile of title page of 1st ed.*

nicht, *adv.*, not, 26, 32, 46, etc.; gar —, not at all; noch —, not yet.

nichts, *indec. pron.*, naught, nothing, not anything, 148, 268, 461, etc.; — als, nothing but.

nid, *prep.* (*dat.*), below, 717. (*A Swiss word*). *Cf. N. l.* 493.

nie, *adv.*, never, 379, 527, 539, *etc.*; noch —, never yet, 2138.

nieder, *adv. and sep. pref.*, low, down, downwards, *21, 2846.

niederbrennen, brannte, gebrannt, *tr.*, burn down, 179, 319.

niederfallen, fiel, gefallen, fällt, *intr.* f., fall down, prostrate one's self, 1919, *159.

niederknieen, *intr.*, kneel, fall on one's knees, *122.

niederlassen, ließ, gelassen, läßt, *tr.*, let down, lower, *137.

niederquellen, quoll, gequollen, quillt, *intr.* f. *and* h., flow down, 1005.

niederreißen, riß, gerissen, *tr.*, tear *or* pull down, 2846, 2863.

niederschlagen, schlug, geschlagen, schlägt, *tr.*, strike *or* beat down, 179.

niederschmelzen, schmolz, geschmolzen, schmilzt, *intr.* f., melt down, 2146.

niedersenden, sandte, gesandt, *tr.*, send down, 1781.

niedersinken, sank, gesunken, *intr.* f., sink down, *119.

niedersteigen, stieg, gestiegen, *intr.* f., descend, 2832.

niederstoßen, stieß, gestoßen, stößt, *tr.*, strike *or* thrust down, 1985.

Niederung, *f.* –en, low land, 697.

niederwerfen, warf, geworfen, wirft, *refl.*, cast one's self down, prostrate one's self, *96, *109, *134, etc.

niemals, *adv.*, never, 587, 588, 2509, etc.

niemand, *pron.*, no one, nobody, none, 490, 632, 1407, etc.

nimmer, *adv.*, never, 1149, 1496, 3045.

nimmermehr, *adv.*, never at all, by no means, 1981.　　　[1276.

nirgend(s), *adv.*, nowhere, 522,

nit, *adv.*, not, 51. *Dialectic, especially South-German, for* nicht.

noch, adv., yet, as yet, still, even, in addition, besides, more, *3, *9, 176, etc.

noch, conj., nor, 1942.

Not, f. Nöte, need, necessity, distress, 156, 171, 678, etc.; in certain fixed phrases as an adverb or a predicate adj., not thun and not sein, be necessary, 136, 505, 3027, 2927; von nöten haben (with gen.), have need of, 349.

notgedrungen, part. adj., compelled by necessity, 1370.

Notgewehr, n. -s, -e, lit. "weapon in need," weapon for self-defense, 646.

Notwehr, f., self-defense, 439, 3176.

nun, adv., now, 99, etc.; as interj., well! why! 68, 507, etc.

nur, adv., only, simply, just, 33, 266, 267, etc.

O.

O, interj., O! oh!, 457, 483, etc.

ob, adv. (in compounds), over, above; prep. dat. (and gen.), on account of, 277, 788, 1014.

ob, conj., whether, if, 46, 135, 233, etc., although, 1158; ob . . . schon or gleich or wohl, although; 2546, to see whether.

Obdach, n. -s, shelter, 713.

oben, adv., above, aloft, in a former place, before, *13, *70, *71, etc.

Oberhaupt, n. -s, -häupter, head, chief, 1217, 3029.

oberherrlich, adj., sovereign, 1832.

obgleich, conj., although, 337, 2407.

Obmann, m. -s, -männer, umpire, arbitrator, judge, 701.

Obrigkeit, f. -en, authority, one in authority, superior, 471.

Ochs, m. -en, -en, ox, 466, 477, 566, etc.

öde, adj., waste, desert, desolate, solitary, 732, 999, 2354, etc.

oder, conj., or, 2714, 2717, 2731, etc.

offen, adj., open, 328, 347, 723, etc.

offenba'ren, tr., reveal, discover, disclose, 292.

öffentlich, adj., public, *2, *23, *140.

öffnen, tr., open, *29, 1070, etc.; refl., open, appear, widen, 959.

oft, adv., oft, often, 502, 1294, 2602, etc.

Oheim, m. -s, -e, uncle, 752, 771, 774, etc.

Ohm, m. -s, -e, uncle, 3164, 3165, 3204.

ohne, prep. (acc.), without, 426, 540, 741, etc.

ohnmächtig, adj., weak, impotent, unavailing, vain, 626, 1038, 2583, etc.

Ohr, n. -es, -en, ear, 60, 750, 822, etc.

Opfer, n. -s, —, offering, sacrifice, victim, 147, 1667, 2444, etc.

Orchester, n. -s, —, orchestra, *71.

ordentlich, adj., orderly, regular, proper, 209.

Ordnung, f. -en, order, 2829.

Ort, *m.* –es, –e, *or* Örter, place, 394, 2448, 2747, *etc.; with pl.,* –e, = Canton.

Öst(er)reich, *n.* –s, Austria; 184, 194, 408, *etc.*

östlich, *adj.,* eastern, *105.

P.

Paar, *n.* –es, –e, pair, 567.

Pair, (*pronounce* pār), *m.* –s, –e *or* –s, peer, 818.

Palm. Rudolf von Palm, friend and accomplice of Herzog Johannes von Schwaben; 2961, 2979.

Papst, *m.* –es, Päpste, pope, 3234.

Paradies, *n.* –es, –e, paradise, 6.

Parricida, *m.* (*Latin word*), parricide, *2, *157.

Parteiung, *f.* –en, faction, schism, 887.

Paß, *m.* –es, Pässe, pass, defile, 2169, 2442, 2934, *etc.*

Pause, *f.* –n, pause, stop, rest, *39, *64, *92.

Pelzwams, *n.* –es, =wämser, fur-doublet, *40.

Pergament, *n.* –s, –e, parchment, document, 244, 1330.

Perle, *f.* –n, pearl, jewel, 916.

Person', *f.* –en, person, character, *pl.,* dramatis personæ, *1; role, part, 811.

Peter, Sankt. Saint Peter; 3233.

Pfad, *m.* –es, –es, path, 732.

Pfaff(e), *m.* –n, –n, priest, 1245, 1746.

Pfalz, *f.* –en, palace, 1324.

Pfand, *n.* –es, Pfänder, pledge, security, trust, 615, 2507.

Pfarrer, *m.* –s, —, priest, *1, 1093, 1296, *etc.*

Pfauenfeder, *f.* –n, peacock's feather, 780.

Pfeife, *f.* –n, pipe, whistle, whistling, 61.

Pfeil, *m.* –s, –e, arrow, bolt, shaft, 1466, 1475, *75, *etc.*

Pferd, *n.* –s, –e, horse, 204, *etc.;* zu —, on horseback, *92, *132, *etc.*

Pflanze, *f.* –n, plant, 592.

pflanzen, *tr.,* plant, 1800.

Pflege, *f.,* care, attendance, 486.

pflegen, *intr.,* be accustomed *or* wont, use, 1112; *with gen.,* Rats —, take council, 339.

Pflicht, *f.* –en, duty, obligation, allegiance, 358, 1208, 1225, *etc.*

pflichtgemäß, *adj.,* conformable to one's duty, as in duty bound, 1358.

pflichtig, *adj.,* bound to, subject to, 1084.

Pflug, *m.* –es, –üge, plow, 476, 478, 567, *etc.*

Pflugstier, *m.* –s, –e, plow-steer, plow-ox, 650.

Pforte, *f.* –n, gate, door, 1012, 2167.

Pfosten, *m.* –s, —, post, 2884.

Pike, *f.* –n, pike, *89, *92, *etc.*

Pilger, *m.* –s, —, pilgrim, 343, 2615.

Pilgerstracht, *f.* –en, pilgrim's garb, 1062.

plagen, *refl.*, be harassed, drudge, toil, 1797.

Platte, *f.* -n, ledge *or* shelf, 2265.

Plaḳ, *m.* -es, **Pläḳe, place,** room, ground, 81, *21, 963, *etc.*

plöḳlich, *adj.*, sudden, *26, 1903, *98, *etc.*

Popanz, *m.* -es, -e, bugbear, 1736.

Port, *m.* -s, -e, port, harbor, 141.

prachtvoll, *adj.*, magnificent, splendid, stately, *71.

prangen, *intr.*, shine, be splendid, flaunt, parade, 29, 779.

Pranger, *m.* -s, —, pillory, 1753.

praſſeln, *intr.*, crackle, 2878.

Preis, *m.* -es, -e, **prize,** reward, 1938, 2642, 2647, *etc.*

preiſen, pries, geprieſen, *tr.*, **praise,** 2322; *refl.*, call *or* account one's self happy, 1083.

preſſen, *tr.*, oppress, 251.

Proſpekt, *m.* -s, -e, **prospect,** view, *48, *84, *105.

prüfen, *tr.*, prove, try, test, examine, 443, 2718.

Prüfung, *f.* -en, trial, test, 1868, 1993.

Puls, *m.* -es, -e, pulse, pulsation, heart-beat, 2456.

Purpurmantel, *m.* -s, -mäntel, **purple mantle,** 781.

Q.

Qual, *f.* -en, pain, torment, agony, 3249.

quälen, *refl.*, torment *or* harass one's self, worry, 1576.

Qualm, *m.* -s, thick vapor, smoke, fumes, 1446.

Quell, *m.* -es, -e, spring, source, fount(ain), 586.

Quelle, *f.* -n, spring, source, fount-(ain), 1696, 1704.

R.

Rabe, *m.* -n, -n, raven, 2832.

Rache, *f.*, vengeance, revenge, 992, 1463, 2112, *etc.*

Rachegeiſt, *m.* -s, -er, avenging spirit, Fury, 3209.

rächen, *tr.*, avenge, revenge, 992, 2596, 2929, *etc.*

Rächer, *m.* -s, —, avenger, 2175, 2995, 3047, *etc.*

Rachgefühl, *n.* -s, -e, feeling of revenge, revengefulness, 990.

ragen, *intr.*, project, stand out, be prominent, *48, 1382.

Rand, *m.* -es, **Ränder,** edge, verge, brink, 2236.

Rank, *m.* -s, **Ränke,** trick, intrigue, 1669. *Now used only in plural.*

Rappersweil. Rappersweil, now Rapperschwyl, town in the Canton St. Gallen on the northern shore of Lake Zürich near its eastern end. *The Counts von Rappersweil are mentioned in l.* 1361.

raſch, *adj.*, quick, swift, **rash,** 470, 484, *78, *etc.*

rafen, *intr.*, rave, rage, 147, 2129, *etc.; pres. part. as adj.*, raving, mad, 2769, *as noun*, madman, 2033.

raftlos, *adj.*, restless, unresting, 1488.

Rat, *m.* -8, **Räte**, advice, counsel, counsellor, council, councillor, 275, 287, 339, 1332, *etc.;* help, what to do, — **wissen**, 2237.

raten, **riet**, **geraten**, **rät**, *tr.* (*dat. of person*), advise, counsel, 141, 301, 685, *etc.*

Rathaus, *n.* -e8, -häuser, town-hall, 1743.

Raub, *m.* -e8, robbery, prey, spoil, 1464, 2497.

rauben, *tr.*, rob, take by force, pillage, 605, 609, 1050, *etc.*

Räuber, *m.* -8, —, robber, 2616, 3165.

Raubtier, *n.* -8, -e, beast of prey, 2165.

Rauch, *m.* -8, smoke, 1422, 2885.

Raum, *m.* -8, **Räume**, room, space, 1914.

räumen, *tr.*, clear, leave, 1430.

rauschen, *intr.* rush, roar, 1554, *etc.; inf. as noun,* *105; rustle, sound, creak, 502.

Rebell, *m.* -en, -en, rebel, 2080.

Rechen, *m.* -8, —, rake, *40.

rechnen, *intr.*, count, reckon, depend, rely, 3230.

Rechnung, *f.* -en, reckoning, account, 1459, 2566.

recht, *adj.*, **right**, straight, true, real, genuine, *58, 1029, 1479, 1739 (respectable), *etc.;* **die Rechte**, right hand, 738, 3288, *etc.;* **zur Rechten**, on the right, *3.

Recht, *n.* -e8, -e, **right**, justice, 309, 488, 702, *etc.;* — **sprechen**, pronounce *or* render justice, 1239, 2760.

rechten, *intr.*, be at law, 1088.

rechtfertigen, *tr. insep.*, justify, vindicate, 3207.

rechtlos, *adj.*, outlawed, 1307.

rechts, *adv.*, on *or* to the **right**, *55, *58, *140, *etc.*

Rede, *f.* -n, speech, talk, words, 148, 250, *etc.;* — **stehen**, answer, give account, 75, 1953; **zur** — **kommen**, be mentioned *or* talked about, 2300.

reden, *intr. and tr.*, speak, talk, 417, 579, 610, *etc.*

redlich, *adj.*, honest, candid, just, 239, 287, *etc.; pl. as noun,* 276; *archaic*, stout, steady, 2248.

Redlichkeit, *f.*, honesty, integrity, 1085.

rege, *adj.*, active, lively, alert, 2435.

regen, *refl.*, stir, move, 677, 2305, 2371.

Regen, *m.* -8, —, rain, 42, 2689.

Regenbogen, *m.* -8, -bögen, rainbow, 975.

Regent', *m.* -en, -en, regent, ruler, 230.

regieren, *tr. and intr.*, reign, rule, govern, guide, 422, 756, 814, *etc.*

Regiment, *n.* –$, –e, power, government, rule, 342, 1014, 1999, *etc.*

reich, *adj.*, rich, *2, 51, 207, *etc.*

Reich, *n.* –es, –e, empire, realm, kingdom, reign, 185, 193, 256, *etc.*

reichen, *tr.*, **reach,** give, extend, *15, 497, *29, 738, *etc.*

reichlich, *adj.*, plentiful, abundant, 345.

Reichsbote, *m.* –n, –n, imperial messenger, *2, *149, 3030.

Reichsfürst, *m.* –en, –en, prince of the empire, 264.

Reichspanier, *n.* –$, –e, **banner** of the empire, 1229.

Reichsvogt, *m.* –$, =vögte, imperial governor, prefect of the empire, *1, *cf. N.*

Reihe, *f.* –n, row, rank, order, line, turn, *40, 1599, *etc.*

Reihen, *m.* –$, —, procession, row, line, 54.

rein, *adj.*, clean, pure, clear, innocent, 968, 1708, 2498, *etc.;* as *adv.*, clear, completely, entirely, 119.

Reis, *n.* –es, –er, twig, 30.

Reisholz, *n.* –es, brushwood, 969.

reisig, *adj.*, travelling, mounted; as *noun*, horseman, trooper, 74, 220, 620, *etc. A poetic word.*

reißen, riß, gerissen, *tr.*, tear, pull, snatch, wrest, 452, 649, 1500, *etc.*

reiten, ritt, geritten, *intr.* [. *and* h., ride, 235, 2670, *etc.;* 220, 2696, *past part.* = *Eng. pres. part.*

Reiter, *m.* –$, —, **rider,** horseman, trooper, *2, 72, 131, *etc.*

Reitersmann, *m.* –$, =männer *or* =leute, horseman, trooper, 1754.

reizen, *tr.*, excite, irritate, provoke, incense, 653, 2010, 2088, *etc.;* charm, *pres. part. as adj.*, 1711.

rennen, rannte, gerannt, *intr.* [. *and* h., run, 448.

Respekt, *m.* –es, respect, 1765.

Rest, *m.* –es, –e, rest, remains, 2465.

retten, *tr.*, rescue, save, 69, 75, 140, *etc.*

Retter, *m.* –$, —, rescuer, savior, deliverer, 154, 182, 1990, *etc.*

Rettung, *f.* –en, rescue, deliverance, 2348.

rettungslos, *adj.*, beyond recovery, irretrievable, 2395.

Rettungsufer, *n.* –$, —, shore of rescue *or* safety, 121.

Reue, *f.*, repentence, 2455.

reuen, *impers. with acc.*, repent, 2775.

Reuethräne, *f.* –n, tear of repentance, 3251.

Reuß, *f.* The river Reuss, bearing this name both south and north of the Lake of the Four Forest Cantons; 1197, 2969, 3242, *etc.*

Reverenz, *f.* –en, bow, **reverence,** 1733, 1820, 1835, *etc.*

Rhein, *m.* -s. The river Rhine; 1329.

Rheinfeld. Rheinfeld, now Rheinfelden, town in the Canton Aargau on the left bank of the Rhine, about ten miles E. of Basel; 1324, 2966.

richten, *tr.*, direct, turn, *98, 2569, *etc.*; *refl.*, straighten *or* raise one's self, *120; judge, 3055.

Richter, *m.* -s, —, judge, 704, 1142, 1217, *etc.*

richterlich, *adj.*, judicial, as judge, 224.

Richterspruch, *m.* -s, -sprüche, sentence, 2751.

Richtmaß, *n.* -es, -e, carpenter's square, "rule and measure," 209.

Riegel, *m.* -s, —, bolt, 506.

Rigiberg, *m.* -s. The Rigi, a group of mountains between the Lake of the Four Forest Cantons, Lake Zug and Lake Lowerz; 2738.

Rind, *n.* -es, -er, ox, cow, *etc.*; *in pl.*, cattle, 203, 898.

Ring, *m.* -es, -e, ring, 1123, *58, *63, *etc.*

ringen, rang, gerungen, *intr.*, struggle, writhe, 2583; *refl.*, struggle, 1511; wring, *13.

rings, *adv. (gen.)*, around, about, 873, 878, 1715; — herum, round about, 2858.

ringsum, *adv.*, round about, 805, 2168.

ringsumher, *adv.*, round about, 826, 1587.

rinnen, rann, geronnen, *intr.* f., run, flow, 1178.

Riß, *m.* -es, -e, rent, gap, 33.

Ritter, *m.* -s, —, knight, 1547, 1599, 1719, *etc.*

Ritterfräulein, *n.* -s, —, noble (young) lady, 938.

Ritterkleidung, *f.*, knight's attire, *40.

ritterlich, *adj.*, knightly, 2024, 2028.

Rittermantel, *m.* -s, -mäntel, knight's mantle *or* cloak, 268.

Ritterpflicht, *f.* -en, knightly duty, 1623.

Ritterwort, *n.* -s, -worte, knightly word, 2064.

roh, *adj.*, rough, rude, 2329.

Rohr, *n.* -es, -e or Röhre, reed, 926.

rollen, *intr. and tr.*, roll, *98, 2761.

Römerkrone, *f.* -n, Roman crown, 1231.

Römerzug, *m.* -s, -züge, procession to Rome, Roman journey, 1134.

Roß, *n.* -es, -e, steed, horse, 2617, 2672, 2764, *etc.*

Roßberg. Rossberg, a castle in Unterwalden, three miles west of Stanz on Lake Alpnach; 77, 130, 547, *etc.*

rosten, *intr.* h. and f., rust, 833.

rostig, *adj.*, rusty, 1024.

rot (*comp.* röter, *superl.* röt(e)st, red, 596, 2171.

ruchtbar, *adj.*, notorious, rumored, known, 101. *Archaic for* rüch=bar.

Rücken, *m.* -8, —, back, 1741, *etc.*; rear, 1814; backing, support, 661, 1843.

rück'springen, sprang, gesprungen, *intr.* s., leap backwards, 1500. *Occurs only in forms written as one word.*

Rudenz. Rudenz, a castle at Flüelen, belonging to the Attinghausen family, from which Ulrich von Rudenz is named; *1, *etc.*

Ruder, *n.* -8, —, oar, 134.

Ruderer, *m.* -8, —, rower, 2231.

Rudolf. Rudolf I von Habsburg, born 1218, Emperor from 1273 until his death in 1291; 3049, 3192, 3263.

Ruf, *m.* -es, -e, call, cry, report, 1010.

rufen, rief, gerufen, *intr. and tr.*, call, cry, summon, 9, 18, 303, *etc.*

Ruffi, *n.* -8, landslide, 2664. *A Swiss word, properly feminine.*

Ruhe, *f.*, rest, repose, quiet, peace, 1395, *71, 1485, *etc.*

ruhen, *intr.*, rest, 2402.

ruhig, *adj.*, at rest, quiet, peaceful, 431, 972, 1112, *etc.*

Ruhm, *m.* -es, fame, renown, glory, 831, 1598, 1677, *etc.*

rühmen, *tr.*, praise, 520, *etc.*; *refl.*, be proud to be, 240, 1136, glory in (*gen.*), 920, boast, 1916, 1936, *etc.*

rühmlich, *adj.*, laudable, glorious, 815.

rühren, *tr.*, stir, move, 789, 1951, *etc.*; beat, *24.

Rui'ne, *f.* -n, ruin, 2426.

Runse, *f.* -n, channel, gully, 1005, *cf. N.*

rüsten, *tr. and refl.*, prepare, equip, arm, 93, 769, 1380, *etc.*

Rütli, *n.* -8. The Rütli *or* Clearing (*a Swiss word*). As proper noun, the traditionally famous clearing on the western shore of the southern arm of the Lake, a little south of Selisberg; 727, 961, 1518, *etc.*

S.

Saal, *m.* -es, Säle, hall, (large) room, *40, 1336.

Sant, *f.* -en, seed, 892.

Sache, *f.* -n, thing, affair, business; cause, 290, 434, 860, *etc.*

säen, *tr.*, sow, 3063, 3081.

sagen, *tr.*, say, tell, 57, 183, 201, *etc.*

Salz, *n.* -es, -e, salt, 1806.

sammeln, *tr.*, collect, gather, 344, 827.

Sammlung, *f.* -en, composure, meditation, devotion, *70.

sanft (*comp.* sänfter, *superl.* sänft(e)st), *adj.*, soft, gentle, mild, *33, 650, 1315, *etc.*; sanft thun, be agreeable, 2712.

Sanft, *indec. adj.,* holy, **saint,** 3233.

Sarnen. Sarnen, chief town of Ob dem Wald or Obwalden, the W. part of Unterwalden, and also name of a castle located there; *1, 558, 624, *etc.*

Sarner, *adj.* Of Sarnen; 2873.

Sasse, *m.* -n, -n, freeholder, inhabitant, tenant, 1401; *in* 1208 *for* Hinterfasse, vassal, bondsman.

Sättigung, *f.,* satisfying, satisfaction, 3014.

sauer, *adj.,* sour, bitter, hard, painful, 1189.

saugen, fog, gesogen, *tr.,* suck, drink in, 990.

Säule, *f.* -n, column, pillar, post, 393.

säumen, *intr.,* delay, linger, tarry, hesitate, 771, 983, 1387, *etc.; inf. as noun,* 2280.

Säumer, *m.* -s, —, driver (of a pack-horse), carrier, 2617.

Saumroß, *n.* -es, -e, pack-horse, sumpter-horse, 875.

Scene, *f.* -n, scene, stage, *3, *5, *etc.; *89, in die — rufend, calling behind the scenes.

Scepter, *n.* -s, —, scepter, 1630, 3020.

Schächen, *m.* -s. The river Schächen, flowing from the east into the Reuss at Bürglen; 1554, *163.

Schächenthal, *n.* -s. Schächen valley; 1550, 3107.

Schädel, *m.* -s, —, skull, 1760.

Schade(n), *m.* -ns, -n, damage, harm, injury, 426.

schaden, *intr.,* hurt, injure, do harm, 79, 252, 1543, *etc.*

schädigen, *tr.,* injure, damage, hurt, 84, 1058, 1775, *etc.*

Schaf, *n.* -es, -e, **sheep,** 42, 898.

schaffen, *tr.,* do, accomplish, 148, 281, 2365 *etc.; procure, 1011; convey, produce, take, get, 571, 1526, 2757.

Schaffhausen. Schaffhausen, capitol of the Canton Schaffhausen, on the Rhein, W. of Lake Constance; 2948.

Schaffner, *m.* -s, —, steward, 758.

Schall, *m.* -es, -e, sound, 123, 968.

schallen, scholl *or* schallte, geschollen, geschallt, *intr.* h. *and* f., sound, resound, ring, 2849.

schalten, *intr.,* rule, hold sway, 309.

Scham, *f.,* **shame,** modesty, 2124.

schämen, *refl.,* be ashamed (of, *gen.*), 783, 840.

schänden, *tr.,* disgrace, dishonor, defile, 2026, 2913, 3183.

Schänder, *m.* -s, —, despoiler, violator, 83.

Schändlichkeit, *f.* -en, disgrace, infamy, ignominy, 1257.

Schanze, *f.* -n, **chance,** hazard; in die — schlagen, stake, hazard, 1435.

Schar, *f.* -en, troop, flock, multitude, 203, 2444.

scharf (*comp.* schärfer, *superl.* schärf(e)st), *adj.,* **sharp,** keen, 2250.

ſcharren, *tr.*, scrape, paw, 43.

Schatte(n), *m.* -ns, -n, shadow, *4, 764.

Schatz, *m.* -es, Schätze, treasure, jewel, 1040, 2598.

Schau, *f.* -en, show ; zur — tragen, display, make parade of, 780.

ſchaudern, *intr.*, shudder, 2016, 3217.

ſchauen, *tr.*, look (at), see, behold, 379, 587, 596, *etc.*

ſchauerlich, *adj.*, awful, horrible, 1504.

ſchäumen, *intr.*, foam, 1005, 1790.

Schauplatz, *m.* -es, -plätze, scene, *162.

Schauſpiel, *n.* -s, -e, spectacle, sight, *71; drama, *on facsimile of title-page of 1st ed.*

ſcheel, *adj.*, oblique, awry, envious, jealous, 270.

Scheibe, *f.* -n, disk, target, 1939.

ſcheiden, ſchied, geſchieden, *tr.*, separate, divide, part, 1158, *etc.; intr.* ſ., part, depart, leave, 15, 953, *etc.;* dahin —, decease, die, 2462.

Schein, *m.* -es, shine, light, appearance(s), pretext, 306, 310, 1635, *etc.*

ſcheinen, ſchien, geſchienen, *intr.*, shine, seem, appear, 2200.

ſchellen, *intr.* (*and tr.*), ring, 1749.

ſchelten, ſchalt, geſcholten, ſchilt, *tr.*, scold, chide, call (derisively), 98, 825.

ſchenken, *tr.*, give, grant, present, 930, 1250, 1610, *etc.*

Scherz, *m.* -es, -e, jest, joke, fun, 2717.

ſcherzen, *intr.*, jest, 1910, 1913.

ſcheu, *adj.*, shy, timid, fearful, *153.

ſcheuen, *tr.*, fear, shun, 1093, 1544.

Scheune, *f.* -n, barn, 203.

ſchicken, *tr. and intr.*, send, 2373, 2711.

Schickſal, *n.* -s, -e, fate, destiny, lot, 327, 1935.

Schickſalsprobe, *f.* -n, trial *or* test of fate *or* destiny, 2901.

Schickung, *f.* -en, dispensation, providence, 2322.

Schieferdecker, *m.* -s, —, slate-layer, roofer, *21, 447.

ſchielen, *intr.*, squint, glance furtively, 2249.

ſchießen, ſchoß, geſchoſſen, *tr. and intr.*, shoot, 1480, 1876, 1886, *etc.*

Schießzeug, *n.* -es, shooting implements, bow and quiver, 2249, 2264.

Schiff, *n.* -es, -e, ship, boat, 424, 2073, 2162, *etc.*

Schiffbruch, *m.* -s, -brüche, shipwreck, 433.

ſchiffen, *intr.*, embark, sail, 1530.

Schiffer, *m.* -s, —, boatman, 132.

Schifflein, *n.* -s, —, little ship *or* boat, 166, 2267.

Schild, *n.* -es, -er, shield, 833, 862.

Schildwache, *f.* -n, sentinel, guard, 1755.

Schimmer, *m.* -s, —, shimmer, glimmer, gleam, 601.

Schimpf, *m.* -es, -e, insult, disgrace, 1754.

Schirm, *m.* -es, -e, shelter, protection, defense, 662, 884, 1031, *etc.*

schirmen, *tr.*, shelter, protect, defend, 186, 695, 1057, *etc.*

Schirmer, *m.* -s, —, protector, 2453.

Schlacht, *f.* -en, battle, 757, 910, 1229, *etc.*

Schlachtschwert, *n.* -s, -er, battle-sword, broad-sword, *58.

Schlaf, *m.* -es, sleep, 2306, 2380.

Schläfer, *m.* -s, —, sleeper, 11.

Schlagbaum, *m.* -s, =bäume, toll-bar, 901.

schlagen, schlug, geschlagen, schlägt, *tr.*, beat, strike, smite, 315, 482, 568, *etc.*; cast, throw, 781, 1435, 2338, *etc.*; *intr.*, strike, beat, *63, 1683, 2166, *etc.*; *refl.*, fight *or* make one's way, 1174, 1484.

Schlaglawi'ne, *f.* -n, (stroke)-avalanche, sliding avalanche, 1781, *cf. N., l.* 1501, *and appendix.*

Schlange, *f.* -n, serpent, 429.

schlecht, *adj.*, bad, low, base, 361, 1737.

schleichen, schlich, geschlichen (*intr.* s. *and*) *refl.*, sneak, slink, steal, 1100.

schlendern, *intr.*, lounge, loiter, be slow, 356.

schleppen, *refl.*, drag one's self along, 366.

schleudern, *tr.*, sling, hurl, dash, 2267.

schleunig, *adj.*, quick, swift, 2379.

Schlich, *m.* -es, -e, secret path, by-way, 711.

schlicht, *adj.*, plain, simple, 1238.

schlichten, *tr.*, adjust, settle, 1137, 1291.

schließen, schloß, geschlossen, *tr.*, close, end, conclude, make, *48, *92, *105, *etc.*

schlimm, *adj.*, bad, evil, 2270.

Schlinge, *f.* -n, loop, noose, snare, 1723.

Schloß, *n.* -es, -össer, lock, 506, *etc.*; castle, stronghold, 457, 708, *etc.*

schlummern, *intr.*, slumber, 1644.

Schlund, *m.* -es, Schlünde, throat, gorge, chasm, abyss, 423, 2138, 2230, *etc.*

Schluß, *m.* -es, Schlüsse, conclusion, determination, 3207.

Schmach, *f.*, disgrace, dishonor, ignominy, 412, 1273, 1299, *etc.*

schmachten, *intr.*, languish, pine, 3112.

schmeicheln, *intr.* (*dat.*), flatter, caress, 1293, 2712.

Schmelz, *m.* -es, enamel, 595.

Schmerz, *m.* -es, *or* -ens, *acc.* Schmerz, *pl.*, -en, pain, grief, sorrow, 588, 622.

schmerzen, *tr.*, pain, grieve, 824.

Schmerzenspfeil, *m.* -s, -e, painful *or* wounding arrow, 2815.

Schmerzenssehnsucht, *f.*, painful longing, 846.

ſchmerzlich, adj., painful, 669.

ſchmerzzerriſſen, part adj., torn or rent with pain, grief-distracted, 2318.

Schmid, m. -es, -e, smith, *1, 1140.

ſchmieden, tr., forge, 1272, 1626.

ſchmiegen, reſl., cling, *104.

ſchmuck, adj., trim, pretty, sleek, 50.

ſchmücken, tr., adorn, decorate, 1714.

Schnecke, f. -n, snail, 356.

Schneegebirg(e), n. -(e)s, -e, snow-capped mountain-range, *84.

ſchneiden, ſchnitt, geſchnitten, tr. and intr., cut, 477.

ſchnell, adj., quick, swift, 192, 222, 227, etc.; rash, violent, 422, cf. N.

ſchon, adv., already, even, surely, no doubt, 71, 196, *21, etc.

ſchön, adj., beautiful, handsome, fine, fair, noble, 49, 53, 208, etc.

ſchonen, tr. and intr. (with gen.), spare, save, regard, 322, 588, 1432, etc.

ſchöpfen, tr., draw, obtain, get, 1218.

Schöpfung, f. -en, creation, 1049.

Schöpfungstag, m. -s, -e, day of creation, 2145.

Schoß, m. -es, Schöße, lap, bosom, 1105, 2492, 2987, etc.

Schranke, f. -n, bar, limit, bound, 1372.

ſchrecken, tr., frighten, alarm, terrify, 1512, 1989, 2572, etc.

Schrecken, m. -s, —, fright, horror, terror, *94, 2990, 3129, etc.

Schreckensſtraße, f. -n, way or road of horror, 3252.

Schreckhorn, n. -s. Schreckhorn, a famous peak of the Bernese Alps; 628.

ſchrecklich, adj., fearful, horrible, 1320; superl. neut. as noun, 3178.

Schrecknis, n. -niſſes, -niſſe, horror, horrible thing, 314, 2813, 3216, etc.

Schreiben, n. -s, —, writing, letter, 3030.

ſchreien, ſchrie, geſchrieen, intr. (and tr.), cry, shout, *91, 1852, etc.; pres. part. as adj., crying, flagrant, outrageous, 1840.

ſchreiten, ſchritt, geſchritten, intr. ſ., stride, step, 27, etc.; past part. for Eng. pres. part., 1562.

Schritt, m. -es, -e, step, pace, 1877, 1883, 1915, etc.

ſchroff, adj., steep, precipitous, 1553, *105, 2159, etc.

Schuld, f. -en, debt, guilt, fault, 584, 1461, 1925, etc.

ſchuldig, adj., indebted, — bleiben, owe, leave unpaid, 2476; guilty, masc. as noun, 2184.

Schulter, f. -n, shoulder, *4, 781.

Schurke, m. -n, -n, wretch, villain, knave, 1761, 1852.

ſchürzen, tr., tie, tuck, gird, 2615.

Schuß, m. -es, Schüſſe, shot, 1888, 1984, 1986, etc.

ſchütteln, tr., shake, *21, *55.

Schutz, m. -es, Schütze, protection, shelter, defense 1214, 2158, etc.;

ȝu **Sᴄ͑uẗ uⁿⅆ Ⅎʳuẗ,** for offense and defense, 742, 1484.

Sᴄ͑üẗ(e), *m.* -eⁿ, -eⁿ, shooter, archer, hunter, 26, 1468, 1473, *etc.*

fᴄ͑üẗeⁿ, *tr.*, protect, shelter, defend, 490, 880, 1808, *etc.*

Sᴄ͑üẗeⁿregeⅼ, *f.* -ⁿ, rule *or* maxim of the archer, 2645.

Sᴄ͑waᵬeⁿ. Schwaben *or* Swabia; *2.

fᴄ͑wäᵬifᴄ͑, *adj.*, Swabian, 1329.

fᴄ͑waᴄ͑, (*comp.* fᴄ͑wäᴄ͑er, *superl.* fᴄ͑wäᴄ͑ft),ₐ *adj.*, weak, feeble. 152, *etc.; superl. masc. as noun,* 328; *pl. masc. as noun,* 436; *masc. sing. as noun,* 2675.

Sᴄ͑wäᵫer, *m.* -ᵬ, —, father-in-law, 2294.

fᴄ͑waⁿeⁿ, *intr. impers. (with dat.),* forebode, 501.

fᴄ͑waⁿt, *adj.*, flexible, swaying, slender, 926, 1416.

fᴄ͑waⁿteⁿ, *intr.*, stagger, reel, toss, 166, *100.

Sᴄ͑warm, *m.* -eᵬ, Sᴄ͑wärme, swarm, 2671.

fᴄ͑warȝ (*comp.* fᴄ͑wärȝer, *superl.* fᴄ͑wärȝeft), *adj.*, black, 1101, 1193, *etc.; neut. as noun,* black spot, bull's eye, 1939, 2646.

Sᴄ͑warȝe Berg, ⅆer. The Black Mountain = the Brünig; 1193.

fᴄ͑weᵬeⁿ, *intr.*, hover, hang, 2236.

fᴄ͑weigeⁿ, fᴄ͑wieg, gefᴄ͑wiegeⁿ, *intr.*, be *or* keep silent, *14, 196, *15, *etc.; inf. as noun,* silence, 420.

Sᴄ͑weiȝ, *f.*, Switzerland; 512, 1611.

Sᴄ͑weiȝer, *m.* -ᵬ, —, Swiss, 537, 749, 1210, *etc.*

Sᴄ͑weiȝeriⁿ, *f.* -iⁿⁿeⁿ, Swiss woman, 3289.

fᴄ͑weⅼgeⁿ, *intr.*, carouse, revel, 1063, 2655.

Sᴄ͑weⅼⅼe, *f.* -ⁿ, threshold, 509, 523, 3193.

fᴄ͑wer, *adj.*, heavy, difficult, hard, grave, great, grievous, 104, 418, 473, *etc.; neut. as noun,* 190, 545, 1523, 2744.

fᴄ͑werᵬeⅼaⅆeⁿ, *part. adj.*, heavy-laden, 2617.

Sᴄ͑wert, *n.* -eᵬ, -er, sword, 1024, 1124, 1133, *etc.*

Sᴄ͑wefter, *f.* -ⁿ, sister, 241.

Sᴄ͑weferfoᴎⁿ, *m.* -ᵬ, ₌föᴎⁿe, sister's son, nephew, 1073.

fᴄ͑wimmeⁿ, fᴄ͑wamm, gefᴄ͑wom₌ meⁿ, *intr.* ᴎ. *and* f., swim; *impers.*, 1983, my head swims.

Sᴄ͑wimmer, *m.* -ᵬ, —, swimmer, 165.

fᴄ͑wiⁿⅆ(e)ⅼiᴄ͑t, *adj.*, dizzy, making dizzy, 26.

fᴄ͑wiⁿgeⁿ, fᴄ͑waⁿg, gefᴄ͑wuⁿgeⁿ, *tr.*, swing, brandish, wave, 645, 1737, 2907, *etc.; refl.*, swing one's self, leap, 2264.

fᴄ͑wöreⁿ, fᴄ͑wor *and* fᴄ͑wur, ge₌ fᴄ͑woreⁿ, *tr. and intr.*, swear, take an oath, vow, 184, 271, 572, *etc.*

Sᴄ͑wuⁿg, *m.*-eᵬ, Sᴄ͑wüⁿge, swing, flight, strain, movement, *71.

Schwur, *m.* -eš, Schwüre, oath, 933, 2399, 2480.

Schwyz. Schwyz, the Canton and its capitol, east of the Lake of the Four Forest Cantons; *1, *3, *etc.*

Schwyzer, *adj.*, belonging to the canton Schwyz *or* Switz, Swiss *or* Switz, 1201; *as noun,* Switzer *or* Swiss, 254, 658.

Schwyzerland, *n.* -eš, -e, land of Schwyz, Canton Schwyz, 967; Swiss canton, 3038, *cf. N.*

sechš, *num.,* six, *40, *139.

sechst, *num. adj.,* sixth, *2750.

See, *m.* -š, -n, lake, *3, 1, 109, *etc.*

Seele, *f.* -n, soul, 236, 477, 823, *etc.*

Segen, *m.* -š, —, blessing, 1800, 2378.

segenvoll, *adj.,* blessed, rich with blessing, 3017.

segnen, *tr.,* bless, 202, 2384, *etc.;* 97, " I blessed his bath for him," *an ironical phrase.*

sehen, sah, gesehen, sieht, *tr. and intr.,* see, perceive, look, *3, 109, 115, *etc.; inf. as noun,* sight, seeing, 586.

Seher, *m.* -š, —, seer, prophet, *121.

sehnen, *refl.,* long, yearn, 843; *inf. as noun,* longing, yearning, 1675.

sehr, *adv.,* very, much, greatly, 486.

Seide, *f.* -n, silk, 779.

Seil, *n.* -eš, -e, rope, cord, 934.

sein, war, gewesen, bin, *intr.* f., be, exist, *3, 10, 16, *etc.;* 2958, wie dem auch sei, however that may be.

sein, *adj.,* his, its, *1, *4, 85, *etc.; pl. as noun,* his people *or* family *or* friends, 1614, 2982, 3066; *neut. as noun,* his territory *or* land, 2982.

seit, *prep.* (*dat.*), since, for, 528, 629, 1248, *etc.; conj.,* since.

seitdem, *adv.,* since, since then, 1199; *conj.,* since, 1736.

Seite, *f.* -n, side, *21, *26, *27, *etc.*

seitwärts, *adv.,* sideways, 2249.

selbander, *pron.,* with one other, together, 2894.

selber, *indec. adj.* (*following noun or pron.*), self, 352, 366, 544, *etc.*

selbst, *indec. adj.* (*following noun or pron.*), self, 119, 139, 262, *etc.;* von —, of one's own accord, 430; für sich —, by itself, 1159; *adv.,* even, 1207.

Selbstherr, *m.* -n, -en, one's own master, 856.

selig, *adj.,* blissful, blessed, happy, 7, 1688, 1700, *etc.*

Selisberg. Selisberg, a mountain and a village on the western shore of the southern arm of the Lake of the Four Forest Cantons; 965.

selten, *adj.,* rare, curious, 2626; *adv.,* rarely, seldom.

seltsam, *adj.,* strange, peculiar, odd, 977, *105, *etc.; neut. as noun,* 1906.

senden, sandte *or* sendete, gesandt *or* gesendet, *tr.,* send, 316, 471, 707, *etc.*

Senn(e), *m.* -en, -en, herdsman, 15, 63. [1006.

Sennhütte, *f.* -n, herdsman's hut,

Sense, *f.* -n, scythe, *40.

Sente, *f.* -n, herd, 2653.

setzen, *tr.,* set, put, 375, *etc.;* stake, risk, 905, 2331, 2891; *refl.,* sit down, *14, 515, *etc.*

Sewa. Sewa, really a town in the Canton Schwyz at the eastern end of Lake Lowerz, but located by Schiller indefinitely in Unterwalden.

sich, *indec. refl. pron., 3rd pers. sing. or pl., dat. or acc.,* himself, herself, itself, themselves; one another, each other; *corresponding to* Sie, yourself, yourselves; *3, 19, *4, *etc.*

sicher, *adj.,* secure, safe, sure, certain, 141, 435, 496, *etc.*

Sicherheit, *f.* -en, security, safety, 613, 710, 2274, *etc.*

sichern, *tr.,* secure, assure, 2056, 2058, 2063.

sichtbar, *adj.,* visible, evident, 2071, 2271.

sie, *pron.,* she, it, they; Sie (*with pl. verb*), you; *frequent.*

Sieg, *m.* -es, -e, victory, 2521, 2556, 2912, *etc.*

siegberühmt, *adj.,* victory-famed, 1600.

siegen, *intr.,* conquer, triumph, 2446.

Sieger, *m.* -s, —, conqueror, victor, 309, 1206.

Signalfeuer, *n.* -s, —, signal-fire, *140.

Sigrist, *m.* -en, -en, sacristan, sexton, *1, 1096, 1749, *etc.*

Sillinen. Sillinen, now Silenen, town and castle some distance south of Altorf, on the right bank of the Reuss; 685.

Simon und Judä (Tag). St. Simon's and St. Jude's day, i.e. Oct. 28th; 146.

singen, sang, gesungen, *tr. and intr.,* sing, chant, *3, *72, *139, *etc.*

sinken, sank, gesunken, *intr.* s., sink, fall, 1564, *98, *100, *etc.*

Sinn, *m.* -es, -e *or* -en, sense, mind, meaning, 213, 342, 637, *etc.;* bei Sinnen, in one's senses, in one's right mind, 138.

sinnen, sann, gesonnen, *tr. and intr.,* think, meditate, intend, plan, 1516, 3118.

Sitte, *f.* -n, custom, habit, manner, morals, 338, 841, 951, etc.

Sitz, *m.* -es, -e, seat, residence, 1236, 1263.

sitzen, saß, gesessen, *intr.,* sit, 217, *etc.;* have one's seat, live, 77, 130, 1081, *etc.*

Sklave, *m.* -n, -n, slave, 1302, 1604.

sklavisch, *adj.,* slavish, 3203.

so, *adv. and conj.,* so, as, thus, then, therefore, 4, 48, 51, *etc.;* 2731, so oder so, this way or that way, whether one will or not; 2755, as *or* if.

soeben, *adv.*, just, just now, 521, 980.

sogleich, *adv.*, immediately, forthwith, 1123, 2074.

Sohn, *m.* -es, Söhne, son, 267, 486, 565, *etc.*

solang(e), *conj.*, so long as, 540.

solcher (solche, solches), *adj.*, *and pron.*, such, 330, 374, 527, *etc.*

Söldner, *m.* -s, —, (mercenary) soldier, *2.

sollen, sollte, gesollt, soll, *intr. and modal aux.*, shall, should, ought, be to, be intended *or* destined to, be said to, 135, 137, 178, *etc.*

Sommer, *m.* -s, —, summer, 16.

sondern, *conj.* (*after neg.*) but, 255.

Sonne, *f.* -n, sun, 587, 609, 759, *etc.*; *gen. sing.* -n, 1107.

Sonnenschein, *m.* -s, sunshine, *3.

sonnenscheu, *adj.*, sun-shunning, light-fearing, 1102.

sonnig, *adj.*, sunny, 14.

sonst, *adv.*, else, otherwise, in other respects, formerly, once, 522, 755, 1082, *etc.*

Sorge, *f.* -n, care, anxiety, 533, 2826.

sorgen, *intr.*, fear, care, take care, 368, 1095, 1443, *etc.*; provide, 3066.

sorgenvoll, *adj.*, full of cares, anxious, 2614.

Sorgfalt, *f.*, care, attention, *115.

Späher, *m.* -s, —, spy, 460.

spannen, *tr.*, stretch, bend, draw, 644, *98, 1996, *etc.*; fasten, harness; *with* von *or* aus, unyoke, 478, 567.

Spannung, *tr.*, -en, tension, attention, excitement, suspense, *32, *98.

sparen, *tr.*, spare, save, reserve, 1463, 2548.

spät, *adj.*, late, remote, 2039, 2915.

Speer, *m.* -es, -e, spear, 2979.

sperren, *tr.*, shut, close, bar, 2777, 2991.

Spiegel, *m.* -s, —, mirror, 972.

Spiel, *n.* -es, -e, play, sport, game, gambling, 406, 2331, 2603, *etc.*

spielen, *tr.*, play, 812, *72, 1923, *etc.*

Spielmann, *m.* -s, =männer *or* =leute, player, musician, minstrel, 2616.

Spieß, *m.* -es, -e, spear, lance, pike, 1848.

spinnen, spann, gesponnen, *tr.*, spin, plot, 242, 1106, 1517, *etc.*

Spitze, *f.* -n, point, top, peak, *3.

spitzen, *tr.*, point, sharpen; prick up, 60.

spitzig, *adj.*, pointed, sharp, 577, 1405.

Spott, *m.* -es, mockery, scorn, 824.

spotten, *intr.* (*with gen.*), mock, deride, scorn, 625.

Sprache, *f.* -n, language, 2021.

sprechen, sprach, gesprochen, spricht, *tr. and intr.*, speak, say, talk, 102, 150, 237, *etc.*; (*with acc. of pers.*), speak with, 2308, 2669.

ſprengen, *tr.*, **spring**, burst, shatter, 1268, 2860.

ſpringen, ſprang, geſprungen, *intr.* ſ. *and* h., **spring**, leap, jump, run, 44, *12, *etc.; past part. for Eng. pres. part.*, *72, *101.

Spruch, *m.* –es, Sprüche, saying, maxim, sentence, judgment, 212, 1934, 3055, *etc.*

Sprung, *m.* –es, Sprünge, **spring**, leap, jump, 329.

ſpülen, *intr.*, wash, play about, 8.

Spur, *f.* –en, trace, track, vestige, sign, 1240, 1550, 2410, *etc.*

ſpurlos, *adj.*, leaving no trace, 426.

ſtaatsklug, *adj.*, diplomatic, politic, 1373.

Stab, *m.* –es, Stäbe, **staff**, stick, rod, *21, 469, 606, *etc.*

Stachel, *m.* –s, –n, sting, goad, 1052, 2675.

Stadt, *f.* Städte, city, town, 32, 883, 1328, *etc.*

Stahl, *m.* –es, Stähle, steel, 577.

Stall, *m.* –es, Ställe, stable, 206.

Stallmeiſter, *m.* –s, —, equerry, master of the horse, *2.

Stamm, *m.* –es, Stämme, **stem**, trunk, lineage, race, 337, 861, 889, *etc.*

Stammholz, *n.* –es, =hölzer, timber, trunk-wood, 208.

Stand, *m.* –es, Stände, **stand**, state, condition, rank, class, 1085, 1141, 1428 (resistance, struggle, trouble), *etc.;* estate, state, canton, district, 2992.

Stange, *f.* –n, pole, *23, *84, 1736, *etc.*

Stanz. Stanz, now Stans, capitol of Nid dem Wald or Nidwalden, the E. part of Unterwalden; 1196.

ſtark (*comp.* ſtärker, *superl.* ſtär= k(e)ſt), *adj.*, strong, 924, *etc.;* *masc. as noun*, 437; *comp. pl. as noun*, 1842.

ſtärken, *tr.*, 3103; *refl.*, be strengthened, 1165.

ſtarr, *adj.*, stiff, rigid, stubborn, 1049, 2782.

Statt, *f.*, place, **stead**, 230, 1866, 2754.

ſtatt, *prep.* (*gen., inf. and substantive clause*), **instead of**, 604, 1109 1797, *etc.*

Stätte, *f.* –n, place, 3138.

ſtattlich, *adj.*, stately, 1561.

Statur', *f.* –en, stature, *40.

Staub, *m.* –es, dust, 2402, 2518, 2773, *etc.*

Staubbach, *m.* –s, =bäche, brook falling in spray, *78, *cf. N.*

ſtäuben, *intr.*, scatter spray, be in spray, 3255, *cf. N.*

ſtechen, ſtach, geſtochen, ſticht, *tr. and intr.*, prick, sting, bite, prompt, 429, 1770.

ſtecken, *tr.*, **stick**, put, set, fix, 1406, *98, 2049, *etc.*

Steg, *m.* –es, –e, foot-plank, bridge, path, 25, 1269, *163.

ſtehen, ſtand, geſtanden, *intr.* h. (*or* ſ.), **stand**, be, 207, 569, 1767, *etc.;* (*with dat.*), become, suit, 53; Rede —, answer, give account, 75; ſtehenden Fußes, instantly, 333; zu . . . ſtehen, stand with or by, 919, 1653, 1726; *pret. subj.*, ſtünde, 1718, 2025.

ſteifen, *refl.*, be stiff, 871.

Steig, *m.* -es, -e, path, *48.

ſteigen, ſtieg, geſtiegen, *intr.* ſ., rise, ascend, mount, go, go down, descend, *4, *12, *21, *etc.*

ſteil, *adj.*, steep, 2255.

Stein, *m.* -es, -e, stone, rock, 359, 670, 2609, *etc.*

Stein. Stein, a castle at Baden; 2965, *cf. N. l.* 409.

Steinen. Steinen, a village in the Canton Schwyz, a little north of Lake Lowerz; *14, 556, 2283.

ſteinern, *adj.*, of stone, stony, 2161.

Steinmetz, *m.* -en, -en, stone-mason, *2, *21.

Stelle, *f.* -n, place, spot, 571, 2759.

ſtellen, *tr.*, place, put, station, 1652; *refl.*, place one's self, take one's stand, *14, *55, *etc.*; stand at bay, 647.

Stellung, *f.* -en, position, *101.

ſterben, ſtarb, geſtorben, ſtirbt, *intr.* ſ., die, 326, 597, 1898, *etc.*; *masc. pres. part. as noun*, *138.

Stern, *m.* -es, -e, star, 1148, *etc.*; pupil (of the eye), 641, 674.

Sternenhimmel, *m.* -s, —, starry sky or firmament, 1154.

ſtets, *adv.*, steadily, constantly, always, 487, 761, 1198, *etc.*

Steuer, *n.* -s, —, helm, rudder, 2155.

Steuerleute, *pl.*, helmsmen, pilots, 2237.

Steuermann, *m.* -s, =männer or =leute, steersman, helmsman, 161 (boatman), 2185, 2195, *etc.*

ſteuern, *intr.*, steer, sail, make headway, 110, 2240.

ſteuern, *intr.*, pay taxes or tribute, 1361, 1362, *etc.*

Steuerruder, *n.* -s, —, steering oar, helm, 1988, 2226, 2248, *etc.*

Steu(e)rer, *m.* -s, —, steerer, helmsman, 2155.

Stier, *m.* -es, -e, bull, ox, *2, 2847.

ſtiften, *tr.*, found, establish, institute, 1154.

Stifter, *m.* -s, —, founder, 3083.

ſtill, *adj.*, still, quiet, silent, unexpressed, secret, 198, 249, 287, *etc.*; im ſtillen, quietly, secretly, 1457.

Stille, *f.* stillness, silence, *92.

ſtillen, *tr.*, still, quench, 1004.

Stillſchweigen, *n.* -s, silence, *93.

ſtillſtehen, ſtand ſtill, ſtillgeſtanden, *sep. intr.* h. or ſ., stand still, stop, 763.

Stimme, *f.* -n, voice, 5, 123, 563, *etc.*; vote, *69.

ſtimmen, *intr.*, vote, agree, suit, 1146, 2657.

Stirne, *f.* -n, forehead, brow, front, 197, 2123, 2760.

ſtolz, *adj.*, proud, haughty, 780, 845, 850.

Stolz, *m.* -es, pride, 812, 920, 2329.

stören, *tr.*, disturb, destroy, 1398.

stoßen, stieß, gestoßen, stößt, *tr. and intr.*, thrust, push, hit, strike, 480, 1303, 2723, *etc.*

Strafe, *f.* -n, punishment, penalty, 472, 2745.

strafen, *tr.*, punish, 2596.

sträflich, *adj.*, punishable, culpable, 464.

straflos, *adj.*, unpunished, with impunity, 2595.

Strahl, *m.* -s, -en, beam, ray, flash, gleam, 2393, 2429, 2558 (bolt).

Strang, *m.* -es, Stränge, cord, string, 1478, 2605.

Straße, *f.* -n, way, road, highway, 2283, 2619, 2733, *etc.*

Strauß, *m.* -es, -e, *and* Sträuße, struggle, combat, 1077.

streben, *intr.*, strive, aspire, 948, *etc.; inf. as noun*, striving, aspiration, 1676, 1681.

Strebepfeiler, *m.* -s, —, buttress, 385.

strecken, *tr.*, stretch, 1663.

Streich, *m.* -s, -e, stroke, blow, 1772.

Streit, *m.* -es, -e, fight, dispute, conflict, strife, 1218, 1425, 2713, *etc.*

Streitaxt, *f.* -äxte, battle-axe, 645.

streiten, stritt, gestritten, *intr.*, fight, contend, dispute, 488, 895, 1129, *etc.*

streng, *adj.*, strict, stern, severe, hard, *79, 2593, 2997.

Strenge, *f.*, strictness, severity, rigor, 1596, 1995, 2637.

streuen, *tr.*, strew, scatter, 892, 1713.

Strich, *m.* -es, -e, line, track, direction, 1018.

Strick, *m.* -es, -e, cord, rope, 2218; snare, 997.

Stroh, *n.* -es, straw, 1036.

Strom, *m.* -es, Ströme, stream, flood, current, river, 697, 1682, 1788, *etc.*

stumm, *adj.*, dumb, mute, silent, 2125, *121, *163.

Stunde, *f.* -n, hour, time, 149, 949, 1705, *etc.*

Sturm, *m.* -es, Stürme, storm, 41, 110, 133, *etc.*

stürzen, *intr.* ſ., fall, tumble, rush, *19, 447, *32, *etc.; tr.*, overthrow, hurl down, 387, *etc.;* cast, hurl, plunge, 797, 1642; *refl.*, cast one's self, rush, plunge, 137, *etc.*

stützen, *tr.*, support, *58.

suchen, *tr.* (*and intr.*), seek, look for, want, 95, 175, 424, *etc.*

Sumpf, *m.* -es, Sümpfe, swamp, 1076, 1265.

Sumpfesluft, *f.* -lüfte, air of the swamp, 2358.

Sünde, *f.* -n, sin, 3222.

Sündflut, *f.*, deluge, 2148.

Surenen. Suren'nen, usually Súr(ĕ)nen, a mountain ridge and

pass between Uri and Unterwalden, leading from Altorf to Engelberg; 998.

füß, *adj.*, sweet, 4.

T.

Tabel, *m.* -ß, —, blame, reproach, 2334.

Tafel, *f.* -n, table, 1063.

Tag, *m.* -es, -e, day, 196, 298, 745, *etc.*; diet, assembly, 1145.

Tagdieb, *m.* -ß, -e, day-thief, time-thief, idler, 358, *cf. N.*

tagelang, *adv.*, for days, 2636.

tagen, *intr.*, dawn, be day, 751.

tagen, *intr.*, assemble, meet, hold a diet, 1111, 1117, 1439.

Tagesanbruch, *m.* -ß, =brüche, break of day, dawn, *140.

Tagesordnung, *m.* -en, order of the day, 1314.

Tagewerk, *n.* -ß, -e, day's work, daily task, 829.

tapfer, *adj.*, brave, valiant, 326, 3027, 3285.

tauchen, *intr.*, dive, 45.

taumeln, *intr.*, reel, stagger, 2787.

täuschen, *tr.*, delude, deceive, 720.

tausend, *num.*, thousand, 1695.

tausendjährig, *adj.*, of a thousand years, 1270.

tausendmal, *adv.*, a thousand times, 2321.

Tegerfeld(en). Konrad von Tegerfeld, friend and accomplice of

Herzog Johannes von Schwaben; 1339, 2961.

Teil, *m.* (*or n.*), -es, -e, part, lot, share; zu teil werden, fall to the lot of (*dat.*), be given to, 1135.

teilen, *tr.*, part, divide, share, have in common, 754, 1388, 2407, 3183, *etc.*

teilhaft, *adj.* (*with gen.*), partaking of, sharing, participant in, 2084.

teilhaftig, *adj.* (*with gen.*), partaking of, sharing, participant in, 2413.

teu(e)r, *adj.*, dear, precious, beloved, 508, 922, 1040, *etc.*; 3184, *superl. neut. as subst.*

Teufel, *m.* -ß, —, devil, 174, *as exclam.*

teuflisch, *adj.*, devilish, diabolical, fiendish, 2581.

Teufelsmünster. Teufelsmünster (*lit.* Devil's Minster), a perpendicular rock on the western shore of the Lake, a little south of Selisberg; 2188.

Teu(e)rung, *f.* -en, dearth, famine, 1168.

Thal, *n.* -es, Thäler, valley, 303, 836, 853, *etc.*

Thalgrund, *m.* -es, =gründe, bottom of a valley, valley, *163.

Thalvogt, *m.* -es, =vögte, governor *or* lord of the valley, 38, (*a personification of driving clouds*).

That, *f.* -en, deed, act, action, fact, 101, 419, 420, *etc.*

Thäter, *m.* -8, —, doer, author, perpetrator, 2950, 3043.

Thor, *n.* -8, -e, gate, gateway, 902, 1409, 1513, *etc.*

thöricht, *adj.*, foolish, 1724.

Thräne, *f.* -n, tear, *33, 842, 1038, *etc.*

Thron, *m.* -e8, -e, throne, 409.

thun, that, gethan, *tr. and intr.*, do, make, act, 80, 98, 136, 138, *etc.*

Thür(e), *f.* -en, door, 502, 506, 607, *etc.*

Thurgau. Thurgau, the Canton, formerly much larger than now; 2432.

tief, *adj.*, deep, low, far, 35, 377, 823, *etc.*

Tiefe, *f.* -n, depth, deep, 9, 117, *etc.;* background (of the stage), *24, *51, *etc.*

Tier, *n.* -e8, -e, animal, beast, brute, 57, 478, 2569, *etc.*

Tiger, *m.* -8, —, tiger, 1061.

toben, *intr.*, rage, struggle violently, 1958.

Tochter, *f.*, Töchter, daughter, *2, 240, 517, *etc.*

Tod, *m.* -e8, -e *and* Todesfälle, death, 69, 73, 91, *etc.;* am Tode, at the point of death, 2115.

Todfeind, *m.* -e8, -e, mortal enemy, 2643.

Ton, *m.* -e8, Töne, sound, tone, strain, *32, *121, *139, *etc.*

tosen, *intr.*, rage, roar, 2137; *inf. as subst.*, *105.

tot, *adj.*, dead, 2122, *etc.; masc. as subst.*, 2304, *122, *139.

töten, *tr.*, kill, put to death, 106, 1264, 1931, *etc.*

Totenhand, *f.*, -hände, 2467, beine kalte Totenhand, thy hand cold in death.

Trachten, *n.* -8, (*inf. as subst.*), endeavor, desire, disposition, 1869.

tragen, trug, getragen, trägt, *tr.*, bear, carry, endure, 192, *21, *etc.;* hold (in fief), 263, 1359; have, entertain, cherish, 548, 3042.

trauen, *intr.* (*dat. or* auf *and acc.*), trust, rely on, 1452, 1810.

trauern, *intr.*, mourn, sorrow, 1716, 2471.

traulich, *adj.*, familiar, cordial, 783.

träumen, *tr.*, dream, 1691.

Träumer, *m.* -8, —, dreamer, visionary, 1904.

traun, *interj.*, faith! forsooth!, 1758.

traurig, *adj.*, sad, sorrowful, 1336.

treffen, traf, getroffen, trifft, *tr.*, hit, 1882, 1888, 1917, *etc.*

trefflich, *adj.*, excellent, choice, 467; *masc. as subst.*, 2337.

Treib. Treib, the landing-place just north of Selisberg; 721, *cf. N.* *3.

treiben, trieb, getrieben, *tr.*, drive, urge on, impel, *21, 367, 468; (*with* Herde *or* Kühe *as obj. understood*), 62, 540;; carry (on), make, do, 406, 541, 723, *etc.;* *intr.* h. *and* f., drive about, drift, 2208, 2268.

trennen, *tr. and refl.*, separate, part, 1295, 1449, 2972, *etc.*

treten, trat, getreten, tritt, *intr.* f. *and* h., step, go, **tread**, *17, *20, *55, *etc.; tr.*, tread, trample, 2769.

treu, *adj.*, faithful, **true**, 199, 255, 851, *etc.*

Treu(e), *f.*, faithfulness, fidelity, faith, 1601, 1602, 1702, *etc.*

treulich, *adj.*, true, faithful, 919.

treulos, *adj.*, faithless, 1603, 1625.

Trieb, *m.* -es, -e, impulse, instinct; love, 848.

triefen, troff, getroffen, *intr.*, **drip**, 3168.

trinken, trant, getrunken, (*tr. and*) *intr.*, drink, *40, 765.

Trommel, *f.* -n, drum, *23, 389, *24.

Trost, *m.* -es, consolation, comfort, 1333, 2092, 2309, *etc.*

trösten, *tr.*, console, comfort, 158, 2309, *etc.; refl.*, be comforted, 2374.

trostlos, *adj.*, comfortless, disconsolate, desperate, 2222, 3185.

trotz, *prep.* (*dat.*), in spite of, 1648.

trotzen, *intr.* (*with dat.*), defy, 1770.

trüben, *tr.*, trouble, disturb, 1704.

Trübsinn, *m.* -s, melancholy, 197.

trügerisch, *adj.*, deceptive, treacherous, 1502.

Trümmer, *pl.*, fragments, ruins, 2543, *144.

Trupp, *m.* -s, -e, troop, *12.

Trutz, *m.* -es, defiance; zu Schutz und Trutz, for offense and defense, 743, 1484.

trutziglich, *adv.*, defiantly, 235.

Tugend, *f.* -en, virtue, 852, 1646, 2024, *etc.*

tugendhaft, *adj.*, virtuous, 672.

tumultuarisch, *adj.*, tumultuous, riotous, *23, *139.

Turm, *m.* -es, Türme, tower, dungeon, prison, 383, 2750.

Turnier, *n.* -s, -e, tournament, 835.

Twing, *m.* -es, -e, strong tower, dungeon, prison, keep, 360, 1391.

Twinghof, *m.* -s, -höfe, strong tower, dungeon, prison, keep, 528.

Tyrann, *m.* -en, -en, tyrant, 497, 720, 748, *etc.*

Tyrannei, *f.* -en, tyranny, 716, 1047, 2123, *etc.*

Tyrannenjoch, *n.* -es, -e, tyrant's yoke, yoke of tyranny, 634.

Tyrannenmacht, *f.*, -mächte, tyrannical power, tyranny, 1275, 2543, 2919, *etc.*

Tyrannenschloß, *n.* -es, -schlösser, tyrant's castle, 2843.

Tyrannenschwert, *n.* -es, -er, tyrant's sword, sword of tyranny, 679.

tyrannisch, *adj.*, tyrannical, 788, 1658.

U.

übel, *adj.*, evil, ill, wrong, 2510.
Übel, *n.* -s, —, evil, wrong, 993.
üben, *refl.*, exercise, practice, 1481, 2645.
über, *prep.* (*dat. and acc.*), *adv.*, *sep. and insep. pref.*, over, above, across, by way of, beyond, about, on account of, *3, *4, 265, *etc.;* überm = über dem, 282; übern = über den, 555; = gegenüber, 725; *adv. after acc. of time*, through, during, *98.
überall, *adv.*, everywhere, 1046, 1115, 1941, *etc.*
überden'ken, überdach'te, über- dacht', *insep. tr.*, think of, reflect on, 218.
Überdruß, *m.* -es, weariness, satie- ty, disgust, 845.
Überfahrt, *f.* -en, passage; um —, to ferry him across, 132.
überhand', *adv., only used in —* nehmen, increase, prevail, get the **upper hand,** 2119.
überlaf'sen, überließ', überlaf'sen, überläßt', *insep. tr.*, leave, give up, give over, abandon, *121 (*past part.*).
überlie'fern, *insep. tr.*, deliver, give up, surrender, 3236.
Übermut, *m.* -s, arrogance, 191.
übernel)'men, übernahm', über- nom'men, übernimmt', *insep. tr.*, take possession of, 481; take upon one's self, 1413.

überra'schen, *insep. tr.*, surprise, 459, 1380, 1442, *etc.*
ü'berschwellen, schwoll über, über- geschwollen, schwillt über, *sep. intr.* j., overflow, 2006.
ü'berse#en, *sep. tr.*, set over, ferry across, 69, 2970.
überste'hen, überstand', überstan'- den, *insep. tr.*, stand, endure, overcome, 2259.
ü'bertreten, trat über, übergetreten, tritt über, *sep. intr.* j., step or go over, 1625.
übrig, *adj.*, over, left, remaining, other, *51; — bleiben, be left, 1351.
Üchtland. Üchtland, formerly a name of the district between the Jura Mountains and the Bernese Alps; 2432.
Ufer, *n.* -s, —, shore, bank, *3, 89, *12, *etc.*
Uhr, *f.* -en, clock, watch, 2567.
Uli. Uli, diminutive of Ulrich; 778, 820, 858.
um, *prep.* (*with acc.*), *adv., sep. and insep. pref.*, around, about, near, concerning, for, with regard to, (*time*) at, *frequent;* um . . . zu (*inf.*), in order to, to, 307, 379, *etc.;* um . . . (*gen.*) willen, for the sake of, on account of, 67, 566, 584, *etc.;* (*with* verdienen), from, at the hands of, 100, 891, *etc.;* ums = um das.
umar'men, *insep. tr.*, embrace, *71, *78, *142, *etc.*

umbrän'gen, *insep. tr.,* press, crowd around, *146.

umfaf'fen, *insep. tr.,* clasp, embrace, *9, 3118.

umgar'nen, *insep. tr.,* ensnare, surround, 878.

umge'ben, umgab', umge'ben, umgiebt', *insep. tr.,* surround, encompass, enclose, *3, *48, 1429, *etc.*

nm'gehen, ging um, umgegangen, *sep. intr.* f., go round, make a circuit, 984.

umher', *adv. and sep. pref.,* about, around, round about, *144, 2990.

umher'bliden, *sep. intr.,* look around, *109, *153.

umher'merfen, *sep. intr.,* observe *or* notice round about, 2250.

umher'fpähen, *sep. intr.,* spy, search, watch around, 1509.

umher'ftreifen, *sep. intr.* f., wander, roam about, 2637.

umhül'len, *insep. tr.,* wrap about, envelop, veil, 2539.

um'fehren, *sep. intr.* f. *and refl.,* turn round *or* back, return, *113, *116.

Umfreis, *m.* -es, -e, circuit, extent, 2650.

umrin'gen, *insep. tr.,* surround, beset, 460, *104.

umfchlie'ßen, umfchloß', umfchlof'fen, *insep. tr.,* enclose, surround, *126.

um'fehen, fah um, umgefehen, fieht um, *sep. refl.,* look around *or* about, 522, *133.

umfouft', *adv.,* in vain, to no purpose, 173, 1732, 1968, *etc.;* for nothing.

umfte'hen, umftand', umftan'den, *insep. tr.,* stand round, surround, *138.

um'wandeln, *sep. tr.,* change, transform, 1263.

Umweg, *m.* -es, -e, roundabout way, circuit, 1740.

umwer'ben, umwarb', umwor'ben, umwirbt', *insep. tr.,* woo, court, 1600.

Unbedacht, *m.* -es, inadvertence, thoughtlessness, 1870.

unbefannt, *adj.,* unknown, 1074, 3238.

unbequem, *adj.,* inconvenient; *neut. as subst.,* 2721.

unbewaffnet, *adj.,* unarmed, 2349.

unbezahlt, *adj.,* unpaid, 2461.

unbillig, *adj.,* unreasonable, unjust; *neut. as subst.,* injustice, 317.

und, *conj.,* and, *1, 7, 31, *etc.*

undurchdringlich, *adj.,* impenetrable, 1687, 2600.

unentdect, *adj.,* undiscovered, 3229.

unerhört, *adj.,* unheard, of; *neut. as subst.,* 402.

unerfättlich, *adj.,* insatiable, 2989.

unerträglich, *adj.,* intolerable, insufferable, 1277.

Ungar, *m.* -n, -n, Hungarian, 2997.

ungeboren, *adj.,* unborn, future, 2132.

Ungebühr, *f.,* impropriety, indecency, 480, 550.

ungebührlich, *adj.*, improper, indecent; *neut. as subst.*, 94.

Ungeduld, *f.*, impatience, *95, 3198.

ungeduldig, *adj.*, impatient, 2807, 2955.

ungeheuer, *adj.*, vast, monstrous, atrocious, 319, 622, 638, *etc.; neut. as subst.*, 1890.

ungekränkt, *adj.*, unvexed, unhurt, in peace, 1927, 2681.

ungerecht, *adj.*, unjust, 1393.

ungereizt, *adj.*, unprovoked, 429.

ungesetzlich, *adj.*, illegal, irregular, 1113.

ungetröstet, *adj.*, uncomforted, 3225.

Ungewitter, *n.* -s, —, (thunder-) storm, tempest, 104, 2229.

ungezügelt, *adj.*, unbridled, unrestrained, 1356.

Unglimpf, *m.* -s, harshness, injustice, outrage, 490.

Unglück, *n.* -s, misfortune, adversity, disaster, misery, 502, 598, 1011, *etc.*

unglücklich, *adj.*, unhappy, wretched, 2762, *etc.; masc. as subst.*, 932, 3157.

unglückselig, *adj.*, unhappy, unfortunate, ill-starred, 457, 949, *etc.; masc. as subst.*, 500; *fem. as subst.*, 2886.

Unglücksthat, *f.* -en, unhappy *or* woeful deed, 3210.

Unheil, *n.* -s, mischief, hurt, evil, 284.

unleiblich, *adj.*, insufferable, intolerable, 421, 535.

unmenschlich, *adj.*, inhuman, cruel, barbarous, 1922.

unmöglich, *adj.*, impossible, 119.

Unmündigkeit, *f.*, minority, tutelage, 3203.

Unmut, *m.* -s, ill-humor, displeasure, indignation, 2462.

unnütz, *adj.*, useless, 2155.

Unrecht, *n.* -s, wrong, fault, 681.

unruhig, *adj.*, restless, troubled, *131.

Unschuld, *f.*, innocence, 324, 951, *etc.; guilelessness, 941.

unschuldig, *adj.*, innocent, 2577.

unser, (uns(e)re, unser), *poss. adj. and pron.*, our, ours, 360, 1053, 1253.

unten, *adv.*, below, down, beneath, *51, *76.

unter, *prep.* (*dat. and acc.*), *adv., sep. and insep. pref.*, under, beneath, below, among, between, during, in, *frequent;* unterm = unter dem, 310, 545; unters = unter das, 652; 1812, among *or possibly* below, *cf. N.;* unter . . . hervor, from beneath, out from under, 2543.

unterbrech'en, unterbrach', unterbroch'en, unterbricht', *insep. tr.*, interrupt, break, 872.

unterdes'sen, *adv.*, in the meantime, meanwhile, *50, *54, *121, *etc.*

unterdrück'en, *insep. tr.*, oppress, 703; *past. part. as subst.*, 1617.

388 VOCABULARY.

Unterdrück'er, *m.* -8, —, oppressor, 1605, 1610.

Untergang, *m.* -8, =gänge, destruction, =fall, 271, 2388.

unterneh'men, unternahm', unternom'men, unternimmt', *insep. tr.*, undertake, 2302, 2538.

unterfteh'en, unterftanb', unterftanb'en, *insep. refl.*, *usually* dare, venture, *but in 234 archaic*, undertake.

un'tertauchen, *sep. intr.*, dive under, 45.

Unterwalben. Unterwalden, the Canton, south of the Lake of the Four Forest Cantons; *1, 100, 279, *etc.*

Unterwalbner, *adj.*, of Unterwalden, 994; *as noun*, inhabitant of Unterwalden, Unterwaldener, 963, 1130, 1525.

unterwegs, *adv.*, on the way, 2153, 2671.

unterwer'fen, unterwarf', unterwor'fen, unterwirft', *insep. tr.*, subject, subdue, 2492, *with dat. refl.*; submit, yield to, 255, 1206, 2731. [spectful, 222.

unterwürfig, *adj.*, submissive, re-

Unthat, *f.* -en, evil deed, monstrous deed, 3011, 3015.

unverändert, *adj.*, unchanged, 1020.

unveräußerlich, *adj.*, inalienable, 1280.

unverbächtig, *adj.*, unsuspected, without arousing suspicion, 1404.

unverlegt, *adj.*, unhurt, safe, 2097, 2314.

Unvernunft, *f.*, unreasonableness, unreason, folly, 2183.

unvernünftig, *adj.*, unreasoning, irrational, brute, 56.

unverschämt, *adj.*, impudent, insolent; *masc. as subst.*, 475.

unversehrt, *adj.*, unhurt, uninjured, intact, 272.

unwandelbar, *adj.*, unalterable, unwavering, constant, 1018.

unweit, *prep.* (*with gen. and dat.*), not far from, *3.

Unwille, *m.* -ns, indignation, anger, *150.

unwillkürlich, *adj.*, involuntary, *70.

unwirtlich, *adj.*, inhospitable, 1151, 2160.

unzerbrechlich, *adj.*, unbreakable, inviolable, 1281.

uralt, *adj.*, very old, most ancient, 841, 1156.

uralters, *adv.*, in most ancient time; von — her, from the most ancient times, from time immemorial, 537. *Cf. N.*

Urfehbe, *f.*, solemn oath (to renounce one's feuds), 2910.

Uri. Uri, the Canton, east of Unterwalden and south of Schwyz; *1, 333, 370, *etc.*

Urner, *adj.*, of Uri, 279; *as noun*, man of Uri, Urner, 983.

Urfache, *f.* -n, cause, reason, 1560, 1576, 1577, *etc.*

Urſprung, *m.* -ß, -ſprünge, origin,
1198.

Urſtand, *m.* -ß, -ſtände, original
state, 1282.

Urteil, *n.* -ß, -e, judgment, opinion,
2018.

urteilen, *tr.*, judge, 1064.

V.

Variation, *f.* -en, variation, *4.

Vater, *m.* -ß, Väter, father, sire,
ancestor, 243, 351, 416, *etc.*;
1156, *gen. pl.*

Vaterland, *n.* -ß, native country,
fatherland, 438, 795, 848, *etc.*

väterlich, *adj.*, fatherly, paternal,
of one's father *or* fathers (= ancestors), 843, 1099, 2954, *etc.*

vaterlos, *adj.*, fatherless, 2385,
2386.

Vatermord, *m.* -ß, parricide, 2953,
3169.

Vätertngend, *f.* -en, ancestral virtue, 691.

ver, *insep. pref.*, *never accented.*

verabſcheuen, *tr.*, detest, abhor, 715.

verachten, *tr.*, despise, contemn,
scorn, 401, 667, 840, *etc.*

Verachtung, *f.*, contempt, scorn,
disdain, 782, 1871.

verachtungswert, *adj.*, contempti-
ble, despicable, 1639.

verändern, *refl.*, be changed, *162;
*4, change appearance.

veräußern, *tr.*, alienate, separate by
sale, 885.

verbergen, verbarg, verborgen, verbirgt, hide, conceal, 172, 556,
etc.; *refl.*, hide (*intr.*), be hidden,
346, 465, *etc.*; *inf.* as *subst.*, 611.

verbieten, verbot, verboten, *tr.*,
forbid, prohibit, 299, 548, 3212.

verbinden, verband, verbunden, *tr.*,
bind (up), unite, 436, 1959, 2400,
etc.

verblaſſen, *intr.*, grow *or* turn pale,
1562.

verblenden, *tr.*, blind, dazzle, delude; *past part.* as *subst.*, 839.

verbluten, *refl. and intr.*, bleed to
death, 2797, 2987.

Verbrechen, *n.* -ß, —, crime, 1102,
2174.

verbreiten, *tr.*, spread, 999, 1034.

verbrennen, verbrannte, verbrannt,
intr., burn, burn up, burn to
death, 2880.

Verdammnis, *f.* -niſſe, condemnation, damnation, 682, 2817.

verdanken, *tr.*, owe, have to thank
for, 1434.

verderben, verdarb, verdorben,
verbirbt, *tr.*, destroy, ruin, undo,
1964, 2020, 2087, *etc.*

verdienen, *tr.*, merit, deserve, 100,
891, 1302, *etc.*

Verdrieß, *m.* -eß, displeasure, vexation, annoyance, 1738.

verdrießen, verdroß, verdroſſen, *tr.*,
vex; ſich (*acc.*) — laſſen, shrink
from, 2636.

Verdruß, *m.* -eß, displeasure, vexation, annoyance, 1965.

verehren, *tr.*, do honor to, respect, revere, 398, 403, 1622, *etc.*

vereiden, *tr.*, bind by an oath, 1363.

vereinen, *tr.*, unite, join, combine, 1664.

vereinigen, *tr.*, unite, join, combine, 2936.

verfallen, verfiel, verfallen, verfällt, *intr.* f., fall to, be forfeited to, 400.

verfangen, verfing, verfangen, verfängt, *refl.*, be caught, 2164; *intr.* avail, 1285.

verfehlen, *intr.* (*with gen.*), miss, fail of, 1995.

verfluchen, *tr.*, curse, 3043, 3181.

verfolgen, *tr.*, follow, pursue, 70, 74, 1488, *etc.*

Verfolger, *m.* -ß, —, pursuer, 2565.

verführen, *tr.*, lead astray, seduce, corrupt, 839, 1635, 2019, *etc.*

Verführung, *f.* -en, seduction, corruption, 821.

vergeben, vergab, vergeben, vergiebt, *tr.*, forgive, 1572.

vergebens, *adv.*, in vain, 869, 1972, 2167, *etc.*

vergeblich, *adj.*, vain, useless, 2825.

Vergeltung, *f.*, requital, recompense, 617.

vergessen, vergaß, vergessen, vergißt, *tr.*, forget, 2323, 2347, 2724, *etc.*

vergiften, *tr.*, poison, 822.

vergleichen, *tr.*, adjust, settle, 2499.

vergraben, vergrub, vergraben, vergräbt, *tr.*, bury, 2110.

vergrößern, *tr.*, enlarge, increase, aggravate, 603.

vergüten, *tr.*, make good, 454.

verhaften, *tr.*, arrest, 1863.

verhalten, verhielt, verhalten, verhält, *tr.*, withhold, conceal, 531; *refl.*, be in a certain state, be, 1242, so . . . alles, 'so it all is.'

verhandeln, *tr.*, transact, 2505.

verhängen, *tr.*, decree, ordain, 2228.

verhaßt, *adj.*, hated, odious, detestable, 1358, 1671, 2534, *etc.*

verhehlen, *tr.*, hide, conceal, 173, 713, 1251, *etc.*

verhindern, *tr.*, hinder, prevent, 2108.

verhüllen, *tr.* and *refl.*, cover or wrap one's self up, hide one's face, *158 (sich, *dat.*), *162.

verhüten, *tr.*, avert, prevent, 86; verhüte Gott, 'God forbid,' 1535, 1893.

verirren, *intr.* and *refl.*, lose one's way; *past part.*, lost, 1498, 3105.

verjagen, *tr.*, drive out, expel, 1368, 1633, 2398, *etc.*

verkaufen, *tr.* and *refl.*, sell, 854, 1605.

verkleiden, *tr.*, disguise, 1062.

verkümmern, *intr.* f., pine away, languish, 2358.

verkünden, *tr.*, announce, make known, 285, 2291, 2679, *etc.*

verkündigen, *tr.* and *refl.*, announce, make known, proclaim, 2071, 2785.

verwalten, *tr.*, administer, execute, 1115.

verwandeln, *tr.*, change, transform, 2573; *refl.*, be changed, transformed, *20.

verwandt, *adj.*, related, kin; *masc. as subst.*, relative, kindred, 1657.

verwegen, verwag, verwogen, *refl.* (*with gen.*), dare, venture, 2416, 2528.

verwegen, *adj.*, bold, daring, rash, 27, 1021, 1505, *etc.*

verweigern, *tr.*, refuse, deny, 785.

verweilen, *intr.*, tarry, stop, 213, *51.

verwirken, *tr.*, forfeit, lose, 1925, 1931.

verwünschen, *tr.*, curse; *past part. as adj.*, cursed, confounded, 1768; *as interj.*, curse it!, confound it!, 177.

verzagen, *intr.*, despond, despair, lose courage, 125, 1987, 2291, *etc.*

verzeihen, verzieh, verziehen, *tr.* (*dat. of pers.*), pardon, excuse, 1870, 1971.

verzieren, *tr.*, decorate, adorn, *40.

verzweifeln, *intr.*, despair, 3194.

Verzweiflung, *f.*, despair, desperation, 456, 2353, 3185.

Verzweiflungsangst, *f.* =ängste, agony of desperation, desperate fear, 646.

verzweiflungsvoll, *adj.*, desperate, 439.

Vetter, *m.* -s, -n, cousin, relative, 1034, 3200.

Vieh, *n.* -s, cattle, beast, brute, 46, 50, 56, *etc.*

viel, *adj.*, much, a great deal, many, *2, 189, 196, *etc.*

vielerfahren, *adj.*, of much experience, very experienced, 241; *pl. as subst.*, 664.

vielleicht', *adv.*, perhaps, may be, perchance, 494, 656, 1316, *etc.*

vielmehr' (*adv. and*) *conj.*, rather, but on the contrary, 3046.

vier, *num.*, **four**, *48.

viert, *num.*, **fourth**, *27, *105.

Vierwaldstättersee, *m.* -s, Lake of the Four Forest Cantons, *or* Lake of Lucerne; *3, *105. [2626.

Vogel, *m.* -s, **Vögel,** bird, 1949,

Vogt, *m.* -s, **Vögte,** bailiff, prefect, governor, 155, 191, 220, *etc.; cf. N.* on **Reichsvogt,** *1.

Volk, *n.* -es, **Völker,** people, nation, folk, 100, 243, 304, *etc.*

voll (*comp.* **voller,** *superl.* **vollst),** *adj.*, full, whole, complete, 65, 203, 417, *etc.;* 1345, seine Jahre — haben (= volljährig sein), be of (full) age; *adv., sep. and insep. pref. with similar meanings.*

vollbrin'gen, vollbrach'te, vollbracht', *tr.*, accomplish, execute, carry out, 85, 2952, 3007; *past part. as subst.*, 218.

vollen'den, *insep. tr.*, end, finish, achieve, accomplish, 564, 693, 1376, *etc.*

völlig, *adj.*, full; *adv.*, entirely, wholly, *48.

Vollmacht, *f.*, full power, authority, 2002.

von, *prep.* (*dat.*), of, from, by, with, concerning, because of; *with family names sign of nobility;* *1, 28, 64, *etc.;* vom = von dem.

vor, *prep.* (*dat. and acc.*), *adv. and sep. pref.,* before, in front of, ago, from, for, with, because of, of, 133, *14, 217, *etc.*

voran, *adv. and sep. pref.,* before, at the head, in front, foremost, *137.

voranziehen, 3og, gezogen, *intr.* f., march *or* go before, 1134.

voraus, *adv.,* before, on ahead, in advance, 2703.

vorbauen, *intr.,* take precautions, anticipate, prevent. 274.

vorbei, *adv. and sep. pref.,* by, past, over, 2086; an (*dat.*) ... vorbei, past, *86, 2186, *etc.*

vorbeigehen, ging, gegangen, *intr.* f., go *or* pass by, *86, 2722, 3092.

vorbiegen, bog, gebogen, *tr.,* bend forward, *101.

vorber, *adj.,* fore, front, *21, *etc.;* bie — Scene, front part of the stage, proscenium, *86, *132.

Vordergrund, *m.* -8, foreground, front, *84.

vorberst, *adj.* (*superl. of* vorber), foremost, in front, most advanced, first, *126, *137, *163.

vorgehen, ging, gegangen, *intr.* f., go on, happen, take place, 545.

vorhalten, hielt, gehalten, *tr.,* hold (up) before, *89.

Vorhang, *m.* -8, Vorhänge, curtain, *3, *139, *163.

Vorhut, *f.,* vanguard; sentinel 60.

vorig, *adj.,* former, preceding, previous, last, *136; *pl. as subst.* *122.

vorkommen, kam, gekommen, *intr* f., come forward, *26.

vorn, *adv.,* before, in the forepart, in front, *20.

Vorschub, *m.* -8, -schübe, aid, help, assistance, 3045.

Vorsehung, *see* Fürsehung.

Vorsicht, *f.,* foresight, caution, prudence, 616, 886.

vorspringen, sprang, gesprungen, *intr.* f., jut out, project, 2253.

Vorsprung, *m.* -8, -sprünge, projection, ledge, *126.

vorstellen, *tr.,* represent, 225.

Vorteil, *m.* -8, -e, advantage, 803, 2251.

vortreten, trat, getreten, tritt, *intr.* f., step forward, 1857.

vorü'ber, *adv. and sep. pref.,* by, past, *134 (*with verb of motion understood*), 3261.

vorübergehen, ging, gegangen, *intr.* f., go *or* pass by, go past, *24, 1763, *88, *etc.*

vorüberlenken, *sep. tr.,* steer past, 2192.

vorübertreiben, trieb, getrieben, *refl.,* hurry past, 2611-12.

vorwärts, adv. (and sep. pref.), forward(s), 325, *51, *54, etc.

Vorwurf, m. -s, =würfe, reproach, 1606.

W.

Wache, f. -n, watch, guard, *84.

wachſen, wuchs, gewachſen, wächſt, intr. ſ., grow, increase, advance, 356, 880, 1793, etc.

Wächter, m. -s, —, watchman, watch, guard, 1860; in 43 = Eng. Watch, as name of a dog.

wacker, adj., valiant, brave, stout, worthy, excellent, 153, 185, etc.; masc. as subst., 169.

Waffe, f. -n, weapon, arms, 302, 700, 1377, etc.

Waffendienſt, m. -s, -e, service with weapons, military service, 1224.

Waffenfreund, m. -s, -e, friend or comrade in arms, 2959.

Waffenknecht, m. -s, -e, servant or man at arms, mercenary, soldier, 1859, *104.

waffnen, tr., arm, 1595, 1977, 2435, etc.

Wagefahrt, f. -en, daring expedition, 1494.

wagen, tr., venture, risk, dare, 135, 136, 162, etc.

Wageſprung, m. -s, =ſprünge, bold or hazardous leap, 2638.

Wagethat, f. -en, deed of daring, 2874.

Wagſtück, n. -s, =ſtücke, daring deed, risk, venture, hazard, 1907.

Wahl, f. -en, choice, election, 328, 815.

wählen, tr., choose, 443, 1213.

Wahlfreiheit, f. -en, freedom of election, right or prerogative of choice, 3022.

Wahn, m. -s, illusion, delusion, 1692.

wahnſinnig, adj., insane, mad, crazy, 943, 2812.

Wahnſinnsthat, f. -en, deed of frenzy, insane act, 3206.

wahr, adj., true, real, genuine, 802, 1162, 1771, etc.

während, prep. (gen.), during, *121.

Wahrheit, f. -en, truth, 572, 1777, 2055, etc.

wahrlich, adv., truly, really, indeed, 974, 2062.

Währung, f. -en, value or standard (of coins); echte Währung, steiling value or worth, 689.

Waiſe, f. -n, orphan, 2735, 2766.

Wald, m. -es, Wälder, wood, woods, forest, 90, 493, 545, etc. Cf. N. 493.

Waldgebirg(e), n. -s, -e, forest-mountains, 687, 1175.

Waldgegend, f. -en, region or part of a forest, *78.

Waldkapelle, f. -n, forest-chapel, 966.

Waldſtätte, pl., Forest Cantons; *2, 804, etc. Cf. N. *3.

Walbung, f. -en, wood, forest, 728.

Waldwaſſer, *n.* -ß, —, forest-stream, 1790.

Wall, *m.* -eß, Wälle, **wall**, rampart, 2437.

wallen, *intr.* ſ., walk, wander, make a pilgrimage, 343, 749, 1163, *etc.*

walten, *intr.*, dispose, manage, rule, govern, 956, 1658; *inf. as subst.*, 2818.

Wälti. Wälti, diminutive of Walther; 1581, 2313.

wülzen, *tr.*, roll, 1589.

Wand, *f.*, Wände, **wall**, 1024, 2639.

wandeln, *intr.* ſ. *and* h., go, move, walk, 2459, 3187, 3280.

wandern, *intr.* ſ., **wander**, go, travel, 607, 733, 1012, *etc.*

Wandersmann, *m.* -eß, =leute, traveler, 212, 1269.

Wand(e)rer, *m.* -ß, —, traveler, 348, 518, *126, *etc.*

wanken, *intr.* ſ. *and* h., totter, stagger, reel, rock, fail, give way, 215, 1982, 2666, *etc.*

wann, *adv.* (*interrog.*), **when**, 182.

Wappenſchild, *n.* -ß =ſchilder, schield, escutcheon, coat-of-arms, 211, *40.

wappnen, *tr.*, arm, 1230.

warm, (*comp.* wärmer, *superl.* wärmſt), *adj.*, **warm**, 514, 595, 759, *etc.*

warnen, *tr.*, warn, 60, 1387.

Warnung, *f.* -en, warning, 2800.

Wart. Rudolf von (der) Wart, friend and accomplice of Herzog Johannes von Schwaben; 1339, 2961.

warten, *intr.* (*gen. or usually* auf *with acc.*), wait, wait for, 105, 106, 306, *etc.;* tend, 1181.

warum, *adv.* (*interrog.*), why, 74, 598, 796, *etc.*

was, *interrog. pron.*, **what**, 68, 70, 76, 3052, *etc.; indef. rel. pron.*, whatever, that which, that, which, 81, 160, 161, *etc.;* = warum, why, 692, 1825, 1856, *etc.;* = all who, whoever, 1481, 1739, = etwas, something, somewhat, some, 159, 563, 1438, 2691, *etc.*

Waſſer, *n.* -ß, —, **water**, 8, 35, 117, *etc.*

Waſſerhuhn, *n.*-ß, =hühner, waterhen, coat, 44.

Waſſerkluft, *f.* =klüfte, gorge of water, water-filled gorge, 2164.

Waſſerwüſte, *f.* -n, **waste** of waters, 2222.

wechſeln, *intr.* (*and tr.*), change, alter, vary, 1506.

wecken, *tr.*, **wake, waken**, arouse, 297, 1644.

weder, *conj.*, neither; weder . . . noch, neither . . . nor, 2067.

Weg, *m.* -eß, -e, **way**, path, road, 26, 173, 348, *etc.*

weg, *adv. and sep. pref.*, **away**, (forth, off, gone), 468, 2739.

wegbleiben, blieb, geblieben, *intr.* ſ., stay away, 1540, 1574, 1575, *etc.*

wegen, *prep.* (*gen. which may precede it*), on account of, for the sake of, 2717.

wegfahren, fuhr, gefahren, fährt, *intr.* f., sail away, pass along, 980.

wegführen, *tr.*, lead away, 1849, *102.

weggehen, ging, gegangen, *intr.* f., go away, (*with* über) go *or* pass over, 167.

wegrauben, *tr.*, abduct, kidnap, 2525.

wegwenden, wandte, *or* wendete, gewandt *or* gewendet, *tr. and refl.*, turn away, avert, *47, *122, 2479.

weh(e), *interj.*, woe! alas!, 180, 801, 1571, *etc.*

Wehgeschrei, *n.* -s, woeful cry, cry of lamentation, 2985.

wehklagen, *insep. intr.*, wail, lament, 1172.

wehren, *tr.* (*dat. of pers.*), prevent, stop, hinder, 234, 2565.

wehrlos, *adj.*, weaponless, defenseless, unarmed, 643, 2030, 2219.

Weib, *n.* -es, -er, woman, wife, *2, 83, 91, *etc.*

Weibel, *m.* -s, —, servant, beadle, summoner, 1126.

weiblich, *adj.*, womanly, feminine, 1711.

weichen, wich, gewichen, *intr.* f., yield, give way, recede, 1378, 1443, 2748, *etc.*

Weide, *f.* -n, pasture, grazing, 14, 59.

weiden, *tr.*, graze, tend *or* feed (a flock), 1003; feast (one's eyes) on, 2813.

Weidgesell, *m.* -en, -en, huntsman, 153.

Weidmann, *m.* -s, =männer *or* =leute, hunter, huntsman, 2708.

Weidwerk, *n.* -s, game, 2628.

weigern, *tr.*, refuse, deny, 1301, 3205.

Weih(e), *m.* -en, -en, falcon, kite, eagle, 1471.

weihen, *refl.*, devote one's self, be devoted, 918.

weil, *conj.*, because, since, 260, 487, 666, *etc.*; while, 341.

weilen, *intr.*, stay, tarry, linger, 3262, 3274.

Weiler, *m.* -s, —, hamlet; as part of proper name, *1, (*indefinitely in Schwyz*); 1076, or Ödweiler, near Rossberg.

weinen, *intr.*, weep, shed tears, cry, 1038, 1338, *121, *etc.*

weise, *adj.*, wise, sage, prudent, 212, 517, 886, *etc.*

Weise, *f.*, -n, manner, way, habit, custom, 1905.

weisen, wies, gewiesen, *tr.*, show, point out, direct, refer, 1332, 2161, *etc.*; 1397, reprimand, reprove.

weislich, *adv.*, wisely, prudently, 2192.

weiß, *adj.*, white, *48, 1778.

Weißland, *n.* -s, Whiteland, the Oberhasli valley; 1193.

weit, *adj.*, **wide**, broad, long, far, distant, 48, *21, 964, *etc.; neut. as subst.*, 1474, 1675; *comp. neut. as subst.*, 2298, something further.

Weite, *f.* -n, distance, 1685, 1914.

weiter, *adv. and sep. pref.*, farther, further, onward(s), on, 349, 380, 1314, *etc.*

weitſchichtig, *adj.*, large, vast, far-reaching, 2727.

weitſchmettern, *sep. intr.*, resound or peal afar, 2849.

weitverſchlungen, *part. adj.*, spreading and tangled, 1190.

welcher, (**welche**, **welches**), *interrog. adj. and pron.*, **which**, what, what a, 296, 327, *etc.; rel. pron.*, who, which, that, *3, *21, *etc.*

Welle, *f.*, -n, wave, billow, surge, 110, 166, 2156, *etc.*

welſch, *adj.*, foreign, *especially* Italian (*or* French), 1222.

Welſchland, *n.* -s, Italy; 519, 1230.

Welt, *f.* -en, **world**, earth, 34, 305, 453, *etc.*

wenden, **wandte** *or* **wendete**, ge-wandt *or* gewendet, *refl.*, turn, *33, *100, 2234, *etc.*

wenig, *adj.*, little, few, a few, 1532, 1911, 1916, *etc.*

wenn, *conj.*, if, **when**, whenever, 18, 19, 20, 73, *etc.*

wer, *interrog. pron.*, who, 70, 126, 127, 225, *etc.; indef. rel. pron.*, whoever, who, he who, 330, 383, 401, *etc.*

werben, **warb**, **geworben**, **wirbt**, *tr.*, obtain, gain, enlist, 686, 706, 718, *etc.; intr.*, sue, woo; *inf. as subst.*, suit, request, 1313.

werden, **warb**, **geworben**, **wird**, *intr. ſ.*, become, get, grow, happen, be, 101, 149, 491, 1854, *etc.; fut. aux.*, shall, will, *etc.*, 41, *etc.; pass. aux.*, be, 101, *etc.;* **mir wird**, I feel, 513; *inf. as subst.*, 2727.

werfen, **warf**, **geworfen**, **wirft**, *tr.*, throw, cast, fling, 321, 377, *26, *etc.*

Werf, *n.* -s, -e, **work**, 355, 524, 723, *etc.;* 2727, **im Werf und Werben**, on foot and in progress.

Werfleute, *pl.*, workmen, *21.

Werfzeug, *n.* -s, -e, tool, instrument, "cat's paw," 716, 1612.

wert, *adj.*, worthy, esteemed, dear, 508.

Wert, *m.* -es, -e, worth, value, 916.

Weſen, *n.* -s, —, being, existence, creature, 590, 645.

Weſten, *m.* -s *or* -en, **west**, *105.

Wetter, *n.* -s, —, weather, storm, 2558.

Wetterloch, *n.* -s, -löcher, weather-hole, 40, *cf. N.*

Wettſtreit, *m.* -s, contest, contention, emulation, 1137.

wetzen, *tr.*, whet, sharpen, 653.

wider, *prep.* (*acc.*), *adv. and insep. pref.*, against, contrary to, 1325, 2502.

Widerpart, *m.* -s, -e, adversary, 1087.

wi'derprallen, *intr.* f., rebound, 2188.

widerſetz'en, *refl.*, resist, oppose, 1844.

widerſte'hen, widerſtand', widerſtan'den, *intr. (dat.)*, resist, withstand, 2601.

widerſtre'ben, *intr. (dat.)*, strive *or* struggle against, resist, 802, 869, 1656, *etc.*

widerſtrei'ten, widerſtritt', widerſtrit'ten, *insep. intr. (dat.)*, conflict with, be contrary to, 2076.

wie, *adv.*, how, in what way, 53, 815, *etc.; conj.*, how, as, like, when, 4, 5, 7, 96, *etc.*

wieder, *adv., sep. and insep. pref.*, again, anew, once more, 168, 499, *etc.*

wiederho'len, *insep. tr.*, repeat, *9, *138, *139, *etc.*

wie'derkehren, *sep. intr.* f., return, 1282, 1331, *etc.;* 64, *impers. refl.*, one returns *or* there is a return.

wie'derkommen, kam wieder, wiedergekommen, *sep. intr.* f., return, come back, 17, 2623, 3097, *etc.*

wie'derſehen, ſah wieder, wiedergeſehen, ſieht wieder, *sep. tr.*, see again, 988, 3210.

Wiege, *f.* -n, cradle, 323, 2154.

wiegen, *tr.*, rock, 2154.

Wieſe, *f.* -n, meadow, *48, 1178, *84. *Cf. N. on* Matten, *3.

wild, *adj.*, wild, 302, 308, 1177, *etc.*

Wild, *n.* -es, wild animals, game, 1804, 2635.

wildbewegt, *adj.*, wildly agitated, tempestuous, 1682.

Wildheuer, *m.* -s, —, gatherer of wild hay, 2738.

Wildnis, *f.* -niſſe, wilderness, 1220, 1267, 1588, *etc.*

Wille(n), *m.* -ns, -n, will, purpose, wish, 395, 752, 1317, *etc.;* um... *(gen.)* willen, for the sake of, on account of, 67, 566.

willkom'men, *adj.*, welcome, 510, 987, 2557.

Wimper, *f.* -n, eyelash, 1962.

Wind, *m.* -es, -e, wind, 1017, 2129.

Windeswehe, *f.* -n, drift-avalanche, 3253.

Windlawine, *f.* -n, wind-avalanche *or* drift-avalanche, 1501.

Windlicht, *n.* -s, -er, torch, link, *48, *55.

winken, *intr.*, nod, make a sign, beckon, 1569, 2029.

Winter, *m.* -s, —, winter, 2637.

wintern, *tr.*, winter, keep through the winter, 1456.

Winterung, *f.*, wintering, 206.

wir, *pers. pron.*, we, 17, 41, 58, *etc.;* wir's = wir es.

Wirbel, *m.* -s, —, whirlpool, 116, 2137.

wirken, *intr.*, work, act, effect, have influence, 1709.

wirklich, *adj.*, actual, real, true, 585.

Wirt, *m.* -es, -e, host, 1007.

Wirtin, *f.* -innen, hostess, housewife, wife, 187, 516.

wirtlich, *adj.*, hospitable, 347.

wiſſen, wußte, gewußt, weiß, *tr.*, know, know how (*with inf.*), 54, 58, 171, *etc.*

Witwenleid, *n.* -8, widow's pain *or* affliction, woeful widowhood, 3035.

wo, *adv. and conj.*, where, when, if, 59, 136, 409, *etc.*; 1218, with *or* from whom.

wofern, *conj.*, if, provided, in case that, 2274.

wogen, *intr.*, wave, surge, roll, 116, 1182.

woher, *adv.*, whence, where, 2945.

wohin, *adv.*, whither, where, 1046, 1652, 2293, *etc.*

wohl, *adv.*, well; indeed, probably, I suppose; 98, 155, 513, *etc.*; lebe *or* lebt *or* leben Sie wohl, farewell, 13, *etc.*; *dat.* wohl thun, do good to, make feel good, 806.

Wohl, *n.* -8, weal, welfare, well-being, 245.

wohlan, *interj.*, come on! well! now then!, 1123, 1936, 3287.

wohlbeſtellt, *adj.*, duly appointed, 1860.

wohlbewahrt, *adj.*, well kept, 2406.

wohlfeil, *adj.*, cheap, 906.

wohlgenährt, *adj.*, well-fed, 204.

wohlgepflegt, *adj.*, well cared for, well regaled, 345.

Wohlthat, *f.* -en, good action, benefit, kindness, 886.

wohnen, *intr.*, dwell, reside, lodge, live, 260, 350, 561, *etc.*

wohnlich, *adj.*, habitable, comfortable, 210.

Wohnſtätte, *f.* -en, dwelling, habitation, home, 2149.

Wohnung, *f.* -n, dwelling, habitation, residence, abode, home, *27, 529, 1008, *etc.*

Wolf, *m.* -es, Wölfe, wolf, 2134.

Wolfenſchieß(en). Wolfenschiessen, name of a noble family of Unterwalden, from the village in the Engelberg Valley south of Stanz; 78, 129, 546, *etc.*

Wolke, *f.* -n, cloud, *3, 33, *4, *etc.*

Wolle, *f.*, wool, 242.

wollen, wollte, gewollt, will, *tr. and modal aux.*, will, purpose, intend, wish, 118, 133, 147, *etc.*; be about to, *14, *etc.*; *pret. subj.*, wollt's Gott, would to God, 1766.

worauf, *adv.*, whereupon, on *or* at *or* for which, 306, *40, 2630, *etc.*

worein, *adv.*, wherein(to), into which, 3036.

Wort, *n.* -es, Wörter *or* Worte, word, 237, 239, 418, *etc.*

wozu, *adv.*, whereto, wherefore, for which *or* what, why, 643, 1651, 1967, *etc.*

Wucht, *f.* -en, weight, 644.

Wunder, *n.* -8, —, wonder, miracle, 1526, 2206, 2271, *etc.*

wunderbar, *adj.*, wonderful, 977.

Wunderding, *n.* -8, -e, wonderful thing, marvel, prodigy, 2668.

wundern, *intr. and impers. tr.*, wonder, 221, 2142.

Wunderzeichen, *n.* -s, —, miraculous sign, prodigy, portent, 2679.

Wunsch, *m.* -es, Wünsche, **wish,** desire, 1597, 3198.

wünschen, *tr.*, **wish,** desire, 63, 248, 672, *etc.*

würdig, *adj.*, **worthy,** 256, 406, *etc.; neut. as subst.*, 953; *masc. comp. as subst.*, 1144.

Wurzel, *f.* -n, root, 924, 1190.

Wüste, *f.* -n, desert, **waste,** wilderness, 1250, 2135, 3215.

Wut, *f.*, rage, fury, 1462, 2331, 2578, *etc.*

wüten, *intr.*, rage, rave, be furious, 314, 697, *etc.; pres. part. as subst.*, 2010, 2532.

Wüterei, *f.*, fury, rage, tyranny, 277.

Wüt(e)rich, *m.* -s, -e, tyrant, bloodthirsty pérson, madman, 99, 181, 615, *etc.*

wütig, *adj.*, furious, raging, mad, 1530, 2344.

3.

Zacke, *f.* -n, tooth, prong, peak, 2144.

zagen, *intr.*, tremble, be dismayed or afraid, 2552.

Zahl, *f.* -en, number, *55, 1119, 2349, *etc.*

zählen, *tr.*, count, reckon, rely on (auf), 435, 438, 899, *etc.*

zahlen, *tr.*, pay, pay for, 904, 1461, 2589, *etc.*

zähmen, *tr.*, **tame,** check, subdue, 3249.

zart (*comp.* zärter, *superl.* zärtest), *adj.*, tender, delicate, gentle, 323, 2998.

Zauber, *m.* -s, —, magic charm, spell, 947.

zaubern, *intr.*, delay, hesitate, *41, 1930.

zeh(e)n, *num.*, **ten,** 734, 1403, 2653, *etc.*

zehnfach, *adj.*, tenfold, 1926.

zehnt, *num. adj.*, **tenth,** 1170.

Zeichen, *n.* -s, —, sign, **token,** mark, *27, *33, 977, *etc.*

zeigen, *tr.*, show, point out, 263, 264, *etc.; refl.*, show one's self, appear, *3, *etc.; intr.*, point at, show (a view), *23, *86, *96, *etc.*

Zeile, *f.* -n, line, *139.

Zeit, *f.* -en, time, 88, 102, *etc.;* eine Zeit lang, for a time, *3, *14, *71, *etc.*

zeitig, *adj.*, early, 1480.

zeitlich, *adj.*, temporal, earthly, 320.

Zell(e), *f.* -en, cell, hermitage, 519, *cf. N.*

zer, *insep. pref., never accented.*

zerbrechen, zerbrach, zerbrochen, zerbricht, *tr.*, **break** to pieces, 631, *144.

zerknicken, *tr.*, break *or* snap across, 926.

zerlumpt, *part. adj.*, ragged, tattered, 1738.

zernagen, *tr.*, **gnaw,** corrode, 3199.

zerreißen, zerriß, zerriſſen, *tr.*, rend, tear, break (to pieces), 1266, 1725, 2013, *etc.*

zerſchmettern, *tr.*, shatter, dash to pieces, 448, 2193.

zerſpalten, *tr.*, cleave, split, 87, 2980.

zerſpringen, zerſprang, zerſprungen, *intr.* ſ., fly to pieces, snap across, 1996.

zerſtören, *tr.*, destroy, ruin, undo, 951, 1718, 2131, *etc.; past part. as adj.* (= verſtört), wild and troubled, *153.

zertreten, zertrat, zertreten, zertritt, *tr.*, tread *or* crush under foot, 2767.

Zeuge, *m.* -n, -n, witness, 1588.

zeugen, *intr.*, witness, testify, 135.

Zeugung, *f.* -en, generation, 3003.

ziehen, zog, gezogen, *tr.*, draw, pull, 116, 873, 937, *etc.; intr.* (*with* an), pull *or* tug at, 476; *reﬂ. and intr.* ſ., go, move, pass, 876, 1161, *etc.; past part. for Eng. pres. part.*, 1468, *163.

Ziel, *n.* -s, -e, limit, end, goal, mark, aim, 536, 961, 1488, *etc.*

zielen, *intr.*, aim, 1887, 1898, 2139, *etc.*

ziemen, *intr.* (*dat.*), beseem, befit, 3073.

Zier, *f.* -en, ornament, decoration, 1348.　　　　　　[*72.

Zimmerart, *f.* -ärte, carpenter's ax,

Zimmermann, *m.* -s, -männer *or* -leute, carpenter, 1514.

zimmern, *tr.*, build, 208, 214.

zinſen, *intr.*, pay tribute *or* rent, 1362.

zittern, *intr.*, tremble, 25, 1495, 1571, *etc.*

zollen, *intr.*, pay toll *or* taxes, 876.

Zorn, *m.* -es, anger, wrath, 481, 626, 786, *etc.*

zu, *prep.* (*dat.*), *adv. and sep. pref.*, to, unto, at, in, by, towards, in addition to, besides, with, for (the purpose of), as, on, too. *3 (zur = zu der), 1 (zum = zu dem), 17, etc.; 1991, ſchieß zu!, shoot on *or* away!; (*after its noun*) towards, 762.

zubringen, brachte, gebracht, *sep. tr.*, bring (to), report, 719.

Zucht, *f.* -en, breeding, breed, herd, 204.

Züchtigung, *f.* -en, chastisement, punishment, 310.

zucken, *intr.* ſ. *and* h., twitch, shrink, quiver, 1962, *98.

zudrücken, *tr.*, close by pressure, shut, 1764, 1908-9.

zuerſt, *adv.*, at first, first, for the first time, 1444, 2530.

zufahren, fuhr, gefahren, fährt, (*intr. and*) *tr.*, carry *or* bring to *or* up; *past. part. used imperatively*, 354.

zufallen, fiel, gefallen, fällt, *intr.* ſ., fall to (one's share), 2473.

Zug, *m.* -es, Züge, march, train, procession, host, 1176, 3272; feature, 2306, *153.

zugeben, gab, gegeben, giebt, *tr.*, grant, concede, permit, allow, 709.

zuge'gen, *adv.*, present, 1120.

zugehen, ging, gegangen, *intr.* ſ., go at, lay on, 2257, *cf. N.;* go to or towards, *26, *162.

Zügel, *m.* -s, —, rein, bridle, *135.

zugleich, *adv.*, at the same time, likewise, at once, *27, 2008, *110, *etc.*

zukehren, kehrte, gekehrt, *tr.*, turn towards, 3215.

Zukunft, *f.*, future, 892.

zuletzt, *adv.*, at last, lastly, last, 139.

zunächſt, *adv.*, next, in the next place, close by, 1408.

Zunft, *f.* Zünfte, guild, 2435.

Zunge, *f.* -n, tongue, language, 300, 1195, 2779, *etc.*

zureiten, ritt, geritten, *intr.* ſ., ride on, 175 (*imper. 2d pl.*).

Zür(i)ch. The city Zürich, capitol of the Canton Zürich, at the northern end of Lake Zürich; 1363, 2435, 2993.

zurück, *adv. and sep. pref.*, back, backwards, behind, in the rear, 2734, 3118.

zurückbleiben, blieb, geblieben, *intr.* ſ., remain behind, *103.

zurückfahren, fuhr, gefahren, fährt, *intr.* ſ., start or shrink back, recoil, *7, *156, 3217.

zurückfallen, fiel, gefallen, fällt, *intr.* ſ., fall back, *121.

zurückführen, *tr.*, bring back, reconduct, reinstate, 2930.

zurückgeben, gab, gegeben, giebt, *tr.*, give back, restore, 2466, 2749.

zurückhalten, hielt, gehalten, hält, *tr.*, hold back, withhold, 2954.

zurückkehren, *intr.* ſ., turn back, return, 2910.

zurückkommen, kam, gekommen, *intr.* ſ., come back, return, *27, *75, *91, *etc.*

zurücklaſſen, ließ, gelaſſen, läßt, *tr.*, leave behind, 2386-7.

zurückſpringen, ſprang, geſprungen, *intr.* ſ., leap or spring or fly back, rebound, 1974.

zurückſtehen, ſtand, geſtanden, *intr.* ſ., stand back, withdraw, 1130.

zurücktreten, trat, getreten, tritt, *intr.* ſ., step back, draw back, *29, *79, *138, *etc.*

zurückwerfen, warf, geworfen, wirft, *tr.*, throw or cast or hurl back, 2189.

zuſagen, *tr.*, promise, 3113.

zuſammen, *adv. and sep. pref.*, together, along with, jointly, *55, 1100, 2370, *etc.*

zuſammenbrechen, brach, gebrochen, bricht, *tr.*, break in pieces or down, 2559.

zuſammenflechten, flocht, geflochten, flicht, *tr.*, clasp closely, 741, *39.

zuſammenführen, *tr.*, bring together, convene, 1152.

zuſammengrenzen, *intr.*, border, meet together, 730.

zufammenhalten, hielt, gehalten, hält, (*tr. and*) *intr.*, hold *or* keep together, remain united, 2447.

zufammenlaufen, lief, gelaufen, läuft, *intr.* f., gather in a crowd, flock together, 1856.

zufammenraffen, *refl.*, gather one's self, collect one's self, *98.

zufammenrufen, rief, gerufen, *tr.*, call together, 635, 2852.

zufammenfinken, fant, gefunken, *intr.* f., sink to the ground, sink down, *101.

zufammenfteh(e)n, ftand, geftanden, *intr.*, stand together, be united, 432, 743.

Zufchauer, *m.* -8, —, spectator, *3.

zufchleudern, *tr.*, hurl towards, 654.

zufchließen, fchloß, gefchloffen, *tr.*, close, shut, 2005, 2993.

zufchnüren, *tr.*, lace up, strangle, choke, stifle, 3124.

zufehen, fah, gefehen, fieht, *intr.*, look on, 2339.

zutragen, trug, getragen, trägt, *refl.*, happen, 2795.

zutraulich, *adj.*, confiding, trusting, 1070.

zuvor, *adv.*, before, 1559, 2875.

zuzählen, *tr.*, count *or* tell (off) to, rent to, 52.

Zwang, *m.* -e8, constraint, compulsion, yoke, servitude, 1353.

zwanzig, *num.*, twenty, 630, 1419.

Zweck, *m.* -8, -e, aim, object, design, purpose, 1994, 1995.

zwei, *num.*, two, 164, *21, 599, *etc.*

Zweifel, *m.* -8, —, doubt, 2540.

zweifeln, *intr.*, doubt, 278.

zweimal, *adv.*, two times, twice, 2072, 2281, 3094, *etc.*

zweit, *num. adj.*, second, *4, *14, *40, *etc.*

Zwietracht, *f.*, discord, 302.

Zwing, *m.* -8, -e, strong tower, dungeon, prison, keep, 370, 372, *140.

zwingen, zwang, gezwungen, *tr.*, constrain, force, compel, subdue, keep down, 373, 2107, 2319, *etc.*

zwifchen, *prep.* (*dat. and acc.*), between, among, 663, 701, 1178, *etc.*

zwölf, *num.*, twelve, 1403, 1419.

www.ingramcontent.com/pod-product-compliance
Lightning Source LLC
Chambersburg PA
CBHW032014110726
47901CB00004B/1082